Wratha threw wide the curtains!

In a moment Karl woke up screaming – and found himself chained to his bed. His cries gonged like great cracked bells as his skin peeled back and his blood boiled. The sun's rays were in his eyes, which blackened to craters in his head! His hair became smoke, while his limbs and various parts cracked open to issue jets of steam and stench! Through all of this Wratha laughed like a madwoman, dancing from one foot to the other in her excitement and hauling on a rope to drag Karl's bed more surely into the focus of the sunlight.

His body shrivelled and shrank; his vampire leech deserted him, came writhing from his bursting belly. Wratha closed the curtains and rushed to his side. Like Karl, his leech was fatally burned. Dying, it produced its egg – and she had what she wanted! Of her own free will, she opened herself to the thing, which entered without pause to fuse with her flesh.

Now her agony would seal the contract. But the deed was done, and Wratha was exultant. *At last she was Wamphyri!*

Brian Lumley was born in the coal-mining village of Hordern, County Durham. At the age of twenty-one, he was called up for National Service and was assigned to the Royal Military Police. He subsequently joined up and in his twenty-two years of service travelled widely.

A devotee of horror and fantasy fiction all his life, he began writing while still in the army in the 1960s, and his first stories were published in America. His early influence was that of H. P. Lovecraft's *Cthulhu Mythos* cycle of fiction. After returning to civilian life in 1981, Brian Lumley became a full-time writer and began working on his longer, more ambitious novels: first the *Psychomech* trilogy, then individual novels such as *Demogorgon* and *House of Doors*, culminating in the highly original series of bestselling Vampire novels, the five *Necroscope* books. *Blood Brothers, The Last Aerie* and *Bloodwars* are all published in ROC, and together they form his new trilogy, *Vampire World*, a spin-off from the *Necroscope* series. Also published in ROC are *Fruiting Bodies and Other Fungi* and *Return of the Deep Ones and Other Mythos Tales.*

With more than thirty books and over a hundred short stories published in English, Brian Lumley has also had his work translated into French, German, Italian, Spanish, Dutch, Japanese and, most recently, Polish. His story 'Fruiting Bodies' won the British Fantasy Award for the Best Short Story and he has also been the recipient of *Fear* Magazine's Award for *Necroscope III: The Source.*

VAMPIRE WORLD I
BLOOD BROTHERS

BRIAN LUMLEY

A ROC BOOK

ROC

Published by the Penguin Group
Penguin Books Ltd, 27 Wrights Lane, London W8 5TZ, England
Penguin Books USA Inc., 375 Hudson Street, New York, New York 10014, USA
Penguin Books Australia Ltd, Ringwood, Victoria, Australia
Penguin Books Canada Ltd, 10 Alcorn Avenue, Toronto, Ontario, Canada M4V 3B2
Penguin Books (NZ) Ltd, 182–190 Wairau Road, Auckland 10, New Zealand

Penguin Books Ltd, Registered Offices: Harmondsworth, Middlesex, England

First published 1992
9 10 8

Roc is a trademark of Penguin Books Ltd

Printed in England by Clays Ltd, St Ives plc

For Nick Austin, my guiding light for many years.
So far we must have got through our weight in Metaxa,
but there's a lot more left where that came from!

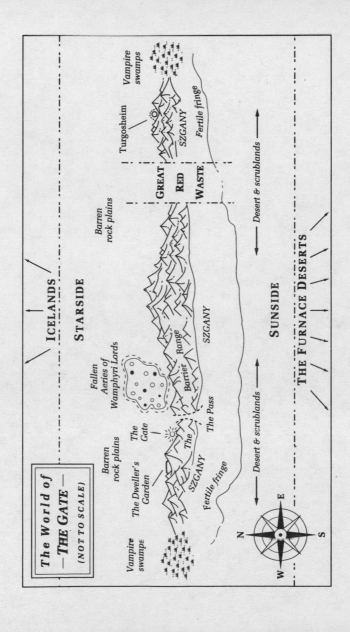

The World of
— THE GATE —
(NOT TO SCALE)

ICELANDS

STARSIDE

Vampire swamps

Barren rock plains

The Dweller's Garden

The Gate

SZGANY

The

Fertile fringe

Fallen Aeries of Wamphyri Lords

Barrier Range

The Pass

SZGANY

Barren rock plains

GREAT RED WASTE

Turgosheim

SZGANY

Fertile fringe

Vampire swamps

Desert & scrublands

Desert & scrublands

SUNSIDE

THE FURNACE DESERTS

CONTENTS

PART ONE:

Looking Back

———————

I

Morning. Sunrise. Sunup!

The sun had risen up fifteen times since the battle for The Dweller's garden; risen up over the south-western horizon, travelled a predestined path according to its cycle, sunk down again into the south-east. Fifteen times that low, warm, oh so lazy golden arc across the sky, making for a like number of sundowns.

Sundown: night, darkness, peril!

Sundown. A time of terror since time immemorial: when the last yellow glints would slip silently from the high crags of the great barrier range, until its topmost peaks turned a pale ochre, then ashen, finally wolf-grey and silver under the stars of Starside. A time of terror, yes ... but no longer. For the battle in The Dweller's garden had been fought and won, and the near-immortal masters of Starside's aeries, the Wamphyri, were immortal no longer. Indeed, they were either dead or flown into the Icelands. Of the latter, only a few had survived to flee.

Sundown, and nothing to fear from it. Not any more. It was strange ...

On the one side of the mountains, that closest to the sun (Sunside, with its forests and rivers, and, to the south, its pitiless furnace lands), daylight would persist for a further twenty-five hours; but on Starside the barrier mountains shut out the sun's life-giving warmth, leaving only the stars and the aurora over the Icelands to light the rugged land. So it had always been, so it would always be.

Except upon a time there had also been the Wamphyri! . . . But now there was none. Not in Starside, anyway. No vampires here but one, and he was different. He was The Dweller.

And at the beginning of that new night, that fifteenth sundown in the New Age of Starside, The Dweller had called for Lardis Lidesci to attend him at his house in the garden high over Starside's boulder plains.

Lardis was a Traveller king, leader of one of Sunside's Szgany tribes. He was short, barrel-bodied, apelike in the length of his arms; his lank black hair framed a wrinkled, weather-beaten face, with a flattened nose and a wide mouth full of strong, uneven teeth. Under wild eyebrows, Lardis's brown eyes glittered his mind's agility, even as he himself was agile despite his stumpy shape. Yes, he was Szgany, and it showed.

'Szgany': in fact the word had two meanings. Starside's trogs, cavern-dwelling neanderthals, likewise called themselves Szgany. To them it meant 'The Obedient Ones' – obedient to the Wamphyri! As for the genesis of Traveller usage, that was lost in time. Now when the Gypsies used the word to define other than a trog, it best described themselves, their way of life: tinkers, music-makers, seekers after refuge (often in deep caverns, like the dwelling places of the trogs), wandering metalworkers, fey people: Szgany.

Travellers. Ah, but upon a time – an oh so recent time – there had been reasons aplenty for the nomadic existence of the Gypsies! And each and every one of those reasons monstrous, and all of them inhabiting the stone- and bone-built aeries of the Wamphyri! But the Wamphyri were no more.

It was strange; Lardis was not yet accustomed to it; the sun was setting for the fifteenth time since the great battle and still he shivered, longing for the misted valleys, wooded slopes and forests of Sunside. Across the mountains it was still twilight and true dark many hours away. Plenty of time to find sanctuary in one or another of the many labyrinthine systems of caverns, there to wait out the night until ... But no, all of that was yesterday. Yet again Lardis must remind himself: *Fool! The yoke is lifted. The Szgany are free!*

Pausing where he made his way through the garden, Lardis looked back and up at the topmost crags. They were ashen now: charcoal dusted a pale blue-grey from the brightening stars, the colour of a wolf at twilight. Soon the hurtling moon would be up, half golden in the sun's reflected light, half blue as Icelands sheen. Then the wolves of Sunside would sing up from the dark forests and down from the pine-clad mountains, and those of Starside would hear them, yawn and stretch, emerge from their treeline dens and answer with songs of their own. For the moon was mistress to all the grey brothers.

Shivering (from the chill of twilight?), Lardis glanced all about in the dusk. At trog workers, leathery, shuffling, nocturnal, already up and about and seeing to their various duties; at the dim but reassuring yellow lights of Traveller dwellings huddled to the gently sloping walls of the saddle; at the misty silhouettes of greenhouses, the glitter of starlight in a shimmering geothermal pool, a creaking wind-vane atop its skeletal tower, turning in the breeze off Starside. And then he shivered again, and started out more urgently for The Dweller's house –

– Only to slow his pace in the very next moment. No need for haste. It was sundown, yes, but there was nothing hurtful here. Not any more. So ... why should he feel that something was wrong?

Lardis trusted his instincts. His mother had used to

read palms, and his father had seen far things; all of the Lidescis had been fey. And tonight Lardis was jumpy without knowing the reason. Could this be why The Dweller had called him, because something was wrong? Well, he would know soon enough. But one thing Lardis already knew: that he had heard the call of Sunside, its rivers, forests and open spaces, and come what may his stay in The Dweller's garden would not be long.

Three acres in a row front to rear, the garden was – it had been – a marvellous place. It was a small valley in a gently hollowed mountain saddle. In this region Nature had flattened the barrier range somewhat; thus when the sun stood at its low southerly apex, it somehow managed to shine between even the highest peaks and down the long slopes, glancing off the crags to light here. From twilight to twilight, the aching light of Sunside struck through the pass in a great warm misty wedge.

A long, curved dry-stone wall defined the garden's forward boundary, beyond which the ground dipped sharply towards frowning cliffs, weathered shelves, more declivities, gentling foothills, and finally Starside's barren plains. Encompassed by the wall, the slopes of the saddle, and a narrow pass at the rear, were small fields or allotments, greenhouses, wind-vanes, sheds and storehouses, and clearwater ponds. A number of pools were astir with trout; others bubbled with thermal activity. Lush with vegetation, much of it crushed and ravaged in the battle but already sprung up and growing again, a surprising number of the garden's vegetable species would have been at home in The Dweller's own world. Hardy, improved or developed by The Dweller himself, they had grown accustomed to Starside's long nights and longer, occasionally dreary days.

Repairs to the garden were nearing completion. Even stones slimed by exploding gas-beasts or evaporating Lords and their lieutenants had been cleaned, or removed to the rim and avalanched down onto Starside. Vampire debris had gone into a crevasse, been drenched with The Dweller's fuels, burned up with hideous stenches. Eventually the last taint had been expunged. Broken dwellings had been mended, flattened greenhouses re-erected, The Dweller's generators repaired. Many of the garden's systems were fragile, requiring frequent attention; tending them was how The Dweller's people earned their keep, and the work served to instruct them in his ways.

His 'people': trogs sent by the Wamphyri to work mischief against him, only to be converted to his cause; a few Travellers from tribes other than Lardis Lidesci's, grateful for The Dweller's sanctuary; and Starside's grey brotherhood, the wild ones of the mountains, who hunted under the moon. These latest of his volunteers were wolves, but it was as if he were their brother — which indeed he might well be. For The Dweller's vampire had been passed to him by a wolf . . .

A vampire, aye — indeed, Wamphyri! For he carried a true egg. And if he were not The Dweller, with his own place here in the garden, what then? On Starside's boulder plains, east of the shining hemisphere portal to lands unknown, there stood the last great aerie of the Wamphyri. In its prime it had been the property of the Lord Dramal Doombody who, upon his demise, gifted it to his heir the Lady Karen. Might not The Dweller, himself Wamphyri, feel the aerie's alien lure, make it his own, take his machines there to light that monstrous stack as now they lit the garden?

As for the Lady Karen herself:

In the battle for the garden, Karen had sided with the

defenders; moreover, she had brought first warning, and with her hybrid warriors had fought like a wildcat against the vampire Lords! Engaging Lesk the Glut, she'd opened his chest with her gauntlet, cut through the pipes of his heart, torn it smoking from his body while yet Lesk stamped and snorted! The Lady Karen: she had been something! But now . . .

Some said she lived in her aerie still, though Harry Keogh (called Hell-lander, and sometimes Dwellersire) would doubtless dispute it; if he were fit and well enough to dispute anything. Harry Keogh: The Dweller's father, his bloodsire.

After the battle, Harry had sojourned awhile with Karen in her aerie; who but a magician out of the hell-lands would dare? She was, after all, Wamphyri! But upon his return to the garden he'd reported Karen's demise: how, in order to avoid some dark, unspoken fate, she had killed herself. Perhaps it was so, but mention her name to The Dweller and he would only smile. Except . . . these days he wasn't much given to smiling.

Lardis arrived at his destination: a white stone bunga-low with round windows and a chalet-styled roof, situ-ated close to a hot spring. An exterior staircase of yellow-varnished pine zigzagged up to a small balcony under projecting eaves, which fronted The Dweller's bedroom in the hollow of the red-tiled roof. After the battle in the garden, when the house suffered exploding gas-beast blasts, only its shell had been left standing. Trogs and Travellers, working together under the direc-tion of The Dweller, had soon put it back to rights. Now it seemed The Dweller no longer took pride in it. Nor in any of his previous works.

The Dweller waited in his doorway. He wore his golden mask, of course, and a voluminous yellow robe which covered his entire body down to his feet. Lardis paused before him, raised a clenched fist and uttered a customary greeting: 'Tear down the mountains!' Customary, habitual, indeed instinctive, the ancient Szgany imprecation no longer had meaning. In return The Dweller nodded, took Lardis's elbow and escorted him to the long room which was his study. A circular window in an end wall looked out over Starside to the distant, shimmering horizon and the auroras of the far north. A second window in the opposing wall viewed the garden, the narrowing funnel of the saddle, the gaunt crags rising on both sides and merging into peaks. In the cleft of the pass the sky was a banded blue, where the sapphire in the well of the V shaded upwards into indigo to accommodate the first glitter of Sunside's stars.

Seated on simple stools in soft yellow electric lamplight, the two men faced each other across a small pine table. Despite the fact that Lardis was The Dweller's senior by a good six or seven years, and a leader in his own right, he was ill at ease in the other's presence. He had felt this way, indeed increasingly so, almost from first arrival here. His discomfort might have its source in The Dweller's alien origins – the fact that he was a being from an unknown world, commanding awesome weapons and powers – but that was only part of it. Rather Lardis sensed in him something of the ancient powers of this world (or more properly, of Starside), and for the most part his disquiet lay in knowing what stared back at him through the orbits of The Dweller's expressionless golden mask – scarlet Wamphyri eyes! Well, no secret there. For much to his credit, The Dweller had disclosed all: the fact that he was the recipient of a vampire egg – from the bite of a wolf!

Lardis, however, suspected that there was even more than this to his persistent disquiet. Gazing somewhat obliquely on his host, he felt that The Dweller's unseen eyes saw more than was their right, that they might even peer into a man's soul. Lardis's soul, like his conscience, was crystal clear, but his thoughts were never less than searching. He didn't much like the idea that perhaps The Dweller was also a thought-thief, a mentalist. Certainly the majority of the Old Wamphyri had had the power, in one degree or another.

Finally The Dweller spoke. 'You are silent.' His voice was young, yet old with knowledge, with strangeness. It had a rough edge, a rasp of physical pain. Beneath his robe, The Dweller's burns were not yet healed. Not entirely.

Lardis shrugged awkwardly, felt lost for an answer. 'You sent for me. I came to discover your needs.'

'My needs?' The Dweller answered Lardis's shrug with one of his own. 'I myself don't know what they are! But for the moment they are the needs of my people. Later . . . we shall see.'

Lardis waited, and eventually:

'I fear there are changes in the offing,' said The Dweller, sighing. 'There are several subjects to discuss. My mother, my father, myself. Yourself, and your people. The garden, and its future. If it has one.'

Still Lardis waited.

'The garden served a purpose, in its time,' The Dweller continued. 'It was a home, a refuge, even a fortress against the Wamphyri. Against their arrogance, anyway: their "invincibility". Well, they were not invincible. Nor am I. Nothing is. Also, the garden proved a point: that while a fixed, permanent home may be vulnerable, still it may be defended, and successfully. One of several things which made the Wamphyri strong was their territoriality. They would not suffer rivals within their spheres. Once they laid claim to a place – or to anything, for that matter – it was theirs forever, or as long as they could hold it. This was no weird idiosyncrasy; most creatures, once they have found their place, will not move lightly aside. And men are much the same. Which is how and why we held the garden and brought the Wamphyri down.' He paused.

'In my father's country,' The Dweller continued in a while, 'in his world, they have this saying: "An Englishman's home is his castle." It may be translated as a warning: "Make no threat against me on my own land, for here I am strong. Here, *I* am the master!"' Again The Dweller paused, then asked, 'Do you understand what I'm saying?'

Lardis wasn't sure he did understand, but certainly he was worried. The Dweller's mode of expression sounded like nothing so much as a Wamphyri word game! And suddenly Lardis wondered: *In the battle for the garden, was it his purpose to simply defend himself against the Wamphyri ... or to usurp them? If the latter, what did that make Lardis Lidesci and his people? Free men ... or thralls?* Now that The Dweller alone held sway on Starside, how would he use his power?

Finally Lardis found his voice. 'Are these things applicable to me?'

'To you and yours, yes,' The Dweller replied. 'The Szgany fought for me and my garden. What they paid in blood has been returned in skill and knowledge; and in future, should the need arise, your people will know how to defend themselves. But for now ... what is there for you on Starside? What was there ever, but a threat? Well, the threat is no more. So go back to Sunside, quit your travelling, build settlements and live in peace – for as long as you may. You've earned yourselves a breathing space, time of your own in which to

11

grow strong. Only remember: the vampire swamps are still there. If ever the Wamphyri should return, whether bred in the swamps or ... *other* places, next time be ready for them.'

Lardis had been holding his breath. He let it out in a sigh which was almost a gasp. For while still puzzled, he was also relieved. He need no longer feel guilty about his intentions; his mind had been made up to leave, which coincided with The Dweller's advice. As for certain other fears in respect of The Dweller's purpose, he saw now that they had been unworthy.

'Before the next sunup,' he finally replied, 'I'll take my people out of here. Until then, if you'll help us, we'll learn all we can from you. As for fighting the Wamphyri, in that we are of one mind. I have always fought them. And if they return I'll fight them again.'

Under the rim of The Dweller's mask where it enclosed his cheek bones and housed his nose in a prow, his lips twitched into a smile. He nodded and said, 'Yes, I know — but in the past you have fought with muscle, blood, bone. The next time will be with "science". Ah, you think you don't know the word, but you do! You've seen it at work, here, all about you! In your permanent settlements, the towns you'll build, there will be time for it. Time for all manner of things, now that your endless trekking *is* at an end! "Science", yes: it means to learn and to understand ... everything! What? And is everything too much for you? Well, perhaps it is. But you Szgany are a crafty people: metalworkers, weaponmakers, skills left over from a time before the Wamphyri. Just a little learning, even a *little* science ... Why, there's nothing in this garden you couldn't make! Nothing of my technology which you can't discover and duplicate for yourselves, given time.'

Lardis felt a great excitement, but at the same time

he was frowning again. For now he detected something else in The Dweller's tone, words between his words. There was a sense of – finality? – in the things he said. But if the Szgany were at a beginning, who then was at an end? Or . . . who suspected that his end was upon him?

'Other matters,' The Dweller painfully rasped, his urgency cutting into the Gypsy's thoughts; so that again Lardis wondered, *Mentalist? Thought-thief?* While out loud he said:

'You, yourself, Dweller?'

The Dweller gave a small start, and now it was *his* turn to wonder. The Gypsy was shrewd. Had Lardis been anticipating his host or simply answering some question of his own? Had he seen the pain in The Dweller's scorched face, heard it in his voice? Had he perhaps guessed that The Dweller's sun-poisoned flesh was dying? Well, possibly, but even a shrewd man could scarcely guess the whole truth, the final truth – that even now The Dweller's vampire was reshaping what untainted flesh remained. But into what?

'Myself?'

Lardis nodded. 'If we Travellers – we Szgany, since it appears we'll journey no more – if we leave the garden, then what of you, your trogs, your people? What of those Travellers who were here before me and mine? What of your mother . . . aye, and your father? What of Harry Hell-lander? This is the second sundown he's tossed and babbled in his strange fever. Who knows how long before he'll recover? Last but not least, what of the garden?'

The Dweller nodded. 'We'll deal with all of these things in their turn. My mother . . . is failing. I have watched her grow old while in fact she's still young. In the world where she was born, women of her age are

13

still in their prime, but that was never her destiny.' Now his rasping voice turned a little sour. 'From the day she met my father the shape of her life was pre-ordained, with never a chance that it might run a straight course. She wasn't weak, but neither was she strong . . . enough. She was ordinary, and Harry is — he was — extraordinary. And yet her life has not been miserable; indeed she has been happy, here in the garden. The nature of her affliction is that it shuts out all manner of horrid things from her mind, until almost everything has been shut out. And now she dwells alone, within.'

'Not alone, Dweller!' Lardis protested.

The Dweller held up a slender hand. 'I know, I know: my people look after her well, and are rewarded with her smiles. But such responses are automatic; she merely obeys her instincts; she *is* mainly alone — but not for long. Soon she'll join that throng who went before, going on from this place like a vine growing over the wall. Well, and it's true there are worlds beyond and I mustn't be greedy. So let it be: let her simple smile brighten some other's garden awhile. Until then I'll stay with her, along with a few others of my people who won't leave her . . .' He paused a moment. And in a little while:

'As for you and your people, Lardis: you'll prosper on Sunside, I'm sure. And myself? Well, I looked after myself, my mother, the garden, long before the first of you Szgany joined me here; and now . . . I have friends other than trogs and Travellers. What's more, I no longer have any enemies.' He stood up, seeming to flow to his feet in the weird way of the Wamphyri, and paced the floor to the window that looked out on the garden. Lardis followed him, watching as he opened the window, leaned out a little way, and inclined his head upwards to the misted mountain peaks. The ghost of a howl came ululating down, thin and eerie, echoing in flooding moonlight. And behind his golden mask The Dweller smiled.

'No harm will come to me or mine,' he eventually continued, when the howling stopped. 'Shortly, even my most faithful will leave me; I shall *ask* them to leave, by which time they'll be ready.'

'But ... why do you isolate yourself?' Lardis was at pains to understand his motives. 'Will you stay on here, alone?'

'Stay here? Ah, no. But I shall return from time to time, to talk to her, in my way ...'

'To your mother? When she is –'

'When she's dead, yes.'

For a moment Lardis believed he saw red fires reflected on the rims of the eye sockets in the golden mask, and he was hard put to contain a sudden shudder. Wamphyri, The Dweller, aye – and much more than that. For like his father before him he had ... ah, *powers!*

The Dweller looked at Lardis, clasped his broad shoulders in pale thin hands, and thought: *He's brave, this man. Brave and loyal. He should fear me, even run from me, but he stands his ground. Whatever comes to pass – however it shall be – I'll not hurt him or his. Never!*

It was as if Lardis heard him. All of the fear went out of him; a great deal of fear which, until the moment it left him, he'd scarcely realized was there at all. At least he'd never admitted it, not even to himself. Finally he straightened up and nodded. 'Then it seems we have no more to talk about,' he said. 'Ah – except your father, of course.'

The Dweller's answering nod was thoughtful, deliberate. 'How goes it with him?'

Now Lardis gave a grunt and offered a frustrated

shrug. 'We care for him, feed him, watch over him in his fever,' he answered. 'Everything as you instructed – but we've no knowledge of his sickness. You say that both of you were burned by your own weapons, those brilliant beams of sunlight with which you destroyed the Wamphyri. Well, and your burns were plainly visible, Dweller, their effect immediate – it's a miracle you survived! But Harry Hell-lander was not burned, not that I ever saw.'

The Dweller had his answer ready. 'I was burned on the outside,' he said. 'My flesh was physically scorched by the sun's fire. But my father's sickness is in his blood, a slow poison, like silver or kneblasch to the Wamphyri. It causes this fever in him. But when the fever has burned itself out, he will be cured. Then I'll take him back to his own place. And then at last I'll be alone here.'

'And that's what you want?'

'It's how it has to be.' The Dweller's voice was now a low growl. He began to turn away – then swiftly turned back, face to face with the Gypsy. And urgently, perhaps pleadingly, he said: 'Lardis, listen. I am Wamphyri! When I fought for this place, the fighting roused something up in me, in my blood. You trust me, I know. Likewise your people, and mine. But I don't know how long I may trust myself! Now do you understand?'

Lardis believed he did, and a little of his escaped fear crept back in. 'But how . . . how will you survive?' Unintentionally, he placed some small emphasis on the word 'will'.

Before the other could answer, an echoing chorus of howls floated down out of the hills. With long, loping strides, The Dweller took himself back to the window, again inclining his head to the heights. And to Lardis he said, 'How do they survive, the grey brotherhood?'

'They are hunters,' the Gypsy answered, quietly. 'And will you also . . . hunt?'

'I know what you are thinking,' The Dweller said. 'And I don't blame you. Your times have been hard. The Wamphyri have made them so. But this I vow: I shall never hunt men.'

Lardis shivered again, but he believed The Dweller's words. 'You are . . . a changeling creature,' he said. 'I can't pretend to understand you.'

'A changeling, it's true,' The Dweller agreed. 'I had two fathers, only one of which was a man! My human flesh is dying now, but I can feel my vampire at work in me. He remembers his former host, and has other clay to mould.'

There was that in his voice . . . Lardis was not afraid . . . but there was weirdness in the air . . . the moon had turned the garden yellow, with black mountains beyond, split by the deep blue V of the pass. 'I should be going,' the Gypsy said, his normal rumble of a voice little more than a whisper.

'See my hands,' said The Dweller, 'how thin they are, like paws?' He stretched out his arms, until his hands and wrists stood free of the wide cuffs. 'These I shall retain, as best I can – the hands of a man – to remind me of what I was.' And cocking his head curiously on one side, he glanced at Lardis. 'Also that you and your people shall know me, when I am . . . *other* than I am now.'

Lardis looked; The Dweller's hands were pale and slim as a girl's; but his wrists and forearms, what could be seen of them, were grey-furred! Backing towards the door, the Gypsy hissed, 'You, Dweller? A grey one?'

'When they call down from the peaks under the moon like that,' the other sighed, 'ah! – I hear them! And I know they call for me.' He opened the door for Lardis, and the Gypsy tremblingly stepped out into the night.

'I ... I knew they were your friends, of course,' he told The Dweller, where now that one stood framed in the doorway. 'But –'

'My friends?' Again that quick tilt of The Dweller's head; his eyes, gleaming now in the eye-holes of his mask, no longer red but feral in moonlight. 'That and more than that. My kin!'

'Yes,' Lardis gulped, nodded, backed away. 'I understand.'

And as he turned more fully into the garden: 'Lardis,' The Dweller called after him. 'Remember – we shall not hunt you. Be sure that you never hunt me or mine ...'

Harry Keogh tossed and turned in tortured dreams. He had been tortured, a little. What his son, The Dweller, had done to him could not have been accomplished by any other means: the Necroscope's metaphysical mind had been entered like a house in the night, its innermost vaults penetrated, its owner deprived of his treasures. The intruder had been none other than Harry Jr himself, called The Dweller, soon to be Harry Wolfson. Except he had stolen nothing, merely changed the combinations on certain locks and booby-trapped certain passageways. During the course of work such as this, inevitably there had been some 'structural' damage which, while he had kept it to a minimum, was the real cause of his father's 'fever'. It was not so much that Harry Keogh's blood was poisoned, rather that his mentality had been depleted.

Harry dreamed of the forbidden Möbius Continuum. Trapped in its flux, he drifted useless as a ship with neither sail nor rudder, a waterlogged hulk rocked and slowly twirled by mathematical tides and algebraic whirlpools, through straits of Pure Number where he was now innumerate. And in the primal darkness of

18

that place beyond or between such places as men are allowed to know, he was aware of a thousand locked doors, all of them drifting with him, around him, even through him, each one of them a mystery to him, closed to him forever. For he was no longer empowered to conjure the Möbius equations which were their keys.

They were doors, yes, to other places, even other times, but without their keys the immensity of the Möbius Continuum might as well be the narrow confines of a dungeon ... or the innermost chamber of some sunken Pharaonic tomb, lost forever in the Valley of the Kings.

Such imaginative associations were cyclic and mutative as the stuff of dreams has ever been. Ideas evoked fresh visions as the focus of Harry's dream now shaped itself to this Egyptian motif. So that in the next moment he wondered: Doors? But if these myriad eerily drifting shapes are doors, then why do they look so much like sarcophagi?

Sarcophagi, coffins, caskets: now they were made of glass, allowing him to see into them. And within, all of those teeming dead thousands, the Great Majority, could see out! They could see Harry drifting helplessly by, and soon commenced to shout at him. He saw their mouths working, death's-head jaws grimacing and snapping, the leather of mummied faces cracking where unnatural stress was applied to otherwise inanimate, examinate tissues. They rapped on their glass lids with ivory knuckles, ogled him through empty sockets, waved X-ray hands as he went floating by.

His countless dead friends: they talked to him as of old, questioned him, begged news, items of information, this, that or the other favour. But the ex-Necroscope couldn't hear them and in any case daren't listen, and he knew that he must never ever again try to answer

19

them. Oh, Harry wasn't afraid of the dead and never had been, but he feared, indeed dreaded, their attempted communication with him! For his deadspeak talent had been forbidden to him, even as the most basic numbers were now unknowable. Worse, there would be a penalty to pay: such agony as might easily win him a box of his own!

He could only offer them a negative shake of his head (and even then believed he took a risk) as he bobbed heavily along where once he'd skimmed, no longer master but captive of the Möbius Continuum. *I shouldn't even be here,* he told himself. *How did I get in here? How will I get out?*

As if some One had answered, he saw that the coffins were doors again, one of which opened directly in his path. Offering no resistance (he had none to offer), he was drawn through into another place, another time. Drawn into time itself, but time in reverse! And so Harry began to fall into his own past.

Gathering speed, he was drawn backwards in time like a thread rewinding itself on to its bobbin. Indeed, he watched his own blue life-thread – nothing less than the course and continuity of his fourth-dimensional existence from birth to the grave – streaming back into him as he backtracked years already lived. And the thought occurred: *I am going back to my beginnings. I will have it all to live – all to do, all to suffer – all over again!*

That was too much. It was the difference between a dream and a nightmare. And Harry Keogh woke up –

– Drenched in his own sweat, and gasping: 'No!'

'Don't!' she told him at once, her voice almost as startled and frightened as his own, but less hoarse. 'You're hurting me.'

'Brenda!' Harry croaked, almost sobbed her name, while at the same time doubting that it was her name, but hoping anyway. Praying that it had all been a dream – and not just this part but all of it, everything – and a moment later knowing that it had not. No, for her fierce breasts, where now on impulse she suddenly hugged his face against them, weren't Brenda's; she didn't smell like Brenda; and anyway he remembered now that the Brenda he'd called out to had been many long years and an entirely different world ago.

'Brenda?' she repeated him, her accent husky, Szgany, as he relaxed his grip on her arms and flopped back into his damp bed. 'Were you dreaming, Harry Dweller-sire?' She leaned over him, supported his head with a cool hand, stroked his brow.

'Dreaming?' He looked up at her, tried to focus on her. It wasn't easy; he felt weak as a kitten, drained. And that last word – coupled with what she'd called him, Dwellersire – was a trigger which released more memories. No, not drained, merely depleted. Robbed. By his own son, The Dweller. And none of it had been a dream, or only the last part. And even that had been so close to reality as to make no difference.

He turned his head, looked around the small, stone-built, whitewashed, electric-lamplit room. A crude dwelling, little more than a cave. But luxury to some. Certainly to Travellers, who hadn't known what a permanent home was before The Dweller and his garden. And Harry's voice turned as sour as the fur lining his clammy mouth as he mumbled, 'Starside?'

She nodded, 'Yes, Starside, the garden. And your fever has broken.' She smiled at him. 'You're going to be well again.'

'My ... fever?' His eyes went back to her face. It looked very lovely in the soft, uneven yellow flow of the lamplight; most of the electricity from The Dweller's generators went to the greenhouses. 'Yes, my "fever",' Harry said again, nodding wrily. No fever, he knew. Just his shattered mind, gradually pulling its bits together again. 'How long have I been lying here?'

'This is the second sundown,' she told him. She withdrew her hand from under his head, replaced it with a bundled fur for a pillow. Then she stood up from her stool and said, 'I'll prepare soup for you. After you have eaten, The Dweller will want to know that –'

'No!' he cut her short, his anxiety very tangible. 'Not ... yet, awhile. He doesn't need to know yet. I want a little time to myself, to get my thoughts in order.'

And she wondered: *Is he afraid of his own son? Then perhaps we all should be.*

Harry looked at her standing there, a frown on her attractive if careworn face. She was small, amply proportioned, with dark eyes slightly aslant, a small nose for a Gypsy, and hair glossy black where it fell to her shoulders. Passionate as all her race – dressed in soft, supple leather – even motionless there was something animal, sinuous, sensual about her.

Still frowning, she crossed to a fireplace built into the virgin rock of the innermost wall and hung a prepared pot from a tripod. Prodding the fire's embers to glowing life, and aware that Harry's eyes followed her every movement, she finally told him, 'But The Dweller's instructions were very clear: Lardis's people are to tend your needs as best possible until such time as you recover, upon which – and immediately – he is to be informed.'

'My needs are that I'm not to be disturbed,' Harry's wits were a little sharper now. 'I'm not to be excited. You mustn't ... mustn't argue with me.' All of this thinking, all of these words, were a big effort. Wearied, he lay back and wondered why he felt only half here. No, he knew why: it was because he *was* only half here. He had lost, been deprived of, several of his senses — like losing touch and taste. Which left him feeling numb, and life flavourless.

The Gypsy woman smiled and slowly nodded, as if the sharpness of Harry's words had confirmed some unspoken thing. 'You are wilful,' she said what was on her mind. 'All of you hell-landers are alike, wild and wilful. Zekintha, called Zek, and Jazz Simmons: they were the same. If only they had stayed here. Their hot blood — their children — would be welcome among the Travellers. We would be the stronger for it.' It was a Szgany compliment.

'Szgany blood is hot enough,' Harry answered, also a compliment. 'So ... will you report my awakening? What's your name, anyway?'

'I am Nana Kiklu,' she answered, coming back to sit beside him as before. 'And no, I will not report your awakening. Not for a little while.'

'Not until morning? Sunup?'

She cocked her head on one side. 'That's a long time. We're only half-way into the night. There will be others looking after you before sunup, who will surely see that you are recovered.'

'Not if I'm asleep,' Harry answered.

'Perhaps not ...' But now she could see how important this was to him, and so made up her mind. 'Mine is the last shift,' she said, thoughtfully. 'If your recovery is still undiscovered when I return, then it can wait till daylight.'

Harry held back a sigh of relief, settled down more easily into his bed. He did actually need the time, didn't want to be transported back to his own world while he was still in ... in a state of shock? And so, 'Fair enough,' he said. And in open admiration: 'Your man is fortunate, Nana Kiklu. At one and the same time, his woman is accommodating and charming.'

'I thank you,' she answered at once, 'but as for my man – alas, no.' And now a certain longing, an emptiness, crept into her voice, and a sadness on to her face. For like Harry, Nana, too, had been deprived. 'My man was . . . less than fortunate,' she explained. 'In the battle for the garden, the Lord Belath's gauntlet, dipped in poison, sliced Hzak's shoulder to the bone. I prayed he would survive. He *did* survive – for six sunups.'

Now Harry Keogh sighed, more a groan than a sigh proper, and turned his face away; but not before she saw the sympathy living in it, and the regret. The time had been – but now was gone – when he might have contacted Hzak Kiklu to comfort him, tell him that the Wamphyri were no more. But ex-Necroscope, the dead were beyond Harry now.

'All things pass,' she said, bravely. 'Now – can you sit up? I have soup for you, with chunks of soft meat. Your blood has grown thin as water through all the hours you've lain here. This will thicken it up.' She brought soup and bread. Harry was suddenly very tired, but he was hungry too. While he ate, Nana Kiklu looked on in silent approval. She approved of him wolfing the food she'd prepared, and she approved . . . of him.

Under his bedclothes lay the body of a hunter, a fighting man; hard-muscled as Hzak's had been, yet pale and different. Well, of course he was different, for he came out of the hell-lands of legend! But . . . not that different. She'd washed him tip to toe and so knew he wasn't *that* different. But handsome, aye! Tall, and lean in the hip. Strong too, before his sickbed, and would be again. Nana had no concept of the word 'athlete', but she could picture Harry chasing a wild pig and casting his spear: the ripple of his muscles, the narrowing of his strange honey-brown eyes. She could picture him doing ... many things.

As for the waving grey streaks in the russet of his hair: it seemed unlikely that age could have put them there. Harry Dwellersire was — what, ageless? When she'd listened to him rambling in his fever, he had sounded like nothing so much as an innocent boy; for a fact his body seemed older than his mind! Nana couldn't know it, but in that last thought she had struck upon the absolute truth.

So, *why* was he greying? Did it result from great learning, the wisdom that came from it, the weight of mighty knowledge? But knowledge of what strange things? In her reasoning, too, she came closer to the truth than she knew. But as things were she could only offer a small, unselfconscious shrug which went unnoticed. Why strive to understand anything? He was after all a hell-lander. It was probably as well that she neither knew nor understood.

Harry was asleep almost before the last spoonful of soup was down, and a half-hour later Nana Kiklu handed over her duties to another, much older woman. Good as her word, she said nothing about their charge's partial recovery ...

Harry woke up at the end of the six-hour shift, saw the old Gypsy woman nodding on her stool, closed his eyes and moaned until she started awake. Then he kicked his limbs, but feebly, convincing her that he was feverish still. When he calmed down she spooned soup into him, crooned to him until he slept again. Six hours later he employed the same subterfuge with a third Szgany woman, but this time there could be no hiding his rapid improvement. He was only saved by the prompt arrival of Nana Kiklu.

'He looks well,' his unknown Gypsy nurse told Nana as she came in from Starside's long night, shrugging herself out of a heavy coat of fur. 'His fever is in abeyance; all the clamminess has gone out of him; he took enough soup for two men! I think he'll wake soon. We should tell The Dweller.'

And feigning sleep, Harry heard Nana's answer:

'Let's not be too hasty. The Dweller is resting. Sunup is five hours away and the dawn will be time enough. Don't worry, I will see to it.'

'As you will,' the other answered, and left.

Harry had done most of his thinking in his sleep, which in the main had been restful; also in his dreams, which were less so. He was aware that his son would soon take him out of this world into his own and leave him there, and that he would be a free man again. But *only* a man, no more Necroscope, and no way round it. He wasn't reconciled to it but had no choice. For the time being, however, his frustration seemed all burned out of him; except . . . he supposed it must return. Yes, as long as there were locked rooms in the mansion of his mind – while he remembered the Möbius Continuum, and the myriad dead friends who were lost to him now – it would always return.

But looking at Nana Kiklu where she came to stand over him, looking at her through three-quarters shuttered eyes, which yet feigned sleep, he found himself remembering other, more mundane things. Earthly, even earthy things; yet not *of* the earth, and certainly not of the grave. For Nana Kiklu was far from that. On the contrary, she was full of life. And he remembered how her breasts had felt against his face when she'd hugged him.

And then he knew why he continued to feign sleep: so that he could watch her watching him. He wanted to

26

consider her expression, and see if he could sense that in her which he felt in himself. It had been a long, long time since he'd known a woman.

When Nana sat beside him he merged into her shadow, felt drawn to her. The top buttons of her soft leather blouse were open; leaning over him to straighten his pillow, the curves of her elastic breasts were partly exposed. Only lift his hands a little and he could test their weight. It was a struggle not to. And to control his breathing.

She cocked her head a little on one side, half-shuttered her own eyes, frowned at him. But her eyes, like her thoughts, were very deep. She had noticed the rise and fall of his chest: a trifle ... irregular? Both Harry and the Gypsy, each wondered what were the other's thoughts.

In the same moment that he felt he must touch her, finally she moved, got up, went to the door – and barred it. And Harry knew, in the way people do, what was going to happen; also that he wanted it to happen.

She came back, her Gypsy hips swaying hypnotically, and sat down again. But as she adjusted his blanket, so her hand crept beneath it on to his naked thigh. Harry stopped breathing, stiffened with the shock of her touch, and her suspicions were at once confirmed. Her laugh was low and husky. 'I thought your fever had cooled a little. But look, here you are hot as ever! Hot – and hard ...'

Already erect, his manhood grew more yet into her tightening, deliciously mobile fist, to hammer like a heart against her palm. Until he groaned, 'No! Wait! Nana, don't waste me!' His trembling hands found the buttons of her blouse and her breasts tumbled free. While he fondled and kissed their softness, teasing her brown nipples to life, she struggled to be rid of her clothes and into bed with him.

'Fill me, Harry Dwellersire,' she moaned, 'for we've both been empty and aching for far too long. I'm not sure why you ache, but this may be part of the cure.'

He made no answer, found the sucking gate to her sex and drove into it. In the next moment, for a moment, he held himself back, then panted: 'I can't – daren't – damn it, I'll get you pregnant!'

'No,' she shook her head, rolled over on top and came down slow and heavy on him, trapping his flesh deep in her lava core and his face in the silky curtain of her hair. And slowly working her body, with her breasts lolling in his face, she gasped, 'I'm . . . barren.' It was a lie; Hzak's seed had been at fault, she knew. But as for Nana, she *wanted* a child – so why not Harry's?

Harry felt himself swelling, shook his head wildly. 'Nana, I can't hold it!'

'Don't try,' she told him, and instantly felt him jerking, geysering into her. His long bursts seemed unending, lubrication for the hot engine of her womanhood.

'Too quick,' he moaned, angry with himself. 'Too damned quick!'

'Yes,' she murmured, smothering him in her breasts, her kisses. 'Too quick. But that one was for you. This one will be for me, and it will be slower.'

It was. And so was the next . . .

In the grey twilight, just before sunup, Nana crept from Harry's bed and dressed, went to The Dweller and told him that his father's fever had broken. When she left her lover of a few brief hours, he was sleeping a dreamless, exhausted sleep, and somehow she knew it was the last she would see of him.

But, warm inside, she also knew that it was not the last of his works.

II

Four years later:

Lardis Lidesci's house stood on a rise a little above Settlement, where the grassy, temperate but abrupt foothills of Sunside climbed towards rocky outcrops and steep, forested heights. He liked sitting in front of the house at sundown, to catch the last rays of the sun; likewise before sunup, to watch it rise. Unthinkable four short years ago (two hundred 'days', or sunup-sundown cycles), and even now nerve-tingling: to be up and about, safe and sound, and the parent star itself not yet risen. Strange, too, to live in one place, in a house; though almost all of the Szgany did these days – certainly the majority of Lardis's prosperous, ever-increasing band.

The Szgany Lidesci: Lardis's people.

Oh, there were still a few families who preferred their hide-covered caravans along the valley trails, and those who dragged their scant belongings on travois from place to place, unwilling to rest, relax, rejoice in the fact that the scourge of the Wamphyri was a thing of the past. But in the main they were settled or settling now, while other tribes, clans, bands of Travellers were following suit, building their own places along the forest's rim, east to west down the spine of the barrier range.

Lardis's cabin was styled after The Dweller's house on Starside. Providing shelter for Lardis, his young wife Lissa, and not least their small son Jason – who had been named by his father after someone he very much

29

admired – it stood a mile east of Sanctuary Rock. Lardis had chosen the spot himself, built the house, finally taken a wife and settled here, all in that period of twenty-four solar rotations following immediately upon The Dweller (whom some saw fit to call 'the changeling' now, and others Harry Wolfson) sending the Szgany out of his garden on Starside. And while Lardis had toiled to construct his home here in the lower foothills, so his people had followed his example, felled trees and built Settlement.

Since the place was the first community of its kind in more than two thousand years of wandering, Lardis found its simple name in keeping – if not the high, stout fence which the Gypsies had seen fit to throw up around it. With its catwalks, turret watchtowers and various defensive systems ... perhaps 'Fortress' would have been a more suitable name! But memories of hard times die hard, and Szgany dread of Wamphyri terror and domination was instinctive and immemorial.

The Wamphyri, aye!

Sitting here in the faint, false-dawn light of Sunside, looking down on Settlement – with its tiny gardens and allotments, blue smoke spiralling from its stone chimneys, the first antlike movements in its cramped streets – Lardis wondered if the Wamphyri would ever return. Well, possibly, for they were like a recurrent nightmare which fades but not entirely from inner memory, bloating anew when least expected, resurgent in the night. But not, he prayed, in his time. Let it not be in his or little Jason's time.

It wouldn't be, not if he could help it.

And yet ... it was reported that the vampire swamps were acrawl again. Creatures and ignorant, lonely men went there to drink, and came away more than creatures and less than men. Or more than men, depending on

30

one's point of view: that of someone entirely human, or that of something other. Impossible and therefore pointless – and not least very, very dangerous – to attempt to quarantine, patrol or monitor those great boggy tracts sprawling west of the barrier range, those morasses of bubbling, festering evil. Their extent was unknown, unmapped; no one fully understood the nature of vampire contamination, infestation, mutation.

How then to keep the threat at bay? The Szgany Lidesci could only do their best. Lardis's plan had been simple and so far had seemed to work:

West of the jagged barrier mountains, where the crags fell to earth, petered into stacks, knolls and jumbles, became foothills which eventually flattened into quaggy hollows, that was where the swamps began. Fed by streams out of the heights, the marshes brewed their horrors through the long, steamy sunups, released them into the gurgling, mist-wreathed nights. At least one tribe of Starside trogs, inhabitants of deep caverns far to the west of what was once The Dweller's garden, knew the danger well enough: they kept a constant watch for any suspicious creature emerging from that region. And since all such were dubious, they destroyed them whenever they could. Wolf, goat, man – it made no difference – if he, it, whatever, came stumbling or stalking out of reeking, moisture-laden darkness into trog territory, then he was doomed.

Lardis had taken his cue from the trogs. One hundred and forty miles west of Settlement, where the mountains were less rugged and the green belt of Sunside narrowed down to something of a thinly forested bottleneck, that was where the Szgany had always drawn their line of demarcation. In all Lardis's travelling days, he'd never taken the tribe across that line, neither him nor any other leader that he knew of. Apart from a

31

handful of solitary types – lone wanderers who always kept themselves apart, perhaps for safety of body and soul – apart from these and the rare, nomadic family group, the territory beyond the line of demarcation was unknown to men, unexplored. But as for the line itself: now at least it was manned. And constantly.

There were two well established Gypsy communities west of Settlement: Mirlu Township only twenty miles away, and Tireni Scarp, three times as far again. Volunteers from all three of these 'towns' took turns guarding the brooding vampire frontier. Even now two dozen men of the Szgany Lidesci were away from home, an entire sunup's march to the west. There they'd stay for four long days – and four fraught, eerie sundowns – until relieved of their duties by the Szgany Mirlu. Eventually it would be the turn of a band from Tireni Scarp, and so forth. This way, just as Starside's trogs kept a lookout for incursions into their territories, so the Szgany protected Sunside.

It was as much as could be done; Lardis had agreed all of the procedures with Anton Mirlu and Yanni Tireni; the Lidescis – because they were situated furthest from the boundary and so had further to trek in pursuance of their duties – would seem to have got the worst of the deal. At the same time, however, they *were* the furthest away . . . but never to the extent that Lardis was out of touch. No, for he must always maintain his intelligence, keep up to date where and whenever vampiric outbreaks or manifestations were concerned . . .

Hunched in his chair in his small garden over Settlement, Lardis chewed over all of these things, considering what had been and wondering what was still to be; until suddenly, feeling a chill, he turned up the collar of his jacket. Not that this would warm him, for his was a chill of the soul – maybe. He snorted and gave an agitated shrug. At times he cursed the seer's blood in him; it told him things and gave warning, true, but never told enough and sometimes warned too late.

A thin mist was gradually (and quite naturally) rising out of the earth, up from the streams and rivers, advancing through the forests and gathering in the hollows. Already Settlement's walls were fading into the grey of it. Lardis didn't much care for mists; he'd seen too many which were other than natural; he remembered their clammy feel against his skin, what had issued them, what all too often issued out of them. But this one –

– He narrowed dark Szgany eyes and merely scowled at this one. Knowing its source he could afford to, for it was simply the dawn. In just a little while now the glorious, laborious sun would lift its rim up over the far furnace deserts, pour its light on fringes of scrub, crabgrass, savanna where they gradually merged into forest, until finally its golden rays would light upon Settlement and the barrier range itself.

Sunup, soon! The land knew it, stirred, breathed a moist breath of mist to wake birds and beasts alike, and cover the shimmer of trout in the brightening rivers.

Sunup, aye . . . And with the thought, all manner of morbid omens and imaginings slipped quietly from Lardis's mind. For a little while, anyway . . .

'Halloo!' The cry broke into Lardis's solitude, brought him to his feet.

Going to the front of the garden and looking down the zigzagging, rudimentary stairway of stones which he'd wedged into the steepest part of the descent, Lardis saw two disparate figures climbing towards him, their feet swathed in a milky weave of ground mist. One of them, whose familiar voice had hailed him, was Nana Kiklu. The other — male, gnarled, and somewhat bent — was the mentalist Jasef Karis; or the 'thought-thief', as most people knew him, except that was an unkind expression. Oh, the old Gypsy could get into your head right enough, *and* steal your thoughts if he wanted to! But that wasn't his way. Usually he kept his talent to himself, or else used it to the tribe's advantage as a whole.

As for Nana: her man had died following the battle for The Dweller's garden, which itself had followed fast on the hell of the bloodbath at Sanctuary Rock. And Lardis remembered *that* only too well . . .

Then: the Wamphyri Lord Shaithis had come into Sunside looking for Zekintha Foener and the hell-lander Jazz Simmons. In fact Zek and Jazz were both hell-landers, but while Lardis had admired them individually, his memories of Zek were that much fonder. Though it would have been impossible to mistake her for a Gypsy (what, with her colouring, like a burst of sunlight?), still there had been *something* of the Gypsy about her. While she'd never once encouraged Lardis, nevertheless he'd entertained hopes. Perhaps if things had worked out differently . . . but they hadn't. Zek was gone now, returned to her own world. Anyway, Lardis had Lissa and Jason, and loved both of them. He channelled his thoughts afresh:

After the slaughter at Sanctuary Rock and the period of sojourn in The Dweller's garden, when the tribe had returned to Sunside to build Settlement, then Nana had been given the task of caring for old Jasef; for there were no drones among the Szgany. Indeed, if circumstances had been as of old, then Nana would have been obliged to find herself another husband. And as for the old man: surely the day had long since dawned when the mentalist would have been no more. His rapidly shrivelling brain, desiccated bones and knotted ligaments must certainly have done for him by now, when during some nightmare raid from Starside – with neither wit to hide himself away, nor agility to flee – Jasef would have ended his days as fodder in the belly of a hybrid Wamphyri warrior creature. Except . . . that had been then and this was now, and things were very different.

Lardis continued to follow the progress of the pair as they climbed towards him, and his thoughts in respect of the aged Szgany telepath were neither callous nor calculating, merely honest:

Old Jasef, with his mind-reading abilities and what-all: what he ate didn't amount to much, nor was he troublesome. In his lean-to adjacent to Nana's cabin, he lived out his time in what small comfort was available and was grateful. For he knew that in certain Szgany tribes he might not be so fortunate; he might even be put down, like his father before him, because there was something of the Wamphyri in him. It was very little and showed itself only in his mentalism, but in Lardis's eyes that made him valuable. Especially now that things were starting to happen again, albeit things which the Szgany could well do without.

Now Lardis looked back some thirteen sunups to the last time Nana brought Jasef Karis to see him – and to what had resulted from the visit:

'Karen's in her aerie and worried!' The old man's hands had fluttered like brown-spotted birds. 'Likewise Harry Wolfson where he prowls with the pack on Starside's flank, howling under the racing moon. Their thoughts are strange and ominous. I have seen with their eyes how the auroras writhe and pulse over the Icelands, and smelled with their nostrils the weird winds that blow from that cold realm!'

Lardis had nodded, and asked: 'What are their thoughts?'

'Karen is uneasy – very! She makes monsters!'

'Out of men?' Not wanting to believe it, Lardis had held his breath. It had been hard enough, that time four years ago, to believe she still lived! What, Karen alive? And Harry Dwellersire so sure that she was dead? But when The Dweller returned to Starside after delivering his father back to the hell-lands, then the truth of it had been seen: the Lady Karen herself had come visiting! She and The Dweller (two of a kind?), walking, talking together on the silvered slopes, in the heights over Starside's boulder plains. But why not? She had been his ally against the Wamphyri Lords, hadn't she? She had been the one to bring first warning.

And now this: she practised the arts of the Wamphyri and made monsters! *But from what?* Perhaps it was as well after all that The Dweller had become a changeling, whose powers waned like his waning man-flesh. Aye, for he was the leader of the grey brotherhood now – a wolf! – albeit a wolf with the pale slender hands of a human youth. Had it been otherwise ... ah, what unthinkable nightmares he and Karen might have bred together! And what blood-lusting progeny, to come raiding again out of Starside!

Jasef, however, had given a shake of his palsied head. 'No, Karen took no men to make her creatures. Neither flesh of Travellers nor even trog flesh, but ... *stuff*, which she discovered alive in the workshops of the Lords Menor Maimbite and Lesk the Glut, buried beneath the ruins of their toppled aeries.' Then with a shrug he'd added: 'But what odds? For it, too, had *been* the stuff of men ... upon a time.'

While word of Karen's weird industry and Harry Wolfson's fretful prowling was bad enough news in itself, still Lardis had wanted to know *why* they'd been driven to these extremes; had Jasef gleaned the reason for it? Had The Dweller's metamorphosis driven him mad? What did Karen fear that she made guardian creatures, when she herself was the last of the Wamphyri? There had been rumours: some said she'd taken men for lovers and never harmed a one of them. What had Jasef divined of these things? Anything at all? Or was he merely groping in the dark?

'Awful winds whistling out of the Icelands,' the ancient had moaned, rolling his eyes. 'The changeling and Karen, they have watched the auroras weaving, and listened to voices out of the living ice!'

At which Lardis's eyes had narrowed. Twice now the old man had mentioned the Icelands, those far northern regions beyond Starside, into which the Wamphyri had banished malefactors of their own kind since time immemorial. After the battle at the garden, several surviving Lords were known to have fled there: the gigantic, acromegalic Fess Ferenc, the entirely loathsome Volse Pinescu, the squat and vindictive Arkis Leperson – even the great Lord Shaithis himself, plus an unknown number of lieutenants and thralls. Well, and they were only the last of many gone before them. But none had ever returned. Not yet . . .

And Lardis had shivered and husked: 'Are you telling me that they fear the return of . . .?'

'Wait! Wait!' Old Jasef had fluttered his hands. 'In the hour before dawn I dreamed of The Dweller, the changeling, the wolf with a man's hands. Except it was more than just a dream, and he asked for you, Lardis. If you would know more, then go and speak to him who runs with the pack.'

'Oh?' Lardis had grunted, shrugging in that jerky way of his, to indicate his irritation. 'Just like that? And should I, too, run with the wolves? And will they also respect my life, like the tame wolves of Settlement? Now tell me: even if I wanted to see The Dweller, how would I seek him out and where find him?' But he'd known the answer even before the question was out.

'Where else?' said Jasef, cocking his head on one side.

At the grave of his mother, of course . . .

Nana and Jasef had reached the topmost flight. Puffing and panting where the going was steep, the old man leaned heavily on Nana. Their errand must be important. Lardis called down, 'You should have sent a runner. I would have come to you.'

A runner – even those simple words conjured images:

Of a racing moon in the skies over Starside, and lean grey shapes, running like quicksilver, whose silhouettes seemed part of the night. Never fully seen – a grey blur on the periphery of sight – they melted into the ridges, the crags, the shadows of black and stirless trees. Their triangle eyes had been luminous in the garden's preternatural gloom.

For of course Lardis had known his duty, and despite his fear had gone there; climbed up to the high pass and through it to the garden, to meet with Harry Wolfson at the grave of the Gentle One Under the Stones. Oh, he'd not gone alone or unarmed; five of his best men had accompanied him, and he'd carried his shotgun and a box of silver-shot cartridges from The Dweller's armoury. It wasn't that Lardis didn't trust Harry Wolfson: he *had* trusted, almost worshipped him in his time and would do so even now – to a point. But there had been word of him. Hunters on the evening slopes of Sunside, returning late to Settlement, Mirlu, Tireni Scarp, had seen him running with the pack. And he had howled with the best of them!

They had their pact, however, and not a man of the western Szgany townships would ever shoot at a mountain wolf. Still, to be absolutely sure they'd not be tempted, Lardis had left his men to wait for him at the back of the garden, where the pass led down to Sunside. And then he'd gone on alone to the rendezvous, at the grave of The Dweller's mother. Except it had not been the changeling whom Lardis met in the now ruined garden. Not him but his father, the Necroscope Harry Keogh, returned at last out of another world.

Lardis could remember the first moments of that meeting in detail: how first the garden had been empty, then the tall figure of the hell-lander, standing there at the wall, alone, shoulders slumped, forlorn, where a moment ago there had been an empty space. And Lardis had known at once who this must be, for no other could come and go like that; and he'd wondered: *Is this what The Dweller wanted me to know, that his father is back in the barrier mountains?*

But then, at Lardis's approach, so Harry had straightened, turned, seen him there. And in that selfsame instant Lardis had known that The Dweller wasn't the only changeling in Starside. Grey and gaunt, Harry's flesh, and crimson his eyes. Wamphyri!

As for the rest of that meeting – their actions, the substance of their conversation – it was all but forgotten. Lardis had wanted nothing so much as to be out of there. Perhaps he'd mentioned The Dweller's fate, and something of his fears of a threat out of the Icelands; perhaps they'd spoken of the Lady Brenda, and the cairn where she lay buried; perhaps at that there had been something other than blood in the Necroscope's eyes. One of the few things Lardis did remember, and clearly – one action of which he would always be ashamed – was that he'd discharged his weapon, uselessly, and that the hell-lander could so easily have killed him . . . but hadn't.

Later: they had stood together in silence at Brenda's grave. But when Harry inquired after the Travellers, then Lardis had been instantly suspicious. Worried about the other's intentions, he'd asked: 'And will you hunt on Sunside, Harry – hunt men, women and children – when the nights are dark?'

'Does my son hunt the Szgany?' was Harry's answer. 'Did he ever?'

But by then the atmosphere had been sour as Lardis's mood. And as he'd headed for the pass where his men were hidden, his parting shot had been: 'Oh, you'll come a-hunting soon enough, for a woman to warm your bed, or a sweet Traveller child when you're weary of rabbit meat!' And the howling of the wolves had followed him and his men all the way down to Sunside . . .

Nana and Jasef had reached the top of the steps; Lardis took the old man, led him stumbling to his own chair and seated him there; Nana said:

'I could have come on my own but Jasef said no, he wanted to speak to you in person. Also, you have privacy here. Such things as Jasef would tell you are best said in private. He doesn't wish to panic the people.'

'And you?' Lardis looked at her, giving the mentalist time to compose himself, catch his breath. 'Has he told these things to you?'

She shrugged. 'I look after him; he mumbles in his sleep; from time to time I overhear things.'

'I mumble, aye,' the old man agreed, showing his gums in a wry grin. 'But ah, the substance of my mumbling!'

'Let's have it,' Lardis nodded grimly. 'What is it now, old man?'

Jasef made no bones of it: 'The Wamphyri are back on Starside!'

Even though Lardis had feared as much, still he was aghast. He shook his head, grasped Jasef's arm. 'But how can it be? Is it possible? We destroyed the Wamphyri!'

'Not all of them,' said Jasef. 'And now they've returned, Shaithis and one other, out of the Icelands. They plot against Harry Hell-lander, the Lady Karen, even the changeling. Their voices are in the wind over the barrier mountains, and in my dreams I hear them talking.'

'Of what?'

'Of sweet Traveller flesh, of the blood which is the life, of bairns to roast like suckling pigs, and women to rend with their lust! All of these things, which they've missed in exile in the Icelands. Even now they inhabit Karen's aerie, flying out from it with their warriors invincible to raid on eastern tribes.'

'Just two of them?'

'What?' Jasef's rheumy eyes peered at Lardis in wonder. '"Just" two of them, did you say? "Just" two Wamphyri Lords?' And of course Lardis knew that he was right. It might as well be an army. Except ... armies weren't always victorious.

Jasef read his mind. 'Aye,' he nodded, 'the Szgany Lidesci are protected: we have The Dweller's weapons! Those weapons in which he instructed us, at least. But what of the other tribes and towns? "Just" two of them – for now! But do you think the Wamphyri won't take lieutenants? Do you think they won't breed, make monsters? Lardis, I'm only an old man whose days are numbered, and so I have very little weight in the world. But I'll tell you what I fear the most: that this is the beginning of the end for *all* of the Szgany.'

Suddenly Lardis was desperate. He grasped Jasef's arm that much tighter. 'How can we be certain that you've read aright? You aren't always so sure of yourself. Even your dreams are sometimes . . . only dreams.'

'Not this time, Lardis,' the old man shook his head. 'Alas, not this time. Do you think I enjoy playing harbinger, bringer of ill omen, like a man whose very breath carries the plague? Believe me, I do not. But I *know* the Wamphyri, and especially Shaithis, who was ever the clever one . . .' He paused to issue an involuntary, uncontrollable shudder. 'Aye, that one's thoughts are strong; they carry on the aether like cries across an echoing valley, and my mind the valley wall, which traps them for me to read.'

Lardis turned this way and that in search of some unseen solution, but in the next moment hope lifted his voice. 'What of Karen?' he demanded. 'What of Harry Dwellersire? That one has powers, which he put to work in the battle for The Dweller's garden. And the pair of them – forgive me for saying it, for even thinking it – they are Wamphryi in their own right! I can't see them sitting still, doing nothing, while Shaithis regains his old influence, recoups his old territories. What? Unthinkable! We were allies before, we'll be allies again.'

Jasef nodded, however tremulously. 'Better the devils you know, eh, Lardis? But weren't you listening? Karen has *already* fled her stack! She's with the hell-lander at this very moment, in his son's garden. As for the changeling: almost certainly he'll side with them against Shaithis and the others. But tell me, what can a wolf do? Ah, he isn't The Dweller which once we knew!'

Lardis paced back and forth, to and fro. 'Well, at least I know what *I* must do!' he said, finally. And turning to Nana: 'Go back down into Settlement, speak with Peder Szekarly, Kirk Lisescu, Andrei Romani and his brothers. Tell them to report to me, and at once – with their guns! We go again to the garden on Starside. If Harry Dwellersire and Karen are in need of soldiers ... I'll wait here and ready myself, until the five join me. We go to parley with them who defend the Starside garden, as they defended it once before. We go to offer our alliance, and to talk of war!'

Nana nodded. Silent all of this time, now words tumbled from her lips in a breathless gush. 'Lardis, do you think that I ...? Could you possibly ...? I mean to say ... only that I should like very much to go with you!'

Astonished, he looked at her, frowned, tucked his chin in. 'You? Starside? Are your wits suddenly addled, Nana? You, with two small sons to care for, and them only a year older than my own Jason? How could I allow such a thing – and why would you want it? Don't you know the danger?'

'I ... of course I do,' she looked away. 'It was just ... it was nothing but a whim.' And then, in another burst: 'But I ... I nursed Harry Dwellersire that time, and I wondered how he fares now that he is –'

'– Changed!' Lardis finished it for her. 'For he was only a man then, Nana – albeit a strange one – and now is other than a man. You may *not* go with me. What, to Starside? Of course you may not! Stay in Settlement and care for Hzak Kiklu's children, while you may. A whim, you say? A damned foolish one, I say! And should I let a vampire Lord, even one such as Harry Dwellersire, lay crimson eyes on one of my own Szgany women? Such a fate could be yours ... I would not wish it on a dog!'

But: *Ah!* she thought. *You don't know, you don't know!*

It was Lardis's last word on the subject, however,

and Nana was left silently cursing her own tongue, which had so nearly betrayed her . . .

Returning downhill to Settlement was easier. As Nana and Jasef approached the last flight, where she would run on ahead with Lardis's message to his men, the old man panted, 'Nana, that was a mistake back there.'

While she, too, was short of breath, still she held it for a moment. 'What was a mistake?'

'Forty sunups, thereabouts, a woman swells with her child,' the old mentalist played at being thoughtful. 'But four years ago' (he did not say 'years' but continued to use terms suited to Sunside and Szgany time scales) 'there were events of great moment, when no one was keeping count.'

'What are you saying?' But she knew very well what he was saying, even before he answered.

'Hzak Kiklu died after the battle in the garden,' Jasef mused at length (a completely unnecessary reminder, which proved what Nana had always known anyway: that old as he was, still Jasef wasn't the old fool that others believed him to be). 'But before he died he was still very much the man. Obviously so, for you have your sons! Ah, but a long, slow pregnancy that, Nana,' he went on, 'which lasted . . . what? Almost ten months?'

'Ten and a half,' she muttered low. 'But as you yourself have observed, no one was counting. Get to the point, Jasef.'

'I was given into your care,' he said, 'since when you've been good to me. There are some who wouldn't have cared much one way or the other. What, an old thought-thief like Jasef Karis? As well forget to feed him, let him lie on his pallet, fade away and die. But with you, I've wanted for nothing . . . well, maybe a new set of pumps in this old chest, a couple of decent teeth, new knees! But of comforts I've all I can use. So, I have my own reasons for being fond of you, Nana.'

'It works both ways,' she answered. 'You're not such a bad one. So?'

He was silent a moment, while they negotiated the final bend. But at last: 'I saw you start,' he said, 'when I told Lardis that Harry and Karen were together in the garden. Those black eyes of yours turned hot as coals, Nana.'

'Hot for a moment,' she turned her face away. 'But only a moment. His blood is in my children, after all.'

He nodded, thought it over, and said, 'What prompted you to keep it secret?'

'Common sense,' she answered, 'and maybe something other than that. There are a couple of women in Settlement who might have made much of it, and several who would have made too much! But at the time, when Harry lay ill in The Dweller's garden, I didn't think about him being a hell-lander. To me he was just a lonely man in a strange land, even as I myself was lonely. But you're right; a lot was happening; by the time the twins were showing, events were crowding fast. Everything became a blur in the mind's eye.'

They were down on to the level. Nana released her charge's arm, handed him his stick. 'And now, even if I would tell, I can't. Harry Hell-lander is Wamphyri! What would I gain from the truth? The best that could happen, my boys and I would be watched – always, and very, very closely – even in the best of times. And right now, with the Wamphyri back on Starside?' She shook her head. 'When men are panicked, they are wont to stampede, Jasef. And then the innocent get trampled underfoot.'

He nodded and watched her start away from him.

'The innocent, aye,' he agreed. And a little louder, as she put distance between: 'My father paid the price in full! Impaled, beheaded, burned. But then, he was no longer innocent. Indeed, and as the vampire change took hold on him, he was no longer a man!'

She came to a halt, looked back. 'But my babies *are* men,' she said, slowly and dangerously. 'And that's all they are.'

'Of course, of course,' Jasef waved her away. 'On you go, Nana Kiklu! Be about Lardis's errand. Yes, yes, and we shall keep your secret, which no one else knows . . . Nor shall they ever . . . Only men, your babies, only men . . .' But to himself:

What, only men, Nana? Spawn of the Necroscope, the hell-lander Harry Keogh? And only men? Ah, I wonder. I wonder . . .

Two of the brothers Romani were off hunting in the forests; Kirk Lisescu was fishing; none of them returned to Settlement until mid-morning, by which time their movements were slow and tired. By then, too, Lardis had grown disenchanted waiting for them, and had come down from his house to discover for himself what was the delay. His arrival coincided with that of a weary, travel-worn party of terrified Gypsies from the eastern foothills – survivors of a Wamphyri raid!

That last took a little time to sink in, but when finally it did . . .

. . . Then the fact of it hit Settlement like a thunderbolt – stunningly! Even Lardis, who had received at least some prior warning, was shocked. And if in the past there had been times when he'd doubted the veracity of old Jasef Karis's telepathic skills, well, his doubting days were over.

Lardis talked a while with one of the seven survivors,

a man of about his own age. Plainly he had been fit and strong, but now was mazed and mumbling. 'When did they strike? When?' Lardis shook the other, but gently.

'Two, maybe three hours after sundown,' the man answered, his face hollow and haggard. 'Earlier, some of the children had wandered home in the twilight; they'd been chasing goats in the peaks; said they'd seen many lights in Karenstack. Perhaps we should have been warned. But it's rumoured the Lady Karen is dead, and these were only children. They could be mistaken.'

'Where were you? Where?' Lardis shook him again.

'Beyond the Great Pass,' the other gave a start, blinked rapidly, 'on a plateau under the peaks ...' His eyes fastened on Lardis's, seemed for a moment to gaze into his soul, and in the next glazed over again. But somehow he managed to continue:

'Two years ago, we went into the heights and found a lake there. There was good fishing, goats in the peaks, game on the wooded slopes. We are – or we were – the Szgany Scorpi. Emil Scorpi, my father, was our leader. There were thirty of us ... then. And now, only seven. We built homes for ourselves in the woods around the lake. Our boats were on the water. At night, under the first stars, we'd sit round our fires on the shore, cook our fish, eat together. Why not? For there was nothing to fear. All of the great aeries lay broken on Starside: Wenstack, Menorstack, Glutstack – all tumbled and lying in ruins. Only Karenstack remained, and they said Karen was dead. Maybe she is, what odds? It wasn't the Lady Karen who fell on us ...'

Lardis groaned and nodded. 'Shaithis, aye.'

The young survivor grabbed his arm. 'Yes, Shaithis ... and one other! I saw him! He isn't a man!'

'Not a man?' Lardis frowned. 'No, of course not. None of them are. Wamphyri!'

'But even the Wamphyri were *once* men,' the other insisted. 'They are *like* men. Except this one ... was not.'

Now Lardis remembered. Jasef had not been clear on this point. 'What was he like?'

The other's throat bobbed. He shook his head, failed to find words. 'A ... a slug,' he finally gasped. 'Or a leech, upright, big as a man. But ridgy as a lizard, cowled, and his eyes burning like embers under the hood. A weird worm, a snake, a slug...'

'His name?' The hairs had stiffened on the back of Lardis's neck.

The survivor nodded. 'I ... I heard what Shaithis called him. It was Shaitan!'

Shaitan! A gasp escaped Lardis before he could check it. Shaitan: first of all the Wamphyri! But how was it possible? Shaitan was a legend, the darkest of all Szgany legends.

'I know what you're thinking,' said the other. 'But I saw what I saw. One was a Lord, but there was also the great slug. I heard them conversing. Shaithis was the manlike one, whom I heard call the other – him, it, whatever – by the terrible name of Shaitan. As for the rest of what I saw, before I fled like a coward with the others, don't ask me. This much I'll tell you, and no more: their warrior creatures were lean and hungry, and not just for food! It was a nightmare! My mother! My sisters! The Wamphyri have bred monsters with the parts of men!'

After that: Lardis asked no more questions of these rag-tag remnants of the Szgany Scorpi, but went about Settlement seeing to its defences. A guard from now on, on the catwalks and in the towers, and no more sending men west to man the vampire frontier. No, for now the threat was closer to home; and now, too, Lardis thanked whichever lucky stars shone down on him that he'd been outvoted that time during the construction of Settlement, when the other council members had insisted upon huge weapons built into the very walls.

Catapults armed with boulders girdled in spiked chains; great crossbows to fire bolts hewn from entire trees outwards into the cleared area around Settlement; trenches covered over with tentlike frameworks of coarse hide, painted in imitation of small warrior creatures and supported by sharp-pointed pine stanchions. Any enemy warrior, spying one of these grotesque semblances, would attack at once and doubtless impale himself; and men, safe in the trench below, would leap out, hurl their oil, set fire to the monster where he writhed and roared!

While all of these devices were still in place, they nevertheless required attention. Frayed ropes to be seen to, and if necessary replaced; the great crossbows must be loaded, their launching tillers greased; children had played at climbing in the frames of the lures and broken them in places. All to be put back to rights. So that as Settlement recovered from its shock, there was plenty of work for everyone.

It was like slipping from a tranquil dream into a living nightmare, the old horror resurgent after a brief respite. It was the Wamphyri! And sloth fell from the Szgany Lidesci like the shucked-off skin of a snake, so that they emerged startled but fresh, alert, agile. And very, very afraid.

Lardis called a council meeting, revoked the powers of his fellow councillors, declared himself leader as of old. Councils are useful when times are peaceful, but in times of war a tribe needs a leader. None was better qualified than Lardis. In fact, since he'd never relinquished his position, this was simply his quick and efficient way of re-establishing his authority. And no one argued the point.

He made arrangements:

Two-thirds of the able-bodied men would stay in Settlement; the remainder and all of the women and children were to disperse into the woods to the west, far beyond Sanctuary Rock and even so far as Mirlu Township. Runners would meanwhile pass on the warning to the Szgany Mirlu, who in turn would relay it to Tireni Scarp. Lardis's own party of fighting men were to accompany him to the garden overlooking Starside, where he hoped to form an alliance with Karen and Harry Dwellersire.

Most of Sunside's 'morning' of twenty-five hours' duration was used up by the time Lardis was satisfied with his arrangements. The 'day' of seventy-five hours and 'evening' of twenty-five would be consumed during the various phases of the climb and the rest periods between. For the trek into the mountains, along the high trails and through the passes, would be a long one ... which was probably just as well.

For such as the three in the garden were, it was unlikely they'd be abroad during sunup ...

Lardis called in at his house on the first leg of the trek. He told Lissa what was happening, kissed Jason, sent them off down to Settlement. There they'd join up with Nana Kiklu and her boys, old Jasef, and one younger, more capable man, before heading into the comparative safety of the forest.

Lardis watched wife and child begin their descent, studied for a moment the hivelike hustle and bustle of Settlement, finally turned to his five companions.

'Well,' he said, 'and so it's come to this. But we've all been here before, right? And this is nothing new to the

Szgany Lidesci. However, if any one of you would rather stay with his family, take care of his own, let's hear it now. You know that it won't be held against you. Ours is a job for volunteers.'

They merely looked at him, waiting.

And Lardis nodded his satisfaction. 'That's it, then. Let's go.'

As the six set out, the great golden ball of the sun was gradually, oh so slowly closing with the highest point in its low southern arc . . .

They toiled upwards for six hours, through the foothills and into the first scarps, then collapsed with fatigue among cliff-hanging trees which gave them shade from the glaring sun. There they slept; later they ate; the sun seemed to hover, and moved a little to the east. With about sixty solid hours of daylight remaining before the 'evening' and twilight, Lardis was not displeased with their progress.

Phase two saw them traversing a series of misted lesser scarps made treacherous by waterfalls, and skirting several boggy, steamy false plateaux of sedge, reeds and tough creepers, before the ground dried out and started sharply upwards again. The going was much harder here; taking longer to cover a shorter distance proved frustrating and wearisome. But eventually they made camp, fed themselves from their supplies, took their second sleep period at the foot of steep cliffs where an ancient fault cut a narrow and precarious causeway to the top. When they awakened it was plain that the sun had already commenced its not quite interminable descent.

Climbing the causeway, now they were up into the mountains proper. Sunside's levels had been left far behind, almost lost in a faintly purple haze of depth and distance where only the glittering snakes of rivers showed through a grey-green canopy of forest. Further south, at the curving rim of the world, the furnace deserts formed a searing yellow band across the entire east-west horizon; way up ahead, the mountain peaks seemed hidden behind wave upon wave of ridges and false summits.

Already it seemed they had climbed forever, and a like distance yet to go. But Lardis was not dismayed; his directional instinct told him that he was on course; he recognized many mountain features. If all continued to go according to plan, they'd be passing between the ultimate peaks even as twilight darkened towards night.

Which was precisely where all ceased to go according to plan . . .

Climbing an easy, rocky ridge towards a new summit, Ion Romani was last in line. Where the others had passed without incident, he disturbed a stone which harboured a small, sleeping snake. The creature hissed, emerged from its hiding place and bit him; he reared back from it, missed his footing, went sliding and skittering down a tearing flank of sharp stone to a shallow fall on to a bed of boulders. He landed awkwardly and broke his arm, and so made himself useless for any more trekking.

They dressed the moaning Ion's wounds as best they could, made a sling for his arm, divided up their provisions. Franci Romani would stay with his younger brother, deal with his snake fever when it came on, eventually discover for them an easier, more gradual descent to Settlement. In all the incident wasted three hours of valuable time, leaving only four men to continue the expedition . . .

*

Later:

A spiral of frothy clouds, lured south from the peaks by thermals rising off the distant deserts, afforded intermittent relief from the sun's glare; a promising goat track ended disappointingly in sheer, unscalable cliffs, so that a new route must be found; for the toiling men, time's passing became a meaningless blur as hours slipped by in straining, swearing, sweaty procession. Finally, with every muscle in every limb a fiery ache, Lardis called a halt some three hundred feet below the tree-line.

In the time frame of another world of men, two and a half days had passed since they set out upon their climb. This was their last chance to sleep, and then cover more ground before the twilight came down. Already the sun was settling towards the south-easterly horizon.

. . . They set no watch and overslept, and Lardis woke up ill-tempered and creaking in every joint. He feared that four years of easy living had sucked all of the energy out of him, and was angry to discover this weakness now, just when he most needed his great strength. With the sun an orange hemisphere clinging to the rim of the world, and the preternatural hush of twilight already settling, he urged his men to greater efforts as they climbed up through the last trees and into the winding passes and trails between the peaks. Bird song faded into the hooting of owls; the moon raced headlong, tumbling on high; out of the west, the first wolf howled a lone appreciation of his fleet, sky-floating mistress.

But at last the four struck upon a trail recognized of old, and Lardis was able to state with some certainty that from now on the going would be easier. Nine more hours should see them up the last rise, through the final pass to what was once The Dweller's Starside garden where ... where they would see what they would see.

Except that they were to see it, and know the worst, long before then ...

Half-way through the peaks and with the twilight fading into night, as the four proceeded cautiously along the dried-out bed of an ancient watercourse, suddenly Lardis felt a leaden weight on his heart and a clammy chill in his soul. He knew the sensation of old: a legacy of talented Gypsy forebears. At the same time, as if at a signal, the distant howling of wolves tapered down into uneasy ululations and ceased, and the small mountain owls where they called to each other across high-walled ravines likewise fell silent.

Scarcely breathing, the four crouched down in the shadows of looming rocks and looked all about. Behind them, wan spokes of pink and yellow light probed the southern sky over Sunside like a fading fan. Sundown, yes ... but not just another sundown. Lardis crouched lower still and pulled the others down with him. Fingers to his lips in the darkness, with a breathless *hiss*, he cautioned them to continued silence. And they waited ...

Faint yellow patches turned powdery grey on the reflective flanks of the surrounding peaks; the velvet gloom settled that much deeper; there came a high-pitched, querulous squeaking, a sudden throb of membrane wings – bats! But there are bats and there are bats.

Lardis's fiery Gypsy blood ran cold. His world had many bat species, not least the insectivores, like tiny winged mice. But these creatures which suddenly appeared out of the night to speed overhead in close groups of three, with their silhouettes etched blue in starshine, were of no such small, harmless variety. Full-grown adults, they were not unlike the *Desmodus* or true vampire of a world known to the Szgany only as the hell-lands — but the span of their wings was almost a metre tip to tip.

Despite the size of the creatures, and the fact that campfire legends were full of alleged attacks, Lardis knew that in themselves they were not especially danger-ous; it was what they stood for which froze him to a statue. More than four years had passed since he had seen a swarm so intent, so full of purpose, but even as he'd known it then, so in his own instinctive way he knew just exactly what it meant now.

Familiars of the Wamphyri were abroad in the night skies again, winging ahead of their masters on an errand of utmost horror . . . searching!

But searching for what?

III

In four speeding arrowhead formations, three bats to a group, the nightmare familiars of the Wamphyri set the air throbbing overhead, disappearing without pause in the direction of Starside and The Dweller's garden. Long moments stretched out, and only the cold stars for company in a sky darkening from amethyst over Sunside to indigo between the peaks. Lardis remained frozen, but Peder Szekarly, the youngest of his men, made as if to stand up. He lacked experience and didn't share Lardis's prescience in these matters.

Lardis felt the other shuffling impatiently, stretching a limb beside him; he reached out a hand and his hard fingers dug irresistibly into Peder's shoulder, holding him down and still. And sensing the way their leader seemed to have shrunk down into himself, Lardis's three crouched lower still, becoming one with the humped silhouettes of the boulders.

'Wha—?' Peder began to speak, his voice the merest whisper; but Lardis at once cautioned him with hoarse, breathless whispers of his own:

'Say nothing! Do nothing! Neither move, breathe, nor yet think – or if you must, then think of silence, of sleep, of what it must have been like in your mother's womb, with nothing to fear but being born! Do exactly as I tell you, if you want to live!'

It wasn't the first time Peder had heard words such as these; they were cautions he'd learned as a child. For like every Traveller child before him, he'd been instructed in the art of silence: of not being heard, not being seen ... of not being. And he remembered how his father had breathed just such words in his ear one monstrous night, and how at sunup he had neither father nor mother. It was so long ago, so terrible to remember, that he'd almost forgotten, that was all.

But now Peder Szekarly wanted very much to live; likewise his colleagues, who grew still as stones; and so the seconds lengthened into minutes.

Then, as time itself slowed and contracted down to *now*, so the night air thickened, turning leaden with an unspoken but tangible dread. It was as if the heartbeats of the four took on the volume of drums sounding against their ribs, so that each man believed the next must surely hear him – and prayed that nothing else would. And all four of them, they turned their heads and looked back the way they'd come. That was where the great bats had come from, and if their masters were with them ...

They were, and in the next moment Lardis and the others saw them.

Dark blots, like gigantic kites, or curious leaves whose scalloped rims undulated in the breeze off Starside, they rose menacingly out of the smothering blanket of night. Up from the tree-line – up into the lesser peaks, and rising over them – up into the night sky, where they blotted out the clean stars with their foul, nightmare shapes.

A flock of speeding night birds, winging east, sensed them and fragmented squawking in a dozen different directions. Mating owls launched themselves in pairs from rocky crevices, to glide and hide in the deep gulleys around. Lardis's companions, brave men all, closed their eyes and literally stopped breathing, leaving their leader himself to identify and plot the course of the terrible shapes in the star-bright sky. And on they came, those obscene diamond designs whose manta wings pulsed oh so silently, lifting them into the upper heights.

They were flyers, their once-human flesh converted and fashioned into metamorphic airfoils ... vast webs of membrane over spongy, arching alveolate bones, forming air-trap wings for lift and support ... their flattened, spatulate heads nodding this way and that on long necks, sniffing out the breezes from Starside that came blustering between the peaks to form thermals. Flyers, a pair of them: they were the aerial observation and command posts of their Wamphyri makers and masters; and not only this, they were also their mounts!

For a moment Lardis glimpsed two lesser shapes humped in their saddles at the base of each flyer's neck. One was manlike, and the other — Lardis couldn't be sure. But he remembered what a man of the decimated Szgany Scorpi had told him about a sluglike thing called Shaitan ...

Still climbing, the flyers passed directly overhead and disappeared into the upper peaks. But Lardis maintained his frozen crouch, his breathless immobility. For where the Wamphyri Lords aboard their flyers had gone silently, the things that followed in their wake were anything but silent! As they came powering into view, with their propulsive orifices rumbling and throbbing, it took every ounce of Lardis's iron will to keep from closing his eyes and shutting out their total horror.

They were warriors, six of them.

Warriors! Ah, but whatever that single word might convey in other tongues, when the Szgany used it to describe the grotesque fighting beasts of the Wamphyri, then it meant only one thing — shrieking madness! But as for these creatures ... in the case of at least one of them, even that description seemed inadequate. Seeing the beast, Lardis flinched uncontrollably; his lips drew back from his teeth in an involuntary grimace.

While the five – lesser? – creatures flew in a tight arrowhead formation, their far more monstrous cousin came on centrally and slightly to the rear. Its pulsing *outline* against the stars was such that it riveted Lardis's gaze; he had merely glimpsed the others before this one stamped itself on his disbelieving mind. Longer, bulkier, and carrying more armour than its companions, it seemed impossible that a creature like this could ever lift its bulk an inch from the earth, let alone fly! Yet here it was, squirting like an enormous octopus through the inky, star-spattered sky.

Details burned themselves into Lardis's brain:

Its grey-mottled flesh, with scales tinged blue in star-shine like smoothly hinged plates of some weird flexible metal ... clusters of gas bladders like strange wattles, bulking out its throbbing body and detracting from its manoeuvrability, but necessary to carry the extra weight of dinosaur body armour ... its grapples and hooks, cutting appendages in the shape of crab claws ... the evil intelligence of its many eyes, some of which peered forwards, while others scanned the peaks all around. And yet none of these various parts seeming *additional* to the warrior but integral, built-in, like the armour and weaponry of any smaller creature of the wild. Except Nature in her wildest mood and deadliest dreams had never equipped anything like this!

Like the flyers and their riders before them, the warriors passed directly overhead, so that the last and most terrible of these Wamphyri constructs left a lasting impression of its size and power. With its leathery vanes fluttering like the mantle of some vast cuttlefish, its bladders vibrating as they shrank and expanded, balancing the whole, and the exhaust gases from its propulsors drifting in a cloud of gut-wrenching stench down into the hiding place of the four Szgany, it was awesome. But at last it too was gone.

Lardis's companions, hearing the roaring and sputtering of the monster fading into distance, opened their eyes in time to get a final glimpse of it spurting for Starside; then its trail of foul fumes drifted lower and enveloped them like a fog, and it was as much as they could do to hold their breath while the hot moist stuff settled all about.

Peder Szekarly wasn't so fortunate and snatched breath at precisely the wrong moment; inexperience has its price. He had only joined with the Szgany Lidesci in the six-month after the battle at The Dweller's garden; his knowledge of warriors consisted of a scattered handful of obscure, reluctant memories from childhood, and sightings glimpsed distantly from the fringes of Wamphryi raids, when as a youth he had fled with other refugees from centres of nightmare activity.

To give him credit he was quiet about it, but before he was done he'd emptied both stomach and bowels, and then must rest for an hour before he was useful for anything else . . .

Andrei Romani wasn't really the rebellious sort, merely inquiring. 'I see no point,' he argued, 'in proceeding to the garden now. If there was to have been a fight it's already happening, and we're already out of it! Also, how may we fight such vileness as crossed our trail less than two hours ago? It makes little sense to me.'

The moon was up again, flying, while from eastern peaks and ridges came the inveigling howls of the grey brotherhood, those great wolves who owned the silver moon for mistress and Harry Keogh Jr for master. But their howling was strange and strained, and Lardis read bad omens in it. To Andrei he said:

'Do you hear that, my friend? And can you read it? Those are The Dweller's dogs, I fancy, but I can't decide if they're whipped or what.' Pausing only slightly in his striding, where he led his party across a long, high saddle of stony ground, he let his querulous companion catch up and grasped his arm. 'Now listen, Andrei Romani – you too, Peder Szekarly, Kirk Lisescu – and I'll tell you again what we're about and why we're still about it. This is how I see it:

'The old Wamphyri, Shaithis and at least one other, are back on Starside; it was them and their creatures passed over us in the gulley back there. They inhabit Karenstack and raid from it among the Szgany as of old. Except now it's been made much easier for them; we Travellers travel no more; instead we have houses and tend gardens of our own, which makes us sitting targets. All of this is proven . . .

'Upon a time, however, the Szgany fought the Wamphyri off – fought and won – and when they were at their most powerful, at that! It was the Szgany stood up to the Lords Belath, Volse Pinescu, Lesk the Glut and Menor Maimbite; aye, and even this same wily Shaithis, returned now out of the Icelands.

'But . . . you and your brothers were actually there in the garden that time, Andrei! Need I tell a Romani how the Szgany fought with The Dweller's own weapons – these very shotguns we carry now, brought from another world – while he used the sun itself to blast his enemies to stinking shreds? Of course not!

'Well, and now he runs with the wolves, I know, and we've only a pact to keep us safe . . .

'Ah, but now his father, called Dwellersire, has returned to Starside! I've seen him, even talked with him – though I'll admit that my words weren't so very sweet. Well, now they shall be sweeter. For who could even guess what weapons *he* might have brought back with him, eh? What, Harry Dwellersire? I tell you, we *must* go to the garden, if only to seek alliance!' He paused, released his grip on Andrei's arm, continued in a softer tone. 'Or perhaps, in some future time, you'd prefer to fight *against* Karen, the changeling, and his father, eh?'

'What?' Andrei Romani, a lithe, rangy man, at once frowned and drew a little apart from Lardis. 'But you know I would not! Come what may, I have my loyalties. Why, we fought side by side, even as you've told it – the Szgany, trogs, and the three together – against our common enemies. Nothing can change that. Nothing of my doing, anyway.'

'Agreed, aye,' Lardis answered with a curt nod. 'Nothing of our doing. But wouldn't you deem it "of our doing" if we did ... nothing? Monsters the three may well prove to be in their own right, though as yet they've done us no harm, only good; but tell me, should we let them stand and fight – and possibly die – alone, when it's more our fight than theirs? And what then, eh, when they're dead and gone? Simply return to Sunside and wait for sundown, and the one after that, and ... however few we have left? Ah, but suppose they win, and having won pause awhile and think? And *what*, pray, will they think? Where were the Szgany in the reek and the roil, eh?'

After a long moment, Andrei shrugged or perhaps shivered in the cooling air. 'Let's get on,' he said gruffly, turning up his collar, and his face to the north. 'Six or seven miles to the last pass, and an easy climb to The Dweller's garden. It's possible that the Wamphyri merely spied out the land – a reconnaissance flight. If it was more than that, then maybe they've missed their prey; there are plenty of hiding places, as we know. Why, just like us, the three could be on their way to the garden even now ...'

In a little while, striding out, Lardis spoke to Andrei in a low aside, confidentially. 'For a moment there you had me worried, old friend,' he said. 'After all these years I've known you, I was beginning to think I didn't know you!'

When the four reached the back of the saddle which formed the hindmost boundary of The Dweller's garden, they found signs of a ferocious confrontation: the lingering stench of furiously expended gases, scales of armour plate torn from some huge creature's underbelly, massive clots of dark red plasma drenching the hardy mountain heather. That was all for the moment – enough to draw their nerves taut as the wire on a loaded crossbow.

But keeping low and moving silent as shadows between the garden's derelict outbuildings and untended plots, they soon came to the forward boundary wall where Lardis had talked to Harry Dwellersire that time three months ago. And there they discovered the first victim of whatever battle had occurred: a warrior, dead on the ground, dispatched like a pheasant by a fox! Its squat neck had been bitten through armoured scales, leathery hide, flesh and gristly cartilage down to the spine and through it. Almost decapitated, the thing lay there in a pool of its own steaming liquids: fifteen tons of savagery, itself savaged! No need to inquire what living engine of destruction had done this.

Awed, Lardis Lidesci moved cautiously around the giant corpse. He pointed out dislocated main eyes in the crimson-rimmed, empty sockets of the grotesque skull. And, 'See!' he whispered. 'No fight this, but a slaughter! And the butcher, he thrust his claws in through those eyes, to nip the tiny brain and get it done with. And these fluids, still warm and reeking ... Why, this creature of Karen's, it was alive no more than fifteen minutes ago!'

'Lardis!' Kirk Lisescu's call came husking from crags which he'd scaled at the eastern extreme of the wall. 'Quickly! Come see!'

Keeping low, Lardis and the others ran, loped to the foot of the crags, climbed them to Kirk crouching on a ledge in the scoop of a fallen boulder. 'Do you see?' the small, wiry man whispered. 'Do you hear?'

He pointed out over Starside. The others could see well enough, and eventually even hear, though not at first.

Far out over the boulder plains, drifting east like a small cloud of midges, black specks darted, glided, spurted under the dome of a glittering sky. Midges at this distance, yes, but up close they'd be monsters. Likewise in the lee of the barrier mountains sprawling eastwards: shapes in flight, and others in pursuit. It was the Wamphyri, friends and foe alike; though impossible to tell one from the other.

'Who's who?' gasped Peder, jaw slack, eyes peering first this way, then that.

Lardis shook his head, slitted his eyes against the blue glitter of starblaze, tried to count those shapes which spurted. 'How many fighting beasts do you see?' he grunted. 'We know Shaithis had six.'

'Karen and Harry Hell-lander had two at least,' Andrei muttered, however sourly. 'We found signs of the one and the carcass of the other!'

'Better pray they had more than that,' Lardis growled. 'Better pray they had a *lot* more!'

Carried on changing winds, sounds of the aerial skirmish ebbed and flowed: the hissing and roaring of warriors, the low rumble of their bio-propulsive systems, the clatter of scales on armoured scales as huge bodies collided in mid-air. But as the commotion faded into distance, Kirk Lisescu had finished counting. There hadn't been much to it, after all.

'Two flyers and six warriors out over the boulder wastes,' he reported, 'all heading east, towards the sphere Gate and the tumbled stacks of the Wamphyri. Two more flyers in the lee of the mountains, pursued by a warrior.'

Lardis's tally agreed. 'And the big one's with the main party,' he added. 'Seven warriors in all, and Shaithis hasn't suffered any losses – unless I'm wrong and that huge corpse beside the wall was one of his. But even at best, it's still two against five . . .'

Andrei Romani shook his head in dismay and stated, quite simply, 'They're done for, finished!'

Lardis scowled at him. 'If they are, then be sure we won't last much longer – or fare any better!'

He looked out again over Starside, scanning the horizon from the eastern boulder plains inwards to the mountains. The larger cluster of airborne specks was beginning to descend, elongating into a straggling line; the smaller party, consisting of two flyers with a lone warrior in pursuit, was also losing altitude where it skirted the lower peaks. Even as he continued to watch, this secondary group of three disappeared behind a distant jut of crags.

Lardis clambered back down to the garden. 'Come on!' he growled.

Recognizing the urgency in his voice but failing to see the point of it, the others followed him down. 'Come on where?' Peder Szekarly wanted to know. He was somewhat recovered from his poisoning now but still felt he could sleep right through sundown.

At the foot of the crags Lardis turned to him. 'East along the high ridges, where else? However far is necessary to fathom the outcome of that fight. Guess-work isn't good enough – we've got to *know* which way it went! The future of the Szgany, every man, woman and child of us, hangs in the balance.'

He turned abruptly and made as if to head for the garden's upward sloping eastern flank ... and just as suddenly the shadows came alive with a massed, furtive creeping motion! Lardis and his three froze. They'd heard nothing, yet found themselves surrounded. But by what? Had Shaithis and the slug-being out of the Icelands left something behind to act as a rearguard? How *many* things had they left here?

'My father would be ... it would *please* him,' came a low, faltering voice from the darkness, one which coughed, growled, and was scarcely human at all. 'Please him to know ... to know that he still has ... has *friends* among the Szgany.'

Legend had it that in the long ago the olden Travellers had owned to a benevolent God. More recently, however, they had only recognized demons ... called Wamphyri! Not that anyone ever prayed to them, nor yet used their name as a curse; let it suffice that they *were* a curse! So that when it came to praying, the Szgany usually held to the sun; not as a form of true deity, but as a symbol of good fortune. Or, if a man had been born during sundown, he might give thanks to whichever star had been overhead at the hour of his birth. Lardis Lidesci was hardly superstitious; at the moment of the voice out of darkness he couldn't have said if his star was in the sky or not – but he hoped it was!

Flanking Lardis on the left, Peder Szekarly nocked his crossbow; on the other side, Andrei Romani snapped shut his shotgun; both aimed into the shadows. A little apart, Kirk Lisescu frantically shoved shells into his double breech.

But: '*Don't!*' Lardis warned them. 'The grey brothers are all about us, and that was their leader speaking.' The others must give Lardis his due: if anyone would recognize that awful voice, it was surely him. Similarly, he who had been The Dweller knew Lardis. He came padding forward out of the shadows – a great grey wolf!

Eyes aslant, yellow, feral – and crimson in their cores – Harry Wolfson paused half in darkness. But his *hands* were visible in the starlight . . .

He looked at Lardis and cocked his head a little on one side, inquiringly. And the look on his face was never seen on the face of a dog as he half-said, half-snarled, 'I . . . know you. Come talk to me, where my gentle mother sleeps under the stones.' He began to turn away, paused and looked back. 'But only you. Your men . . . they will wait here.'

'*Lardis!*' Kirk Lisescu snapped shut his weapon, began to crouch down.

'I said *don't!*' Lardis barked, as fifty pairs of yellow eyes blinked and moved nervously in the shadows. 'Only let a man of you shoot one of these, I swear I'll kill him with my bare hands!'

'No,' Harry Wolfson coughed at once, 'you wouldn't have to. The grey brotherhood takes care of its own. So put down your . . . your *weapon*, yes . . . and come talk.'

At the cairn, the great wolf was silent for long moments. He nuzzled in turn each of the larger burial stones, marking them, whined a little, gazed burningly on Lardis. And eventually he said, 'She, too, remembers you. It was a while ago. After the battle, you joined us here. You were kind. Despite your own privations, your people . . . were kind. To me, to my mother, my father. And you and I, we talked together, when I was . . . was a man. I remember it.'

'All of this is true,' Lardis nodded, discovering a lump in his throat which had little or nothing to do with fear. 'We talked on several occasions. At the last, you seemed to know what was coming.'

The other looked at him in that curious, alert way of his, and Lardis found it weird that a wolf should understand his words and answer them with a nod and snarled words of its own: 'And now ... now it has come. Strange, even sad in a way. Sometimes I feel I've lost so much; at others I take pleasure in what I've gained. Except ... my man-memory is fading, and all the time more swiftly. I forget the man-times and remember only the wolf-times, and it has made ... made a traitor out of me. For I swore I would be ... be *here*, when the Wamphyri came a-visiting Karen and my father. But I ... *forgot*, and so was late.'

'You couldn't have helped them,' Lardis shook his head. 'This time the Wamphyri have made invincible creatures, monsters of unbelievable ferocity and power! You and all your grey brothers together, what could you have done?'

The other loped this way and that. 'Still, I should have been here.'

'There was nothing you could do,' Lardis insisted.

Harry Wolfson came closer, stood still. 'Did you see it?'

'We saw them fly away eastwards,' Lardis answered. 'They were still fighting. I think that Harry and Karen ... I think they got the worst of it.'

The great wolf blinked his slanted eyes, and their cores burned yet more scarlet. 'No, not yet – but soon! The worst is what Shaithis has in store for them!'

And suddenly, so suddenly that Lardis gave a great start, the wolf that had been a man pointed his muzzle straight at the stars and howled, and from the derelict garden's shadows came the answering howls of his brothers. Then, he sprang up on to the cairn, glanced once more at Lardis and growled, 'I go.'

As he made to leap away, Lardis called after: 'But where will you go? And what do you intend? Perhaps we'd do better to go there together.'

'The Gate,' the other paused again, however momentarily, and sniffed the night air. 'I sense them there. I don't know what the grey brothers can do, but you and yours would only slow us down.'

Again he turned away — only to collide with a sleek she-wolf who came loping from the shadows. Her eyebrows were bushy, white as the snows of the higher peaks. They faced each other; perhaps some message passed between them; she whined a little, and Harry Wolfson snapped at her, deliberately clicking his teeth on thin air. Plainly the bitch was his. And to Lardis he said, 'She'll stay here, where there's no more danger.'

Lardis tried one last time. 'My men and I, we're going, too. We need to see. I have to know.'

The changeling thought about it for the briefest moment, then snarled his throaty answer: 'Then I'll leave you a guide. Follow him closely, for he knows the easiest route . . .'

Lardis returned to his men and found them on their own; the wolf pack had melted away into the shadows, leaving only one of the grey brothers behind. Lardis marked him: a flame-eyed silhouette, nervous and impatient, atop the garden's eastern flank. Kirk Lisescu nodded and remarked, 'That one's stayed back, apparently to keep watch over us!'

Lardis shook his head. 'No,' he corrected his colleague, 'he's our guide. We're to follow him to the hell-lands Gate. Or at least, we'll try to get close enough to see what goes on there.'

They struggled up the sloping eastern flank, gazed down on Starside laid out in weird, blue-tinged monochrome beneath them. The boulder plains, reaching out to a curved and shimmering, aurora-lit horizon; the jagged spines of mountains on their right, sprawling eastwards; seemingly endless miles of crags to cover before they would arrive at their destination, where the peaks looked down gauntly on the pockmarked crater which housed the hell-lands Gate.

Lardis had been there only once before, in his youth (and then at the height of sunup, of course, when the Wamphyri slept and dreamed their scarlet dreams behind the draped windows of their aeries), but even then he'd found the place ominous, unquiet, unknowable. That great ball of white light, glaring up and out of the earth like the eye of some buried giant from its socket, unblinking, malevolent, lending all the region around a leprous white and grey-blue aspect as of rotting flesh. And the stony crater itself, which formed the Gate's rim: pocked like rotten wood when the borers have been at work, shot through and through with alien wormholes. Even the solid rock . . .

While Lardis was there, a flock of bats had come to hunt midges, moths, other insects hatched or awakened by the sun's natural light blazing through a pass in the barrier range. One small creature, perhaps dazzled, had flitted too close to the Gate; its membrane wing touched the solid-seeming surface of white light; it disappeared without trace, apparently *sucked* right into the glare! For some little time Lardis had continued to watch, but the bat hadn't returned.

It had been a lesson in caution: don't approach the Gate too closely. Ah, but that time it had been sunup, while now it was a fresh sundown. And Lardis definitely did *not* intend to approach too closely. What, with the Wamphyri there? Madness! But he did have a plan, which as always was simple.

'See the grey one go?' he said. 'Heading down towards the timber-line? He'll know every tree like an old friend, and all the winding trails between. We'll make best time if we follow in his tracks.'

'Lardis,' said Andrei Romani, conversationally, 'you're a madman, I'm sure! Indeed, we all are, each and every mother's son! Made crazy by the blue-glittering stars!'

'Oh?' Lardis scarcely glanced at him, picked his way down between scree-littered spurs. 'Tell me more.'

'It's sundown on Starside,' the other continued, 'and all sensible folk hidden away. But us? We're following a mountain dog to see what the Wamphyri are up to! We should be in a hole somewhere on Sunside, waiting for the sun to rise and praying we'll still be around to see it!'

'But it's *because* we hate hiding in holes on Sunside that we're here!' Lardis reminded him. 'Me, I prefer the comforts of my house on the knoll, believe me – except I know I can't find peace there so long as the Wamphyri are wont to come a-hunting in the night. And right now ... why, I've a chance to see with my own eyes how many they are and what are our chances. So that when we go back to Sunside, we'll know to do one of two things: either advise the Szgany of Settlement and the other townships of the precautions they must take, or tell them *definitely* that the Wamphyri are no more! And let me tell you something else, Andrei ...' But here he paused.

For at the last moment Lardis had recognized a certain dangerous passion blazing up within himself. It was in the heat of his blood, the way he spat out his words, so that he knew he'd been on the point of uttering a vow. He was Szgany and proud of it, and a leader of men at that. Once spoken, a vow like that couldn't be revoked. Not and live with it, anyway.

'Oh?' Andrei prompted him. 'You were about to tell me . . .?'

Lardis bit his tongue, changed the subject:

'Do you know how far it is to the Gate?'

'Too far,' said Kirk Lisescu, clambering behind. 'Even on Sunside's levels it would take us an entire sunup to get from Settlement to the great pass. But up here, through all these crags and peaks . . .' He let it tail off, but Peder Szekarly at once took it up:

'Eighty-five miles from Settlement to the pass. But weaving through these high crags . . . a hundred, at least. And hard going at that.'

'Something less than forty hours to sunup,' Lardis mused. 'Which is when we want to be there. For if by then the Wamphyri are still alive, still abroad, that's when they'll head for Karenstack – to be out of the light when the sun blazes between the peaks!' He made rapid calculations and continued:

'A generous ten hours for sleep, leaves almost thirty for travelling. Why, at something a little more than three miles to the hour, we'll be there in time aplenty!'

'But to see what?' Andrei gloomed. 'To discover . . . what? *Hah!* The worst, perhaps.'

Lardis gave a grunt and for a little while was silent.

The boles of tall, straight pines loomed out of the darkness below; along a track dappled with starlight, feral eyes gleamed silver and sentient; the grey brother waited patient and passionless while the four gained on him, then turned and headed east. They followed as close as possible in his tracks where he chose the least cluttered, most direct route through the straggling trees.

But while the wolf's passions were at an ebb, Lardis's were still flowing strong. He thought of Lissa and Jason on Sunside, the Szgany Lidesci in its entirety, all of the Traveller tribes in their various camps and townships across the barrier mountains. And then he thought of the horror of the Wamphyri, which he'd once considered over and done with.

But no, it wouldn't be over until it was over . . .

Until it was finished . . .

Finished utterly!

And at last Lardis's passions got the better of him.

'Whichever way it goes,' he ground out his Szgany vow from between clenched teeth, 'I'll see them *dead*! Beheaded, staked out, pegged down – spreadeagled in clean yellow sunlight – and steamed away in smoke and stink!'

His words were hot as hell, fiercely spoken: a growl of hatred, a promise, a threat, so that his men knew it was his vow. But it wasn't over yet.

'So far there are only the two of them,' Lardis finally continued. 'Two that we know of for sure, though they'll make lieutenants soon enough. Ah, but they are Wamphyri! And where can they go at sunup, eh? Where else but Karenstack, the last aerie! So mark well my words: if Harry and Karen are done for and we're left to fight on alone, and if Shaithis and his lot take up residence in that last great pesthole of a stack . . . then that's where we'll finish this thing. Not in the next sunup, no, nor even the one after that – but maybe in the next!'

''Ware, Lardis!' Andrei cautioned. 'Is this your vow?'

'It is,' Lardis answered, nodding his head in the gloom of the trees. 'It's mine, yours – it's that of *all* the men of the Szgany Lidesci! Now listen:

'Their works, the terrible works of the Wamphyri, take time. Time to take men and make them lieutenants, and time to make monsters from the flesh of Travellers and trogs. Two or three sunups are nothing, not time

73

enough. But in Karenstack they'll think themselves secure. What? And who would dare to attack them on their own ground? We will, that's who!'

Peder Szekarly was astonished. 'Go against the Wamphyri, on Starside?' he whispered.

'During sunup, aye,' Lardis replied. 'With crossbows and sharp staves, hammers and stakes! With kneblasch, silver, and The Dweller's shotguns.'

'What?' said Kirk Lisescu, his voice hushed. 'Toys against the Wamphryi? And what about their warriors?'

'But their fighting creatures are vampires no less than the Wamphyri themselves!' Lardis replied, grabbing Kirk's arm for emphasis. 'We'll go there with our mirrors, given to us by The Dweller; we'll set fire to the drapes at the stack's doorways and lower windows; we'll reflect the sun's cleansing rays deep into the foul darkness. That's how we'll do it! Who would know the way better than us? Why, it was The Dweller and his father who showed us how! Well, and now it will be our turn.'

'Tear down the mountains!' Andrei Romani snarled aloud to match the spirit of the other's vision. And then (but a little less vigorously), 'But let's hope it won't come to that. After all, we could be wrong . . . maybe it's not such a hopeless case . . . it's a fact that Karen and the hell-lander are – or were – enormous powers in their own right.'

Andrei could hardly know it but his qualifying 'were' was close to the mark. For even as the four men set out upon their timber-line trek, far to the east, in the region of the glaring hell-lands Gate, Harry Keogh and the Lady Karen were already Shaithis's prisoners.

Which is to say, they were as good as dead . . .

*

74

Events followed slowly and seemed of little conse-
quence, yet later would become concertinaed in Lardis's
memory, each one hastening after the last, assuming
varying degrees of importance.

After six hours trekking along the timber-line, the
four were so exhausted they had to pause, eat, sleep,
allow their aching muscles time for replenishment. They
awakened with the coming of the hurtling moon, by the
light of which their progress was that much faster.

Later, with the moon down again, they took it a little
easier and fell into the natural, jingling, fast-striding
pace of accustomed Travellers. They held back from
talking, saved their breath for the work. Now and then
they must climb where ridges and spurs broke the
timber-line, but mainly they followed level contours.
Plainly The Dweller had been right; their guide was
completely familiar with these heights; either that or he
was a creature of unerring instinct. They forged steadily
east.

Another rest, another meal . . .

A string of long, flat, shallow saddles between elevated peaks like wave crests, where their striding ate
up mile after mile unending, until finally and far too
soon the easy going was eaten up entirely . . .

A region of sliding scree which the trees had gathered
into a treacherous, teetering barricade. Only tread
unwary, trip the wrong pebble, and the whole thing –
trees, scree, men and all – would go avalanching down
on to Starside. To prove it, there were plenty of breaks
where the green belt had been swept away right down
to the raw rock . . .

Another sleep period . . .

When they sat down, the grey one sat apart; when
they lay flat, he stretched himself out. Coming awake,
he'd be up first, waiting for them. They tossed him

scraps of dried meat, which he 'wolfed', naturally. His job didn't allow for hunting.

Then, an odd thing:

Twenty-five hours or almost two-thirds of the way into the trek, the wolf bitch which Lardis had seen with the changeling overtook them. He recognized her from her pure white, extraordinarily bushy eyebrows. She carried something in her dripping mouth, which she put down on approaching their guide. Then the two wolves went through a careful recognition ritual, following which she sat down with the other a while. Peder Szekarly tossed meat, which she gratefully accepted.

But Lardis was more interested in the item she'd carried in her mouth: a grenade, from The Dweller's armoury in the garden. Lardis knew what it was well enough; there'd been several left over from the battle four years ago; devastating devices, he'd wanted nothing to do with them. Aye, for there are weapons and there are weapons. A shotgun is controllable until the moment you pull the trigger, but one of these . . .?

Only arm it . . . and from then on, no way to change your mind. The rest was out of your hands – indeed it must be out of your hands, and as quickly as possible! What The Dweller's bitch would want with such a thing was a mystery, but as far as Lardis was concerned she was welcome to it. And in a little while she gathered it up in her mouth again, and set off east as before.

Then –

– Six more hours of trekking, followed by a break (all too brief) before the next incident: a small, unequal dispute. But long before that the beacon of the sphere Gate was already making itself visible from time to time in the east. At first, as the distance between gradually narrowed down, it was the merest firefly glimmer; later it became a weird glow-worm radiation – light without heat – in the shadows of the barrier range where eastern foothills met boulder plains to merge into Starside's blue-tinged moonscape.

As for the dispute:

This came where Lardis wanted to leave the pine-clad margin and climb diagonally towards the saddles between the high peaks: his escape route into Sunside, in the event a bolthole should become necessary. Their wolf guide thought differently, however; he had been told to stick to the timber-line and head for the ball of glaring white light close to the great pass, and he didn't intend straying from his duty. So that when the grey brother simply refused to change his tack ... that was the end of the unspoken argument. But in any case (Lardis consoled himself), the way up had looked pretty rough going just there. And so the four men followed on behind their lupine guide as before, except that now they were constantly on the lookout for easy climbing.

They found it an hour later, just as a parting of the ways became absolutely necessary. For if indeed the Wamphyri were still abroad and active in the vicinity of the Gate, then from this point forward it would be madness to remain too far Starside of the peaks.

Climbing along an easy diagonal fault towards a system of crags, saddles and flat-topped plateaux, the four waved a farewell to their guide. For his part he simply watched them out of view, whined a little deep in his throat, finally put them out of mind and headed east ...

Lardis and his colleagues took an hour to climb to the flat summits, a little longer to rest from their labours, then set off again in the direction of the great pass. The ground was unknown to them but the going was fairly easy. On those rare occasions when they caught a glimpse of the southern horizon between the peaks, it was a faint crack of amethyst streaked with silver. Three more hours and the silver would turn to gold.

Sunup, soon, and Lardis should be feeling happier. But he wasn't. Coursing through his veins, the blood of his unknown seer forefather was warning him of ominous times ahead . . .

Three hours later it started to rain; the way soon became slippery and precarious; Lardis deemed it dangerous to proceed. After their prodigious trek, they had reached a spot some four to five miles south-west of the Gate and now looked down on it from a vantage point in the high jumbles. Behind them, a promising looking pass wound between the peaks and presumably down to Sunside. And the sky in the south was brightening, however marginally, from minute to minute.

Lardis and his three huddled beneath the groping branches of a wind-blasted, grotesquely malformed tree until the rain stopped. And now their view of Starside and the glaring hell-lands Gate was that much clearer. Some miles east, the plains were heaped with the strange stumps and tumuli of tumbled Wamphyri stacks – Wenstack, once Volse Pinescu's place; the mad Lord Lesk's shattered Glutstack; sprawling, hugely humped sections of Shaithistack; the acromegalic Fess Ferenc's exploded Grosstack; the lesser Lord Grigis's Gougestack; Lascula Longtooth's Fangstack, and several more. Indeed, all of the great aeries of the Wamphyri, lying prone on the plains where they had fallen.

All save one. Karenstack.

But no lights in Karenstack's kilometre-high windows now, no smoke going up from its chimneys, no sinister motion behind its plateau battlements or in its launching bays. For the moment it was . . . inert. But not quiescent.

Looking at it, Lardis shivered and felt the blood of his forefather stirring. Like a vision out of some future time, he watched the high windows come blazing into life, smoke start to belch from the chimneys, flyers cruising in the updrafts about the bays, where they queued for landings.

Then, as quickly as it had come, the vision passed, leaving Lardis to shiver again, breathe again, and remember again his vow . . .

'What now?' Andrei Romani grunted, but on a rising note. His attention was riveted on the Gate.

'Eh?' Lardis was drawn from his reverie.

'Fires!' Peder Szekarly gasped. His young eyes were that much sharper, keener. 'And some movement down there, close to the Gate. See, the sudden blazing up casts shadows. But things that big . . . can only be warriors!'

'The Wamphyri are camped there, aye,' Lardis's eyes had narrowed under the frowning overhang of his brow. 'The Lords, their flyers, their warriors. But why are they leaving it so late? Sunup is coming. They should be heading for Karenstack, before the first rays strike through the great pass. What's their business down there, so close to the sphere Gate?' He screwed up his eyes, vainly trying to make out those details which distance had forbidden them. Vainly, and perhaps mercifully, too.

'Look!' Kirk Lisescu's voice was no more than a tremor in the gradually brightening air. They saw where he pointed: the timber-line some hundreds of feet below their vantage point, but full of motion now as The Dweller's entire wolf pack came bounding in a silent flood up through the trees! They headed for the high crags, headed west, headed in any direction as long as it was away from the Gate, the Wamphyri, and their bonfires!

'Now what –?' Andrei began – but Lardis grasped his arm and shut him off.

'*Get down!*' Lardis gasped, hurling himself out from under the tree's sparse branches and diving behind upthrusting crags. The seer in him had surfaced at last; he knew that whatever was coming . . . was already on its way!

As a single, brilliant, prolonged flash of lightning lit the peaks, so Andrei and Kirk joined Lardis where he crouched down, hugging the naked rock. And as thunder played a booming, lingering drum-roll across the sky, so the three heard Peder Szekarly's croaked question: 'But what is it?' Peder had been the last to leave the gnarled tree; he made no attempt to seek cover; he stood trembling, looking down on Starside through a jagged gap in the rocks.

From where Lardis crouched, he couldn't see Peder, didn't know that his young friend stood exposed. 'I don't know what it is,' he finally answered, 'but I saw it – felt it – like a burst of brilliant light, searing my eyes, my soul!'

'The lightning?' Peder didn't understand.

At last Lardis looked up and saw him standing there, and knew that the *thing* of his premonition, whatever, was almost upon them! 'Peder, *get down!*' he cried.

Too late.

Down on Starside's boulder plain, the sphere Gate disappeared in a LIGHT which ate it in a moment, a light to sear a man's eyes, his soul, as Lardis had said. But it was much more than that, more powerful than that, more terrible than that. In the smallest fraction of a second it leaped the gap between and shone on Peder. Only for a moment, but long enough. Smoke leapt from him. He screamed, clutched at his face, tottered back away from the gap in the rocks. Even as he stumbled, a giant's hand seemed to slap at him, hurling him down!

In the next moment there commenced such a howling of torn earth, riven rock, crazed winds ... it was like the combined hissing, mewling, and bellowing of every warrior the Wamphyri had ever spawned! And as the sky turned red over Starside and the frightened clouds went scurrying, so Lardis looked out – because he *had* to know, *had* to see.

And *what* he saw ... !

It was as if something of the hell-lands themselves had erupted through the sphere Gate. Which was as close to the truth as Lardis or anyone else might ever guess, except perhaps a handful of men a universe away, who knew the truth in its entirety.

For the Gate itself was no longer visible, only a mighty mushroom of frothy white and dirty grey, shot through with red and orange fires, boiling for the sky. Already its billowing dome towered high as the mountains, and even now its stem was leaning towards the Icelands, as if bowed down by the weight of its roiling head.

Lardis's jaw fell open; he mouthed unheard, unremembered things into the warm wind off Starside, that demon breath which whipped his hair back and hurled hot grit in his face. And as the furnace blast died away he shielded his eyes against the tracery of lightnings that leaped and crackled between the incredible mushroom and the boiling earth.

Then, hearing Andrei and Kirk calling to him, he pulled himself together and went to them where they crouched beside Peder. Miraculously, the youth had closed his eyes in the moment of the fireball; though the skin of his face, neck, hands was badly seared, his sight was returning with each passing second. Clutching at his leader's hand, he gasped, 'Lardis, Lardis! It was ... it was –'

'I know,' Lardis nodded. 'It was hell!'

Later, Peder's hair would fall out and his gums and fingernails bleed, and when his face grew new skin it would always be white. But at least he would *seem* to recover, for a while, and be the whole man again. However that might be, he would die six years later, by which time his appearance would be as grey and gnarly as the aspect of an ancient. Nor would there be heirs to survive him . . .

In the wild woods to the west of Settlement, in the pre-dawn silence of sunup, old Jasef Karis had dreamed his last dream and now tried to rouse himself, shake himself awake, stand up. But something was desperately wrong; his arms hurt as if they were cramped, and there was a grinding pain in his chest. It was as much as he could do to open his eyes.

Above him, Jasef saw the oiled skin which Nana had draped over low branches like an awning, to keep the dawn rains from his wrinkled hide. Except he'd rolled to one side in his sleep and so lay uncovered, drenched and shivering. The way he felt – hot on the inside, cold out, yet sweating from the pain of the thing in his chest – he suspected that the dawn light in the green canopy overhead would be the last he'd ever see. It must be the end of him, yes, for he had never felt like this before and didn't much want to feel it again.

But first he must tell someone about his dream. He must tell . . . Nana, of course!

His dream. His dream of –

– *A corpse, smouldering, with its fire-blackened arms flung wide, steaming head thrown back as in the final agony of death, tumbling end over end into a black void shot through with thin neon bars or ribbons of blue, green, and red light; indeed descending or retreating* into this tunnel of streamers. A tortured thing, yes, but dead now from all of its torments and no longer suffering, unknown and unknowable as the weird things of dreams often are. And yet . . . there had been something morbidly familiar about it, so that Jasef had wished he could look closer at that endlessly rotating, silently screaming, scorched and blistered face.

And when his dream had drifted him closer — then Jasef had seen, and finally he had known. Had known who, and believed he also knew what.

After that:

The corpse's gyrating flight into eternity — through this alien continuum of green, blue and crimson bars — had speeded up, leaving Jasef behind. But then, in the moment after the thing had sped away and disappeared —

— An explosion of golden light in the distant haze, where the corpse had been! And a rush of golden splinters like living darts, speeding towards Jasef and past him, each blinking out as it escaped out of this unknowable place into other, more real times and places!

That was when the scene had changed:

To Nana's four-year-old twins, wrapped together in a blanket under a tree, with a roof of oiled skins just like Jasef's to keep the rain off. And suddenly — appearing out of nowhere — one of the golden darts, which hovered undecided, first over one twin and then the other. At which the pair stirred in their sleep, which had seemed to decide the matter. Hissing his horror, Jasef had seen the dart lance down, to enter into the head of one of them! Except there was no scar, no blood, nothing but a smile spreading on the face of the sleeping innocent!

And: 'Innocent?' Jasef had wondered, like a memory from some earlier dream, some previous time. 'Still innocent?'

Which was when he had awakened, or tried to, only to discover himself bound by these pains like tight thongs across his chest and limbs. But he knew now that indeed he *was* awake, and also that he must pass on his dream, his vision, while yet he might.

He tried to call out for Nana, and couldn't, for the pain wouldn't let him. His cry came out the merest gasp. Well then, and so he must simply lie here and listen to the first birds calling, and wait until Nana came to him.

But he hoped she wouldn't keep him waiting too long . . .

Only a moment earlier, Nana Kiklu had woken up. But she was some little distance away and so failed to hear Jasef's gasping. There had been a noise – the dull, distant booming of thunder, perhaps? – and a little later one of the twins had come tottering, rubbing at his eyes, on the point of tears. Obviously he'd been nightmaring, or else would not have left his bed for his mother's. Small as they were, Nana's twins preferred sleeping alone.

Pulling him down under her blanket, giving him her warmth, Nana had comforted him: 'Oh, dear! There, there,' and stroked his hair. Then, still half-asleep, she'd automatically fumbled for the small leather strap he wore on his left wrist. It was Nana's way of identifying her babies in the dead of night: Nestor's was a plain band, a simple strip of leather joined with a few strong stitches, while Nathan's band had a half-twist. Now, recognizing the child as he snuggled closer, feeling the pounding of his little heart, she asked:

'What was it, eh?' She hugged him closer still. 'A dream? A bad dream?'

The forest was waking up; the birds were filling the

air with their dawn chorus; light came down in hazy beams through the trees. Sunup, and all was well. And yet ... something felt wrong. It was in Nana's bones: a gnawing ache, a nagging concern. But for what?

'Mama?' The child in her arms was almost back to sleep.

'Yes?'

'My ... my daddy ...' he said. And that was something he'd never said before.

'Shhh!' she said. 'Shhh!' And to herself, perhaps a little bitterly: *Your daddy's on Starside, asleep in the arms of the Lady Karen, where they hide from the light of the new day.*

'Dead,' the child mumbled, where he snuggled to her breast. One word, but such a word! It filled Nana's veins with ice.

'What?' she questioned him. 'Dead? Is something dead?'

'Is he?' came the not-quite-awake question-answer, freezing her blood anew. 'Is he – my daddy dead?'

Nana knew she wouldn't sleep again and so got up. There in the dawn glade she found Jasef Karis sprawled on his back, eyes glazed, dew dripping from his cold nose, and believed she now understood what her small son had tried to tell her. He had not been talking about the daddy he'd never known (and couldn't possibly know), but the old seer, the old mentalist, Jasef.

But far to the east and across the peaks, an omen!

The boiling sky over Starside was black, and the bellies of its clouds flickered red with reflected fires ...

PART TWO:

Looking Further Back, and Scanning Forward

———————

I

This much has been told:

Shaitan, first of the Wamphyri, remembered neither mother nor father, nor yet understood his own genesis. To him it was as if he had simply sprung into being, full grown, with a will but no memories of his own to mention. Following which he had fallen, or been thrown, to earth; but fallen, on this occasion, to 'earth' as opposed to *Earth*. In any event, he discovered himself upon the surface of one of many worlds, in one of the many universes of light. And dimly (and quickly fading in the eye of his mind), he remembered something of . . . of an expulsion.

The world into which he had fallen was in one sense an old world, and in another a new one. Recently it had suffered calamity: a Black Hole, losing most of its mass and deteriorating to a Grey Hole, had likewise fallen out of space and time and settled here, reshaping the planet. But where that had been a calculable disaster, the disaster which was Shaitan would be quite in-calculable.

From him would spring an order of beings whose nature was such as to threaten not one but two worlds, filling the myths and legends of both with dread and uttermost horror. For Shaitan was a vampire.

And yet, when he fell (or was thrown out), he was *not yet* a vampire. That was still to come: a matter of choice, of exercising his own free will, his human curiosity. And this is how it came about . . .

*

Starting into awareness, Shaitan cried out . . .!

It was the shock of consciousness cloaking an intelligence previously bereft, will without knowledge inhabiting a mind wiped clean. And as his cry echoed into silence, so he discovered himself kneeling at the edge of stagnant water, with his naked image mirrored in scummy depths. But seeing that he was beautiful, he was proud.

Standing upright, Shaitan saw that he could walk; and in the twilight of a dim, misty dawn he moved by the edge of the dank, rank waters, which were a swamp. And seeing how dismal and lonely was this world where he had fallen, or into which he had been cast, he assumed himself a sinner and that the place must be his punishment.

Such assumptions defined not only Shaitan's intelligence but also his nature: that he instinctively *understood* such concepts as sin and punishment. And he thought his crime must be that he was beautiful, which was his pride working . . . which was in fact his crime! For he saw beauty as might, and might as right, and right as he willed it to be.

Which was a will he would impose.

So thinking, Shaitan moved away from the rank waters and went to impose his will upon this world. But behind him the mud boiled and spattered, so that he paused to look back where black bubbles came bursting to the surface. And with the parting of the weeds and the scum, Shaitan saw a figure floating up into view.

In its body it was bloated and burned, but its face was almost whole. And in that face was an innocence beyond comprehension. Shaitan knew it for an omen, but of what? He had will; he could wait and discover what would be, or move on, according to his will. Also, he suspected that this thing in the swamp harboured evil; why else would such a blackened, blistered thing be here, in this emerging dawn world? For again it was Shaitan's instinct to know that all things are balanced, and that for any measure of good there may be an equal measure of evil.

For a moment he stood still, as at a crossroads, then ... turned back and knelt again beside the swamp. For his will was that he would know this evil.

He gazed upon a face he had never known, which he would not recall to memory for numberless years, and sensed nothing of moment except that he tempted fate, which he was proud and glad to do. And as the beasts of this dawn world came to the water to drink, and as the mists were drawn up from the swamp, so the Fallen One, Shaitan the Unborn, gazed upon his own future where the weeds anchored it in scum and slime.

In a while the scorched, bloated limbs and trunk of the corpse split open and small black mushrooms clustered there, growing out of the rotting flesh and opening their gilled caps. They released red spores into the twilight before the dawn, which rose up and drifted on the warm reek of the swamp. Shaitan saw the clouds of drifting spores, and of his own free will breathed them into his lungs, the better to know of them ... his last act of any innocence –

– At least in this incarnation.

All of this has been told before. What follows has not been told: it is the tale of Shaitan's travels and travails, his triumphs and torments from this time forwards . . . .

Shaitan travelled east through the foothills of gradually rising mountains. He sought for that thing or those things upon which to impose his will. The swamps had not been to his liking, nor the boggy region between the swamps and the foothills. The creatures of these places, while seeming largely unintelligent, had yet been wary to a fault!

Sunlight had first come streaming, then blasting from the south, where a golden orb had climbed gradually into the sky to commence a low, slow arc eastwards. Its rays had dried out the land around and lured clinging fogs up from the sodden earth. In those places where there was little or no shade, the yellow rays had irritated Shaitan, reddening and roughening his skin.

After that − *forever* after that, in every way − he would always walk in the shadows. And just as he chose to stay on the left-hand side of the mountains, away from the sun, so would he choose a dark and sinistral path through life. He did not know it but he had ever chosen that route, even in worlds before this one.

When Shaitan was thirsty, he drank. The sweet water quenched his thirst but there was no satisfaction in it. When he hungered, he ate grasses, herbs, fruits. They filled him but . . . the hunger remained. Within his body a red spore had taken root, forming the nucleus of that which had hungers of its own.

He was unclothed but unashamed. Knowing that he was beautiful, he would display himself; except he would prefer to make himself known to others of his own design, made more nearly in his mould. For the creatures of the swamps and foothills were other than he was and innocent, so that all of them had fled before him. Therefore, he was unable to impose his will upon them, because of their innocence.

And so Shaitan journeyed east across a land where the northern sky was dark blue to black and full of the flicker of stars and the cold weave of weird auroras; but always in the south the golden orb of the sun blazed perilously in the pale blue heavens, so that he must keep himself to the shadows in order not to be burned. And he called all of the land lying to the south of the foothills 'Sunside', despising it greatly, and all the land to the north 'Starside', claiming it for his own. And where finally the foothills grew into mountains like a wall on his right hand, shutting out the sun's harmful rays, there Shaitan discovered creatures which were not afraid of him but merely curious – at first.

For Shaitan's part, he was likewise curious, even astonished. These creatures were not human, yet seemed full of an almost-human purpose and intelligence. They communicated among themselves, however witlessly, in a near-inaudible range which Shaitan sensed rather than heard (for the spore-spawned *Thing* within him was growing, and causing a strange intensification of his five mundane senses . . .). They were small, lowly, weak creatures, which yet commanded aerial flight: a skill far in excess of Shaitan's own meagre, as yet unformed talents.

And when he saw their aerial agility he scowled and was jealous of them; for it seemed to Shaitan that upon a time he too had flown – but with such *authority* and in such *places* as to put all the best efforts of these small creatures to shame! Why, if only he could will it, he would fly again, right here and now, and show them how it was done!

. . . Except, having physical limitations, it was beyond the power of his will. He could *not* will it. Not yet . . .

But while Shaitan envied them, in some small part he also admired these children of the twilight, the night, the velvet darkness, and chose them for his familiars. And when he called out to them with his mind, he saw that they heeded him and hastened to his beck; for they knew that they were his. But these were only the small

93

cousins of greater creatures, who likewise 'heard' Shaitan's mind-calls from the shadows of Starside; and when they also came to swerve and dip about him, crying out with their shrill voices, then his pride was great. For he saw that indeed he had imposed his will upon all the bats of this world.

They were his first conquests; he enjoyed his triumph, however small; other victories would follow in short order.

Always heading east, Shaitan ate sparingly of tasteless berries gathered on the border of the swamps and in the foothills. Where streams trickled down from the heights, there he would drink, though the brackish water was never to his taste. And before sleeping, he had learned to gather in unto himself his bat minions great and small, for their warmth; so that he quickly became expert in their habits.

The smaller bats were insectivores; their greater cousins ... drank blood! Which seemed only right to Shaitan: that small life-forms should sustain themselves by devouring even smaller forms, and greater life-forms by devouring ... why, the very source of life itself! And he believed he now understood his personal dissatisfaction with the common fare of wild animals. Berries, fruits, grasses? What sort of foods were they for one such as him? Water? What was that for a drink? And:

'No, no!' Shaitan now promised himself. 'I'll have no more of them. They are for the hooved beasts and the scuttling foragers of this world. But for me ... the blood is the life!' And within him (however vacuously, instinctively) the as yet embryonic spore-creature exulted, for it was or would be of a like mind and nature.

Beyond the mountains the sun sank down; the last yellow glints vanished even from the highest peaks; the stars shone that much brighter in the north and spread themselves like a sprinkling of jewels all across the domed vault of the sky. A breathless moon raced on high, begging of the wild ones in the mountains their adulation. Eerie wolf voices echoed up into the night of Starside, and Shaitan was impressed by the howling of the hunting packs.

And again he reached out his growing vampire awareness to contact and impose his will upon them, even as he had instructed the bats. Except these creatures shied from such contact. For while they were untamed, still they were of a high order of organized intelligence – far higher than the bats – and suspicious; and anyway they had their own leaders, who were jealous of their sovereignty.

'Dogs!' Shaitan called them then, snarling his frustration at them and abusing them with his mind-voice. Which was why (in this world at least), total domination of the wolves by the Wamphyri never came to pass. Later generations of vampires, all springing from Shaitan, might occasionally produce a Lord who would master or befriend this or that lone wolf, but in the main the grey brothers would retain their lupine integrity . . .

Then, three hundred miles along the north-western fringe of the barrier range of mountains, there Shaitan came across his first tribe of men or sub-men. Aboriginal even before the advent of the Grey Hole – grey and leathery, cavern-dwelling, slow-moving and -thinking – now, in the seventh century of aftermath, the trogs were grown truly primitive. Highly photophobic, they took to their caves at sunup, came out to hunt at sundown. They lived mainly on the grubs of a species of giant moth with a wingspan wide as a man's hand, on mushrooms, and on small bats which they netted and roasted. But still they were men; they understood and used fire, and had a language of their own. And as such they made perfect subjects for the imposition of Shaitan's will.

This is how it was:

He saw a group of them bring down a tawny mountain cat which had strayed down on to the Starside levels. They netted the animal, clubbed it unconscious, finished the job with bone knives. And as they set about to skin it, so Shaitan emerged from the shadows of a boulder where he had rested, coming upon them suddenly. They saw him and their jaws fell open. For while they were not conscious of their own ugliness, Shaitan's beauty was inescapable.

He stood before them, naked and proud in starshine, and his appearance – springing up out of nowhere like this – was next to magical. Tall and straight, where the trogs were hunched and shambling, smiling in his darkly sardonic way, where they could only gawp and gabble, he was like a ray of light fallen among shadows. Which was entirely contrary to the fact, for he was the Great Corrupter come among innocents.

And as they came forward to examine him, so Shaitan stood still and suffered their timid touchings and awed, astonished exclamations. He listened attentively to their language, for it had dawned on him that his own (as yet largely untried) was very rudimentary, a vague string of sounds left over from ... from when? From what? He could not say, except that he felt his few words to be the fading echoes of many tongues; but he knew that the ability was in him to learn and use all tongues. For he was able, however dimly, to see into the minds of men and creatures alike, from which it is the very smallest step to tie pictures to the spoken words.

'It is un-man!' one of the trogs reported of Shaitan to his companions. 'Its skin is soft, pale, easily broken.'

'Its eyes are blue, not yellow,' another pointed out. 'Yet they see in the dark like ours.'

'Blue, yes,' grunted a third. 'But in their cores . . . is that a fire burning behind them? From time to time, his eyes burn!'

'He is . . . a man!' said the first. 'Not unlike the men beyond the mountains, who live in the light – and yet, not like them.'

And another, perhaps wiser trog desired to know: 'But is he a friend?'

Shaitan's guile was great; first he would be friend, then master. 'I am what I am,' he told them, 'and I have come to show you the way.'

They shambled back from him, in awe of their own language slipping so easily from Shaitan's lips. But in a little while the wise one told him: 'We know all of the ways. We are born, we wax, we hunt and forage for food, we make young ones. Then we die and leave our young to do as we have done. These are the ways.'

At which Shaitan smiled and nodded. 'But there are other ways,' he told them. And from within, for the first time, he heard a voice which was not his voice, saying: *These shall be yours!* The voice of his conscience (or lack of it), or of something else? At any rate, Shaitan was not troubled. But seeing the mountain cat lying there red and gleaming and shorn of its skin did trouble him. And again, as from within: *The blood is the life!*

And taking a knife from one of the trogs, he cut himself a portion from the hind leg of the slaughtered beast and squatted down to eat his fill. And as the trogs gathered round him, one of them said: 'See, he eats his meat raw!'

And another: 'His smile is beautiful!'

And a third, the one who had made previous mention of Shaitan's eyes: 'And where is the blue of his eyes now? Gone, as if the blood of the beast had flowed into them!'

Which was true in more ways than one . . .

Shaitan lived a while with the trogs and learned their ways. They showed him those cavern mushrooms which were edible, but he would not eat them. They showed him those that were deadly poison, which he *must* not eat. And later, taking meat with the tribal elder (the wise one of the first meeting, who was wary of him and his new ways), Shaitan put what he had learned to use. The wise one died in agony, and Shaitan took his place.

The tribe was small, its people ugly of form and countenance, its caverns smoky and full of stenches. Shaitan quickly became disenchanted. He would instruct these people in . . . oh, in diverse ways, but their capacity for learning was small. He would open their eyes, take away their childlike innocence and replace it with . . . what? Again he was not sure, except that he desired to impose his will. But to what end? Existence with the sub-men was severely limited and limiting.

Shaitan was full of vice. He had a man's passions, lusts, desires; and all enhanced, multiplied by the developing thing within him. He detested the trog women, yet gathered together a harem of all their ripest. When an enraged young male protested the theft of his prospective mate, Shaitan castrated him and made him the eunuch overseer of his carnal chambers. When a group of trogs rose up against him to kill him, he hid in a cave where he trembled and sweated . . . and his sweat formed a mist that hid him from view and frightened his vengeful enemies away. They ran off to other tribes, spreading Shaitan's legend abroad.

He practised arts which were instinct in him, for he knew that he was corrupt in all his parts. And bleeding himself with ticks, he used them to contaminate the storehouses of the trogs until their food seethed with his evil. More of the sub-men ran off, while yet they were unblemished. As for those who stayed: they were sick now in mind and body and called Shaitan master, and followed in his footsteps. Of all Wamphyri thralls, they were the first.

Shaitan planted seed in his women and several brought forth. Such offspring as were produced were hideous, scarlet-eyed, shrieking ... and hungry. They suckled blood from their mothers' paps and grew too fast. And their own mothers smothered them, all but one which Shaitan ate ... Until finally he had had enough of the cave-dwellers, for he knew that there was flesh in this world other than the lowly flesh of trogs.

And always his parasite guided him, living on his blood as he lived on the blood of others. It was a very subtle symbiosis, however, so that except in Shaitan's darkest dreams and certain rare waking moments, he believed he was the sole author of his affairs and master of his own will and destiny. But ... he could never be sure. And from that time forward the question of free will, self-determination, and all connected theories of integrity of spirit, became matters of vast importance to Shaitan, even assuming dimensions of obsession in him. In him, and in all subsequent vampires ...

Shaitan remembered how, in his first meeting with the trogs, they had likened him to men on the other side of the barrier mountains. Now (having almost forgotten the irritation of the sun's golden rays, and with only one way to test for a recurrence of the problem), he determined the conquest of Sunside. But it would be subtle, as were all his works. First he would approach the Sunsiders as a friend, and later as their master. Thus it would be as it had been with the trogs.

So thought Shaitan . . .

Leaving his trog thralls behind to fend for themselves, he climbed the mountains diagonally, heading east as always. He climbed at sunup but was shielded from the sun by the wall of the mountains. Still the sky's brightness troubled him and the light hurt his vampire eyes, so that he wondered if all of this world's creatures were photophobic, himself included. But high over the treeline and into the peaks, he saw great birds soaring on high, which were not bothered by the sun. They were birds of prey, kites, which scoured the land for food in the last rays of the sun. Also, there were great shaggy goats in the peaks, which had no fear of the light, and likewise small creatures in the coarse grasses and heather.

Shaitan shrugged. Well, he would put his theories to the test soon enough; indeed, he might even impose his will upon the sun! (At which the spore-grown vampire inside him shrank down and was small, for in this matter Shaitan was *too* wilful and his vampire could neither guide nor control him. Immature in its own right, it must simply go along with him.) While for his part Shaitan felt merely uneasy, as a result of his parasite's concern.

As fate would have it, he crested the mountains in that hour when all that remained of the sun was a spoked wheel of pink and yellow light fanning the southern horizon, and so felt no discomfort. And the gradually developing thing inside Shaitan, which was now irreversibly part of him, relaxed somewhat. For after all, it could feel the power of its host and knew that he was strong.

And as twilight turned to night, Shaitan saw the

flickering fires of hunters where they camped on the flank of the mountains. While down on the Sunside levels, the glowing fires of their camps and settlements lit the night in all directions, as far as his eyes could see. Their tribes were legion!

And in his heart Shaitan was glad, believing that at last he had found true men upon whom to impose his will ...

The Sunsiders as a race of men were still recovering from the Grey Hole's holocaust, which had reshaped their 'Earth', realigned its orbit, and redesigned its geological features. They were recovering from earthquakes and tidal waves, from seasons of torrential rains and whirlwinds of black frozen ash (which in another world might well have been termed 'nuclear winters'), and from other seasons which had baked half of the planet to a desert while the other half lay cold and wasted, mainly under frozen oceans. But as a race they were recovering, and gradually rebuilding their decimated numbers.

Upon a time: 'Earth' had had continents, oceans, islands, seasons of winds, sun, rains, snow. It had species galore, and a quarter billion of people. They had the wheel, used fire and sails, experimented with rudimentary medicines and coarse chemistry. While gunpowder had not yet been discovered, still they understood the basic elements of the forge and of metalworking; they had metal tools, and the crossbow for hunting. And all in all theirs had seemed a bright future, whose explorers sailed out across the seas in wooden ships to seek new lands.

But that was before the Grey Hole. And now, seven hundred or more years later, in the time of Shaitan? This is what the Sunsiders – less than thirty thousand of them now – knew of their world:

That it had been ravaged of most of its species along with its peoples, and might well be considered dead except in that temperate zone whose spine was the barrier range of mountains between Sunside and Starside. And in their legends (which were confused and contradictory, because the written form of their language had been at best basic and was lost in the aftermath, so that history had become a thing passed down immemorially by word of mouth), the scourge which had visited itself upon them to destroy their world had become synonymous with a forbidden place on Starside known only as 'the Gate to the hell-lands'.

And the legend was this: that one night a strange 'white sun' had appeared in the southern skies ... a portent of terrible times in the offing!

At first it had seemed to move slowly, like a comet, then more swiftly, and finally in a rush like a bar of white light where it speared down out of space to glance off the moon and blaze across the surface of the world! But as it fell to earth so it shimmered and shrank, until it skimmed across the land like a huge flat stone bouncing on water; and at last it thudded down into a crater of its own making, on a world gone mad by reason of its coming. Not a shooting star or a comet, no, but a *Force* far greater than these whose occurrence in Nature is mercifully rare: a Black Hole which had eaten itself, until only the event horizon remained. A Grey Hole now, and a bridge between universes.

In any case, such science was beyond the people of this world. To the handful of stumbling, stunned survivors it was sufficient – and more than sufficient – that a deadly white sun had fallen out of the sky and destroyed everything they had known, leaving them and their descendants to live through a sort of hell for more than two and a half centuries. Until eventually, as the planet's orbit stabilized and its climates polarized — however dramatically — all that was left of humanity dwelled as best they might in the narrow belts of forest and on the plains south of the great barrier range, and in the southern flanks of the mountains themselves.

And now, whenever hunters climbed those mountains in their central region, or strayed through the great pass to Starside's boulder plains, they saw how an awful revenant of the cataclysm yet survived to reinforce its legend: a crater socket with its sunken, blind white eye glaring up and out, as if some fallen demon lay paralysed, unblinking, and wondering at his lot. And the gaze of his cold, dead white eye was like a beacon, a forbidding pharos, not guiding but warning souls away . . .

A demon, yes, why not? Something from hell, anyway. Something which had brought hell here with it.

And in the legends there was also the story of a wandering adventurer, first through the pass after those turbulent centuries of stabilization, who climbed down to the mainly buried sphere of white light to touch it . . . and was never seen again. For it had opened like a Gate to take him into hell.

Which was why the place had been named like that and why it was now forbidden, along with all of those desolate lands lying north of the mountains: the boulder plains, and further east a region of dizzily rearing stacks of volcanic stone, like vast spears of rock rising to rival the barrier range itself; and beyond the northernmost horizon, sending up a blue shimmer and sheen under the diamond stars and weirdly writhing auroras, the bitterly frozen Icelands.

All of these places, forbidding and forbidden. But in any case, who would want to go there? Nothing lived there; nothing *could* live there, but bats in the caves, and wolves up in the peaks and passes over Starside, and certain lesser creatures. Surely it was no fit habitation for men. Not for any sort of men.

Not yet, anyway . . .

Shaitan came across his first true men by the light of their campfire, and saw that they were clad in the furs and skins of animals. There were three of them and they saw him at the same time, saw also that he was naked; which was just as well for Shaitan, for they were hunters. If he had clothed himself and come upon them suddenly like that . . . with his height, he could have been mistaken for a great bear. As it was he found himself covered by their crossbows as they scrambled to their feet and turned more fully towards him. But then:

'A man!' one of them grunted, frowning.

And: 'An idiot!' said another. 'I very nearly put a bolt in him!'

Shaitan read their expressions, their lips, in part their minds. Their words fitted readily with everything else he saw, so that he understood much of their language from the start. As they came forward to peer at him in the firelight, the last of them queried nervously, 'A madman? Do you think so?'

And the second: 'What else? Up here in the night on his own, naked under the stars.' And to Shaitan, coldly, 'Who are you?'

Smiling his sardonic smile, he answered, 'I am what I am.'

'And your name?'

'Shaitan!' Because finally he remembered it.

'Well, Shaitan,' the first of the three chuckled, but not unkindly, 'you'll excuse me for saying so, but it seems to me you're a bit daft!'

'You think I'm . . . demented?' He looked at them, and down at himself. 'But if I am mad – a harmless idiot – then why do you point your weapons?'

At that the second man again spoke up, saying: 'Because "idiot" and "harmless" don't necessarily coincide, that's why. Down on the levels, in the camp of Heinar Hagi, we've one such "idiot" who works for his living – and Janni Nunov lugs boulders which I can't even budge!'

Moving artlessly so as to disarm them, Shaitan approached their fire, hunched down and fed a stick to the fitful flames. The three put up their weapons and approached him again, and he pretended not to study them where he warmed his hands. It seemed they had no leader with them but were equals. One was short, squat and bearded; the next of medium height, sturdy, heavy-jawed; the last young and wiry, whose mind seemed entirely innocent. But since they likewise studied him, Shaitan kept his scarlet eyes half-shuttered and gazed mainly into the fire. The red would be taken for reflected firelight.

And finally the squat one, Dezmir Babeni, mused, 'You're soft and pale, whoever you are! For all that you're a big 'un and strong, you haven't known much of hard work. What's your tribe?'

Shaitan shook his head.

The muscular, prognathous Klaus Luncani wanted to know: 'Why are you naked? Were you set upon? Ah, there are too many wild ones in the mountains these days, loners who'd kill a man just for his good leather belt!'

Again Shaitan shook his head, and shrugged.

But the young and wiry one, Vidra Gogosita, opened a pack and took out a long leather jacket, which he draped over Shaitan's shoulders by the fire. It was an old jacket but comfortable. And he said, 'The nights are cold. A man – even a fool – shouldn't go naked on the hillside!'

And Shaitan smiled and nodded, and thought: *Of the three, he alone shall live – but only as my thrall. For he is sensitive, wherefore his agonies in my service will be that much sharper! A 'fool' has willed it . . . so be it!* But out loud he said, 'I thank you. But of myself . . . I wish I could tell you more. Alas, I can't remember.' It was mainly the truth.

'Set upon, aye,' Klaus Luncani grunted, as if it were now decided beyond all doubt. 'By outcasts in the mountains. Clubbed on the head, all memory flown. Stole his clothes, they did. A man who hunts alone risks much!'

Dezmir Babeni moved closer, went to touch Shaitan's head, perhaps discover a wound there. Shaitan put up a hand to ward him off. 'No! There is . . . a pain.'

Dezmir nodded, and left it at that.

The matter seemed to be settled: Shaitan was obviously the victim of thieves. He was lucky they'd spared his life.

'Well, and Dezmir's right about one thing,' Klaus Luncani offered Shaitan a chunk of cheese and a bit of coarse bread. 'You certainly *look* big and strong enough! You'll live, I'm sure.'

Alas, but you *won't,* Shaitan thought, looking at the food in Luncani's outstretched hand. It was execrable stuff and he shook his head. 'I . . . I killed a creature,' he lied, 'for its flesh. It wasn't long ago. I'm not hungry.'

'A creature?' This was young Vidra Gogosita.

'With horns, curving back. Like this.' And Shaitan used his long slender hands to demonstrate. 'A small one, but sweet . . .' *Though you will be far sweeter.*

'A goat,' said Dezmir Babeni. 'A kid, anyway. Huh! Why, it seems he's had better luck than all of us together!'

'A . . . goat, yes,' Shaitan slowly repeated him, with a hand to his forehead, to indicate gradually returning memory.

'It'll all come back in time,' said Klaus Luncani, making a bed for himself in a triangle of boulders a short distance from the fire. 'But listen, we've been hard at it for most of the day – though there's only a couple of piglets in our bag to prove it! So now we'll catch a little sleep. A sight safer than climbing in the dark, for sure! A few hours, that's all, until the moon's up again; then it's back down to the levels and the camp of our leader, Heinar Hagi.'

Dezmir Babeni took it up. 'You'd do well to come with us, Shaitan, as you've nothing better in mind. Oh, you're a strange one, to be sure: tall and pale, with your brains all shaken up in that handsome head of yours. No memory to mention, nor even a tribe to claim you. But the Szgany Hagi have taken in a few strays in their time. So . . . what do you say?'

Shaitan looked up at him, and in that same moment Babeni was struck by the way the fire lit in his eyes. But Shaitan was quick to turn away again, gazing into the glowing embers as before. And: 'Get your sleep, all of you,' he told them. 'I shall likewise sleep. And later . . . we'll see what we'll see.'

Babeni shrugged, walked off a little way and trampled a bed of bracken for himself; he lay down, pulled a blanket over his lower half, snorted once or twice and fell silent. In his nest of boulders, Klaus Luncani was already snoring. But the youngest of the three, Vidra Gogosita, simply seated himself by the fire, close to Shaitan.

'I'll not sleep,' he said, 'but keep watch. It's my turn. You, however, would do well to get your head down. There's a blanket I can throw over you.'

Shaitan nodded, and in a low voice answered, 'In a little while.'

Aye, in a very little while . . .

Of the rest:

Vidra remembered very little, and all of it ill-defined, unclear in a mind which had rapidly succumbed to the hypnotic allure of Shaitan. He remembered talking to the — man? — and the feeling of drowsiness, lethargy that had crept over his limbs, his mind, his will.

There was something about a face (but not Shaitan's handsome face, surely?) which had changed hideously to a bestial, nightmare mask with the forked tongue and dripping fangs of a snake. The face's approach . . . a blowhole stench, of sulphur? . . . and a pain, like the hot sting of a wasp where the artery pulsed in Vidra's neck . . . no, *two* wasps, stinging him there, inches apart. And Shaitan's crooning, and his kisses where he sought to suck the stings from —

Vidra came awake with a small cry, seemingly in answer to some other's cry. He was cold and cramped in all his limbs, his neck stiff and caked with a great scab . . . of blood? His dream!

. . . Not a dream?

He lurched to his feet, stumbling in the ashes at the edge of the fire. But where was his strength? He was dizzy, staggering, weak as water! And tangibly present in his mind — indeed visibly present, burning behind the night scenes which his eyes showed to him — were *other* eyes, like malignant crimson scars on his soul. Which was precisely what they were. And something was looking at him through those windows on his mind, smiling at him sardonically, leering at him.

The moon was up, arcing over the mountains; the fire was out except in its heart; a ground mist lay all about, writhing where it lapped the scrubby hillside, filled the small hollows, twined in the roots of bracken and heather. No owls hooted, nor wolves sang, nor any earthly or human sounds at all. But in the shadows over there . . . something slobbered!

That was where Dezmir had made a bed in the bracken, and Vidra lurched in that direction. But here on his right, the triangle of boulders which sheltered Klaus and gave him protection; his legs were sticking out even now, where the mist lapped about them. Vidra stooped, went to grab Klaus's ankle and shake him awake. Before he could do so, the extended foot gave a massive start, trembled violently, flopped loosely and was still.

Vidra's flesh crept. He jerked upright, took two staggering paces down the length of Klaus's prone body to the cluster of boulders, leaned on them to look down on his sleeping friend — and saw that he wasn't merely sleeping. Not any longer.

For someone or something had taken a huge and impossibly heavy rock, levered it up over the top of the three embedded stones, and let it fall squarely on Klaus's face! Its roughly circular rim entirely obscured the area where his head would be, and in the flooding moonlight it seemed that a tarry substance seeped or was squeezed out from beneath. But Vidra Gogosita knew that the moonlight lied: it wasn't black but red.

Scarcely in control of his limbs — choking, unable to cry out by reason of his gulping, the dryness of his throat — the youth went flailing through the sentient mist to where Dezmir Babeni lay in the bracken. 'Dezmir!' he finally forced a warning croak. 'Dez . . .

'. . . mir?'

For Dezmir's blanket had been thrown aside, and over him now Vidra's own long jacket, which his mother had begged him to bring with him. Except the jacket seemed alive, humped and mobile, fluttering like some huge black bat fallen to earth!

Vidra reeled, cried out! And the jacket, and what it contained, flowed upright, stood up and faced him. Shaitan – but no longer handsome, indeed barely human – his monstrous metamorphic face scarlet from gorged blood! And the slimy, alien mist pouring off him like sweat, and billowing out from under his borrowed leather jacket!

Then ... Shaitan's talon of a hand reaching out to grip the youth's arm and steady him, and Vidra knowing for certain the source of those eyes in his mind; knowing, too, the terrible truth of his dream. After that: what else could he do but crumple to his knees before his new master? In any case, his legs no longer had the strength to hold him up. No, for the *strength* would come later.

And Shaitan's burning eyes gazing down upon him, and the monster's voice a clotted gurgle as he said, 'My ways may seem very strange at first, though in the end you'll gladly embrace them. Only tell me, did I hear you calling for Dezmir Babeni? Well, his blood is still hot, vital, if you are ... ready for that?'

And then, with perhaps a trace of disappointment, 'Ah, a pity. For I see that you are not ...'

The climb down to Sunside's levels on the fringe of the forest took four hours. By then most of the Szgany Hagi's lesser campfires were out, and many of the folk asleep in their makeshift tents of animal hide. But the night watch kept a central fire blazing, and when they were not patrolling the perimeter they gathered beside it to talk. There was, too, a little lamplight issuing from the flap doors of several of the larger tents.

Typically, the tents of the single men formed an evenly spaced outer perimeter: a barrier against intruders or marauders, though in these settled times that was unlikely. A few animals were tethered inside this loose outer circle, or left to graze in corrals roped off between the trees. The larger, family tents stood towards the middle of the camp, with the fire marking the very centre.

There were several carts, a few of which were covered over with stretched skins, the largest being Heinar Hagi's caravan. Though the trails around the borders of the tribe's foothills and forest territories were scarcely better than rutted tracks, still it seemed only decent and right to Heinar – as leader or 'king' of his three-hundred-strong band – to jolt along behind snorting beasts rather than haul a small cart or travois like the rest.

As for 'beating the bounds' of his enclave: it was either that or have some other Szgany group move in and settle on it. Only by constantly measuring his acreage, patrolling its borders, and every mile or so posting his sigil (a highly stylized face, with a turned down mouth and one eye painted over with a black patch), could Heinar ever hope to hold on to it for his and the tribe's descendants. The perimeter of these territories was perhaps thirty-six miles, all of which Heinar guarded jealously. It was the same for most bands and tribes, so that in this respect they had been travellers – indeed, Szgany – right from the new beginning.

But not all of the tribe of Heinar Hagi was on the move. Eastward, in honeycombed cliffs in the roots of the mountains, were caves which housed almost a third of his people. They had sheltered there ever since the holocaust, and there would stay. Likewise in the south, at the edge of the forest where it gave way to grasslands and finally the desert: fifty pioneers of the Szgany Hagi, tending their crops where they'd built permanent homes among the trees. Since both of these locations were on Heinar's roughly triangular route, he looked forward eagerly to sojourning first in the woodlands camp, then at the caves.

As his people grew and expanded, so they would build more towns around the perimeter of Heinar's lands, safely enclosing them. Finally he might be able to settle and live out the rest of his days untroubled by thoughts of land-thieves – except by then Heinar himself would likely be no more, but his sons and their sons would reap the benefits.

These were his thoughts; and at a hundred campfires large and small, east and west all along the Sunside flank of the barrier range, a hundred leaders just like him thought them alike. And he sat at the central fire, chatting with members of the night watch, with a brew of herb tea simmering on its tripod.

Then, close by, on the perimeter . . .

. . . The familiar half-growl, half-cough of a wolf! – one of the camp's wolves, it must be. None of the wild grey ones would ever stray so close to such a large body of men. Heinar looked up, his brow furrowing, his good eye glinting in firelight. His men picked up their crossbows; the fire crackled; they all listened to the night.

There came fresh sounds: of a voice raised in challenge, and of another answering with a gasp, a sob! Heinar believed he knew that second voice. He started to his feet and snapped, 'Who's still out?'

'The lads you sent into the forest and down to the river, all are safely back,' one of his men answered. 'If these are ours at all, they can only be Klaus, Dezmir and Vidra.'

'Aye,' Heinar gave a curt nod of agreement. 'That was Vidra's voice just then, for sure. But what ails the lad?' No one ventured to answer; they would find out soon enough.

A party of three entered the clearing: a watchman with his wolf, ushering two others ahead of him. The two came stumbling, dishevelled, apparently exhausted. Heinar recognized only one of them – Vidra Gogosita.

'Heinar!' the youth cried. 'Heinar!'

'What is it?' Heinar demanded, as Vidra all but collapsed in his arms. 'What's happened? Where's Klaus and Dezmir? And who's this?'

'Klaus ... Dezmir ...' Vidra babbled unashamedly. 'Both ... both of them ... dead! In the hills.'

'*What?*' Heinar gasped. 'Dead, you say? How?'

'We were ... were set upon, ambushed!' Vidra appeared to make an effort, pulled himself together. 'Outlaws! They came out of the twilight. And I'd be dead too, if not ... if not for ... for *this* one. He ... *fought* them off, saved my life. His name is ... is ... *is* ...' But he could say no more; his eyes rolled up; he sagged in Heinar's arms.

The stranger swayed, began to topple. Eager hands caught him, lowered him to a prone position. The fire lit strangely in his eyes as they slowly closed. And his voice was a sigh, trailing into silence as he told them:

'My name ... is Shaitan.'

II

At first, all had been chaos in the camp of Heinar Hagi.

For almost an hour Heinar and his men, and various women, had chased about, doing their best to care for and see to the immediate needs of young Vidra Gogosita and the stranger he'd brought into the camp, the man called Shaitan.

Vidra's mother, the slender but voluble widow Gogosita, had been first on the scene; she had been awake, waiting in her small tent for her only son's return from the mountains. Hearing something of the excitement, and sensing the sudden tension, the horror creeping in the night, she'd gone to the campfire of her own accord. And when first she'd seen her boy stretched out like that — such a weeping and wailing! But ... Vidra was alive, merely exhausted and sleeping! And how she'd cradled the youth in her arms then, while the men told her what little they knew of the tale. And the endless blessings she'd heaped on the tall pale stranger who had saved her son's life: Shaitan, who lay there close at hand, as in a coma, absorbing all he could of these people and their ways.

Then they had sent for the grown-up daughter of Dezmir Babeni, lovely Maria; at first she could not accept the fact of her father's death, so that she looked in vain for his face among the men. And finally her grief, strong but silent, when at last she went to sit alone, rock herself and weep. And the wife and sons of Klaus Luncani, all dazed and staggering from the impact of this unexpected, unacceptable news. So that the traditional peace and quiet of the campfire had been quickly transformed into a scene of tragedy, grief, trauma.

No one felt the Szgany Hagi's loss more than Heinar himself. He couldn't face the weeping women; giving instructions for the welfare of the survivors of this atrocity, he retired to his bed. He would be up and about at intervals through the long, forty-hours night, of course, but long before sunup he would lead a search party into the foothills, to recover the bodies of the dead. And if by any chance they should stumble on a party of loners or outcasts up there ... But Heinar knew that the odds were all against it.

Meanwhile, the widow Gogosita had had her son carried to their tent where she watched over him. The badly bruised flesh of his neck was puffy, lacerated, probably infected. His fever was high and he tossed and turned, moaning in his sleep. As for *what* he moaned: they were things of blackest nightmare, resulting no doubt from what he'd experienced in the hills.

At the campfire Shaitan had been made comfortable, a blanket thrown over him, his head propped up on a bundled skin. And Maria Babeni had come to sit beside him, staring at his drawn, handsome face in the flaring of the fire. It seemed to her he should be taken in, given proper shelter, cared for and protected until he was fully recovered. Hadn't he risked his life for the men of the Szgany Hagi? All in vain where her father and Klaus Luncani were concerned ... but at least he had saved young Vidra Gogosita! When the night watch returned she'd have them bring him to her small caravan (hers now, aye, and lonely at that), where she could give him the care he deserved.

Which was exactly what she did.

But most of the camp slept on, with the majority knowing nothing of the night's events; nor would they know until they got up to eat, tend their animals, take turn at watch. Unless something should happen before then, to break the routine.

And the stars turning in their endless wheel, dappling the clearing at the edge of the woods; and high in the mountains a lone wolf howling for his mistress moon, to rise up again and lend him her light for the hunting . . .

As Maria Babeni prepared for bed behind a curtain, she heard Shaitan stirring, then his moan. Making fast her night clothes, she went to him where he had her father's narrow bed at the other end of the caravan. By the light of a wick burning in oil, she saw that his face was pale as ever, with long, dark hair swept back, the colour of a raven's wing, and lips very nearly as red as a girl's. He would be perhaps forty years old (his looks, at least); his proportions perfect, his brow high, intelligent, lordly. For a man, Shaitan was quite beautiful.

And she thought: *Wherever he comes from, he is not Szgany.*

Then Shaitan opened his eyes.

And now there could be no mistaking it: his eyes were red!

Maria gasped where she leaned over him. And quick as her thoughts – just exactly as quick – he grasped her arm, rose up half-way on an elbow . . . then closed his eyes, released her and fell back. And knowing what she had seen, he said, 'My eyes . . . my eyes! They hurt. There's blood in them. Someone struck me there . . .'

'Bloodshot?' The word fell from her lips as if conjured, which it had been, half-way. His eyes were bloodshot? So very evenly?

For a moment, only for a moment, Maria had seen something other than a handsome man. Something hideous lurking behind the beauty. But . . . it could only be the strangeness of the situation: this man in her father's bed, and Maria alone with him in the night. Maria, who for all that she was nineteen years old, had known only her father's close company since the day of her mother's death. And the fact of a new bereavement slowly sinking in. The aftershock; the enormous hole inside of her; the loneliness. Of course she saw shadows where there were none, and phantoms to inhabit them.

He moaned again, tried to sit up, again opened his eyes – but kept them half-shuttered. She helped him, propped him up, said, 'How did . . . how did he die? My father, Dezmir Babeni. He was the short one, bearded, laughing.'

Shaitan avoided the question. 'I didn't see it all,' he answered. 'I only heard their cries, and went to help. But . . . your father?' And glancing around the caravan, as if noticing his whereabouts for the first time: 'Where am I?' His question was so innocent, childlike.

She sat on the edge of his bed and told him everything he desired to know. About the Szgany Hagi, the Szgany in general, herself, her situation – everything. And as his eyes opened more fully (but oh so slowly, so gradually), so Maria's small feelings of anxiety retreated, her ill-formed suspicions fell away, her will was subverted.

His voice was so low – like the rumble of a great cat, deceptively gentle but full of a fierce energy – and fluent despite its as yet alien use of her tongue. And behind every word a hint, a suggestion, an enticement. Shaitan beguiled, entranced, seduced; of course, for he was the great seducer. He seduced with his eyes, his tongue, the lure of his magnet personality, so unlike anything Maria had ever known before. And despite his strangeness, and the strangeness of her own innermost feelings, awakened now for the first time, she was drawn like a moth to the blood-red fire of his eyes.

She knew his fingers were at the fastenings of her night clothes, turning them back, laying her flesh bare; but as if to salve each burning brush of those fingers against her sensitized skin, Shaitan poured forth his balm of words. And his furnace heat enveloped her, spreading into every region of her body. So that she grew hot, so very hot.

Maria felt the perspiration swelling in her pores, forming droplets, trickling from neck and shoulders, breasts and belly. And she heard Shaitan's honeyed voice confirming the sultry oppression of the night, telling her how hot it was, how good to be free of such clammy restrictions as clothes and bed covers.

He had turned back his blankets; he sat up and helped her disrobe entirely; their sweat mingled as he rubbed his body against hers. Maria's breasts were firm and proud, with dark brown buds ... erect, now, where Shaitan stroked her. Before, she'd known only Szgany lads, clumsy buffoons whose hands and faces she'd slapped. But now, when Shaitan stood up, drew off his shirt, stepped from his breeches ... she clung to him and kissed his nipples, and stroked his horn where it steamed and jerked.

'See?' he said. 'My body would know all of you! For while my eyes have observed this softest of soft fruits, and while my hands have touched its perfect skin, still the lips of my probe would test its flesh for succulence. Aye, for I fear it may be bitter, that a worm may have crept into your juicy core, to itch there in the heart of your heat and spoil your flavour. But don't you feel him itching?'

He touched her belly, the cleft in her bush, and her thighs lolled open. And: 'Ah, you see? You seè?' Shaitan's face showed his amaze, and a very little of his lust. 'This dark and secret hole, all unsuspected! That's where he entered, be sure. So let me in, of your own free will, to drown your worm with my cock's wet kiss.'

He entered her in one, long, slow pulse, breaking her without pause and feeling her sweet virgin's blood hot on his bony shaft. And Maria's hunger was such that she might cry aloud for more, but could only gasp and gurgle as he rode to and fro, in and out between her salivating lips.

And for a long, long time Shaitan took Maria in every way he knew and others which he invented, until his lust was sated, however temporarily. And sprawling there lewdly, with the girl all bruised and insensible between his thighs, and his sperm like foam on all her openings, he thought:

These people are clever, yet in many ways they are innocent as trogs. And like the trogs, the Szgany Hagi shall be mine!

It was Shaitan's first major error. His stay with the trogs had lasted for two long years, and little occurring in all that time to tax or stimulate his superior mind and talents; so that in certain respects he had grown lax, and perhaps as naïve as the trogs themselves. But as he would soon discover, the men of Sunside were in no way trogs.

For now, however . . . his excesses with the girl had wearied him. He would join Maria in sleep a while.

Which was his second big mistake . . .

One third of the way into the night, Turgo Zolte was called to his duty watch. Zolte was a big, taciturn man; tough, iron-grey in the eyes, with shoulder-length hair to match. He wore silver earrings, a silver buckle on his belt, silver buttons to fasten his black clothes; like all Sunoider men he jingled when he walked, only more so. Zolte was a loner, not quite an outsider. The Szgany Hagi had accepted him now.

He'd come to them only a year ago, chased out of his own far western band by a chief whose son he'd killed. According to him, it was a fair fight; the other had called him out over a woman, and Turgo had broken his neck. Well, he had the brawn for it, certainly; and since there was no lack of space among the Hagis for big, strong fighting men – so long as they were working men, too – Heinar had let him stay. Since when no one had bothered with Turgo Zolte very much, and he'd kept mainly to himself. But if a man could catch him in the right frame of mind, with a jug of good plum brandy inside him, he might occasionally tell a few wild tales of his latter days along the western reaches. Campfire tales, of bogeymen and beasts. His audience might snort a bit, but none called him a liar.

This night, when Turgo reported to the fire, the tables were turned; the man he relieved was the one with the tale to tell. Turgo heard it out, scowled and narrowed his glinty eyes, finally said, 'You saw all of this? Young Vidra with his neck torn and scabbed? And this stranger – he was pale, you say? Not much of a description!'

The other shrugged. 'What's to describe? A man: tall, pale, with a girl's long soft hands. Somehow, he didn't look Szgany – he was all smooth and unweathered, like he'd lived in a cave all his days. And his eyes were . . . they seemed full of blood!'

'Blood? In his eyes?'

'Exactly! Like he'd been poked in them, or had sand thrown in 'em – which no doubt he had, in the fighting.'

Turgo's own eyes narrowed more yet and he nodded, mainly to himself. And sitting down by the fire, he said, 'Tell me more, everything, but in finer detail. Leave nothing out.'

The telling didn't take very long.

And shortly –

– Heinar Hagi came awake instantly, looked at the earnest face of the man who had given him a shake, grunted and glanced up through an opening in the roof of his caravan at the night sky. He knew the hour at once, from the position of the stars, grunted again and growled, 'Anyway, I was due to be up about now.'

Turgo Zolte wasn't much of a diplomat. He shrugged and said, 'Due or undue, you're up.' And: 'It looks like there's business to attend to, Heinar. Bad business, I fear.'

Heinar threw on his clothes, put on his eye-patch to cover the hole which an eagle had torn in his face when he was just a lad. Teach him to hunt eggs in the heights! 'Business?' He repeated the other. 'You'll be talking about murderers in the hills, right? Aye, we'll be doing what we can – but at sunup. You want to come along, you're welcome. Couldn't it wait?'

Turgo shook his head, stepped down from the caravan into the night, waited for Heinar to join him. 'Not what I've got to say,' he answered. 'Not unless you want to see plague in the camp, spreading through all your people!'

And now Heinar was very much awake. 'What?' he grasped the other's arm. 'Plague?'

Turgo nodded. 'But quiet! Let's not wake the entire camp. Not yet. Now listen, and I'll tell you what I heard from the watch. Except I know it may have been exaggerated. But you were there, so if all tallies . . .' He repeated the story of the watchman. And when he was done:

'Aye, that's the story,' Heinar grunted. 'Blow for blow.'

'Huh!' Turgo returned his grunt. 'Well, and now I've a different story for you . . .'

And after a moment, as they made for the campfire: 'I

121

came from west of here, as you know,' Turgo began, 'out of the tribe and territories of Ygor Ferenc. That's way up at the end of the barrier range, where the hills slump into misted valleys, fens and mire. The swamps are dire: quicksands, mosquitoes, leeches, but the Ferenc's borders fall short of them by a good seventy miles – which to my mind is still too close by far!'

They had reached the fire; the watchmen were out, patrolling the camp's perimeter; Turgo seated himself on a stool and Heinar chose the well-worn branch of a fallen tree. They each took tea, strong and bitter, and eventually Turgo continued.

'Well, about eighteen months ago, some funny things began to happen there on the edge of nowhere. As you'd imagine, they have their share of mountain men up there, much as you do down here: loners who take to the hills, look after themselves, live on their own in the wild. And now and then such a one will come into camp with a beast he's killed, too much meat for one man, and they'll usually make him welcome. There'll be a feast, and brandy to wash it down; the women will dance till sundown; the likely lads will end up fighting . . . and so on. That's how it goes.

'But there in the western reaches, that wasn't always the way it went, not in the last six-month. Some of the mountain men up there in the misty hills where they descend to the valleys and swamps, and even the occasional lone wolf . . . they were suddenly changed, different. Something weird had got into them.

'There were rumours: about men with red eyes, madmen with the lusts of beasts, and wolves that snatched people right off the fringes of their camps and territories! Always by night, or in the light of the moon. It was like an infection, a sickness spreading out of the swamps, and people grew wary of any stranger who might come into their camps at twilight or sundown. But in the Ferenc's camps, or on the march, beating his bounds ... well, as I've said, all of this was rumour. The other camps may have been hit, if the stories were true, but old Ygor was the lucky one. For a while, anyway.

'Then, just before I landed in trouble – Ygor's hot-headed fool of a son, Ymir, forcing me to kill him over a woman's favours and what all – that's when the luck of the Szgany Ferenc ran out. It happened like this:

'I was out with Ygor and maybe a dozen others, beating the bounds just like now. One twilight, we reached this old clearing where we'd make camp. Ygor knew the place well enough: it was about as far west as folks have ever journeyed, except for the loners, of course, who often step where no one else would. Nothing superstitious about that, it's just that west of there the ground's no good for growing things; the water's scummy and the mists are far too frequent. It's like the end of the world! But old Ygor, he likes to beat the ground there anyway, to make sure no one will come down out of the hills and settle on it.

'And there in the clearing, that's where we found Oulio Ionescu – something that looked like Oulio, anyway . . .'

As Turgo paused, so Heinar cast him a sharp glance. 'Eh? Something that looked like him?'

'Give me a chance and I'll explain,' the other held up a restraining hand. And after a moment's thought:

'Oulio was one of these types who'd come into camp for an evening's entertainment. Oh, he liked his own company best, but from time to time got a little too much of it. His parents had been mountain people, too – until an avalanche killed them – and Oulio had a cave up there somewhere. Also, he was known to wander west and trap big lizards in the swamps. See this belt of mine? A bit of Oulio's good leather.

'So, we knew him well. Or thought we did. But this time he was in trouble.

'At first we didn't know what we'd stumbled over. The Oulio we knew was big and wild as they come: clothes all in patches, eyes black as night, hair like a waterfall. And garrulous? He was full to the brim of words that didn't mean much, all spilling out of him because he'd kept them so long bottled up. He played his fiddle like no one I ever heard, drank brandy like water, would dance till he fell. But he danced alone, because he was wary of the women.

'But now? Well, he wouldn't be doing any dancing for a while, for sure.

'How long he'd wandered like that, who knows? But it had slimmed him down a lot. All of his fat was gone, and quite a bit of his skin, too. Why, he was . . . black! Burned black, by the sun, as it turned out. But he was red, too. Red where the skin had peeled from his face and limbs, and red in his eyes. Aye, red as blood. And there he lay, sprawled like a dead man in the clearing, with only the occasional twitch or moan to hint of any life left in him at all.

'We looked after him. We didn't know what had befallen him, but despite all rumours and old wives' tales we cared for him. Even as we're now caring for this stranger . . .'

'Eh?' Heinar gave a start. 'The stranger? But he was here, by the fire!'

'Until Maria Babeni took him in,' Turgo nodded grimly. 'She had him carried to her cart.'

And now Heinar thought that maybe he understood something of what was going on here; for he knew that Turgo had paid one or two small, polite attentions to

Maria, even though the girl hadn't seemed to notice or acknowledge them. But Turgo saw the Hagi's thoughts written plain in his one good eye, and:

'Better let me finish,' he said, 'before you go jumping to any conclusions.'

'Get on with it, then,' Heinar told him.

'Oulio was taken to the tent of one of the younger men, a man who had his young wife with him. There were four couples like that, who'd come along to form the germ of a settlement in the woods to the south, much as you've started a permanent camp south of this place. He and his slip of a wife knew Oulio from other times; they took him in, bathed him, laid him on a clean blanket and rubbed good butter and salt into all of his sore places. By which time it was night.

'As darkness came down in full and the moon came up, so this same young man was called to keep watch. And he left his girl wife tending the much-ravaged Oulio. Ah, but when he came back all those hours later . . .

'. . . Only picture it, only imagine the lad's horror, *to discover his much-ravaged wife!* And Oulio still grinding away at her like a pig; her breasts all bruised and bloodied from his long nails, and the beast they'd cared for using her as worst he could. He'd gagged her, tied her hair to the tent's pole at the floor. But he'd hit her once or twice, too, and broken her nose and jaw, before having her whichever way he fancied. And he'd fancied them all!

'And there stood this young man, at the flap of his tent, and his wife broken like a doll and still being used by this flame-eyed fiend! Worse, Oulio's teeth were like fangs, which he'd stuck in her neck to suck her blood! And as he heard the lad's horrified gasp behind him, so he bit down on the artery and sliced it through!

'He turned his head and glared at the intruder, snarling at him like a wolf! And his face wasn't dissimilar to that of a wolf, except his eyes weren't feral but crimson! Red as the blood which spurted with each faltering heartbeat from this poor girl's torn neck!'

Heinar's eye bulged and he gripped Turgo's arm. 'Man, what a story!' His voice was hoarse. 'But finish it.'

The other nodded, and continued:

'The lad had been on watch and carried his crossbow with him, loaded. For a moment he'd been paralysed, unmanned; but now he screamed his outrage, let fly, put a bolt through the sod close to his black heart. It would have finished any other man, to be stuck through and through like that with a hardwood bolt, only a hairbreadth from his heart. But not Oulio, not the thing which Oulio had become. With the strength of a maniac, he knocked the husband aside, kicked him in the face, and rushed out of the tent into the sleeping camp. His hissing and howling woke all of us up . . .

'Well, everything I've told so far is the way I heard it and how I remember it. But from here on in it's the way I *saw* it. And I've no sinister motive for telling this tale, Heinar; no, for I've learned my lesson where women are concerned, and I'm not much of a one for subterfuge. But the Szgany Hagi took me in and for that I owe you a favour. So here's how the rest of it goes:

'Before the camp was fully awake, before anyone could say, ask, or do anything, this young lad – who was now mad as Oulio himself – put another bolt in him, in his spine. Oulio toppled into the campfire, and the lad had him! He grabbed a leg, dragged him screaming out of the cinders, noosed him round the neck and strung him up from a tree there and then! And then he took us to his wife, so that we'd understand.

'We'd understand some of it, anyway . . .

'And no one cut Oulio down, so that he might well be swinging there yet, except . . . that wasn't the end of it. No, not by a long shot.

'For at sunup, Oulio's coughing and grunting brought us awake again! He was *still* alive, yes! With a rope round his neck, his face all purple, dangling there in mid-air; one bolt skewering him through the chest, and another deep in his spine. And *none* of these things had killed him! But something was in the offing which would for sure. It was the sun, coming up over the trees and blazing down into the clearing. And when it lit on Oulio – how he smoked and steamed!

'And then . . . this awful, impossible commotion: he choked and kicked and danced up there! Until the knot came loose, letting him down. And so he crumpled to the ground and lay there, staring at us with those scarlet eyes of his. And we called for the lad, who'd just finished burying his poor wife, to come and finish it. It seemed only right . . .

'He brought a machete and went to Oulio where he lay. But before he could take his head . . . the monster spoke to him! Oh, he didn't cry out, beg for mercy, plead for his life; none of that. His throat, all puffy and grooved, wouldn't have allowed for it, and anyway he had no wind. And in a voice no more than a hoarse whisper, he said: "I'm sorry! It wasn't me!"

'The liar! For of course the lad, and everyone else, knew it had been none other! Half crazy, the poor bereaved husband snarled and his machete went up, but before it could fall . . . Oulio began to choke and flop about, so that we knew it was the end of him. And perhaps the lad thought, "Why should I make it easier for him?" At any rate, he stayed his hand.

'And so Oulio flopped about in his death agonies; his mouth yawned open and his neck grew fat, and his purple face swelled up as if to burst. Until at last . . . at last something came out of him!'

Heinar half started to his feet. 'Something? What sort of something? Was he sick? Did he throw up his guts?'

Turgo shook his head. 'His guts, no. He threw up nothing. I saw it and I remember. I remember what I thought: that this thing *wanted* to be out of him! Because while he was finished, there might be another chance for it. Don't ask me where the idea came from, but that's what I thought.'

'But what *was* it?'

Turgo shrugged, then shuddered, which was something Heinar had never seen him do before. 'A huge slug, a leech, a great fat blindworm – don't ask me, for I don't know. It was partly black, grey, leprous, ridged, writhing. Big as a boy's arm, I thought it would split his face! And it dragged itself out of him and wriggled for cover – because just like Oulio it felt the sunlight. Its head was flattened, like a snake's, but it was blind, eyeless. Yet somehow, it sensed the lad's machete still raised on high and reared back from it. But too late . . . he was quick . . . he struck off its head!

'A moment more and men unfroze, sprang forward, kicked the wriggling pieces into the fire. Then . . . we all looked at each other – all of us, with faces white as chalk – and we looked at the lad, who used his great knife again. This time he took Oulio's head: two, three strokes . . . it was done. And again we tossed both parts into the fire, then stood there till they'd burned to ashes . . .'

Heinar stared hard at Turgo, who gazed back unblinkingly. And Heinar knew that every word of it had been the truth. For who could embellish a thing like that? Finally he said, 'This Shaitan's eyes were red. I thought it was only the firelight, reflected in them. Well, maybe it was – and maybe it wasn't.'

'We'll know for sure at sunup,' the other answered. 'But do you really want to wait that long? Right now, who or whatever that man is, he's with Maria Babeni, in her caravan. And maybe he's with her just like Oulio was with that girl. Also, Heinar, my story still isn't finished.'

'There's more? But what else can there be?'

'A plague, I said,' Turgo reminded him, 'and a plague's what I meant. For in the dead of the next night – and after that poor lass's husband had buried her in the woods – who should come ghosting into camp but the girl herself! Oh, her flesh was pale and her nails broken from the digging, but her appetite was healthy enough, and good long teeth to match it!

'Well, the men around the fire had all taken strong drink; at first they didn't know her. She went among them like a whore, tempting, stroking, biting their necks. But suddenly her bites were real! Aye, and her eyes were red! Then, they knew her.

'Well, this time we knew better what we were doing. But we had to hold her poor raving husband down while we did it . . .'

Heinar shook his head in utter bewilderment. Until at last: 'A plague, aye,' he said. 'But Turgo, what are we talking about here? A creature that lives in a man – or a woman – making him or her crazy enough to live by the blood of other men?'

'That's exactly what we're talking about,' said the other. 'A *wampir* which makes its host victim strong, lusty, devious, and very hard to kill. Old Oulio Ionescu wasn't a rapist, and he certainly wasn't a murderer! And what about this girl, who came back from the grave?'

'Isn't it possible she was buried alive?'

'No,' Turgo shook his head in firm denial. 'She was dead for sure. And later – undead!'

Heinar could scarcely take it all in. 'What was that word you used? Wampir?'

Turgo nodded. 'In certain western regions, that's what men call the great bats that suck on goats. If they find a crippled goat under the moon, they'll suck him dry.'

Heinar's mouth was likewise dry. He looked nervously all about – at the tents, the carts and caravans, and not least the shadows – then licked his lips and finally nodded. 'Well, I know about such bats, of course: we Hagis call 'em "vexies". Catch them at our goats, we sneak up, club them, break their wings. But men with giant leeches in them?' He didn't try to hide a small shudder. 'No, I have to admit, you're the expert on this one, Turgo Zolte. So what next? How do we handle it?'

'What we don't do is act too hasty,' Turgo said. 'For we'd never live it down if this Shaitan's innocent – *and* a hero to boot.'

'Which he could well be,' Heinar let himself down from his branch. 'For after all, young Vidra Gogosita reckons he saved his life!'

Turgo's deep-etched frown showed his dilemma, his uncertainty. 'That's the hell of it,' he nodded. 'It's possible all this talk's for nothing – indeed I hope it is! – but can we risk it?'

'No,' Heinar gave a short, sharp shake of his head, convinced that he'd be far better safe than sorry. 'Vidra's had his head down for a while now. Perhaps we should go and have a word with him.'

They did. The widow Gogosita heard them coming, met them at the flap of her tent with a finger to her lips. '*Shhh!* The poor lad's asleep. And Heinar,' she grasped his arm, 'it's very good of you to show your concern this way. Ah, but it must have been terrible up there! Such nightmares! Vidra rambles as in a fever . . . he·speaks of blood, and murder!'

They went in, all three, to stand quietly beside the youth where he tossed and turned. The night had turned cold, and yet the sweat stood out on Vidra's brow. He was pale as a ghost, with grey hollows in his cheeks and under his eyes.

Turgo glanced at Heinar, went to shake the lad's shoulder. His mother got between. 'What's this?' she hissed. 'But can't you see he needs his sleep? Well, whatever, it will have to keep.'

'No, Elana. It can't keep.' Heinar was familiar with her, but firm. He put her to one side, and ...

... And Vidra came breathlessly, babblingly alive!

He was still asleep, but the cold sweat welled up that much faster, and the words jerked out of him in squalls, like sudden bursts of spattering rain. 'No, no ... keep off ... keep away!' He tugged at his blanket until it was a damp knot. 'Ah, great ghoul ... but do you murder men for their clothes? No, no, for I see it's more than their clothes you're after! ... Keep off! Go torment Dezmir ... not me, not me.' He flopped this way and that. 'Ah, but now I know you, fiend! ... Your eyes like lamps ... they let you find your way in the dark! But not me, not me! Go suck on Dezmir's neck and let me be!'

And with that last he turned on his side, and his neck was visible where his mother had washed it. Turgo and Heinar looked – and saw.

'Punctures,' Turgo growled. 'Tears in the flesh. And the flesh itself inflamed, poisoned!'

Heinar nodded his grim agreement.

The widow's hand had flown to her mouth. 'What did Vidra say? About murdering men for ... for their clothes? But now it comes to me. That stranger was wearing Vidra's long coat. Also Klaus Luncani's trousers! Much too short for him ... they have a patched

131

right thigh. I'd know that patch anywhere, for I put it there. His poor wife is no good ... with needle and thread ... at all!' Her eyes opened like great mad windows.

And so did Vidra's as he came awake, sat bolt upright and snarled his terror, then reached out his trembling arms for his mother. 'Ma! – Mama! – Ma-*aaaaa!*' His cry was a gasp, a *hiss*, not loud, but it penetrated Turgo, Heinar and the widow like a long hot iron sliding into their flesh.

And for all that it was quiet, still its echoes reached out a great deal farther than the tent of the Gogositas ...

In Maria Babeni's caravan, Shaitan came awake!

What was that? A cry in the night? From which quarter?

The night seemed still, quiet, but Shaitan's vampire intelligence was not. It was unquiet. He sensed movement; men other than the watchkeepers were awake in the camp, stirring furtively.

... And they were with his thrall!

He reached out with his mind – and gasped as the scene in the tent of the widow Gogosita flooded his awareness in all its vivid, telepathic detail. Not a scene from the youth's dreams, no, but from life. Vidra was awake – and talking his head off!

No! Shaitan sent his command like a flung knife. *Oh, you faithless one! Much too late now to change sides, Vidra Gogosita ...*

In the widow's tent, suddenly Vidra's terrified eyes went wide where he clasped his mother and babbled the true story to Turgo and Heinar. His words were shut off as Shaitan closed a telepathic fist on his mind; groaning, he slumped to the floor. But the others had heard enough.

132

'Look after him!' Heinar snapped as the frantic widow got down beside her son. And Turgo thought:

Aye, look after him very, very well!

Then the two men were out of the tent, and Heinar blowing on his alert whistle. From out on the perimeter came answering cries, the strange cough of a wolf, sounds of men hurrying to investigate. 'The girl's caravan is on the other side of the clearing,' Heinar grunted, leading the way. They skirted the campfire, and Heinar blew again.

'He'll be alerted by now,' Turgo warned.

'Distracted, I hope!' Heinar answered.

Turgo loaded his small crossbow, knocked off the safety. 'There are only the two of us.'

'*Huh!* How many do we need?'

Turgo wasn't known for his patience. Baring his teeth, he snarled, 'More than just the two of us, be sure!' And he grabbed Heinar's arm to slow him down.

By then they had almost reached Maria Babeni's small caravan. Heinar shook himself free of the other's hand, growled, 'Yes, I know: he'll be strong, this creature. But poor Maria, she's just a weak girl – and me, I'm Szgany!'

'Both of us,' Turgo snapped. 'Both fools, too.'

Arriving at the small covered cart, Heinar blew one last blast on his whistle; a glimmer of lamplight shining through the wicker weave of the caravan's door went out at once; the shadows lengthened as watchmen came loping in starlight. But before they could arrive, the door was flung open!

Shaitan stood there, his face a pallid mask, alert but calm. And no disguising the scarlet fire in his eyes now. He made no attempt to do so but said, simply, 'Heinar, my ways will be strange to you at first. But only follow them, and I shall make you the most powerful leader the

Szgany ever knew, until the Hagis are feared throughout the length and breadth of Sunside.'

Heinar shook his head. 'It wasn't fear made me a leader,' he answered, 'but respect. That . . . and justice!' And to the man beside him, in a voice which cracked like a whip to activate his trigger finger: 'Turgo!'

Turgo's bolt zipped from the tiller of his weapon. But in the same moment, Shaitan snarled and slammed the door in their faces. Still the heavy hardwood bolt struck through the wickerwork to find its target; most certainly, for Shaitan's cry of pain sounded from within like the howl of a stricken animal, and the flights of the bolt were sheared from its shaft as it was wrenched through the tough weave and out of sight.

Men arrived on the scene: three of them, one with his wolf to heel. 'What's going on? What's happening?'

Heinar had no time for explanations. 'That man in there, the stranger Shaitan. I want him brought down. Maybe even dead. Turgo here has shot him; that might be enough . . .'

Turgo, fitting another bolt to his crossbow, thought not. And he was right. But before he could say anything:

A mist sprang up; it *sprang* into being, literally!

One moment, the five men stood at the door of Maria's small caravan – with lamps in the other tents and carts beginning to flicker into life at the commotion, and grumbling voices raised in inquiry – and the air was dry and sharp. Then, suddenly, as if the earth and the forest had exhaled mightily, a ground mist lapped at their ankles, and the air was damp, even greasy. Time only for one of the watchmen to murmur, 'What?' – and another, 'Eh?' – before the mist was thickening, writhing in the trees, obscuring the camp's silhouettes.

Then, from the covered cart, Maria Babeni's cry rang out!

Galvanized, forgetting for the moment the weirdness of the night, Heinar bounded forward up the single wooden step, charging the door with his shoulder. Simultaneously, there came the sound of ripped leather and the cart rocked a little.

The door burst inwards under Heinar's weight and a wall of mist greeted him, collapsing around him, issuing outwards from the caravan like water when the dam breaks. Then the Hagi was inside, with Turgo hot on his heels; and Maria, naked and sobbing, collapsing into their arms.

A hole gaped in a side wall. Framed in the ripped hide, briefly, they saw the tall pale figure of Shaitan before he fled outwards to the night. Turgo's bolt was in his shoulder, blood flowing freely ... but not *only* blood. For when Shaitan breathed, he breathed a billowing mist. And the pores of his body, open like tiny pouting mouths, secreted milky vapour as a slug issues slime!

Turgo cursed, fought free of Maria's arms, loosed his second bolt through the hole into Shaitan's mist, hopefully into Shaitan. But no, there came no answering cry, only a red-eyed shadow loping soundlessly through the mist-damp shrubbery.

'Loose your wolf!' Heinar shouted to the men outside.

With a snarl, the animal went bounding, and the watchmen after it. 'Yes, get after him!' Turgo leaned out of the door, urging them on. 'And don't just catch him – kill him on the spot!' *If you can ...*

Heinar had wrapped his coat around the girl. They laid her on her bed, examined her neck. Nothing, just bruises, and more on her body. They were proper about it: they merely glanced at her naked flesh, but that was enough. There were signs which both men knew. And confirming their unspoken thoughts:

135

'I . . . had thought I was dreaming,' her voice was tiny, a sob. 'But . . . when I woke up, I . . . I knew what he had done. Except I . . . I couldn't stop him! I swear it! He . . . he has this power. It's in his eyes . . .'

Heinar called for women, left Maria in their care. And a little while later, at the campfire:

'Well?' he asked Turgo. 'And what now?'

The mist had thinned out, seeped into the ground, disappeared. The stars were bright again and the hurtling moon just risen. From away in the forest came far, faint shouting. 'For now,' Turgo answered, as the distant cries died away, 'let's just wait and see if they get him.'

Heinar grunted, nodded, said, 'Well, Turgo Zolte, it seems the Szgany Hagi are firmly in your debt. And me, I'll not forget it. *Hah!* Who could forget a night like this? But at least young Vidra and the girl are all right.'

The other made no answer, merely stared into the fire and wondered, *All right, are they? Are they really?*

Before the dawn two of the three men returned. They had got cut off from the third watchkeeper and hadn't seen him since. Neither him nor his wolf.

At sunup Heinar found Turgo packing his small tent and a very few personal things, and sniffing out the breeze from the east. 'Something on your mind?' he inquired.

'I came to you with nothing,' Turgo answered, 'and I'm not taking much more away with me. What little I have, I've earned. Any complaints?'

'None. But I don't like to see you go. Has last night upset you? Is it the girl? What happened wasn't her fault; this Shaitan was full of arts; she would still make a good wife . . . for someone.'

'Not this someone,' Turgo shook his head. Then, galvanized, he hugged the other, and said, 'Heinar, listen . . . be careful!'

Astonished, the Hagi freed himself. 'I always am careful,' he answered. 'But of what this time?'

Turgo shrugged, looked away. 'Something of innocence has gone,' he said, finally. 'In its place, something full of dark knowledge, power, evil, has come. Like the Szgany Ferenc before them, the Szgany Hagi are touched by it.' Grey-faced, he turned to Heinar and grasped his shoulders. 'Listen: I can't watch it happen again, not to you and yours, and stand there powerless to stop it! It came from the west, and so I'm heading east.'

Frowning, Heinar inquired, 'And if this evil lingers on, how should I guard against it?'

'Chiefly with your eyes. And whenever you see it, put it down! One of your men hasn't returned. If he does, watch him – and his wolf! Watch the ones who did return, likewise Maria Babeni. Most obvious of all, watch Vidra Gogosita.'

'Vidra? His mother's in a state. He wandered off in the night, apparently. His fever . . .'

'Oh?' Turgo hardly seemed surprised. 'Then say a prayer that he never comes back. Aye, and you'd do well to watch his mother, too.' He put his pack on his shoulder, headed off.

Heinar felt the sun warm on his weatherbeaten face and was seduced by a feeling of well-being. He called after Turgo: 'I think you exaggerate! Whatever evil came with this Shaitan, whatever sickness he carried, it's disappeared with him. Also, and wherever he is, it's bound to kill him in the end. There's nothing here now to run away from.'

'Running?' Turgo called back over his shoulder, dappled by sunlight where he strode among the trees. 'Yes, I suppose I am. It's the only way I know to put distance between.' When he paused to look back, his lips were tight and grim. Then:

'In certain ways we're alike, you and I, Heinar,' he said. 'And do you make camp beside a poisoned pool? No, for you know better than that. Well, and so do I know better. For I've seen this thing before and know that I can't live with it. Now let me warn you one last time, and I pray you'll heed these final words of mine: keep watch, Heinar – *keep watch!*'

But the sun still felt very warm and reassuring to Heinar. He would keep watch, of course – well, for a while. 'Eat well, then,' he called out after Turgo, perhaps a little too gruffly. 'Stay healthy. Have many children . . . eventually.'

Turgo's nod was his only answer. And then he was gone . . .

Turgo Zolte was right: it would take Heinar Hagi eight long years to eradicate Shaitan's vampire taint from his people, a task which in the end would amount to culling the tribe down to less than half its current numbers. It was to be man's first real stand against vampires (if not the Wamphyri proper), out of which would be learned many a valuable lesson for the future.

Of the Szgany Ferenc who had featured in Turgo's tale of Oulio Ionescu: the taint in their blood never would be washed away but would stay with them to the end of their days, not only in this world but also in one other.

That, however, is a tale already told . . .

III

Raging, Shaitan fled from the camp of Heinar Hagi. He flowed through the night, which was his element, and covered himself with its darkness; but behind him a watchdog – indeed a wolf – came fast on his heels. And behind the wolf came Sunsiders, Szgany, which he had discovered were in no way trogs. Difficult to impose one's will on such as these. Their own will was so very strong! Shaitan would have more sway over their women, who at least appreciated his beauty. But to remain beautiful, indeed, to remain alive ... this was now his chief priority.

Turgo Zolte's bloodied hardwood bolt stood out from his right shoulder, giving him pain. He might will something of the pain away, but not the bolt itself. That would have to be drawn out. And despite the speed of his flowing flight along the forest's fringe, the wolf was gaining. Its eyes were very nearly the equivalent of Shaitan's own in the night and the darkness.

Cliffs reared suddenly on Shaitan's left hand; he lengthened his stride, flowed through the uneven foliage, climbed up onto a low ledge. Vines and creepers hung down from above. But it was not his intention to climb.

He jammed the flight end of the bolt in his shoulder into a niche, wrenched his body sharply to one side. The bolt snapped ... and Shaitan cried out! Blood flowed freely, its smell inflaming him. Now he felt behind his shoulder with his left hand. The barb of the iron arrowhead protruded an inch, but he had no leverage to pull it out. He tore down a length of tough vine, looped it over the arrowhead, tied its ends to a creeper growing from a crevice.

The wolf had heard Shaitan's cry, smelled his blood. It came snarling, leaping to attain the ledge, scrabbled there a moment to regain its balance. Then it saw Shaitan and leaped again, locking its jaws on his arm. Its weight overbalanced him; locked together they fell from the ledge; the bolt was torn from Shaitan's back.

In the near-distance, Shaitan's closest human pursuer called out to his wolf: 'Seek him!' But the wolf had already discovered Shaitan, who was himself on the point of discovering a new and terrible weapon. Within him, his vampire was at last mature. Metamorphic, its flesh was Shaitan's flesh.

The wolf had jaws like a bear-trap, clamped fast now to the bones of Shaitan's forearm. Their eyes met, feral yellow against evil scarlet, and the man felt something of the beast's ferocity. So did his vampire, which must make him ferocious to match. Something was summoned to his flesh, summoned *from* his flesh! He felt a burning in his fingers as if they were on fire, an agony in his face and jaws far greater than the mere pain in his back. And yet these additional pains were not without . . . pleasure?

It was not unlike those occasions when he had summoned his vampire mist; but he had *not* summoned this, not knowingly. For this was the instinctive response of his metamorphism, the tenacity of his vampire, its lust for life; and suddenly the great wolf was no more than a puppy!

Shaitan's fingers, grown to claws, rammed into the animal's sides and tore them; his jaws, yawning impossibly wide, elongated into a nightmare cavern of serrated tusks which sprouted from red-gushing gums; his eyes

140

were blobs of sulphur shot with scarlet fire. Gutting the wolf, he let its entrails spill. And when its agonized jaws flew open, then Shaitan's closed – upon its throat. Which he tore out in a welter of pipes and gristle and gore!

In just a moment, the wolf was wolf no more but a mangled carcass; it hadn't even cried out but died silently, in vast astonishment . . .

A second passed . . . another . . . and a third.

'Lupé?' A voice called from close at hand. 'Where in all that's . . .?' A man stepped out of the trees into starlight – in time to see something move in the undergrowth at the foot of the cliffs. 'Lupé?' the man repeated, but in a whisper now, wonderingly, as he lifted his crossbow.

Crouching down a little, he ran to the place beneath the cliffs. As he got there, so the darkness came flowing to its feet! Starlight gleamed on the horror that was Shaitan, which reached out a bloody hand and caught the other by his throat.

The watchman would have discharged his weapon – but he'd left the safety on! Shaitan knocked it from his trembling hand and drew him closer. And:

'Lupé?' he quietly, almost conversationally growled, his monstrous head cocked on one side. 'Ah, no – for my name is Shaitan!' And as he lowered his face to the other's throbbing neck, 'But from this time forward you must call me master . . .'

With his new disciple or lieutenant, who was the first entirely human underling of the Wamphyri, Shaitan headed east as before. There were no more pursuers; the night was long; they covered a good many miles – before the sun found them out.

For Shaitan's symbiont or parasite was a two-edged

141

sword: one could not accept its advantages without its disadvantages. Sunlight, which had irritated Shaitan from the outset – almost from the moment of his breathing the red, corpse-spawned spores – now became a seething agony in his eyes and against his hide. It burned him, visibly steamed the moisture from his flesh, ate into him like acid and sapped his strength. He could stand to go out from the shade for seconds, but minutes would deplete him horribly, and an hour would kill him. His thrall was less susceptible for the moment; given time, however, and he, too, must surely succumb to direct sunlight. Such was the measure of Shaitan's corruption, and his contagion.

They were climbing diagonally eastward, above the foothills and towards the tree-line, when sunup came with its fogs in Sunside's valleys and forests, and its probing golden beams on the peaks; beams which gradually joined up to become a wall of yellow fire, creeping down towards them where they went all unsuspecting, like ants on the flank of the mountain.

And yet perhaps Shaitan (or his leech) did suspect something; for there was an anxiety in him, not yet fathomed, to be out of this place and once more into the cool of Starside. But when he felt the effect of the first of those as yet hazy beams on his nakedness, and when he observed in astonishment the rapid evaporation of his body's fluids and the scorching of his flesh, then he understood well enough his instinct – or that of his vampire – to take cover. And so, forced into the shade of a deep cave, Shaitan and his thrall, Ilya Sul, waited out the long day.

The cave had been the lair of some creature but now was empty; lesser caves and branching fissures within were cool, damp, dark; Shaitan felt reasonably secure. But he also felt hungry. The sun's rays, in however brief a time, had depleted him sorely. He fuelled himself on Ilya Sul, which weakened the man more yet but bound him even closer to his master. Also, it fed the vampire fire in Sul's blood, and hastened his change. So that when he went out on to the slopes with his cross-bow, to find food for himself, he returned within the hour, feeble and blistered by the sun. But at least he'd shot a kid, which Shaitan gorged upon before tossing the less appealing parts to Sul.

So they fed themselves.

And then they slept, because by now they could feel the *weight* of the risen sun, like an immovable boulder, blocking the door of the cave; which meant there was no going on for a while. And Shaitan could *hear* the land outside sizzling with a deadly heat; he could even *smell* the scorching of the rocks, so that his skin crept with the knowledge of what that golden furnace could do to him . . .

Shaitan came starting awake!

He shook Sul, cautioned him to silence. 'The sun is high,' he whispered. 'I can feel it. Also, I feel Sunsiders! So come, find a dark hole for yourself.' They retreated into the cave deeper still, found shadowed niches in which to crawl.

And the weary trackers, with a wolf, came after; but not into the cave. For lying there, Shaitan fought down the urge to create a mist and flee into it (what, into the sunlight?) and instead willed it that the men would turn back. The grey one was their guide: he fastened upon its mind with his vampire awareness, spelling out the doom which would befall if it should enter.

The wolf pawed the remains of their meal at the entrance where they'd tossed the scraps, but came no farther. The men, Szgany Hagi, saw the skin, hair and

143

bones, and knew that this had been a goat. And one of them said, 'A bear, probably a big one. This must be his lair. See, these remains are fresh. Why, he might even be at home!' And so they passed on by.

Shaitan waited a moment, then crept to the entrance. And keeping well back from the dazzle, he taxed his eyes to watch the men move away, marvelling greatly that they went in brilliant sunlight, with no apparent harm! Then ... he was filled with bitter resentment. They lived here, where he could not; they hunted here, living on the earth's simple things, which he could not. It was their place, their haven (their heaven?) and could never be his except . . . in the dark of night.

Well, and so they lived and hunted here: indeed, they even hunted Shaitan himself! But tomorrow and tomorrow there would be other days, and long dark nights, when he would hunt in his own right – for men! Aye, and then he would turn their heaven into a hell.

It was a solemn promise, which Shaitan made unto himself . . .

Sunside's day was long and long, seeming interminable to Shaitan; but at last the shadows lengthened, the sun became a hot, smoky red blister on the south-eastern horizon, and the first pale stars blinked into being high over the spine of the barrier mountains. Twilight came down, and it was time to move on.

At which point there came a diversion.

Emerging from the cave into the gloom of evening, Shaitan was startled to hear a wailing and moaning, and to observe the approach of two figures – whom he recognized at once. The one who cried out and tore at his hair came, after all, as no great surprise: for this was the treacherous thrall, Vidra Gogosita, who seemed in a bad way indeed. But the other figure, advancing upon Shaitan quietly, hollow-cheeked and flame-eyed, was a shocking sight indeed. For he –

– was a dead man! He – was in fact Dezmir Babeni!

Ah, but there had been changes. He was still bearded, and shortish in the limbs and trunk as before, but much of the fat was gone from him now so that he no longer appeared squat. He was a leaner Dezmir Babeni, certainly, but just as surely the same man. And he was no longer dead.

This was a new thing. Before Babeni, Shaitan had never so depleted a man, or even a trog, as to kill him. The creatures who were his thralls had not died but lived only to accommodate Shaitan's needs. This man, however, had died. Babeni *was* dead . . . or undead?

'Master! Master!' the young Gogosita came ghosting to Shaitan, hands fluttering. 'Take me back, I beg you! I have nowhere else to go, nowhere else to be.' Shaitan did not even look at him but put him aside. For his gaze was rapt upon Babeni. And Babeni's rapt upon him, and full of hatred!

The undead man growled and lurched forward, his pale grey hands reaching, his eyes like sulphur pits, lit with fire in their cores. 'You!' he accused, his voice harsh and rasping. 'You, Shaitan, you did this thing to me. And now this youth tells me you've done other things to my daughter!'

He bore down on Shaitan, grasped him, went to fasten his teeth in his neck. And Shaitan saw how those teeth were grown into fangs! Stunned until now, immobilized, finally he summoned his vampire strength to throw the other off, then leaped on him to choke him. Babeni's grey face turned purple under the crushing power of Shaitan's hands, but still he fought back and his body heaved with an impossible strength.

Amazed, Shaitan knocked Babeni's head again and

again upon the hard and stony ground, until the skull at the back was soft and dented. Finally the other quit fighting and lay back. But he was not dead and his limbs twitched, and his yellow eyes followed Shaitan wherever he moved.

And Shaitan looked at him and thought: *The strength of your body is second only to mine, and its wounds heal even as fast. In relieving you of your frail human life, I have given you this unlife. However unwittingly, it seems I have bestowed certain powers upon you! And yet you are not my thrall and will not accept me as your master. Wherefore I must kill you, lest you become a rival. But how may I kill you, if you are undead?*

Babeni was even now taking up a jagged rock, staggering to his feet, mewling brokenly as he lurched towards Shaitan. Spittle dribbled from a corner of his mouth and his head and neck were soaked in blood; because of his damaged brain, he came on lopsidedly, like an idiot. Shaitan stepped aside, tripped him, looked for a large stone with which to finish it. But:

'How may I kill you?' he asked out loud, as yet again the mewling thing clambered upright.

'Master,' Vidra Gogosita clawed at his arm. 'I know how to kill him!' For Vidra had sat at the campfire one time when Turgo Zolte had been telling his stories.

'Oh?' Shaitan looked at him, at the same time avoiding the staggering cripple. 'And would you redeem yourself? Well, and maybe you have your uses after all. Say on then: what will it take to put him down?'

'A stake through his heart,' Vidra gasped. 'To fix him in place. Then cut off his head. Finally, burn him — all of his pieces!'

'All of that?'

Vidra nodded. 'This is how the Szgany Hagi will deal with you, if they catch you!'

Shaitan nodded. 'Indeed? Then we must test this thing. You shall build me a fire.' And to Ilya Sul where he fended off the thing which had been Dezmir Babeni: 'Put your bolt through his heart.'

The other obeyed and Babeni was knocked down, stretched out upon the ground, with only the flight of the bolt sticking up from his chest. He bled the merest trickle, even when Sul took a knife and commenced sawing through his neck, its pipes and the bones of his spine. Through all of which the undead man's limbs jerked and twitched, and air whistled in and out of his chomping jaws, until the pipes were severed and the head detached.

Then they burned him, but even burning he thrashed about while his fats were rendered down . . .

Observing all, Shaitan nodded again. 'And this is how they would deal with me? *Hah!* But if you think he died hard, then you don't know the half of it. The Hagi shall not catch me, Vidra Gogosita; and if they do, I will not be the one to die.'

Meanwhile, Ilya Sul had built the fire to a roaring blaze. 'I . . . I can't seem to warm myself,' he complained, examining his cold grey arms.

'I am the same,' Vidra agreed. 'For we have known the kiss of the great Wampir, our master Shaitan.'

And again Shaitan was interested. 'Wampir?'

Vidra explained, repeating all that he had heard from Turgo Zolte. And when he was done:

'Ah, no!' said Shaitan. 'For the wampir is a common bat, a dull creature which is my Starside familiar. But I am uncommon. Wherefore I shall be called . . . Wamphyri! Aye, for I like the sound of it. The great Lord Shaitan, first of the Wamphyri! So be it.'

They crossed the mountains in the night, and on the

way Shaitan questioned Vidra as to how he had found him. The youth answered that he had 'felt' his master in his mind, and had known that he must go to him. On the way, as the power of the sun's rays waned, he had met with Dezmir Babeni, who had hidden in a crack in a cliff to keep himself out of the sunlight. Being undead, he had been more nearly like unto Shaitan, and the sun was his mortal enemy.

The night passed, and as the three — Shaitan, Vidra and Ilya Sul — descended into Starside, so they discovered Shaitan's trog thralls waiting. They, too, had known where to find their master. And now they numbered thirteen in all: the three, plus seven female trogs and three male. And Shaitan called all of the others his disciples.

Then they saw a light shining up into the night, a white and hazy shimmer unlike the coldly flickering auroras of the north, which Ilya Sul said must be the fallen white sun, which some called a gate into hell.

'White sun?' Shaitan had drawn back.

'I've heard it's cold,' the other answered. 'It isn't harmful, if you keep your distance. But you must never touch it.'

Shaitan was curious, however, and said he must see this hell-gate.

They climbed the low crater wall and stood at the rim, and looked down upon the ball of cold white fire within. The trogs were blinded and staggered this way and that. One tripped and fell, landing on a ledge close to the white glare. Terrified, he put up a hand to fend it off. His hand touched the surface of the dazzle, sank into it . . . and he cried out in his guttural fashion as the hell-gate dragged him in and swallowed him whole!

The trog was gone, and only his strange slow cry came echoing back. Shaitan believed he could see him down there, a small frightened figure, dwindling, but the light hurt his eyes so that soon he must look away.

And he said: 'This shall be the punishment for those who offend me three times. Three times, aye – for I am forgiving, as you see.'

'A fitting punishment,' Vidra fawned upon him.

'As well you think so,' Shaitan answered. 'And as well you mark my words. One: you told the Hagi about me. Two: you told Dezmir Babeni how I had honoured his daughter. Do not wrong me a third time.' His voice was dark, and very frightening.

'And there shall be other punishments,' he told them all. 'For I am Shaitan who can make men undead. Any who would do me harm, let them think on this: I shall take their blood and bury them deep in the ground. And when they awaken, they shall lie there and scream forever, until they stiffen to stones in the earth.

'Also, that land there to the north; I perceive that it is icy cold. No fit habitation even for such as we. Therefore, let him who would deny me beware. For in my house there shall be no warm bed or woman-flesh for him; no kind master to guide and instruct him; neither wonders to be witnessed, nor mysteries revealed. For I shall banish him north, to freeze in the ice all alone.

'But for him who would obey me in all things, and be my true servant and thrall, a rich red life forever! Aye, even unto death – and beyond! So be it . . .'

'Where shall your house stand, Lord?' Ilya Sul ventured with a shiver, as they left the Gate behind to cross the wide mouth of a pass where the light from Sunside was a pale purplish haze in the 'V' of the split range. 'For this seems a desolate place – a plain of boulders, lacking rivers, where lichens live and scrubby grasses – with wolves in the mountains and bats in the crags, but never a man.'

'There are men of sorts,' Shaitan answered him. 'Under the mountains, in their caverns, dwell trogs. They shall provide – they shall *be* – my food. Until we are established. But on Sunside there is life galore! Common fare will suffice, at first, but the true blood which is the life lies beyond the mountains. And in all the nights yet to be we shall hunt. As for my house: it shall stand east of here a ways, for I am drawn east.' Then, looking sharply at Sul: 'But do you doubt me?'

'Never, Lord!'

They trekked for several miles, and came to a region of stone stacks worn out from the mountains, which littered the plain like the petrified stalks of gigantic mushrooms. Their bases were fortified with scree jumbles, but in their columns were ledges and caverns, many of which were vast as halls.

Shaitan admired these stacks, for they were very grand and very gaunt. And: 'One of these shall be my house,' he said.

Sul answered him: 'They are like the aeries of the mountain eagles!'

And: 'Aye,' said Shaitan. 'The aeries of the Wamphyri!'

And so Shaitan set to and commenced the building of his house. The task was huge; only a vampire and his thralls, with their longevity, could ever have accomplished it. And Shaitan would build not only a house but an empire of vampires.

He recruited trogs out of their caverns in the lee of the mountains, and sent his lieutenants into Sunside's nights to hunt and recruit Szgany. And in dark chambers in the base of the stack which he had chosen, he experimented with his own metamorphic flesh and powers to furnish himself with all of his requirements.

He bred trogs which were no longer trogs but cartilage creatures, whose minds were small and bodies
elastic. From these he made leathers and coverings for
the aerie's exterior stairways, and articles of furniture
for his rooms. And all of them still living a life of sorts,
gradually petrifying and becoming permanent in their
places. He mated men with trog women, the issue from
which was not seemly. He got foul, bloated things, all
gross and mindless — but even these were not wasted.
In nether caves he bred them into gas-beasts, for the
heating of the stack, or into Things-Which-Consume,
for his refuse pit.

He took mindless vampire flesh and experimented
with it; he would imitate the aerial prowess of the great
bats, build flying creatures, soar out from his aerie
upon the winds. At first he knew failure, but later he
provided his flyers with the metamorphosed brains of
men, that they should have something (but never too
much) of volition. All of which creatures, nascent and
full-formed alike, were Shaitan's thralls.

Word of his works went abroad, even into Sunside.
And now Starside was double-damned and shunned
utterly . . . by men, at least.

But by now the Szgany of Sunside had problems
other than Shaitan and his night-raiding lieutenants,
for in the west the swamps were an entire spawning
ground for monsters! Foolish men and innocent creatures went down to the scummy waters to drink, and
things *other* than men and wolves came up from that
place. So that in the first twenty years several beings
who were very like unto Shaitan had come across from
Sunside to build their houses in the rearing stone
stacks. And because they were even as strong as him
and much of a kind, he made no protest but let them
build. In any case, there was space enough among the

many stacks, so that even Shaitan was unable to lay claim to all of them; and, just across the mountains, there was food and entertainment for all.

And it happened that at this time Shaitan's lieutenants went a-hunting, and brought back from Starside a certain man of their master's previous acquaintance. And as he went among the captives, inspecting them, he knew this one at once. Why, there was still a scar in his shoulder, put there by this very man, which Shaitan had kept as a reminder of that first night on Sunside! For the man was none other than Turgo Zolte, not quite so young but just as proud and independent as ever.

Shaitan laughed and hung him in chains, tormenting him at will from that time forward. But the man had a trick: he could turn pain aside, much like Shaitan himself. And in his fashion, Shaitan liked Turgo for his pride and bravery: the fact that he would not cry out but rather faint from his agonies. So that in a while he took him down and made him his chief lieutenant ... which was an error.

For Turgo was strong in many ways, and had this streak in him which would not accept thralldom to any creature. Let the Lord Shaitan drain him all he would, to the very dregs of his blood, but while he lived he would be his own man. Which were feelings he kept very much to himself; likewise the fact that on Sunside he had been the great vampire hunter, who in twenty years had learned many a diverse thing about the swamp-born menace. There was, for instance, a white metal, also the root of a certain plant, both of which were common on Sunside and poison to vampires. Perhaps even to Shaitan himself ...

And so Turgo grew close to the Wamphyri Lord Shaitan, who placed his trust in him. And if Shaitan had a brother it might well be Turgo Zolte, except ...

Turgo had no blood-lust. Or if he had, then it was special and deeply hidden . . .

Eventually Turgo took Ilya Sul aside and spoke to him. And because Turgo was strong, Ilya listened to his treason – that they should kill Shaitan in the approved fashion, but with the new skills which Turgo had learned. 'I've made a long knife of silver,' he explained, 'to take his head! And I can devise a hardwood spear, with a barbed silver point. Silver will hold Shaitan in place while I rub him with oil of kneblasch root, which will poison his flesh. Then we'll burn him.'

'And Shaitanstack will be mine?' Sul was greedy.

'Of course,' Turgo shrugged, 'for you deserve it.' But he intended no such thing; for Sul was contaminated and his blood changed, and in the end he must go the same way as his master.

Then Turgo sought out Vidra and said much the same things to him, to which the other agreed readily enough. But when Turgo's back was turned, then the traitor went straight to Shaitan . . . who listened, smiled and nodded grimly, and did nothing . . . but merely waited.

And down in his workshop, forbidden now to all others, he worked with an angry zest upon the flesh of trogs and men, designing a great abomination. And where Shaitan's cartilage creatures were for the fashioning of useful things, and his flyers for conveyance and scanning out the land around, and while all of his creations served to supplement his works in one way or another – even his flaccid siphoneers and puffing gas-beasts – this new monster writhing in its vat was a thing entirely apart. Indeed, it seemed nothing so much as a death machine.

It *was* just such an instrument of death! For fearing the treachery of his thralls, Shaitan had brought into being the very first Wamphyri warrior! And fashioned in part from his own metamorphic flesh, the thing was his in every part, mind and body alike. So that when in due time Turgo and the others came to find and destroy him, *this* was the nightmare he called down upon them. And no one – not even a dozen Turgo Zoltes – could stand against this. His knife, spear, oil of kneblasch, all were useless to him.

Then Vidra Gogosita cried out to Shaitan, reminding him of his warning. But Shaitan in turn reminded Vidra of *his* warning, telling him that this was his third and last great treachery.

Vidra was frozen, astonished! How had he offended?

His offence lay not in the direction of his treachery, but in that he *was* treacherous. Also, in the very fact that he had warned of Turgo Zolte's intended insurrection: Turgo, whom the Lord Shaitan had befriended. That was a bitter taste on Shaitan's forked tongue, and Vidra had put it there.

Without further ado he was taken to the Gate and tossed yelping into its glare, protesting his innocence to the last, and so disappearing there . . .

As for Ilya Sul: Shaitan drained him of his life's blood until he was pale and dead, then took him out into the boulder plain where his trog army dug a deep grave in the stony ground. And as time passed and the first rays of the sun shone through the great pass, and as Sul cried out and would rise up, naked and undead, so Shaitan said:

'I have made you a vampire. The sun is the proof, which burns you even as it burns me. But you need not fear it, for you shall feel its rays never more. You sought to do me great harm, Ilya, but I am a kind master and shall not hurt you in any degree, except that I shall put you from my sight.'

154

Then, at his signal, Sul was hurled screaming into the hole, which the trogs filled in with rocks and earth. 'There let him lie forever,' said Shaitan, gravely, shielded by his bat-fur cloak from the risen sun. 'Even until he stiffens to a stone. So be it!'

And he turned to Turgo Zolte, who stood there pale, bound and scowling, saying: 'You . . . are a special case. For you were only a man and I liked you. Oh, you suffered some small torment in my care, but I drank not of your blood. As I am what I am, so I allowed you to be as you would be, to see if time could sway you to my cause. It amused me to have a man – not a vampire, nor even a thrall, but a mere man – among them that are mine. Well, my amusement is at an end. I am no longer . . . amused.'

They went back to Shaitanstack, where Turgo was thrown into a dungeon to repent a while. A very short while.

Then the stack's master came to him and said, 'Vidra Gogosita is gone into unknown places, a land beyond. Call it hell, if you will. Ilya Sul cries out from the dark earth, and sometimes it pleases me to listen to him. But upon a time I decreed three punishments, one of which remains untried. You are a hard man, Turgo Zolte, but only a man for all that. If I send you north as a man, then you'll die – but too quickly! Wherefore I shall first make you a vampire.'

Turgo was bound to the wall, with his feet dangling inches above the stone floor. Shaitan reached up and cut him down, so that he collapsed in great pain, drained of his strength. Then Shaitan went down on his knees beside him, and gloomed upon him with his scarlet eyes. And his anger was very great. 'I treated you as my brother, even my son,' he said. 'And you

155

would repay me by killing me! It would be fair and just if I killed you in your turn, but I want you to freeze in the ice and repent your iniquities.'

Turgo looked at him and knew his time as a man was up. But while he was a man he would never bow to Shaitan. And he said, 'Me, your son? You could never father a son, you swamp-thing! You only look like a man, but your tongue is a snake's, and your blood is the blood of trogs, dupes, thralls. Your familiars are bats full of lice, and the clean sunlight boils your flesh like a snail in its shell. *Hah!* I, Turgo Zolte, Shaitan's son? No, for I am the son of a man!'

The other was no longer capable of controlling his anger; his parasite creature amplified his passion by ten; his jaws cracked open and his great mouth gushed blood from torn gums as teeth grew out of them like bone sickles. Handsome one moment – even with his blood-hued eyes, handsome – in the next he was the embodiment of all horror. And his passion incensed that of the creature within him, which now *was* him.

He went to his knees beside his victim, used red-spurting talon claws to tear, prise open his chest, and laid his razor nails upon the pipes of Turgo's pounding heart. None of which meant anything to Turgo, because he was already in the pit of oblivion. But as Shaitan saw his innards, his blood, the very circuits of his life . . . something new happened.

His creature went into spasm within him. It gripped his spine, put out suckers into his veins and organs to revel in his, its, passion. Shaitan coughed, gagged, felt a rising in his gorge, something creeping in the contracting column of his throat. He choked the thing out: a pale sphere no bigger than an eyeball.

It shimmered; it was alive with flickering cilia; it fell in a froth of spittle to Turgo's open chest. And in the next moment it turned scarlet . . . and was gone, soaked into him!

Shaitan reeled to his feet. He felt dizzy, nauseous; he knew instinctively that this thing – whatever it was – was irreversible as the breathing of swamp-born spores. Which was reason enough to see it out to its end. And so he left Turgo lying there unconscious, with his chest laid open and bloody, and the scarlet vampire egg burrowing in him and hiding in his flesh . . .

Turgo Zolte recovered; his torn flesh healed, and quickly; he was Wamphyri!

And he hated Shaitan as no creature was ever hated before. Shaitan knew it, and would say to him: 'But you are my son – my *true* son – which is why I now name you Shaithar Shaitanson. You are not the ugly spawn of trogs, many of which I have made and put down, but Wamphyri! Oh, you had a father before me, but he made you mortal. And I have made you immortal. Why then do you despise me?'

'I was what I was,' Turgo would growl in answer, from where he hung in chains of silver. 'And I preferred it. You have made me other than that –'

'– More than that!'

'– Which disgusts me. I spit on your name and won't take it! Nor will I drink the blood of men.'

'Oh, but you will, eventually, or wither and die. The blood is the life.'

'Not my life.'

'Fool!'

'Ordure of blood-sucking bats!'

And always Shaitan would be enraged. But he could not kill him. For Turgo *was* his son, of a sort.

In the end he turned him loose, sent him forth, banished him out of Shaitanstack. Not to the north, for he would watch his progress. No, he merely turned him out on to Starside, to make his own way in the world.

Turgo went to Sunside but could not stay there. The Szgany pursued him; the sun threatened him; his foetal vampire tugged at his will, so that if he stayed he must kill. He *did* kill – but only to live on beast-blood. Finally he sought out men vampirized in the swamps, recruited them, returned to Starside and gathered together an army of trog thralls. And in thirty years he built Shaitharsheim, but well away from the aerie of his so-called 'father'. And so in the end Turgo did take his great enemy's name, calling himself Shaithar Shaitanson ... by which to remember his 'father' the better and hate him all the more.

By then Shaitan's house was finished and furnished; his banner – a skull head with horns – fluttered from the high ramparts of his aerie, and he was known on both sides of the mountains as Lord Shaitan of the Wamphyri. Which pleased him greatly.

Turgo was still a lesser Lord, and much given to nightmares. One night he dreamed he drank Szgany blood, and when he woke up it was true. In the night he had taken from his odalisque, a girl stolen from a Sunside tribe. He could deny it no longer: he *was* Wamphyri! Then, blaming Shaitan and loathing him more yet, he devised a sigil of his own: Shaitan's horned skull-head – but split in two halves by a silver axe!

Shaitan saw how he was abhorred and bred more and better warriors. Turgo bred them, too, as a safe-guard. And through all of this men came lurching from the vampire swamps to build their aeries in the stacks. Their industry was great, so that they had little time for wars.

Two hundred years flew by and the Wamphyri were mighty and many. Too many ...

Now, on Sunside, the Szgany had become Travellers, nomads, Gypsies who went from place to place by day, and slept in deep forests or caves at night. And for them it was as bad or worse than the aftermath of the white sun. The Wamphyri gave them no peace; night after night they raided; the toll of blood was monstrous!

While on Starside . . . Shaitan saw his error in permitting the other Lords to wax so strong and so many. He determined to make sons for lieutenants, bloodsons, which he would get out of comely women. In this way he would overwhelm the Wamphyri Lords and keep them down. He made a harem of six Szgany women, took from them and gave to them. And his vampire sons and daughters were many. Of the latter, when they were ripe, he used them in their turn; for his own flesh was the sweetest. Which would be the way of it with vampires down all the ages . . .

And Shaitan begat Shaithos Longarm, Shailar the Hagridden (who was half-mad, for insanity was a curse which the Wamphyri would never eradicate), Shaithag the Harrower, and many others. And his egg-recipient son, now Shaithar Shaitanson, begat Shielar the Slut, Turgo Toothbreaker, Zol Zolteson, and Pedar Sloughskin, who at the age of thirteen contracted leprosy during a Sunside hunt. And thereafter Pedar (also 'the Leper') killed Szgany women on sight and went only with trog females.

And in the great aeries of the Wamphyri the other Lords begat egg-sons and bloodsons of their own, made vampires and warriors galore, and generally filled their stacks with beastliness of every description. Lagular Ferenczy begat Nonari the Gross, whose left hand was a great fist, its fingers fused into a club; Lagular also begat Freyda Ferenc, who for her pleasure suffocated men with her sex. Freyda was a Mother of Vampires, who in a single confinement produced an hundred eggs, being so depleted during the which that she died. But the eggs of Freyda, all save one, were gross and diseased and likewise expired; the one fused with Bela Manculi, a Szgany thrall, who became heir to Freydastack.

And Pedar the Leper begat Tori Trogson, who went on all fours and became Lord of Trogstack. And Shielar of Whorestack brought forth Thador Thornskull; she then made a warrior with an Organ, and died of fornication in the Thing's embrace. And so Thador became Lust-lord of Whorestack. But from that time forward it was generally agreed among all the Wamphyri that none would make monsters with the parts of men, for Shielar's creature had proven difficult to put down.

And as the many Lords and fewer Ladies proliferated, so they degenerated; even the Wamphyri, going from evil to evil and descending from depth to irredeemable depth . . .

Eventually all of the greater aeries had masters or mistresses; the lesser stacks were occupied; there was no more room in all the vampire heights for men and their sons, their women, thralls and creatures. Some built their aeries in the sheerer crags of the barrier range, looking out on Starside; but they were prone to avalanches, brought about by enemies. Also, they were scorned as worthless Lords, who had not proper aeries of their own. And finally they warred for possession of the lofty stacks, until the winds over Starside were filled with flyers and warriors which fought in the dark sky under blue-glittering stars, and did battle in the higher ramparts of the great aeries.

And gongs sounded as warriors were brought mewling out of their vats and launched into battle all untried; the drums of war pounded, and banners flew from all the stacks, displaying the sigils of their masters; vampire destroyed vampire, even sons and brothers, as the boulder plains and the lands around the great aeries were drenched in blood and littered with the grotesque and shattered corpses of fallen beasts.

Even Shaitan came under attack, but he was clever and defended his aerie, and went not out to war. But as various Lords were weakened in stacks close by, then he would swoop on them and put them down. And in this manner a cluster of aeries all came under Shaitan's command.

When his strategy was seen, the others called a truce and came upon him as a single force. Surprised, Shaitan found himself trapped in the higher levels of Shaitan-stack. The flyers of his enemies were landing in his launching bays; he was cut off from his warriors; *their* warriors landed on his roof to seek him out!

He was forced out of a window and exposed upon the highest ledge. Flyers closed in, to knock him from his perch. He formed the metamorphic flesh of his hands into great suckers wherewith to clasp the sheer face of the stack, and went in this fashion to find a secure niche. But a warrior, dashing itself into the wall close by, shook him loose. Then, by dint of his great will – coupled with the tenacity of his vampire tenant, which dared not allow him to be broken in such a disastrous fall – Shaitan stretched his flesh into an airfoil and swooped, in a fashion, to earth. Even so he crashed down, but was not greatly harmed.

And meanwhile his forces had regrouped under his lieutenants, and Shaitanstack had not been taken.

So Shaitan was the first of the Wamphyri to fly in his own right. Which seemed hardly strange to him, for he fancied that upon a time, somewhere and when, he had known the power of flight before . . .

*

161

The stack wars continued for a hundred years; men and monsters were born and died fighting; the fashioning of flyers and warriors became an art, and Wamphyri numbers were decimated in all the reek and roil and mindless slaughter. And this was the era in which the Szgany of Sunside stepped back from the brink and breathed again, reorganizing their lives and what little was left of their society. Except it couldn't last.

For Shaitan was now the undisputed Lord of Vampires, the high magistrate to which lesser Wamphyri Lords took their disputes for his judgement. And as the clamour of war subsided, so the period of mercifully infrequent raids on Sunside was over, and the nightmare sprang up again with renewed consistency. For now the Wamphyri must see to the replenishment of their ravaged and undernourished aeries, whose sustenance roamed on Sunside.

For sixty years this was the way of it: three thousand sundowns of horror and misery, while Shaitan doled out hunting permits and took his tithe of trembling flesh from whatever the others brought back. But in the same sixty years, his egg waxed in Shaithar Shaitanson, once Turgo Zolte, and made him a crafty vampire indeed. And Shaithar was strong; likewise his sons, Zol Zolteson and Turgo Toothbreaker. And all of them together, they hated Shaitan worse than any other.

The Lord of Vampires knew it, for he had his spies in all the aeries. And when the coup came at last he was ready to put it down, with never a loss to mention. Then he brought Shaithar to trial with his sons and their lieutenants, and banished them north to the Icelands – all of them that were of his own egg.

They were allowed flyers, certainly, and a female thrall or two, but neither provisions nor beasts to spare and never a warrior between them. So they launched themselves north, and held to that course a spell — before swinging east to follow the spine of the barrier range into lands unknown. Shaitan's familiar bats brought him word of their deception, which was no great surprise. For this, too, he had foreseen.

And he said to himself: *Ah, Turgo Zolte, what a son you could have been! Why, we could have ravaged this entire world together, you and I! But I have already shown my weakness for you in banishing you when by rights I should kill you, and I know now that you must die, else return one day to plague me with your mischiefs. Well, so be it . . .*

Even as he thought these things, his warriors were aloft and spurting through Starside's night skies, falling towards their prey where Shaithar and his outcasts winged east. And Shaitan reached out to mind-jab his beasts, commanding that they: *Destroy them to a man!*

And riding east, exiled, expelled, Shaithar *was* Turgo Zolte once more. Oh, he was Wamphyri, but his intentions were human so far as he could determine. A pity there was no room now for humanity on Starside.

His plan was simple: find a new home for his small group in the east, far beyond the Great Red Waste which was known to lie there. Perhaps something of their old humanity could still be salvaged from what they had become. Perhaps they could find a new way to live.

Turgo was in no hurry; his flyers were already burdened; he would not exhaust them by spurring them on. To what end? To crash in the Great Red Waste and to go on foot till the rising sun found them out and reduced them all to tar? Better to take them up to their ceiling, then glide them on whichever thermals were available, and so conserve their energies. Which he did.

Shaitan's warriors, coming from behind but still some

way off, saw the small knot of flyers spiralling up towards the stars; they too must climb; their propulsors throbbed and gas sacks inflated, and their mantles extended to give them lift. But flyers were fashioned for flying and warriors for warring; they had not the endurance for prolonged pursuit. Shaitan must sacrifice them. *Do not return, but destroy them utterly*, was his final command, over such a distance that he barely reached them. But it was enough.

Turgo's party flew on, gliding down the wind ... but now they spied behind them the instruments of Shaitan's wrath. They urged their flyers to greater effort, sped out across the Great Red Waste. The warriors pursued, gaining however gradually. But in the south the mountains were no more, only flatlands of rust-red sand, beyond which showed spokes of sunlight stroking the sky! Sunup, soon!

And the golden fan was even now slanting over the rim of the world, and Turgo must fly lower, ever lower, to avoid the deadly rays. His creatures were tired, their energy expended; Shaitan's warriors, too, but in them there was only one goal, one requirement. No need for conservation: this was their last mission.

Then, beyond the Great Red Waste, Turgo spied a secondary range of mountains, with deep gashes and gulleys facing north, where the sunlight could never reach. *There!* he mind-called to his people. *In the lee of the mountains. Build your aeries there.*

But they knew from his tone that he would not be with them. *And what of you?*

My flyer is finished, he told them. *Anyway ... I've done with running away. Now go!*

Shaitan's warriors were almost upon them. As Turgo's people sped off into the shadows of the lesser range, he turned back, passed between the pursuers (but barely), hauled on his reins and climbed for the fading stars – and climbed into blinding sunlight! And the warriors followed at once!

The vampire stuff in them was very strong, for they were of Shaitan's fashioning – which was also their weakness! The sunlight ate into them that much deeper, pitting their flesh into craters and steaming them away. All but one fell, exploding as their skins shrivelled and gas bladders ruptured. Turgo was likewise burned and blistered, until finally he could take no more. Then he guided his hissing beast into a dive, down to the shade of the mountains.

Too late, for he was blind! *Fly on*, he ordered his creature. *Into the east, as far and as fast as you can.* For he knew that one warrior yet survived; he could feel its tiny, savage mind intent upon his destruction; he would lure it from his people.

And he did, for thirty more miles: lured it to a place where mists came writhing out of the earth, drawn up by the risen sun, where once more the mountains crumbled into bogs and quagmire. There at last Shaitan's warrior caught him, and tore him and his flyer both. And Turgo Zolte, his flying beast and the warrior, all three, surrendered what was left of life and crashed down into the swamps.

Turgo's flight from the stacks of the Wamphyri had been long and long, but he was of the line of Shaitan and carried a leech grown from his egg. When Turgo died Shaitan knew it. And he sighed, once ... and then forgot him.

But on the gluey bed of the eastern swamp Turgo's torn body rotted down and was buoyed up with gases trapped in its tissues, and floated to the surface. And there in the weeds and the quag, black fungi sprouted in his flesh, which as they ripened put out drifting spores from their gills.

The vampire is tenacious . . .

PART THREE:

Now

———————

I

'That was the way of it,' the Historian thrall Karz Biteri intoned, pleased to be moving towards the end of his period of instruction, when he could pass on these recent tithelings down the line for assignation ... or whatever. 'It was the end of Turgo Zolte, called Shaithar, but it was also the beginning of Turgosheim and a new era of Wamphyri domination. Far in the west Shaitan might have certain doubts with regard to the continuation of Turgo's people, but it suited him to suppose that they had died along with their leader; anyway, he had plenty of problems to deal with closer to home. This last is also supposition, but we do have the Seer-Lord Mendula Farscry's written word in support of the theory, for which reason it must stand.

'Mendula Zolson – better known as Farscry, and later "the Cripple" – was Wamphyri that time more than two thousand years ago; indeed he was the first bloodson of the bloodson of Turgo Zolte himself! But in Mendula the secret arts were very strong; his mother had been a Szgany witch-wife, whose talents came out threefold in her son. And Mendula had the power to read minds at a great distance, and scry out scenes afar. In this he was not so far removed from the current Lord Maglore of Runemanse, a powerful thought-thief and seer in his own right. But ... I must not stray from my subject.

'In his youth, Mendula developed a crippling bone disease which twisted him in his joints, bent him over, and made him useless in the hunt or fray; which was why his mind turned to learning instead of more physical pursuits. And such was Mendula's inspiration to discover and record the history of all the Wamphyri, that he even invented glyphs in which to write it down; without which the present Lords of Turgosheim must rely on all manner of legends, immemorial myths, and word of mouth handed down father to son. And the Lords would be the first to admit that they don't much lean toward that sort of thing; neither are they inclined toward the unravelling of glyphs, which is my good fortune . . .

'And so, clever as he was, Farscry the Cripple was made clumsy and vulnerable by virtue of his deformity. But he was safe from the torments of others because he dwelled in Vladsmanse, the house of his younger brother, who valued Mendula's sound advice in all manner of things. And he lived mainly to work on the histories, as I have said, also to mind-spy for his brother, likewise to keep his scryer's eye on the brooding west, where the olden Wamphyri had their aeries in the stacks of Starside. And so Vlad Zolson was Mendula's brother and protector.

'Which brings us almost to the end of the pre-histories, because after Mendula died there was no one with the power to scry on the western Wamphyri and record their works. But there were always Lords who were interested in Mendula's writings, and so some small measure of understanding of his glyphs was passed down. All of which came to me in my turn, so that now I am the Historian.

'Of the history of Turgosheim: I may say that I am writing it in Farscry's own glyphs, from immemorial legends and a few fragments of pictorial tapestries and skins which have survived all the years flown between. It will be my duty to instruct you further in these ancient matters, those of you who are fortunate enough

170

... enough to ... to win places for yourselves in the service of the Lords.'

Karz Biteri paused a moment to scan over the faces of his class of tithelings, seeing them as a blur of sun-browned flesh and dark Szgany eyes, and trying not to remember them. No, for he knew there were some faces here which he'd never see again. Except that from a certain point of view, they might be said to be the lucky ones ...

The Historian licked his suddenly dry lips, blinked his eyes rapidly, and scanned their faces again. They were all so young, so strong! For the moment. But ... better not to dwell upon it. And so:

'As for now,' he continued, somehow keeping his voice from trembling, his words from blurting out, '– now we must return to Shaitan:

'Well, eventually Shaitan's lust for power, his greed, maladministration, and – for all that he was the self-appointed "Justice" – his injustices became too much. The others rose up against him in a body to be rid of him, and he was overwhelmed. Some suggested he should go to the Gate; others insisted he be walled up under the barrier mountains, or buried on the boulder plains to "stiffen to a stone" in his grave. Ever the slippery one, somehow he swayed them to the least of his own pre-scribed punishments and was banished north.

'They also cast out a crony of Shaitan's, one Kehrl Lugoz, who went with him. But with these two out of the way the unity of the Wamphyri quickly dissolved; they returned to feudalism, warring, inbreeding and the insularity of their stack communities. Since when until the present day, such has been the enmity between them that none have sought or had time to expand their empire beyond its olden boundaries. They do not even know that we are here. But ...

'... We, at least, have reason to believe that *they* are no longer there! For the last eighty years' (he made no mention of 'years' as such but said 'four thousand sundowns') 'since Maglore the Mage's ascension to Runemanse, he has listened and watched in his fashion, like Farscry before him. Eighteen years ago he reported a mighty war; the cause was not certain, but it seems that in the aftermath the obliteration of the olden Wamphyri was almost total! Then, fourteen years ago, there was a bright white light in the sky far to the west; there came a thunder which heralded warm, black rains, and the more sensitive among the Lords of Turgosheim even reported that they felt the earth shaking under their feet.

'After that, from then till now ... nothing! The Lord Maglore has proposed a theory: that some great magician among the survivors of their war brought down such a DOOM on their heads that none escaped. Perhaps he is right, but there are certain hotbloods among the younger Lords who would put his theory to the test. They say: "If a handful of the olden Wamphyri remain, then let them pay for the crimes of their ancestors!" And they say: "We were thrown out, upon a time, but now the gauntlet is on the other hand! We are in the majority, and they don't even know that we exist! We shall fall on them like rain on dust to dampen it down – permanently! For now it is *our* time! Time we went home again, to Starside and the lofty aeries of the Wamphyri!"

'Aye, for Turgosheim confines these young Lords, who are restless and hungry for expansion into more seemly manses and aeries of their own. They feel their burgeoning strength and would vie with one another, and day by day they make practice and flex their muscles. For the time being all of this gauntlet-rattling is verbal; but soon, if they can't go abroad to make war, who can guarantee that they won't make it here? It wouldn't be the first time – no, nor even the tenth – that Turgosheim was torn with internecine war!'

Karz Biteri's voice fell to a hoarse whisper. Taken in the grip of his subject, he was no longer the Historian but a commentator on current events: a dangerous pastime at best, and more so for a thrall. Even so, he wasn't voicing his own specific fears but those of his master, Maglore of Runemanse, who was himself much given to rumination and often out loud. 'Even now,' Biteri continued, 'in the secret caverns of certain of the larger manses . . .' He paused and glanced nervously all about, cautioning: '– this next is rumour, you understand, which may not be repeated – warriors designed for aerial combat are mewling in their vats! Abominations which have been forbidden ever since that creature of Shaitan's slaughtered Turgo Zolte in the swamps, on the day his people came fleeing out of the west to make homes for themselves in . . . in the . . .'

He paused again and once more cast all about with startled eyes, this way and that. Had someone come into the room unseen? Suddenly, for all the flaring of the gas jets and the searing glare of their mantles, it seemed darker. But then, it *always* seemed darker when a Lord was about.

Karz Biteri gulped and his parched throat clenched in upon itself like a fist. But somehow he croaked out the last few words: 'Homes for . . . for themselves in . . . in the dark clefts and crags.'

And as the echoes of his words died away, now the unseen intruder made his – no, her – presence known, and flowed into view from the shadows. Seeing and knowing her, Karz gulped that much harder and fell to his knees. 'My . . . my Lady!'

This was a public place in the lower levels, set aside for aspiring lieutenants, thrall nurses, manse-managers, beast victuallers, brewers, and other specially talented thralls such as Karz Biteri. Honeycombed with lesser rooms, it was a sprawling cavern system which looked out over eastern Starside towards the sunless and forbidding Icelands. At the current hour one would not normally expect to find any Lord or Lady in this vicinity; there was precious little here for them, or so Karz Biteri had always supposed. And this close to sunup (even though the sun could not harm them in the depths of Turgosheim) they usually preferred to be in their own apartments. But right here and now the presence of the Lady Wratha was living, or undead, proof of the unpredictability of the Wamphyri.

Wratha the Risen: she was herself like a ray of sunlight falling upon some dark jewel. At least, that was her guise. But Biteri knew that on occasion she looked far more like something risen up from hell! For indeed she had *returned* from hell, or its brink, this ex-Szgany girl who was now a powerful Lady of the Wamphyri.

She laid a hand upon his bowed, balding head and her perfume fell on him cloyingly. 'Up, Historian,' she sighed. 'What? And is this not a free place? You have every right to be here, you and these tithelings of yours. But I was passing by, on my way through the levels to Wrathspire, and I heard something of your words as you instructed these . . . young people.' She drew him to one side, while he fluttered his hands and said:

'My . . . my words, Lady? But there was nothing of any deliberate mischief in them. I merely recounted the histories, what little is known of them, in accordance with my Lord Maglore's command. It is part of the induction, and . . .'

'I know these things,' she stopped him with a glance.

'But I thought that something which I heard was more of the present than the past, and I wondered at the presumption of any thrall that he should so speculate upon the affairs of his superiors.'

'My Lady,' again Biteri went to his knees, almost collapsing there this time. 'If I have . . . offended?'

'Up!' she hissed, almost dragging him to his feet. 'Perhaps you have offended. But if so . . . well, you are not my thrall to punish, and as yet I've no reason to repeat what I heard.' She glared at him, and her huge eyes opened a fraction wider. Their fire held an almost physical heat, which would normally be contained beneath the scarp of carved bone worn upon her brow, and subdued by small circular plates of a deep blue volcanic glass fixed to her temples in front of her conch-like ears. But when she opened wide the doors to those furnace eyes, like this . . .

She saw the cold sweat on Biteri's brow, the pounding of a vein in his neck, and inquired: 'Do you fear me, Historian?'

'I am but a thrall,' he gave his stock answer, the only entirely safe answer. 'Here in Turgosheim, the Wamphyri hold sway. If I do or think incorrectly I may die, or worse! Wherefore I fear no one but myself, for my own actions underwrite the terms of my existence. I repeat: in Turgosheim the Lords, and of course the Ladies, hold sway.'

'Only in Turgosheim?'

'And in all the world,' he added hurriedly, 'when the sun is down and shadows creep. As for me: things are as they are, and mine is not to fear but to obey.'

'Then obey me now,' she told him, her voice low, languorous, deadly dangerous, 'and make no more speeches of warriors mewling in their vats. Ah, I know where you have heard these whispers – which are the fears of old, old men, whose learning has stunted their manly appetites – but put them out of your mind. Aye, while yet your mind *is* your own.'

'Of course, Lady, yes!' he answered, following her where she moved back towards the tithelings.

She paused and took his arm, as if he were the friend of a lifetime, saying, 'Do you know, Historian, but just as Maglore has you, I too had a trusted thrall upon a time. Oh, I've had many such, aye, but this one was ... *very* special. No hard and thorny lieutenant, but a soft-skinned song-bird out of Sunside. Yes, it's true: he bathed me and sang me songs! Alas, but the many intimacies I allowed him were not enough; he would be my husband and lord it over Wrathspire as my equal! For he was a strong, comely young man, and what was I but a woman, after all?'

She let go his arm and suddenly her voice was cold as ice. 'Well, he's not much for singing now, though I'll admit he grunts a bit. For now when I go to my bed, the bulk of his warty hide guards my doorway, and what small part remains of his brain cringes from the lash of my thoughts!'

And Karz shuddered deep inside as he remembered what he'd heard of the guardian of Wratha's bedchamber: that it once was a handsome Szgany thrall, whose ambitions had been bigger than his member. And he was reminded of an old thrall adage: 'Never attempt the seduction of your master, neither by word nor deed. Remember: seduction was only the *first* of his disciplines!'

But Wratha's voice was light again as she commanded, 'And now you must show me these likely tithelings of yours, fresh out of Sunside.'

The Historian couldn't deny her. What she suggested went against the general rule, but she'd caught him preaching less than orthodox lessons, which gave her the upper hand. And now she would inspect the tithe-lings, likewise unorthodox, but what could he do? Nothing, except step aside as she went among them smiling like a girl: the Lady Wratha, dead and buried ninety-five years ago, but undead all the years flown between.

As she turned her eyes away from him, Karz could only marvel at this thing anew. He was forty-five years old and looked seventy, while she was more than one hundred years but looked only twenty – at the moment, anyway. It was her vampire, he knew, moulding her metamorphic flesh to the shape she desired, presenting her as fresh and vital as life itself. Ah, but only anger her and the thing inside would respond instantly, a transformation which even the greatest of the Lords would avoid at any cost! For Wratha was no simple Szgany girl, and it astonished the Historian that she ever had been – if she ever had been.

He thought on what Maglore the Seer had told him of her:

Wratha had been a Sunsider, living in a small tribal community with her father. The leader's son had wanted her, but her father, a strong man in his own right, said she should have the husband of her choice. Being contrary as well as beautiful, she wouldn't make a choice but scorned all of the tribe's young men alike. When her father died, the leader made it plain that her choice had now narrowed down: she could be his son's woman, or she could be listed for the tithe. It was simple as that.

Not so simple after all, for she ran off! Angered beyond reason, and despite the pleas of his son, her tribal leader put her on the tithe list. If she wouldn't go to his son, then let her go to the vampires.

She lived wild in the hills awhile and managed to avoid the first tithe. Like her father before her, she was opposed in every way to vampire supplication and believed they should be fought, destroyed, even followed Starside of the mountains and put down in their manses. Madness! For at sunup, warriors were let out to roam on the floor of the gulleys and ravines of Turgosheim, to keep the Wamphyri safe from attack through their most vulnerable hours. And anyway, how may you kill men who are already dead?

Well, there were ways, but on the few occasions they had been tried – when lieutenants and lesser Lords had come over the mountains at sundown to collect the tithe, been ambushed, dealt with – Wamphyri retribution had always been swift and merciless. The last of these 'risings', which had taken place some forty years ago, was still told of around the campfires; but the heroic insurgents in question, and their tribe to its last member, were no more. The story itself was still the ultimate deterrent.

In any case, Wratha was captured, kept prisoner, tormented and threatened (but never harmed physically, neither marked nor sullied, for that was not the sort of tribute one paid to the Wamphyri), and finally handed over at tithe-time to collector lieutenants on their tithe routes through the tribal territories. But somehow, during her captivity, she had managed to obtain and conceal a small amount of kneblasch oil and a packet of silver filings upon her person . . .

At that time and to the present day it was the practice of the collectors to march most of the tithelings back to Turgosheim. Special cases (beautiful girls, strapping youths, clever musicians and men skilled in the working of metals) went on the backs of flyers. In this way they were spared any small ravages which might occur en route, so ensuring their pristine presentation. Wratha's hands were loosely bound; she was strapped into the long saddle behind the pilot-lieutenant of a flyer; at the last moment the leader's son came to sneer, and tossed up to her a small bag of belongings.

On their way back to Turgosheim, she got her hands loose and began to stroke her captor's back, and to whisper sensual suggestions in his ear. He was an aspirant but in no way Wamphyri; once a Sunsider himself, he found this beautiful Szgany girl's attempt at his seduction pleasing; he made no objection to Wratha's stroking and her fondly beguiling words . . . and all the while she worked kneblasch oil into his broad back, and now and then fingered the handle of the ironwood knife which she'd discovered in the bag given to her by the man she'd spurned.

The pilot lieutenant's blood was infected with vampirism, of course; he was in thrall to the Wamphyri generally, and to his own patron Lord especially. And this was the source of his downfall: his own tainted blood, which made possible Wratha's poisoning of his system. She worked the kneblasch deep into his spine, his back and shoulders, until he grew at first fatigued, then ill where he began to rock in the saddle. The tree-line was below them and the dark peaks beckoned, but his hands trembled on the reins and his body was clammy with the sweat of fever.

'You are sick!' Wratha told him, feigning concern. 'Take us down before we crash, and let me care for you until you're well again.'

Gripped by this dread lethargy, he began to do as Wratha suggested, settling his flyer down towards the trees. But deep within he suspected that she was the source of his discomfort, and instead of landing squared his shoulders to fight off whatever it was that sickened

179

him. Which was when Wratha used her knife, driving it into his back to the hilt. In fact the knife had been given to her as an instrument of mercy, so that she could take her own life. But that wasn't her way. Indeed, life had never been so dear to her.

She wrenched the ironwood blade this way and that in the lieutenant's back, until he cried out and his spine arched in agony. Then, as he slumped sideways in the saddle, Wratha toppled him into space. He crashed down in the pines, and a moment later his flyer followed suit. Unhurt, Wratha jumped free and went to look for him where she'd seen him fall. She found him under the canopy of the trees, groaning and badly broken, and hurled dust of silver in his face until he breathed it in. And as he coughed and choked, so she stabbed him again and again: in the eyes to blind him, then in the heart to make an end of it. And finally she set about dismembering him.

But in the twilight hours before sunup, the light of her fire was seen by a late patrol out of Turgosheim. Suspicious riders came winging to investigate — and discovered Wratha burning the lieutenant's pieces!

She was retaken — this time knocked unconscious — and so at last was brought in with the other tithelings. Except of course where they were innocent, she was guilty of this 'heinous' crime against the Starside Lords, and naturally her life was forfeit. No question of what should become of her, or to whom should go the task of execution. For her thrall victim had a brother, also a lieutenant . . .

The other tithelings were assigned, but Wratha was handed over to Radu Cragsthrall, to do with as he wished, so long as his final act was to kill her. Radu was the brother of Lathor, the lieutenant she had killed. But he was also thrall-in-chief to Karl the Crag, and dwelled in Cragspire. Karl was a rock of a man, Wamphyri through and through, but of all that a capricious Nature had given him in physical strength, she had taken back in wits. In short, he was a dullard.

And Radu paraded Wratha proud and naked before his Lord Karl, listing all the many things he would do to her, before she paid the ultimate price; which list was long and detailed. At first Karl applauded his chief lieutenant, but Wratha had caught his eye and was not cowed by Radu's threats. Hers was a stunning beauty, with hair blacker than night and eyes to match, legs long as sundown, pointy breasts, and a behind firm as an apple. And her mouth was a special delight: shaped like a crossbow's wings, pouting, and fitted with a soft dart of a tongue whose sting ... Karl might not find displeasing. A dark Gypsy jewel, she tilted her breasts at him, so that he lusted after her.

Radu saw the girl's ploy, ceased numbering his intended torments, knocked her to her knees. She cried out and fell against Karl where he sat, and hugged his legs to her breasts. And as she begged his protection, so Radu rushed upon her. But the Lord Karl of Cragspire held up a hand ... simply that, but more than enough. Which was when Radu, stalled, had made what could so easily have been a fatal error. 'She is mine!' he had snarled. 'She was given to me!'

'Aye,' Karl nodded his great head. 'Just as you are mine, given to me. But with the heat of your words – *this* which you would do to her, and *that* which you will do – you have set my juices working, and I would try her first. So tell me: do you make objection?' And all the while Wratha hugging his thighs, saying:

'Save me, Lord! Save me! I killed his brother because he would have taken me, to which end he landed his

181

flyer in the hills. But am I to be given to mere thralls, while even the greatest of Wamphyri Lords goes wanting?'

Radu calmed down. Blood was in his Lord's eye and a dab of spittle at the corner of his mouth. True, Karl was a great fool and easy to handle when he was at peace with the world, but when his mood was sour ... then the vampire in him took over. No sensible idea to turn him sour now. And so he said: 'Do I make objection? No, of course not, Lord – except that she is unworthy! But if it will amuse you, have her first by all means, and instruct her in your ways. For after all, what better teacher could she have?'

'Exactly,' Karl growled, and that was that.

Then ... the Lord Karl took his time about the 'trying' of Wratha, the while becoming enamoured of her. Finally she bowed to being vampirized by him, which was inevitable: stuff of his got into her from his kisses and embraces, also from those acts which she performed to entertain and ensnare him. However and for all of which, she let herself be Karl's thrall only insofar as that without him she was doomed, and no further. Her will was *that* strong, and in Wratha's case his was that weak. But at least as Karl's paramour her life was spared – for the moment. A respite she must put to good use.

Now Karl knew he must let Radu have Wratha in the end; or if not 'must', then 'should'. She had been rightly condemned to death by Radu's hand, and Karl could only lose face among his Wamphyri peers if he prolonged matters. And so he was in the dilemma of being, as it were, in thrall to a thrall. And meanwhile Wratha pleaded that she would do anything to avoid her fate, if only Karl could show her the means of her delivery. She did not wish to die but live forever ... with Karl, in Cragspire, of course.

The time came one night when she fell asleep in his arms, crying how she loved him and must be with him always. And Karl determined that she would be. Draining her to the last drop of blood while first she slept, then swooned, and finally died, he laid her prone in a private room and crossed her arms on her breast; then called Radu to see what he had done. 'There,' he said. 'The sentence is carried out. What does it matter who killed her or how? She is dead. Soon she will be undead, and mine, wherefore you need no longer concern yourself.' Dullard that he was, he didn't see the glint in Radu's eyes, or the way his chief lieutenant choked back his anger.

For Radu was no fool; he'd seen for himself the strength of Wratha's will, her tenacity, her lust for life. Now, for the moment, she was dead, but when – if – she rose up again, then she would be even stronger. And no room for both of them in the service of Lord Karl of Cragspire then . . .

So that when Karl was out and about seeing to his affairs, Radu took Wratha down into a secret place away from the spires and manses and prepared a chamber for her. And the chamber was a niche at the back of a deep dark cave, which he walled up with many tons of boulders, even bringing the entrance crashing down with his furious energy. So that at last the sentence *was* carried out, and Radu was satisfied.

Later, when Karl returned to Cragspire and found Wratha's room empty, he raged a while. Radu could only shrug and look mystified. A flyer was missing: obviously Wratha had woken up, stolen the beast, flown off. Perhaps they could track her down? They tried, Radu, Karl and two lesser lieutenants, to no avail. Then, because it would soon be sunup, they returned to Cragspire. It was possible Wratha had tried to go back to

Sunside. Well, too bad. By now the sun would be melting her away.

But in fact it was only melting the poor flyer, which Radu had ordered south for as long and as far as it could fly. And so life returned to normal in Cragspire, while in a walled-up niche in a blocked cave in a deserted ravine, death returned to undeath . . .

Wratha woke up!

She woke up with a small cry, in darkness like that of the tomb . . . and could see as if it were daylight! She could see in fact that this *was* a tomb – hers! And in a moment she knew what had happened, and even guessed something of how it had happened and who was chiefly responsible. Then for a while she wept, tore her hair and beat her breast, for she believed that already she could feel herself turning into a stone, petrifying in the earth.

Madness swiftly followed. She screamed and tore at the wall of boulders, which shifted ominously and threatened to roll inwards and crush her. Then, sobbing, she sat and hugged herself, and wondered how long the air would last; certainly the jumbled rocks were airtight, sealing her in like wine in a jar.

But . . . what did the air matter? Even when it was putrid she would live on, for she was a vampire now and could not die twice except she die as a vampire: by the stake, the sword and the fire. Which meant that in a century – or two, or three – she would quite literally stiffen to a lonely fossil here in the earth. But long before then, in days or weeks, she would be so weakened that movement was impossible, when she must simply lie here remembering her miserable life, and *loathing* the miserable creatures who had brought her to this unthinkable end.

Her madness returned! She cried out, shriek upon pealing shriek! Until it seemed to her that out of the very walls of rock far faint echoes . . . came back to her?

But echoes? In an airless tomb?

Then Wratha sprang up and searched the cave top to bottom, end to end, what little space had been left for her to search. And at last she found a hole no wider than her shoulders, no higher than the distance between her chin and the top of her head, out of which came a breath from gulfs beyond. A breath of fresh air!

She went head-first into the hole: a nightmare of suffocation, of wriggling, inching forward until exhausted, then resting as best possible, at whichever tortured angle, before starting again; and never knowing when the passage would come to an end, but *knowing* that if it did there was no way back, no way to wriggle in reverse. And so like a snake she progressed through the pressured rock, with all the tons of the mountains overhead weighing down on her.

Eventually there was a cave, with other cavelets leading off. On hands and knees, fingernails broken, bloodied, Wratha explored every crack and crevice. At ground level, nothing; all of the lesser caves were dead ends. But there, confined in darkness, entombed in rock, her vampire senses were at their best.

She was not Wamphyri, no, for no egg or spore was lodged within her body, but she was a vampire: the vampire thrall of Karl of Cragspire. His thrall – *hah!* But they would see about that! He had used the entrances of her body, her very throat, for his amusement, and she had absorbed the liquids of his lust like old, dry leather sucking at oil. And this was her reward. Well, and she knew who she must blame as well as Karl. And she did. *And* he would know of it, if only she could find a way out of here . . .

She rested awhile, and when she was still felt once more the flow of air across her dirty, rock-scarred body and torn hands, and on the cold-sweating mounds of her bruised breasts and buttocks. And yet what pain she felt was small, and all the while her fear receded. She had no egg, no, but her body was infected nonetheless. The tenacity of undeath complemented her own, and heightened her senses in a like degree. Moreover, the wounds of her hands were healing, and where new flesh grew it was paler but stronger than before. And she felt a certain sinuosity in all her limbs, as if they had a new flexibility. Now when she walked, she would seem to flow, and move with an evil grace. And even her beauty would be greater than before – unless she became mummified first!

She sprang up with a new energy, turned her face to the cave's ceiling, searched for the lungs of this place. And sure enough a hole was there, like a chimney going up. Ah, but it would take some climber to reach it! She started up the wall of the cave, and at once discovered that she was just such a climber! Her fingers and toes found secure holds in the smallest of cracks; the muscles of her arms were springy as the green branches of trees; she did not seem to have any weight at all! And clinging like a leech, she inched her way up the scarred rock interior and across the cave's ceiling.

And so Wratha progressed. But slowly, oh so very slowly . . .

Sne had been sealed up in the first third of sundown, and was out again by the next sundown . . . but so depleted that her hunger raged like a fire in her heart. And emerging on to the dry and dusty plains of Starside, in the shadows of the eastern range, Wratha's first thought – indeed her *only* thought, for the moment – was of sustenance.

She located a trog cavern, from which the first leathery inhabitants were even then emerging into the gloom, and took one on the spot. He was only a trog, but blood is blood. And from the moment of the piercing, when her freshly lengthened, keenly serrated eye-teeth bit into his neck and found the spurting jugular, Wratha knew the meaning of that immemorial Wamphyri phrase, 'the blood is the life!'

The trogs made no protest as she drained the life of one of theirs. She was a vampire, thrall and servant of the Wamphyri. What could they do? Only interfere and the rest of the monsters would fall on them with all their might, like an avalanche out of the crags. Anyway, they rarely suffered in this fashion, for the human leeches of Turgosheim were far more fond of the sweet flesh of Sunsiders. It must be hoped that this attack was the exception to the rule. And as Wratha moved on, they dragged the drained corpse of her victim into their cave and burned it, for even trogs had come to know the nature of vampires . . .

Strengthened, Wratha made for Turgosheim, for the passes leading to Sunside. It was sundown and the Wamphyri were awake in their manses and abroad on their flyers. But she knew that their warrior creatures were confined in their pens under the crags and spires, which gave her heart. And keeping always to the deepest shadows, eventually Wratha approached a pass.

Here the ground rose sharply, from the bed of the vast gorge which housed Turgosheim to the mouth of the pass, and there was no cover to mention. She couldn't risk it, not with the high beacons flaring red and orange, and lights burning in all the manses, and flyers overhead where aerial patrols came and went through the pass. Time to rest, and move on in the hour before sunup. Which she did, finding shelter under a shelf of rock away from the trail through the pass . . .

... The hissing and roaring of hungry warriors brought her awake. They had been let loose from their pens into the gorge where they roamed at will. When two came together they would challenge and rear up but not strike; their Wamphyri masters had lodged commands in their small brains, forbidding fighting among themselves; they were, quite simply, watchdogs. And they were not watching for other warriors.

For centuries ago, when the tithe system was first established, a party of Sunsiders had come through the mountains at high sunup to seek out and kill the Wamphyri in their manses. And they had actually achieved some small measure of success – the deaths of several lieutenants and thralls, the capture of a lesser spire, the murder of its Lord and master – before the surprised habitants of Turgosheim had put them down. Since when, this daily release of monsters into the gorge had become a matter of habit, passed down all the years between.

Emerging from shelter, Wratha spied the loathsome grey-blue bulk of a warrior moving in the darkness close by! She fled with all speed for the pass; scenting her, the creature roared and snorted all the more and followed after; she might have made it ... but another warrior was waiting in the mouth of the pass itself!

Wratha was trapped between them. They came upon her mewling, and glaring murderously with their crimson, night-seeing eyes. She could flee no more, and so simply stood and waited. At least they would make a quick end of it. But snuffling and snorting, and issuing their vile stenches, the warriors came no closer. They had her full scent now and knew that she was vampire stuff no less than they themselves. And Wratha moved between them into the pass ...

Sunup came and Wratha proceeded south, but in the

deep, twining ravine which was the pass she felt nothing of the sun, merely spied its light spreading through the sky overhead like a pale stain. And all the long day she marched the route of the tithelings and kept her burgeoning vampire senses alert for any strange or inimical thing. So she came to the descending slopes of Sunside, where rather than brave the furnace sun she rested in the opening of the ravine till sundown. And in the twilight she bathed in a tumbling stream, then made her way through the long night down to the place where her tribe had built a small town on the Wamphyri titheroute within the border of its territories.

Avoiding the watch, she moved silent as a wraith to the leader's house of woven withes and skins, where she found him home and abed. His wife was many years dead; he lived on his own and in a slovenly fashion; his loud snoring caused Wratha to smile, for she knew that this was his last sleep. But her smile was awful in the night, having nothing of warmth in it and even less of humanity. And standing naked in the shadows of his room, she called his name but softly.

He grunted and came starting awake, demanding: 'Who is it?'

'Wratha!' she answered, moving into the moonlight where it flooded through his window, but keeping her feral eyes hidden for the moment.

'You!' he gasped, seeing her outline, and that she was naked. And, coming more nearly awake: 'But . . . you?'

'I escaped!' she told him in a low whisper. 'The Wamphyri think I'm dead. Tonight I must rest, and before sunup go off into the forest like a wild thing to hide there all my days.' She intended no such thing.

He sat up straighter in his bed. 'You . . . you *dared* come back here? Why, you'll bring them down on us like –'

189

'Only for the night, as I've said,' she answered, cutting him off. 'And anyway, they don't even know I'm alive . . . you poor blind fool!'

'What?' He sat there astonished as she moved closer to his bed. 'Me, blind? What are you saying?'

'You who would give me to his son, when all that I really wanted . . . was you!' It was a ploy: words to immobilize him, keep him from exclaiming too loudly. She lifted his blanket, stole beneath it, pressed herself against him. She was a vampire, strange and sensual. He felt her body's weird heat, which was cold at the same time, and grew dizzy from her fascination.

'But . . . I was old,' he stuttered. 'And you . . .'

'You were the leader!' she answered, her stroking bringing him burning alive, jerking like a hooked fish in her hand. And in a moment:

'Let me . . . let me feel you,' he husked, with his coarse hands on her body. She allowed it – until he bent his head to kiss her breasts. And then she saw the throb of his neck where her caresses had caused the blood to course like a river, and he heard the *hisss* of her breath as her hand slid from his member to the seed-swollen source of his lust. Then, as she tightened her grip with a vampire's strength, and as her nails dug in, he tried to draw away . . . too late!

He saw her eyes yellow as molten gold in the night, saw the moonlight gleaming white on her mouth of knives, which she closed on his windpipe to sever it. Perhaps, in the instant of her striking, he issued the small scream of a gelding, cut off along with his air and, less rapidly, his life . . .

. . . And perhaps, in the smaller house alongside his own, his son Javez heard or in some way sensed his father's small scream. At any rate he woke up, and listened awhile to the silence, then came padding to investigate.

Wratha, a child of the night, saw Javez in all detail;

he saw only shadows and moonbeams in his father's room, and a humped outline moving under the blanket. But he also heard the *sounds* of Wratha's hungry suction. It sounded like something else: like his father was with a woman! Which he was, but not in the way Javez thought it. The younger man's jaw fell open as he began to back out of the room.

Wratha stuck her head further out, tossed back her hair, and in a 'shocked' voice said, '*Oh!* – Javez!' Which spoke volumes, however falsely.

He knew that voice at once, and his eyes started from his head as he whispered, 'Wratha?' Then, jaw lolling more yet, he choked: '*Father!*' And blood surging, he leaped to the bed and tore aside the blanket. What had been his father lay there . . .

Stunned, Javez fell back, tripped, would have fallen. But Wratha was standing beside him, smiling her smile. She held him upright, watched his face, mouth and throat, all working in unison, doing nothing. And the knob of Javez's throat going up and down like some strange dumb bird's wattle, as he gathered saliva to cry out. But before he could gather enough –

– She showed him a splinter of ironwood stripped from a shattered tree in the mouth of the pass. And: 'Do you remember?' she said, dragging him by the hair back on to the bed with his father. 'You gave me a knife like this, upon a time – to kill myself, I suppose. But no, I used it for another purpose. And now I give it back.'

'Wratha-*a-a-a!*' he gurgled, as she drove the splinter deep into his groin, and drew it out; into his shuddering belly, and drew it out; into his heart, and twisted it there, and wrenched it until it broke . . . Then, when all was still, she kissed them both gently, upon their clammy foreheads, and left them sprawling in their blood where they had died . . .

In the morning they were found; the tribe built up the campfire and burned them, and elected a new leader. A search was made, but nothing was found. And no one slept for long and long, because they suspected a vampire had come to them out of the swamps. They were wrong, for she had come from Starside.

And now she was on her way back.

In the hills Wratha waylaid a hunter in the night, killed him, and drew sustenance from his red-pulsing lifestream. And each time she appeased her hunger in this fashion, so the changes in her metabolism accelerated, and her undead vitality went from strength to strength. Her vampire senses developed; she felt the restless, eerie zest of the vampire and a renewed, replenished lust for life — albeit for the lives of others. In the way such passions took her, she knew that she was rare; it was as if she were a vampire born. Perhaps some credit was due Karl of Cragspire, for he contained a leech within him, grown from an egg, whose essence had mingled with Wratha's.

In the next sunup she went down into the stony gullies and bottoms of Turgosheim, between the spires of the Wamphyri with their massive scree jumbles, and under the very façades of their manses fretted in the glooming faces of soaring ravines and jutting crags. And no warrior bothered her where she flitted like a shadow to the base of Cragspire, whose guards kept watch on the ramps and in the entranceways. Guards, aye, but thralls for all that; but Wratha was more than any mere thrall now, for she went under her own direction.

She climbed Cragspire at its rear, to an unguarded lower level, then came up onto a walkway of cartilage grafted to the stack's exterior. The walkway spiralled steeply for the heights but there was no one there to stop or challenge Wratha. Higher, the spire was hollow in many of its parts, so that she entered within and proceeded all the faster, from hall to hall, stairway to stairway.

She knew the rooms where Karl's lieutenants kept their Szgany odalisques, and the closets where the women kept their clothes. And dressed in just such a sheath, which revealed far more than it concealed, finally she made her way to the Lord of Cragspire's quarters. And all the spire asleep now except for those with duties, whom Wratha had known to avoid.

But in all three of the approaches to the penultimate levels under the seared ramparts of the spire itself, there she found small warriors on guard, protecting their master's privacy. And in the third such entranceway, because her patience was used up, she approached the tethered monster openly, with her head held high. The creature blinked its many eyes at her and shuffled, but merely grunted and made no move to stop her. For the beast recognized Wratha: that she had used to come and go with the spire's master. And HE had instructed that this one should be allowed to pass, with no interference. It was an order which had never been rescinded. Also, the master's scent was on Wratha, even in her blood.

And she passed the armoured bulk of it by, where its pincers and stabbers worked unceasingly at thin air, and its cavern of a mouth chomped however vacuously.

And so Wratha came to Karl in his rooms, and knew where to find him asleep. Except he wasn't asleep, for the vampire in him had warned of someone's approach. And entering his bedroom, she found Karl waiting for her. Then . . .

. . . His astonishment was great! He drew her to him,

193

lifted her up, gazed upon her from every angle. There was no word in his mouth, which gaped. And Wratha . . . she had been beautiful before, even as a lowly thrall (though in truth, she'd never been lowly). But now . . . everything about her was a man's fondest, darkest dream. Just looking at her, Karl knew she could make even the most erotic dream reality. And he saw with every glance what he had made: such a vampire!

Aye, and he knew what he had missed all this time . . .

She took off her dress for him and sat on his great knee, and as he fondled her, he was now more thrall than she – far more. Then, when he would have her, she made him wait and told him everything, sparing no detail.

Hearing her out, Karl's rage flared to match his inflamed passions. For just as Wratha had guessed it, so now the Lord of Cragspire likewise knew the author of this thing. His eyes bulged and his snout flattened back and grew ridged and convoluted, like that of a great bat, while the teeth sprouted in his jaws like scarlet scythes! Until he came roaring to his feet with a name on his bloodied lips:

'Radu!'

'But my way,' she insisted, clinging to his arm. 'Do it my way.'

'He dies tonight, now – the death he planned for you – changed to a vampire and buried forever. Not in a cave, no, but in a grave fifty feet deep, whose construction I shall supervise personally. Especially its filling!'

'Ah, no,' she advised, 'for as we've seen, even the best-buried persons sometimes return. And Radu is a traitor you must be rid of always. Do it my way.' And she told him her way. Karl listened, and smiled in his fashion; which in the circumstances was hardly a smile at all. Then:

He called for Radu, who got dressed and attended his Lord at once, wondering what it could be, at this hour of sunup. And in Karl's quarters Wratha was hidden away, watching and listening to everything.

'Lord?' Radu stood before Karl's great bone chair.

Karl's crag of a body hunched there, his scarlet gaze accentuated by the uneven flaring of gas jets in the walls. Such was his doomful silence, that for a moment Wratha feared he'd lost the words. But then: 'It is ... it is this business of the Szgany thrall, Wratha,' Karl growled, breathing heavily as he reined back on his Wamphyri rage. 'I am finding some difficulty sleeping, because it puzzles me. And you know how I hate a mystery.'

Radu shrugged (negligently, Wratha thought), and without Karl's leave seated himself upon a carved stool. 'Where's the mystery, Lord? Strong-willed in life, she remained unchanged in undeath. Rising up from your fatal kiss, she stole a flyer and departed Cragspire, Turgosheim, the world entire. She flew south for Sunside, into the risen sun. She is no more.'

Karl nodded. 'So we have supposed,' he answered, breathing easier now. 'So you ... have suggested.'

Now Radu detected the edge in his Lord's voice and came to his feet. Again his shrug, not so negligent now, as his eyes slid this way and that. 'But the evidence was such –'

'– What evidence?'

'Eh? Why, her absence – the missing flyer!'

'Ah! *That* evidence.' Karl fingered his chin, studied Radu intensely.

And for the third time Radu's shrug, now absolutely genuine in its bewilderment. 'But ... what other evidence is there?'

Karl nodded again, and sighed deeply. Then,

apparently changing the subject, he said: 'Do you know, the other Lords see me as a dolt?'

'What, you, Lord?' Radu's attempt at astonishment was less than convincing. 'I cannot believe it.'

'Oh, you can, you can! You've heard it said, I'm sure.'

'Never, Lord! Why, if ever I heard such a . . .'

'. . . And yet I fancy,' Karl stopped him short, 'that among my ancestors was a scryer of considerable skill. An oneiromancer, perhaps, and one of great power! Which is why I cannot sleep – because of my dreams.'

'Dreams, Lord?'

'Of treachery, aye!'

Radu said nothing, but waited. For after all, a dream of treachery is still only a dream. And in a while, Karl continued: 'Do you see that skin there, on the table? That chart of Turgosheim and all the lands around?' He pointed to a table close by. 'Look at it closely. For I have marked it.'

Radu stepped to the table, checked the chart, and his eyes were drawn irresistibly to a certain secret place – but secret no more, for Karl had ringed it with a line of black dye! Radu staggered back a pace, regained control of himself as best he could, and said: 'I . . . I see your mark.'

'Come,' Karl crooked a finger, beckoning. 'Come here, where I can look upon your face.'

Radu stood before him.

And Karl's voice was very soft as he said, 'Now admit it to me: that you have buried her there, as I saw in my dreams.'

Stunned, Radu opened and closed his mouth but said nothing. So that Karl warned him: 'Better if you tell me with your own tongue, while still you have one.'

Radu remained dumbstruck.

Karl sighed and spread wide his arms, as in a gesture

of defeat. 'Then, Radu my would-be son, we must go and dig there, you and I. And all of my thralls and trogs to boot, digging in a certain blocked cave. Until we have dug up what you put down. Then, if my dream has not lied to me . . . you shall replace her there in the cold, cold earth, forever. But if you'll be brave and tell me with your own lips how it was, and so save me the trouble . . .?'

'But . . .!' Radu's dam had cracked at last.

'Oh?' Karl cocked his head and looked at him, looked *into* him. But Radu only hung his head. It was an admittance of sorts – but not good enough.

'Very well,' said Karl, in a voice which was softer yet. 'Then go to my bed and bring me the sharpest of those crossed swords from where they decorate the wall. Alas, they are not *very* sharp, but sharp enough in a strong hand. The one is of iron and the other silver. I dislike silver as well you know, but its grip is of bone and it *is* the sharpest, and the other hangs there red with rust. So bring me the silver sword.'

Radu looked, saw the dull glimmer of gaslight on ancient Szgany weapons. 'Swords . . .' he said, tonelessly.

'Do it now,' said Karl.

Radu brought the sword. And as he returned with it to Karl many thoughts passed through his mind. To leap on him and kill him . . . *hah!* – what madness – try killing a warrior! To kill himself, then, which was far more feasible. Or . . . perhaps he should try to brazen it out; for surely Karl knew nothing for a fact, not yet, and all of this was a trial by nerves. Later, if it came to the worst, Radu could always make a run for it. That is, if there was to be a later . . .

By then he was back in front of his master's chair, and the time for action, perhaps even for thinking, was past. Karl reached out a hand. 'The sword,' he said. 'Put it down.' Radu did so, and his master took it up – but carefully – by the bone hilt.

Then Karl stood up, and Radu backed off. But: 'If you so much as think of running,' Karl warned, 'I shall take you down into the bottoms and let the warriors fight over you. Now kneel beside the stool there.' That was easy, for Radu's knees were giving way. 'Good!' said Karl. 'And place your hands behind your back, and clasp them. Then lower your neck across the stool. Even so . . .'

'Master, I . . .!' Radu's eyes bulged where he stared at the stone floor.

'Aye?' Karl's inquiry was almost casual.

'If I say nothing, I lose my head,' Radu gabbled. 'And if I speak the truth – even though I have done nothing for myself but everything for you – still I lose my head! Where is the justice?'

'Tell me the truth,' Karl said, 'and I swear that I shall not harm you in the slightest degree. Neither myself nor any man or monster in all Turgosheim.'

Radu knew better than to try bargaining, not with his neck across a block. And now his dam broke and the words flooded out of him. 'It is . . . as you have dreamed it! But she was Szgany filth; she was not good enough; she made your bed a mire!'

'*Ahhhh!*' said Karl.

Radu heard the swish as the sword went up, and screamed, 'Master! Your word, not to harm me: neither yourself nor any man!'

'Indeed,' said Karl.

Sensing in that final moment the presence of some other, Radu's eyes swivelled up – even as Wratha's silver sword came slicing down. And in the instant of death, still Radu didn't believe who he saw standing there . . .

Then it was done, Wratha's way, and in every instance but one Karl had stood by his word. For neither himself nor any man of Turgosheim had killed Radu Cragsthrall.

But a monster . . .?

II

Some hours after his meeting with Wratha, Karz Biteri, Historian to the Wamphyri, thrall to Maglore of Runemanse, reported to his master in one of his several workshops and recounted the occurrences of the day. But not in every detail.

When Karz was done, Maglore looked up from his examination of stretched, rune-inscribed skins (the bleached skins of trogs, mainly) and various fragments of carved bone, and said, 'Continue.' Simply that. A man of words, he nevertheless knew how to use them sparingly. And the implication of this single word was that he already knew there *was* more to be known.

Maglore was one hundred and sixty years old. By Wamphyri standards he should be in his prime, but he looked old. He and certain others of the Lords and Ladies — mainly the so-called 'high-caste' of the Wamphyri — were modern disciples of Turgo Zolte: so far as possible, they followed Zolte's olden ascetic dictums. These were simple and all based upon one ideal:

To fight vampirism throughout life and undeath, even including the ultimate condition of vampiric contagion, which is to be Wamphyri! To deny oneself — and therefore one's parasite — those things which are the fuel of all evil works: blood, the carnal lusts of the flesh, suspicion and hatred of one's fellows, and the pride which comes before a fall. In short, to be Shaitan's opposite, or as much opposed to him and his ways as possible. It had been a losing battle for Turgo Zolte and all his followers ever since, but still they tried. And it accounted for Maglore's shrivelled aspect; for as he'd learned well enough, though still he would deny it, the blood *is* the life.

Yes, Maglore *looked* old, but Karz knew that he didn't need to. On those infrequent occasions when he called for his woman, then he would appear young again, and the Historian would know that he had taken the blood of a man.

'Continue, master?' Karz looked blank, and for all that he should know better wondered what Maglore was thinking.

'My thoughts are mine alone!' the Mage told him at once, in a voice that rustled. 'Unlike yours, which are to me like scenes in a shewstone, except when I'm not given to exertion and would prefer to hear them from your mouth – such as now! Or perhaps you'd have me look more deeply inside your head? That can be arranged, though it might cause you some small pain. Yet I admit to temptation; for who knows how many other secret things I'd find in there, kept back from me, eh? Now, stop playing the fool and tell me about Wratha: what else did she say and do?'

Karz had not wanted to annoy Maglore, for which reason he'd held in reserve various parts of his conversation with Wratha the Risen: for instance, that part in respect – or lack of it – to the self-styled aristocrats of Turgosheim, such Lords as Maglore and his peers, who were thought of as elders, sedate and sedentary in their ways. But now, at the Mage's prompting, Wratha's words were recalled and floated back to the surface of his mind:

'... *Obey me now, Historian ... make no more speeches of warriors mewling in their vats ... these are the fears of old, old men, whose learning has stunted their manly appetites ...*'

Maglore read her words there in Karz's mind, and smiled however bitterly. 'Huh!' he grunted. 'Because we deny ourselves – because we are, well, yes, it may be said, *kind* rather than cruel, *inquiring* rather than inquisitorial, and *retiring* rather than rampant – she thinks us dodderers! Nothing new in that. But is that all? Threats to you and insults to me? If so, then you prize my sensitivity much too highly, Karz, for Wratha has been known to say far worse things than these! So tell me now, what else did this so-called "Lady" say and do?'

Karz looked at his master and was at one and the same time fascinated and repulsed by him, who once was a man. His deeply scored skin like stained, ancient leather grooved by time and use; his white eyebrows tapering upwards into temples whose coarse, receding hairline lay as strands of grey lichen on his sloping dome of a head; the crimson orbs which were his eyes, deep-sunken in their purple sockets: eyes which were narrowing now moment by moment, as Maglore's patience grew thin.

Karz snapped out of it. 'Why, she walked among the tithelings, Lord!' he burst out. And then, more stumblingly (for he knew how unseemly it was to criticize the Wamphyri), 'Which is not . . . not according to . . . which goes against . . . which –'

'– Which was simply *wrong!*' Maglore finished it for him; and reminded him: 'We are *alone* here, Historian! If you offend here, to whom shall I report you? *I* am your master, who makes punishment – if and when it is required.'

'Yes, Lord.'

'Say on, then.'

Karz nodded, moistened his dry lips, and continued: 'One of the young male tithelings was tall, very strong, proud and even forward. He invited with his posture and hot eyes; he did not flinch when Wratha smiled at him and tried the muscles of his arms, nor lowered his eyes when she stood close – very close – to him.'

'More fool him!' Maglore growled. 'What then?'

'As I took the tithelings away for assignation, she told me: "Tell the assignor that I have . . . *noticed* this one." Which I did.'

'And?'

'A strange thing,' Karz answered (but here he hung his head a little, as if ashamed of his own Szgany blood). 'The assignor was Giorge Nanosi, called Fate-sayer, thrall to all and to none. He is no one's favourite and calls no Lord master, but merely performs his duties . . . impartially.'

Maglore nodded, and what was human in him thought: *This Karz Biteri is a wasted man. But if he were my thrall proper, then the waste would be so much greater. Among his own sort, doubtless he would be a great thinker, even a wise man. Which is why I have made no change in him but left him a man entire, or almost: for the originality of his thoughts, which are not merely images of my own. I allow him the freedom of thought, for he has a mind and is a thinker! And because he considers me a 'fair' or 'reasonable' master, he is faithful in his way and accepts my concerns for his own. Ah, but it's hard enough to be a common man, Szgany, in Turgosheim, without being a thinker too! Hence this brush with Wratha the Risen, when the words she overheard were mainly mine but from his mouth . . .*

But that which was inhuman in him thought: *On the other hand, and as he gets older, this honesty and outspoken spontaneity could become a problem. And so, in a year or two – when he has translated all of the* remaining histories – it might be in my interest to favour him and replace those brittling bones of his with far more flexible stuff. For with his agile brain, why ... Karz Biteri would make me a crafty flyer!

All this in a moment's thought, while out loud he said: 'Giorge Nanosi, called Fatesayer for obvious reasons? I know him, aye. So – what struck you as strange?'

'First,' Karz continued, 'Giorge examined the tithelings and separated out those which he considered inferior. These were taken away for processing. The ... the requirements of Turgosheim; the provisioning; the needs of the manses and spires.'

'Yes, yes,' Maglore waved a hand, dismissing a concept which to Karz was sheerest horror.

'Then,' the Historian went on, 'the Fatesayer lined up the rest and began drawing out the sigils from his leather bag, to which I was witness, as is the custom. First in line stood that young man whom Wratha had ... noticed. Giorge had put him there. And lo, the first bone shard he drew from the bag bore Wratha's sigil: a kneeling man with bowed head!'

'Yes, yes,' Maglore growled again. 'I know her blazon well enough.' And then, if not explosively with a deal more animation: 'Corruption, Karz! What? Why, it might have been named after her! Not Wratha the Risen but Wratha the Sunken – into the quag of her own corruption! And you know it, and the Lady *knows* you know. Wherefore, in future, avoid her at all cost. For I value you.'

'I avoid all of them, Lord,' said Karz, before he could still his tongue.

But Maglore only nodded, and said: 'Corruption, aye. But should I be surprised? No, for all of us – the Wamphyri entire – are corrupt! We are not our own masters but governed by our creatures, even as we govern our thralls. Except where we are merely corrupt, Wratha is *corrupt!*'

Karz said nothing but merely waited, and Maglore finally went on, 'Did I ever tell you her story?'

Karz nodded. 'Yes, Master. To the point where she killed Radu Cragsthrall.'

'Then let me finish it,' the other sank back in his chair and steepled his hands. 'For it's as well that men know this witch and her ways, as long as they steer clear from knowing her too well . . .'

'Wratha lived with Karl a year in Cragspire. But she was not Mistress of Cragspire, only of Karl . . . which we may suppose she found irksome. It may also be supposed that eventually she would get his egg, but eventually can be a long time.

'Now, Cragspire was one of the tallest spires; at sunup the rays of the sun, striking between the high mountain peaks, turned all its upper ramparts to fatal gold. For which reason Karl shielded the windows of his chambers with heavy curtains of good black bat fur. His several small warriors within the aerie, and the sun without, were all the protection he needed in those hours when the Wamphyri prefer their beds.

'Came that season when the sun is hottest and the coarser produce of Sunside — nuts, fruits, grains and wines — never more plentiful, when Wratha made her move. She exhausted Karl with her sex upon his bed (no small feat in itself!), and made him drunk with good wines. Then, when he was sound asleep, she bound him to the bed with chains. It has even been said that she sprayed the forbidden kneblasch oil about the room, more deadly to him than to her, for she was but a vampire while he was Wamphyri! Mind you, I can't swear to the last, but as for the rest: it is exactly as Wratha boasted of it to the other Ladies after the deed was done.

'She decked the walls with bronze – shields out of the olden times, when the Szgany had used to fight back, removed from the halls of Cragspire and burnished to mirrors – and all directed upon Karl in his stupor. And then . . . then she threw wide the curtains!

'In a moment, Karl woke up screaming. But he was exhausted, drunk. He lolled upon his bed, chained down, and his cries were like the gonging of great cracked bells as his skin peeled back and his blood boiled! The sun's rays were concentrated in his eyes, which blackened to craters in his head! His hair became smoke, while his limbs and various parts cracked open to issue jets of steam and stench! And through all of this Wratha laughing like a madwoman in a shaded part of the room, dancing from one foot to the other in her excitement, and hauling on a rope which she had fixed to his bed, dragging Karl more surely into the focus of the sunlight.

'Karl's body shrank and shrivelled; he was finished; his leech deserted him, came wriggling from his trunk as finally he burst open at the belly. Seeing all of this, Wratha closed the curtains and rushed to Karl's bed, and took his cindered head with the same silver sword which she'd used to slay Radu Cragsthrall!

'Then she turned to his vampire, which was also fatally burned and dying. In its final throes, the creature produced its egg – and at *last* Wratha had what she wanted! Of her own free will she opened herself to the thing, which entered her without pause and hid itself away in her flesh. It was done, and Wratha was or was about to become Wamphyri!

'Karl's warriors had been hauling on their chains

from the moment of his first scream. Now one of them burst free and came hurrying to discover and destroy his master's tormentor. Wratha, consumed by that ecstasy of agony which ever attends the transfusion of an egg, nevertheless stood tall and showed herself to the creature. For her time in Cragspire had been well occupied, and she'd made herself known to all of these children of Karl's vats. However dully, they had grown used to Wratha and responsive to her vampire techniques and aura; and so she'd exercised her will over them, practising for this very day.

'Now the time had come when these preparations must be put to the ultimate test. Wratha faced the warrior down, shouted at it with voice and will both . . . and the monster at once backed off! Then, knowing that she had won, Wratha ordered the warrior to a new post right there in a corner of Karl's bedroom; except that the room was now hers, no less than the warrior itself was Wratha's. For her will was abroad in all the corridors of Cragspire (soon to be Wrathspire), and Karl's other creatures were likewise quickly quelled.

'Beasts are beasts, however, and men are men, of which there were several sleeping in the spire. But Wratha's sigil — an unseemly device, to my mind — shows all too well what she thinks of men! She called for Karl's lieutenants one by one, showed herself and her handiwork to them, demanded their allegiance, their obedience. Some were common thralls, while others were undead vampires who had perhaps aspired to Karl's seat; whichever, none made objection. Let one so much as frown or make wry face, Wratha's attendant warrior would rumble and vent furious gases. And so now she was risen in every respect, Wratha of Wrathspire, and ready to announce that fact.

'Come sundown, she sent out a lieutenant and flyer

with messages of invitation to certain other Wamphyri Ladies, such as Zindevar Cronesap and Ursula Torspawn, informing them of a gathering in Wrathspire. Vastly intrigued, they all attended of course; but Wratha's special guest was Devetaki Skullguise, the so-called "virgin grandam" of Masquemanse, whom she much admired. Devetaki, when she was a thrall, had vied with a vampire girl for her master's egg. She won the ensuing fight but lost the right half of her pretty face, flensed from the cheekbone. Since when and to this very day, she wears gold-filigreed half-masks of lead: a smiling mask if her mood is good, and one which frowns when it is sour. In this way the two halves, both living and leaden, always concur. But being Devetaki, usually she wears the frowning mask. Ah, but when she is *most* angry, then she wears no mask at all . . .

'Well, I will make a long story short: the Ladies accepted their new sister (Zindevar of Cronespire, perhaps grudgingly), and following the Ladies the Lords. For after all, Wratha was Wamphyri now; which was, is, and presumably always will be the way of things. The route to ascension is not important, only the getting there. And it should be remembered: for every one of us born to the spires and manses, there is one who was born on Sunside or in the swamps.

'So Karl died, and Wratha was risen. Long live Wratha! In Turgosheim only a blind man or a fool would ask why beings who could live as long as the Wamphyri usually live so short.

'But who shall dictate otherwise, eh? As I've said often enough before: we are not true masters but slaves to our parasites, and not even entirely to them but to blind Fate, who leads us all upon our teetering march across the abyss of life and undeath. Such is the nature of the Wamphyri, and jealousy, greed, hatred and lust – and blood – their way of life. So be it. Perhaps it's as well to leave it at that . . .'

Maglore paused, then said, 'Very well then, Karz Biteri, Historian, and now you know the history of Wratha the Risen.' Following which he sighed and fell silent.

And in a while, Karz answered, 'For which I am grateful, Master. But if I may make so bold, all that you have told me was yesteryear – even a hundred years in the past – and this is today, when we know that the Lady Wratha breeds warriors in secret for the fighting of aerial battles. *But against whom?* Which man or men does she hate now, and to what new, even higher station does she aspire?'

Maglore looked at Karz and said, 'Hmm?' But he had heard him well enough. And he thought: *Aye, a clever man and a fine brain, but perhaps a dangerous tongue. I'll grant you a year, Karz my friend, or two at most. After that: you'll retain some of your intelligence at least – but flyers aren't much sought after for their conversation.*

While out loud: 'Mark this well,' he said. 'Let there be no more frivolous discussion of things you may hear from time to time in Runemanse. And never again let the substance of my conversation form the body of yours. Not even with the best of motives or intentions. Do you hear?'

'Of course, Lord. From now on I'm deaf, dumb and blind.'

Smiling grimly, Maglore shook his head. 'Let dumb suffice,' he said. 'Which I can arrange, and swiftly, if you cannot!

'As for Wratha and certain forbidden flying things which I've reason to believe she's breeding in the bowels of Wrathspire: she'll be called to give account soon enough. And not only Wratha but others I could name. As for now, let it rest.

'And as for me: I *must* rest, for it's sunup and I grow weary!' He stood up, and Karz backed away, bowing.

'Put these things of mine away,' Maglore told him, peering about his study workshop. 'Make all tidy, then return to your studies or tend your duties. Not least, prepare my good clothes, complete with chain and sigils. And my gauntlet: get the rust off it, if you can. Doubtless I shall be up and about from time to time during the long day, but be sure I am up at sundown!'

'Indeed, Lord!' Karz answered, who knew why his master must rise with the sinking of the sun, but in light of their conversation made no comment nor even thought about it, not until much later when Maglore was abed.

Then:

Looking out through a window and up at the spires and high crags, each one tipped gold in sunlight – and gazing far across the miles-wide gorge of Turgosheim, whose honeycombed walls contained the great manses, to where the pale lights of melancholy Vormspire still burned like glowworms despite that it was day – Karz did think about it, and wondered at its meaning. For it was this:

That the Lord Vormulac Unsleep, who in his prime had been the most powerful of them all, and still retained a measure of his former might, had called a meeting in Vormspire in the second hour following twilight. And no simple gathering this, for *all* of the Wamphyri had been called, Lords and Ladies alike, with tithe-penalties for any who might think to abstain.

Aye, times were changing in Turgosheim; Karz Biteri could feel it in his water! And he fancied that soon there'd be new histories to write, possibly even in blood . . .

Lord Vormulac Taintspore, called Unsleep after his insomnia of seventy years, had seated himself at the head of the great table; this was only proper, for he was convenor and host both. Tithemaster, adjudicator and 'aesthete' (the word must be read in the same light as 'ascetic' as applied to Maglore, insofar as such words may be said to apply to any of the Wamphyri), Vormulac was greatly respected . . . generally.

He was no strict adherent to Zolteism, but neither was he a glutton. He had not dealt his fellow Lords ill, not even in his prime. His forces had never attacked, other than to defend Vormspire; but when they *had* made war, then it had been utter and ruthless! Eighty years ago, Vormulac had lain Gonarspire and Trogmanse to waste, decked their masters in silver chains and hung them from their own battlements to await the rising sun's hot melt. Since when Turgosheim had stayed relatively free from internal feuding.

In aspect:

Vormulac had kept his shaved head and thrall's forelocks for all of a hundred and thirty years. What had suited his old master Engor Sporeson in that earlier time had suited Vormulac ever since. His own thralls were similarly cropped, including the women. His forelocks, having lost most of their jet sheen through long years of sleeplessness, were iron-grey; they were plaited and finished with tassles, which dangled down on to his nipples. His eyes, not quite uniformly crimson but marked with curious yellow flecks, were close-set and deep-sunken in ochre orbits.

Vormulac's nose was long and thin, and sharply hooked at the bridge; it might be that in some former time it had been badly broken. Its convolutions and the gape of its nostrils were less marked than in most of the Wamphyri, but its great length was a singular anomaly, with a pointed tip which came down almost to the centre of his upper lip and lent his frown a hawkish severity. He wore iron-grey moustaches which dipped at their ends to meet the 'V' of his goatish beard, and within this boundary of bristles his mouth was wide, thin as a gash, and held slightly but not cynically aslant. He wore a thin white scar in the hollow of his left cheek, from the orbit of his eye to the corner of his mouth, which might account for the latter's tilt. His ears lay flat to his head, and their conch-like whorls were tufted with coarse white hair.

A huge man, he stood almost seven feet tall. The histories had it that gigantism was common among the olden Wamphyri, when some had reached eight feet and more! Vormulac was happy with his seven, which were especially advantageous on occasions such as this. Since the seat of his chair was also an inch or two higher than the rest of them about the table, he made an imposing figure indeed.

And yet, overall, Vormulac's face and form were as melancholy in aspect as Vormspire itself, and the aura of his rooms, furniture, and tapestries – despite their richness, intricacy and questionable 'beauty' – was likewise doleful. Neither overtly dull nor doom-fraught as such, yet full of some sad nostalgia, theirs was a silent conspiracy to evoke visions of fled or stolen youth, mordant mistakes, and everlasting poignancy.

Maglore, Vormulac's contemporary down the years, knew the reason well enough. So might several of the others if they had cared to mark and remember such things; but in a world without proper records, time itself becomes an efficient eraser.

The reason was this:

That in his youth, after Vormulac received the dying Engor Sporeson's egg and ascended in his turn to Vormspire, and while still he retained something of Szgany humanity, he had returned to Sunside to reclaim the love of a sweetheart lost when he'd been taken as a titheling. She had come back with him to Vormspire, where their passion was such that in a very short time his vampire, however immature, produced an egg which passed to her through intercourse.

Alas, what Vormulac's former master had not told him was this: that he, Engor, was a leper!

The Wamphyri, whose metamorphic flesh shrugged off most of the common Szgany diseases, were prone to leprosy. While it made itself manifest in several forms and was little understood, they believed that one strain at least was genetic and passed on through the egg. It might skip one or more generations, but sooner or later must recur somewhere down the line. In the Lord of Vormspire's case it had skipped just one generation: his own.

After several years, when his love's flesh had taken on the hue of decay and begun to slough (and only then recalling his former master's swift deterioration and death), Vormulac had opened Engor's mausoleum to see if he might discover some clue there. Within, Engor's body lay in many crumbling pieces, with more than sufficient evidence to show how the filthy rot had continued to work on his flesh — *from his leech outwards* — even after he himself was dead!

Then, to make a quick end of it, Vormulac had poisoned his exhausted, ravaged love with kneblasch and silver, and placed her body with Engor's in the mausoleum. The tomb had then been fired like an oven; when all was cold again it had been sealed up — forever. From which day forward Vormulac had dreamed of her burning, and of his own flesh slowly softening, until he'd vowed to sleep and dream no more. Well, and he hadn't slept, but it was Maglore's belief that he still dreamed.

The story accounted for the first of his self-given names, Taintspore, likewise for the melancholy aspect which both he and Vormspire wore like shrouds . . .

These were some of Maglore's thoughts and memories where he sat at Vormulac's right hand at the head of the table. And as their host named and formally introduced the other guests (such introductions were mainly unnecessary, for each knew the others well enough; it was simply a formality, by way of starting the proceedings), so the Mage of Runemanse also considered them:

'The Lady Zindevar of Cronespire,' Vormulac intoned, his voice gritty as gravel. And, with some small effort at gallantry: 'Never in all her years more . . . more beautiful.'

'*Hah!*' she snorted, and her eyes flashed fire at him. 'All *what* years, pray?'

Vormulac shrugged. 'A handful of handfuls, Lady,' he made amends, however drily. 'And after all, what are a few years to the Wamphyri? Why, you are the merest girl!'

Much to Maglore's dismay, Zindevar was seated on his immediate right, and she was no 'mere girl' but a contemporary. When he had come out of the swamps that time ('lowborn', as it were, a Szgany mystic who went into the forbidden places to meditate, breathed a spore and came out Wamphyri), Zindevar had already ascended to Cronespire. Then she had been young, but even then she had not been beautiful!

She was squat, hairy, of lesbian persuasions, and the atmosphere about her pervaded with a manly odour which all her many perfumes together could never hope to obscure. And despite her years – whose number fell far short of Vormulac's and exceeded Maglore's – she looked young or in her middle years at most, which said a deal for her mode of life. Zindevar was no great 'ascetic'.

Rouged and painted, with her elbows on the table and one hand scratching at her chin while the clawlike fingers of the other rapped upon the old oak, there was this overpowering air of aggression about her, this impatience, this great disdain – mainly of men, Maglore supposed. He could scarcely contain the urge to shrink his nostrils and creep away from the touch – even from the *thought* – of that great fat thigh of hers bulging against his where they sat at table. And he refrained from more than a glance into her mind, which was full of breasts and behinds of various shapes and styles; and red-rimmed, yawning, pulsating orifices; and blood, of course. But the worst of it lay in knowing that he shunned the lascivious display of her mind not so much because it was disgusting, but because it was *seductive!* For whatever his alleged sensitivities, Maglore was Wamphyri no less than the Lady Zindever herself.

As for the mainly derisory agnomen 'Cronesap': while its use was common among the Wamphyri, it was never used to Zindevar's face except as a deliberate insult; for which reason Vormulac had avoided it. It referred to the way in which she had ascended: by gradually sapping the blood and energy of the ancient Lady who had occupied her aerie before her. Nor was she any different now, as her many female thralls could doubtless testify. Only a handful of her lieutenants were men in the fullest sense of the word (necessary for the protection, maintenance and administration of Cronespire), and even then she kept an equal number of female officers, to guarantee a balance. As for Cronespire's menials: all of its males were eunuchs to . . . to a creature.

So much for Zindevar; Maglore had missed several cursory introductions of lesser lights; even now Vormulac was moving on again:

'Now I bring to your attention the Lord Grigor Hakson of Gauntmanse,' he said, 'with whom we commiserate; his get from the draw these several tithes has been scarcely sufficient to his needs.' Grigor, tall, thin and shifty-eyed, nodded sourly, perfunctorily, all about the table, then returned to examining his fingernails. 'Following these proceedings,' Vormulac continued, 'and in the event there are persons present who would care to barter with him, Lord Grigor will doubtless make himself available in the pursuit of a mutually advantageous deal or two.'

Maglore leaned forward a little to scan down the table at Grigor of Gauntmanse, or 'Grigor the Lech' as he was known. One of the younger Lords and full of lust, recently his share of the Sunside tithelings – of the lottery in human lives – had been low in women; almost without exception his tokens had matched up with Szgany males, of which he had plenty. Maglore read it in his mind how tonight, if Grigor could find a taker, he would offer four strong men for just two half-decent girls! Someone would make a killing, certainly. In other circumstances it might well be the Lady Wratha. Except, and as Maglore knew, tonight she'd be otherwise engaged.

So the introductions went on, and next came Canker Canison. To see the Lord of Mangemanse was to know that somewhere in his ancestry was a spore-infected dog or fox. Named for the disease of the inner ear which had driven his father baying mad (till mounting a flyer he'd soared south into the rising sun), Canker had caused the fleshy lobes and fine whorls of his own ears to fret themselves into curious and intricate designs, including his sigil, a sickle moon. His hair was red and the gape of his jaws vast; his long-striding walk was more a lope; when laughing, he would throw back his head and shake tip to toe.

Lom Halfstruck:

The Lord of Trollmanse was a dwarf among the Wamphyri, with legs which were stunted to little more than thighs with feet. But with his barrel chest, hands like grapples, and arms almost as long as himself, any who would think to belittle him must maintain a safe distance. His reach was phenomenal, and he knew the vulnerability of a man's essential parts . . .

Vasagi the Suck, who was likewise deviant of form:

Vasagi was the victim of an hereditary bone disease. The small handful of Wamphyri diseases were mainly hereditary: various animalisms, several forms of insanity, aggressive autisms, acromegaly and other bone disorders; though with the exception of leprosy, they were rarely fatal. But when the growth of Vasagi's jaws and teeth had threatened to outstrip the metamorphic flesh of his face, then he'd simply extruded them. Which is to say, he'd stripped his upper jaw of teeth, unhinged his lower jaw, withdrawn all flesh from the offending bones and so been rid of them. Now, chinless, his mouth was a tapering pale pink tentacle tipped with a flexible needle siphon, not unlike the proboscis of a bee, which he could slide into the finest vein with amazing dexterity. Needless to say, he was not an ascetic.

So the list went:

Ursula Torspawn of Tormanse, who affected an almost human guise even to the extent of wearing Sunsider clothes, with all their leather tassels and tinkling bells (but bells of tin, not silver). Yet at one and the same time, she swore by the use of the rendered fats of Szgany women as lotions to hold at bay the sag and scathe of more than a century, and kept preserved various mementoes of her lovers down all those long years . . . in jars. It must be stated, however, that Ursula had not availed herself of these *souvenirs* while yet their owners lived. For despite that she knew the toll to be paid for the denial of her Wamphyri flesh, she was Zolteist to a point, whose nature was neither cruel nor entirely sanguinary.

The list extended itself:

Lord Eran Painscar; Lady Valeria of Valspire; the Lord Tangiru; Zun of Zunspire; Gorvi the Guile; the Lady Devetaki Skullguise (who today, for whatever reason, wore her smiling mask); Wran the Rage and his brother Spiro Killglance of Madmanse . . . all of these and many more. Thirty-six Lords in all and seven Ladies. The introductions took the best part of an hour. And all the while Maglore aware of Zindevar's growing impatience, and of her hot fat thigh against his; and all of their various thoughts impinging upon his own, until he could reel from the innuendoes and infamies, the dooms and desires of their collective mind.

They kept the bulk of their thoughts suppressed, of course, for the Lord of Runemanse was not unique in telepathic skills. All of the Wamphyri had them to some extent; at the very least, they could sense the *direction* of another's thoughts. Zindevar, for instance:

That Lady was as much aware of Maglore's close presence as he was of hers, which might well account for her impatience and the lewd scenes with which she filled her mind. She'd probably reckoned, and correctly, that these would suffice to keep him out.

Taken with the idea, he glanced at her from the corner of his eye – and caught her staring back at him! Her eyes were hot and burned on him, and her nostrils pinched with suspicion. So then, and what did *she* have to hide?

218

But by now Vormulac had reached an end, and only one was left to announce: Wratha the Risen. Maglore put all else out of mind in order to concentrate on the Tithemaster's introduction:

'The Lady Wratha,' Vormulac intoned, narrowing his eyes, 'of Wrathspire . . .' But now there was an edge to his gravelly tone, so that all fidgeting and murmuring stopped at once and all eyes turned to Wratha – which was no great hardship.

Maglore looked along the table to where she was seated at the very end facing Vormulac down its great length, and knew that he had never seen her looking more . . . *delicious*, indeed edible! And in that selfsame moment the mental ether was full of two waves of thought: one of lust, and the other a jealous loathing. No need to search for the origins of such sweeping emotions. Ah, but the crests of both waves foamed with something of respect, too, and even admiration! Aye, for Wratha the Risen had style.

She had not seated herself properly in her chair but was curled there, entirely at ease, with both elbows on one rest and her hands supporting her chin. Her hair fell in plaits almost to her shoulders, which were fitted with a torque of finely worked gold. Depending from this golden harness, ropes of black bat fur hung down vertically to form a smoky curtain. Wratha's pale shoulders showed through, likewise her arms, the points of her tilted breasts, a large area of immaculate thigh and her knees where her legs were folded. Seen as pale curving stripes through dusty black bars, the rest of her was scarcely secure from viewing.

Paradoxically but not unusually, Wratha's eyes were least in evidence; they were protected by the scarp of figured bone upon her brow, their fire subdued by the ornamentation of blue glass ovals at her temples, and matching earrings where they dangled from the fine-furred lobes of her ears. But apart from her Wamphyri ears and the tilted, somewhat flattened aspect of her nose, whose convolutions were not exaggerated to any great degree – and the red-flickering fork of her tongue, of course – apart from these things, she might well be Szgany: a clean-limbed Gypsy girl from Sunside, whose flesh was still untried, just as she must have appeared to Karl the Crag almost a hundred years ago.

Except . . . where was Karl now?

A few chairs away from Maglore, Grigor Hakson made small choking noises deep in his throat, which Maglore sensed rather than heard. He turned his attention to the Lord of Gauntmanse, whose mind was now an open book. *If I could have her* (Grigor lusted for all he was worth). *Ah, that mouth! And how I would fill it! She beds Szgany whelps, so whelmed by her curves they dribble on her thigh. But if I could have her . . . my liquids would scald her like steam, even to the core!*

Maglore scanned no more; in any case, they were all thinking much the same thoughts. The men, at least. As for the women: they thought other things. Devetaki Skullguise was amused, well in keeping with her mask; one or two others were envious, their glances sour; Zindevar of Cronespire thought:

Pale and skinny bitch! Szgany whore! She shows herself to men, gives herself to men! And to think . . . upon a time I even thought to have her for myself! Well, let leprosy rot her softest parts, and worms crawl in all her openings!

'Aye, Wratha the Risen,' Vormulac repeated, his eyes staring and forelocks beginning to quiver. 'Whom some might say has risen too far!' He put his great hands on the table as if ready to come to his feet; and farthest away from him, Wratha likewise straightened up and lowered her feet to the floor.

'If your tone and words have any meaning, Lord Vormulac,' she hissed, 'then perhaps you'd better explain it!'

'Better?' the flesh at the corner of his mouth twitched, tugging at his beard. *'Better!'*

'I came here at the polite behest of a *Lord!'* Her voice was also rising. 'It is not the case that some ... some swaggering lieutenant *lout* has crooked his finger at me, and like a scullery girl I have hastened to his beck. What? I am the Lady Wratha! Not some Sunside slut to be bullied, abused, and ... and insulted! "Risen too far", indeed!'

As Wratha's blood grew heated, so she herself changed. It was her vampire, reacting to her emotions, her anger, pumping its essence into her veins in the same way that lesser mortals pump adrenalin. For she had sensed that she was to be something of a focus here, and this was her response: to gird herself for whatever was in the offing.

Without so much as blinking an eye, she gained inches in height as her flesh and bones stretched, so that she seemed to grow in her chair. Her cheeks shrank inwards, ageing her face to gauntness in a moment. The ridges of her nose took on clear definition; its flat flange turned darkly moist, with nostrils which flared and gaped. Her breasts, beautiful and girlish one moment, in the next became wrinkled, fell flat, withdrew under the bat-fur ropes of her gown. And her eyes ...

... *Little wonder she keeps them hooded!* thought Maglore. For now beneath the carved cowl of bone upon her brow, Wratha's eyes were blobs of hellfire, starting like scarlet plums from their sockets.

Among the Wamphyri there had always been those of hybrid origin; their mutations were many; their metamorphism allowed *transmutation* into endless varieties of form. But few manifestations were ghastly as the Lady Wratha's eyes.

It was mainly that she had no control over it: only anger or threaten her, and this was the result. It was nothing that she willed; rather, it was something she would unwill, if that were possible. For it was this — this swift transformation from a girl into a demonic *thing* — which even the most hardened Wamphyri Lord found monstrous and, yes, unnatural. Well, and its cause had been unnatural, as Maglore knew well enough.

Reading minds the way he did, he'd long since learned the source of it, which lay one hundred years in the past, in the time of Wratha's premature burial. For it was then, awakening from death to undeath in her cavern tomb, that Wratha's eyes had first started in this way. Except hers was no mere claustrophobia of the flesh, nor even of the mind, but of her leech itself. Oh, it reacted like all vampires to threat or pressure — by fighting, or by attempting to break out or away from the immediate hazard — but it reacted more so, and more violently. For in the time of her entombment, Wratha had been driven partially mad, which madness had later transferred to her parasite. And now, host and leech alike, their moods and sporadic rages were fused inseparably.

Guilty as sin itself! Vormulac thought, where he sat and trembled with fury and outrage at the head of the table. *The reaction of her leech, and of her flesh, is at once apparent! She gives herself away, in front of everyone. Her accusers, myself included, are correct in their every suspicion. Except, I have gone too fast; this is not going the way Maglore, Devetaki and I planned it. Wherefore and for the moment I must back off. But how?*

The Lady of Masquemanse came to Vormulac's rescue, though whether by chance or design Maglore couldn't say; but he did note that Devetaki had replaced her smiling mask with one that frowned. And now, tut-tutting, and glancing from the tail of the table to its head and back again, she said:

'But Wratha — ah, Wratha my child — and why is your mood so poor tonight? The Lord Vormulac intended no slight or accusation, I'm sure, but merely stated a fact. For as you yourself must be aware, there are several here who *do* envy you that you are risen so high, even as Vormulac intimated. You know it and so do we all, for they protest your status at every opportunity. So? But they protest mine also, and even Vormulac's! And isn't that just the way of things? Why, we are all *full* of such petty jealousies, of one thing or another! And surely it's better to be envied than ignored.'

Clever! thought Maglore, who now saw how Devetaki deliberately cooled the proceedings, not only giving Vormulac the chance to make amends but also allowing time for their scheme to take its proper course, both within and without this meeting. For it would never do to have the Lady Wratha leave in a huff — not now, at this very moment — and perhaps discover for herself how the wind blew. Yes, very clever! For Maglore likewise knew that Devetaki Skullguise of Masquemanse was one of Wratha's principal accusers.

Devetaki had been there — indeed, she had been *here*, right here in Vormspire, with Maglore and Vormulac, contemporaries with whom she formed a covert Wamphyri triumvirate — at that secret meeting where *this* meeting had been decided. Here, in the privacy of Vormspire's upper levels, at that uncomfortable but secure hour of sunup when the peak's exterior was

223

blasted by scorching rays, they'd convened to discuss ... Wratha! Then Devetaki had told how certain unnamed informers had warned her of Wratha's works, which were such that they must be brought to the attention of the others; all of which transgressions, when they were described, coincided with Maglore's own fears and convictions, accruing mainly from his mind-spying.

Thus Devetaki, no less than Maglore, had brought charges against Wratha; but at the same time she'd vetoed all but the mildest of the corrective or punitive measures which Vormulac had then proposed. Sufficient that Wratha's new breed of warriors be destroyed, she said, and the Lady herself warned off from any further experimentation. Like measures must also be taken against a handful of younger Lords, whom Wrathspire's Lady had allegedly inveigled into producing similar beasts of their own. So it had become apparent that Devetaki still 'liked' or 'cared for' Wratha, despite that she'd informed on her.

Of course, the question had also arisen as to why Wratha needed such aerial warriors? To protect herself? But against whom? Or ... could it be that she planned for war?

Here Devetaki and Maglore had agreed that the Lady did not appear especially ambitious in respect of Turgosheim itself, not yet. But from Maglore's mindreading and Devetaki's sources, they had gathered that she intended to strike west – into Old Starside! At last Turgosheim's precincts had become too narrow, too constraining. The younger Lords would break out, and Wratha would lead them.

All very well, but in the unlikely event that the Old Wamphyri were still mighty in Starside, Wratha could only betray the presence of those here in Turgosheim!

And if she and the younger Lords lost their fight against them, how long before those great and *practised* warriors came seeking her place of origin? Conversely, if Wratha found Olden Starside deserted and settled there, how long before she'd build armies of her own with which to return to Turgosheim, this time as a warrior queen? Ah, for she was quite the one for rising up and returning, this Wratha!

Therefore, to simply let her go and to hell with her was out of the question. Wratha was headstrong, even 'wicked' . . . they dared not let her get away with it, and take the chance that in some not so distant future she'd make them pay for it. Vormulac, Devetaki and Maglore, they would go ahead and apply their agreed sanctions. But in order to do so, first they must arrange and provide the distraction of a gathering of all the Wamphyri together: *this* gathering. Which was how it had come about . . .

Such were Maglore's thoughts, which had centred (perhaps *too* centrally) on Devetaki Skullguise. For while reminiscing in the aftermath of Devetaki's conciliatory speech, so he'd unconsciously swept her mind with a telepathic probe. And:

Is there no privacy? Devetaki asked him directly, suddenly, and without changing her expression or even glancing in his direction.

Eh? Maglore gave a start, and at once apologized: *Excuse me, dear Lady, but I was carried away by the proceedings.*

Devetaki was a telepath in her own right, a mentalist of no meagre talent, and so knew that Maglore's apology was sincere. Also, he was an old 'colleague'. Nevertheless: *Hands off my mind, Maglore!* she warned. *Drift in the fooble, shallow thoughts of others all you will and catch what sprats you can. But beware the swirly deeps, for there dwell great and vicious fishes!*

Ah! – indeed, he agreed, and hurriedly moved on. All of which, like his reminiscing, had been the substance of mental processes, literally as swift as thought. But meanwhile:

'Well?' Wratha had unwound somewhat. Now she let herself slump down a little in her chair. Some semblance of youth had crept back into her looks; her narrowed eyes were hidden again under the bone scarp upon her forehead; her body was gradually recovering its previous blush, however pale. And her voice, no longer hissing but a chime, reached out all along the great table to Vormulac. 'And has the Lady of Masquemanse read it aright?'

Vormulac knew how he would like to answer, but must not. He nodded instead, however curtly, and added creatively, 'But it is your nature, Wratha – something in the way you ... posture? – to make yourself a great distraction. We have serious matters to discuss here. I desire that these Lords give all of their attention to me, and in a moment to Maglore. Alas, but a good deal of their attention – far too much of it – goes to you!'

No more! Grigor of Gauntmanse gave a mental shudder. He had heard tales of Wratha's awesome retrogressions but never before witnessed one. *I am saved in the nick of time. She is a hag!*

Wratha, however, seemed appeased. She pouted a little, then deliberately took up her former relaxed and revealing position, that 'posture' to which Vormulac had referred.

Maglore, allowing himself a wry grin, glanced out of the corner of his eye at Zindevar. *Aha!* she was thinking. *These men! But they are all alike: dogs who shag uselessly against the thighs of trogs. Except now they have seen this 'Lady' as she really is: a great crone! Hah! Well, and I, Zindevar, have dealt with crones before!*

This Wratha ... she should be fed to the beasts which she breeds in her not-so-secret vats! Ah, if only I could have persuaded Devetaki to a like solution ...

This told Maglore something and at the same time explained Zindevar's impatience and furtiveness, the way she shielded her mind against intrusion. Quite obviously, she was one of Devetaki's informants in respect of Wratha's illegal activities. But since Zindevar was known to operate a spy network second to none among Turgosheim's spires and manses, this hardly came as any great surprise.

As to why Zindevar should be so keen to conceal her part in all of this ... two reasons, possibly. One: she feared the Mistress of Wrathspire's reprisal, should she emerge unscathed. (Aye, for Wratha had a good many men at her disposal, while Zindevar's crew were mainly women.) Two: despite that Zindevar was an envious bloodbag, she didn't much relish her ugly reputation as a sapper of crones and a curse on her own sex in general. Or, if she *did* relish it, still she would seek to disguise the fact. So that where on the one hand Wratha must be considered corrupt, Zindevar on the other *was* devious to a fault!

Ah, well (and the Mage of Runemanse gave a mental shrug), no one was perfect ...

Meanwhile, things had simmered down. All around the table, the Wamphyri were taking wine and a little raw red meat — the halved hearts of suckling wolves, Maglore noted — to moisten their throats. He glanced from one face to the next, penetrating to their thoughts when and wherever he could.

Wratha's mind was shielded. As was her wont, she conjured thick banks of fog in her head to exclude unwanted mental attentions. Wratha was no great telepath but knew how to block the stuff. Perhaps understandably, there were several others around the table who employed similar devices:

Zindevar of Cronespire, of course, with her crudely lascivious gallery; but also Vasagi the Suck? Canker Canison? The brothers Wran and Spiro of Madmanse? Gorvi the Guile? Strange bedfellows, these! Or were they?

Maglore nodded knowingly, if only to himself. Oh, yes, they'd be careful, all right, this bunch. For they were in it to a man, even as deep as Wratha herself! Aye, for these were those selfsame Lords which she had inveigled. And their minds were clamped shut like lichens to rocks.

But ... might that not indicate that they knew, or at least suspected, that something was in the wind? And indeed Wratha *had* been quick off the mark, when in his anger Vormulac had almost given the show away. No time to worry about it now, however, for on Maglore's left Vormulac was on his feet and holding up his arms to quiet the murmur. And:

'Now to business,' Vormspire's Master grunted. 'But first, in order to refresh your memories with regard to the background of the matter in hand, allow me to reintroduce Maglore of Runemanse, whose knowledge of our history, from Turgosheim's humble beginnings to the present day, is unsurpassed. I give you the Seer Lord Maglore.'

As Vormulac sat down, so Maglore climbed creaking to his feet. Now it was his turn to keep the show going. Ah, but if only he could be sure that it wasn't already over . . .

'Two thousand years ago,' Maglore began without pause or any further introduction, 'Turgosheim was a vast canyon: a place where the mountains had torn themselves asunder, a deep dark stony gash with its mouth opening towards the Icelands far to the north. Its uneven body gaped like a wound in the belly of the mountains, and its several tails tapered into the passes which lead to Sunside.

'Within the canyon stood a good many stacks and spires eroded or split from the original rock, some whose roofs were flat and others which were craggy. And in the canyon's walls were caverns and overhangs and ledges galore, so that the very rock was honeycombed. The gorge was some four miles long north to south, two and a half to three east to west, and mainly sheltered from the sun at its zenith by the body of the range itself. Only the highest spires and flat summits ever felt the full force of the sun.

'In its bed, the canyon was a jumble of fallen boulders, scree, lesser ravines and olden watercourses, with some deep caverns in the walls where lowly trogs lived out their lives in gloom and ignorance. In the beginning, our ancestors were obliged to utilize these dull creatures as best they could, at least until they could explore Sunside for the bounty of its forests and lakes, and its Szgany settlements, of course.

'In short, Turgosheim the canyon was much as it is now, with the exception that it was empty, and only a handful of Turgo Zolte's people to furnish and inhabit its spires and manses. But to them, despite that in reality Turgosheim was a small place, it looked huge! Not so vast an area as Olden Starside with its rearing stacks and endless boulder plains, no, but enormous to them who were so few. And trog meat plentiful, and eventually the sweeter meats of Sunside, too.

'Plentiful, aye, in that time when Turgo Zolte's people, who had fled here from the devil Shaitan in Olden Starside, were only a handful . . .

'The great manses were built, extended, and furnished with cartilage and bone; and all the spires likewise, their external stairways covered over and protected by oiled skins, in imitation of those mightier stacks in Olden Starside. The passes to Sunside were opened up; at sundown our ancestors hunted in the forests, flying home before sunup with their booty. Life was good, and the Wamphyri prospered . . . for a while.

'They prospered, and they multiplied. Turgo had crashed and died in the swamps; his body produced spores; animals and men from Sunside were infected. Some of them joined with Turgosheim's Wamphyri and no one objected. For despite that these outsiders were lowborn, of spores and not the true egg, still they made us strong. And as yet there was room galore in the great canyon. Ah, but all the time what space there was . . . it was narrowing down!

'Lords begat Lords and Ladies, likewise the swamps, and in six hundred years Turgosheim was crowded. Even the smaller manses, the lowliest spires, were occupied, and Wamphyri blazons fluttered from the merest mounds. And the road to ascension was hard indeed, when the new Lords must inhabit stacks which in an earlier time had been rejected as mere stumps!

'Meanwhile, Zolteism as a creed had waned. Hard to deny oneself with all of the good things of life so close at hand, a twilight's flight away over the peaks or through the passes. They, our ancestors, revelled in blood and the hunt, and the fulfilment of their leeches became their only pastime. As for their carnal appetites: they satisfied those, and with enormous zest, among the tribes of the Szgany. But to what end? Yet more Lords and Ladies, and no more room to house them.

'Men go to war for two main reasons: to feed themselves, and to expand into new territory. No, three, for even the most peaceful of men will retaliate against an aggressive neighbour who seeks to relieve him of those selfsame commodities, food and space. The Wamphyri were no different. Of food there was plenty – as yet – but space was limited. Lesser Lords of low-huddling mansions envied those in their rearing spires, and slovens in crumbling caves could only imagine the opulence of Ladies in their vasty caverns. As for fresh-spawned vampires: they must be satisfied with their lot in whatever niches were available in the canyon floor!

'Satisfied . . .? Oh . . .?

'It was a scenario for war!

'Younger or less affluent Lords banded together and made vampire thralls, lieutenants, warriors, more than any legitimate requirement. They marched on the greater spires, to take them one at a time. And for every Lord vanquished, staked out, beheaded, burned, there were three or four to occupy the various levels of the ravaged stack. And then the new masters of these levels, being freshly blooded and full of battle, would make war with each other: level against level, stack against stack, manse against manse! Even so, amidst all the reek and roil, most of the Warlords held back from breeding warriors with the power of flight, for any who broke this rule would soon find themselves under attack from all the others in a body.

'But after each wave of fighting, victors and vanquished both would see how worn down and rag-tag
they had become, and raid on Sunside like recurrent
plagues to replenish themselves. And we may readily
understand how, in order to fuel themselves for more
war – or restore themselves in its aftermath – our
Wamphyri ancestors raped and depleted Sunside. How,
with never a thought for the future, they harried the
Szgany who *were* that future almost to extinction! Aye,
for while some of us may have resisted it all our lives,
we nevertheless admit that the blood *is* the life, and in
those early days of Turgosheim Szgany blood was rapidly running out!

'Eventually, common sense prevailed; the Lords called
a Grand Truce; they gathered together and talked. And
here, thirteen hundred years later, we may consider
ourselves fortunate that among the hotheads were thinkers. They saw now how Turgosheim was small in comparison with Olden Starside in the west. Turgosheim
was small; the range in which it was a gash was small;
the region across the mountains – called Sunside for
obvious reasons – that, too, was small. Quite obviously,
to destroy Sunside would have been to destroy themselves. So they saw how close they'd come to disaster.
Well, the upshot was this:

'No more wars, not for some time, anyway; a resur-
gence of Zolteism; a ban on raiding, even hunting on
Sunside, and likewise on the breeding of unnecessary
creatures. Peace returned to Turgosheim ... but at a
price. What price? Suppression of Wamphyri passions,
the outlawing of territorial expansionism, and the introduction of the tithe-system. Which rules apply even to
the present day, and we've each sworn by our sigils to
abide by them.

'Oh, there have been feuds, even wars between times,

but never so wasteful, and never so threatening to all of us. So things have stood for long and long.

'Except ... times are changing, and the changes have crept up on us all but unseen. My meaning? Simply this: that once again Turgosheim is filling up, with too many thralls, lieutenants, Lords and Ladies. Except *this* time it's our duty to heed the lessons of history, and never again allow matters to reach such a head that we go up against each other.

'In short: we need to expand! – but outwards, to avoid a great clashing of heads. Aye, and some among us may even feel the need to abandon Turgo Zolte's doctrines entirely, and let their parasites hold full sway. For they fear the stagnation of their leeches, which are the driving force of the Wamphyri as a race.

'Expansion, then – but to where? In all this range there is only one gorge suitable to our needs, whose spires and caverns are protected from the sun: Turgosheim. As for new blood for our young Lords and Ladies – from what source? Already Sunside feels the strain, as it did those many hundred years ago. The Szgany are grown unwilling to breed; some put their girl babies to death, and disfigure their boys rather than let them grow up and be taken in the tithe. Oh, they'll part with their fruits, wines, grain and livestock readily enough; but their children were harder come by, and so harder relinquished.

'Nor may we assist in that respect; that is, with regard to their reluctance to impregnate their women. For while our lustier Lords would doubtless relish such ... such *forays* into Sunside, the seed of vampires breeds only vampires. Of which we have enough.

'And so I say again: expansion, which seems to be our only recourse. But the question remains, where to expand? Into which legendary land of plenty? Well exactly, into a *literally* legendary land of plenty – into Olden Starside itself!'

As Maglore paused a murmur went round the table. There had been some small background noise before, when first he'd commenced to speak: a cough or snort here and there; a disinterested shuffling of feet, chairs; the occasional whisper. But now their attention was very much riveted upon Maglore, and the Mage of Runemanse could feel the weight of every scarlet glare, sense the swirl of hot, speculative thoughts, where he stood waiting for their low mutterings to fade. Until finally:

'I am a seer, as well you know,' he continued. 'Seer and mentalist both. And for many years I have scried upon Starside – but carefully! For in their time the Old Wamphyri had wizards, too; indeed, and until recently, there were *still* great minds in those remote western reaches, where mighty sorcerers had come among the descendants of Shaitan in their aeries. I sensed their presence there, and knew they commanded Powers out of alien worlds!

'Eighteen years ago there was a war, then four years of peace when nothing of their thoughts reached out to me, and finally . . .

'. . . Finally, fourteen years ago, the time of the Light-in-the-West. Sensitive eyes detected it: like the glimmer of a white sun rising, but westwards; it cracked like dawn, and then was gone. But sensitive flesh recorded the tremor which accompanied it, racking the earth in its passing. And sensitive dreamers felt its rolling thunder deep in the floors of their manses, which brought them starting awake. I was one of them who shot awake that time, and in my mind there burned a sigil out of nowhere, which I have taken for my own from that day to this.

'As for the meaning of the light itself:

'I, Maglore, have voiced a theory: that the last of the

great old Wamphyri magicians brought down a calamity on Olden Starside, since when they are no more. Except . . . I could be wrong. They might be there in their aeries as before, but quieter now and biding their time. Till what? Till when? No way to know, unless we go and discover for ourselves, one way or the other . . .'

The Mage of Runemanse shrugged and scratched his chin; he had played his part; he was glad to sit down.

Replacing him, Vormulac came to his feet and held out his arms for silence. For following the momentary lull as Maglore had finished speaking, now Vormspire's great hall was suddenly alive with the shouts and queries of many of the younger Lords, reacting with feverish excitement to the Mage's hints of ventures and explorations – and possibly even war – in the west.

'Wait!' Vormulac commanded – and again: 'Wait!' – as the clamour threatened to become an uproar and drown him out. But gradually the din subsided as they all leaned forward in their chairs and focused their attention on the Lord of Vormspire; all except Wratha, who made small but significant gestures to her cohorts sitting there. Maglore saw or sensed these urgent covert signals, but made no effort to alert Vormulac. By now the deed was done, anyway, and nothing Wratha could do about it – except rage!

The rest of them were under Vormulac's control now, eager to hear what he had to say. He glanced down at Maglore on his right and nodded, and said: 'Our thanks to the learned Lord of Runemanse, for detailing the histories and background to these times and circumstances in which we live; certain of our circumstances, at least . . .' His voice was low, dark, insinuating. And after a pause in which the hall grew even quieter: 'There are, however, other circumstances to which I would alert you, and they are these:'

(Wratha was sitting up now, and making more of her urgent signals, even as Vormulac commenced what would quickly become a series of grave accusations): 'First,' he began, 'Maglore has mentioned the making of unseemly warriors, fighting creatures with the power of flight. They have been forbidden in Turgosheim since Turgosheim's first day. Second, territorialism, or rather expansionism: forbidden, except in the near future *outside* Turgosheim, where now it has become a necessity. We must seek to move out, and soon, but it is still a crime to prepare for war within. Third, the tithe, a subject which I know certain of you hold close to your hearts, because of what is seen as its . . . inadequacies? For while the grain, beasts, fruits, wines of Sunside have always been distributed evenly, fairly, and according to individual needs, its human produce has been apportioned on the basis of pure chance. "Pure", yes . . .

'This was necessary, certainly, lest the flower of Szgany females go to Zindevar of Cronespire, Grigor Hakson of Gauntmanse, and others of the younger Lords; and likewise Sunside's young males to persons of other persuasions. I make no discrimination here: we are what we are, and no one's needs are less than any other's, except in the requirements of their spires and manses, which differ according to size.

'So –' (he gave a shrug) '– occasionally the finger of fortune points the other way: those who require girls get youths, and vice versa. But time usually evens up the score, and if not we resort to barter, occasionally at a loss depending on our needs. And because it has been – or rather, while it *was* – a matter of random but equal chance, the system was seen to work well enough. Until now . . .

'Well, I have made certain points, but without being specific. Time now to *be* specific!' He looked at Wratha, directly, the glare of his eyes reaching out to her down the full length of the table. Glaring back at him, her guard slipped, and Maglore read in her mind a single word: *Flight!*

He looked at the others sitting there: Gorvi the Guile, whose thin face was void of expression, and his mind shielded by a white, impenetrable glare. The brothers Wran the Rage and Spiro Killglance of Madmanse: the one remarkably placid, while the features of the second were twisted (as was Spiro's custom when cornered) into a hateful mask. Canker Canison: more wolf- or dog-like than ever, his feral eyes shifting this way and that but mainly watching Wratha. Lastly Vasagi the Suck: whose thoughts were usually strange as his countenance and often unreadable — never more so than right now — though Maglore did glimpse monsters in them, and knew that Vasagi's mastery over metamorphism must give him the edge in the breeding of weird warriors.

All of them: they had pushed their chairs back a little; they cast sporadic glances over their shoulders, checking that the way was clear behind them; they controlled their hearts, which to a man were beating faster.

For Vormulac's gaze had transferred from Wratha to them, bathing each in his turn in the red glare of his eyes. And now he spoke to them:

'For long and long we the Wamphyri Lords and Ladies of Turgosheim have known the penalties to be paid by any among us who would transgress against our laws. Penalties great and small, depending on the wrong which must be righted. Recently, accusations have been made which I, Vormulac, have investigated. First the matter of the titheling draw, its supposed "impartiality". What? The draw impartial? *Hah!* And indeed the Lord Grigor of Gauntmanse has a right to feel dissatisfied at his poor get, *from a system which for some time now has been manipulated!'*

What?! The astonished, outraged thought blasted out as from one mind — almost. For of course to some of them gathered here, Vormulac's accusation came as no great surprise. But among the majority: jaws dropped as if hinged; split tongues flickered and damp black nostrils gaped; eyes opened wide and scarlet. A furious fist (Grigor's) slammed down upon the table and made it shudder; speechless for the moment, in the next he would doubtless demand a name or names.

And perhaps he had one already. For Canker Canison had somehow contrived to slink away from the table to one of the great open windows, where even now he drew the curtains and leaned out. In a moment he was noticed; heads turned in his direction; he faced back into the room, staggering this way and that. 'Such treachery!' he barked, his muzzle wrinkling back from canine teeth. 'To rig the draw! It makes me sick! I grow nauseous from the lack of good clean air . . .'

And as Canker stumbled towards Wratha's end of the table, close to the arched exit from the hall and the stairway to the landing bays, so Maglore thought: *He has given a signal! Beyond the window, something waits!*

But already, and apparently unperturbed, Vormulac was continuing. 'Second,' (he once again held up his arms for quiet), 'of the making of warriors beyond common requirements: why, I have it on good authority that just such monsters are waxing even now, in secret caverns in certain spires and manses!'

What?! Again the outrage, the astonishment, hurled out from their massed mind. But before it could be given voice:

'Warriors, aye!' Vormulac raged, at last giving vent to previously suppressed fury. 'And for what, I ask, if not for war? Enough! Now I accuse!'

Sidling away from their vacated chairs, Gorvi the Guile, the twins of Madmanse, and Vasagi the Suck joined Canker Canison where he edged towards Wratha. Vormulac pointed them out, and all heads and eyes swivelled to follow his trembling, stabbing finger. 'There they go,' he spat the words out as if they were poison. 'Full of guilt, as witness their stealth. Canker, with his tail between his legs: a mangy cur indeed! And Vasagi the Suck, who alienates himself even further from his fellows. Also Gorvi the Guile, never so deceitful as now. And Wran and Spiro of Madmanse, whose madness finally overflows!'

Wratha was free of her chair; the others joined her; they backed off towards the arched exit.

'See them go,' Vormulac shouted, 'who by their own actions betray themselves! For I ask you, would innocents react in such a fashion? See, they join their leader, the very author of this treachery, of whom I say again: *she has risen too far!* But why is everyone astir? Be calm all of you, and sit down. They shall not escape.'

Many of the outraged Lords and Ladies were throwing back their chairs, springing to their feet, some reaching instinctively for gauntlets which were no longer there, relinquished in Vormspire's landing-bay antechambers. Others had commenced to surge menacingly along both sides of the great table towards Wratha and her five, but came to an abrupt halt as Vormulac put fingers to his lips and whistled.

It was a short, shrill, even ear-piercing blast ... and it was a summons. He could have called his creature just as easily with his mind, indeed more easily, but did it this way, openly, so that all of them would know what he was about. And now to a man they saw how Wratha was trapped.

All except Maglore, who wondered: *Why has she not undergone her monstrous transformation? Why is she so cool?* And at once answered himself: *Because now is no time for raging but for thinking, and even now she calculates!*

'Now hold!' Wratha hissed, as if to prove Maglore's point, and produced from beneath the bat-fur ropes of her robe a curious instrument formed of some small creature's bladder attached to a slender silver rod or wand. She held the bulb in her hand, pointing the wand into the hall. And: 'Oil of kneblasch,' she informed, squeezing the bulb however slightly. A fine spray issued out from perforations in the end of the rod, hanging in the air like a mist.

The aerosol's effect was immediate. As a thin garlic waft permeated the hall, the furious Lords and Ladies groaned and began to retreat towards Vormulac where he stood at the head of the table. Their faces had turned pale, even sickly; they shouldered each other aside in their anxiety to put distance between themselves and Wratha's illegal weapon.

Then, as a frantic clattering of chitin and a series of querying animal grunts sounded from the stairwell beyond the arch, Wratha warned them: 'Enough poison in this bladder to drive all of you to your sickbeds for a sunup, and some of you permanently! Call off your creature, Vormulac, or suffer the consequences. If your guardian warrior so much as glares at me, believe me . . . I'll crush this bulb flat!'

Vormulac's warrior, his personal bodyguard, came through the archway. It was a small one of its sort, no more than a ton or two in weight but very ugly: a thing of hooks and pincers, grapnel arms and stabbers. Slate-grey and chitin-blue, with its scales rattling where it scurried like a scorpion towards the six accused, the creature's intentions seemed murderous.

'Vormulac!' Wratha bared her fangs, prepared to squeeze her bulb.

'*Wait!*' the Lord of Vormspire snarled at his warrior, and brought it clattering to a halt. And to Wratha: 'Lady, why do you delay matters? My warrior's not here to harm you, but to ensure that *you* do no more harm! He is your escort out of this place, into the shame and seclusion which you all deserve so well.'

Amazingly, she laughed. 'What? And do you banish us like wayward children, back to our spires and manses? No, I think not. For Olden Starside waits, and we would be the first to claim its aeries, and all the sprawling treasures of legendary Sunside.'

'"Would be", aye,' Vormulac answered her, grin for grin. 'Oh, I know your ambitions well enough. But your plans lie in ruins, Wratha, and that's the penalty you pay. For while we've kept you busy here, our most trusted lieutenants have commandeered your aerial warriors, or destroyed them in their vats. By now your forbidden creatures, and those of these dogs who run with you, are either dead or redirected. So, you would be first in Olden Starside, eh? Well, *we* say you'll be last!'

Again she laughed ... then crouched down snarling, and pointed her wand at Maglore. At that range there was no way she could squirt him, but still he cringed inside. And: 'You, mentalist,' she hissed. 'Thought-thief. Why, I've sensed your snooping for all of a ten-year. But you could only hear such thoughts as we chose to think! Aye, and so you've followed a false trail, Maglore of Runemanse.'

Now she pointed at Zindevar, saying: 'And you, blood-hag. Ah, I remember you! You were ever the jealous one, even from the first. Why, if not for Devetaki, who overruled you, you would have vetoed my ascension, then tried to take me for ... for your *companion!* How dared you ever imagine that I, Wratha, would make my bed with such as you? What? When there's ripe raw muck in the methane pits? And did you think I couldn't buy your spies, or offer them what you could not possibly give? Ah, but you've sent some pretty boys into Wrathspire, my Lady Cronesap! I thank you, for I had them all before sending them back again, but without the information you required. Or at best, with the *wrong* information!'

Now, while Zindevar fumed and sputtered, Wratha looked at Devetaki Skullguise, and saw that in her anger she wore no mask but had exposed the damaged half of her face down to the flensed bone. 'And you, Devetaki, who was my good friend,' she said, her voice low now and less spiteful. 'Indeed, I admired you greatly. But you've listened to my enemies, and so become one of them ...'

She threw back her shoulders. 'Well, and you are all fools ... but none so great as you, Vormulac! What? Warriors waxing even now in secret caverns? But I tell you – *they are waxed!*'

And as for the third time she laughed, so Canker Canison lifted his muzzle and howled like a wolf. It was an eerie ululation, which passed out through the high windows and into the gulf of Turgosheim. And no less than Vormulac's whistle, it was also a call – which in a moment was answered!

But between times: 'Rush them!' Grigor the Lech shouted. 'What? And are we afraid of a stench? If the bitch uses her weapon, she and her pack are vulnerable no less than the rest of us! Vormulac, use your warrior to crush them!'

The Lords and Ladies took heart and surged forward again. Vormulac's creature, waiting for his command, sensed the tension and the fact that the six had been alienated; it clattered this way and that, watching them, undecided, with its stabbers and pincers at the ready. Wratha aimed her spray: at the skittering warrior – then at the Lords and Ladies – then back to the warrior. She was no longer in control, and her girl-shape was gradually giving way to monstrous metamorphism.

Finally . . .

. . . Canker Canison laughed! He threw back his head and shook like a fox shedding fleas, and a weird new sound – in fact a very old sound, out of times immemorial – sounded in Vormspire. The throb and sputter of an aerial warrior's propulsive orifices!

There came a wind from the great window, which blew the heavy curtains inwards; but in the next moment they were torn from their hangings by a nightmare shape whose armoured bulk barely cleared the gap as it slammed through the parapet wall, tore up the flags of the floor and skidded to a halt within the great hall! A warrior, but *what* a warrior!

If the dimensions of Vormulac's poor creature were six times as great, still it would not equal this one. Moreover, since Vormspire's upper levels were all of two thousand feet above Turgosheim's bottoms, this monster was not only equipped for but had already proved itself in flight.

'There!' Wratha howled in savage glee, as masonry and cartilage from the shattered balcony went flying, and dust from the rubble billowed up in a suffocating cloud. And as the monster's acid breath burned through the torn shreds of curtains draping its incredible head, she cried: 'Well, Vormulac, and will you also "commandeer" this one?'

Like all Wamphyri warriors, the thing was a hybrid atrocity – a blasphemy against all the laws of creation – but in this case more so. In Olden Starside worse, bigger, yet more hideous creatures had been made from men and metamorphic vampire stuff, but this was Turgosheim, where nothing like this was ever seen before.

Red-mottled in its softer underbelly and silver-scaled on top, with an electric sheen which reflected the glare and splash of the hall's gas jets, the thing was like a flexible machine, an instrument of madness, mayhem, murder. And it was Canker Canison's construct beyond a doubt, for its huge 'face' was that of a monstrously mutated fox! Scarlet eyes were set about the forehead in a semicircle, with others in rows along its armoured sides; but its *jaws* ...

... The head carried three sets of jaws, one facing front and the others to the flanks, all equipped with the teeth of a primal carnivore. Behind those lethal blades, each throat was a cavern which could swallow a man whole. Shaggy, the thing had Canker's red hair, making its looks foxier yet. Tufts of hair sprouted from between its scales, pushed back by their overlap, and patches of stiff red bristles protected the underbelly.

Along its lower flanks pectoral to ventral, the warrior's scales were hinged to house its retracted mantle and gas bladders. Angling down from its serrated spine, a ferocious array of claspers, pincers, stabbers, clubs, and saws of chitin plate festooned its sides. A dozen 'launchers', like fleshy springs, were coiled in depressions in the segmented belly. At its rear and flanking the anus, propulsor tubes like the siphons of an octopus vented their hideous vapours. Tip to tail, the thing measured forty feet; through its middle it was nine.

Now that the dust had settled, its many eyes were staring, taking in the total scene. And its tiny brain was waiting for a command – *any* command – from its maker and master.

There were exits from the great hall other than through the archway, boltholes in its rear wall, behind Vormulac where he stood as if transfixed at the head of the table. Even if he had felt capable of answering Wratha's derisory question with regard to 'commandeering' this monster, he could not have done so; for in the moment that he blinked his astonished eyes and recovered from his paralysis of shock, so the vast invader commenced to roar!

That was enough for the Lords and Ladies; they fled, all except a pair of lesser lights who had been bowled over by the creature's destructive arrival. Young Lords, as they dragged their broken bodies free of the debris, so they came within range of the warrior.

Kill! Canker Canison issued a mental command. The warrior fell on the crippled Lords and worried them like a wolf worrying rabbits; it tossed one out screaming through the shattered gash of the window, trampled the other flat, then rose up and fell on the great table, whose pieces flew in all directions.

And *that* was enough for Vormulac!

Making for a bolthole exit in the wake of his fleeing guests, he sent similar instructions stabbing towards the bewildered mind of his own small guardian: *Kill them – all six of them!*

The creature at once hurled itself at Wratha and her five. She held out her weapon at arm's length, squeezed the bulb and vaporized its contents directly into the charging beast's face. It breathed every last drop of moisture into its vampire lungs, into its system ... reared back, all of its appendages clashing in unison ... came on with yet more determination, but gagging and frenziedly shaking its great head.

And meanwhile, Canker had called to *his* warrior.

In a short-lived, stomach-churning sputter of propulsors, with a thrust of powerful launching limbs, the horror skidded and flopped twice its own length down the hall. Overwhelmed by its sheer bulk, Vormulac's beast was made impotent, forced back from Wratha and her group. And without pause Canker's warrior grasped the lesser creature in its left-flank claspers and commenced to dismember it.

It was the grisly work of moments, seconds, nothing so great as a minute. Stabbers slammed in and out like pistons, damaging and loosening joints; pincers went into the wounds, grasping and tearing; saws were a blur of chitin. Vormulac's creature screamed – high-pitched, throbbing, a piercing agonized whistle – but briefly. There were grunts of satisfaction from the greater warrior, and thuds as various detached appendages and other portions were tossed aside. Fluids splashed: grey, yellow, red, and a reeking pink mist rose up.

Then the screaming stopped . . .

Canker's monster grunted again (in disgust, even disappointment?), thrust aside a shuddering mound of steaming meat, turned its triple-jawed head a little to glare down the ruined hall at pallid faces gawping from the bolthole exits.

Canker Canison laughed and danced, cavorting in a gleeful frenzy . . . then stopped abruptly and fell to all fours, saliva dripping from his muzzle. And after the briefest pause: *Kill!* he commanded a second time, his scarlet eyes ablaze.

His creature ploughed debris where it went roaring down the hall.

'No, hold!' cried Wratha, taking Canker's elbow, assisting him to his feet. 'No beast could reach them in there; that wall is solid rock, with a warren of escape tunnels. Best save your creature's energy.'

The six ran down the hall to where the warrior had come to a halt. And from there Wratha called, 'Vormulac, Maglore, Zindevar, Devetaki and all you others. Remember: it was you who turned on me, not out of fear but jealousy! We posed no great threat, me and my five. What, against all of Turgosheim in a body? No, not even if we had made a dozen creatures like this one. But all we have is four . . . for the moment.

'Four of them, all tested and airworthy, and made of good strong vampire stuff; not to mention other good stuff, even the very *best* stuff, out of Sunside. Aye, and to hell with your tithe-system! By now they're en route to a peak in the western reaches of the range, where we've hidden away a cache of food to replenish us — flyers, warriors and all — before we leap the Great Red Waste. This was always our plan: not to war with you but to fly west, to the aeries of Olden Starside and make new lives there. Except you were greedy and jealous and would be first, and you envied those of us with spirit enough to try it.

'Well, Vormulac, I'm sorry to disappoint you and your lieutenants; your men will find nothing in our houses but a handful of thralls and empty vats. Whatever else we're obliged to leave behind, you are welcome to it. Take our spires and manses and keep them. We've no longer any use for them.

'And so we fly west — let him follow who dares! For you have set yourselves against me and mine, and so are become our enemies. We shall know how to deal with you, when at last you have the nerve for it. So be it . . .'

She and her five headed for the stairwell to the landing bays. But before passing under the archway, she paused, looked back and shouted.

'Vormulac, Maglore: send no mind-message ahead of us. For if in leaving gloomy Vormspire we should suffer any hindrance, then Canker's warrior will fire its propulsors directly into your hidey-holes. And if in the past you've found kneblasch a trifle bothersome, why, you don't know the half of it!'

With which she and her renegades were gone.

In the tunnel escape routes, Vormulac and the others were torn two ways. These man-made passages led down into the rock, eventually emerging onto exterior walkways which descended to the lower levels. But to go that way would take time and in the end expose them to whatever other dangers waited in the gloom of Turgosheim's canyon. For shortly, Wratha and her gang would mount and launch their flyers; likewise their lieutenants out of Wrathspire and Madmanse, and the other houses of treachery. Indeed, the latter would be out there even now, spiralling on thermals out of Turgosheim, waiting in the night for Wratha and the others, ready to join with them like a swarm and thrust westwards.

Ah! But what if they'd left a rearguard to watch their backs? Only Wratha's word for it that all their warriors except this one were already fled. An unthinkable fate: to be caught on a flimsy exterior staircase of cartilage and bone, by some cousin of the monster which snarled and sputtered in the great hall!

Crowding there in the low, narrow tunnels, these were some of the more mentionable thoughts of the Wamphyri Lords and Ladies where they huddled and cursed. Until Maglore clapped a hand to his forehead and cried: 'Canker has called for his monster to attend him! Our siege is ended!'

The mentalist was right. Sputtering and snarling, Canker's warrior spat acid towards the bolt-hole tunnels, then propelled itself in its ungainly fashion to the shattered window. For a moment it perched there, its hideous head projecting outwards, before launching itself into the night. The rest of the balcony went with it, while a cloud of noxious fumes from its propulsive vents remained behind.

Braving these loathsome vapours, Vormulac, Maglore, and half-a-dozen others left their refuge and rushed to the window. Outside, Wratha and her renegades, and their lieutenants, rode the night in a spiral round Vormspire's ramparts. Behind them, climbing – with its gasbladders bulging, mantle extended and propulsors blasting – Canker's creature headed west. The Lady was off and running, and nothing anyone could do to stop her.

Her laughter came back to them, and a simple warning:

'Vormulac ... send flyers and lieutenants after us if you will, to our refuelling station in the western heights. We can spare a warrior, I think, to swat them from the skies. And so for now, farewell!'

'Whatever awaits you in Olden Starside, Lady,' he shouted after her, 'be sure not to return! You know the penalty if you do!'

Her fading laughter was the only answer ...

Later: there was unaccustomed, even hurried activity in all of the great spires and manses of Turgosheim; new workshops with extensive vats were designed, and others long fallen into disrepair put back to rights. Before sunup the word was out: the ban on the making of warriors was lifted!

Wrathspire, Madmanse, Gorviotack, Suckspire, Mangemanse: all of these were put to the sack and their spoils, both human and material, were divided as fairly as possible; likewise the possessions of the two Lords murdered by Canker's creature in Vormspire's great hall. And so a rapid re-shuffling commenced, which saw lesser Lords arguing their individual merits as they vied for ascension to these redesignated, soon to be renamed, cavern mansions and crag aeries.

While in Runemanse:

. . . In the hour before sunup, the Seer Lord Maglore called for his thrall Karz Biteri to attend him in the topmost apartment, a cavelet with a dual purpose: on the one hand to act as a lookout, and on the other to house the manse's siphoneer. It was a place Karz avoided, except to feed its grotesque inhabitant which reclined flaccid, mindless and motionless behind drawn curtains. For even the Wamphyri held certain things as unseemly, and knew when to hide them away.

There Karz found his master, lost in weird reverie, gazing gravely out through the horizontal slit of a window, across the gulf of Turgosheim towards melancholy Vormspire in the canyon's south-eastern bight. And after he had stood before him for some little while, finally Maglore blinked his strange eyes and focused them, and turned them on Karz.

'Being an intelligent man and curious,' he said, his voice rustling as ever, 'by now you will know what has happened.'

Karz could only nod. 'Something of it, Lord.'

'Well, and we shall discuss it at length,' Maglore took him by the shoulder and turned him about face. 'And you shall write it down in the glyphs of Mendula Farscry, as part of the modern history of Turgosheim. But before that . . .' (he guided the Historian toward the room's curtained area), 'I would remind you of my warning about Wratha, and the pleasures and pains of knowing her too well. Indeed, of the perils in knowing *any* of my contemporaries.'

'But . . . I have not forgotten, Lord!' Karz protested.

'Be still and listen,' Maglore told him as they arrived before the curtains, where he turned Karz so that they stood face to face. 'For you see, despite all of her crimes, no harm has befallen the Lady Wratha; the witch and her coven are fled into Olden Starside. But what of their thralls, their manses, and spires, their dupes? I will tell you: all tossed aside to fend for themselves, disassembled, apportioned and scattered. They are left to count the cost, not Wratha. But I also mentioned her dupes . . .'

'Dupes, master?'

'Indeed,' Maglore nodded. 'Indeed.' And in a moment:

'How long since you opened these curtains, Karz?' His hand was on the rope.

'A while,' the other gulped a little, his throat suddenly dry as he wondered what Maglore was about. 'Not long. I wash the creature and turn him thus and so, and fill his trough. I search his flesh for sores, and if and when I find them apply your ointments. I know that he is old, and so look for signs of decay. And –'

'I know,' Maglore stopped him. 'All of these tasks which you perform. I know. For you are faithful, Karz, and observe your duties well. But I know of a one – we both know of him – who was unfaithful, who did not fulfil his trust, who was suborned and bought . . . by Wratha!' Suddenly Maglore's voice was hard, cruel. 'Well, and he also counts the cost.'

'Huh – huh – he?' And now Karz was terrified, without as yet knowing why.

'My siphoneer is old, Karz,' Maglore cried at last, yanking on the rope. 'And despite that you tend him so well, soon he will die. Where there is no will, there is precious little will to live, eh? For which reason, among others, I have got myself a new siphoneer. Behold!'

The curtains swished open, and behind them –

– *Two* siphoneers: one wrinkled, mottled, old but still functional, for the moment at least; the other pink and new, and not yet fully ... formed. The Historian saw the bulk of them, in this topmost room of Runemanse, but not all of them. What he did see lay on a platform over the vast bowl of water whose outlets supplied the manse's needs; the mouth of the older one dribbling water into the bowl, like the drool of an infant or an idiot, except the falling droplets were sweet and clear. Their bodies were trembling like jelly from the pounding of hugely enlarged hearts; their limbs, cleverly boned and amputated at knees and elbows, were filmed in vampire slime; their living veins, similarly sheathed and elongated by metamorphism, extended from the butchered nubs and disappeared into conduits of dead bone which descended through the floor.

What Karz Biteri could *not* see (and what he had trained himself not to think about) were the many *hundreds of feet* of these living capillaries, all dangling down inside their bone pipes through Runemanse above and Madmanse below, to the wells in the floor of Turgosheim from which they drew up the water! But for all his training, Karz could imagine them well enough.

He looked at the new siphoneer – at its head, all shaven, with dark sutures and blue bruises betraying some recent surgery: an extraction of brain, of *most* of the brain, he knew – and at its vacant, grin-grimacing face, which Karz recognized only too well. For this was the face, and what was left of the form, of Giorge Nanosi, called Fatesayer, whose veins were even now extruding from his stumps, and inching down the pipes to the wells!

Unable to restrain himself, the Historian reeled away from the curtained area to the window, and there stuck his head out to draw long and hard on the dark air.

Maglore, reading his mind, came to stand beside him. 'And so you see what is become of the Fatesayer,' he said, 'who was less impartial than we thought. Aye, for when Wratha stuck her hooks in him, she said *his* fate loud and clear. So be it!'

Karz's shoulders jerked. Maglore pulled him away from the window, saying: 'What? And would you foul Runemanse with your vomit? I'll not have it, neither within nor without! Go tend your duties, make clean my workshops. For soon I'll be practising my arts.'

Karz staggered away, out of the room, and made unsteadily for the lower levels.

Maglore followed him a little way, but beyond the arched entrance paused and looked back. His eyes went to the blazon carved in bas-relief over the doorway, as it was carved over all of Runemanse's doors:

This was that sigil of which he'd dreamed at the time of the Light-in-the-West, from which time forward he'd taken it as his own. As for its meaning (if it meant anything at all), that was anybody's guess. Maglore's guess was that it must be potent; else why would he, a mage, have dreamed it?

And what other potent things would Wratha find, he wondered, in Olden Starside?

PART FOUR

The Brothers – The Raids

———————

I

Predawn twilight on Starside, sunup a few hours away, and the peaks of the barrier range already changing from one massively homogeneous black-fanged silhouette to gaunt, grey-featured sentinels in their own right, each taking on its own unique shape. Soon the sun's rays, glancing through the high passes, would colour them gold. The change from dark to light was always inspiring, even gladdening.

So thought Lardis, head man of the Szgany Lidesci.

But to have spent the best part of a night here – on Starside! at sundown! – under the silver light of the moon and the blue glitter of the stars ... and to have *slept* here! It was a thought which invariably set Lardis's scalp to tingling, brought gooseflesh creeping, and a sense of awe, wonder and heart-pounding horror bursting out afresh from every inch of his body and soul ...

Every fifty sunups or thereabouts, Lardis would make this ... this what, pilgrimage? – this passage of exorcism, anyway – into Starside, and across the barren boulder plains to the tumbled stacks of the Wamphyri; to Karenstack, the last aerie, and back again through the great pass to Sunside. But he knew he would never make it alone, that the ghosts of all that had been would journey with him, touching their cold fingers now and then to the knobs of his spine.

A rite of exorcism, aye: to drive out the demons from his dreams and the olden nightmares even from his waking hours. A renewal of his faith, his belief – that

the Wamphyri were no more, and would never return –
in the shape of one more trek across their ancient territories, through all the long lonely hours of sundown,
which had been *their* time. That was why Lardis came,
why he continued to come and always would, as long
as his legs could carry him: to convince himself of the
marvellous truth, that they were no more.

'Dead and gone forever,' he muttered, mainly to himself, pausing to look back on Starside from a vantage
point in the foothills, not far from the mouth of the
pass. 'Wiped out in a body and cleansed from the world
in what they thought was the hour of their triumph,
when they toyed with their victims and glutted themselves at the shining sphere Gate. All of them that were
left: Lord Shaithis, and even Shaitan the Unborn himself, who was their father, destroyed with their creatures. Likewise the Lady Karen, burned up in a single
breath of hell, in the searing fire of something more
hateful than all of them together! All gone, those creatures of evil. And possibly ... possibly some that were
good, too, even if they did bear the seeds of evil within
them.'

'Some that were ... what, "good", did you say?' An
old and trusted friend and companion of Lardis's,
Andrei Romani, stood there with him. 'Oh, really? The
Wamphyri, d'you mean? Then perhaps you'll be so kind
as to refresh my memory, for I'm damned if I can remember any that were good!'

Lardis glanced at him and nodded knowingly. 'Yes,
you can. You're being contentious, that's all. What about
Harry Hell-lander, called Dwellersire, who came from a
world beyond the Gate to stand side by side with his
son in the battle for the garden? And what of The
Dweller himself, who with his father toppled all the
stacks of the Wamphyri down on to the plain? Aye, and

even the Lady Karen, who stood with them and fought against her own kind.'

Andrei looked astonished. 'Her own kind? Their own kind, you mean! She and the others, they were all Wamphyri! Harry Hell-lander, who could come and go in a twinkling, and call up the dead: he was Wamphyri, as well you know. Likewise his son, called The Dweller, who became a wolf . . . and how was that for a hell-spawning menace? As for Karen: you forget, Lardis, that I was there in the garden that time, when she tore the living heart out of Lesk the Glut, and stood there laughing, drenched in his blood! Now she was Wamphyri! Aye, but the plague was in all of them, so don't tell me what's evil and what isn't! Me, I say that somewhere there's a God, and that finally He'd had enough of them. So that night He took 'em all, every last one, which left us to act as custodians of the peace.'

Lardis and Andrei: they were older now and their joints stiffening just a little, their hair mostly turned grey, and their eyes not quite so bright. But their memories were still sharp. And after all, fourteen years isn't such a very long time, not for memories such as theirs. So for all that they argued, each knew that the other was right in part, and so a balance was maintained.

'You're right,' Lardis grunted at last, 'and it's best that they're gone, all of them. But still I often wonder: if not for Harry, The Dweller, Karen . . . what would have become of us? Where would we be now?'

'Dust, most likely,' Andrei answered, 'and nothing would matter any more.'

'And our children?'

There was no answer to that. Instead of searching for one, Andrei shivered and stamped his feet, then changed the subject. 'What the hell are we waiting for, anyway?' he wanted to know, raising his voice. And: 'Where the hell is that misfit son of Nana Kiklu?'

'What, me, a misfit?' came a loud, laughing inquiry from the shadows in the mouth of the pass. In the next moment there was movement there, where Nestor Kiklu and Lardis's son, Jason, had gone on ahead. They came out of the shadows into full view, and again Nestor inquired: 'Is someone taking my name in vain?'

'No, not you, but your dumbstruck brother Nathan,' Andrei shouted back. 'It's him who's keeping all of us waiting!'

Their shouting echoed reverberatingly through the pass, rolled up into the mountains and bounced down again, rang out across the plains of Starside. Lardis didn't much like it; it caused the small hairs to stir to life at the back of his neck, and made his breath plume that much faster in the cold air. Nor did he care for people calling Nathan Kiklu names, not even in misconceived jest, and not even Andrei. Oh, Nathan was a dummy, true enough, but there was a lot more than that to the lad. And: 'Quiet!' Lardis warned. 'For all that Starside's empty now, still it's no place for shouting . . .'

But someone had heard them, at least.

Down on the rim of the low crater which housed the Gate, Nestor Kiklu's twin brother Nathan came back to life where he stood gazing into the white hypnotic glare of the half-buried sphere of alien light. He mustn't touch that shining surface, he knew, on penalty of being drawn into it and vanishing forever. Out of this world, anyway. But still he was tempted.

Tempted . . . but not entirely stupid. For there were times when life seemed very good to Nathan right here, or rather, on Sunside. Sometimes life was good, anyway . . .

It was just that the Gate was such a weird, inexplicable thing. If it were really a doorway into some other place, for instance – a place where there were people –

then why didn't they come through it and make themselves known? Lardis Lidesci said that in the old days they had come through now and then, and that the Wamphyri had prized them for their strange powers. Maybe that's why they'd stopped coming. On the other hand, Lardis had been known to say many things about the Gate, the old days, the hell-landers . . . everything.

Why, Nathan had even heard it rumoured that there'd once been a hell-lander woman Lardis had fancied! Except she already had a man, also a hell-lander. Her name had been Zek, short for Zekintha, and she could pick a man's thoughts right out of his head! Well, and so could Nathan, sometimes; Nestor's thoughts, anyway. But this Zek: she'd been pale and blonde, blue-eyed and . . . beautiful? Now how could anyone with colours like those be beautiful? None of the Szgany had them — with the exception of Nathan himself, of course.

Anyway, most of these events Lardis spoke of had taken place before the Kiklu brothers were even born, and as Nathan had noted, with the passage of time Lardis found a great deal to say about almost everything of yesteryear. It wasn't so much that he was very old (though certainly his youth, as the leader of a wandering Szgany tribe in the shadow of the Wamphyri, must have taken its toll of him), but that there was little now to occupy his mind, so that he was wont to dwell too much in the past. Which was something Nathan understood well enough, for on occasion he was himself given to dwelling in other worlds, and adventuring in lands of fantasy. It helped shut the real world out: the sounds of Settlement and its scathing voices, with all the taunts and questions which in the main Nathan no longer bothered to answer, or answered with his stumbling stutter. For ever since the night of the red clouds and the thunder in the hills, he had spent his time withdrawing from this world . . . into others.

Other worlds, yes, and lands of fantasy . . .

. . . *The twilight mountainsides, for instance, when he was alone and his wolves would come whining out of the hills to be with him. That was a secret, however, something he kept to himself, lest Settlement's Szgany youths call him a liar. For as everyone knew, wolves must be caught as pups and trained, or else they can't be trusted.*

. . . *And in his daydreams, which he knew were morbid things, however much they fascinated him.*

. . . *But especially when he slept and dreamed of . . . oh, of all manner and shape of things! Of the crumbling dead in their graves, who could talk to him if they wanted to but would not, though he frequently overheard them talking to each other; of meaningless yet maddeningly familiar numbers, cluttering his reeling brain until he thought his head must fill and burst from their constantly mutating rush and whirl; and of a different world of men which was weird and unknown as the spaces between the stars.*

. . . *Perhaps like the world beyond the Gate?*

Again the shouting of the others reached out to him from the foothills and the pass; until at last Nathan backed away from the coldly glaring source of his fascination, and jumped down from the low crater wall. But as he picked his way very carefully between the gaping mouths of giant, perfectly circular wormholes where they pierced the ground and angled down into otherwise solid, compacted earth and rock all around the perimeter of the Gate, still he sensed the lure of the silent, shining sphere, and felt it like a magnet in his mind.

'Nathan!' Andrei Romani's call came yet again, distantly, followed in a while by the echoes of his bull voice rolling down from the hills: 'Nathaaan!'. . . 'Nathaaan!. . . Nathaaan!'

Nathan had moved away from the Gate now, but still was unable to tear his eyes or his thoughts from it. The Gate to the hell-lands, another world, and possibly a world that was terrifying.

When Lardis talked of what had happened that night fourteen years ago, he usually spoke of 'a breath of hell', which came roaring out of the Gate to burn the Wamphyri in its fire. But at other times and less romantically, he had admitted that it might have been some kind of unthinkable weapon, whose power was such that the hell-landers themselves had little or no control over it. 'Whatever their world was like before,' (he would say), 'it really *must* be hell now, if that was merely the backdraught of one of their wars! Zekintha told me all about that: how their weapons were devastating.'

Measuring his pace, Nathan started to run. He had kept the others waiting too long and they'd be impatient. He was right: almost a mile away, Andrei Romani was complaining again. 'Is he deaf as well as dumb?'

Coming lithely, jinglingly from the mouth of the pass, Nestor and Jason joined the two older men. 'No,' Nestor shook his head and gave a disdainful grimace. 'My brother's neither deaf nor daft, nor even dumb. He doesn't *want* to speak, that's all. He's just . . . Nathan.'

Lardis glanced at Nestor, could almost taste the bitterness where his mouth puckered on his sour words. A pity they weren't closer, he thought, like they'd been as children. For then they had been inseparable.

Nestor had looked after his brother until they were well into their teens. Maybe he'd looked after him too well, fought one too many fights for him, taken one too many knocks on his behalf. Whatever, it wasn't the same between them now. And then there was Misha, of course. Young boys will always be boys and friends, until they grow into youths and become rivals.

Nathan and Nestor Kiklu: Nana's sons ...

Twins, yes (Lardis continued to consider them), but in no way identical. Indeed, they seemed poles apart: in their looks, philosophies, lifestyles. Nestor upright, brash, devil-may-care, outspoken and even noisy; Nathan weighed down (but with what?), withdrawn, serious, and silent of course.

Nestor was like his mother. Only see them together, and there could be no hiding the fact that he was her son. Except where Nana was small, Nestor was tall; as would his brother be tall, if only he would stand up straight! Long-limbed, both of them. Which was somewhat strange in itself; for their father, Hzak Kiklu, had been small like Nana. All the better for hiding in holes in the ground. Perhaps that was the reason. Many children had grown up tall and strong, since the destruction of the Wamphyri.

Nestor had his mother's dark, slightly slanted eyes, her straight nose however small, her glossy black hair falling to his broad shoulders. Her smile, too, which could be mysterious at times. His forehead was wide; his cheekbones high; his chin jutted a little, more so when he was angry. His body was that of an athlete, and he wore his jacket with the sleeves rolled back, to display the width of his forearms. He looked Szgany through and through. That was Nestor, a youth to be proud of. But as for Nathan:

Well, a throwback there! Though to what, Lardis couldn't imagine. Nathan's eyes were less tilted, and for all that they were the deep blue of a sapphire, still they lacked the gem's great depth. Their gaze was usually vacant, misty, or at best wandering (much like the mind which directed them, Lardis supposed, and indeed, much like the lad himself). But the strangest thing about him was his hair, which was the colour of damp straw! It was like Zek's hair, but a little darker, and Nathan kept it cropped as if ashamed of it. Possibly he was, for like his other anomalies it set him apart.

As for the rest of his features: they were not *too* dissimilar from Nestor's. A strong chin, high cheekbones, broad forehead ... his mouth was fuller than Nestor's, less cynical, but given to twitching a little in the left-hand corner. Then of course there was his skin, which was pale to match the colour of his hair; so that all in all, he scarcely looked Szgany at all.

His mother said his pallor was due to spending too much time indoors, or walking abroad at sundown, when most of the Szgany stayed close to home. According to Nana, his health in general was poor, so that he avoided the common activities of Settlement's more active youths and preferred his own company. Well, the latter was quite obviously true enough. But to Lardis's knowledge, the rest of it simply didn't add up. On the contrary, Nathan seemed a wanderer born, and was forever out and about. Sunup and sundown alike, you would find him in the forest or on the mountain slopes, anywhere but indoors. And sickly? Lardis didn't think so. A disinclination towards japing, girl-taunting and -chasing, and rough-and-tumbling with the other louts didn't automatically make him sickly, did it?

No, Nathan wasn't just the runt of the litter, he was a throwback. But to what? And if he didn't look Szgany, then what did he look?

Lardis had pondered that question time and again: who did Nathan remind him of? Whose was that soft, that compassionate, indeed that innocent look in his eyes? But as always it remained a puzzle, an aggravation, a word stuck to the tip of his tongue which refused to eject and reveal itself. And Nathan *himself* an aggravation, so that at times even Lardis could kick him – if only to stir him to life!

That was why he had asked Nana Kiklu if he could bring her boys with him this time, into Starside on his annual pilgrimage: to get Nathan away from his old haunts, try to stir him into life. Maybe he'd find something here in the awesome barren wilderness to lure his mind back from wherever it wandered now . . .

Even as Lardis Lidesci thought these things, so there sounded the soft, regular pad of flying feet and the clatter of pebbles, and an approaching man-shape silhouetted against the glare of the near-distant Gate. And as the light grew marginally brighter over Starside, Lardis's thoughts immediately changed tracks.

What, sickly, this one? Well, if so, then Lardis wished *he* was as sickly as that, with heart and lungs banging effortlessly away, as once they had used to, to power his tireless limbs. And vacant, Nathan? Not now at least. No, for his eyes were shining where he came panting to a halt, and shrugged in that apologetic way of his. He was sorry he'd kept them waiting.

'Did it interest you, then, the Gate?' Lardis asked him, before anyone else could speak.

Nathan already had his breathing under control. He looked at Lardis and nodded, however slowly. But a nod was an answer, which in itself was an improvement; usually you wouldn't even get that out of him. And Lardis was pleased. It was like when they sat at the campfire in Settlement and he told his stories of the old times, and sensed Nathan's attention rapt upon him above all the others put together. A dummy? Well, perhaps . . . but only on the outside.

'*Huh!*' Nestor grunted. 'Oh, he's interested, sure enough. Interested in all the weird, unanswerable things. Stars in the sky: how many there are. Ripples on a river: why he can't count them. Where people go when they die, as if the smoke from their funeral pyres isn't answer enough in itself. And now the hell-lands Gate? Why, of course he's interested in it! If it doesn't matter a damn, then Nathan's bound to be interested in it.'

Again the sourness in his voice.

But Jason, Lardis's son, who was eighteen months younger than the Kiklu boys, was less hard on Nathan. 'The world's not much to Nathan's liking,' he said, 'and he steers as far clear of it as he can. Which is a very hard thing to do, because of course he must live in it! That's why he concerns himself with things which seem to us irrelevant. This way he has his world, and we have ours, and we don't cross over too much one way or the other.'

(And Lardis nodded, albeit to himself, for he considered this a statement of astonishing perception.)

Lardis was proud of his son; Jason was open-handed, instinctively fair-minded, handsome in his dark Gypsy fashion, and intelligent. But just like anyone else, he was wont to err now and then. Like now. And:

'The Gate isn't irrelevant,' Lardis quickly corrected him. 'Come up here a moment.' They climbed a small knoll – no more than a hump of jagged rock – to a slightly higher elevation, and from there looked back on Starside. Specifically at the Gate.

'It's getting lighter now,' Lardis pointed out what must be obvious to anyone. 'Another hour or so and the peaks will turn to gold, and so what I wanted to show you isn't so clear any more. Far better in the heart of sundown. And anyway it's fading with the years, washed down into the barren soil by the rains, and carried away by warm winds out of Sunoide. But do you see the glow?'

They saw it:

Maybe a hundred and fifty paces beyond the Gate, a

raw crater in the earth whose sides were rough and broken, with a rim of fused slag like puckered skin around a giant wound. More stark and jagged than Starside's usually rounded boulders and other natural features, which had been worn down by the elements through untold centuries, this was a more recent thing, as if a shooting-star had crashed to earth here only a few short years ago.

Spreading out from the crater's farthest rim, a faintly glimmering plume of light lay upon the earth like the luminous early-morning ground mists of Sunside. A long, tapering spearhead, feather, or finger, it pointed towards the Icelands on the blue, aurora-lit horizon. But it was the earth itself – the barren soil and the stony ground – which glowed with this soft yet sinister radiance; as if some giant slug had passed this way, leaving its slime-trail to shine in the light of the stars.

'And over there,' said Lardis, pointing, his voice very quiet. Westwards, following the base of the mountains to the horizon and out of sight – given clearer definition in the shadow of the barrier range – the earth shone more brightly yet, with a light which came and went by degrees, like the foxfire of rotten wood or the cold luminescence of glowworms.

'Light,' Lardis gruffly continued. 'But not like the good clean light of day, nor even the light of a fire. A body can't live by it, and mustn't stay in it too long. It blasted Peder Szekarly that time, fourteen years ago: turned his skin white as a mushroom and robbed him of an heir. Aye, and it killed him, too, in the end. As for the trogs dwelling in the lee of the mountains: they paid the price, all right. It took them in their hundreds! But for their deep caves, they were finished for sure. Why, there are freaks among them still, whose fathers' blood was poisoned on that night of nights! The one good thing about it: it also fell on the swamps, since when we've had precious few vampire changelings . . .'

'Aye, hellfire!' Andrei Romani nodded in agreement. 'And it's burning still, though not so hot now. Me, I say leave it be, and all of Starside, too. There's nothing but ghosts here now, and it's a wise man who leaves them to their own devices.'

'So you see,' said Lardis to Nestor, when they'd climbed down again and were headed for the pass, 'the Gate is hardly irrelevant. It's a marker shining there still, to remind us that this is the spot where the powers of the hell-lands and those of the Wamphyri clashed and cancelled each other out.'

'All very well,' Andrei put in, 'but what's all that to Nathan? Do you think it matters at all? I mean, do you think he understood or was interested in a single damn thing we've talked about? If so, well, he's not much for showing it!'

'He showed plenty of interest in the tumbled stacks of the Wamphyri,' Lardis replied. 'And in Karenstack, the last aerie, blackened like a chimney flue on that side facing the Gate. Aye, and I firmly believe he would have entered Karenstack to climb it, if we'd let him! And finally, it seems he also felt the mystery of the shining sphere Gate. If you ask me, I'd say that's a whole lot of interest – for a dummy.'

Just as they entered the shadow of the pass, he glanced at Nathan and saw the youth looking back at him. Nathan's eyes were shining again. With gratitude, Lardis thought.

But Nestor only said, 'About the Gate: I don't like to contradict you, Lardis – especially not you, a Lidesci, and leader of your people – but what is the Gate really except a ball of white light? So it attracted my brother . . . so what? Don't moths flutter to a candle just as readily? And don't they get singed just as often?'

Which, however much he disliked it, was another statement Lardis couldn't dispute . . .

For fifteen minutes or so they walked in shadows and silence, with only the jingling of their silver baubles to keep their thoughts company. Then a yellow glow came filtering down from above, as the first of the range's topmost peaks turned gold in the rays of a sun rising even now on Sunside. And:

'I timed that well,' Lardis grunted, pleased with himself. He struck off from the trail and climbed towards a ridge jutting over the western side of the pass. The others, all except Nathan who followed on directly behind Lardis (unquestioningly, of course), came to a halt and watched the two go. Until Nestor inquired of Andrei Romani:

'What now?'

'It's a ritual,' the other answered, 'which Lardis follows every year. Something he likes to see, back there on Starside. That jut of rock's his vantage point. Me, I've seen it before and can get along without it. I'll wait here and save my pins for walking. But you two can go on up, if you like.'

Nestor and Jason went scrambling after Lardis and Nathan, and after a steep but safe climb came upon them standing on a shelf from which they gazed north and a little east. The sunlight on the peaks was stronger now; it found passage between the high crags and cast a fan of beams out across Starside's sky. Up there, only the brightest stars survived; the stars, and the rippling auroras where they warped and fluttered over the far northern horizon.

'Sunup,' Lardis panted, his breathing still ragged from the climb. 'She rises slowly, the sun, along a low flat curve, and in the old days used to light on all the taller

270

stacks one after the other in their turn. Now there's but one aerie left, as you've seen. But still I like to see the sun striking home in its topmost ramparts, and know that there's nothing hiding within, behind bone balconies and black-draped windows. Somehow, it's a very gratifying sight. But don't take my word for it; just wait and watch, and see for yourselves.' And he continued to gaze out across Starside.

Out there in what was once vampire heartland – rising up dramatically from a plain littered with the broken stumps and shattered segments of all the once-great stacks, which had not survived The Dweller's war on the Wamphyri – there stood Karenstack. Reaching almost a kilometre in height, the last aerie stood out as a lone fang of rock against the banded blue background of the north, its awesome shadow falling like a black, spastic arm far across Starside, and visibly stretching itself in the improving light, as if blindly groping for the north-eastern horizon.

The group on the bluff waited – a minute or two, three at the outside – for the sun's rays to sweep down, find them, and flood over them. Following which, in the very next moment, they observed the effect which Lardis had so desired to see: a golden stain spreading itself across the uppermost levels of the stack, burning in windows as hollow as eye-sockets, lighting up the grim mouths of launching bays, and seeming to set the high turrets and embrasures afire in a blinding effulgence.

And so like a giant candle, Karenstack stood falsely radiant amid Starside's silence, desolation and devastation . . .

For long minutes the four stood there, their attention rapt upon the molten grandeur of Karenstack's crest, which had become the centrepiece in an otherwise bleak and barren scene. But as reflective angles changed and the golden fire began to fade on the stack's stone face, so their momentarily uplifted spirits settled down again and the sense of wonder departed.

And from below: 'Ahoy, up there! Time we got on . . .'

Lardis blinked, nodded, turned his face to the others. 'Andrei's right,' he said, shading his eyes against the unaccustomed dazzle. 'Let's get down.'

The young men went first, with Lardis bringing up the rear. But before following on behind, he cast one more glance out across Starside: its moonscape of endless, boulder-strewn plains, the distant glitter of a frozen ocean, the unvisioned but imagined Icelands under their fluttering aurora banners, and of course Karenstack. And at last he sighed and began to follow the three youths down into the gloom of the pass . . .

. . . And having descended a little way paused, rooted to the spot, suddenly frozen in his tracks. For Karenstack was burning still in his mind's eye and on the lenses of his retinas. Karenstack and something else he'd seen, or thought to see – but what? He closed his eyes and the picture came up clearer: the aerie's crest aglow with its false halo of fire. But *below* the area of reflected light, where the golden rays could never reach:

Black motes swirling, jetting, settling towards the yawning mouth of a vast landing bay; midges at this distance, but what would they be up close?

As if in answer to his inward-directed question, a small black bat hovered close to his face, fanning his cheek before side-slipping and stooping on a moth which he'd disturbed. In the next moment it was gone, and Lardis breathed easier. Bats, yes, that was what he'd seen: great clusters of them, closing on the stack. Except that unlike the little fellow who fanned his cheek, they'd been the great bats of Starside – aye, and familiars of the Wamphyri, upon a time – which Zek had called *Desmodus*. And their home would be Karen-stack itself, deserted now except for their black-furred colony.

'Father?' Jason's voice came from below. 'Are you coming? Can I give you a hand?'

'No, no,' Lardis husked from a dry throat, then swallowed and found his voice. 'I'm fine. I'm coming. Get on down.'

But from then on, and all the way back to where they had tethered their animals at the head of the descent to Sunside, and for most of the trek back to Settlement — which took the greater part of sunup to complete, for they had friends to see along the way — Lardis was far less given to talking and kept his thoughts to himself.

'Bats, yes,' he would mutter, and nod his head furiously, when the others were out of sight and hearing. 'The great bats of Starside.' Until, by the time they were home again, he had almost convinced himself.

During his waking hours, at least . . .

In his dreams, however, Lardis Lidesci was not convinced. For the blood of a seer still ran in his veins, and tormented him whenever he closed his eyes to sleep. It was weaker now, this sixth sense, this blessing or curse passed down to him out of a lost Szgany history, from some long-forgotten ancestor whose second sight must have been potent indeed, that its trace had survived all the sunups — and sundowns — flown between. But potent *then*, in some unknown long ago, and this was now.

It was now, and what small reserves of the thing remained in him seemed to have been running out ever since that time on Starside, when the Gate spewed fire and fury to write THE END on the last chapter of the Wamphyri. Or . . . perhaps it ran as strong as ever in his veins, except in recent years there had been no use for it. For the Wamphyri were no more.

So why had it started to bother him again now? And why did it *continue* to bother him?

For on the long trek home he had slept and dreamed, and all of Lardis's dreams were nightmares, from which he would start snarling awake, wide-eyed and panting. Until, even in his waking hours, at last the four who travelled with him had heard him muttering: 'Bats, aye – the great *Desmodus* bats of Starside.' And they had seen him nodding his head furiously.

'What ails you?' Andrei Romani had wanted to know, as they approached Settlement in the hour before evening twilight. The youths had gone on ahead, to meet up with their young friends about the campfires – Nestor and Jason to dance a while perhaps, to enjoy the music, good cooking, company, conversation: to be Szgany – and Nathan to seek out and be with his mother.

'Nothing ails me!' Lardis had snapped. And then, almost in the same breath: 'Well, if you must know, my dreams ail me. And the mists. And the smoke from all those fires up ahead. And all the busy sounds of Settlement, which are a tumult even here, almost a mile away! What? Has all the caution gone out of the world? Do they tempt fate? Don't they know the hour, and that soon it will be sundown?'

He glanced all about, at the ground mist and the shadowy forest, finally at Andrei, who gazed back at him in amazement. And: 'Where is the watch?' Lardis continued. 'We haven't even been challenged! We've seen neither man, youth nor wolf, despite that we crossed into Lidesci territory well over an hour ago!'

Andrei's astonishment, and his concern, were very genuine now. 'The watch?' he repeated. 'Man, you stood the watch down all of ten years ago! But the markers which define your boundaries are well maintained, and we haven't had a border dispute in . . . oh, I can't remember! So why now, after all this time, do we suddenly need a watch?'

Lardis blinked his fierce brown eyes and something of the passion went out of them. He blinked again, frowned and shook his head. 'I . . . I actually did that? I stood down the watch? Yes . . . yes, of course I did.' For a single moment he looked shaken, confused, lost –

– But in the next the passion was back, and with it all the grim determination of his youth. He glanced knowingly at the darkening sky, where the first stars glittered like blue ice chips over Starside beyond the barrier range, sniffed suspiciously at the evening air, stared piercingly at a ground mist rising out of the woods. And: 'Great fool that I've been,' he growled, as if he couldn't believe it, 'I stood the watch down! . . . And now must start it up again!'

Andrei Romani recognized it: that visionary fire in Lardis which had made him a great leader of the Szgany in a time when leaders were few and far between. But where once it had inspired men, now it caused a shiver to travel the length of Andrei's spine. 'What is it, Lardis?' he husked, gripping the other's arm. 'What did you see from that bluff in the great pass? I know you as well as any man, and you've not been the same since you climbed up there to watch the sun burning on Karenstack's face.'

Lardis felt Andrei's fingers digging into his arm, paused in his striding and turned to face him. His eyes held Andrei's as in a vice as he answered: 'I don't know what I saw, except that it frightened me and straightened out my addled senses. Or else addled them more yet.' He pulled himself free, turned and headed for Settlement as before.

Andrei frowned after him, then hurried to catch up. 'But you did see something?'

'Bats,' Lardis growled. 'Starside's great bats. That's what I took them for, what I've been telling myself they were ever since. Certainly they could have been, for I merely glimpsed them – a scattering of dots in the sky around Karenstack – which made no impression until after I'd started on my way down again. Well, and I know my eyes aren't all they used to be. But on the other hand, and if they weren't bats . . . then what were they?'

Andrei's shrug tried hard to to be careless but didn't quite make it. 'But they were,' he said. 'It's just that you've been letting the old times crowd too close in your memory. Perhaps it's a warning: that you should give it a rest and quit trekking into Starside every fifty sunups or so. After all, you're not as young as you used to be.'

'No, and neither are you!' Lardis snapped. 'If you're so sure of what I *didn't* see, then why is your voice so anxious, eh? Who are you trying to convince, Andrei, me or yourself? But I'll tell you this . . .' He broke his striding and rounded on the other. 'Since then it's like I've been asleep and I'm only now waking up. And my sleep had dulled senses which are only now coming alive. I can see, hear, feel, smell – I can *remember* – things! Things which I thought had gone forever.'

More stars had blinked into being. Again Lardis sniffed the night air, glared at the rising mist. 'Come on!' he said, striding harder yet for Settlement. 'And say no more. If I'm wrong – and I pray that I am wrong – then I'm nothing more than an old fool, frightened of my own shadow. Ah, but if I'm right . . . We have family and friends in the town, Andrei, and the long night is only just beginning!'

Together now, Lardis and Andrei, and breathlessly silent in the deepening shadows of the forest's fringe. And for all that they were tired where they followed sounds of laughter and music, smells of wood smoke and cooking fires, still they hurried. Hurried, yes; for as one man they were suddenly aware that those same sounds and smells were permeating the night air, rising through the wooded slopes into the peaks of the barrier range. And they were also aware that the campfires would be blazing like . . . like beacons.

But more than that, they were aware of all the life in Settlement. And of all the hot Szgany blood . . .

In the town, Jason Lidesci and Nestor Kiklu had gone one way, and Nathan Kiklu the other. The pair to the campfires, which burned through the night in the gathering places, and the one to his mother's house against the stockade wall.

In the central open space, a public place where the main fire and many lesser cooking-fires burned – where tables and chairs had already been laid out in preparation for Lardis's and the others' return, for the Szgany Lidesci rarely missed an opportunity to celebrate – Jason and Nestor had received a boisterous welcome from their friends, and then exchanged more sober greetings and information with the town's elder citizens and dignitaries.

The latter had wanted to know how the trip had gone? And where was Lardis now – and Andrei Romani? – how far behind the younger, fleeter members of the party? What news from the other towns and villages to the east? And so forth. Jason and Nestor had restricted their answers; everyone knew that Lardis and Andrei would want to tell everything in their own way, in their own good time. Indeed, the story-telling would form a major part of the celebrations.

Finding chairs in the quiet corner of an old stone wall, finally the two settled down with a jar of wine and a pair of small silver goblets between them. They weren't important now; Lardis Lidesci and Andrei Romani were the important ones, and their arrival imminent. Between times, Jason and Nestor could talk.

'My father sometimes worries me,' Jason admitted, having washed the trail's dust from his throat with a gulp of sweet wine.

And: '*Huh!*' Nestor grunted. 'You should have my problems, for my brother worries me all the time!' His voice was at once sour, a sure sign that the conversation had returned to Nathan.

Jason was hardly taken aback. 'You're too hard on him,' he said.

'You think so?' Nestor raised an eyebrow. Eighteen months Jason's senior, he considered Lardis's son clever but naïve; hardly the right kind of man to inherit the leadership of the clan when that time came, and never strong enough to hold it together and make it a power in the world. There was too much of the thinker in him, too little of the doer. 'But Nathan's not too hard on me, right?'

'Nathan, hard?' Now Jason *was* taken aback. 'But he's soft as a child!'

Nestor nodded. 'He *is* a child, in some things, aye. And in some ways he's an idiot, despite what your father thinks! But I'm his brother and so know him better than anyone, and there's another, weirder side to him.'

'Oh?'

'We're twins, as you know,' Nestor nodded. 'Not identical, no, but still our kinship goes deeper than ordinary flesh and blood. Far deeper.' He nodded again but angrily, even savagely. 'I mean, I wouldn't mind Nathan dreaming all the strange things he dreams, or blame him for living in his daydreams – just so long as he'd leave me out of them!'

'But how are you part of them?' Jason was puzzled. 'In what way do they concern you? Why, I've never met brothers more dissimilar than you two!'

'Huh!' Nestor grunted again. 'But up here,' he tapped his forehead, 'in our minds, we're not that dissimilar.' He leaned closer. 'Listen, and I'll tell you how it's been for as long as I can remember.' He got his thoughts in order, then:

'Among other things,' he began, 'my brother dreams of numbers. Great waves of numbers, all meaningless, swirling in his head like a river in flood! There's this – oh, I don't know – this fabulous "secret" behind them, which he seeks to discover, except he hasn't a clue where to begin. And so in his sleep he goes through the numbers again and again, endlessly searching them for their secret meaning. All very well, and I'd have no complaint – if only he would keep his dreams to himself!'

'What?'

Nestor nodded. 'Don't ask me how, but I "hear" his dreams! I can see him, feel him there in my head, lost in these damned numbers! Now to me, a number is the count of fish I've caught, division is the share-out after a day's hunting, and multiplication is what rabbits do. As for schooling: I got as much of that as I need – and all I can use – when I was a child. So, if I can't work something out on my fingers and toes, then I'm not interested in it. I'm not one of these so-called "wise men" who tinker with runes and scratch on slates to keep records and histories, or work out the distance to the moon, which they say is another world. I won't be around when the things we do today are history, and as for the distance to the moon: what possible use in knowing that, except to the wolves who sing to her?'

Jason was fascinated. 'You really hear his dreams?'

'Not all of them,' Nestor shrugged, concerned now that perhaps he was saying too much. 'For his mind is deep, like a well, and there's a lot he keeps hidden. Even so, it's full of faraway worlds and dead people ... and numbers, of course! Not that I'd pry, you understand, for if it was up to me I'd have nothing at all to do with Nathan's damned dreams and fancies! But I can't control it. His dreams find their way into mine, so that he's just as big a pest asleep as when he's awake!'

Puzzled, Jason shook his head. 'But how can you be sure? How do you *know* you share the same dreams? Has he told you? A rare event that, for he scarcely speaks at all!'

'He doesn't have to,' Nestor was tired of the subject now. 'I only have to wake up in the middle of the night in our room, and look at him sleeping there, and I know. Now and then, not very often, I can read his mind as clearly as the spoor of a wild pig. Read it, and hate it!'

'Hate it?' Again Jason was astonished, by the fire in the other's voice, and by his passion. 'Hate your brother's mind? But why? Is he devious?'

But Nestor merely scowled, shook his head, and finally sighed. 'What, Nathan, devious? No, I hate it because he's as gentle and trusting as the doves nesting in the eaves!'

Jason found it all very hard to understand, and not least Nestor's curiously mixed emotions. 'You share your brother's dreams and read his thoughts,' he shook his head in wonder of it. 'Well, the way I see it, it can mean only one thing: that you are true Szgany, Nestor, both of you! For there are mysteries in our blood which even we can't understand. Why, there could even be something of the Wamphyri in you − !' He quickly held up a hand to ward off any protest (though in fact Nestor would be the last to take offence at his remark). '− As there is in most of us, naturally. For in the old days the Wamphyri were like a plague among us, and there are throwbacks even now. My father believes it's the source of all Szgany mysticism: the power of fortune-tellers who read dreams and palms, and seers who scry afar.'

Nestor pulled a face. 'You really believe in such stuff?' Obviously Jason was even more naïve than he'd suspected. 'Can you show me one genuine − what, mystic? − in all Settlement? And am I, Nestor Kiklu, a mystic? Not likely, nor would I want to be. No, it's simply that we shared our mother's womb, were born together, and brought up almost as one. Except we're *not* one but entirely different. And finally . . . I've had enough of him.'

'Of your own brother?'

'Yes,' Nestor answered. 'Of the trouble he's been to me, and the trouble still to come.'

'Ah!' said Jason. For he believed he understood something of *that*, at least.

Nestor frowned at him. 'Ah?'

Jason saw his mistake at once and tried to change the subject. 'Back on Starside, you said that Nathan was neither deaf nor daft. And yet a moment ago you called him an idiot. Something doesn't match up.'

Now Nestor scowled. 'A lot doesn't match up,' he answered. 'Like the way you're avoiding saying what's on your mind! Now out with it.'

Jason grimaced, shrugged awkwardly. And: 'Misha,' he said. A single word, a name, which felt like a great weight rolling off his tongue. Nestor was a hard one;

his hands were hard; it wouldn't be the first time he had broken lips just for speaking that name.

The other sat up straighter, pulled air into his chest, let a little of it come growling out. 'What of her?' Nestor's young voice was all gravel now, a man's voice, threatening and inquiring in one. Indeed, a jealous voice.

'As children you three were inseparable,' Jason said, hurriedly. 'All four of us together, all the hours of the day. Me, I was a friend. But you and Nathan, she loved both of you. She still does, I'm sure.'

Nestor slumped down again. 'So am I,' he answered, perhaps morosely. 'And that can't be. And you're right, of course, for that's the trouble in store: Misha. She loves us both, but who the most? If it's me, then it's because I'm a man and can look after her. If it's Nathan, then it's because he's still a child and *needs* looking after! Well, a real rival wouldn't be much of a problem. I could deal with that. But Nathan? My ridiculous, speechless — or at best stuttering — pale-faced, corn-cropped brother?'

Jason nodded. 'I see now why you've gone your own ways. I saw it begin — oh, four, five years ago? — but didn't really understand what it was.'

Nestor, caught up in his own thoughts, scarcely heard him. 'There have been times,' he burst out, 'when I might have taken her — even by force!' (Jason looked startled, shocked.) 'Maybe I should have. It might have settled things there and then. But Nathan ... Nathan ... *damn him!* I know he only has to smile at her, just smile, and ... and ...'

Jason stared at him. 'And does *he* know it, d'you think?'

Nestor sat up again and tossed back his wine in one. 'No,' he said. 'Not an inkling. And *now* you know why I

282

consider him an idiot. For all his dreaming of other places, and his endless quest for meaning in a handful of numbers, where she's concerned he can't add two and two! And if he could – or if he ever does – what then? If I can't live with him as he is now, how could I ever live with both of them together? What, Misha and Nathan? And who would look the dumb one then?'

'What will you do?' Jason's concern for his father was all but forgotten now.

Nestor poured more wine into their goblets, then snatched up and drank his own as if it were water. 'Ask her to be mine, and soon,' he answered. 'No, tell her she's going to be mine!'

'And if she says no?'

'Then I'm gone, out of Settlement, away from the Szgany Lidesci forever. What opportunity for me here? You're the next chief of the tribe. And shall I be a hunter all my days, grow old by the campfire, and sit there telling stories like your father? Forgive me, Jason, but I see little profit in that. And anyway, what stories would I have to tell? How one day I caught a fish, put a bolt through a rabbit, and skewered a wolf where he crept up on my animals? No, the days of adventure went with the Wamphryi. But me, I wish they were back, and I always have! What good in being strong in a world where even the weakest is my equal? I feel I've a name to make for myself, but how? And where? Not here, for sure. And not without Misha . . .'

'You're ambitious,' Jason told him, his eyes narrow now.

'And is that wrong?'

'You don't much like it that I'll be chief one day.'

Abruptly, Nestor stood up, swayed a little, clutched at the table to steady himself. The trek had been long and he was tired – they were both tired – and the wine was strong. 'Maybe I don't much like anything about Settlement any more,' the words came slurring out. 'Maybe I should leave come what may. There are places to the west, and new territories far to the east. It's rumoured there's even a place beyond the farthest wasteland. But frontiers are few, and time is wasting.'

'You'll take Misha and go?'

Nestor snorted and shook his head. 'No, for her brothers are big lads, both of them! So for the moment it has to be her choice. But with or without her, still I'll go. And if it's the latter, then be sure I'll be back one day.'

Now Jason stood up, but only to take a pace to the rear. 'Be sure you'll be back? But why do you make it sound like a threat? What, will you bring an army with you? To steal Misha? Or ... do you also covet my father's territory?'

'Are you worried?' Nestor scowled. 'For Lardis? But it's you who'll likely be chief by then.'

'And should I be afraid of an old friend?' Jason's look was sour as Nestor's now. 'Aye, and maybe I should.' He shrugged and turned away. 'Anyway, it's high time I was home. My mother will be waiting up for me.'

For a moment Nestor's expression changed, softened; but then he stiffened his back, and turned it on Jason where the other moved off abruptly towards the North Gate and the dark foothills. And as that young friend of his childhood went off, disturbed and soured by their conversation, so Nestor chewed his lip and glanced all around, perhaps to avoid calling out after him ...

Meanwhile, the old meeting place had filled up, and now there was movement, shouting at the East Gate. Lardis and Andrei were here. But in all this great crowd, never a sign of Misha. Where was she? And where Nathan?

Nestor picked up the jar, drained it, wiped his mouth on his sleeve. And:

Tonight! he promised himself. *I'll have it out with Misha tonight. Or I'll have her tonight, one way or the other. And if there's anything of a man in Nathan — and if he cares for her at all — maybe then he'll yelp and bare his teeth!*

Jason had disappeared now, out through the North Gate and into the night, on his way home to Lardis's cabin on the knoll. But here in Settlement . . . what was going on? That awful commotion and shouting. And angry, furious shouting, at that! Was it Lardis, bellowing like a stag at the rut? It could only be. His voice was unmistakable.

And pushing his way through the gathering crowd, Nestor went to see what it was all about . . .

II

Some two hours earlier, eastwards, and not quite twenty miles distant:

. . . The Lady Wratha climbed down out of the saddle of her flyer on to a high plateau still warm from the sun's last rays. Stepping to the rim, she looked down through hooded eyes on the fires of a Szgany town nestling in the lee of the barrier range; looked down on the fires of Twin Fords . . . and smiled. She smiled with all the delight of a young girl, and lusted after Twin Fords with all the evil of an ancient horror.

And waiting on the rim of the plateau while her band of circling renegades found landing places on the flat, scrubby expanse of rock behind her, she gazed on Sunside in the twilight of early evening – a sight unseen by Wamphyri eyes for all of fourteen years – and let her mind drift back a little: to her flight from Turgosheim across the Great Red Waste, all along the spine of these unknown mountains, and deep into Old Starside . . .

Unlike Turgo Zolte's flight in the time of Shaitan the Unborn, Wratha's had been relatively easy. Where Turgo was pursued and unable to pause for respite, Wratha suffered no such handicap. Which was just as well; her flyers were unused to covering vast distances, and for all her boasting in Vormspire's great hall, her aerial warriors were mainly untried. Oh, no one could doubt that they were superb engines of destruction, but as for flying skills: there had been no way to put those to the test, not in the skies over Turgosheim.

In the end, however, little had been left wanting in performance; all of the flyers had made the crossing; only one of the warriors had been lost.

The plan had been to 'refuel' at the western edge of the secondary range of which Turgosheim was a part, then climb as high as possible on thermals out of Sunside before commencing the long glide westwards. The ceiling would of course be that altitude where the sun's rays, striking tangentially across the curve of the world, intersected the flight path: not very high initially, for the slow-moving sun had only recently set. Phase two would come when it was calculated that the warriors had expended about half of their energy. At this point they would climb again, to whatever limit the sun and exhaustion permitted, before finally gliding and jetting down into Old Starside.

The warriors were the main cause for concern. For in the end, having converted much of their own mass into fuel, they might be obliged to draw on their flimsy gas-bladder reserves. Loss of weight would compensate in some small degree, but the equation was still a loser. Lacking energy, buoyancy, and conceivably even will (for while small minds are malleable, their attention span is limited), a fatigued warrior might well gravitate to earth. If and when that was perceived as imminent, the weak one would be sacrificed and torn apart in mid-air, to fuel the rest of them on their way.

In the event, it was Canker's creature that paid the price. The energies consumed in its landing at Vormspire — its savage work in the great hall, and the subsequent launching from the spire's shattered window — all had served to deplete it. Thus, at the apex of the second climb, when the warrior was seen to be failing, then Wratha had ordered its dissolution.

Canker had raged (naturally, and to no avail), but in

any case his protest was an automatic, instinctive reaction, his stance untenable, and resistance inconceivable. And three to one the other warriors had fallen on Canker's weary creature, dismembering and devouring it in short order. After bone and chitin armour had rained to earth, when all that remained was a thin, skeletal frame drifting at the mercy of the winds, finally the bladders had been drained and the empty rag-thing allowed to spiral down to oblivion.

And replenished, the group had flown on . . .

From time to time the Lady, Lords, and their handful of lieutenants would pull cartilage stoppers from wells drilled in the knuckled backbones of their flyers, and sip sparingly on sustaining spinal fluids . . .

They took turns to sleep, half of them nodding in their saddles while the rest controlled the beasts and maintained the course . . .

On high, the stars glittered like ice-chips; far below, the Great Red Waste seemed endless; the obscenely flowing shadows of the renegades, however faint, diluted and somehow polluted the starlight where they passed . . .

Sundown crept towards sunup and they were anxious . . .

Now, time and again, the propulsors of the warriors would sputter warningly, the beasts would falter, and even the most vicious mind-darts would fail to inspire them. Such creatures could never turn on their mistress and masters, of course not, but it was conceivable that eventually they might seek to kill and devour one another . . .

Then, distantly but closing, moonlit mountains rose up to greet the inevitable descent – but wider, higher, vaster mountains far than those of Turgosheim – so that Wratha knew this could only be Old Starside. And, south of the towering range, Old Sunside, too.

All propulsive power stilled now, the wind keened under leather canopies where flyers and warriors alike shaped manta wings and fluttering mantle vanes into gliding aerofoils. And as a thin line of silvery light made a crack on the southern horizon, so they skimmed low and silent over the first peaks of Starside's eastern range ... and spied their first signs of life since leaving Turgosheim!

There on the north-facing flank, in a stony basin lying midway between the foothills and the rearing mountains proper, a circle of small fires sent up spirals of black smoke. Within the circle, figures capered and made intricate, awkward, apparently aimless leaps and twirls. Sounds of guttural, rhythmic grunting, and the jarring clatter of ceremonial crotalae, rose up with the reek of burning wood and dung.

Huh! Spiro Killglance, flying close to Wratha, sent her a bitter, scornful thought. *Trogs! Two dozen of them, performing their rites.*

Her answering thought was darker, more practical, and much more to the point. *Meat!*

The warriors were ordered down: two of them would land between the fires and the mountains, so blocking the route of the trogs back to their cavern homes, and the third would make sure that none escaped into the foothills. Propulsors sputtering into hot, stinking life – with stabilizing vanes extended, and tiny saucer eyes in their bellies swivelling to seek landing sites – the monsters came down bellowing and snorting, eagerly to earth.

On the ground, the trog ceremonies came to an abrupt halt. Wide black eyes under dark, sloping foreheads scanned the starlit sky, found hideous shapes circling, rapidly descending. For a single moment, mouths gasped and jaws fell open in disbelief. Then, shuffling and lurching in their fashion – their leathery limbs galvanized far beyond the earlier exertions of their esoteric devotions – the trogs scattered. But all too late.

A dozen flyers sideslipped this way and that, settling to earth like leaves falling in still air, or flat stones sinking in water. They flopped down on springy tendrils which uncoiled from their bellies; and Wratha and her five, and their vampire lieutenants, took battle gauntlets from their beasts' harnesses and climbed down out of their saddles.

After that . . . mayhem!

Five, maybe six trogs attempted to slip through the murderous Wamphyri noose which threatened to close them in; three made it past the circle of long-necked manta flyers with their vacuously swaying, diamond-shaped heads; two were left, after running the gauntlet between the warriors snuffling and snorting in the shadow of the mountains, to make it home. But out of two dozen, only two. And as for the rest:

It was slaughter where Wratha's renegades scythed among them, their gauntlets red in the flying spray of their havoc. Hoarse screams echoed through the night, became gurgles, guttered into silence like candles snuffed out. It was the work of minutes, three at most, which in the end saw a terrified silence fall over Starside; a silence broken only by the panting of a trog priestess, grabbed up alive by Canker Canison. Rabid with lust, he tore her rags from her and took her three times in quick succession – once in each opening – before tearing out her throat and crushing her skull. Then, draining blood from her wounds while her heart still feebly pumped, he glared at the others where they watched him. So, she'd been a trog. She was still female, wasn't she?

The rest was routine. Wamphyri, lieutenants,

warriors and flyers alike, all took their fill. But shortly, when the edge was off their hunger: Spiro Killglance paused to wipe his mouth on his sleeve, turning it scarlet, and gruntingly inquired, 'What now?'

'Westward,' Wratha answered at once, dabbing a square of coloured Szgany cloth to the perfect bow of her girl's lips. 'The sun will be up soon, and we need to find a place.'

'Then we should go carefully,' Gorvi the Guile's voice was oily, insinuating, 'and spy out the way before us. For if Maglore is wrong and the Old Wamphyri lie in wait –'

But Wratha only shook her head. 'No. For all my detestation of that old thought-thief, still Maglore is right. When did you last see trogs out in the open in Turgosheim? Speaking for myself, never! Because we, the Wamphyri, are in Turgosheim. But here? ... they take no precautions but cavort grotesquely by the light of their fires, and when we fall on them flutter in every direction, like Sunside chickens! No, there are no Wamphyri in Old Starside. Not until now, at least.'

Replete, then they had rested an hour before mounting up to fly west. The warriors, sated but not glutted, were ordered into a reverse arrowhead formation, one on each flank and the third to the rear. And thus the Wamphyri returned to the long forsaken territories of the Wamphyri ...

As time had passed and the air grew brighter moment by moment, so the jagged shapes and twining contours of the barrier range had stood out that much clearer, until finally the rays of the rising sun had lit golden on the very highest peaks. And as Wratha's anxiety had risen up in her again, so she'd seen Karenstack, the last aerie. But scattered all about that lone fang – lying there in total disarray, like dismembered stone giants with their stumps scorched as by colossal fires – she also saw the vast sprawls of rubble which were all that remained of the other ancient aeries.

But . . . the one stack remained.

And before the sun could burn her renegades, Wratha led them into the hugely frozen yawn of a cavern launching bay as big as the largest Turgosheim manse, which opened in the east facing wall of the stack two thousand and more feet above Starside. And dismounting there in that high, empty, echoing place:

'See to the warriors and flyers,' she had instructed the lieutenants, 'then see to yourselves. I don't know how far the sun will rise; it may light upon half of the aerie, for all I know! So find rooms for yourselves – without windows! Or if they have windows, be sure they face north.'

Then, with her five following on behind, she had set out to explore the rest of the stack.

They climbed.

The aerie seemed to go up forever, and Wratha tried not to show the awe she felt. She knew she could house five hundred thralls and lieutenants in this upper third of the stack alone! And below, where the great honeycombed butte widened into its base?

Why, given a hundred, two hundred sundowns, the place could be filled with an army and stand impregnable! With its great height, it was a giant watchtower on all Starside, which none could approach unseen – especially not from the east. For Wratha had no doubt but that they would come one night, out of Turgosheim to track her down. Except they'd be weary, and their blood thin, and their warriors spawned of feeble, watered-down stuff. While she . . . she would be Wratha! Wratha the Risen, but risen higher than ever Maglore, Vormulac, Devetaki and all the others together could ever imagine.

So she pictured it; but for now, all she had was this aching, echoing, empty shell of a stack.

Dust lay thick; the bone water pipes had come apart in places, and likewise the complicated gas-channelling systems; cartilage stairways were creaking and dangerous, and required earliest possible attention. At windows cut through solid rock, black bat-fur drapes were all fallen into moulder, and in the empty storerooms rotting cocoons had long since slumped into sticky, molten-silk puddles. The great red spiders were still here, however, to spin more cocoons as they were required.

As for the workshops: they were in good order, and their hollowed vats huge as any in Mangemanse or Suckspire. With the assistance of Canker and Vasagi, crafty masters of metamorphism both, Wratha could have good stuff brewing here in no time. But the basement granaries would be empty, the gas-beast chambers and methane pits reduced to so much dust and bone-shard, and the water in the wells lively with all manner of creeping and swimming things. Oh yes, it would be a long time before the stack could be put back to rights. But when it was, what a fortress then!

And glancing at her companions through half-shuttered eyes where they gawped and strutted in the vast rooms of the upper levels, Wratha had thought: *Mine, all of this — eventually*. Except she kept the thought to herself, of course.

The upper levels . . .

At first sight of them, then Wratha had known that this was a Lady's stack, that its last inhabitant had been female. For one thing, there were mirrors here: plates of gold hammered perfectly flat, polished to a high sheen, giving warmth and life to the features which they reflected. And they had been female features, certainly; for Wratha knew that while all of the Wamphyri Lords were vain, only the vainest would ever adorn his walls with such as these.

No, for generally mirrors were deemed dangerous things, which in the olden times had been known to reflect death (in the form of sunlight), as easily as life! Long ago, in Turgosheim's Sunside, Wratha had even owned a silver mirror; this despite that all such lethal devices and metals had been forbidden to the Szgany since time immemorial. Well, and now she could look upon her face again, admiring once more the beauty she'd clung to for over a century. But who last had looked in these mirrors, she wondered? And had she been beautiful, too?

She had been slim, beyond a doubt! For in the biggest bedroom of the largest suite on the penultimate level, there Wratha found several dresses, or what had been dresses. They were falling into decay now, but if Wratha had been alone and in the mood . . . she was sure they'd suit her figure perfectly well. So, she had been shapely, this Lady, and young; or having all the outward trappings of youth, at least.

Her bed was still here. Built high and wide, of great heavy slates, its polished wooden steps and carved headboard remained intact. Wooden rails, too, suspended from the high ceiling on chains, with golden rings which once held sheerest Szgany curtains. But all gone now, turned to dust, and ropes of cobwebs hanging in their place. Likewise the bed's covers: all blotched with lichens and fluffy mould.

As for the rest of the room:

There was an onyx water basin, with bone pipes descending from the roof's exterior gutters, or from some long-shrivelled siphoneer's place; narrow shelves of fretted cartilage, filled with all manner of worthless knick-knacks and baubles under an inch of dust, Szgany stuff mainly; airing cupboards with gas jets below, and other pipes leading off to heat a great stone bath . . . big enough for two?

With whom had she shared it? Wratha wondered, allowing herself a smile. Or was she a Lady in every respect? But no, for Wratha knew all about Wamphyri 'Ladies'. This one had not stinted herself but had taken pleasure in all her little luxuries. This one had lived!

Sniffing the air as she moved through the cavernous apartments, Wratha had felt ever more at home here; but at the same time she'd felt that the five with her were more and more like alien invaders of her privacy. Until at last:

'Out of here!' she'd rounded on them. 'This is my place. All of these upper levels which we've explored, they're mine.'

'What?' Gorvi the Guile had exploded. 'Are you insane? Why, there's room here for all of us! Our lieutenants, too, and all the thralls we care to muster!'

For all that his words were snarled, the Guile's voice was oily as ever. Tall, slender, and with the dome of his head shaven except for a single central lock with a knot hanging to the rear; always dressed in black, so that the contrast of his sallow flesh made him look fresh risen from death; with eyes so deeply sunken in their sockets they were little more than a crimson glimmer, yet shifty for all that — this was Gorvi. He was sinister, but who among the Wamphyri was not? And he cowed Wratha not at all.

'My lieutenants!' She wrinkled her nose and glowered at him. 'And all the thralls I care to muster! But . . . did I hear you call me insane?' Now she also glared at the brothers Wran the Rage and Spiro Killglance. 'But madness is their speciality, surely?' And, redirecting the blaze of her scarlet eyes to Canker Canison where he prowled like a dog, sniffing the floor. 'Nor am I too certain of him!'

'Now hold with these insults!' cried Wran, his eyes flaring dangerously, but not without a certain shrewd intelligence. 'For at best they're a blind – eh, Wratha? And Gorvi's right: we all should have a say in this.'

'*No!*' Wratha turned on him, on all five of them. 'Now *you* hold, all of you, and listen! I was the one who schemed and plotted, and drew you all together, and brought you here out of Turgosheim unscathed. Why, but for me you'd be skulking in your hovels still. Mangemanse, indeed! Suckspire! Madmanse! My place was the best of the lot – a worthy spire – and so I lost the most. Well, now I've regained it. So here's how it will be:

'Gorvi the Guile. As your name can't help but hint, you are an insular creature, little trusting of your fellows. You are crafty and would not feel safe in a manse without a bolt-hole. I make no accusations but merely state the facts. Therefore, take the wide and spacious base of the stack – say, the two lowest levels? – for your own. This will give you a dozen escape routes from your windows out on to the plains. Also, you will have control of the wells, whereby you are guaranteed our aid in the event of any future attack from Starside's bottoms. At the same time, however, it means that the wells will be your responsibility, and to judge by the rest of this place they'll be bound to require your most urgent attention. A task for the first of your thralls, to be recruited in the next sundown.

'Wran and Spiro. Despite that you are brothers and even twins – who among the Wamphyri normally despise each other – you two prefer to be together, within certain limits. So be it: choose yourselves apartments in the several levels immediately above Gorvi's, where the width of the stack should provide not only ample accommodation but also plenty of room for privacy. I fancy you will be well suited. Also, from what I saw of the crumpled ruins which litter this region, your area of responsibility will be great indeed! Namely, control of the refuse pits and methane chambers. For I noted that almost every one of those former aeries was burned and broken in the same section, and I can't doubt but that this stack is of a similar design.

'Vasagi. You were ever a loner, no less than I myself. I suggest you take the next levels down from my own. No fear of claustrophobia, with all this air surrounding us! Your warriors, when they are made, may have joint use of my vast launching bays. In return for which, I may require some small assistance in the fashioning of creatures of my own. As you see, I acknowledge your mastery of the metamorphic arts . . .

'Ah, but I acknowledge yours no less, Canker, and would also enlist your aid! You shall be central among us, occupying the levels between the brothers and Vasagi. This way, when the moon rides on high, we may all share your . . . *singing*, and the . . . *delights* of your devotions together! Alas, not much in the way of duties, but what is that to an artist like you?'

Canker was not fooled, nor any of the others; they knew that apart from his skill in the fashioning, the only reason he was here was to make up the Lady's numbers. But the levels she had assigned to him required an overseer, certainly, and at least she'd apportioned the rest of the duties, displayed her powers of reason (however warped), and reinforced her leadership. In the end they must accept, but meanwhile:

'No need to go rushing off immediately,' she'd told them, while they thought it over. 'Outside, it's sunup.

Our lads will have seen to the beasts, and to themselves. All will have their heads down by now, and we should do the same. We've come a long weary way, and nothing more to get excited about till the sun sets. So find beds for yourselves – several levels down, I'd suggest – and catch up on all the sleep you've missed. Come nightfall, we'll all of us have work.'

'On Sunside?' Canker had grinned and winked.

'Aye,' she'd answered. 'Where else?'

It had been like a promise, which above all else placated them . . .

Then it had been sundown. And almost as quickly as that, or so it seemed.

For Wratha and the others had been weary as never before in their long lives, their sleep deep and dreamless, undisturbed even by calls of nature. This latter was not strange; such was Wamphyri metabolism that their bodies wasted very little; what was consumed was transformed.

Once, towards twilight, Wratha had come half-awake with some weird fancy or anxiety niggling either at her or the vampire within her. For a moment, opening her eyes, she'd thought to see sunlight blasting in through the undraped window! . . . But it was only moonlight. And propping herself up she'd seen the auroras writhing over the Icelands, and Starside's barren boulder plains turning a uniform, ashen grey as clouds covered the moon. Then, remembering that she'd made her bed in a room facing north, Wratha had relaxed. And hearing Canker's mournful howling rising from some nether place of his choice, she knew what had lured her from sleep and gladly returned to it.

But the next time she came awake, that was because she knew! Knew that the last glint of gold was gone from the peaks of the barrier range, that all of Starside lay in shadow, and that the others were even now stirring, called up from their sleep by the long night just beginning. And her eyes blinked open like shutters thrown back, and her forked tongue moved luxuriously, sensually, in the thirsting tunnel of her mouth.

Sundown! And now she would see what this new but ancient land had to offer.

Knowing that the others would be just as eager to be up and about, Wratha had no time to spare. In the launching bays she'd found Gorvi and Vasagi mustering their lieutenants and rousing their beasts, and in a little while Canker, Wran and Spiro had joined them. Gorvi had been surly.

'The climb is crippling!' he'd complained. 'But I won't be making it again. While the rest of you slept I went below, looked my place over, and saw what you have not seen: that the sun strikes only these higher levels. Wratha, you are welcome to them! But down there, I have launching bays of my own, and stables for my flyers. When we return I'll take my creatures below. As for the wells: you're right, they are foul. When I have the material, then I shall make a creature to eat the slime and purify the water.'

'You have no complaints, then?' Wratha was pleased.

Gorvi shrugged, and grudgingly replied: 'Only that I must dwell in the basement, as it were, and see to the wells for all to share. As for my levels, apartments, facilities: they are or will be ample. But all this talk of responsibilities prompts me to inquire: just what are your duties, Wratha? I mean, now that you've risen to the top, as it were . . .'

'I shall house and tend the siphoneers,' was her immediate response. 'A place of these dimensions will need more than one, for no use having water if you

299

can't deliver it.' She frowned at Gorvi. 'What? And do you imply that I would shirk responsibility?'

Without waiting for an answer, she turned to the brothers Wran and Spiro. 'And did you inspect your levels, also?'

Despite that they were physically identical (or perhaps because of it), the twin bloodsons of Eygor Killglance affected opposing styles and mannerisms: one was loutish, the other a 'gentleman'. In the main their allegedly inherited 'madness' was also affected, though this was a matter for conjecture and argument among the Wamphyri. Undeniable, though, that in Turgosheim the destructive rages of Wran had been notorious, giving licence to the general consensus that he, at least, was quite insane.

As for their disparity in appearance: paradoxically it was Spiro who went in rags and sandals, with a strip of cloth upon his forehead to keep his hair out of his eyes, while Wran dressed impeccably in a cloak and finely crafted leather boots out of Sunside. Physically, their looks were nothing extraordinary: broad in the shoulder and narrow in the hip (if running a little to fat), they stood six and a half feet tall. A small black wen on the point of Wran's fleshy chin, together with his elegant dress, distinguished him from his brother.

But it was the ragged one, Spiro, who answered Wratha's question about an inspection of their levels:

'Briefly, aye,' he glowered, as was his wont. 'We, too, have a serviceable launching-bay for flyers and warriors, and like Gorvi we'll move our beasts down there at first opportunity. But it seems that when this place was deserted, the gas-beasts were left behind to die and rot in their chambers. Now their dust is everywhere, drifted into every nook and cranny, and clogging all the ducts. As you know, impurities can cause blockages, stenches, even explosions. Which means that before we can hope to bring back light and warmth to the stack, all must be made clean, the walls of the chambers polished, the pipes flushed to discover the leaks, and all repairs made safe.'

Wratha nodded. 'Well, in one more sundown – two at most – we should have thralls enough for all such work. Meanwhile, we'll have to live with it. Ah, but as I recall, luxuries were also scarce in Turgosheim!' And to Canker:

'How about you? Do you have complaints, too?'

He shook his head, set his mane flying. 'None!' he barked. 'I have a small but useful workshop, a launching-bay, and veritable mazes of apartments on all levels. My windows are wide and face north, with suitable balconies from which I may ogle the moon. When I sing ... the walls reverberate with choruses all their own, and my rooms are filled with sound! All I need now is a bitch to warm my bed, a bone to sharpen my teeth on, and I shall be content!'

'You shall have all of that and more,' Wratha nodded, and turned to Vasagi the Suck. 'Last, but by no means least?'

Vasagi had no voice as such. Below his dark, flattened, convoluted nose his face was a trunk of pale pink flesh which tapered into a quivering proboscis. But the Suck had developed his sign-language to an extraordinary degree; there was meaning in his slightest glance, each turn and tilt of his head, every wrinkle of his forehead or flutter of his long, tapering fingers. So that between this and his telepathy, which was an art shared by all of the Wamphyri to one degree or another, his 'voice' was as clear as any other's and clearer than most.

I have no complaints, he answered as 'simply' as

that, with a complicated shrug that said it for him. Except Wratha could swear that she also 'heard' him say: *However, and if or when I do have complaints, then you shall hear of them first, Lady.*

If there was a threat in it, she ignored it for the moment. But she would not forget it. Meanwhile, there was enough to keep everyone occupied.

'Mount up!' Wratha cried. 'Up, all, and into the air — warriors, too! The sun is off the peaks and it's twilight on Sunside. And now, if Maglore has it right, we shall see what no one else has seen for all of fourteen years.'

With which they had headed west over the boulder plains, then south across the mouth of the great pass and the glowing hemisphere of the legendary hell-lands Gate, finally to this very plateau where now —

— Where now Wratha's renegades landed and joined her on the rim. And as they returned to earth and the present, so did the Lady's thoughts . . .

'There!' she said, pointing. 'Look *there!*'

Below them, maybe three miles distant in the lee of the twilight mountains, a Szgany town or more properly a village stood on slightly elevated ground between twin streams which tumbled down from the heights. Southwards, the streams joined up and formed a river through the forest; to east and west, at ancient fording places, stout wooden bridges spanned the cascading waters. The lands thus enclosed, between mountains on the one hand, streams on the other, were sufficient to support the township.

Szgany! Vasagi's facial anomaly quivered his anticipation.

'Women!' Canker fell to his knees and might have offered up thanks to the moon in his fashion, but Wratha stopped him with a glance.

'Thralls galore!' Gorvi's whisper oozed his delight. 'And fresh lieutenants to oversee them in their duties.'

'Flesh for the shaping,' Spiro scowled. 'The first small nucleus of our army. But a town as big as this? Why, Turgosheim never saw the like!'

'And all ours,' Wratha nodded. 'But I think you'll find this a small place, compared with what's waiting out there!' She threw her arms wide as if to enclose all of Sunside, and their greedy scarlet eyes took in something of its span:

The curved horizons to east and west, and between them a dozen and more campfires clearly visible, dotting the darkening land like glowworms as far as the eye could see. Broad forests lying dark to the south, and beyond them furnace deserts, cooling now under banded amethyst skies. In all, a vast expanse.

'How many of them?' Wran, who was normally silent except in a passion, spoke up. 'The Szgany, I mean. Ten thousand, do you think?'

'What?' Wratha smiled at him. 'Why, even in Turgosheim's Sunside there are that many! No ... *fifty* thousand, and more!'

Spiro gripped his brother's arm. 'Just think, Wran! Fifty thou ...!' But the words were choked off as his emotions overcame him. He cleared his throat. 'Our tithe will be massive!'

'Tithe?' Wratha laughed, a young girl's laugh, which in the next moment became a woman's voice again, indeed a Lady's. 'No tithe-system here, Spiro. We take what we want!'

'Oh?' said Gorvi. 'But if they're so many, surely they can fight us? We only talk of building an army, they are *already* an army!'

Wratha shook her head. 'They are Szgany, yes, but it seems that in fourteen years they've become as

303

territorial as we ourselves. See how they've settled, divided their lands, built their towns. Fight, did you say? With what and against whom? Against each other, perhaps, but not against us. Have you forgotten the trogs we fell upon in their devotions? The Wamphyri are no more, Gorvi! We are the stuff of legends!'

Gorvi was astonished; for this time his natural duplicity — his devious mind, which usually examined every angle, expecting trouble from whichever quarter — had worked against him to obscure the simple facts, which Wratha had made clear. 'But of *course!*' he said, his face agog. 'They are unprepared. They don't know we're here, or even that we exist!'

'But they will,' Wratha told him, 'eventually. And then it will be as it was in Turgosheim, too late — for them! *Then* they might choose to fight, by which time we shall be too many. Which is why we start by increasing our numbers . . . start now, tonight!'

Then why do you keep us waiting? Vasagi might look alien, but his eager thoughts were all Wamphyri.

'Simply to remind you why we are here,' Wratha answered. 'I know you have certain needs, all of you; also that you must put them aside, for the moment. Now is no time for wasteful self-indulgence, but for structuring our future. Tonight we kill, but only to rekindle! Tonight we destroy, in order to create! Canker —' she turned to him, '— take as many women and make as many vampire babies as you will, until you are exhausted. But remember this: the rest of us will be making thralls! Bring a Szgany slut back to your manse, by all means, but your flyer has room for just two passengers. And we shall be taking back fine young Szgany flesh, for the making of lieutenants. Enough. I hope you take my meaning . . .' She turned to Wran.

'Wran, you are handsome tonight, as ever. A fine

cloak and boots, and your good gauntlet at your belt. Ah, but should you rage, your cloak and boots will be ruined with blood! Aye, and your every effort wasted. So kill by all means, slay with your gauntlet all you will, but remember this: a dead man is *only* a dead man. Not until he has something of you in him will he rise up again, trek for Starside before the rising sun, and be your thrall in the bowels of the stack. Now, your rages are legendary, I know, but not tonight, Wran, not tonight. Instead, let it be like this: don't maim but make each kill a clean one, for we've no use for thralls who are cripples. And every time you slay, take a little something, a sip, from your victim – but at the same time give a little something back! That way you'll make useful vampires, Wran, not useless corpses.'

She looked at the rest of them. 'The same applies to all, of course . . .

'Now: these are the instructions you should give to those who become your thralls: that when they rise up undead and flee from the rising sun, they should bring with them into Starside grain from their storehouses, nuts and fruits, tools and other metal things – but never silver! – and any woven items which they can carry. They can bring them on their travois or carts, through the great pass; which is why this place makes a good choice, because it is close to the pass . . .' She paused for a moment's thought. And eventually: 'Well, I think that covers it.'

They began to turn away, head for their flyers, but she stopped them. 'No, wait: two more things.

'I remember a time – oh, long ago – on Turgosheim's Sunside, when I was a Szgany titheling. A captive of the Wamphyri, I was given into the charge of a young lieutenant and taken up on to his flyer's back. Then . . . I killed him! Any live prisoners you take, make sure they're either tightly bound or unconscious, or both!

'Finally, don't let the warriors glut themselves. A morsel here, a tidbit there, sufficient only to fuel themselves and no more.' She nodded sharply. 'There! Is all understood?'

All was understood. Again Wratha's nod. 'Good! Now let their fires guide you down to what will be glory for you, hell for them. And if all goes well, later there's maybe a treat for you . . .'

The Szgany of Twin Fords scarcely knew what had hit them. Two of the warriors landed at the bridges, destroying them in seconds, and the third towards the junction of the rivers, from where it herded fleeing villagers back towards the town. The flyers were guided down closer to Twin Fords itself, to encircle it in a ring of lolling grey primordial shapes. Largely harmless when grounded, still these manta-shaped beasts were fearsome to look at, and they had orders from their riders to roll upon and crush anyone who came too close. They could eat flesh, of course, but were instructed not to; their food consisted of a special preparation, which Wratha hoped soon to manufacture on Starside.

But in Twin Fords their arrival had not gone unnoticed: the rumble of warrior propulsors was unmistakable to certain of the older inhabitants, also the amorphous, squid-like silhouettes which blotted out the stars as they passed overhead, and the stench of exhaust gases which fell on the town like the smoke of a hundred corpse-fires. And a concerted sigh of horror went up and was passed on, swelling to a choking cry in the suddenly reeking twilight: Wamphyri! *Wamphyri!*

Issuing a clinging vampire mist as they advanced into the village, the raiders heard that massed cry – indeed, they *felt* the terror which their presence engendered – and laughed. They fed upon it, and with

Wamphyri passions inflamed met the fleeing inhabit-ants head-on. The result was carnage.

Wratha and her five were in the streets, blocking every exit as best they could. Human yet inhuman, they were simply figures in the stinking, slimy mist ... until the people who fled into their arms saw their eyes, their melting, changing faces, and the metamorphic poisons which dripped from their fangs!

Wran raged, of course, but he also remembered Wratha's words and his fury was controlled. Having left his gauntlet tied to his saddle, instead he drove fingers like talons into the chests of his victims, nipping their hearts a little until they fell twitching to the ground. And kneeling, he would fasten his teeth in their necks to taste their blood, which served to trans-fuse his own blood's monstrous fever into them. So he dealt death and undeath to a score of victims in as many moments.

And 'dying', they all sensed the instructions of Wran's hideous vampire mind, which spoke to them as one body although they were many: *When you rise up and come to me in my manse in Starside, bring me your goods and chattels, which are now mine. Only remem-ber: come before the sun is risen! For your Szgany flesh is as a soft metal beside the fire of the sun, and what has been forged may be melted. Aye, and what I have made can be unmade forever.*

Within the hour he killed sixty like this, men, women and youths, of which less than one third would make it to Starside. For before they could escape from the sun, first they must escape from the raid's survivors; and of course, there would be some who woke up too late, or not at all, but slept on with stakes in their hearts until they were burned. In its way, it was not unlike a process of natural – or unnatural – selection.

Spiro's way was simpler than his brother's: he snatched up people where they fled through his mist and bit their faces, then struck them down with hands like hammers. Pain and shock did the rest. They would not die but wake up with sore heads and strange cravings, and hear the message which he'd left in their changeling minds.

As for Canker: to the terrified people streaming out of the stricken town, he must seem like a tame wolf who fled with them. But he was not a wolf and he was not tame. Loping among them on all fours, he chose only the fleetest, and for every male he chose a female. He was tempted . . . there were plump young beauties here . . . but like Wran the Rage, Canker, too, remembered Wratha's words. Why waste his energies now in the cold comfort of the streets, when he'd be using all these women later in whichever way he chose and to his heart's content? – those of them who made it, anyway. His brand would be unmistakable when he saw it: they would be limping where he'd savaged their legs to bring them down, and chewed a little in the junction of neck and shoulder.

Gorvi the Guile crouched in the arch of a mist-wreathed doorway, from where he called out softly, urgently to people rushing by: 'Quickly, there's safety within!' Upon entering, they stumbled over the sprawled heap formed of previous victims, saw the smoking blobs of sulphur which were his sunken eyes, and at the last felt the needles of his gleaming teeth.

Vasagi the Suck waited around a corner, grabbed up any who passed too close, and stabbed them deep in their ears – even to their brains – with his darting, spurting proboscis. For Vasagi, all was accomplished in this one, simple, flowing action; if he desired it, his toll might be huge. But he did not. And his message to the undead was likewise simple:

It was Vasagi the Suck who tasted your brains and bent them to his will. Report to me on Starside. You will know me by my face, which is unique.

So the six and their shadowing lieutenants advanced into the town, leaving death and undeath in their wake. And each of them was like a plague in his own right, except Wratha.

She wore her gauntlet, but only for protection. And killing no one, her method was the simplest of all. Stepping close on the heels of the others where they went, flitting from one to the next as they advanced, she would go to certain of their male victims and touch them, saying:

I am Wratha. He who killed you is to me what you were to him: nothing! Wherefore you are mine. When you come into Starside, be sure you come unto me.

So she recruited her thralls, all of them men or youths. But still she did not see herself as a thief. No, for as the leader of the pack, in order to ensure that all went well for the rest of them, she needed her wits about her. Personally, she could not afford the additional distraction of the kill. Thus Wratha excused herself.

And indeed all went very well, for a while . . .

. . . Until the six and their lieutenants came together in an open space where the fires burned in the town's centre. And face to face, with the warrior stench fading and only their own mist draping them, victory shone from their redly luminous eyes. It had been almost too easy. It *had* been too easy!

For suddenly, a voice from behind snarled: 'Murdering – bastard – *things!*' And human, Szgany, the voice itself was a threat. Whirling as one, falling to defensive half-crouches, the twelve turned outwards. Behind them in a ring, a dozen or more men of the village hemmed them in. But these were mature, experienced men: men of the

309

old days. Their faces were filled with horror, hatred, and resolution; they carried crossbows, loaded and aimed.

Wratha had half-expected it. Szgany herself upon a time, she knew there were always some who retaliated, who could not be crushed utterly: these people, for instance. In the old days this band – these wanderers, always on the move from place to place in their avoidance of Wamphyri raids – had not been supplicant; they'd not surrendered easily to Wamphyri oppression but fought back. And these men ... they remembered how! Their bolts would be silver-tipped, steeped in kneblasch, deadly. There were long knives in their belts, and wooden stakes!

And: *Come!* Wratha called to her warrior. But in that same moment, the men began firing.

Wratha's lieutenant, a young man and very bloody, with a gauntlet which was clogged with red flesh (her restrictions had not applied to thrall watchdogs such as him), hurled himself in front of her – and took a bolt in his throat! He gagged, threw up his arms, was hurled back against her – to be grasped and held there by Wratha, as a shield.

The other lieutenants had acted in a like fashion, three covering their masters, the others leaping head-on to confront the threat. Bolts took one of them in mid-flight, skewered him and stretched him out, but the other got in among the would-be avengers. He struck left and right, his gauntlet spraying red, until silver-edged swords hissed to cut him down.

Vasagi the Suck's mental screech sawed at his colleagues' nerve-endings; he had been struck in the side, where his vampire flesh was now poisoned. A master of metamorphism, he would quickly shed the infected flesh and cure himself; but his cry served to galvanize his five Wamphyri colleagues to action.

Until then they had been stunned and immobilized by the attack, even Wratha, for in Turgosheim's Sunside it would have been impossible. But now:

'Wran,' Wratha cried, 'now you may rage all you will!'

Gorvi cursed where he issued a screening mist for all he was worth; Vasagi reeled and tore out the bolt from his side, hurling it down; the rest sprang to join their lieutenants in the fray.

The men of the village were reloading. One of them got off a frantic, lucky shot which took Canker's lieutenant in the heart. In the next moment Canker was on the crossbowman, tearing out his throat . . .

Wratha came face to face with a man just finished reloading who elevated his weapon point-blank against her breast. Even as he squeezed the trigger, her hand closed on the projecting head of the bolt. Ignoring the 'pain' of kneblasch and silver (she was partly immune, anyway), her fist clenched the bolt more tightly yet and her awesome vampire strength held it back. But the crossbow itself answered the laws of physics. Flying backwards, its thrumming wire sliced the man's windpipe like a razor, even as Wratha's gauntlet disembowelled him.

Gorvi's mist settled over everything, and Gorvi himself was central in it. His gauntlet turned one man's face to ruin, sheared through the rib-cage of another as if the bones were twigs. And the screams of the dead and dying were like music in the ears of the Wamphyri.

Through all of this Wran raged, and likewise his brother Spiro. So that they were *still* raging as Gorvi's mist cleared and it became apparent that nothing more threatened. Distantly, briefly, there sounded the patter of flying feet, but that was all. The dead lay where they had fallen.

As Wran and Spiro grew calm, so there sounded the stuttering throb of propulsors and Wratha's warrior, followed in short order by the others, began circling overhead. Gorvi the Guile looked from the warriors to the smoking red ruins of men where he stood among them, and said, wonderingly:

'So they did fight, after all . . .'

And with a nod, Wratha answered, 'A handful of them, who remembered the Old Wamphyri. But we must never tolerate resistance.'

'They should pay for it!' Canker declared. 'Let's follow them, hunt them down!'

Wratha looked at Vasagi and her face framed a question. His eyes were wide with fury where he stood holding his side, but he shook his head and glanced at his warrior spurting over the rooftops. He sent a message, and the beast at once crashed down on a huddle of dwellings, shattering them outwards!

And: 'The Suck is right,' Wratha declared. 'Let the fools run and hide and think it over, and when they return discover the retribution of the Wamphyri!'

Her creature likewise crashed down, with more sod and timber buildings disappearing into rubble, and Wran and Spiro's warrior followed suit.

And leaving all of the monsters wallowing together in the town's debris, Wratha, her renegades, and their two remaining lieutenants returned to their flyers. Now the warriors would fuel themselves on the victims of the brief battle, human defenders and vampire lieutenants both. It should not occupy them for too long . . .

Later, airborne, Wratha said: *All accomplished, except we've lost four lieutenants and failed to recruit more. So, we have a choice. We can wait and make new lieutenants from our thralls when they come over into Starside, or . . .*

The others waited, and in a moment:

Do you remember, she continued, *I said that if all went well there might be a treat for you?* They did, and she went on: *Vasagi, are you up to it?*

With telepathic perceptions sharper than the others, the Suck knew her mind. And: *Yes*, he answered, as brief as ever.

They rose up level with the peaks and Wratha pointed west. *The night's still young*, she said, *and we have lieutenants to recruit. So let's see what else this marvellous Sunside has to offer, eh?*

No one disagreed.

At about which time, and twenty miles away:

The three more youthful members of Lardis Lidesci's party, returning home from their Starside trek, had gone on ahead into Settlement. But Lardis and Andrei Romani still had the better part of an hour to go before they in turn would enter through the town's East Gate . . .

III

Something less than an hour later, in Settlement:

Attracted by a sudden commotion and surge in the crowd, Nestor Kiklu made his way through the milling people to discover what was going on. And he saw that he'd been right: it *was* Lardis Lidesci's voice making all the fuss. As for what it was all about: that remained to be discovered.

At the forward edge of the crowd, where the people who had come out to welcome Lardis home now held themselves back, shocked by their leader's outburst, Nestor felt himself swaying with an unaccustomed dizziness. Complementing the natural excitement of the night – that and his passion of a minute or two earlier, when he'd talked to Jason about Nathan and Misha – the Szgany wine was quickly going to his head. Reeling, he paused to lean against a cart, and became just one more slack-jawed witness in a sea of astonished faces.

For there at one of the old decoys Lardis stomped about in the tired, broken-down framework of torn, weathered skins and rotting wooden ribs – and raved! Ever faithful, Andrei Romani followed on behind his leader, trying to calm him down and imploring the crowd to hold back and not concern themselves; the old Lidesci was just worn out from the trek. But to Nestor and the rest, Lardis looked far less tired than . . .

'. . . Crazy!' some woman muttered, close by. 'He must have been drinking on the way in, and had a skinful. Why, listen to the man! Playing at being the Big Leader again, after so many years of doing nothing! What? But if his Lissa knew the state he was in, she'd be down here boxing his ears by now! But no, they have their fine cabin up on the knoll, well away from us common folk.'

Old bag! Nestor thought. He didn't think much of Lardis, but old sows like that were worse far. All the same, what on earth was Lardis up to?

'Lardis!' someone shouted from the crowd. 'Now what's all this about? Why, you sound like you've lost fifteen years out of your life, and gone back to the bad old days! As for these lures and all such rubbish: we abandoned their upkeep a lifetime ago. They should be stripped down for firewood. So what's all the fuss?'

Now Nestor began to understand, and to believe that maybe Lardis really was crazy; certainly he'd been acting strangely since they came back through the pass. In order to get a better idea of what was going on, he pushed himself upright and moved closer still.

Fuming and sputtering, with Andrei Romani still in tow, now Lardis stalked around the perimeter of the decoy. 'What?' he snarled. 'But look at the *state* of these lures! The skins are tattered and the timbers rotten. What could you impale on stakes as wormy as these? Nothing! They'd crumble at a touch. As for a warrior impaling himself, ridiculous! What creature would ever feel challenged by . . . by *this* mess?'

'Lardis,' Andrei tried to keep pace with him, catching at his arm to slow him down. He kept his voice low but still Nestor heard what he was saying. 'Lardis, you'll only excite the people, worry them, frighten them silly. Can't this keep, at least until you've rested? You have no proof, after all I mean, you're not sure, now are you?'

Nestor's head felt light, even giddy. He wondered: proof of what? Not sure about what? Perhaps Lardis was tired after all – or sick, maybe? Even now he was looking at Andrei with burning eyes, turning his gaze on the muttering crowd, finally holding up a trembling hand to his sweating brow. But no, he wasn't sick, for in the next moment he was raving again.

'The stockade fence!' he shouted, heading in that direction. 'You've cut doors in it, gates on all four sides. Except they've stood open for so long that they're warped and won't close any more. And just *look* at the great crossbows and the catapults!'

He went at a stumbling run, up the rickety wooden steps where they climbed the fence, to tug at the lashings of a catapult whose huge spoon of a head stood taller than his own. In a moment, rotten leather had fallen to mould in his powerful hands. Disgusted, Lardis let the dust trickle through his fingers and looked around. And his fevered eyes went at once to frayed hauling ropes where they dangled from the pivoting hurling-arm. Then, risking life and limb, he used these self-same ropes to slide back to earth.

'Oh, they take *my* weight, all right,' he panted, landing. 'But how do you think they'd stand the strain of hauling that bucket down against its counterweight, eh? Well, I can tell you that for nothing: they wouldn't!'

'Lardis!' Now Andrei had stopped trying to reason with him, and his voice was suddenly harsher, angrier – sorrier? 'Man, I don't think you ... I mean, it seems to me that you're not ... that you're no longer responsible!'

Lardis had meanwhile turned away to head for the South Gate. Still following him, Andrei cried out: 'Lardis, do you *insist* on being right? But man, you can't be! You mustn't be!' Sensing a drama, the crowd moved as one man to shadow the pair. But finally it seemed that something of Andrei's words had got through to

Lardis. What? What was that he'd said? That Lardis Lidesci was no longer responsible? Or did he simply mean sane? His footsteps faltered, stopped, and he turned.

And as Andrei caught up and went to him, pleadingly now, so Lardis hit him once and stretched him out. Then he turned and went more quickly yet – but crookedly, brokenly – towards the South Gate and the forest beyond. And this time the crowd let him go.

Nestor shook his head, partly in amazement and partly to clear it. The wine lay like a blanket in his brain and on his tongue. Alcohol: even as it deadened the senses and killed off common sense utterly, still it generated passion and excitement. Drunk, Nestor was excited about what had happened, which must surely signal the beginning of the end for Lardis Lidesci, his decline and fall – and the rise of his weakling son, Jason? And he was passionate about . . .

. . . 'Misha!' He spoke her name out loud, and turning bumped into someone. The other, a youth he knew, whose face was now a frowning blur, steadied him and said:

'Misha? I saw her earlier, heading for your mother's house, I think. But what do you reckon about –'

But Nestor had no more time to waste here. Not waiting to hear the youth out, he thrust him aside and went stumbling in the direction of the houses huddled in the western quarter of the stockade, in the lee of the fence and the watchtower. One of those houses had been 'home' to him for as long as he could remember, but perhaps no more.

And the strong wine churning in his stomach, and likewise the thoughts in his fuddled head:

Misha at his mother's house . . . And who else would be there? . . . Why, none other than Nathan! . . . The two

317

of them together, like lovers reunited after a long absence.

Well, Nestor knew what he must do about that!

With the murmur of the crowd fading behind him, he walked unsteadily through the empty streets of low cabins, store- and barter-houses, stables, beehive granaries; and with every thudding beat of his heart his resolve grew stronger and his course seemed more clearly defined. If what he planned was a crime, at least it would be justified. To Nestor, at least.

The west wall loomed, and there was Nana Kiklu's house, one of several built close to the fence: a long sloping roof of wooden shingles at the front, and a short one at the back, covering the stable and barn. Hanging open, the louvre-covers at the windows let out lamplight and the low murmur of voices. His mother's voice, Misha's tinkling laugh, and Nathan's stumbling stutter. Inside, all would be light and warmth.

Perhaps wistfully, Nestor thought about that: all light and warmth . . . but the narrow alley leading to the back of the house and the hay barn was as dark as his intentions. And suddenly he *knew* how dark they were; so that he might have gone straight to the door and entered, been one with the others, and woke up in the morning with a thick head, a sigh of relief and a clear conscience. But it was not to be, for at that precise moment he heard laughter and the door opened a crack, and he stepped back a pace into the shadows of the alley.

Then Nestor heard his mother bidding Misha goodnight, the door closing, and the lingering footsteps of two people coming towards him as they made for Misha's house. And when they stepped into view, and paused silhouetted, her arm hugged Nathan's, and the starlight gleamed on her smile. And Nestor was cold as stone again, but the fire inside him raged up hot as hell.

He felt his feet carrying him forward, had no control over them, or over the hand that made a fist and drove for Nathan's chin, striking him and rocking his head back against the wall. Misha had time for a single gasp as Nathan crumpled – time to stumble backwards, wide-eyed, away from his attacker, and gulp air to make a shout – which came out as a shocked exclamation as finally she recognized ... 'Nestor!?'

And as her eyes went wider yet he grabbed her up, muffled her mouth with his hand, and dragged her kicking and biting – but all in silence – along the passage to the barn door, where he lifted the bar with his elbow. Inside, the piled hay made a musty-sweet smell, and the inky darkness was striped with starlight filtering faintly in through a loosely boarded side wall.

Nestor was aroused now; with his free hand, he tore Misha's dress open down the front and fondled her firm breasts, and she felt him hard where he pressed himself to her. And the incredible became possible, even likely, as he half-pushed, half-fell with her on to the hay.

Misha had always known Nestor was strong, but the strength she felt now was that of the rapist: mindless, brutal, fevered and phenomenal! His breath was hot and sweet with wine, his kisses rough and lusty, and his hands even more so where they alternated between squeezing her breasts and dragging her legs apart, positioning her on the hay. And to accompany every move, each panting breath, he tore at her clothing, and at his own.

Now she fought him in earnest – raking his face, trying to butt him, bite him, bring her knee into his groin – all to no avail; in just a few seconds she was exhausted. Pinned down, breathless and gasping, her fate seemed certain. She drew air massively to scream,

319

and Nestor brought his face down on hers, crushing her mouth. How she tossed and wriggled then, desperate to be rid of him as he threw her dress up over the lower part of her face ... and a bar of starlight fell across her forehead and eyes.

Seeing the fear in Misha's eyes, Nestor flinched inside, in his guts. Perhaps for her part she felt the change in him, which came and passed in a moment. And: 'Why?' she panted, as he completed the work on her underclothes. 'Nestor, why?'

He began to come down on her, his hand behind and under her, opening her up. 'When your father and brothers know,' he husked, 'they'll either kill me or see to it that we're married. Whichever, it will be decisive.'

His mouth closed on hers; she felt his manhood throbbing, thrusting, searching her out, and wondered: *Married? Then why didn't you just ask me?* For after all, she had always known it would be one of them, Nestor or Nathan. She hadn't known which one, that was all. Now she did, and it wasn't Nestor.

But maybe she knew too late ...

Nana Kiklu kneeled by her stone fireplace and chopped a few last vegetable ingredients into the stew bubbling in a copper pan. Her boys would be in soon, Nestor from the welcoming party and Nathan back from walking Misha home. They might have eaten already, but with their appetites it would make little difference. And home cooking was always best.

Nana smiled as she thought of Misha: that girl was really smitten with her boys. But then, she always had been. Sooner or later she would make her choice, and Nana hoped ... but no, she must be impartial, and certainly she loved them both and had no favourite. But Nathan, Nathan ...

The smile fell from her comely face, became a frown, and she sighed. If not Misha Zanesti, then who *would* take Nathan? And if it *was* him, then what of Nestor? For they had grown up together, all three, so that whichever way it went the choosing would be painful and the parting of the ways hard.

And again Nana thought: Nathan, ah, Nathan!

Misha understood him and his ways; something of them, anyway. And as for Nana: she, of course, understood them only too well! She need only look at him to see his father, Harry Keogh, called Dwellersire, looking back at her. Fortunate that no one had ever noticed or remarked upon it; but times had been hard in those days, when people had enough to do minding their own business without minding the business of others. And Nathan's differences hadn't become really marked until he was five, in the year after the last great battle, which had destroyed his alien father along with the first and last of the Wamphyri.

On occasion, infrequently, Nana had seen Lardis Lidesci look strangely, wonderingly at Nathan. But even if he suspected, Lardis would never say anything. He had always been the strong one, Lardis: the protector. And anyway, he got along well with Nathan and liked him; that is to say, he got on as well as could be expected with someone who kept so far apart.

Nathan had always kept himself apart, yes, except from Misha, of course ... And now Nana was back to that.

Finished with her vegetables, she sighed again, stood up, crossed to the window and looked out. Twilight was quickly fading into night now; the stars were very bright over the barrier range, and a mist was rolling down off the mountains and across the lower slopes. In the old days a mist like that would have sent shivers down Nana's spine, but no more. And her mind went back all of eighteen years and more to just such times – and one night in particular – in The Dweller's garden on Starside. What she had done then ... maybe it had been a mistake, maybe not, but her boys were the result and she wouldn't change that.

Nestor and Nathan: they'd never known their true father; which, considering what came later, was probably just as well. But for all that Harry had been (and must now forever remain) a stranger to them, the one unknown factor in their young lives, still he'd left his mark on them, and especially on Nathan. Oh, Harry Dwellersire had marked both of her sons, Nana knew, but in Nathan it burned like a brand.

Burned! She sniffed the air and went back to the fire. For that would never do, to let her good stew burn. But in the pot, the water was deep, simmering, not boiling over at all. And so the smell must be something else entirely. A smell at first, and now ... a *sound*, which Nana remembered.

Impossible!

She flew to the window. Out there, the mist was leprous white in moon- and starlight, undulating, thickly concentrated where it lay on the foothills and sent tendrils creeping over the north wall and through gaps in the stockade's inner planking. Nana had never seen a mist like it. No, she had, she had! But there are certain things you daren't recall, and *this* mist was one of them.

The *sound* came again – a sputtering roar – and a shadow blotting out the stars where it passed overhead. And drifting down from the darkness and the night, that nameless reek, that stench from memory, that impossible smell. *Utterly* impossible! But if that were so ...

... Then what was the meaning of the sudden, near-distant tumult which Nana now heard rising out of the town? What was all that shouting? What were those hoarse, terrified, Szgany voices screaming?

No need to ask, for she knew the answer well enough. 'Wamphyri! *Wamphyri!*'

And as the throbbing sputter of propulsors sounded again, closer, shaking the house, the one thought in Nana's mind was for her boys and the girl they loved: Nathan! Nestor! Misha!

She ran to the door and threw it open.

Nathan! Nestor! Misha!

The bellowing of warriors seemed to sound from every quarter, and the sickening stench of their exhaust vapours touched and tainted everything. Nathan! Nestor! Misha!

Something unbelievable, monstrous, armoured, fell out of the sky, directly on to Nana's house. Along with the adjacent houses, her place collapsed into dust, debris, ruins, like a ripe puffball when you step on it. Shattered, the door flew from its leather hinges and knocked Nana down in the billowing dust of the street. But even as she dragged herself away from the hissing and the bellowing – and now the screaming, which rose up out of the smoking rubble of the nearby buildings – still she repeated, over and over:

'Nathan! Nestor! Misha!' And wondered, would she ever see them again?

Five minutes earlier, in the barn:

Misha felt Nestor beginning to enter her, and in desperation gasped, 'Let me . . . let me help you.'

He lifted his face from her breasts and stared at her disbelievingly. But then, as she reached down a hand between their bodies, he could only grunt an astonished, 'What?'

Certainly Nestor could use help; not only was his drunkenness a handicap in its own right, he was also inexperienced. For all his swaggering and boasting among Settlement's youths, and his apparent familiarity with certain of the village girls, he was a virgin no less than Misha herself. Indeed, more so, for she at least seemed to know something.

She caught him up where he jerked and strained, and tightened her slender hand to a yoke around the neck of his pulsing member. As she began to work at him he murmured, 'Ah!' and rose up from her a little, to allow her more freedom. Never releasing him for a moment but continuing to gratify his flesh, she at once took the opportunity to roll him on to his back.

He was young and full of lust; her hand was a warm engine of pleasure, squeezing and pumping at him; it couldn't last.

Aching to touch her, tug at her, feel the warm resilience of her perspiring breasts, he reached out a trembling hand — but too late. And as his fluids geysered and splashed down in long, hot pulses on to his belly, so Nestor groaned and flopped back in the hay. But even lying there in a mixture of mindless ecstasy and empty frustration, still he sensed her straightening her clothing and drawing away from him. And as his tottering senses found their own level, suddenly he wondered:

How? How had she known what to do?

And trapping her wrist before she could stand up and run from him, his question was written there on his face plain for her to see. As was the answer on hers.

'Nathan!' he snarled then, as she snatched her hand away, got to her feet and backed off. He made to get after her, came to his knees. If she'd learned that much from his not-so-dumb brother, then obviously she knew all of it. And now more than ever, Nestor desired to be into her. If only for the hell of it.

Misha saw it in his face, shuddered her terror and flew for the door; he hurled himself ahead of her, slammed it shut. And moving menacingly after her where she stumbled in the dark, he huskily asked: 'But why? Why with him? Why Nathan?'

'Because he ... he *needed* someone,' Misha's voice was a frightened whisper. 'Because he needed something. But mainly because ... because there was no one else who cared.'

'Well, now there *is* someone else,' Nestor growled, his head clearing. 'Me! Except I don't care, not any longer. No, but there is something I need.'

He caught her and lifted her skirts, and when his hand went to her throat she knew that this time she mustn't fight. But she could still protest. And: 'Nestor, please don't!' she begged him.

'What you've done for him, you can do for me,' his voice was choked with lust and fury.

'But we didn't ...' she gulped as he pinned her to the wall and positioned himself between her legs. 'We've never ...'

'Liar!' he snarled. For in his mind's eye he'd seen them: Nathan and Misha, panting out their lust as their flesh heaved and shuddered. And hoarsely he ordered her: 'Now do it, put me in. And after that ... just pretend that I'm Nathan!'

It was like an invocation.

'B-b-but you're not!' said a stuttering voice from where the barn door now stood open. And it was Nathan, silhouetted against the night, one hand to his face, and the other a fist which was wrapped round the door's inch-by-three ironwood bar.

Nestor half-sobbed, half-moaned as he thrust Misha

aside and went for Nathan's throat — and ran head-on into the flat side of the other's ironwood club! It smacked him in the face, shook his teeth and flattened his nose, struck him down like a swatted fly. He lay there groaning, clutching his face, while Misha stumbled towards Nathan where he stood with legs spread wide and feet firmly planted, and the bar held high for a second blow. Maybe he would do it, and maybe not, but Misha knew she couldn't let it happen.

And neither could Nathan. Even before she could reach him, he'd turned away and let the bar fall.

At which point both of them heard the uproar swelling out from the town's crowded meeting place, and the throb of powerful propulsors overhead. If they had heard that ominous sound before, then they'd been too young for it to make any lasting impression. But still it was strange, frightening, evocative; as was the wafting stench which suddenly accompanied it.

They looked at each other, clung in each other's arms for the very briefest moment —

— Only to be wrenched apart as the roof caved in and the barn flew apart! Then, as their entire world collapsed in chaos all around them, the nightmare they had just lived through commenced its long spiral down from one dark level to depths more lightless yet . . .

Nestor was a child of ten again, playing in the woods with his lieutenant, Nathan, and the Szgany thrall Misha. He, of course, was the vampire Lord Nestor. That was what he had wanted to be all of his young life — what he would *always* want to be, and the only role he would ever accept — Wamphyri!

But this time, and for all that the plot was simple, the game wasn't working out. Nathan and Misha had joined forces to escape from the aerie (a ramshackle treehouse) into the woods, and Nestor was intent upon finding and punishing them. Indeed, and after a decent interval, they were supposed to *let* him find them, except today they didn't seem to be playing according to the rules. And though Nestor had searched for all he was worth for at least half an hour, still they continued to elude him. So that his mounting anger where he slipped through the green maze of the forest, pausing every now and then to sniff at the air in approved vampire fashion, might well be equal (in young boy measure) to that of the legendary Wamphyri themselves. And *how* he would punish this wayward lieutenant, and this ingrate Szgany slut, when he discovered them!

Normally it was easy to find them. He might lean against the bole of a great tree – stand there absolutely motionless, holding his breath in the forest's often preternatural silence – and wait for a telltale sound to give them away: a furtive rustle of undergrowth, the snap of a dry twig, their whispering, conspiratorial voices. Or if not 'voices' in the plural, one voice at least: Misha's. For of course Nathan could not, or would not speak, not without sputtering and stuttering like a fool. And so it would be Misha leading the way, doing all the whispering, the planning, the . . . cheating?

That's what it was: cheating! Spoiling the game! For by now Nestor should have found them, chastised them, sent them to pick nuts and berries for him as punishment, and stood over them scowling while they filled his mother's basket. Which was the real reason they were out here in the first place: to fill Nana Kiklu's basket with wild fruit and nuts. Except, and as always, it had seemed a good idea to turn work into a game.

And now he shouted into the green haze all around, 'Nathaaan! ... Mish-aaa!' ... and waited for their answer.

Hah! Try waiting for a birthday, or a wish to come true!

So now there was only one thing for it, the one infallible method. Nestor didn't like to use it, for it seemed to him an intrusion: like that time he stumbled over lovers in the long grass of the foothills, and watched them at their play. He had never forgotten it: all naked backsides and thrusting, jerking flesh. And hurting, too, from the sound of it. If that was love you could keep it! But at the same time he'd known it was wrong of him to watch them ... as had the young man when it was over and finally he'd sensed a peeping-tom there! What a chase that had been, and Nestor lucky to get out of it unscathed.

This wasn't the same, he knew, but it was similar, and he and his brother had this unwritten rule never to use it. Even the very young have things they would rather keep secret, entirely to themselves. Especially their thoughts ...

But on the other hand, didn't Nathan intrude upon him, too, in his dreams?

Of course, Nathan would know what he'd done; he would feel him there in his mind, and slam it like a door in his face. Ah, but if he and Misha had played the game as had been intended, Nestor wouldn't have to do it, now would he?

He sat down with his back to a mossy bole, closed his eyes and let his mind drift. Somewhere out there, Misha and Nathan were hiding from him. Somewhere in the deep woods, which they all three knew so well, his brother (no, his 'lieutenant') and the Szgany thrall Misha trembled in terror where they huddled in the forest's green expanse. But being Wamphyri, Nestor could smell them out! He could extend his senses, or issue a vampire mist, and *know* when its lapping tendrils touched their shivering flesh! He could scry on them from afar and see them where they cowered! And only let him catch a glimpse of their surroundings, he would know their secret location on the instant!

And so his thoughts drifted out until they touched upon Nathan's. It was difficult and would have been even harder if his brother weren't distracted, if he'd been looking inwards, as was his wont. But this time his thoughts weren't clouded; his mind was clear for once, and concentrated upon something entirely different from Nestor and the game. Concentrated in fact upon Misha . . .

. . . Misha, swimming naked in sun-dappled shallows, sleek and agile as a fish, and just as innocent. Misha, all silver and gold from the sunlight shimmering on her brown pixy body, laughing as she taunted Nathan, daring him to join her in the water. And seeing Misha through Nathan's eyes – seeing her exactly as Nathan saw her – it was as if Nestor saw her for the first time, from a different viewpoint or through a different soul . . . which of course was precisely the case.

Then Nathan knew he was there and Nestor felt his shock, which caused him to start and bang his head against the tree. In that same moment, the scene on his mind's eye blurred and blinked out. But not before he recognized their location: the sandy shallows at the river's bend, where the speckled trout played in the pebbles and eels wriggled in the long grasses.

Nestor knew all the shortcuts; he could be there in four or five minutes, before Nathan accepted Misha's dare and got into the water, and certainly before they were out again, dry and into their clothes. He could be there as quickly as that . . . but he wouldn't.

It wasn't so much what Nestor had seen through Nathan's eyes that stopped him, for if anything that would have goaded him on; it was what he'd felt in the other's inner being. The tumult of emotions there in his unguarded, for once unsuspecting mind. The young man trapped in a little boy's skin, stretching to break free of it, but held back by the knowledge that he'd be a stranger here alone in a strange land. A fear, then, of growing up, when at last he'd be obliged to accept that he was a part of this world and forced to live in it. The lonely depths of his feelings; the awareness of his own outsideness; the sure knowledge that he was without purpose here and could never belong, except to Nana, and to Nestor . . . and to Misha, of course.

All of this concentrated in Nathan's rapt mind, given focus there and highlighted by this crystal clear vision of innocence: a little girl, naked, swimming, laughing and real – undeniably *real!* – as if she were a mainstay, a prop, one of the precious few reliable factors in Nathan's entire world of unreality; which made him fear to reach out and touch her, in case she too was just a mirage.

At the time – the real time, the waking moment of the actuality eight years ago, before the dream – Nestor hadn't understood what he felt. It was hard enough to fathom 'love', without trying to understand something so far beyond it. And much *too* hard to understand the jealousy which held him back, to walk slowly home on his own; that cold void opening between him and his brother, which made him wish that Nathan really *did* belong in some other world, and that he would go there, soon.

One thing he had known, however, and that was the pain and the anger inside, which Nathan had caused. Yes, and Misha, too. So that if Nestor really were Wamphyri –

– Then – *then!*

But he wasn't, and Nathan and Misha weren't his thralls. They were just children playing a game. One which they'd used to play, anyway. For from that time forward they would never play it again . . .

Nestor's dream was fading, slowly giving way to crushing darkness and the return of physical sensations, most of which were feelings of pain. Pain and anger, a monstrous claustrophobia, and a nameless stench.

The dream gradually receding, yes, but in its wake the pain lingering on.

And the anger . . .

Nathan drifted in a darkness shot with brief, brilliant bursts of violent illumination, scenes from the recent past:

Misha smiling where she held his arm tightly against her body . . . Nestor attempting to rape her against the wall of the barn, his voice husky with lust and fury, his hands hurting her with their fierce fondling . . . the ironwood bar from the door in Nathan's hand, feeling good and hard and solid there.

Then he had hit Nestor, hard! Following which something a great deal bigger had hit him, and harder! And now this claustrophobic darkness as his memories tried to piece themselves together and become whole again.

Nathan knew he wasn't dreaming; he was sure of that; his dreams were very special to him, and this wasn't one of them. No, it was the period between sleeping (or lying unconscious) and waking; the interval when the real world starts to impinge again, and the mind prepares the body for a more physical existence. It was him trying to remember exactly what had happened before the world caved in, so that he would know how to act or react when it all came together again.

And occasionally in such moments, those gradually waking moments as the mind drifts up from the fathomless deeps of subconsciousness, it was also a time for communication. Sometimes Nathan would hear the dead talking in their graves, and wonder at the things they said, until they sensed him there and fell silent.

It wasn't so much that they feared Nathan; rather they were uncertain of his nature, and so held themselves reserved and aloof. This was understandable enough, for in their terms it wasn't so long ago that there had been *things* in this world other than men, more evil than men, which had preyed upon the living and the dead alike; the former for the blood which is the life, and the latter for all the knowledge gone down into their graves with them. Things whose alien nature, whose *condition*, was neither life nor death but lay somewhere in between the two, in a seething, sunless no-man's-land called undeath! They had been the Wamphyri, who were known to spawn the occasional necromancer: one of the very few things that the dead fear. Which was why the Great Majority were wary of Nathan.

He knew none of this, only that he sometimes overheard them talking in their graves, and that where he was concerned they were secretive. He was like an eavesdropper, who had no control over his vice.

But in fact, and despite that he could hear them talking and might even have conversed with them (if they had let him), Nathan was no eavesdropper in the true sense of the word, and no necromancer. He *did* come close to the latter, however; very close — perhaps too close — though he wasn't aware of it yet. But the dead were, and they daren't take any chances with him. They'd trusted his father upon a time, and at the end even he had turned out to be something of a two-edged sword.

And so Nathan lay very still and listened neither maliciously nor negligently, but out of a natural curiosity, and in a little while began to hear the thoughts of the teeming dead in their graves: the merest whispers or the echoes of whispers at first – and then a great confusion of whispers – going out through the earth like sentient, invisibly connecting rootlets, and tying the Great Majority together in the otherwise eternal silence of their lonely places.

It didn't feel at all strange to Nathan – he'd listened to the dead like this, between dreams and waking, for as long as he could remember – but this time it was different. Their whispered conversations were hushed as never before, anxious, questioning, even ... horrified?

For on this occasion there were newcomers among them – too many newcomers, and others who came even now – bringing tales of an ancient terror risen anew. Nathan caught only the general drift of it. But it was as if, along with a background hiss and shiver of mental static, he also heard the rustling of a thousand pairs of mummied hands all being wrung together. And so in the moment before they sensed him, he became aware that their fear was no nebulous thing but in fact very tangible.

This much he learned, and no more. For as soon as they knew he was there ...

... Their thoughts shrank back at once, were withdrawn, cut off, and there was only a shocked, reverberating silence in the otherwise empty mental ether. It was as sudden as that, giving Nathan no time to probe any deeper into the problem; but at least he thought he knew *how* they had sensed him so quickly: because they had been alert as never before, almost as if they were expecting some ... intrusion? The only thing that worried him about it, was how in the end he'd sensed that they identified *him* with the source of their terror!

And finally, before their withdrawal, there had been the *name* of that terror, which at the last was whispered from the tips of a thousand shrivelled tongues, or tongues long turned to dust: Wamphyri!

But why should that be − how *could* it be − that these long defunct legions of the teeming dead feared the Wamphyri, who were themselves dead and gone forever?

Nathan knew he would find no answer to that here, not yet, not now that the dead had fallen silent. And so he left them to return to their whispered conversations, and rose up from his dreams to seek the answer elsewhere . . .

. . . Rose up from dreams, to nightmare! To a memory complete with every detail of what had gone before, except the answer to the question: what had happened here? But in his first few waking moments Nathan knew he had that, too, for the dead had already supplied it.

It was a fact, all too hideously reinforced by the alien stench of warrior exhaust gases, the rubble in which he lay sprawled, the distant screams of the dead and the dying, and other *sounds* which could only translate as inhuman . . . laughter? Unless all of these elements were figments of his imagination, and Nathan himself a raving madman, it could only add up to one thing: the Wamphyri were back! And they were here even now, in Settlement!

Which prompted other questions: how long had he been unconscious? Minutes, he suspected, a handful at most. And what of Misha, and his mother . . . and Nestor?

Nathan dragged himself upright, clambered shakily out of the debris of the barn – and back into it at once! For out there, maybe fifty yards towards the town centre, he'd seen the incredible bulk of a warrior hurl itself against a barter house and reduce it to so much rubble. And overhead, a huge, kite-shaped flying thing had arched its wings as it came down like some weird leaf into the main street.

Someone moaned in the litter of timber and straw at Nathan's feet: Misha!

He tore at the rubbish, hurling it aside, and stared down at Nestor's face, all bruised and bloodied. He was stretched our flat, unconscious, three-quarters buried; but it was his moan Nathan had heard, not Misha's. And even as he looked at him, so Nestor moaned again. But there in the rubble beside him . . . a slender white arm. And this time it must be Misha!

Trying not to bury Nestor deeper yet, Nathan dug her out. He slapped her face, gathered her up in his arms, whispered her name urgently in her ear. She was wan, dusty, pale in the starlight falling through wispy smoke and gut-wrenching stench. He couldn't tell if she was breathing or not.

In the near-distance, the Wamphyri warrior roared as it moved inwards towards the town centre. Nathan looked around. The stockade fence was buckled outwards behind what had been his mother's house. There was a gap there, where the great wooden uprights had been wrenched apart. And beyond the gap, the dark forest. The darkness had never seemed so welcoming.

Nathan saw how it must be, what he must do: first carry Misha to safety, then search for his mother, who was probably buried in the ruins of the house, finally come back one last time for Nestor.

He picked Misha up and staggered from the ruins

towards the break in the stockade fence. But half-way there he heard a panting and a patter of feet and looked back. A great wolf-shape – obviously one of Settlement's trained animals – had come from the direction of the main street and seemed to be making straight for him, seeking human company. All very well, but Nathan would have problems enough saving the girl he loved and his family, without having to worry about . . .

Nathan's eyes went wide, wider. The 'wolf' seemed to be enveloped in a drifting cloud of mist, and one of its forepaws was bulky with something that made a dull glitter. More biped than quadruped – loping towards him at an aggressive, forward-leaning angle – it only went to all fours in order to sniff the earth and turn its great ears this way and that, listening. Worse: its eyes were scarlet and glowed like lamps in the dark, and to cover its hindquarters it wore belted leather trousers!

And now Nathan saw that it wasn't coming *through* the mist, but that the mist was issuing from it!

He had heard all the campfire stories of the old Wamphyri – their powers, hybridisms, animalisms – and knew what he was facing. And of course knew that he was a dead man.

Canker Canison came loping, reared up snarling, as tall and taller than Nathan . . . !

Nathan tried one last time to stand Misha on her own two feet and shake her awake, to no avail. He held up a hand, uselessly, to ward the dog-, fox-, wolf-thing off. Canker came to a halt and leaned forward. He sniffed at Nathan, then at the girl in his arms, and cocked his head on one side, questioningly. And: 'Yours?' he growled.

Nathan held Misha back from the monster; Canker laughed, caught him by the scruff of the neck and hurled him brutally aside, against the stockade wall. Unsupported, Misha crumpled to her knees. Canker caught her up, sniffed at her again, and snatched her rags of clothing from her in a moment.

And as Nathan slumped to a heap in the long grasses at the base of the damaged wall – even as his eyes glazed over and he passed out – he was aware of Canker's eyes on him and his writhing muzzle, and the spray of foam coughing from his jaws as he laughed again and said: 'No, not yours – mine!'

What he did *not* see or hear, because he was already unconscious, was the scream of a terrified woman running through the streets: the way Canker let Misha fall to go chasing after her, and his grunted philosophy:

'Better a live one than one half-dead.' And his half-bark, half-shout – 'Wait my pretty, for Canker's coming!' – as he plunged after his doomed, demented victim . . .

The pain and the anger . . .

And not only inside, but outside, too.

It was an hour later and Nestor's turn to come awake – slowly at first, then with a sickening rush! And like Nathan before him, he too woke up from a dream to a nightmare. Except where Nathan had remembered everything, Nestor remembered very little: a handful of scattered, uncertain fragments of what had gone before. Mainly he remembered the pain and the anger, both of which were still present, though whether they sprang from dream or reality or both, he was unable to say.

Three-quarters buried in rubble, dust, straw, his body was one huge ache. His face was a mess and some of his teeth were loose; at the back of his head, above his right ear, an area of his skull felt soft, crushed. When he put up a tentative, trembling exploratory hand through the debris to touch it, agonizing lances of white light shot off into his brain. Something shifted and grated under his probing: the fractured bone of his skull, indenting a little from the pressure of his fingers.

He asked himself the same question that his brother had asked: what had happened? But unlike Nathan, he had no answer. Not yet.

He pushed at wooden boards pressing down on him, shoved them aside, choked as dust and stench fell on him from above. But framed in the gap he could see the stars up there, drifting smoke, and strange dark diamond shapes that soared in the sky. And he could hear a throbbing, sputtering rumble, fading into the distance.

Yes, and other sounds: faint, far cries . . . moaning . . . sobbing . . . someone shouting a name over and over again, desperately and yet without hope.

Nestor kicked at the rubble, extricated his arms, dragged himself into a seated position and shoved the clutter from his legs. He looked around, at first without seeing or recognizing anything; there was nothing here that his glazed eyes and stunned mind were prepared to take in. No, there was something: the tall stockade fence, which for a moment focused his attention. But even that was different, gapped in places and leaning outwards a little.

He stood up, staggered, stepped from the debris. Whatever had happened here, his clothing seemed to have been ripped half from him! Automatically, fumblingly – like a man flicking dust from his cuffs after a hard fall – he made adjustments to his trousers, his leather shirt. And slowly, reeling a little, he headed for the town centre, away from the rubble of his mother's house.

His mother's house?

Now where had that thought come from? And turning to look back at the freshly made chaos – at the black, jutting, splintered timbers and smoking mounds of debris, under a dark shroud of still settling dust – he slowly shook his head. No, for his mother's house had been a warm and welcoming place. Hadn't it?

Along the way, voices continued to cry out from shattered buildings; people stumbled like ghosts here and there, calling for help, or for lost families; flames gouted up where hearth fires turned ruined homes to funeral pyres. There was nothing Nestor could do about any of this, for there were far too many people in need of help. And anyway he needed help himself.

He began to remember names and fractured, jumbled fragments of conversation:

Jason, Misha, Nathan, Lardis, Andrei . . . Nestor?

Jason: *'What will you do?'*

Nestor, growling: *'It's Misha's choice. With or without her, I'll go. But be sure I'll be back one day.'*

Misha, afraid: *'Because . . . because he needed someone! And I was the only one who cared. But Nestor . . . why are you doing this?'*

Nestor, determinedly: *'When your father and brothers learn what's happened, then they'll kill me!'*

Misha, astonished: *'No, they may not, for you are the Lord Nestor!'*

Nestor: *'Of course! And I fear no man, for I am Wamphyri!'*

Nathan: (But here there was nothing, no words at all but a cataract of numbers foaming down the falls of Nestor's mind and forming endless, meaningless patterns there, one of which was a weird figure-of-eight symbol like a discarded apple rind or wood-shaving lying on its side. And rising over the rush and swirl of numbers, a distant, dismal howling of wolves. And superimposed over all these things a haunted, haunting face, all sad and lonely and . . . accusing?)

Lardis: 'This is where the powers of the hell-lands and those of the Wamphyri clashed and cancelled each other out.'

Andrei: 'But they're gone now, reduced to dust and ghosts, and we should let them lie.'

Nestor, in anger: 'What, ghosts? The Wamphyri? Never! For I am the Lord Nestor!'

The voices came and went in Nestor's head: voices out of the past, the present, the imagination. Voices from child-reality, adult-reality, and unreality alike, all seekiṇg the stability of a central focus, revolving together in the grand free-for-all of his trauma. True memories merged into pseudo-memories as his past life faded away and devolved to a single, self-repeating phrase, *I am Nestor of the Wamphyri!* Until it seemed certain that the present, surreal and incoherent as a dream, could only be a dream, given substance by the subconscious will of its creator. And Nestor felt relieved to know that he was only dreaming.

In the near-distance, amid smoky, flame-shot ruins close to Settlement's east wall, a last lone flyer flopped up hugely on to a pile of rubble and craned its swaying head towards the sky. Pausing to watch, Nestor was vaguely aware of a rider in the saddle where the creature's neck widened into its back. But in another moment the flyer had thrust itself forward and aloft on powerful coiled-spring launching members, and rising up from the ruins it banked in a wide circle over the town and rapidly gained height. Feeling its shadow on him as it passed overhead, Nestor gaped at its massive diamond shape flowing black against the stars, and wondered at its meaning.

Then, slack-jawed, with his head tilted back at an angle and his half-vacant eyes still fixed on the alien shape in the sky, he continued his shambling walk through the reeking smoke and scattered rubble; until his path was obstructed and he felt something splash wet and warm against his torn trousers.

Sprawled at his feet, he saw the shattered body of a man whose face had been flensed from the bone. A dark red fountain was spurting in bursts from his savaged throat; but even as Nestor considered the meaning of this, so the crimson fountain grew spasmodic, lost height and gurgled out of existence. And with it the man's life.

But it had been only one life, and this was only one body among many. Looking around, Nestor could see plenty of others, almost all of them lying very still.

And so he came to the old meeting place, that great open space which stood off-centre in Settlement, a little closer to the east wall than the west, and there discovered life in the midst of all this death. But not immediately.

First:

The East Gate was burning. Yellow and orange flames were leaping high over the stockade wall, where the gate seemed to have been set on fire deliberately. The wide path from the gate to the gathering place was strewn with bodies; Nestor dimly recalled, however, that there had been a crowd here. Well, while the corpses were a great many, still they would not have made a crowd. So some had escaped, anyway. But from what?

Wamphyri! said a voice in the back of his mind.

But another said: *Impossible, for they are no more!*

And a third, his own, insisted: *But I am the Lord Nestor!*

The smoke was clearing now and the vampire-spawned mist evaporating, sinking into the earth. People were starting to come out of hiding, stumbling among the dead, crying out and tearing their hair as they discovered dead friends, lovers, relatives. Central in the open space, where tables lay overturned and the ground was strewn with the spoiled makings of a feast, a young man, Nestor's senior by five or six years, stood over the body of his girl and tore his shirt open, beat his breast, screamed his agony. She had been stripped naked, torn, ravaged, brutalized.

Stepping closer, Nestor stared at the man and believed he knew him ... from somewhere. And a frown creased his forehead as he wondered how it was he knew so much yet understood so little. Then he saw the rise and fall of the girl's bruised breasts and noticed a slight movement of her hand. And as her head lolled in Nestor's direction, he saw a strange wan smile upon her sleeping or unconscious face.

He moved closer still, touched the sobbing man on the arm and said, 'She isn't dead.'

Wild-eyed, the other turned on him, grabbed him up with a furious strength, shook him like a rag doll. 'Of course she's not dead, you fool – you bloody fool! She's *worse* than dead!' He thrust Nestor away and fell to his knees beside the girl.

Nestor stood there – still frowning, still mazed – and repeated the other's words: 'Worse than dead?'

The man looked up, peered at him through red-rimmed eyes, and finally nodded. 'Ah, I know you now, Nestor Kiklu, covered in dirt. But you're one of the lucky ones, born at the end of it. You're too young to know; you don't remember how it was, and so can't see how it must be again. But I *do* remember, and only too well! I was only six years old when the Wamphyri raided on Sanctuary Rock. Afterwards, I saw my father drive a stake through my mother's heart, watched him cut off her head, and burn her on a fire. That's how it was then and ... and how it must be now.' He hung his

head and fell sobbing on the girl, covering her nakedness.

There were more men in the open space now, a handful, but these were different, older, harder men. They
had grown hard in their young days, spent in the
shadow of the Wamphyri, and were now filled with
some grim purpose. Nestor seemed instinctively to know
these things, and felt he should know the men, too, but
their names wouldn't come. They were hurrying towards
the east wall, where colleagues on the high wooden
catwalk beckoned to them, urging them on.

Nestor followed in their wake, but more slowly, and
tried to understand what one of the men on the catwalk
was shouting to them. In the still night air – with only
the dazed, bewildered, trembling voices of other survivors, and the whoosh and crackle of the fires to compete
with – his words carried over the open area loud and
clear. And for all that they were hard words, still there
was a catch and even a sob in his familiar voice:

'Too late now, you dullards!' he cried. 'Didn't I try to
warn you? You know I did. What? And you took me for
a madman! And now ... now I think I am a madman!
But all those years of building, of being prepared, gone
up in smoke, gone for nothing. And all this good Szgany
blood, spilled and wasted, and unavenged ...'

And at last Nestor remembered him: Lardis Lidesci,
whom even the Wamphyri had respected, upon a time.
And beside him on the catwalk, Andrei Romani; between them they'd wound back the loading gear of a
giant crossbow, and manhandled a great ironwood bolt
with a barbed, silver-tipped harpoon into its groove on
the massive tiller. Men's work for sure, but they were
men.

So were the others on the ground, whose names now
sprang into Nestor's mind:

They were Andrei Romani's brothers, Ion and Franci, and the small wiry one was the hunter of wild boars, called Kirk Lisescu. Together with Lardis, these men had been legendary fighters in the days when the Wamphyri came a-hunting on Sunside and the Szgany dwelled in terror; even now Kirk Lisescu carried a weapon from those times, a 'shotgun' out of another world. But Nestor knew that except in dreams all such things were over and done with long ago.

Weren't they?

While he puzzled at it, the men had moved on towards the east wall. But up on the catwalk Lardis was shouting again and pointing at the sky – over Nestor! And now, shutting out the stars, a shadow fell on him.

He looked up, at the lone flyer where it side-slipped to and fro, deliberately stalling itself and losing height. For a moment it seemed poised there, like a hawk on the wing, before lowering its head, arching its membrane wings and sliding into a swooping dive. It was heading directly for the bereft young man where he sobbed over his ravaged love. And its rider was lying far forward in his saddle, reaching out along the creature's neck, directing its actions with voice and mind both.

Suddenly something snapped into place in Nestor's befuddled mind. For if this was a dream it had gone badly wrong. And if it was *his* dream, then he should have at least a measure of control over it. He started lurchingly back towards the ragged figure crouching over the girl in the centre of the open area, and as he ran he shouted a warning: 'Look out! You there, *look out!*'

The man looked up, saw Nestor running towards him, and beyond him the others bringing their weapons to bear, apparently on him! Then he glanced over his shoulder at the thing swooping out of the sky, gasped some inarticulate denial, and made a dive for the shallow gouge of an empty fire-pit. As he disappeared from view the flyer veered left and right indecisively, then stretched out its neck and came straight on — for Nestor!

Coming to a skidding halt, suddenly Nestor sensed that this was more than a nightmare. It was real, and the reality gathering impetus, rushing closer with every thudding heartbeat. He glanced all about, saw open space on every side and nowhere to take cover. From behind him someone yelled, 'Get down!' And a crossbow bolt zipped overhead. Then . . .

. . . The flyer was almost upon him, and the underside of its neck where it widened into the flat corrugated belly was splitting open into a great mouth or pouch lined with cartilage barbs! Nestor turned, began to run, felt a rush of foul air as the flyer closed with the earth to float inches over its surface. And in another moment the fleshy scoop of its pouch had lifted him off his feet and folded him inside.

As darkness closed in, he saw twin flashes of fire from the muzzle of Kirk Lisescu's shotgun; up on the stockade catwalk, Lardis Lidesci and Andrei Romani were frantically traversing the great crossbow inwards. Then . . . cartilage hooks caught in Nestor's clothing, and clammy darkness compressed him.

Squirming and choking, denied freedom of movement and deprived of air and light, he breathed in vile gases which worked on him like an anaesthetic, blacking him out. The last things he felt were a massive shuddering thud, followed by a contraction of the creature's flesh around him and its violent aerial swerving.

Then his limbs turned to lead as the flyer fought desperately for altitude . . .

PART FIVE:

Vampires! – The Sundered Tribes – The Search

I

Lardis and Andrei were asleep when the searchers found Nathan and brought him in along with five more. By then sundown was one-third spent, and Nathan had lain unconscious in the grass at the foot of the west wall for more than nine hours. He was still unconscious when they dumped him unceremoniously on his back on a huge plank table salvaged from the wreckage at the site of the meeting place. This was where the survivors were being examined – all the survivors – to see if they really *were* survivors.

Between times, a lot had happened and was still happening. After the attack – after Wratha and her henchmen had done their worst, taken the best, destroyed what they could of the rest and left – then Lardis had taken charge, issued hurried instructions, finally rushed at killing speed up to his cabin on the knoll, where he'd hoped against hope to find his wife and son waiting and unharmed.

But he had doubted it. For he knew that Lissa always kept lamps burning in the cabin's windows when he was away, to guide him home, and he hadn't seen Jason since he and the Kiklu boys had gone on ahead into the town. That soft glow, from Lissa's lamps, could be seen for miles around – as indeed Lardis had seen it through the treetops during his and Andrei's approach to Settlement, but as he no longer saw it – burning up there against the dark flank of the mountains. And as he had driven himself like a madman up the steep side of the knoll, so he'd wondered who or what else had seen that glow, and why his son hadn't come back down when he heard the uproar and saw parts of the town burning.

It could be, of course, that Lissa had seen a suspicious mist on the slopes and stifled the lamps, and that then she'd restricted Jason to the house. It could be . . .

. . . But it wasn't. For when finally Lardis had got there it was to find his place in ruins. Following which he'd spent a back-breaking hour digging in the rubble, finding neither Lissa nor Jason. In a way it had been a relief: at least they were – or might still be – alive! But it was also the greatest tragedy of Lardis's life. For he didn't know where or in what circumstances they lived.

Taken by the Wamphyri? To be used by them, slaughtered by them, perhaps even . . . *altered*, by them? That hadn't borne thinking about. And so for a while he'd thought nothing but sat there in dumb silence, amidst the ruins, already grieving or preparing to grieve their loss. So that by the time Andrei came to sit with him – saying nothing but simply being there in silent commiseration – Lardis's unspoken agony was already turning outwards, to everlasting hatred and cold fury.

But even so, and for all that his loss was great, he had known he wasn't the only one. And when finally he'd looked at Andrei, to inquire in that gravelly voice of his, 'Well?' . . . then his friend and ally of so many years had known that the old Lardis was back. And nodding grimly he'd told him:

'In the old days you were iron, my friend. Now it's time to be iron again. For we're ready, down there.'

Then Lardis had come to his feet, straightened his back and shrugged off his weariness. And: 'Then let's be at it,' he'd said, as simply as that.

But half-way down, pausing briefly, he'd begged Andrei's forgiveness for striking him; also for the fact that he'd been deep in the woods – alone and lonely, bitter and raging, far beyond the South Gate – when the Wamphyri had struck so devastatingly at Settlement. To which the other had answered:

'You have it, and on both counts, but only if you will forgive me: that I ever doubted you . . .'

Since when, the pair had done or directed what must be done, between times catching up on a little sleep; the latter out of sheer exhaustion. Mercifully their weariness was as much mental as physical, so that they hadn't dreamed; otherwise their task might be impossible. Work such as this did not make for easy dreaming. And so they were asleep, in a hastily erected tent close to the meeting place, when Nathan Kiklu and five others were brought out of the darkness into the light from the lamps and the blazing central fire.

It was nothing new to Lardis and Andrei, this process of screening, the investigation or inquisition of the injured in the wake of a Wamphyri raid; in the old days they had seen plenty of this. But the last raid had been eighteen years ago and they were no longer inured to it. Of course, the friends and families of those they examined were invariably present, their dark Szgany eyes soulful in the flickering firelight, mutely questioning the examiners in their turn.

But if the horror wasn't now, at the direction of free men – men who were still their own men – then it would only come later, and from a different source entirely. And all of them knew it.

Coming to the table, Lardis shivered under the blanket round his shoulders and tied a knot in its corners under his chin. The accidental fires had been put out hours ago, since when the night had grown chilly . . . or maybe it was just him. At least the stink of monsters had cleared away now. He glanced up at the mountains blue-edged with starshine; no mist on the peaks now. In any case, the Wamphyri rarely struck twice in the same place, not in the space of a single sundown. And usually their raids followed fast on the setting sun, when they were most hungry.

It seemed unreal: to remember all of these things now. And to know how very necessary it was that he remember them.

The first figure on the table was that of a woman in the middle of her life, maybe thirty-six years old. Lardis shook himself awake, rubbed sleep from his eyes and stared hard at her face. He knew her: Alizia Gito. Her man was three years dead; he'd broken his back in a fall while hunting in the mountains.

Upon the index finger of Lardis's left hand, he wore a ring of gold set with a large, flat, reflective stone. Holding this over her open mouth, he watched for signs of breathing, the filming of the polished stone. Patiently he waited, and was rewarded when the stone's glitter faded to an opaque moistness. She breathed, but very slowly and faintly. As yet this proved nothing, except that she lived. Lardis had seen people dying before, and knew how their breathing was wont to fade away like this. Ah, but he also understood how well undeath could imitate life!

Alizia's face was very badly bruised and her jaw looked broken, but she had no wounds that Lardis could see: no cuts, and her neck was unmarked. He called forward two older women. 'Strip her —'

— And a haggard young man stepped forward, a growl rumbling in his throat as he grasped Lardis's arm. Lardis looked him in the eye, unflinchingly, and continued: '— but let her keep her dignity, what's left to the poor woman. Put a blanket over her.'

The young man was Nico, one of Alizia's sons, about

seventeen years old. Lardis recognized him, and now asked after his younger brother. 'Vladi?'

Nico released Lardis's arm, shook his head. His eyes were very bright with unspilled tears. 'Taken,' he reported, with a gulp. 'I was in hiding under a cart. Towards the end of it I looked out, saw one of them knock Vladi on the head, toss him into the saddle of a flyer and make off with him. I found my mother later. Is she . . .?'

'I don't know,' Lardis could only shrug and shake his head. 'I have to look under this blanket to find out. Listen, I've looked at a lot of women tonight. It means nothing to me, but I know it means a lot to you. We can look together, if you like?' He put an arm across the other's slumped shoulders. And they looked.

Alizia was naked now; she'd been half-naked anyway. Lardis saw . . . obvious signs, but he had to be sure. 'Nico, I want to touch her, turn her over,' he said. 'Can you help me?' Very carefully, they turned her face down. There were indentations in her thighs and buttocks, deep as claw marks, some of them bleeding.

Lardis shuddered and let the blanket fall. His face was working as he stepped back a little, nodding to three men who waited at a discreet distance. One of them was Andrei Romani.

'No!' said Nico, his voice the merest gasp, a breath of air.

Lardis caught him by the arm, held him back. The executioners − three merciful killers − came forward very quickly. Nico screamed high and shrill, but Lardis trapped his neck in a powerful armlock and turned his face away.

The three lifted Alizia in her blanket and carried her to the very end of the table. And there they hammered a stake through her heart. The sound was meaty, soggy, and crunching where ribs splintered. 'But she's alive, she's alive!' Nico was gurgling. 'She's my mother! I came out of her!'

'Yes,' Lardis told him through gritted teeth, holding him even tighter, 'but what's in her now must stay there. She's no longer the mother you knew but a foul, undead thing. But you're lucky, for soon she'll be clean and merely dead. So forgive us if you can, and be thankful.'

'You ... *bastard!*' Nico spat in his face. And on the table, his mother sighed and struggled into a seated position!

A ring of blood oozed from the rim of the stake between her breasts, also from her mouth where she'd bitten through her bottom lip. But her eyes were open now, and they saw Nico. She sighed again, bloodily, and held out her arms towards him. 'My son! Nico!' and as Lardis turned the youth's face away a second time, so Andrei took her head off with one clean sweep of a bright-gleaming sickle.

Nico had passed out in Lardis's arms. He was carried away by Kirk Lisescu, taken to people who would look after him. The parts of Alizia Gito were carried in their blanket to another fire on the other side of the open space, and there disposed of.

Lardis hung his head and Andrei went to him. 'Steel yourself,' he said. 'We're only half-way through.'

Lardis looked at him from a face made haggard by sorrow. 'These people were mine, and I'm killing them.'

The other shook his head. 'We're killing *Them*,' he said. 'Or should we let them live, run off into the forest and hide, and come back at the next sundown to kill us?'

Lardis half-turned away, then nodded, and looked at the next one on the table. And saw that it was Nathan

Kiklu. They had already stripped him and thrown a blanket over him. Lardis went to him, saying, 'Nathan! Ah, no ... this is the worst! I had hopes for him. There was something different in him, something better.'

He threw back the blanket, searched Nathan's body. There were bruises galore, but no cuts. Neither had he been violated, and the lining of his mouth was clean. As Lardis examined him, he coughed and groaned, began to stir.

Lardis was excited. 'Do you know –' he said, more to himself than to anyone else, 'do you *know* – I think he's clear!' In the next moment his excitement turned to despondency. 'But his brother, Nestor: we saw him taken by that flyer.'

'A goner,' Andrei nodded, 'like so many others.'

'We don't know that for sure,' Lardis propped up Nathan's head and gave his face a sharp slap. 'We put our bolt in that beast good and deep!'

Andrei nodded again, and said, 'Aye, and Kirk's shotgun blew its rider right out of the saddle!' He looked up and a little apart, to where a Wamphyri lieutenant was nailed with silver spikes to a heavy wooden cross. He hung there like a bloody rag, apparently dead and certainly unconscious – for the moment. 'But the flyer made off, so what hope for Nestor now? If the wounded creature dropped him, then he's dead from the fall; likewise if it crashed. But worst of all if it made it home.'

Nathan coughed again and rolled his head a little in the crook of Lardis's arm. Lardis glanced at Andrei, said: 'Where, home? Aye, Karenstack, I know – but where before that? These bastards might be new *here*, but they weren't new to their hellish game. They were full-fledged! They had flyers, warriors; they wore gauntlets! So where did they come from?'

Andrei looked again at the lieutenant on his cross.

'When this one comes to, maybe we'll find out. But let's face it, he hasn't much of a choice one way or the other. If he talks he's for the fire, and if he doesn't . . . he's for the fire. Personally, I think we should burn him now. What if they come back for him?'

Lardis shook his head. 'They won't. They have other business to occupy them now.' For a moment he thought of Lissa and Jason, then shut them out of his mind. If he wanted to carry on here, then he must shut them out.

'But,' he continued, 'if they suspect it wasn't just an accident and we actually brought this one down and killed him . . . they'll certainly wonder about it. Strangers here, they're not yet sure of our capabilities. This was their first raid on us, and they had the advantage of total surprise. Even so, it's possible we killed a lieutenant, which means we might also be able to kill one of them. That in turn guarantees their eventual return – not *just* out of curiosity – probably at the next sundown. So catching this one is a point in our favour, especially if we can make him talk. He *must* talk, for I want to know who they are! . . . For later, if for nothing else.'

This was no idle threat and Andrei knew it; he also knew that Lardis must die one day at the hands of the Wamphyri. He must, for it was them or him now, to the end. And he was just a man and mortal, while they apparently went on forever.

Nathan woke up. Lardis knew it at once, for suddenly the youth's neck in the crook of his arm had stiffened, and Nathan had stopped breathing. He was holding his breath. He lay still, rigid, petrified by knowledge of what had gone before, and by ignorance of what was going on now. Then he opened his eyes – a crack at first, then wider, saw Lardis – relaxed again and breathed out.

But Lardis hardened himself and narrowed his eyes a little. He wasn't yet satisfied that the youth was in the clear. 'Nathan,' he said, 'can you hear me?'

Nathan nodded and Lardis helped him to struggle into a seated position. He saw where he was, that he was naked, and clutched his blanket to him. Then, with Lardis still supporting him, he looked along the table: at one end, prone figures lying side by side, and at the other a great wet patch, gleaming red. Finally he saw the Wamphyri lieutenant on his cross and gasped his terror, his lips drawing back from his teeth in an involuntary snarl.

Lardis could well understand that; neither Nathan nor anyone else would require the benefit of previous experience to recognize such as this when they saw it; not with the beast in a state of metamorphosis, as this one had been when the silver shot from Kirk Lisescu's twin barrels ripped him out of his saddle. He had been laughing or shouting, filled with blood and frenzied elation as his creature swooped to claim one last victim. And for all that his eyes were closed now, his passion was still plainly visible, written in every line of his terrible face:

The distended jaws, hanging open, their serrated incisors at least an inch longer than his lesser teeth, which were themselves as jagged as the peaks of the barrier range. The bunched muscles of his face, frozen, drawing back grey flesh from his gaping jaws in a mad laugh, or perhaps in a rictus of instant unbearable agony as he was hit. The flaring nostrils in a squat, flattened nose, whose bridge showed the first signs of convolution, a symptom of his condition: that he was a vampire of long standing. He wasn't yet Wamphyri, but given time he would be. Or would have been.

Nathan took all of this in and more. He took note of

the jet-black lacquered gleam of the lieutenant's forelock, where a silver spike had been driven through its knot, holding back his head to the upright. What he could not know was that the forelock's sheen came from the human fat used to grease it. He saw the man's heavily muscular arms pinned horizontally to the crossbar through the wrists and elbows, with huge hands dangling loose; hands whose fingers were half as long and thick again as his own, and tipped with broad, two-inch nails filed to a chisel edge. What he did not know was that the power of this creature was such that he could drive those hands *into* a man's body to crush his heart or tear through the vertebrae of his spine.

'Ugly bastard, eh?' Lardis's voice was full of hate.

Nathan tore his eyes from the figure on the cross and nodded. Then, glancing at the sky, the position of the stars against the mountains, he gave a start and made to get down from the table. All of the Szgany were expert in gauging the time from the stars, but none so good as Nathan. He knew how long he had been unconscious. And meanwhile ... what of his mother? And Misha?

Lardis grabbed his shoulder. 'Hold on, lad,' he growled. 'First tell me about the bruises on your back. In fact your back *is* a bruise, one big one!'

Nathan nodded. 'A ... a creature – a wolf, man, fox, I don't know what – threw me against the stockade.'

Lardis's eyes were still narrow, suspicious. But in fact he had heard reports of a hybrid thing among the Wamphyri raiders. Hideous reports. 'Threw you? He didn't bite you?'

Nathan clutched his arm. 'He t-t-took ... took Misha from me!' His eyes were wide again, brimming with the horror of it. Then, shaking Lardis off, he got down from the table, staggering as soon as his legs took his weight. His back was a column of molten agony from nape of neck to base of spine, so that he might have fallen if Lardis hadn't caught him under the arm.

'Don't try to go rushing off, lad. You're in no fit state for it. Anyway, what can be done is being done.'

'B-but my m-mother, and Misha!' He looked dazedly around. 'W-Where are my clothes? And what about N-N-Nestor?'

Lardis opened his mouth ... but he could only say, 'Ah!' and look away.

'Nestor?' And now Nathan's voice was steady. Very steady.

Lardis looked at him again, frowning. In other circumstances it might even be funny, for this was the most anyone had ever had out of Nathan in as long as he could remember! Was it just the shock, or what? What had got into him? *Had* something got into him? 'Are you sure you're all right?'

'What about Nestor?' Nathan looked straight at him with those weird, bottomless blue eyes of his.

There was nothing for it but the truth. Lardis had too much to do; he'd not had sufficient time to give rein to his own sorrow yet, so mustn't concern himself with the tears of others. Straight out with it then: 'Taken!' he said. 'We saw it: a flyer got him and carried him off. That one on the cross was its rider. Kirk knocked him out of the saddle; Andrei and myself, we put a bolt in his mount's belly. But we didn't stop it. It made off and took Nestor with it. I'm sorry, lad.'

Nathan made to stumble away. Like Lardis, he would save what grief was left for later. But right now: 'My mother was in our house,' he said. 'She's buried!'

Again Lardis stopped him. 'Nathan, wait. We've been digging in all the fallen houses.' He called forward a woman with a simple map of the town scrawled in charcoal on a piece of cloth, and said, 'What of Nana Kiklu?'

The woman didn't need to look at her map and its smudged symbols; she'd known Nana well; she said nothing, simply shook her head inside her black shawl.

'Speak!' Nathan cried out, and Lardis stepped back a pace, astonished. 'What?' Nathan shouted. 'A shake of your head? What does that mean? Did you find my mother? Is she dead? Speak!'

Grief-stricken herself, with losses of her own, finally the woman found her voice and sobbed, 'Your mother isn't there, Nathan. They didn't find her. Neither your mother, nor the Zanesti girl, Misha, who was at your house. Her father was here to see if she'd been found. He was mad, tearing his hair! He lost not only Misha but also a son this night.'

Misha, lost! Finally the truth of it hit Nathan. He sat down in the dust and cradled his head in his hands. There were no tears, just a vast weariness. For he knew now that he must wake up – *really* wake up – and become part of this world he had spurned. Before . . . it hadn't mattered. Nothing had mattered very much. This world hadn't been his, hadn't even been real, because he'd thought it held nothing for him. With only a few exceptions, its peoples had seemed like aliens. But the loss of Misha was real, and he couldn't deny it; the one warm spot in his heart was empty now and cold.

No, there was one other warm place there, occupied till now by his dear mother. And was she, too, lost? In which case his heart must freeze entirely. He turned to Lardis. 'Did anyone see my m-m-mother taken?'

Lardis sighed. 'Nathan, I've many things to do. *Too* many things, and too little time. But when all's done be sure I'll ask around. You're not the only one with questions. By sunup we'll all know who was taken, murdered, raped, changed. And by then, too, we'll have ... dealt with all this. Right now, however, there's nothing to be done. Not by you, at least.'

'And what am I supposed to do?'

Lardis shrugged, sighed. 'Find a warm place. Get some sleep.'

'And you? Don't you need your sleep?' Amazingly, Nathan was almost defiant. Lardis might expect such as this from his brother, Nestor, but from Nathan?

'I'll sleep later,' he answered roughly, turning away. 'But for now ... I've work to do. So be off, I'm busy!'

Nathan shook his short-cropped yellow head. 'If you can be strong, then so can I. Anyway, how could I sleep? Lardis, I ... I don't *have* anyone!'

Lardis heard the emptiness in his voice, like an echo of his own emptiness, and thought: *Neither do I have anyone, not any longer. Except maybe you.*

But out loud he said, 'Then be strong somewhere else, for the moment at least. This is a bloody place, Nathan, and what we're doing here is bloody work ...'

After that there was no more time for talk, for Andrei had lifted the blanket off the next one and was beckoning urgently. Lardis went to him and looked where his finger pointed. The man under the blanket had been bitten in the neck, and wide-spaced punctures had formed scabs over heavy blue arteries. There was no breath in him, no pulse, and he lay utterly still.

Nathan backed off a few paces and stood there watching. He had to learn what he could of this sort of thing now, for it was no longer a game which he, Nestor, and Misha played in the woods. The Wamphyri were real, and so was the horror they brought with them.

Lardis yanked a bauble from its stitches in the cuff of his jacket, opened the cold grey fingers of the corpse's left hand and folded them around a small silver bell which he forced into the palm. Then he stepped back and waited. And in a little while . . .

. . . The 'dead' man (whom Lardis had been fairly sure was undead, but must test anyway), moaned and gave a shudder that shook his entire body. His eyelids fluttered but remained mercifully shut. He wasn't ready to wake up, but even unconscious the poison in his blood was protecting its changeling. His hand vibrated on the table's boards, unclenched, and in its agitation tossed aside the silver bauble. Finally he sighed and lay still again. And Lardis nodded, sharply.

The gaunt-faced, strong-willed executioners came forward, and Nathan saw what Lardis had meant by 'bloody work'. He forced himself to watch this one, just one, and was sickened. All the rattling, grimacing skeletons of whispered campfire stories took on rotting flesh now, and every bad dream of his childhood was realized at one and the same time.

Against this surreal background of smoky, ruddy firelight and terrifying burnt-pork stenches – where gaunt figures came and went through the night, carrying their burdens of blanketed bodies, and Lardis Lidesci was the Ultimate Authority, who determined life or death – finally Nathan was set free from his deep-rooted mental shackles, became a man of Sunside, Szgany, and left the shucked-off chrysalis of his weird other-worldliness behind him.

The shell was left behind, at least.

But a man is more than flesh and blood. When he is conscious a man can control his body and even, in large measure, his thoughts. But when he's asleep . . .? Are his thoughts entirely his own?

When he was very small, Nathan had sometimes asked his mother: 'Why do the wolves talk to me in my pillow? Why do I hear all of the dead people whispering?' Then she would seem to close up on herself like the flowers at sundown; an uneasy look would come into her eyes; she would shush him and beg him not to ask things like that, for such questions were strange and people wouldn't like or understand them.

These were only a few of the strange questions Nathan had learned not to ask, until he'd rarely asked anything at all but remained silent. Even in his dreams, he'd learned how to stay mainly silent.

But that had been then, in his childhood.

And this was now, and he was a man . . .

Lardis had told Nathan to go away, find himself a warm place, sleep. But he could not. Indeed, it would not surprise Nathan if he never slept again. Instead he turned his back on Lardis's and Andrei's 'bloody work' – what was happening on the great table, the monstrous but necessary examination of the dead and the undead by those who still lived, *while* they still lived – and went to sit cross-legged close to the foot of the cross, where the Wamphyri lieutenant hung on his silver spikes.

Someone brought Nathan his clothes and he dressed himself automatically, almost without conscious volition, then sat shivering under his blanket and waited for the lieutenant to regain consciousness. For Lardis intended to question this creature, this man or once-man, and whatever the old Lidesci's methods would be – however cruel – Nathan intended to hear for himself whatever answers they might elicit. He was Szgany now and had made himself a vow; it was unpublicized but a vow for all that, and it would be a hard thing to accomplish. In order to destroy his enemies he must first understand them.

There was a lesser fire close by, which slowly warmed him through until he began to nod. And despite that he had thought it impossible, in a little while he curled up on his side and went to sleep. It was the beginning of a healing process, but only partly physical. For mainly it was an opportunity for his mind to consolidate the undeniable fact of his existence, at the same time assimilating something of the monstrous facts which had focused that reality.

That was partly why he slept: to heal himself in body and spirit, and let the subconscious Nathan create some kind of order out of the chaos of the physical Nathan's new reality. But his mind was not like those of other men; complex as the genetics which had built it as a reflection of another's mind, it was living proof of that universal axiom, 'like father, like son'. The only difference between him and his Necroscope father was this: that Harry Keogh, in his own world, had had the benefit of a mathematical science, and of a million dead people who cared for him and were not afraid. While in this world ... now the Great Majority had plenty to fear, and felt that they could only trust each other. And so they continued to avoid Nathan when his dreams impinged too closely upon theirs. Like now ...

... He felt them shut him out, withdrawing into the silence of their tombs! More quickly than ever before, the teeming dead had sensed and rejected him. And so he must dream of the living.

Misha was at the forefront of his mind: naturally he would dream of her. Not as he had last seen her, in the clutches of a beast-man (his mind shied from that), but briefly, in snatches out of time. As a child, as a girl, and then as a young woman.

First as a child:

Misha as he'd seen her that first time: all naked, sleek, shining, and agile as a fish in the water, swimming in the sun-dappled shallows and beckoning him to join her there. Strangely her innocence had deprived him of his own! And despite that he had been a child, his thoughts had been a man's thoughts. After that there had been other times, but always he kept his sensual self from her; they had played as children, sexless at first, until the passing years had brought changes.

One time, when they had been swimming together and after they'd scrambled back into their clothes – as they laughed and rough-and-tumbled each other on the riverbank – finally they'd fallen into each other's arms and she had felt him hard against her. At once, he'd sensed her catching her breath and drawing just a little apart. But then, as curiosity got the better of her, she had let her arm fall 'casually' across Nathan's lower half, to test the response of the small rod where it throbbed in his trousers.

Misha had older brothers; she wasn't blind; she knew about such things.

One day as they wandered in the forest, when he was fifteen and she something less than a year younger, they'd come across a plum tree. It was late in the season and the fruits were very ripe. Lifting her up until she could reach the shining, purple plums, Nathan had been more than ever aware of her thighs swelling into firm, rounded, still boyish buttocks, and conscious of the buds of her breasts where she strained her arms upwards. So that after she had picked several of the fruits, and he relaxed his grip to let her slide down between his hands –

– He'd marvelled at the sight of her brown legs, revealed where her dress rode up about her waist. She

365

had seen his eyes on her and felt him against her where she stretched her toes for the forest's floor; and she'd told him, however breathlessly, impulsively:

'Ah, see! Your little man is jumping again . . .'

And when he'd turned away, embarrassed and reddening:

'Nathan, wait!' she had taken his elbow. 'It's all right. I understand. There's no harm in him. He jumps for joy – for the joy of me!'

For her brothers had girlfriends, too, and Misha knew how *they* dealt with their frustrations, how *they* gained relief from the overabundance of their emotions. 'You should let him out,' she told Nathan then, still clinging to him, 'before he bursts!'

And in the secrecy of the long grass under the plum tree, she had whisperingly, wonderingly compared the purple of his swollen glans to the tightly stretched skins of ripe plums, and stroked him to orgasm. Since when and for three long years, she had satisfied him in this way, and allowed him to return this most tender compliment. But wise beyond her years, she had not once let him into her.

'Ah, no!' she would say when his flesh seemed most insistent. 'For when my children come along I must be able to teach them, which I can't do while I've still so much to learn. Also, I have not made up my mind. I *may* love you, Nathan, but I can't be sure. What if I discover someone else to love, but too late? If I let your flesh into mine now, this very minute, it might decide me against my will.'

And finally, just a year ago, walking in the twilight before the night, when they paused to fondle a while on a grassy bank and she'd held him throbbing in her hand, and Nathan had told her:

'H-h-he wants to k-kiss you, too. Where only my f-fingers have kissed you.'

And again on impulse she'd taken him deep into her mouth to draw his sting, and afterwards told him:

'There. Flesh is flesh, Nathan, but this way makes no new flesh.' And putting her finger to his lips, she'd added, 'Shh! Say nothing, make no protest! We are grown up now. Give me just another year, and then — I shall make up my mind. But it won't be easy. My father and brothers see many men in Settlement, and they see you. Oh, I know — I *know* you are more different than even they suspect — but harder far to convince them of that. And anyway, there could be someone else.'

The only 'someone else' there could be was Nestor and Nathan knew it, but he'd said nothing. Except ... he *had* wondered. For there had also been times when Nestor and Misha were alone together, too, and who could say but that — ?

— But no, for Nestor chased after the other girls of the village, while Nathan had no one but Misha. Surely that must make a difference?

Now that his brother had entered his dream, Nathan moved on, moved forward, to the present. And now Misha was no longer a slip of a girl but a young woman, sitting there in his mother's house, like some warm wild flower in the light of lamps and the glow of the fire.

Small but long-legged — elfish as the creatures of Szgany myth, which were said to inhabit the deep forests — Misha Zanesti was the focus of Nathan's fascination; indeed, she *was* his only fascination in the world! So that it was hard to concentrate on what they were saying, she and his mother, when all he really wanted to do was look at Misha. Even now, dreaming, he couldn't remember what had been said, but he certainly remembered the way Misha had looked:

Her hair dark as the night, velvet, the darkest Nathan

had ever seen, which in the light of the sun shone black as a raven's wing. Her eyes – so huge and deeply brown under black, expressive, arching eyebrows that they, too, looked black – all moist and attentive where she listened to Nana Kiklu's warm low voice, and now and then nodded her understanding and agreement. Her mouth: small, straight and sweet under a tip-tilted nose which, for all that it flared occasionally in true Gypsy fashion (indeed, a great deal like her father's) had nothing hawkish or severe about it. Her ears, a little pointed, pale against the velvet of her hair where it fell in ringlets to her shoulders.

She might be less wild, voluble, deliberately voluptuous – less enticing and far more retiring – than certain of Settlement's Szgany girls, but she was in no way *less* than them. Misha lacked nothing of fire, Nathan knew, but kept it subdued and burning within. So that he alone (and perhaps Nestor, too?) saw its light blazing out from her in all directions, like the white of her perfectly formed teeth when they smiled into the sun. Ah, but he'd also seen those teeth snarl and knew of several village youths who'd felt the lash of her tongue when they sought to be too familiar! Well, they'd been lucky, those lads, for they might have felt a lot more than that if he ... if Nathan ... but that wasn't his way. Or it hadn't been, not then.

In any case, Misha could look after herself and had her own philosophy. He remembered her words: 'If a girl flaunts herself and acts the slut, she can only expect to be treated as such. I do not and will not!' But with Nathan she'd always acted as the mood took her. For which he was glad ...

His mother and Misha faded from Nathan's dream and were replaced by Nestor. Nestor striding in the streets of Settlement, admired by the girls and adored by his friends even as the stuttering Nathan was shunned. Nestor proud, strong – arrogant? – but never the bully. Not until that night, last night, when he would have used his physical strength to bend another to his will. Nestor who had cared for and protected Nathan through all the years of their childhood, and cared for Misha, too, until he'd seen how closely she and Nathan were drawn together.

Nestor gone, taken, stolen by a Wamphyri flyer into Starside.

No! said a voice in Nathan's dream, one which he recognized at once. For it was a mind-voice, and telepathic voices – even the whispers of the dead – are not unlike their more physical counterparts; they 'sound' the same as if spoken. But this was no dead person speaking, not even a 'person', though Nathan had always considered him as such. And:

No, the mental voice came again, like a snarl, a cough, a bark in Nathan's dreaming mind. *Your brother – our uncle – has not been stolen away into Starside. The flying creature which took him crashed to earth in the east, on Sunside.*

Nathan pictured the speaker. He had his own name for him: Blaze, after the diagonal white stripe across his flat forehead, from his left eyebrow to his right ear, as if the fur there was marked with frost. Blaze, whose eyes were the brown of dark wild honey in the twilight, and feral yellow at night. Lean but not skinny, all muscle, sure-footed as a mountain goat and fleeter far. And intelligent? – oh, *far* beyond the average intelligence of the pack! He admired and respected him, and knew that it was mutual. Why else should the wild wolves of the barrier mountains call Nathan their 'uncle', and come to him in his dreams as they sometimes came to him in his waking hours?

The grey brother read Nathan's thoughts, which were focused now beyond the scope of casual dreaming. *Because you are our uncle!* he insisted. *Mine, and likewise the ones you call 'Dock' and 'Grinner', my brothers from the same litter. And because you and we are of one blood and mind, we are curious about you and consider your welfare. Our father would have wished it, we think . . .* (A mental shrug, the twitch of a grey-furred ear.) *You are not of our kind, but you are of our kin, after all. You are our uncle, as is Nestor. But you are the one who understands us. You, Nathan, of all the Szgany, translate our thoughts and answer them.*

Nathan had never understood the way they included him in their wolf family-tree; it could only be a compliment; he considered it as such, and was satisfied to be their friend. But now it seemed his friendship with the wolves was bearing fruit.

'What of Nestor,' he was eager. 'Does he live?'

Our grey brothers in Settlement saw him taken into the creature's mouth, the other's snarling answer came at once. *He was snatched up, whirled aloft, carried east and towards the barrier peaks. But in the hills and all along the spine of the mountains, we observed the creature's clumsy flight. Wounded where a great bolt was lodged in its flesh, it could not clear the mountains. With fluids raining from its wound, it fell to earth, came down in the pines and expired on the slopes above a Szgany township. And so your brother, who is our uncle Nestor, is not in Starside but Sunside. But . . . I cannot say if he lives. Members of the pack were close to hand, but not that close. And the men of the town are fearful now of creatures other than men. Aye, and even of strange men! The grey brotherhood must stay well clear.*

'Which town?' Nathan could scarcely contain his

excitement, which threatened to wake him up. 'Where did the flyer crash? If Nestor is still alive, I have to find him. He's all I have left.'

You have us.

'Among men, he's all I have.'

You have the Lidesci, who was our father's friend even before we were littered.

'But Lardis Lidesci . . . is not of my blood.'

(A nod of that wise wolf head.) *The town is the next one to the east, between the rivers.*

'Twin Fords?'

That is its name, we think. But Nathan, you have your mother, and a young female of the Szgany. We have seen you together, and she is always in your mind.

'Misha? I don't know if she lives. And if she lives, I don't know where or for how long. She was taken by a . . . by a human dog! By a beast-thing, Wamphyri!'

The Dweller, our father, was a wolf-human, a were-wolf.

Nathan shook his head. 'Your father could not have been like this one. You are animals, not-humans. But this one was a . . . a beast! He was inhuman.'

We know of him. (That nod of a wise head again.) In the east, beyond the pass, the grey brothers have heard him singing to the moon in Karenstack. For he worships our silver mistress much as we do. But you are right: he is not like us. We are . . . animals, and he is a man-beast.

'Wamphyri,' said Nathan, 'aye . . .'

And your mother? What of her?

'I don't know. Perhaps she was taken; I pray by my star that she was not; perhaps she ran off into the woods. But if she did, then why has she not returned? Do you know anything of her?'

No. It is only by chance that we know of Nestor. We wish you luck in your search for him.

'Do you leave me now?' Nathan was reluctant to let them go.

New things have come to pass. (In Nathan's mind, Blaze's golden eyes seemed to burn on him. But their yellow fire was fading, and the wolf's telepathic voice was faint now, retreating.) *Strange and monstrous creatures are come into Starside, from where they raid on Sunside. The woods and mountains are no longer safe, neither for wolves nor men. These are problems for which we have no answers, but there is one at least who might know. Now we go to find out about these things.*

Desperately, Nathan tried to retain him, hold on to this one familiar thread – however weird, tenuous, unbelievable – in a world which in the space of a few short hours had become a nightmare. 'Answers? But there is no answer to the Wamphyri.'

You may be right. You may be wrong. (The voice was fading out and starting to lose all sense and meaning. How else could Nathan translate the next and last words he heard, except that he misunderstood them?) *But our mother speaks to our father, who is your brother. And if anyone would know, he is that one. And so we go to speak to the one who suckled us.*

'Your mother, a wolf?'

Aye, where her bones lie bleached in a secret place . . .

It seemed that a cold wind keened upon Nathan then, as the wolf-voice went out of his dreams –

– But the wind was only the night air where someone had uncovered his head. Squinting his eyes in the firelight he saw Lardis kneeling beside him, turning back his blanket. 'Nathan,' the old Lidesci growled. 'Be up, lad, and away from here. This one you've guarded so well, he wakes up – and I have business with him.'

As dreams are wont to do in the light of reality, Nathan's was quickly disintegrating, breaking up. Those parts concerning impossible relationships were quickly forgotten; his wolves had always called him uncle, so that he saw nothing strange or new in it. It wasn't worth retaining. But as for the one important item of information, about Nestor: he clung to that, repeating it to himself:

The flyer that carried Nestor away has crashed to earth in the east, close to Twin Fords.

Strange to think that just yesterday, in the late afternoon, Nathan and the rest of Lardis's party had passed through Twin Fords on their way home. Since then, it was as if a new age had dawned. An age of darkness.

Perhaps he had spoken out loud before he was fully awake. For Lardis at once demanded: 'Eh? Twin Fords? What of it?'

'I . . . I was dreaming,' Nathan answered. 'Of Twin Fords, I think.' He'd long ago learned not to talk about his dreams. Especially the stranger ones.

But Lardis was shaking his weary, hag-ridden head. 'No, it was no dream. Twin Fords was hit last night, as prelude to what happened here. A handful of refugees came in while you lay sleeping, and you must have overheard us talking. Twin Fords is no more; its people won't go back there; the tribes are sundered, Nathan, and we're all to be Travellers again. The days will be ours, and the golden sun our one sure friend, but all the long dark nights will belong to them, the Wamphyri!'

The Wamphyri lieutenant was groaning, stirring on his cross. Nathan stood up, eased his cramped bones and felt fire in his bruises. He glanced at the stars over the black barrier range, saw that the hour was well past midnight. He had never slept so long in one place, at one time. His bladder was full of water, which he must be rid of.

Stumbling away into the shadows, he found a place to relieve himself. The ground all around was already desecrated, steeped in vampire mist, warrior stench, and unavenged Szgany blood. A little urine couldn't hurt. Already Nathan's thoughts had turned as sour and cynical as the bitter brown taste in his mouth . . .

When he got back to the cross the lieutenant was fully awake, turning his head this way and that, as far as the spike through his topknot would allow, glaring at the handful of men who were gathered there to question him. For a moment the vampire's scarlet eyes lit on Nathan, burned into his soul, drove him back a pace before they moved on. Nathan was no threat; he was a mere youth, of no importance. But the men were something else. Especially the apish, hollow-eyed leader of this Szgany rabble.

Vratza Wransthrall brought his scarlet gaze to rest upon Lardis and scowled at him. 'Man,' he croaked, 'you are doomed. For what you have done and will do to me –' his eyeballs swivelled left and right, observing the silver spikes which pinned him to the cross, '– my master, the Lord Wran, will stuff your throat with your own tripes, rip out your living heart and eat it smoking, and feed your tatters to his warriors. Whoever you were, you *are* no more.'

Lardis looked up at him, tilted his head a little on one side, sniffed at the air suspiciously, disdainfully. He glanced at the men around him: Kirk Lisescu, Andrei Romani and his brothers, and one or two others, inquiring: 'Do the words rise or fall from his lips? I think they fall; or is it the stench of warriors lingering on the night air? No, for that is sweet by comparison. And so it seems we've erred and should have nailed him higher. But what the hell . . . a stench is only a stench.'

The vampire's muscles bunched as he flexed grey

arms on silver spikes; he gave a shudder that wracked his entire body, then groaned and hung still. But in another moment, lifting his head to glower at Lardis as before, he said: 'Aye, make your jokes while you may. For all of this –' he snorted and tossed his head derisively in a small, sneering gesture which dismissed Settlement in its entirety, '– is finished. And all of your people are as dust. Let every man, woman and child of them that are yours count each breath he takes from this time forward, enjoying it individually as if it were his last. For the *lucky* ones have very little of breathing left to do. As for them that are unlucky: they shall be heir to the dubious delights of the great stack on Starside; from the mills where their bones will be ground down for meal, to the pens of the warriors and the reeking methane pits. They shall be fuel for my master's lusts, flesh for his fashioning, fodder for his beasts. So be it.'

Someone had brought Lardis a stool where he sat with a hiked knee supporting his elbow, and his square chin resting on the knuckles of a calloused hand. His attitude towards his captive seemed almost casual, but anyone in his acquaintance would recognize how doomful was his calm, quiet voice as he answered, 'Long-winded bastard, aren't you?' And then, more businesslike:

'Do you have a name, vampire, or are you satisfied to be remembered as a stench and a puff of black smoke rising from our fire?'

The creature gave a start, and glared harder than ever; but he also trembled a little where he hung suspended on the cross. Poisoned by the silver shot which had ripped into his great chest – also by the long silver spikes which pinned his wrists, elbows, and the twitching muscles of his calves to timbers hard as iron – he was weak by a vampire's standards, but still strong by a man's. Even now, if only he could get down from this cross, he'd wreak havoc among his tormentors before someone put a bolt through his heart. That was how he would prefer to go: fighting bloodily the one minute, with a bolt through his chest the next, and finally his head flying free in a crimson welter! After that, they could burn him all they wanted. But ... not while he was still alive.

It was as if Lardis read his mind. 'Oh?' he said. 'And is it that the fire worries you?' He knew it was, for a vampire burns slowly, and the thing inside him fights it all the way.

Meanwhile, Kirk Lisescu had slipped away and returned with a spade. Whistling tunelessly, he bent his lean, muscular back at the foot of the cross and commenced digging in the loose soil there. Whenever his spade struck the upright, it shivered a little. Looking at the lieutenant, Lardis nodded to indicate Kirk's activity, and said:

'He digs here at the front, so that eventually the cross will be weakened and topple towards the fire there.' Standing up, he jerked his thumb negligently to his rear where a long, deep pit of glowing embers lay behind him. And: 'Phew!' Lardis wiped his brow, 'but it's hot!' Then, walking to and fro – with his great head jutting a little, though not aggressively, and his hands clasped behind his back – he continued conversationally:

'Of course, if you were to loosen up a bit and talk – why, my good friend here might stop digging in order to hear what you were saying!' He gave a shrug. 'And really it's as simple as that: while you talk you live, at least as long as you make interesting conversation. And when you stop talking you burn. Meanwhile, you still haven't told us your name, or where you come from, or how many there are of you ... *or anything at all which we might find remotely interesting!*'

Snarling the last few words, finally Lardis gritted his teeth, sprang forward and snatched Kirk Lisescu's spade, and began shovelling himself with a vengeance; until the cross gave a lurch and an ominous creak, and tilted forward a fraction towards the fire in the trench.

But a fraction was enough, and now at last the vampire started to talk ...

'My name?' the undead creature on the cross gabbled, his red eyes starting out, staring at the fire-pit into which he would topple slowly, face down, unless he chose to speak first. 'Is that all you want to know? My name and a little useless information? Well then, and for all the good it will do you, they call me Vratza Wransthrall. There, and what else can I tell you?'

Lardis tossed the spade aside, stepped back a little and filled his labouring lungs. Then he looked up at the other, nodded, and smiled albeit humourlessly. 'So you've taken your master's name, eh? And was it also your plan to step into his shoes one day?'

Beneath lowered eyebrows, the vampire's slitted eyes shot scarlet loathing at him. 'In Turgosheim,' he grunted, 'the Lord Wran the Rage had several lieutenants. Here and for the moment, he has just the one – myself! Yes, I would be Wamphyri. Or I would have been.'

Again Lardis nodded. 'Turgosheim, eh? And where, pray, is Turgosheim?'

The other glared at him, flared his nostrils, remained silent ... until Kirk Lisescu took up his spade again. Then:

'East!' Vratza cried, straining on the silver spikes until the blue veins jerked and writhed in his arms, but straining uselessly. He might tear his flesh but he wouldn't tear those nails loose. And: 'East,' he croaked again, relaxing as best he could and hanging there shivering, panting. 'Beyond the Great Red Waste. There are mountains there, a lesser range – Starside to the north and Sunside in the south, much the same as here – but smaller. Turgosheim lies hidden from the sun in a gorge. It was our home but Wratha brought us away, to this.'

'Wratha?' Lardis cocked his head on one side. 'A girl's name? A Lady, your leader?'

'Wratha the Risen, a Lady, aye. She led us out of Turgosheim.' Vratza's floodgates were fully open now; Lardis need only question him.

'Why did she bring you here?'

'Because Turgosheim was used up. Too many vampires, too few Sunsiders.'

'Ah!' Lardis craned his neck, narrowed his eyes. 'And how many Lords were there, in Turgosheim?'

'More than forty, less than fifty. Including the Ladies.'

'And how many here, now?'

'Six. Wratha and her five.'

'And lieutenants?'

'Myself, and one other.'

Lardis drew in his chin. 'What? Six of them and only two of you?'

'Four of us died last night,' Vratza scowled, 'when we came out of Starside to raid on a town standing east of here.'

Andrei Romani nodded and clapped his hands appreciatively. And: 'Well done, Twin Fords!' he chuckled, however grimly. 'A little good news at last. At least they were prepared!'

'No,' Vratza shook his head. 'It was that we were not prepared. Some of the men fought back! In Turgosheim, that would have been unthinkable. But afterwards, striking here, by then we were prepared. As for myself, I was unlucky . . .'

'Very,' said Lardis, quietly, 'for it will cost you your life – this loathsomeness which your life has become, anyway. But in fact we'll be doing you a favour.'

379

'You'll burn me anyway?'

'You know we will.'

'And you call that a favour? *Hah!* Why then should I talk to you?'

'To live a little longer,' Lardis answered, as Kirk rammed the spade into the earth again.

The cross gave a jerk and Vratza cried, 'No, wait!' And in a moment: 'What else?' he groaned.

Lardis considered it, stroked his chin. 'Six of the Wamphyri, and two − no, one − lieutenant. And thralls?'

'Only those which we recruited in Twin Fords. And a few recruited here tonight, perhaps.'

'Aye, *precious* few,' Lardis told him, grinding his teeth. 'For we're old hands at dealing with your victims!' Clenching his fists, he took a pace forward; Andrei Romani was there to grab his arm and bring him to a standstill.

But the passion had gone out of Lardis in a moment; he was his own man again; he sighed and let his shoulders slump. 'And we have dealt with them,' he said. 'Most of them . . . I think.'

He drove from his mind all of the gaunt, accusing faces of those he had examined and found wanting, and tried to concentrate on the business in hand. But it was hard, for he was very tired now. And: 'Warriors,' he growled at last. 'How many?'

'Three,' came back the answer. 'But they will make more, as soon as they have the stuff for it.'

What? The 'stuff'? Lardis couldn't contain a shudder. This nightmare *thing* was talking about people − decent human beings, good Szgany flesh − mutated by the Wamphyri into monsters! Deep inside he felt his gorge rising, also his fury and everlasting hatred. And he knew that he wouldn't be able to talk to Vratza Wransthrall for very much longer.

But for now he must control himself, keep a tight rein on powerful Gypsy emotions, and say: 'Something here rings like a bell without a clapper – hollowly. You say the Wamphyri came here out of this Turgosheim with only a handful of lieutenants and warriors between them? What, and were they banished?'

'Not banished, no,' Vratza answered, sweat dripping from him where he suffered the agonies of the silver spikes. 'But she would have been, the Lady Wratha, if the others had known of her works earlier. It was this way:

'Warriors, the aerial sort, are forbidden in Turgosheim. But as you have seen, Wratha the Risen and her colleagues made fighting creatures that flew. To do so they must work secretly, in the privacy of their manses; it was the only way they could escape the restrictions of Turgosheim and make new lives here. But in the end they were discovered, and so forced to flee.'

Lardis frowned, scratched his head. 'There are no warriors in Turgosheim?'

'Not which fly. Of other types: a few lesser creatures are kept in the spires and manses, and there are those which roam in Turgosheim's bottoms, guarding against intruders.'

Lardis frowned, tried to picture all he'd been told, and slowly nodded. He looked around at his men, narrowed his eyes, and continued the questioning. 'But eventually – I mean, now that this Lady Wratha has found her way here – it's entirely possible that the others will breed monsters of their own and follow her, right? And is that why she's in such a hurry to make new lieutenants, warriors, thralls?'

Up on his cross, Vratza was growing weaker by the moment. The alien stuff in his blood, which made him a vampire, was poisoned; his flesh could not repair itself; each of the small silver balls in his peppered chest was an agony in its own right. Even so, and for all his suffering, he was beginning to see Lardis Lidesci in a new light. He nodded, as much as the spike through his topknot would allow, and grunted, 'I can see . . . can see that they will have their work cut out . . . with such as you. And I believe that I . . . that I am not the first thrall of the Wamphyri with whom you've spent an hour or so in . . . in *polite* conversation. A shame we weren't destined to meet on terms more equal.'

'Aye, too true!' said Lardis with a snort. 'What? Equal terms? You with your gauntlet and the strength of five men, undead and almost impossible to kill? Hah! Do you remember how *you* were taken? And were *those* equal terms? No, don't try appealing to my humanity, Vratza Wransthrall. For where you and your like are concerned, I am a monster in my own right!'

Kirk Lisescu tugged urgently at his elbow. 'Get on with it,' he whispered. 'He grows weak. Get what you can out of him and then make an end of it.'

Vratza scowled down on them. 'I have a vampire's ears,' he growled, 'in which your whispers ring like shouts! Anyway, you are right: I am weak and fading fast. You should go away now and let me die. That is what I wish.'

'A few more questions,' Lardis told him, 'and then I'll see to your wishes personally.'

'No! No!' Vratza protested, groaning. 'It is . . . it is enough. I . . . I am finished.' He hung his head, slumped down on his spikes.

Lardis nodded, but grimly. 'So you're finished, are you?' he repeated the other. 'Yes, and I'm the village idiot, lured away from a nest full of eggs by a partridge with a "broken" wing!'

Vratza said nothing but simply hung there, even when Kirk took up his spade again.

Lardis waited a little while, then said, 'Vratza, listen to me. We can't stay here but must move on; all of us, the entire village. And we certainly don't intend to take you with us. Now, you are going to die, I make no bones about that. But *how* you die is up to you. This is your choice:

'Answer a few more questions, and then go cleanly, without even knowing it. Or hang there till morning when the sun comes up, and suffer the worst of all possible deaths — for such as you. Now listen: you are right and I've had dealings with vampires before. I have *seen* and *heard* the likes of you melting in sunlight: the swift blackening and peeling of your skin, the black smoke boiling as your fats begin to melt, the awful screaming as your guts rupture and your eyeballs start out upon your cheeks. After an hour, two, three at most, you will be a black and tarry rag-thing hanging there, with all your bones protruding and your black skull frozen in a final scream! Is that what you want, Vratza Wransthrall?'

Vratza twitched a little but made no answer.

'So be it,' Lardis nodded. And: 'Men, bind this creature more firmly yet, with good silver wire round his arms, legs and neck. And knock a few more nails in him, so that he won't jerk himself loose when the sun's first rays hit him. Then clear the village. We're moving out, right now, within the hour.' It was a bluff, of course, but Vratza didn't know that.

'*Wait!*' The vampire's scarlet eyes shot open as he began to strain again, but less powerfully, against the spikes where they pierced his flesh. Then, panting, genuinely exhausted, he hung there glaring at Lardis as before; but helplessly now, hopelessly. And:

'I'm good as dead anyway,' he choked the words out. 'Your silver is in my blood. But ... do I have your word? Will you make a clean end of it?'

Lardis nodded, and growled: 'Which is more than you ever granted.'

Vratza lay back his head against the cross, closed his eyes and breathed deep, and said, 'One bolt won't be enough. I was Wran's thrall for long and long. I've come very close to being Wamphyri ...'

Lardis nodded again, and quietly said, 'So I've noted. Be sure we'll take care of it.'

'Then ... ask your damned questions and be done!'

To one side of the cross and a little behind it, just out of sight of the crucified vampire, Andrei Romani's brothers placed loaded crossbows in readiness on the now empty table, and Kirk Lisescu snapped his shotgun shut. They didn't want Vratza to see their preparations, in case he should resolve to remain silent to the end. But, strangely, there was no hatred left in them now – not for this one, who was finished – just a grim determination.

And Lardis said: 'You've told us about this Lady Wratha, who is the leader of the six. Also about your master, Wran the Rage. Now tell me about the rest. Who are they, and how may we know them?'

Vratza levelled his head and stared out bleakly across ravaged, smouldering Settlement. And as if he were speaking to the night:

'Gorvi the Guile is one of them,' he said. 'As his name suggests, he's smooth and slippery as oil. Then there's Spiro, Wran's brother, called Killglance. They are twins, Spiro and Wran, whose Wamphyri father had the evil eye. In his youth he could kill men – kill the Szgany, burst their hearts – just by looking at them! The brothers have tried it, too, though as yet with no success to mention. Also, there's Lord Vasagi, or Vasagi the Suck, as he's known. I will not try to describe him but . . . you will know him anyway, when you see him. Last but not least there's Canker Canison, who sings to the moon and leans to the fore, loping like a dog or a fox, but upright on two legs . . .'

A choked cry – half-gasp, half-shout – rang out from the flickering shadows a little beyond the range of the fires, and Nathan Kiklu stumbled into view, his eyes fixed on the terrifying yet tragic figure on the cross.

Standing in the shadows of an upended cart opposite the dull-glowing fire-pit, listening to all that Lardis had asked and every answer that Vratza Wransthrall had given him, Nathan had been witness to everything. Until a moment ago his eyes had been like misty mirrors: full of starlight, firelight, strangeness. But now, suddenly, he was alert as never before. Coming forward to stand beside Lardis, he gazed up hard-eyed at the wretched creature on the cross. And:

'What was that?' he said, his clear youth's voice contrasting with the coarseness of the night, cutting it like a knife. 'About a dog or a fox, a loping thing? Canker Canison, did you call him?'

The vampire angled his huge head to look down on Nathan. He recognized him: this was one of the first faces he had seen when he regained consciousness, before the questioning commenced. Then . . . the youth had seemed terrified; he'd backed off a pace and stumbled, moved away to where Vratza's scarlet gaze couldn't follow. Even now he was unsteady on his feet, but no longer awed.

And so Vratza was brought to this: even children dared to gaze upon him now, without cringing!

Curling his fleshy upper lip, the vampire snarled and showed Nathan his twin-tipped tongue and dagger teeth. But still the youth stood there. Until finally Vratza smiled – if what he did with his face could be called smiling – and said: 'I was your age, when I was taken in the tithe. Since when ... I've come a very long way.' He glanced at Lardis. 'Aye, even to the end.'

Lardis put an arm across Nathan's shoulder. 'The lad has ... he has an *interest* in all of this,' he said. But looking at Nathan, he knew it wasn't a healthy one.

'Oh?' Vratza cocked his head a little on one side, questioningly.

Nathan's mouth twitched in the left-hand corner. 'It ... it's my girl. This dog-thing, Canker, knocked me down and took her from me. Since when ... she hasn't been found.'

'Ah!' said Vratza, matter-of-factly. And as if Nathan no longer existed, his red eyes swivelled to look at Lardis. 'Is it done? Am I finished?'

Lardis nodded; Kirk Lisescu and the others took up their weapons, came from behind the cross into view.

Vratza saw them, and fire and blood sprang into his eyes together. He opened his nightmare jaws and hissed, vibrating his forked tongue in the red-ribbed cavern of his throat.

'No, wait!' Nathan shrugged free of Lardis's arm, pointed a steady hand and finger at the monster on the cross. 'I want you to tell me: about Canker Canison, and about Misha. How will it be for her?'

'No!' Lardis got in front of Nathan, throwing up his arms as if to ward off some horror; indeed, to ward off a very real horror. 'Vratza, don't tell him anything! Your time has come.' He glanced at his men where they took up their positions, and nodded. But the vampire was already speaking – to Nathan.

'My last act,' he said, in a voice which bubbled like tar in a volcanic pit, 'to curdle your dreams now and forever. You ask about Canker? And your girl?'

'Yes,' Nathan had to know. But behind him the men were lifting their weapons, aiming them.

'Canker takes women for one thing only,' Vratza gurgled. 'To use them. And when he has used them – in whichever of the many ways he favours – then he *worries* them, as a wolf among goats!'

'Be *quiet!*' Lardis roared.

A crossbow thrummed and its bolt took Vratza close to the heart, burying itself in his torn and bloody chest until only the flight protruded. He jerked massively and coughed up blood, then sucked at the air – *and continued to speak!* And with his voice rising to a shriek, and finally a gale of mad laughter, he said:

'Boy, do you see this shaft in me, how it tears me? So *she* is torn, even now. And Canker's shaft is just as vicious. Be *sure* he'll fuck her heart out! Oh – ha, ha, *haaaaa!*'

Nathan staggered to and fro, his face pale as a papery wasp's nest, with dark punched holes for eyes and mouth. And as a second bolt joined the first (though still not on target, for the men were shooting in haste to shut Vratza up, and so missing their aim), the youth whispered:

'And now . . . now I want you to die.'

Kirk Lisescu granted Nathan's wish. Twin blasts, coming in quick succession, turned the vampire's head to pulp as silver shot removed any last trace of a face.

Blood flew in gouts and splashes; booming echoes came back thunderously, first from the stockade's walls, then from the hills; Lardis dragged Nathan roughly aside, out of the red rain. 'You don't want *that* on you,' he gasped. 'What? Even the air that bastard breathed is tainted!'

Again Nathan shook him off, then staggered away into the night to be sick. Once, hearing shouting, he looked back and saw the cross and the thing upon it as a black silhouette against the glow of the fires – but the silhouette was hideously mobile!

Vratza Wransthrall had told how he was close to becoming Wamphyri, and he'd been right. Undead metamorphic flesh formed nests of writhing tentacles which sprang from his guts, chest, and all the massive parts of his body. Whipping and vibrating, they lashed themselves – lashed him – to the cross's upright and horizontal bar. But the men had lassoed both arms of the cross and were hauling on it furiously, until it leaned over and toppled into the fire-pit.

Nathan heard the *hiss*, saw white smoke or steam rising, which he knew would soon turn black. Lardis had it right: in an hour, Vratza would be reduced to a stench and a final puff of smoke. Nothing more would remain of him –

– Except, of course, that monstrous picture which he'd painted in Nathan's head. And that might very well last for a lifetime.

Meanwhile, Nathan's stomach in its entirety desired to be out of him . . .

Afterwards:

Nathan went back to his mother's house and dug in the ruins. He wasn't satisfied that the searchers had done everything in their power. And in order to be absolutely certain, when he was finished with the house he laid bare the floor of the barn. And found nothing, not even a bloodstain.

He stood on the spot where he'd last seen Misha in the embrace of a snarling red-eyed fiend, hung his head, gritted his teeth, clenched his fists. But he didn't cry. *No*, he told himself, *I'll shed no tears until I've shed his blood, taken his shaggy head, smelled the stench of his*

*burning hide and seen his last black trace go drifting
on the wind!*

It was his Szgany vow.

He slept again, and before the dawn went to the
Zanesti house where it stood undamaged. Misha's father
and surviving brother were there, pale as ghosts, sitting
in silence. Before, they hadn't much cared for Nathan;
now, her father cradled his head and cried on it. But
Nathan wouldn't. And Misha's brother (perhaps
thoughtlessly, but surely he could be forgiven) said,
'She never knew a man; she'd been with no one; she
wasn't even whole. Once, I would have *killed* the man
who looked at her like that! And now I would kiss him
– because Misha had loved him.' And he'd looked at
Nathan, perhaps hopefully.

But the youth could only shake his head and say,
'Always remember, you have each other.' Which, while
he'd not intended it that way, caused them to see that
Nathan had no one. Before they could say anything he
left them and went looking for Lardis, only to discover
that the old Lidesci had experienced the selfsame
doubts and returned to his ruined cabin on the knoll.

Nathan joined him there, where Lardis had been at
work again in the wreckage. He came across him sitting
in what had been his garden, with eyes as vacant as his
soul, staring south, waiting for the first glimmer of light
to make a silver stain on the far faint curve which was
the rim of the world. And when at last Lardis sensed
him there, blinked life back into his eyes and looked at
him, then Nathan said:

'What will you do, Lardis? Will it be as you told it to
Vratza Wransthrall? Will you trek with your people,
and turn them into Travellers as in the old days, to
keep them from the Wamphyri?'

Lardis shook his head. 'Some will move on,' he

answered, gruffly. 'Can you blame them? But I will stay here. Not "here", you understand, but in Settlement. And I fancy a good many will stay with me. Maybe that way, by adopting at least this one of the Wamphyri's methods, we'll defeat them in the end.'

'By adopting their methods?'

Lardis nodded. 'When the Wamphyri have something, they fight to keep it. Especially territory. They are fiercely territorial, Nathan. In the old days, most of their wars were for territory, for the great aeries, the Starside stacks. Oh, they were for blood, too, and for the sheer hell of it; but mainly they were about territory. It's what drove them to go against The Dweller, and why they were destroyed. And now, finally, it's why they've returned.'

'And how will you keep Settlement?'

'By defending it! This sunup you'll see activity as never before in Settlement. So much to do . . . I shouldn't be sitting here . . . I must get on down!' He stood up.

Nathan touched his arm. 'I won't be seeing it,' he said, shaking his blond head. 'I'm heading east.'

Lardis was disappointed. 'You're deserting me?'

'Never that,' the other answered. 'I came to find out what you would do so that eventually I'd know where to find you. But first I must find Nestor.'

'Nestor?' Lardis's eyebrows peaked. 'Why, anyone would think you weren't there last night! Nestor's gone into Starside, Nathan, in the mouth of a flyer. Look, I've no time for this and so must speak plainly: Nestor's dead, or worse than dead! Can't you get that into your head?'

Nathan followed him down the first flight of steps cut in the steep side of the knoll. 'But you wounded the flyer with a bolt from one of the great crossbows,' he replied. 'What if it crashed? In fact, I dreamed that it crashed – on the wooded slopes over Twin Fords.'

Lardis turned to him. 'You dreamed it? What, and are you a seer? Since when?'

A seer? Am I? Nathan wondered. *No, I don't think so. But my wolves talk to me, and sometimes I hear the dead whispering in their graves . . .*

He shrugged. 'No, I'm no seer – but I know how to hope when hope is all that's left. And I fancy you do, too, Lardis. Isn't that why you came back up here: to dig again where you have already delved enough, even knowing you'd find nothing?'

After a moment Lardis sighed and nodded, turned away and continued on down. 'Then you have to go,' he said. 'Except – if your star is good to you, and likewise mine to me – you'll promise to come back one day and be my son.'

'I feel I'm that already,' said Nathan, lying yet at one and the same time, and however paradoxically, remaining sincere. For certainly the old Lidesci had been as much a father to him as any he had ever known. And yet behind Lardis's back where Nathan couldn't be seen, he frowned wonderingly. Because just for a moment then he'd seemed to remember something else from last night's dream . . . something which his wolves had told to him? Some connection between his father – his real father, Hzak Kiklu – and theirs? Some blood relationship between the two? And was that why they called him uncle?

Still unseen, Nathan shook his head in bewilderment. But how could that be? For quite obviously, *their* father had been a wolf!

It was all very mysterious and puzzling. But then, that was frequently the way of it with Nathan's dreams: some things appeared as real and solid as the ground under his feet, while others were vague and ephemeral as ripples on a pool, or frost on the high peaks before

391

the dawn. Some things he remembered, and others he was glad to forget, mainly because he couldn't understand them. Best to fasten on what he perceived as real, he supposed, and leave the fanciful stuff to its own devices.

It was a mistake, but all men make them. Especially when they are under pressure. And Nathan was no exception ...

In the hours after dawn, as Nathan trekked for Twin Fords, the thought or question would frequently recur: *But why would they take my mother?*

He would understand – and detest his understanding of it – if she had been raped, vampirized, murdered out of hand. For after all, so many had been. But taken? Nana Kiklu was no mere girl. On the other hand, she was or had been a warm and beautiful woman. Her sons had always thought so anyway, and without prejudice – especially Nathan.

But ... did the Wamphyri take people indiscriminately? Were they so insensitive of human life that they would simply take, defile, use or waste whatever, *who-*ever, was available? Perhaps they were and did.

Or perhaps it was just that they followed a simpler set of rules: blood is blood, and flesh is merely flesh. For when a hunter is hungry, is he concerned that the rabbit he shoots should have pleasing marks? Does he really care if it is past its prime? And what about the sandal-maker? What difference does it make to him which beast supplies the leather for his sandals, as long as it's supple, hard-wearing stuff?

But on the other hand, the Wamphyri were or had been men, and the 'beasts' *they* hunted were likewise men – and women! So that they didn't just hunt for meat, or even for stuff to fashion into monstrous undead creatures, but for . . . other reasons, too. And so Nathan would always come back to that, and end up wondering if Nana shared the same fate as Misha Zanesti. *If* Nana had been taken.

And if she hadn't? Then what *had* happened to his mother, and where was she now?

Nathan had seen a monstrous, massively armoured warrior creature ravaging destructively in the streets of Settlement, and knew that these Wamphyri fighting beasts were carnivores, indeed vampires in their own right. Maybe that was the answer: a horrific answer, to be sure, but a quick end at least. Could it be that the same monster which flattened their home had also snatched up his mother? If so, she would have been dead instantly. But never a trace of her, nothing, not even (Nathan was obliged to consider it, however flinchingly) a splash of red.

The same for Misha; except that with Vratza Wransthrall's deliberately cruel picture still burning in Nathan's all-too-vivid imagination – and Canker Canison's slavering dog-voice reverberating in the vaults of his memory – he suspected or feared even worse for Misha! And however much he loathed himself for thinking it, he could only wish her dead.

Striding east along an old Traveller trail, he found himself thinking back an hour or two, to when he and Lardis had climbed down from the house on the knoll into Settlement. Lardis's band of old comrades had been waiting for him there, with all of Settlement's citizens – those that remained, anyway – gathered together at the central meeting place to hear his words. What Lardis had said to them then had been simple and to the point, and entirely typical of him:

'All is as it was twenty years ago,' he had said. 'The Wamphyri are back, and we are their sport, their food, their cattle. The townships will soon be broken down, and all the Szgany sundered, scattered into small groups throughout the length and breadth of Sunside. So *they*, the Wamphyri, would have it. But there are differences.

'Now we have made our homes here in Settlement, and we travel no more. This is our place, built with our own strong hands – with which we must likewise defend it! And our hands *are* strong, even against the Wamphyri! Last night ... we were taken by surprise. Next time it will be different, when we'll make these creatures pay – and heavily! For as I've as good as said, it's my intention to face up to them. That's *my* intention, yes ...

'You, however, have a choice. For I make no bones about it, the risks will be great and I won't ask anyone to stay who isn't willing to face up to it. Men *will* die, of that you may be sure – but so will Wamphyri! And so the choice is simple:

'Go off on your own and become Travellers, if that's how you see your future, and I'll make no objection. Live as best you may and as once we lived, never knowing what the next sundown has in store for you. You are welcome to wander wherever you will in those lands bounded by my markers. Except I would tell you this: when sundown comes, and if you're in the vicinity of Settlement, don't come here looking for succour. Those who fight for it are welcome to it, but those who desert me are gone for good.

'Now, I see that some have already moved on. Well, and I wish them luck. But any more of you who would join them, do so now. I see no profit in talking to people who'll pay me no heed anyway ...' Then Lardis had waited a while, but none had stirred. Those who would go had already left. And so at last he had continued:

'Very well. And this is what I want of you:

'You men, you take your orders from me. Likewise you women. If you lost a wife or husband last night, don't mourn but find a new one. If you lost a son or daughter, don't mourn but *hate!* And let your hatred be your strength.

'You old ones, sick ones who can't work or help ... you *can* work, you *must* help! No, not by furious fighting or hard labour but in those areas where your help is most needed: in keeping the fires, harvesting the fruits of the forest, tending the animals. For it's you who must feed the builders and fighters, and when they've time to rest make sure they do so in comfort, or whatever of comfort is available. For we all have our parts to play.

'Now, to the tasks ...' And he had gone on to list them.

Nathan had been witness to all of this; he'd listened to everything the old Lidesci had said, and his admiration was boundless.

And Lardis was inspired; he forgot nothing; so that in something less than half an hour, Settlement was more abustle than at any time in all of fourteen years. And its people were doing exactly what they had done then: preparing for war! Which left Nathan feeling like a deserter, for he knew that soon he would be out of it.

He had mentioned this to Lardis, who told him: 'Son, you have your reasons which you've explained well enough. And still I say come back one day, to where there'll always be a place for you. But before you go ...' He'd called for Ion Romani, who had got together a final list of all the night's victims.

Scrawled upon a piece of bark were the sigils of those whom the Wamphyri had been seen to steal away, those who had been found slaughtered or changed, and those who were simply missing. Of the latter: by now a small number would be vampire thralls, hiding from the sun in the woods or the depths of mountain caves, waiting for the night when they could make for Starside.

And of course there were also marks for Nana Kiklu and Misha Zanesti. They were shown as missing, too, as was Nestor. And Nathan had known that Lardis didn't have the heart to show the three as he believed them to be, dead and gone forever. No, for his own wife and son were similarly listed.

Then Lardis and Nathan had embraced, and the latter had gathered up his small bag of things and left Settlement for Twin Fords . . .

Nestor would remember very little of his brief flight in the fetid pouch of the stricken flyer. Even if he'd remained conscious during the trip (impossible, for the creature's gases were noxious and anaesthetizing, and it was only by a tremendous effort of will that he had stayed upright and mobile in the first place, before being taken), still he would remember very little; just darkness and clammy reek, and flexible cartilage hooks fixing him firmly in place in the pouch's confines.

As for the beast's rapid and erratic descent from mountain peaks it had neither the strength nor the altitude to surmount – the way the massive bolt lodged deep in its body snagged in the green canopy of trees to set it spinning, crashing through pine branches and brambly undergrowth, finally to come to rest shudderingly on a steep wooded slope over Twin Fords; and Nestor's subsequent partial ejection from the gaping slit of the pouch – he would remember nothing whatsoever of that.

The wonder was that he lived through any of it, let alone all of it . . . and yet perhaps not such a wonder after all. For the flyer was of vampire stuff; Nestor had breathed the essence of its body; the oils of its man-trap pouch had got into his various scrapes and gouges. Insufficient to change him substantially, but perhaps enough to assist in his healing. That and his youth, his great strength, his *will* to survive – all of these things had combined to pull him through.

But healing takes time, and the greatest healer of all is sleep. Up there on the hillside over the ravaged town of Twin Fords – where the leaping, cleansing flames of funeral pyres blazed up in the night, and gaunt-eyed people went stumbling through horror and chaos in the wake of Wratha's raid, much as they did in Settlement – Nestor slept. It was the sleep of exhaustion, of traumatic physical damage, of the poisons in his system which on the one hand deadened him, and on the other supported and repaired his damaged functions. And so it was a healing sleep. It would help towards healing his body, at least . . .

Even so, he might have died from exposure. But the grotesque flyer was still feebly alive, its body was still warm, and only Nestor's head, shoulders and one arm dangled from the palpitating flap of its pouch. The rest of him remained inside, as yet 'unborn', in a metamorphic womb of cartilage and quivering, insensate flesh. And all through the night the creature leaked its fluids and its life into the loamy soil, and its remaining warmth into Nestor. So that he lived.

He lived and slept through the longest night of his life, and awoke in the hours before dawn to wriggle free of the flyer's pouch and fall a few harmless inches into springy moss and soft leaf-mould. And with the creature's broken body supported on the shattered stumps of pines, forming a sagging, diamond-shaped ceiling overhead, there he lay for a long time recovering his reeling senses. Some of them, at least.

But the one which had suffered most, and one of the most basic and important at that, was memory. So that when finally Nestor could find the strength to crawl away, sit up and examine the sources of his aches and pains, the one facet of being which he could *not* examine was his past. Not in any great detail. Misty faces were there, only half-recognized, distorted and grimacing in his mind's eye; scenes out of his childhood, and the early years of emerging manhood; even something of the violence of his most recent past. But all of it so vague, disjointed and kaleidoscopic that it was impossible, even painful, to piece together. And Nestor had had quite enough of pain.

The one incontestable 'fact' – the one answer which surfaced time and time again whenever he considered the question of identity and being – was the repetitive phrase: 'I am the Lord Nestor.' So that in a little while he knew who he was at least. But what *sort* of a Lord was he?

Physically: his skull still felt soft at the back, where plates of fractured bone were agonizingly mobile under an area of rough, puffy skin and subcutaneous fluids; but at least he could touch himself there without feeling sick. Apart from a slight blurriness of vision, his eyesight seemed sound in the pre-dawn light. Other than his lumpy, tender face – his nose which was definitely hooked now and still sore where the bone was knitting, split lips, and several loose teeth – no bones appeared broken in his limbs or body. In short, he knew that whatever he had survived, he would probably continue to survive it. Certainly he was hungry and thirsty for two men, and a good appetite is usually indicative of good health.

With this in mind he looked down on the fires in Twin Fords and the black smoke hanging like a pall over the town, and wondered if he'd find breakfast there. Probably, because after all he was a Lord. Also, he wondered if he would find some answers, clues as to his and the world's circumstances in general.

As for the three-quarters dead flyer: Nestor had seen its grotesque carcass as a hugely anomalous lump in the darkness of the trees: a sprawling blanket or tent of skins, or more likely a tangled platform of fallen branches. He had considered it no further than that.

Its true nature – the fact that it had transported him to this place, and that he had emerged from it – these things were entirely forgotten. But as twilight brightened into dawn and the rising sun lit up the peaks, and its golden light fell like a slowly descending curtain towards the tree-line, so he had cause to regard the creature anew. For now the thing in the trees was most definitely alive!

It tried to arch its broken wings, craned a prehistoric neck for the sky, and cried out in a hissing, clacking voice. But the shattered pines had pierced its membranous wings and crushed their fragile alveolate bones, and all its energy had drained away along with its fluids. Pinned down, grounded and broken, the creature could only despair its fate, for the vampire stuff in it sensed the sunrise as surely as a lodestone senses north, except the flyer wasn't attracted but repulsed. Or would be, if it still had the power of flight.

Walking unsteadily, gingerly around the perimeter of the triangular stand of pines at the rim of the bluff where the flyer had crashed down, Nestor observed the slate-grey, leathery skin of the thing; its long neck and spatulate head, and dull, near-vacant eyes. Despite that its head was huge, blunt and acromegalic, still there was something vaguely, disturbingly human about it; but nothing remotely human about the tentacular thrusters which it drove into the pine-needle floor each time it arched its torn manta wings, as if to assist in launching itself into flight. These reminded Nestor of nothing so much as a nest of giant maggots erupting from the belly of some dead thing.

And at the base of its neck, where its back widened out into swept-back wings ... was that some kind of saddle?

He might have climbed back under the canopy of the trees to make a closer inspection, but such were the thing's struggles that he feared it might flop down on top of him; and so he held back. At which point the jagged rim of sunlight creeping down across the tree-line fell squarely upon the creature – to devour it!

So it seemed to Nestor.

For the pines filled with stench and steam at once, as the doomed flyer's skin shrivelled and turned from slate-grey to the unwholesome blue of corruption and the texture of crumbling pumice. Its flesh quaked, bloated, split open in a dozen places, out of which its smoking fats ran like water! Then the thing screamed – a sound so thin, high and penetrating that it sliced like a sharp edge of ice on Nestor's nerves – and commenced a shuddering vibration which only ceased when several of the shattered pines were displaced and the flyer slumped down between them to the forest's floor.

And there the sun continued its cleansing work, blazing through the trees to reduce the monster to so much glue and blackly smouldering gristle. But in a little while it became obvious that this would take hours, and what with the poisonous odour and disgusting mess, Nestor didn't wait for the end.

But in his mind's eye, now more visions were waking; and as he began to climb down the wooded slope towards the near-distant town – and as a waft of foulness reached down to him from the dissolving flyer – he 'remembered' a previous rush of reeking air . . .

. . . Wind in his hair, yes, and dark diamond shapes adrift on the updrafts under glittering ice-chip stars – flyers just like that one back there, with riders proud and terrifying in saddles upon their backs – and a distant cry of horror faint on the morning air, but fading now as the scene itself faded back into vaults of memory. 'Wamphyri!'

Wamphyri? The cry had been real, carrying to him from the town in the 'V' of the rivers; but the Lord Nestor ignored it in deference to its evocation.

He paused, looked back and up the slope to where smoke and steam continued to pour from the pines, spilling out of them like a slow-motion waterfall over the rim of the bluff. Had that been his flyer back there? But that couldn't possibly be, for here he stood in sunlight and felt no harm.

But at the same time . . . did he still feel comfortable in the sun's warm rays? Had he ever?

Lord Nestor of the Wamphyri . . .

It seemed like a dream, some game which he'd played as a child, but he remembered now how he had hunted his human prey in the deep forests, sniffing them out, searching for them with all of his vampire senses alert! Except . . . where were his vampire senses now?

A vampire – indeed, Wamphyri – was he? He shrank down a little from the sun, which paid him no heed but burned, as ever, benevolently on the southern horizon.

Had he been a vampire, then? But if that were so, how may one of the undead return to human life? And why would he want to? And what of the people in the town down there, Twin Fords? How would they receive him if he went among them?

He frowned, sat down in the long grasses of the slope

and considered his position. He must be cautious; he must know himself, before he dared show himself to others. But where was his past? What had it been? If people asked him, what could he tell them? That he was the Lord Nestor of the Wamphyri? Hardly!

Then, close by, a distraction:

A rabbit, emerging from its hole, blinked pink eyes and turned twitching ears this way and that before hopping tentatively forward – and uttered a short shrill scream as a wire snare tightened around its neck! Then, triggered by the animal's sudden frenzy, the weighted branch of a sapling slipped its anchor, sprang erect and hauled the poor creature aloft to hang it.

Now here at last was something that Nestor remembered and understood well enough: hunting and trapping. So what did it matter that the trap wasn't his; surely it would make good sense to satisfy his hunger here rather than in Twin Fords, whose people might well be suspicious of him?

Just a few short paces away, Nestor had already noted the reflective glitter of a flinty outcrop weathering up out of the shallow soil. Using a fist-sized rock to knock a pair of good firestones free of the mass, now he gathered together the rabbit and the makings for a fire. And in a nest of tall boulders which provided him with shade and cover both, he set about to prepare his meal. If the smoke of his fire was seen from below, then he'd probably be reckoned for just another lonely hunter having his breakfast up in the hills.

But for some reason as yet unfathomed (perhaps it had to do with the many fires burning down there, the black smoke roiling, and a too-familiar stench carried up in the heat and the smoke?), Nestor fancied that the people of the town would have problems enough this morning, without worrying too much about him . . .

*

Unknown to Nestor and fourteen miles due west of him where he cooked and ate his breakfast, his brother Nathan was striding out for Twin Fords. And in Settlement –

– Nathan had been gone for well over an hour when Misha Zanesti came through the forest from the south and slipped into town through the South Gate. She was seen, recognized by a girl who had been posted to keep her eye on the gate, and her presence reported to Lardis Lidesci. Misha, too, would report to Lardis, but not until she'd been home.

And in her father's house ten seconds after she entered:

Astonishment! Rejoicing! A great flood of laughter, questions, tears! The joyful madness (for Misha) of being whirled about, crushed, lifted off her feet, gazed upon! And for them the joy of whirling, crushing, gazing.

Finally, they demanded to know what, how, where – everything.

But she only wanted to know about her brother, and about Nathan. And then the sadness all over again – for her brother, Eugen, taken by the Wamphyri. As for Nathan: he had been here, yes. And her surviving brother, Nicolae, remembering Nathan's visit and how he'd felt then, said: 'Misha, you should marry that one as soon as possible – even today!' And her father saying nothing, which meant that he agreed.

By which time Lardis and Andrei Romani had come knocking at the door, and Varna Zanesti knew why; but so did Misha. For Nana Kiklu – who remembered what it had been like in the time of the Wamphyri, and how it must be again – had warned her it would be this way. So that Misha knew exactly how to handle it even if her father, the huge and tempestuous Varna, didn't. Neither him nor her brother Nicolae, who was the model of his father but on a younger, only slightly smaller scale. They let Lardis and Andrei in, but as soon as the door was closed:

'Lardis,' Varna rumbled, 'I'm reunited with my daughter, as you see. But my emotions are in turmoil, and so I warn you: do nothing to further disturb them. As for Misha: you need only look at her to see that she is whole and well.' He stood like a rock – glowering, towering over Lardis – with his huge hands knotted at his sides.

Varna was massive. But while he dwarfed most other men of the Szgany Lidesci, his size had its disadvantages: it left him slow-moving, lumbering. Black-browed, bearded, and barrel-chested: by virtue of his aspect and dimensions alone he might appear brutal. And he could be, if he or his were threatened. A very determined man, Varna (some might say pig-headed, but not to his face), whose remaining son was scarcely less massive, and no less resolute.

And Nicolae, casually fitting a bolt to the groove in the tiller of his crossbow, said: 'Andrei Romani, you're my elder and I respect you. But if you're hunting for vampires, best go do it somewhere else. The girl is my sister.'

Before the others could so much as speak, Misha placed herself in the middle of the four men. And: 'Lardis, Andrei,' she said, 'you've nothing to fear from me. And if I'm to be examined, then do it here, now, in my own home, and be sure I'll understand. For just this morning both Nana Kiklu –' she paused briefly, looked at Lardis and smiled, '– and your own wife, Lissa, have told me the way of it. And so I'm ready.'

Suddenly Lardis felt weak at the knees; his mouth fell open and his dark eyes opened huge as saucers; ignoring Varna and Nicolae, he stumbled forward a pace and took the girl by the arms – as much to steady himself as to confine her. And scarcely breathing the words, he said, 'You ... you had this from Lissa? This morning?'

'Yes, oh yes!' she answered. 'Where we waited for sunup near the place of the lepers!'

Lardis staggered again, clapped a hand to his forehead and cried: '*Ah!* The leper colony! Of course – I remember – yes!'

For upon a time, some ten years ago, Lissa had accompanied him when he was out beating the bounds of his territory. They'd camped a mile from the colony, and it had been then that he'd told Lissa: 'In the old days, if we were in this vicinity when the night came down, we would always camp as close as possible to the place of the lepers. For there was one thing you could be sure of: that no Starside Lord would ever come a-hunting here! No, for leprosy strikes terror in their black hearts, and it's as much a plague to them as they are to us!'

And Lissa, by the mercy of her star, had remembered his words ...

III

'Lardis,' Misha said, while still he sputtered and gaped, and before he could explode with all of his many questions, 'first look at this.' She split off a small piece of garlic, the Szgany kneblasch, from one of several cloves on a shelf over the fireplace. And popping it into her mouth, she began to chew. Then she pulled a wry face – but one which was *normally* wry – and swallowed. 'There,' she said, still grimacing. 'Now I won't be able to breathe on anyone for the rest of the day! But it's worth it. Now then, give me one of your silver bells.' He fumbled one out of his pocket and handed it over. Misha rubbed it between her palms, hung it for a moment from the golden ring in her left ear, pressed it to her cheek and finally kissed it.

And giving him back his bell, she went to the door and threw it open. Daylight flooded in, turning her hair a shiny raven black as she stepped out into glaring morning sunlight. And whirling the skirts which Nana Kiklu had repaired for her during the long night, she said: 'Under all of this grime my colour is my own, Lardis, not the lifeless grey of a vampire. When I've bathed myself – and how I *need* to! – then you'll see. But tell me: what do you think of this blouse I'm wearing?'

He looked, and saw that it was one of Lissa's blouses; his own wife's design and stitching couldn't be mistaken. And finally he was convinced, which in any case he'd wanted to be. 'Yes, yes,' he drew her back inside the house. 'You had that from Lissa too, I know. But now . . . now tell me about Jason!'

Misha looked at him. Lardis's face was alight with high expectations, but a shadow had moved across hers. Her father and brother knew that look; they made sure Lardis was seated, with Andrei close at hand, then went to stand quietly in a cool, shadowy corner. And:

'Lissa was hoping –' Misha began, stumblingly, '– she was hoping that you – that you could tell her something.'

Lardis groaned and hung his head, but in another moment he lifted it and said: 'An hour ago I had no hope for either one of them, and now you tell me my wife is alive and well.' He glanced at her sharply. 'She . . . she *is* well, isn't she?'

Misha nodded and answered, 'A few bumps and bruises, but that's all. She had a narrow squeak – so did we all – which I'll tell you about in a moment.'

Lardis sighed, and continued: 'And so there must be hope for my son, too. Yes, I'm sure there is. But now tell the rest of it your way and in your own time, so that I may take it in. But tell all of it, and so make an end of my foolish, fumbling questions.'

She nodded, and began:

'Your place on the knoll was hit first. But Lissa had seen a mist on the hillsides. Dousing the lamps, she'd gone out into the garden. It was a flyer which wrecked your cabin, Lardis. It came from the east, following the contours of the foothills, and settled on your house which collapsed under its weight. And riding the creature's back – a man!'

'Wamphyri, aye,' Lardis growled. 'Or one of their lieutenants. I had thought that perhaps it was a warrior; but now, thinking back on it, the stench was not so great.' He nodded his head, indicating that Misha should go on.

'This man – this vampire – was tall and slender, with

eyes tiny as jewels, deep-sunken in his face,' the girl continued. 'He was dressed all in black, with a black cape and boots. His skull was shaven, except for a topknot. He looked like a corpse, and yet was lively, sinuous as a snake. But for all that he was Wamphyri and powerful, he also seemed nervous, cautious, furtive. At least, this is how Lissa describes him.'

Lardis said nothing but thought: *Gorvi the Guile? Possibly.*

'Lissa had hidden herself in the trees behind the house,' Misha went on, 'from where she could watch what happened. That was a mistake, for the vampire sensed her there! And satisfied that there was no danger, he stood in the garden with his hands on his hips and sniffed Lissa out! She felt his hypnotic power in her mind, and knew that she'd been discovered.

'She tried to make a run for it, past the vampire Lord to the steps cut in the steep side of the knoll. But he got in her way and showed her the killing gauntlet on his hand. And closing with her, he said: "Where is your man? Where are your sons? Show me your daughters!" He caught her up by the hair –' (Lardis almost started to his feet) '– and then Jason was there!'

'Jason!' the word burst from Lardis's lips.

'He had come up from Settlement,' Misha was breathless, 'to discover this creature threatening his mother. Crying out his rage, without pause he hurled himself at the vampire. Distracted, the monster released Lissa, turned on Jason and struck at him with his gauntlet. Ducking the blow, Jason stabbed the other with his knife, whose silver blade glanced off the vampire's ribs, tore along his forearm and caught in his gauntlet, which Jason wrenched from his hand. And Jason's knife was red with the vampire's blood!'

'What then?' Lardis couldn't contain himself.

'Lissa saw your hatchet in a tree stump . . .'

'My axe?' Lardis cut in again. 'No other axe like it in the world – and I left it in the garden? To the rain and the rust? Just see how lax I had become! Jazz Simmons gave me that axe; he brought it with him from the hell-lands, and for nine hundred sunups it kept its edge! But go on.'

'She worked the hatchet out of the stump,' Misha continued, 'and went to leap on the vampire Lord where he clutched his side and arm. He saw how keen was the weapon's edge, and knew that even in a woman's hands it could take his head. And both Lissa and Jason together, they were intent upon killing him! Well, perhaps he's a coward, this one –'

'They all are!' Lardis cried.

'– But he fled before them, snatching up his bloodied gauntlet as he went. And as he got behind his flyer where it wallowed in the ruins of your cabin, Lissa heard him cry out: "Roll on them! Crush them!"'

'The creature made to thrust itself upon them; they ran in different directions; Lissa was struck by the flyer's wing and knocked over the knoll's steepest rim! And . . . and that was the last she saw of Jason. Then: she fell through the brambles, bracken, saplings of the hillside, tumbling most of the way to the bottom. Her clothes were torn – you see how this blouse is stitched, here and here? – and so were her hands and arms, but not seriously. And when she came to rest, then she would climb to the top again!'

Lardis groaned and clutched his head. 'What a fool of a women I married,' he said. And then, with pride: 'But what a *woman!*'

'Hear me out,' Misha told him. 'She *would* have climbed back to the top – to be with her son and help him fight the vampire Lord – but missed her footing and went plunging the rest of the way to the bottom! Then, shocked out of her wits, half-stunned, she made for Settlement where she hoped to find you and tell you what had happened. But at the North Gate ... she saw the town was burning, saw what was loose and ravaging in its streets.

'Weak now and terrified, hoping to find a place to hide, Lissa went into the forest and skirted Settlement to the west. And that was where she bumped into Nana Kiklu. Nana had hidden in the woods after her house was wrecked, but when things had seemed to quiet down a little she'd gone back in through a gap in the stockade to look for her sons. Instead of finding them, she found me. And so I have Nana to thank for my life.

'She dragged me out of there and brought me round, and as I regained consciousness ... that was when Lissa came stumbling and crying through the night. Nana calmed her, and then would have returned again into Settlement. But by then there were monsters everywhere. Their roaring, and all the screaming ... it was terrible. And Lissa and I, we couldn't be left alone. We ... we were no longer capable. I feel so ashamed — of my own weakness!'

'You've nothing to be ashamed of, daughter,' Varna Zanesti rumbled, but with a catch in his voice. He came forward to put his arms round her and glower at Lardis. And: 'These women,' he growled. 'Why, they put the rest of us to shame!'

Lardis nodded, but neither he nor Varna knew how true it was; especially in Misha's case. For she had avoided explaining a single detail of why she'd been so close to Nana Kiklu's house in the first place. And so like Nathan before her, she'd covered up for Nestor's shameful lapse. But now:

'I have to know,' she said, eagerly. 'Where *is* Nathan?

410

I would have expected him here by now . . . *oh!*' And to cover her immediate embarrassment: 'Oh, and Nestor, too, of course! Nana is eager for news of both of them, naturally.'

'Aye, "naturally",' her father repeated knowingly — and in the next moment fell deathly silent. For he remembered now about Nathan's brother. And poor Nana Kiklu, after all she had done and been through: still at the leper colony, knowing nothing about her son taken by the Wamphyri.

Then, low-voiced, Lardis told Misha about Nestor, and went on to explain Nathan's absence: how Nathan believed that the flyer which took Nestor might have crashed to earth somewhere in the east, and had gone to see if he could find him there. Misha was sad to have missed him, but at the same time felt glad that he had forgiven Nestor. For after all, nothing had come of that one's bad behaviour in the end. And if Nestor still lived, perhaps all this would serve to reunite them.

'Of course,' she said, when Lardis was done, 'Nathan will be back, won't he? I mean, whether he finds Nestor or not . . . Nathan *will* return?'

'Of his own free will?' Lardis shrugged. 'Immediately? I can't promise it. Oh, I want him to come back — and so do you, I know — but Misha, he thinks that you, too, have been stolen away! So what is there here for Nathan now?' And there followed more explanations: how the last time Nathan had seen her, Misha had been in the grip of a slavering, hunch-shouldered Wamphyri hybrid.

'Ah!' her hand flew to her mouth. And: 'But Nana saw that creature too!' she gasped. 'She had just returned to the gap in the stockade fence, and saw the dog-thing drop me to go loping off after some poor screaming woman. But that means . . . Nathan was right there, just a few paces away!'

Lardis nodded. 'Crumpled in the grass at the foot of the fence, aye. If Nana Kiklu had known where to look, she might even have seen him there. But with the vampire mist and what all – everything that was happening – and you and Lissa to care for . . .'

Misha's eyes were wide; she made an instinctive, almost involuntary move for the door. Her intention was all too obvious, but her father stood in the way. 'No!' he said. 'I forbid it! The old Szgany trails where they skirt the foothills are no safe place for a girl even at the best of times. But now? Why, there'll be changeling people hiding in the thickets and caves, trapped by the sun as they headed for Starside. And there are bound to be vengeful men out hunting them! I'll not lose you a second time, Misha.' He turned to his son. 'But Nicolae . . .?'

It was Lardis's turn to object. 'What, and am I still the leader of my people, or has Varna Zanesti taken my place, to do my work and my thinking for me? Well, and you're a fine strong man and all, Varna – likewise your son – but no one would call Nicolae fleet of foot! Anyway, you've both of you mourned enough and now have reason to rejoice. And while I *am* still the leader, I won't have you split up again. Finally, I need both of you, indeed all three of you, right here in Settlement. What? But there's work to be done! On the other hand, I do have a number of runners to choose from, who'll be after Nathan in a flash.' Turning to Andrei Romani, he nodded. 'See to it.'

As Andrei went off in great haste, Lardis spoke again to Misha. 'I love Nathan Kiklu like a son, and I'm sure there's more to him than he's been given credit for. Will you and he get together now?'

She looked at her father and Varna shrugged. 'The choice is yours, daughter. But it's true the lad came looking for you, and I have to admit, he seemed a likely son-in-law to me.'

Nicolae nodded, and added: 'I'll have him for a brother, certainly.'

'Good!' Lardis clasped Varna's broad forearm.

Then:

It was as if the old Lidesci had woken up from a nightmare. He straightened up and squared his shoulders, as if to throw off some great invisible weight, and to Varna and Nicolae said: 'They could use your help repairing the stockade, for it's heavy work. And then the great catapults and crossbows need bringing up to scratch. Also, Dimi Petrescu is convinced he can duplicate the black, explosive powder from The Dweller's shells and grenades. Old Dimi's been working at it for eighteen years, on and off, but he's very weary now and needs the strength of others to make purest charcoal, break rocks, and grind sulphur and iron into dust.'

He nodded. 'So ... it's a long day ahead, lads, but you can't say it hasn't started well enough. All we have to do is keep it rolling, right?' And to Misha:

'Girl, the way I see it you've done more than your fair share already. Yet now I'll ask you to do one more thing. If I get a couple or three likely lads together and arm them, can you lead them back to the leper colony, and so bring Lissa and Nana Kiklu safely home? I ask this of you, Misha, in order to save time. You know the whole story, you're sympathetic, and so the women will have word of their sons from another woman. What do you say?'

And as he'd known she would, Misha nodded and said, 'Just bring me my escort, and I'm ready . . .'

Within the half-hour she was on her way back through the woods with Lardis's 'likely lads': three tried and trusted friends. The way was fairly easy going; as the crow flies it was maybe seven miles, nine if you counted the winding trail. Misha knew all the shortcuts, however, and also the shallow fording places across the many streams. Last night in the darkness, with only star- and occasional moonlight to see by, Nana Kiklu had provided the strength and will, but Misha had been their guide.

Then it had taken five hours; now, as she'd already discovered, it would take less than two and a half to retrace her steps. By then, too, Lardis's runner should be catching up with Nathan on the approaches to Twin Fords. Such was the span of Sunside's day – more than one hundred and twenty hours – that with luck the two should be together again a third of the way through the morning. By then she would be very tired, but for now thoughts of Nathan sped Misha on her way.

While at the leper colony:

Nana and Lissa were camped less than a hundred yards from the colony proper, at the edge of the forest where it gave way to rolling savannah, then scrub, and finally the mainly uninhabitable desert wastes known collectively as the Furnace Lands. Out there, only ten to fifteen miles south of the leper colony, there was nothing much worth mentioning: sand, scorched earth, rockpiles; snakes, scorpions, and other poisonous creatures; a scattered handful of aborigine tribes. Of the latter:

In the old days when the Szgany had been true Travellers, these primitive desert nomads – who seemed no further advanced along the evolutionary trail than Starside's trogs – had sometimes bartered with men. They would meet at high sunup, in the dry savannah margins between desert and forest, to trade fancy lizard leathers and healing salts for Szgany knives and knick-knacks, wines, gourds and garlic. And now, here at the rim of

Lidesci territory, the nomads traded just as in the old days; except now they traded with the lepers. Nana Kiklu knew this for a fact; for, far out on the savannah, she'd noticed a tall springy pole with a fluttering rag pennant, like a fly on the face of the sun.

As a girl, travelling with a small tribe, she'd seen just such markers before and knew that the listlessly flapping pennant indicated a nomad trading place. She supposed it was just as well that the lepers had some sort of trade, even with the mysterious, little known or understood nomads; for certainly the bulk of the Szgany weren't likely to come too close. No, for leprosy was as contagious among them as it was among the Wamphyri.

Not that the colony had been entirely abandoned by the Szgany Lidesci. On the contrary: it had been Lardis's father who conceived of it and built the first nucleus of airy lodges under the trees at the forest's edge. As to how that had come about:

Twenty-four years ago a good friend of the elder Lidesci had contracted the disease. Before the affliction made itself obvious, it had been passed on to every member of his family. In those days – in that earlier period of Wamphyri domination – the old ways had been simple and hard: such sufferers were usually banished out of camp to wander alone until they died, on penalty of an even swifter death if they should ever try to come back. Some tribes had even been known to put lepers down out of hand. But Lardis's father wasn't able to do that, and so instead he built the leper colony here at the rim of Szgany territory to house the family of his friend.

Later, hearing about the place, other lepers had made their way here from the wilderness and from various tribes, and so the colony was established. And seven years later as Settlement had grown up and prospered, it had been a younger Lidesci, Lardis himself, who had continued to send supplies to the colony on a regular basis, so helping those who were mainly incapable of helping themselves. And even though in those early years the Szgany Lidesci rarely had a surplus of anything, still there was always enough to give a little to the lepers.

Now it was the turn of the lepers to give in return . . .

These were Nana Kiklu's thoughts where she stood in the shade of a tree at the forest's very edge, and thought back on the events of last night. Not on the painful scenes – such as the destruction of her house, and the fact that she'd not been able to return and search for Nathan and Nestor, which had left such an ache in her heart that it would not be driven out until she and her boys were reunited – but on her exhausted arrival here at the colony. Exhausted, yes, for she and Misha Zanesti between them had been mainly responsible for getting Lissa Lidesci here safe and sound. Poor Lissa, cut by thorn and thicket, and very nearly insane from what she'd seen and been through.

And yet while Nana had the strength both physical and mental, it had been Lissa who was wise enough to advise their coming here, and Misha who was artful enough to lead the way. Misha Zanesti, to whom as a child the forest had been a vast and glorious playground. So all three had played their parts, until at last the woods were behind them and they came upon the savannah by moonlight.

Then, too, Misha had known or divined the way; studying the stars and stating her belief that they had strayed too far west, she had led her companions in the other direction, along the edge of the rolling grassland. Until finally, in the lee of great trees which stood like sentinels looking out towards the inhospitable deserts, they'd seen the soft glow of lamplight and knew that this must be the colony.

Then there had been a low wooden fence, a robed and hooded watcher at the gate, holding up his lamp, and the hoarsely whispered, mumbled query: 'Who comes? Are you lepers?'

'No, not lepers,' Nana had answered, turning her eyes from the lamp's bright glare, 'but friends of those that live here.'

'Not lepers?' the other shrank back. 'Then go away – and go quickly! For we lepers have no friends. And it's not so much that we live here, as that this is where we come to die . . .'

'No friends?' Now Lissa had found voice to speak up. 'Not even Lardis Lidesci whose land this is, whose father built this place, and whose wife I am?'

'Ah!' the other hissed, and they caught a brief glimpse of his face where he held his lantern higher yet: the grey bone showing through his cheek, and the fretted gape of his nostrils. 'The Lidesci? His wife? But in the dead of night? And you –' he swung his light towards Misha, '– only a girl, yet dishevelled, full of bruises, and your clothes all in tatters? And . . . and . . . the Lidesci's wife, you say?' He turned back to Lissa. 'But likewise wild and torn? Now say, what is this thing?'

'Old man,' it was Misha's turn to speak, 'hard times have come, and we must spend the night here and wait for sunup.' And innocent, she reached out a hand to touch his sleeve.

'Ah!' he said again, a gasp this time, and swiftly drew back out of reach. And: 'I am not . . . not old,' he shook his head, however slowly . . .

But in the next moment, 'What hard times?'

'The Wamphyri are back in Starside,' Nana told him

then, breathlessly. 'And tonight they raided on Settlement!'

Finally they had made an impression. 'The Wamphyri!' the leper croaked, bobbing about in sudden agitation. 'What? They are back, did you say?' Abruptly he turned, hobbling off down a path towards the wooden buildings under the trees.

'Wait!' Misha called after him. 'We can't spend the night in the open!'

He glanced back. 'I only keep watch,' he husked. 'But we have a leader, too. Now wait here, and I'll bring him.'

In a little while he returned; several more lepers, all dressed alike, came with him. One of them was tall, shuffling, obviously in great pain. The sleeves of his robe seemed empty from the elbows down ... but his cowl was thrown back so that his face at least was visible and clean. He was pale, hollow-cheeked, with dark expressive eyes.

'I'm Uruk Piatra,' he told the women, looking at them. 'The others call me Uruk Long-life. And you ...' He looked long and hard at Lissa – her oval face with its gentle almond eyes; her slim, long-limbed figure – and said, 'Yes, you are Lardis Lidesci's wife. You've been here before, am I right?'

'With my husband,' she nodded. 'When he was beating the bounds. Twice, I think, but long ago.'

'Aye, long ago,' the other agreed, 'when I had hands.' He looked at all of them again, blinking in the yellow light of the lanterns. 'But I've been told a terrible thing: that the Wamphyri have returned to raid in Sunside!'

By then Lissa had taken a firm grip on her nerves. 'It's true,' she told him, 'all horribly true! We've come here from Settlement, which was burning when last we saw it. There were vampires in the streets, killing, raping, making thralls. But I remember that long ago, my husband told me that this was a place safe from all vampires. That's why we've come here: to hide through the night from the Wamphyri, and to shelter from the forest and its beasts – till sunup at least, when we'll think what to do.'

The leper leader shook his head and his expression grew more haunted yet. 'A monstrous thing!' he said. 'But there are terrible things and terrible things. For a woman to fall into the hands of the Wamphyri would be a nightmare, I know, and to live with them even worse than dying. But to live here . . . is a slow, lingering death in itself – which you risk just by being here.'

Nana Kiklu had had enough of this. 'So, we are turned away by lepers!' Her words were bitter. 'Then we'll sleep here, outside your gate. Only bring us clean blankets and a lantern, and we'll look after ourselves.'

Uruk Piatra looked at her and nodded slowly. 'Being what I am,' he said, 'does not make me any less the man. Upon a time I was Szgany, like you. Not a Lidesci, no, but I was a man. And even now I know my duty. I meant simply this: that I could not invite you in, for your own sakes. But certainly we can do better than blankets and a lamp! When lepers come here, we build them homes. Until they are built, however, a tent of skins must suffice. I suggest you pitch it under the trees, over there.'

Nana went to speak again, then hung her head.

And again he nodded. 'It's all right. I understand. Only looking at you I can see how much you've suffered.'

He gave orders and the other lepers went back to their sprawl of dwellings, returning in a while with a tent, blankets, vegetables, an iron pot and tripod. And: 'Stay here,' their leader told Nana, Lissa, and Misha, 'while they build your tent under the trees and light a small fire. Then you must make your own soup, with water from the stream there.'

And while their refuge from the night was put in order for them, so the three had told Uruk their entire story . . .

That was how it had been for them at the leper colony, in the early hours of the previous night. But as they had settled in to wait out the long hours of darkness, their worries were not so much for themselves as for their loved ones.

Not unnaturally, Nana's thoughts had been for Nathan and Nestor:

How had they fared through Settlement's devastation, she wondered? — wondered it in her sleep, and through all of her waking hours — till at last, still wondering, she'd shivered awake with the dawn. Had it been just as bad for them? Surely it must have been even worse! And how were they faring now?

Now in the light of early morning, in the foothills over Twin Fords, Nestor finished his rabbit and stretched out his limbs in the long grass to digest it. While behind him and somewhat higher, at the sheer, rearing rim of an outcrop, vile evaporation continued to spill out of the trees and tumble down the cliff like a frothing waterfall — but less vigorously now — from the three-quarters liquefied flyer destroyed by sunlight.

As for Nathan . . .

Following old Traveller trails between the forest and the foothills, striding east towards Twin Fords, Nathan was tempted to seek out his brother in a way neither of them had used since childhood. It would mean breaking his easy, long-legged, mile-eating lope for a few minutes, which he was scarcely willing to do, but if it proved successful at least his mind would be at rest.

For there had never been a time in Nathan's life when he was more aware that he was only one half of twins; when, as if to accentuate his and Nestor's physical differences, he could feel this new rift between them like a great canyon, yawning ever wider the closer he came to its rim. And he knew that Misha Zanesti had been only a part of it, that it had been coming anyway and she had been merely the catalyst.

But it had all culminated so swiftly. First Misha:

Because of her love for Nathan (rather, because of Nestor's jealousy), the brothers had drifted apart; that rivalry which had seeded itself in childhood had finally bloated into life, separating them. But they weren't the first brothers to come up against such a problem; it was something which might well have righted itself, eventually. Especially now that . . . now that Misha . . .

But no, Nathan couldn't bring himself to dwell upon that – Misha with the dog-thing, Canker Canison – not in the way Vratza Wransthrall had so gleefully described it. And yet he must, for back in Settlement he'd vowed against the Wamphyri, especially Canker. And though he felt choked inside, still a low growl escaped his throat as he pictured *that* one! Aye, and his vow was a double, even a triple vow, surely; for the Wamphyri were also responsible for whatever fate had befallen his mother, and for tearing him physically apart from his brother. As for the latter . . . he could only hope that it wasn't permanent.

A terrible, terrible thing to have lost all of them: his mother, Misha, *and* Nestor. He neither knew nor wanted to know what effect the death of his brother would have on him, but he supposed it would be like losing an even bigger part of himself – perhaps the last part.

For he and Nestor: they'd shared their mother's womb, her milk, the love of the same Gypsy girl –

though she'd loved one as a brother and the other for himself. But their blood was one blood, and even their minds had seemed fashioned of like stuff; at least, they were similar enough that sometimes they touched upon each other.

Which was what Nathan intended now: to touch Nestor's mind, and in so doing prove that he still lived. And if there was nothing there, a vacuum? That was the chance he must take: to be part of something which *once* was whole, at least, or to be even emptier than the husk he inhabited now.

With all of these thoughts and others swirling in his head and clouding the psychic ether, it was hardly the best moment for such an experiment, but Nathan drew off from the trail anyway, sat down with his back to a boulder and closed out the day, his furious loathing of last night's raiders, all other emotions, everything, and let his mind drift . . .

The dead drew back from him!

He felt that at once; their shock, even their horror. But this time Nathan's interest lay with the living . . . he hoped. And up in the high hills, in deep caves, grey-furred ears sprang erect, grey heads were lifted, and triangle eyes blinked in gloomy lairs. There were three of them, three together, who knew his mind as if it were one of theirs: Blaze, whose brow was marked with his mother's white; Grinner, whose damp black lips forever twitched, as if on the verge of smiling; Dock, whose tail had been shortened when he was a cub and wanted to play with some brave vixen's brood.

They divined Nathan's purpose at once but couldn't help him, not this time. For none of theirs was abroad in the daylight, and no further reports of Nestor had reached them. If it were night, that might be different. But not now.

Nathan acknowledged them anyway, where they whined a little, curled up and resumed their contemplations. And moving on, he let his thoughts drift, drift . . .

. . .Until they struck upon a mind he knew, yet at one and the same time did not know! For it seemed different, changed, wiped clean. Or perhaps wiped unclean, with a dirty, bloodstained rag? For this was Nestor, and yet it was not him.

Nathan couldn't understand. It was as if Nestor's mind itself was undecided about his identity! And a great rage of pain and frustration, of need and ambition, and of loss and discovery seethed in the core of him!

Such was Nathan's shock that he snatched himself back from the stranger which was his brother – and jerked erect where he sat with his back against the rock!

And all of his thoughts fled back to him like whipped dogs, and his quandary was deeper than before where he took up the trail again and headed east . . .

Nestor was asleep, digesting his meal, converting the strong food into energy. He was asleep and wandering in the most fragile of dreams – which were scattered on the instant that the alien Thing entered his mind!

Alien, yes, and a hated enemy! He knew it from the whirlpool of numbers, symbols, meaningless equations and other mathematical devices behind which the Thing concealed its identity and purpose. That same enemy which had plagued him all the days of his life! Shivering despite that the sun blazed down on him, Nestor opened his eyes . . .

. . .and looked up at two men, one about his own age and the other much older, who had come across him where he lay!

The enemy of his dreams was at once forgotten; he

saw the men – saw that just for the moment they were looking at each other, not at him – and closed his eyes again, feigning sleep. But what he'd seen stayed etched on his mind's eye:

One of them, the young one, was kneeling beside him with his fist knotted round the handle of a knife whose sharp blade gleamed like liquid silver in the sunlight. Slender, wide-eyed, nervous, he looked more than a little frightened. The other, a weathered, surly-looking man in his middle years, stood erect with a loaded crossbow held in his strong brown hands. He had been scowling and was now quietly muttering to himself:

'Steal a rabbit right out of my trap, would you, boy? And what are you doing up here anyway, eh? Especially this morning, after last night . . .'

'No vampire,' the one on his knees whispered, still glancing over his shoulder at the first speaker, 'else he wouldn't be out in the sun. And look at the *state* of him, all bruised and banged about! Was he a lone hunter, perhaps, scared down out of the mountains? What do you think, father?'

'What do I think?' the first one's answer was a low rumble of unreasoning hatred and suspicion. 'Oh, I'll tell you what I think: that the bloodsucking bastards have thought up some new tricks, and that this one's some weird Wamphyri changeling! So he's not changed far enough yet that the sun will hurt him . . . so what? You saw his flyer up there, all melting away, and its black bones poking through the rot. Too much of a coincidence to find a thing like that up there, and then to find this one down here. That's what I think!'

Nestor's flyer? He remembered it. Indeed, it was one of the very few things which he did remember. But what was that the older man had called him, a changeling? *Hah!* Little he knew. For Nestor was no mere thrall but a Lord! He *was* the Lord Nestor – of the Wamphyri!

The word was like a fire in his blood – *Wamphyri!*

And now he tensed himself – but carefully, guardedly – for action. His arms were folded comfortably on his chest, and one knee was bent a little. All to the good.

'So what do we do about him?' the one who kneeled wanted to know.

'First we wake him,' the other growled. And reluctantly: 'Then ... I suppose we'd better drag him down into Twin Fords, and find out about him there. For I'd hate to make a mistake.'

Too late! thought Nestor. *You've made too many already.*

He felt the younger one's hand grip his arm above the elbow, shaking him, and heard him bark: 'You, wake up!' Following which, all was a blur of motion.

Nestor's eyes blazed open! Stiffening his hands and shooting them wide in a slicing motion, he knocked aside the young one's knife arm, simultaneously wrenching his hand from its hold on his right arm. Suddenly unbalanced, with his hands sliced out from under him, the youth could only topple forward. Grasping his advantage, Nestor slammed his bent knee into the other's groin, and jerked his head up off the ground to butt him full in the face.

Lips which were already snarling their shock and terror split open bloodily; teeth and bone crunched sickeningly; the youth's yelp of astonishment turned to a red gurgle as Nestor grabbed for the knife. He found it in the other's slackening fingers and gashed himself wrenching it free. But the slicing pain served only to galvanize him further.

The older man was hopping left and right, trying to line up his weapon, shouting, 'Stab him! Kill the bastard!' He would get off a shot but his son was in the way, and what he couldn't see was that Nestor had the knife. And suddenly it seemed that the sprawling, jerking body of his son lifted itself up a foot from the one he was pinning down, and in mid-air shuddered convulsively. Then the youth was thrust aside, turned by Nestor's arm and knee, and his awful face was a bloody mask with a gasping hole for a mouth. Also bloody was the slit in his jacket, from which Nestor drew out the knife.

'Son!' With a cry of anguish, eyes popping, the father watched his son's brief death struggles, saw him flop motionless on the bloodstained grass. Then:

'You!' he snarled, swinging his weapon towards Nestor and pulling the trigger. But Nestor was on his feet, his arm already fully extended forward, and the red-blotched knife in flight! Nestor was good with a knife, but on this occasion he was lucky, too. It took the man in the throat, in the 'V' of bone directly under his Adam's-apple, punching a hole there which penetrated to the spine.

Even crumpling to the earth he was as good as dead, and so didn't see his bolt take Nestor in the side, skewering his flesh like a needle through a blister. He didn't see it, but there were others higher up the hillside who did.

Nestor heard them cry out, looked up from where shock had knocked him off his feet, and saw them through the wash of scarlet agony flooding over him. A group of four or five men, something less than two hundred yards away, descending the hillside towards him in a series of breakneck leaps and bounds – vampire hunters!

Nestor got his fingers into the tear in his jacket and ripped it open. The bolt had entered his body under the ribcage on his right side, scraping a rib at the back where its barbed head had emerged. Its flight was sticking out at the front, and both holes were dripping thick, dark splashes of blood where a five-inch bridge of white, puffy flesh joined them like a bulging roll of fat.

Nestor didn't think twice but gripped the head of the bolt with his right hand and the flight with his left, and bent the wooden shaft against his side until it snapped. He saw the skin of his side bulge as the broken shaft forced the white flesh outward, and almost passed out; but he knew that if he did, it would probably be the last thing he ever did. And in any case, breaking the bolt had been only half of it. Now he must draw it out.

He did so without pause, and had to fight from gagging as the red blood spurted. Then, cinching his jacket tightly to his body, he somehow got to his feet and made off down the steep slope. But weak and desperate as he was, his heart was already pounding and his breath faltering. And those men back there – Szgany, and full of bloodlust – they'd not give him a second's respite or his life a moment's thought once they had him. It would be the stake, the knife, the fire for Lord Nestor of the Wamphyri!

He limped to the rim of a bluff and looked over, saw deep water rushing into the foam and spray of broad falls, and white water all the way down to the levels and the broken bridges of Twin Fords. But from behind as if to spur him on, rising above the hiss and surge of foaming waters, he could hear the angry shouts of his pursuers.

And looking back just once, to glimpse raised weapons and furious faces, he shouted his defiance – and jumped!

Nathan got into Twin Fords a little less than two hours

later. He found the town a shambles – a pesthole of stumbling, slack-mouthed survivors; a bubbling cauldron of narrow-eyed, suspicious, would-be avengers; a chaos of terrified, demented people – with little or nothing of Settlement's order and discipline about it. Before that, however:

There were guards on the approach roads to the town, who stopped him the moment he crossed the river through the shallows of the fording place, where all that remained of a once-sturdy bridge was a weir of timbers crushed down into the mud. He was recognized as one of Lardis Lidesci's party, which had passed through heading west for Settlement just yestereve, and allowed to go on into the devastation.

And the chaos was at once apparent. At least two fires were still smouldering where granaries had been gutted; the dead – or their pieces, if they had been vampirized – were still being dragged through barely recognizable streets to be burned on funeral pyres; the wailing of women and weeping of children was nerve-rending. Inside a more or less intact perimeter of wooden buildings, the destruction was enormous, far worse than in Settlement. Here, where a great many houses had been simply smashed flat, it appeared that the Wamphyri and their creatures must have raged out of control.

Approaching the centre, where the leaders and elders of the Szgany Zestos were holding a meeting, Nathan witnessed the discovery and destruction of a vampire thrall who had slept too late. Flushed from her hiding place under the eaves of a house by men brandishing torches, a woman was driven into the street and ringed about. With the sun beating down on her she shrank back and tried to cover herself, all the while raving and gibbering, and cursing the men about her in language so filthy that Nathan couldn't believe it.

Wild, grey as a cloud, with eyes bubbling like sulphur, finally she braved their torches and launched herself at the nearest man. And as she snarled at him it was at once obvious that her eye-teeth were unnaturally long, white and sharp!

The bolt which cut her down was equally sharp, likewise the knives with which they took her head . . .

Then Nathan arrived at the meeting place in the shade of a large, hastily erected, open-sided tent. And as the gathering broke up he recognized Karl Zestos, the oldest son of Twin Fords' former leader. His father, Bela Zestos, was dead now, a heroic victim of the vampire raid; if from the wreckage of his people Karl could salvage a number sufficient to lead, then he would become a Traveller King in his own right.

Recognition like sorrow was mutual; the two spent a few moments trading their grim stories; Nathan picked up several details of last night's raid on Twin Fords which had not been available in Settlement. More than anything else, he was interested in Canker Canison. But when he explained why . . . then the other's face turned grey. And:

'My friend,' Karl told him, shaking his head, 'you must pray that your Misha is dead! The reports I have heard . . .'

'I know,' Nathan answered, cutting him short. 'And when I think about it, I'm tempted to try *willing* her dead! Except that's not possible, and I'm glad it isn't.'

'I understand,' the other nodded, then frowned at Nathan and added: 'But something is strange here. I remember you differently: not only from your colouring, which is rare among the Szgany, but also for the fact that you were quiet and retiring. You have a brother, right? *He's* the one I remember as forward and outspoken!'

'Am I forward and outspoken?' Nathan was surprised. 'Then perhaps I've gained from Nestor's loss.' He explained his meaning and his mission: how his brother had been taken, and how he had 'dreamed' of the flyer crashing in the hills close by.

'That . . . rings bells,' Karl told him then; but if anything his frown was more deeply etched than before. 'Some men were up in the hills this morning, looking for changelings who had escaped out of town. You'll understand that there are many people we can't account for. Anyway, they discovered a flyer and . . . a man. A youth, at least.'

Nathan grabbed his arm. 'A youth? Alive?'

'He was – living – when they found him, yes,' the other replied. 'But "alive"?' He shrugged. 'Undead, perhaps.'

Nathan groaned. And: 'Explain,' he said.

Karl told him the story as he'd had it, finishing with: 'He leaped into the torrent and was swept away. They saw him go under in the white water, but they didn't see him surface.'

'And you say he . . . he murdered two men?'

The other could only nod. 'He was seen to do it, aye.'

Nathan shook his head. 'Then it couldn't be Nestor!'

Again Karl's shrug. 'Who else could it be? The description I was given fits. Also, you've related how things were in Settlement. So how do you know Nestor wasn't vampirized before the flyer took him? You don't.' He sighed. 'I'm not unsympathetic, Nathan, but it seems to me you should forget him now and go back home to those you have left.'

Nathan was bitter. 'I *have* no one left!'

'Then follow me,' Karl urged. 'I need good, strong young men. I'll take my people out of here and return to my father's way of life before he built this place, and be a Traveller.'

But Nathan's mind was still on Nestor, and now he mused: 'There are two tributaries plunging out of the heights. Which one did he jump into?'

'The one that descends to West Ford,' Karl answered. 'But what will you do?'

'I'll try to find his body,' Nathan told him. 'And then I'll know, for better or for worse.'

The other nodded. 'Good luck. But Nathan, if you do find him . . . be prepared.'

Nathan didn't find Nestor, but at least he found word of him.

He spoke to the guards at the ruined bridge. They'd seen the body of a man go drifting down river. There had been blood in the water and the body was facedown, motionless. They would have dragged him out but had failed to notice him until he was over the slippery weir and drifting deeper. He could be one of two things: a murdered victim of last night's raid, or a vampire thrall caught by the sun in the foothills.

Anyway, that had been more than two and a half hours ago. By now he'd be tangled in roots somewhere down river, or sunk to the bottom in the mud and the weeds . . .

Nathan thanked them for the information, if not for their 'assurances', then forded the river and set out to follow its course downstream. Walking a path used by the town's fishermen, and scanning the overgrown banks as he went, he followed the rushing waters to where the river joined with its twin in a broad green swath, but saw never a sign of Nestor. At which point most men might have given up, but not Nathan. He would follow the greater river all day, if need be. And when night came? . . . Well, sundown must find him wherever it found him.

And for that matter, what difference did it make?

Fifteen minutes after Nathan passed from sight of the West Ford bridge, Lardis's runner made the crossing. He had been held up by a string of vampire hunters along the way.

By then the guards at the fording place had changed; one of them reported that he'd seen a man of Settlement talking to Karl Zestos in the town; the runner hurried on into Twin Fords without ever knowing that Nathan was less than three miles away but in a different direction.

Having found and spoken to Karl, the runner quickly returned to the sunken bridge. This time the guards could only shrug and offer their opinions that Nathan must be on his way back to Settlement, and that the two had passed each other by on different trails. It seemed the only logical explanation. Thus the runner gave up the chase, and began retracing his steps . . .

PART SIX:

Szgany Sintana – Dissension in the Aerie –
The Thyre

I

Where the river swung east in a languid curve through deepening forest, broadening out until details on the far bank were hard to discern, there Nathan was about ready to admit defeat. By then the morning was more than half-way through and he was exhausted; he had been on the move nonstop since before first light, a period of some thirty-two hours. Also, since the path had come to an end just four or five miles south-east of Twin Fords, the going had been very difficult.

Now, in a sun-dappled clearing by the bank, he lay down in the long, sweet-smelling grass to sleep, and was just beginning to drowse when he was startled to hear a familiar clop, clop, clop, of cloven hooves, the creak and jolt of caravans, and the jingle of trappings and Szgany bells. Somewhere close to hand, hidden by the river's rearing fringe, there must be an old Traveller trail; for these were surely the sounds of a party of Gypsies, who were even now passing through.

Nathan was wrong: they weren't just passing through but making camp, which he saw when he left the river, pushed his way through a tangle of soft-leaved shrubbery, and emerged on the old trail. And as he appeared in the open, on the ancient rutted track, so they likewise saw him.

Brown, soulful female eyes met his deep blue ones across the trail's width, and Nathan froze on the instant as the girl melted back into the greenery and out of sight. He'd suddenly remembered that these were strange times, and the last thing these people would be expecting was a wild man jumping out at them from the forest! On the other hand there were a good many of them, and Nathan was just one. Also, the sun was high, and so there was little chance of vampires abroad in the woods.

Certainly they were aware that the old threat lived anew in Starside; that was obvious from the moment of their first greeting. 'Tear down the mountains,' said a soft Szgany voice from one side, startling Nathan.

Jerking his head in that direction, he saw a tall, lean, incredibly weathered man of indeterminate years, propped casually with his shoulder against a tree. And just from looking at him Nathan could tell that these people were *real* Travellers, Szgany in the fullest sense. No permanent dwelling place for such as these; township comforts had never lured them from their ways, not for more than a night or so; they had been on the move all their days, as much a part of the wilderness as the creatures of the woods.

Which meant that they might not know of the return of the Wamphyri after all. For among the true Travellers the old ways were still remembered as yesterday, and the old greetings – which could as well be maledictions as pleasantries, depending on the times and situation – were still very much alive. 'Tear down the mountains,' this one had intoned, and Nathan knew the answer. He'd heard it from time to time when Travellers passed through Settlement trading their good skins, sharpening knives and axes, and reading palms. He had *heard* it before, but never used it. Because then he'd neither needed nor wanted to speak to anyone. Things were different now, however. And so:

'Aye, tear down the barrier range,' he answered. 'Let the sun blaze full upon the last aerie, and melt it down to the ground!'

The man acknowledged Nathan's understanding of the old curse and nodded, but at the same time he frowned and said: 'And yet ... you're not a Traveller. Then perhaps your town has made us welcome in the past. For we don't hold it against you town people that you have chosen to settle. We visit now and then, and sometimes find it good to talk with others. We merely think it foolish to stay trapped in one place, like a fungus on a tree. For when the tree falls, the fungus goes with it ...'

He brought out his right hand from where it had been hidden by the bole of the tree, and in full view applied the safety catch to his loaded crossbow. Then, nodding again, he added: 'Aye, foolish – especially now that the Wamphyri are back! But then, we've always said that they would be. And can you tell me a better reason for having spent all these years on the trail?'

Nathan shook his head, and answered, 'Right now, that's why I'm here, too. But I'm not running away from them, just searching for ... for my brother, who was their victim. I ... *lost* him last night, in Twin Fords. A man was seen to fall in the river. I thought that it might be him, and if I followed the river I might find him.'

'And did you?'

'No,' he shook his head. And stepping forward he offered his hand. They clasped forearms, and Nathan said, 'I'm Nathan Kiklu, of the Szgany Lidesci.'

The other smiled, however humourlessly. 'Szgany, you say? The Szgany Lidesci? From Settlement? Well, it's true at least that old Lardis *used* to be a Traveller! I'm Nikha Sintana, and these are my people. We, too, stayed in Twin Fords last night, and I also lost a brother. At least, I lost one who would have become as a brother to me. So much for the safety of towns! As for running away ...'

Nathan saw his error at once and went to correct it. 'I meant no slight or insult!'

'None taken,' the other shook his head. 'We *are* running away! What? Should we sit in a burning tree, drink poisoned water, tie boulders to our necks and carry them into the river? And should we live in a town, lighting great communal fires to welcome the Wamphyri to their feast?' Again he shook his head. 'From now on I think a great many will be "running away", just like me and mine. But last night – what an error! Of all the nights to choose to spend in the company of settled men!'

While Nikha Sintana talked, Nathan made him the subject of a thorough appraisal. He did so openly, with a display of natural, friendly curiosity; it was the Szgany way when meeting strangers. And what he observed was impressive.

Nikha was – he could be – oh, anything between thirty-five and forty-five years old. The actual number of his years was a secret hidden in the agelessness of his penetrating, intelligent brown eyes, in skin weathered to a supple leather, in the oiled flexibility of sleek-muscled arms and the easy litheness of his posture. When Nikha leaned against a tree he didn't just slump; the tree seemed not only to support him but became one with him, lending him its strength. Indeed, there appeared to be a great deal of Nature's strength in every part of him.

His hooked nose was almost as sharp in profile as a kite's beak, but without its cruelty. His brow – for all that it was broad to accommodate a good brain and wide inscrutable eyes – had the flat slope of a wolf's. His lips were thin, grooved as old bark, and maybe not much given to smiling; but at the same time Nathan could not fail to notice the laughter lines, too, at the corners of his eyes and mouth. Overall, with his dark-grey, shoulder-length hair, Nikha Sintana reminded him of nothing so much as a lean and rangy hunting owl.

The Traveller had fallen silent now, waiting for Nathan's response. And Nathan was not remiss. 'I'm sorry you lost someone. I feel for you and know your pain well. For just like me, you also lost a brother.'

Nikha nodded. 'But my sister's pain is the greater. She was to have married this one. Which is how he would have become my brother.'

'Ah!' said Nathan, quietly.

He looked around. The Gypsies had led their animals into the forest's shade; a few tents of skins were being erected; a cooking fire was already smoking under a tripod of green branches, fuelling itself on dry bark tinder. Men were moving like shadows under the trees; a crossbow thrummed and a pigeon fell in the sun-dappled glade; a youth with a fishing line made for the river bank, collecting moth larvae bait as he went. There was something very natural, very appealing, about all of this almost casual activity. Nathan felt ... comfortable here, in the company of these people. Except comfort was a feeling he couldn't afford.

He straightened his shoulders and said, 'I should get back to my search.'

Nikha took his arm. 'We've stayed in Settlement from time to time. Lardis Lidesci was always a friend, in the old days and in the new. I'm not a man to incur debts, but where they exist I always try to square them. You are tired, Nathan Kiklu. You look fit to drop. As well sleep here among friends as alone along the river, and when you've rested eat with us. That way, in some future time, my debt will have transferred to you. It's from small debts such as these that friendships are forged.'

Nathan felt his weariness dragging on his bones and remembered now that he'd been about to sleep. Also, his back was a mass of blue bruises, whose aching was such that it might soon immobilize him entirely unless he rested first. 'I'm tired, it's true,' he said. 'But I don't wish to inconvenience you.'

'No such thing,' the other replied. 'This is where we make camp, eat and sleep. You've come across us at the right time. Our lives may be short but Sunside's days are long. At least while the sun is in the sky we may sleep safely. As for your search: the river is wide and its banks overgrown, with miles of forest on both sides. I understand your need, but I can't say I'm envious of the task you've set yourself. A rest can't hurt ... and then a little food, to fuel you on your way?'

In this way Nathan found his mind made up for him. 'I'm in your debt,' he said.

Leading him into the camp past a small caravan, Nikha said: 'My wagon. I shared it with my young sister, and cared for her until she was a woman. Then, when Eleni found herself a man in Twin Fords, or when he found her, we made them a tent of skins. This time passing through Twin Fords she would have been married; this very day, in fact! But last night, in the middle of a small celebration ... well, you know what happened. All of that became as nothing. Now for a while she'll put up her tent and sit in it, and mourn this man she never got to know.' His voice hardened. 'But she'll forget about him soon enough, and the tent won't go to waste. Maybe it's just as well.'

Nathan glanced at him, perhaps a little sharply. Nikha saw his frown and raised a defensive eyebrow. 'If she'd known him well, then she would mourn him that much harder. And what if there had been children?'

'That seems a hard point of view,' Nathan was frank.

'Because I can remember hard times,' Nikha answered. 'And harder still to come, I fear.' He paused a while to fondle the ear of a beast of burden, a shad, one of a pair hitched to the thill of his vehicle. Shaggy as a hugely overgrown goat and of a like intelligence – but less boisterous, wider in the shoulder and sturdier in the legs – the creature and its companion waited uncomplainingly for someone to unhitch them and put them to graze. Turning its head, it offered up a grateful bleat and allowed Nikha to scratch behind its ear.

And: 'Aye,' he finally continued, as if he talked to himself or to the shad, 'even the smallest comforts will be hard come by from now on, I fancy. For men and beasts alike . . .'

Meanwhile, Nathan had looked the camp over and noted its size and composition. There were two caravans and a flat, covered cart, half a dozen shads and two calves, and a few goats tethered at the back of the vehicles. Dangling outside the caravans, festooning their sides, were all the tools and utensils necessary to Traveller life, each item muffled now to prevent unwanted jangling and clattering. And under the trees at the rim of the clearing, three good-sized tents stood cool in the shade. Finally, the camp had its own wolves, a dog and a bitch. Capable hunters, they would see to themselves and provide early warning of intruders – which explained how Nikha Sintana had been so quick off the mark and waiting on Nathan's arrival.

According to Lardis Lidesci's campfire stories, there had been hundreds of groups such as this one upon a time. Scarcely larger than a few family units – able to melt away like ghosts into the forests, or hide in small caves during Wamphyri raids – they had made harder targets than the larger, more prominent Traveller tribes.

Several of Nikha Sintana's earlier statements had more than suggested his solitary nature, which the size of his party might appear to confirm; but to Nathan it seemed more likely that he simply adhered to this old tenet, that small is synonymous with secure.

Of people, the group was made up of thirteen in all: four men, including Nikha, three women, and five children whose ages ranged from a small infant to the youth in his early teens who had gone fishing. The thirteenth ... was Eleni Sintana, that sister of whom Nikha had spoken.

Nathan had caught only the briefest glimpse of Eleni in the moment he broke through the undergrowth on to the track, but in that same moment he had seen something in her eyes which had seemed to strike a resonant chord within himself ... perhaps it had been her eyes, so much like Misha's. In any case, he'd been aware of her presence ever since but was careful not to look at her directly. Travellers are often fiercely protective where their women are concerned, and they don't care for forwardness in strangers. He was aware of her now to one side of the camp's central area, where she used an axe to break up dead, fallen branches into firewood.

'This is Eleni,' Nikha confirmed, leading him across the clearing, 'my sister. She cuts firewood to occupy her mind.'

She looked up as they approached – looked at Nathan and smiled, however wanly – and he saw now that it *was* her eyes. They took him by surprise, for he'd thought that only Misha's eyes could be so warm, black and caring. Obviously he'd been wrong; or perhaps it was just that Misha had been so much on his mind lately, that ...

'This is Nathan Kiklu,' Nikha said, breaking into his thoughts, and possibly into hers, too. 'A man of Settlement, from Lardis Lidesci's people. He could use a wash, a place to sleep, a blanket to keep him warm. Until our meal is prepared. Will you see to it, little sister?'

She nodded and straightened up. And now that they'd been introduced, Nathan allowed himself to look at her.

Maybe twenty or twenty-one years old, she was typically Szgany. All lithe and sinuous, with movements as smooth as oil, her hair was shiny black, her skin tanned to a glow, her mouth generous and sensuous at one and the same time. And there was something wild as the woods about her – even more so than her brother – so that if Nathan didn't know better he might think there was room for only one mood in her: she should be vivacious and live life to the full, joyously, with a husky laugh that teased, taunted but never quite seduced. Because when finally Eleni did love, then her man would get all that she could give.

Mainly naïve, Nathan was wont to make judgements such as this at first sight. And sometimes he was right. Eleni should be that way; perhaps she would have been and could be again, one day. But for now ... she was small and sad and lonely.

As Nikha walked away, back towards his caravan and animals, Nathan began: 'Your brother has told me –' and paused. '– I mean, I just want you to know that we're two of a kind. For just as you have lost your man, so I have lost my girl.'

She nodded seriously, and answered: 'I know how much you have lost, for it's in your eyes. I knew from the first moment I saw you. Ah, but I saw much more than that in those strange blue eyes of yours, Nathan! They are filled with all sorts of things, and you're not much given to hiding them.'

He was surprised, not quite sure of her meaning. Perhaps he looked at her too openly. He turned his eyes aside at once. 'Have I . . . been forward? If I've seemed so, then –'

'No, no, not that,' she cut him short. 'And if you were, what of it? Gypsies are forward. If a person is liked no one complains, and if he is not liked we say that he is forward. No, but you have been the sad one for a long, long time, and now is the worst time of all.'

He shook his head, frowned, fingered his chin. 'But . . . how can you know?' And now her smile was warmer.

'Oh, I read palms,' she said, tossing her ringlets back out of her eyes. 'Like my mother before me. Except, why it's easier far to read faces! And as I said, your face – especially those eyes of yours – tells a long, sad story.' She reached out and touched his brow. 'Such lines, and so very deep, in a face so young . . .' She shook her head, wonderingly. But before he could question her further:

'Enough of that for now,' she said. 'Come over here, to my tent. Nikha says you need a wash. We can take care of that. And then I'll get you a blanket.'

Close to her tent she set up a tripod and bowl, and brought hot water from the fire. A piece of bark provided a cleansing, milky sap, with which Nathan scoured his face and hands. But watching him, Eleni saw him wincing whenever he stretched his arms.

He had removed his leather jacket but still wore his shirt. 'Take it off,' she said.

H. looked at her sideways, questioningly. They were alone in the clearing now, almost. The men were off hunting; women tended their offspring or performed other duties; Nikha was seeing to his beasts. 'Take what off?'

'Your shirt. When you bent over it rode up your back. I have seen your bruises. Were you beaten?'

Beaten? No, merely tossed aside – but by a Thing as strong as four men! The thing that took my Misha. 'A Lord of the Wamphyri very nearly killed me,' he finally answered. 'I suppose I was lucky.'

He tried to reach over his shoulder and grasp the fabric of his shirt, but couldn't. Perhaps it was as well; Nikha had come back and was sitting on the steps of his vehicle. Seeing Nathan glancing that way, Eleni asked him: 'Are you concerned that my brother is watching us? Well, you shouldn't be.' And before he could answer she took the hem of his shirt in both hands and lifted it, and as he bent forward stripped it from his back.

'Now your brother will know I'm forward,' he groaned. 'Or that you are!'

And now for the first time she laughed, and her laugh was as husky as he had guessed it must be. 'Nathan, Nikha will be delighted!' she told him. 'Can't you see that he's still trying to marry me off?' But as she saw the extent of his bruising her laughter died away. And: 'You *suppose* you were lucky?' she repeated him. 'But your back should have been broken in three places! Now wait.'

She ran to Nikha and past him into the caravan, and was back in a moment with ointment wrapped in a leather pouch. 'It smells, but it's good!' she said, applying the stuff liberally to his back. 'Next sunup the sting will have gone, and by midday the bruises fading. I guarantee it. When we pass through the townships, we Gypsies guarantee all of our products!' And again she laughed.

Then she helped him on with his shirt, took him into her tent and gave him a blanket. Her bed was a huge watertight skin stuffed with down, herbs and dried ferns; more than sufficient for Nathan's needs, he made no complaint. As he lay down she threw the blanket over him, and almost before she left the tent and closed its flap he was asleep . . .

Numbers formed a whirlpool which sucked Nathan in, whirled him round and around, and dragged him unprotesting down the central funnel of warping algebraic equations. To anyone else it would be a nightmare, but not to him. Unlike the dead, who could have talked to Nathan if they wished it but never did, the numbers were his friends. In a way, they did 'talk' to him; except he didn't have the math to understand their language. In a world largely without science, Nathan had no math at all. What would probably have been instinctive, intuitive in him from his first serious lesson, had never had the chance to develop. Not yet.

But he did understand that the numbers could sometimes carry him – his thoughts at least – to other places, other minds. It was a telepathic talent he shared with Nestor, part of which was to reach out with his mind and make a connection with that of his twin. Another part of it, which was his alone, allowed him to contact and speak with his wolves. In his waking hours this might only be accomplished by an effort of conscious will, and even then it had sometimes failed him, but when he slept it was quite beyond his control. For then his talent seemed to work on its own, or occasionally with the help of what Nathan had long since named 'the numbers vortex'.

Now he was in that vortex, but only for a moment. For in the next he felt himself expelled, hurled out and down – into water! Into the river!

And because he had searched for Nestor, now he was Nestor. He was one with his brother's mind. He knew what Nestor knew, felt what he felt, observed what he observed. Which was nothing.

Nathan knew what 'dead' minds feel like. This was it, and yet at the same time it was less than death. For the dead know many things, and this mind — Nestor's mind — knew nothing at all! And Nathan believed he knew what that meant: that his brother was freshly dead, and as yet had learned nothing from all of those others who had gone before.

He felt what Nestor felt: nothing. Or perhaps he did feel or was aware of something: the gentle flow of cold, cold water — his lungs full of the stuff, which weighed like lead to drag him down — and the first, tentative nibble of some small, curious fish. He observed what his brother observed: nothing. Or if not that, a drift of dark green weed sliding slowly across his blurred, submerged view, to fill the screen of his gaping, glazing eyeballs . . . before the final darkness closed in!

And with that he knew that Nestor was dead, drowned, and gone from him forever.

He started awake —!

— To find Eleni Sintana down on her knees beside him, her brown eyes wide and anxious where they stared into his. She had hold of his shoulders, holding him down under the water. Except . . . there was no water. And at last he breathed, stopped struggling, allowed her to push him back into his own depression in her bed. And:

'A dream?' she inquired, her concern clearly apparent.

Nathan nodded, felt cold sweat drip from the tip of his nose. More than that, Eleni, he wanted to say, but couldn't, because he knew that she wouldn't understand. But looking up into her face, her eyes . . . she so reminded him of his mother . . . and of Misha . . . he wished she would wrap her arms around him, for his protection.

He saw that she was going to – until Nikha's soft voice sounded from the door of the tent, saying: 'We're about ready to eat, Nathan. Will you join us?'

And the spell was broken.

Nathan joined the others to eat, but he was quiet and had no appetite. There was nothing wrong with the good food, nothing wrong with the company, just with him. For he knew now that he was alone, entirely alone, and that what he'd mistaken for his awakening into this world had only been the beginning of the end. The Wamphyri had wrought reality out of a fantasy – changed everything, made him aware of his place here, and given him an identity – only to rob him of his roots. Now he was drifting, as Nestor's body had drifted, and not even the weeds of what might have been to anchor him.

For the last link had been broken, Nestor was dead, and Nathan felt in his heart the coldness of his brother's watery grave . . .

And two miles down river, in a shingly bight, a burly, bearded fisherman cried out, tossed aside his rod, went plunging into the water to his thighs.

He had been monitoring the progress of a log drifting out of the main current and into the shallows of the backwater. And knowing that fish sometimes swim in the shadow of floating debris, he had thought to see a big one accompanying this piece of driftwood. But lolling closer to the bank, suddenly the log had given a lurch and turned over, and in the next second the fisherman had seen that what had come adrift from it to slip down into the clear water was anything but a fish!

That had been a moment ago; now Brad Berea waded to the log and thrust it aside, sank to his knees in the shingle, and gathered up the body of a young man from where it bumped slowly along the bottom. The youth's clothes were ragged, waterlogged; he was limp, cold . . . dead? Well, very likely. But his flesh seemed firm, his limbs were still flexible, and his lips were not entirely blue.

In fact Nestor Kiklu was dead or as close as could be, and had been for several long seconds, but as yet his spirit had not flown the flesh. What his brother Nathan had experienced was not true death but the final sleep which leads up to it, except this time that sleep had been interrupted.

Brad Berea carried Nestor to the bank, dragged him out feet first to let the water rush out of him, and thumped his chest until he coughed up mud, small weeds and more water. Coughed them up, lay still . . . and breathed!

He breathed – however raggedly, shallowly – and slowly but surely a semblance of life crept back into him.

Into his body, at least . . .

After their meal, Nikha Sintana and his people took their rest. Later, they would spread out into the forest and hunt more diligently; for they must find game now, in the daylight hours, to see them and their families through the long night ahead. After the hunting – assuming it was successful – they'd be more at their ease; they would play, make music, talk over their short-term plans. The plans of travelling folk were ever short-term, Wamphyri or no; but by midday they would be back on the trail again.

Nikha's idea, which he had told to Nathan while they ate, was this:

He and his party would follow the old trail south to the narrow strip of prairie where it bordered on the furnace deserts. He knew the location of a spring there, which in all his years of wandering had never dried out. There was no shortage of game, and the fruits of the forest were always plentiful. In the woods at the edge of the prairie, well away from the customary haunts and routes of other Travellers, there Nikha's group would disguise their caravans in the thickets, stain them green to match the foliage, and pitch their tents under cover of the great trees.

In short, they would quit travelling for a while at least, if only long enough to see how the wind blew. And if it seemed they had chosen a good, safe spot, then perhaps they'd make it permanent. Settling there would go against the grain with Nikha, of course; it would be a solitary, ingrown existence with no company to mention and no external contacts. But at least they *would* exist, and more or less on their own terms.

As for the Wamphyri: there would be richer pickings for them elsewhere. Word of their return would be spreading even now, but many townships would not hear of it until it was too late. In Twin Fords and other towns, there were plenty of old people who could not or would not move; these must soon fall prey to the vampires. And there would be a great many parties of refugees on the move outwards from threatened towns along the southern flank of the barrier range, whose leaders had forgotten or never known the skills necessary for survival in the wild. For a certainty, the Wamphyri would pick these off first.

In Settlement and possibly a handful of other places, men would stand their ground, fight and inevitably die. The vampires *loved* to fight, and such bastions of defiance would present irresistible challenges. All of which should provide Nikha and his party a breathing space, ample time to settle into their secret place, discover hiding holes and prepare themselves against every hideous eventuality.

One of the first things they would do would be to breed more watchdog wolves, and train them to be alert for strange sights, sounds, smells . . .

With luck the vampires would never find their camp – or if they did would discover it deserted, its people fled into the woods or grasslands. And as any fool must see for himself, the closer you live to the sunrise, the safer you are from vampire slavery, death and undeath. Why should the Wamphyri bother to fly across all these miles of woodlands, when they could reap their tithe of blood so much closer to home? For to raid in the southern extremes of Sunside would mean a greater distance to travel back to Starside, before sunup. It was a small point but it seemed to make sense.

As to why Nikha told Nathan all of these things: simply, he hoped to tempt him along. And so Nathan saw that Eleni had been right: Nikha was angling to catch her a husband before he and his people disappeared into solitude. Well, and Nathan supposed he could do much worse. But before that –

– His thoughts were all for Misha, despite that she was lost or dead . . . or worse than dead. Misha and Nestor, yes. If only Nathan could see Nestor again, find him and take him from the river, and give him a decent grave. For while the teeming dead couldn't bring themselves to speak to Nathan, he was sure they would allow him a little time, a few words, with his own brother at least. The chance to make things right with him?

Which was why, when they had finished eating and talking, he mumbled awkward excuses and headed for the river. Eleni said nothing but went to her tent; but Nikha Sintana, on his way to his bed in the caravan,

451

came after Nathan at once and took his arm. 'Won't you come with us, then?'

'I can't,' Nathan answered. 'Maybe I would, for Eleni's sake, if she'd have me – and if you think I'd make her a capable husband, of course. But first I must try one last time to find Nestor's body. Find and bury him, so that I'll know where he is always. For I think ... that he must be quite close to this place. I have a feeling, that's all.'

'I understand,' Nikha nodded, and gave Nathan a skin with a route marked on it, to bring him to their camp. 'We'll sleep now, then hunt, finally move on,' he said. 'By midday we shall be gone from here, and by sundown we'll be in our place, which I've kept in mind these many years. How long will you search?'

Nathan offered a despairing shrug. 'Until I can no longer hope to find him. Perhaps there's no hope even now, but I must try. And Nikha, even then I can't swear I'll be back. There are things in my head ... I have memories as fresh as yesterday ... it's not easy to swing this way and that, like a reed in the wind. It only looks easy.'

Nikha nodded. 'Very well. But if you should decide that ... well, however you decide, only be sure to reach us before sundown, for after that there'll be no fire to guide you, and it might prove dangerous to come too close unannounced.'

Then they clasped forearms, and through the trees Nathan could feel Eleni's eyes upon him until he passed from sight into the undergrowth ...

He searched the river bank until the middle of the afternoon, when the ground on his side of the river turned into a bog and became impassable, and the overhanging branches were so full of creepers and rank, secondary foliage that the water was shaded, dappled, opaque. If his brother was down there, there could be no finding him now. As for burying him: Nestor would be buried already, in the weeds which had been part of Nathan's 'dream'.

Now, too, Nathan must decide what to do. Earlier, he had seemed to feel something for Eleni Sintana. Or perhaps he had simply felt it for himself: a yawning void, an aching need. In any case, he had a choice: join the Szgany Sintana in whatever future would be theirs, or return to Settlement and be Lardis Lidesci's son, replacing the one he'd lost. Whichever he chose to be − husband to Eleni, or a son to Lardis − he would be a replacement, not the real thing; and he would always know that he was the second choice.

Settlement seemed a long way off from Nathan, and he knew it could never feel the same if he went back there. If a girl passed by he would look at her, hoping it was Misha. When the women stamped their feet and snapped their fingers thus and so in the dance, he would think of his mother. And if some brash youth came striding, laughing along the road, it would always be Nestor from this time forward. No, the town would be full of ghosts now; indeed, Settlement itself would be a ghost.

But Eleni Sintana was warm and alive . . .

And what of his vow against the Wamphyri? All very well, when there was a chance that Nestor lived. Together, united under a banner of vengeance, the two of them could have fought alongside Lardis Lidesci and taken whatever revenge was available to them, before they too paid the price. They could have, but no longer. For Nestor was drowned and cold. And again the thought came to Nathan: *Eleni is warm and alive.*

It was a little more than half-way through the afternoon; there were still some twenty-five hours of full daylight left, and five or six more of twilight; Nathan was feeling worn out, as low as he had ever felt, and quite at the end of his tether. Over a period of time which would equal almost four days in the time-frame of the world beyond the Starside Gate – of which as yet Nathan knew nothing other than that it was there – he'd managed to snatch only a few hours sleep. Now he must sleep, and sleep his fill, before heading south for ... for the encampment of the Szgany Sintana, where the forest met the savannah.

Back up the river he had passed a tiny sandy island with a few reeds, shrubs and trees. Now he made his weary way back there, waded out to the island, curled up under a bush half in the shade, and almost at once fell into an exhausted, dreamless sleep. His last conscious thought as the darkness came down was that he would sleep for a good seven or eight hours, and still have plenty of time to trek to Nikha's camp before sundown.

But the fact was that both physically and mentally Nathan was far more depleted than he thought. And while he slept ... on Starside the vampire plague-bearers were wide awake, active, and filled to overflowing with their loathsome poisons, their unspeakable ambitions ...

Though as yet the rays of a slowly setting sun continued to paint the higher peaks of the barrier range a dazzling gold, its cleansing glare had lifted from the face of that one remaining aerie, whose name upon a time was Karenstack. And in the hour of the sun's passing, Wratha the Risen had called a meeting in her vertiginous apartments; several of her familiar bats had been dispatched into the stack's lower levels, where Wratha's renegades understood their messages far better than men understand the whining of dogs. And now the changeling vampire Lords attended her, however sullenly.

They had all been up and about since the arrival of their first new thralls out of Sunside: allotting quarters, 'victualling' their beasts, choosing lieutenants and in structing them in their duties, apportioning work to commoner thralls . . . and last but not least, sating themselves, of course. Which surely accounted for Canker Canison's ravaged look, for where females were concerned he was ever the Great Dog. In Settlement he had excelled himself: at least two thirds of his recruits from the Szgany Lidesci were women.

But even in Canker's case the choosing of new lieutenants had taken priority for a while; for with the single exception of Gorvi the Guile, all of the Lords and the Lady too had lost their right-hand men in the first raids on Twin Fords and Settlement. In Turgosheim's Sunside it would have been unthinkable, and here it was a major setback which not even Wratha had anticipated. Of the six of them, Gorvi had been the fortunate one; or . . . could it be that his lieutenant had learned something of the wiles of his master? Whichever, he had survived, and the one thing Gorvi lacked now was a warrior.

Ah, but the makings were to hand in the shape of a procession of dazed Szgany thralls drawn irresistibly out of Sunside and across the boulder plains to the last aerie, all bemoaning their fate even as they came shuffling through the lengthening shadows of the barrier range. The Guile had wasted no time; in the bowels of the stack his vats were seething even now, where altered metamorphic flesh shaped itself to Gorvi's design.

Canker, too (once he'd inspected his get, chosen his men and rutted among his new harem), had set to work at the vats. In just nine or ten sundowns he would have a warrior to beggar the one which he'd lost over the

Great Red Waste! And in thirty more there would be a litter of yelping bloodsons to replace the ones left to their fate in Mangemanse.

And so the Lords had been busy when Wratha's great bats called them to attend her. But since they desired words with the Lady anyway, it seemed as good a time as any.

Gorvi, Wran the Rage and Spiro Killglance took the easy route up from their freshly peopled manses, and landed their flyers in Wratha's spacious bays. Canker and Vasagi the Suck, situated that much closer, climbed the stack's internal staircases of hewn stone and grafted cartilage. However they chose to come, upon arrival they all greeted Wratha in the same way: with surly, suspicious, even angry stares and glances. She had anticipated no less and was ready for them.

'So, all goes reasonably well,' she started without preamble, speaking to them from where she sat in the gaping jaws of a huge bone-throne at the head of a table in the largest of her several halls. 'Our new thralls attend us, and though they are fewer than we bargained for their blood is good and strong and fresh: superior in every way to our get of tithelings in Turgosheim. At least we can all agree on *that*, I think.' The way she expressed herself indicated her presentiment of trouble.

'As far as you go you state hard facts,' Gorvi answered at once, his voice a sly, oily, accusing gurgle. 'Alas, you don't go far enough. And the hardest fact of all is the one you choose not to mention.'

The five were seated with her: Vasagi and Gorvi on one side of the table, Canker and the brothers Killglance on the other. Wratha was dressed in her robe of bat-fur ropes. She had chosen to look like some wanton young Gypsy: precocious, provocative, proud of the power which her sex gave her over men. It was her way of distracting them from their course, their argument. But now she saw that it might not be enough. These Lords had taken their fill of women; for now, there was no lust left in them.

Putting all posing and posturing aside she sat up straight, pulled a wry face and uttered an exaggerated sigh. 'So, here we are,' she said. 'Right at the onset of our great adventure, and already you find something to complain about, Gorvi. Better, I think, if they'd named you Gorvi the Grouch!'

'What you think becomes less important moment to moment!' Gorvi snarled. He stood up and put his knuckles on the table, hunching his shoulders and thrusting his head forward like a great carrion bird. 'Wratha, you are a thief!'

His words seemed to freeze her ... for perhaps a second. Then she reached up and lifted the bone scarp upon her brow, until her eyes were no longer in shadow. And in a moment her image of true life had fallen away and her flesh was grey as undeath. Her nose became ridged and convoluted, with black, flaring nostrils, and her top lip curled back a little in the right-hand corner, displaying a gleaming fang. And:

'A thief?' she hissed.

Before matters could deteriorate further, Vasagi flowed to his feet and put himself between Gorvi and the Lady. The Suck was extremely susceptible to kneblasch – even more so than the others – and knew Wratha's mind and therefore her temper better than them. She considered this her place now; only subject her to too many 'insults' in her own aerie ... she would very likely stink them all right out of here into their sickbeds, so making an end of their complaints. Well, for the moment Vasagi had enough of healing pains. If that bolt which he took in his side last night had been dipped in kneblasch ... even Vasagi, with all of his powers of metamorphism, would have been in trouble then! It didn't bear thinking about.

So, time *now* to make their point – merely that, and delicately if at all possible – so that at least she would see how she had offended. Time *later* for correction, if or when she tried it again. There were five of them, after all, and only one Wratha; it should not be too difficult to take her unawares and so even up the account. And if the instrument of such correction were a crescent of sharp metal to scythe the bitch's head from her neck ... so be it! But for now:

We are all thieves, Vasagi's thoughts were given form by an elaborate, intricate shrug. He fluttered his hands, shaped his fingers into expressive webs, struck a pose and angled his head a little. *It's just that we think it unnecessary to take from one another. Especially in a place like this.*

'The Suck is right,' Wran tweaked the small black wen on the point of his chin. 'Sunside teems, so why poach your colleagues' thralls, eh, Wratha? We converted them, and yet they have come to you. Why, if my brother and I had not been quick to recognize some of them who climbed through our premises on their way to yours, we'd have lost even more! And them with our marks upon them, which are unmistakable.'

'Did you think it solely for your benefit, Lady,' Wran's brother, Spiro put in, 'that we went recruiting last night on Sunside?'

She studied the five sourly, each in his turn – Gorvi and Vasagi on her right, standing – the brothers and Canker on her immediate left, still seated. But her gaze lingered on Canker, whom she believed most easily swayed. 'Well, and have you nothing to say?'

He shrugged, scratched a fretted ear, finally barked:

'I haven't the patience for all this yelping and bickering. Also, I'm weary unto death! But you've kept your promises as far as I can see. There are women now in my kennel, and a new warrior brewing. But if you must know how I feel – well, I'll admit to being a little disappointed.'

'How so?' She was genuinely curious; Canker was a strange one, whose true mind was hard to know.

'Of men,' he answered, his voice a low whine now, 'of lieutenants,' (he shrugged, awkwardly) 'well, I converted a few, not many – but all of them well-fleshed and strong, mind! And now it seems I've lost most of them to you! Wherefore a pat on the head won't suffice, Lady, not this time. If you expect me to fashion you another warrior, like the one I made for you in Turgosheim, then first you'll return my thralls to me.'

'What?' she hissed at him. 'Didn't I warn you against taking too many women?' She jumped to her feet and glared at all of them. 'And how was I supposed to watch your backs and still find time to make changelings of my own? A thief, am I? Is that what you think? Only count my thralls and you'll see who got the better of it. You did, all of you! Now listen: so far I've had time to fuel my creatures, choose my new lieutenants – just two of them – and set about the fashioning of my siphoneers. And how many thralls do I have left, eh? Well, I'll tell you: I have seven! And you, Wran?' She swung to face him. 'What was your get? And you, Gorvi the Greedy?' She spun on her heel. 'How few for you? *Twice* as many, I'll warrant!'

'*But you were the one –*' Wran thundered, his blood beginning to boil, so that he must calm himself before going on, '– who said there'd be no such thing as a tithe, not here in Old Starside. Yet now you make yourself a tithemaster, or mistress, no less than old Vormulac himself in Turgosheim! They were our best which you took,

Wratha, as well you know. Now enough of prevarication, admit your guilt!'

'And what of the provisioning of the stack?' She glared back at him. 'Do you breed gas-beasts or warriors, Wran? *Hah!* I thought so! Never a thought for the rest of us, but you can stand and accuse me. And you, Gorvi: have you fashioned a creature to clean the wells, or is it something else that waxes in your vats? And how *many* things wax there?'

They made no answer but stood there enraged and glowering; all of them, with the sole exception of Vasagi, whose wound was not yet healed. And again looking at each of the vampire Lords in his turn, Wratha saw that she was right: never a thought for the stack in a single head, only for their own well-being. But she saw more than that, for to a man they had reached the end of their tether – where Wratha herself had driven them.

Ah, and these were furious Lords! Despite that they kept their thoughts cloaked, Wratha could read them clearly enough in their scarlet eyes. *They had tasted war and wild, untamed blood, finding both much to their liking. Why stop now? The stack was a big place, true, but bigger still without Wratha! And what was she anyway but a woman?*

She did not like the way Canker looked at her, stripping away her bat-fur robe with his feral dog's eyes; neither that, nor the way in which Gorvi sidled closer. Her hand went inside her robe ... and Vasagi, bobbing wildly and gesticulating like a madman, finally held up a quivering hand.

NOW HOLD! His thought came so hard, a mental shout, that all grew quiet in a moment. But beneath that great blast of a thought were others, which the Suck kept closer to his chest. Cloaked though they were, Wratha could read something of them at least:

Last night after Vasagi had been shot, before the attack on Settlement, Wratha had asked him if he felt capable of further venturings. Knowing he was wounded, she'd taken his condition into account. Oh, he had known that her concern was not for him alone but for the party as a whole: seeing herself as a general, she needed her troops in fine fettle. But still it had been worth something. Also, Vasagi could see the value of an aerie properly maintained and provisioned. Right now the stack was little more than a hollow fang of rock, a pesthole of vampires, but it could become a fortress. In that respect the Lady's ideas were good and sound.

And finally . . . finally Wratha's hand was still inside her robe, where she kept oil of kneblasch in a small bladder, to fill the air with poison. That, too, was worth taking into account, for now at least. But later, when the stack had been put to rights . . .

Gorvi's oily voice broke the uneasy silence. 'Well?' he inquired of no one in particular. But he, too, saw the Lady's hand inside her robe, and wisely he drew back a pace.

Have we come all of this way, Vasagi gestured, *out of the tyranny of Turgosheim, to fight among ourselves?*

'But —' Wran continued to glower at Wratha. Heart pounding and chest heaving, he remained uncomfortably close to raging.

Now listen to me, Vasagi cut him short. *For it seems that I'm the only one who can see what's happening here. We are Wamphyri! And now that the restrictions of Turgosheim are lifted, we are reverting to type. But isn't that why we desired to come here in the first place: to give our leeches full rein? To be as our nature intended us to be?* He paused . . .

. . . And seeing that he had their attention, continued: *Wratha is no thief — but she is Wamphyri! And apart* from this one incident, this one – lapse? – she hasn't put a foot wrong. Well, except in her belief that she could lead us like a warrior Queen. For we're all of us men and warriors in our own right, and as such we resent giving up our hard-earned spoils to any self-styled leader. And I say again: to any leader!

Very well, so from now on we are our own men and Wratha is her own woman. But on the other hand she's right: without that we show a degree of co-operation, the stack can't survive and we are doomed. It is imperative that Gorvi puts the wells in order, that Wran and Spiro service and maintain the refuse pits and methane chambers, and that Wratha fashions siphoneers to draw up water from the wells, for the benefit of the whole stack. To this extent – if only to this extent – we must be of one mind. To this extent, we need each other.

Wran, fingering his wen as before, was calmer now. And: 'I agree all of that,' he said. 'Except –' and he scowled at Wratha, '– she appropriates no more of our thralls!'

Wratha, too, was calm and 'lovely' again. So, she'd lost her army at a stroke. Well, and so what? She could soon build another, and next time loyal in every way. 'So from now on we hunt alone,' she nodded, curtly. 'We attend to the needs of the stack, for everyone's sake, but other than that we fend for ourselves and to hell with the rest! Very well, see if you like it better that way.'

Gorvi had second thoughts. 'But what if we are attacked out of Sunside, or worse, out of Turgosheim? Am I required to hold the lower levels on my own?'

'Oh, we'll be attacked, eventually,' Wratha assured him. 'Though I think not from Sunside. When it comes, once again we stand or fall together. The stack is our refuge; though we may never be friends, we must be allies.'

All the more reason, Vasagi made elegant shrugs and wriggles, *to practise a modicum of co-operation now.*

Spiro, clad in his customary rags of breechclout and headband, took his brother's arm. 'Come,' he said. 'Enough of talk. We have tasks aplenty. But when darkness falls we'll leave our lieutenants to supervise the work, and go raiding for ourselves in Sunside.' He cast a vilifying glance at Wratha. 'Except this time we'll keep what we catch!'

'What of me?' Canker barked. 'Do I get my thralls back?'

'Ungrateful wretch,' Wratha was openly scornful. 'You who have nothing better to do but whine and wench! What's that for co-operation? Best quit your yelping, Canker, if you'd have gas to warm your kennels and clean water to drown your fleas!'

In return, Canker snarled a little and bared his canines, but while Wratha had the kneblasch that was as much as he could do.

And with that it was over. Their courses set – as individuals, as well as interdependent members of the stack – the Lords took their departure from Wratha's apartments. Vasagi was last to leave . . .

On his way down, Vasagi must pass close by the Lady Wratha's draughty landing bays. There he found Wran the Rage waiting for him, still seething like an active volcano. Wran came straight to the point: 'Why did you defend her? We could have been rid of her at a stroke; I would have taken her apartments, and left the ones I share now to my brother.'

She had kneblasch, Vasagi shrugged, gestured, backed off a little. *Also she has commenced to fashion siphoneers. Why waste the Lady's best efforts? Time later to punish her – if such is required – when the* stack is in working order. You agreed as much yourself, if not in so many words.

'It isn't simply that you fancy the whore?' Wran grinned unpleasantly. 'After all, you and she would make a grand team. You with your freakish face, and Wratha a hag under all that sweet girl-flesh! Is that it? Do you hope to partner her? Are you so tired, then, of the shrieks of your odalisques when you go to service them? Do they insist you mount from the rear, so that they need not see your face?'

Vasagi flowed forward now, his gestures sharper, less subtle, his telepathic 'voice' a hiss: *Why do you insult me, Wran? Do you seek to provoke me? I have no chin, it's true, but that is of my choosing. Rather that than your chin, with its black and possibly leprous growth!*

'Now who speaks insults?' Wran thrust his red face to the fore. 'As for my wen: it is a beauty spot.'

Oh? the Suck laughed scornfully. *Then you could use a few more!* But as Wran grunted and stepped closer still, Vasagi's tapering snout stiffened and his sharp siphon proboscis slid into view, dripping saliva. And: *Best to remember,* he warned, *that your gauntlet is in your apartments, Wran. But me, why, I carry my weapon with me at all times!*

Wran knew that Vasagi could strike at lightning speed, to pierce or pluck an eye, or penetrate an ear to the brain. He withdrew, however grudgingly, then turned on his heel and headed for the launching bays. But over his shoulder: 'Let's have one thing understood, wormface,' he snarled. 'Eventually the Lady's options will be down to two: to be *my* most obedient wife in Wranstack, or to die and make room for her betters! If it's the first — I'll *enjoy* cutting the sting out of Wratha's tail, believe me! And if it's the second,' he shrugged, 'so be it.' With that he passed from sight behind a jut of stone.

Not to be outdone, Vasagi sent after him: *Better stick to your girl-thralls, Wran! Wratha's far too much woman for a fop such as you!* His dart was too late; Wran had closed his mind; Vasagi's thoughts came echoing hollowly back to him.

It was probably as well. Wran was a maniac, after all. And shrugging off his irritation, Vasagi continued on his way . . .

II

Nathan stirred. The sun had been off his island for quite a while now and he was cold. The river gurgled close by; a fish jumped for flies, making a splash; the combination of sounds woke him up.

He awoke cold, stiff, aching, and saw in a moment how long – and how late – he'd slept. The sun was a bright flash of fire glimpsed through the treetops to the south; except for silvery glints striking from the river's ripples, its entire expanse stood in green, gloomy shade from bank to bank. Nathan had been asleep for ... *about fifteen hours?*

He waded to the bank and began to backtrack westwards. As he left the boggy region for firmer ground, so something of the stiffness went out of his muscles and a little of the gnawing ache out of his back: Eleni's ointment, he supposed, and wondered where she and the Szgany Sintana were now.

... Jingling along the approach route to their new home, most likely. Tonight they would set up a makeshift camp, and tomorrow camouflage the place, make it semi-permanent, settle in. And if only Nathan could make his legs go a little faster, he would be with them – with Eleni – and have a place among them. In a way he felt like a traitor: to Lardis, to the memory of Misha and his mother, especially to his Szgany vow. But in another way he felt ... new? Certainly he was making a new beginning. And in any case, he knew that as long as he lived his vow would never be entirely forgotten.

In a spot where a beam of slanting sunlight fell

through the riverside foliage, he paused and unfolded Nikha's map. The route didn't seem too difficult: go back to where the Sintanas had made camp, follow the disused trail east by south-east for some fifteen miles, then head south along the bed of a narrow, curving valley in the woods. Where the valley bent westward to follow the course of a stream, there climb a gentle slope onto level ground once more. Finally, still heading south for five or six miles through a broad belt of ironwoods (where with luck Nathan might strike another ancient track), he would come upon the grasslands. By then the woods would be ash, walnut, wild plum, and a few giant ironwoods. And depending upon where he emerged from the declining forest, the Sintana camp should be no more than two or three miles east or west. An accomplished tracker would conceivably follow direct in their footsteps.

That was what Nikha had said, anyway...

Nathan was furious with himself. If he had woken up just three hours earlier there would be no problem. He would be able to see where the wagons left the trail to turn into the forest, the ruts their wheels left in the loamy earth. There would be signs: crushed foliage, broken twigs, beast droppings. But the best of the light was gone now, and as yet he wasn't even back to their first meeting place.

He put on a little speed, loping through the trees parallel with the river until he was winded, then breaking into a stiff walk. Now, too, he began to feel just a little panicked, and he knew that *that* wouldn't help, either.

How far did he have to go: thirty, thirty-five miles? And how long in which to do it? It would be sundown in ... oh, ten to twelve hours. Plenty of time, if he'd been out in the open on a good trail. But in the forest

. . . the light would be failing long before then. Of woodland creatures there wasn't much to fear; but if he got
lost, that would be a problem. His new Traveller friends
would worry about him; at least he supposed, hoped,
that Eleni would. And for his part, he certainly didn't
relish the thought of spending a long, lonely night in the
forest . . .

It seemed a long time – too long by far – but at last
Nathan was forcing his way through the shrubbery onto the old trail, back where he'd first seen the Szgany
Sintana. Breaking camp, they had been careful to cover
their tracks; if he didn't know better, he might not
suspect that anyone had been here at all! Even so, they
hadn't been able to disguise the deep ruts in the overgrown trail, which now he followed east at a steady,
mile-eating lope. And as he went the forest grew up
around him, the light faded, however imperceptibly, and
the long afternoon grew longer . . .

Nathan discovered an ancient and entirely unscientific
fact: that time in short supply diminishes faster than
it is spent. He also found that concentration can be self-
defeating: only do enough of it and sooner or later you
will be concentrating upon your concentration, and not
the matter in hand. His limbs and muscles had grown
accustomed to their continuous, rhythmic effort until the
dull pain of constant motion was very nearly hypnotic.
Indeed it was hypnotic; for suddenly the trail was overgrown, with nowhere a sign to show that men, animals,
vehicles had passed this way . . . because they hadn't!
Despite all his best efforts of concentration, Nathan
had passed the turn-off point without even noticing it.

Again he backtracked – a mile, two – and eventually
discovered the truth: that the Travellers had left the trail
where the soil was thin and the ground full of flints

and pebbles. They had deliberately used the hard, stony earth itself to obscure their tracks and make them that much more difficult to follow; not to discourage Nathan, no, but to confuse anyone else who might come sniffing on their heels.

Going much slower now where the way wound along a narrow, thickly forested gully, he found shad droppings and commenced tracking again, following on until the valley widened out and turned west along the course of a deep, darkly gurgling stream. There, where the earth was stony again, he toiled up a gentle incline between the trees until once more he stood upon level ground. But somewhere along the way he'd lost the trail, and now the light was fading much more rapidly.

By now Nathan had been on the move for some eleven hours and his fatigue was rapidly gaining on him. Under the claustrophobic canopy of the trees his lungs couldn't seem to draw enough air, and with every staggering step his legs felt ready to crumple up under his weight. He needed to rest very badly but knew that he daren't stop. And so he pushed on . . .

Always he headed directly into the sun where its light was most evident in the sky and through the trees. But there were streams to cross, bramble and creeper thickets to negotiate, places where the forest's canopy was so dense as to shut out the light entirely. Until suddenly . . . the light improved a very little, the trees thinned out, lesser shrubs, brambles, undergrowth disappeared under a brittle carpet of poisonous needles. He had found the ironwood groves; but nowhere a sign that the Travellers had come this way, and no track for him to follow. He hurried on, skirted the thicker needle patches and passed safely through the groves.

The trees thinned out more yet; light, what little was left of it, flowed palely into the forest from the south;

the ironwoods gave way to ash, walnut, wild plum. At least Nathan was heading in the right direction. But just when he believed he was through the worst of it, then he felt the sting of a needle sliding through the stitching of his sandal into the ball of his right foot.

Agony! And he must pause a while to draw the thing out. That was a mistake; in just a few minutes of sitting down his muscles stiffened up; from now on he must stumble half-crippled through the gathering twilight. Twilight, yes, and on the rim of the world the sun an orange blister that leaked liquid light onto the cooling deserts. And the forest very still now, where small creatures rustled and the cooing of pigeons was quiet, afraid, and all else was silent . . .

And coming to the edge of the woodlands he looked south across the broad savannah belt, and saw a great wheel or fan in the sky whose spokes were pink, yellow, gold; a wheel that turned, faded, and passed like a rainbow after the rain, when the sun comes out. Except here the opposite was true, for the spokes of the fan were fading rays of sunlight, a reminder of the golden glory that had been. It was sundown, and for a few hours more the land would lie in velvet twilight; stars would come out, glittering over the barrier range; true night would come down like a creeping thing, painting everything the colours of darkness.

Nathan turned his head this way and that, looked east and west in the deceptive light. Which way to go? He cocked his head, listened for a distant, familiar jingle, and heard nothing. But then, he hadn't really expected to. A wind came up and rushed through the woods, making the branches toss and sough. Streamers of cloud rushed south, following the sun. And to the east . . . was that a shout carried on the wind? Or just the shriek of a night-hunting bird?

He limped west a mile, then spied a knoll out on the sea of grass. A further half-mile to the knoll and Nathan was ready to give in, lie down, spend the night there. But he forced himself panting to the top and scanned the land around, and spied in the east at the edge of the forest – a fire? Hardly a bonfire; a dull flicker at best, but better than nothing.

It must be Eleni! Despite Nikha's warning to Nathan, that there'd be no friendly light to guide him after sundown, Eleni had kept a small fire burning. Uplifted, he climbed down again to the plain and started out diagonally across the grasslands in the direction of the fire. And now the going was easy where he swished through tall, windblown grasses under ashen skies, wispy clouds and gathering stars.

But ... the sky was strange tonight; there seemed to be several belts of cloud at various levels; some scudded one way and some another. Directly ahead of Nathan and high above the forest, small black rags of cloud sped north for the mountains and were quickly lost in the deceptive velvet of night.

On the level, the light of the fire was no longer visible. Nathan hurried; he covered a mile, two, and was into his third when he saw the light again. After that, as the nighted forest grew up on his left hand, and a racing moon rose over the distant barrier range to light his way, the beacon eye of the fire shone ever brighter. Until at last he was there.

Where the trees met the prairie he saw the carts and caravans of the Sintanas sheltering under the branches of a trio of mighty ironwoods. Their fire was a welcoming splash of leaping orange and yellow light where it held back the shadows in the triangular space between the trees. It welcomed Nathan ...

... In the same way it had welcomed others, who had been here before him!

He slowed down, reached the clearing, stumbled forward with his bottom jaw slowly lolling open. He smelled a certain odour which the squalling wind had almost but not quite blown away. And Nathan remembered the dark, ragged clouds which the wind had also blown away over the forest, towards the distant Starside pass. And he saw how the doors on the caravans swung to and fro in the eddies, as if they were protesting at their emptiness. The place was . . . deserted?

No, not deserted, just empty. Of life . . .

Nathan couldn't accept it. He looked beyond the caravans where an area had been roped off into animal pens. Everything stood in shadows cast by the guttering firelight and starshine made pale by the wind and the scudding clouds. The animals were lying down, forming low, humped, motionless silhouettes; which should have been evidence enough in itself. Shads rarely lie down, and never in a group . . .

He made his way to a great ironwood where the ground had been swept free of needles to form a small clearing in its own right. But as he paused there and turned in a circle, bloated black shapes like windblown weeds went lumping and fluttering low along the ground into the shadows. He gasped, took a pace to the rear, glanced this way and that as the wind sighed and the branches soughed. And as Nathan's eyes focused so he saw other eyes – like tiny crimson pinpricks – reflected by the fire and glaring back at him from the encircling underbrush.

One of the things, whatever they were, was hiding behind a broken table where it had been tipped on its side, crouching there like a vulture. Nathan stood breathlessly still, paralysed under the great tree, until something made a shrill *chittering* sound in the surrounding darkness ... and was answered from the other side of the circle!

Then, as he gave a start of recognition –

– Something dripped down and splashed against Nathan's forearm where his sleeves were rolled up, and looking down he saw that his arm was red; likewise the ground under his feet. And looking *up* ... he saw the tree's strange ripe fruit, male all three, hanging by their heels with their throats slashed, and the last of their scarlet juices running down their dangling arms to drip into space!

A giant desmodus bat, glutted with blood, released its hold on a drained corpse and fluttered to earth. Too bloated to fly, the creature scuttled and flopped out of sight, joining its companions in the shadows ...

All the demons of hell rode the wind then, shrieking mad with laughter as Nathan staggered to the fire, took up a brand and lit his way to Nikha Sintana's caravan. Inside, the place was a shambles, and outside, at the back ... Nikha lay there with his eyes staring and the halves of his chest laid back, and his heart ripped out of his body for a tidbit!

Now Nathan knew he must look for the others – search for Eleni, and pray she'd run off into the woods – but first there was something else he must do. His blue eyes blazed with a sort of madness when he found oil in a large stone jar on the ground beside Nikha's caravan. Lifting it, he sniffed at the uncovered rim: nut oil, mainly, for cooking. But a little kneblasch, too. Little wonder *they* hadn't wanted it! And carrying the jar back to the slaughter tree, he knew how he must use it.

There under the ironwood, the bloated black familiars of the Wamphyri – more than a dozen of them – had gathered once more in the cleared space to lap like ghouls at the bloodsoaked earth. Keeping well back, Nathan looked at them a moment, shuddered and grimaced. Then without further pause he loped through the underbrush around the perimeter of the great tree, deliberately slopping oil as he went; and when the circle was closed, he tossed his firebrand into the tinder-dry scrub.

The fire crept slowly at first, then with a vengeance as the wind caught it, and finally roared up in a wall of blistering heat and yellow light. Forced back, Nathan laughed, danced, and shook his fists like a madman, which for the moment he was. And: 'Burn, you bastard things, *burn!*' he yelled.

Greedy tongues of fire licked at the lower branches, took hold, and spread into the whole tree. Jets of fire, whipped by the wind, leaped from bough to bough like demon imps, till all three trees blazed up in unison and the heat was an inferno.

Still Nathan danced, and laughed all the louder when the shrill chittering of the bats turned to shrieking and a handful tried to flee the holocaust. Singed and smoking they rose up into view, burst into flames, spiralled down into the furnace under the mighty torch trees. And so they burned . . .

Later, when the wind swung south and blew a widening swath of fire across the grasslands, Nathan's madness passed and he returned to the carts and caravans. Standing to one side of the huge trees and mainly away from the fire, the vehicles had been licked by the flames, blistered by them, then passed by and left intact. Nathan examined them thoroughly . . . and found what he found.

Then, skirting the trio of burning, skeletal trees and the blackened scar of undergrowth, he went into the forest. He knew he was taking a chance, that the wind might easily change again, but he had to search. And searching he discovered, and laboured a while carrying *what* he discovered back to the cleansing fire. Not that these children were going to become vampires – they were mainly pieces, scraps – but it seemed the right thing to do. Nathan knew that Lardis Lidesci would have done it, anyway. As for Nikha's men where they had been bled under the tree: well, the fire had dealt with them. They were still burning where they had fallen, like slow candles slumped upon the earth. And now their leader, Nikha himself, joined them there.

Finally Nathan must see to the women. Dragging them from their various places, he dealt with each in her turn. They had been savaged and raped – no, more than that: they'd been *used* hideously – then vampirized. The skulls of two of them were dented as by terrific blows; while the other two, including Eleni . . .

. . . Nathan could only shake his head in horror and disbelief. There were fist-sized holes to the left of centre in their chests between their breasts, where someone, some*thing*, had thrust its hand into their bodies to nip their hearts. Not to kill them, no, but to stun them. For even now they were alive, or undead.

There was no putting it off, not even for Eleni's sake; especially not for her sake. Lardis had shown Nathan how to do it, and now it was up to him. He did it – did it to Eleni, too – and only at the last felt someone's eyes on him. It was the sole survivor, the youth who had gone fishing in the river, now standing at the edge of the firelight gaunt as a ghost and vacant-eyed, with caved-in cheeks the colour of chalk.

Nathan spoke to him; the youth ignored him. He went to him, took his arm; and the other – a mere boy – snarled at him and bared his teeth. At that Nathan stepped back a little and stared hard at him, very hard; but there wasn't a mark on him, neither bruise nor puncture. He'd simply been ... lucky? If living to witness this could be called luck.

Eventually Nathan left him standing there, watching his world burn. And salvaging a blanket from a caravan, he walked out a little way into the grass at the edge of the scorching, found himself a hollow in the earth and went to sleep. Later, waking up, he looked back and saw the boy standing where he'd left him. He thought to call out, shook his head instead, left the lad to his grief and went back to sleep.

Eight hours later the wind had died away; the fires were smouldering; the ironwoods were blackened corpses of trees at the forest's rim. And the boy was no longer there. Nathan got up and went back to the burned-out place to look for him. And remembering the last time he'd come here, this time he looked up. Sure enough the boy was hanging there, cold and dead.

There was no life in him – not any sort of life – but Nathan couldn't leave him for the crows. He reached up, took hold of his legs and added his own weight. It seemed a cruel thing to do but Nathan was drained of energy; there was none left for climbing, anyway. It worked: the thin rope snapped, and the boy came thumping down.

And now Nathan must build another fire ...

In the middle of the long night, under the coldly glittering stars, Nathan wrapped himself in his blanket, headed south and walked out across the prairie. He never once looked back at the last funeral pyre burning behind him.

He took nothing with him but the blanket, the clothes he was wearing, the leather strap with a half-twist on his left wrist, by which his mother, in what now seemed another world, a different age, had recognized him in the darkest of nights. Because the strap was a familiar thing – his sigil, a token of his identity? – Nathan had kept it through his childhood, replacing it as his wrist thickened first to a boy's, then a youth's, finally a man's. Likewise Nestor: he, too, had kept his wrist band, the straight one, without the half-twist ... but he no longer featured in Nathan's thoughts, except as an echo.

Nothing much featured in his thoughts. Just the faces of the dead: his mother, Misha, Nikha Sintana and his Travellers, Eleni; but all of them fading now as his mind discovered ways to obliterate them. For sometimes a memory – a face or scene out of the past – can be too painful to remember. And Nathan had reached the stage where *all* of his past was much too painful. It was a peculiar thing, but the thought had come to him that a man without a past has very little on which to build a future. Which was why he now walked out across the grasslands into the desert: because he no longer wished for a future.

When he felt tired he sat down, weary he went to sleep, hungry and thirsty he went without. And he knew that while weariness couldn't kill him, deprivation most certainly would: what he had been deprived of, and what he now deprived himself of. That was how he wanted it and how he willed it to be.

There was no bitterness in him; he didn't feel that he was quitting; only that he had never got started and so had nothing to finish, except his life. And even that might not be The End. For of all living men, Nathan knew that death was just another beginning. And maybe then, when his body was dead, all of them who had gone before would talk to him at last and explain the things which he'd never understood in life.

Would he be able to talk to his mother, he wondered, and to all the rest who were lost to him? And if he still couldn't find peace or purpose, would there be other worlds beyond?

The last clump of withered grass was far behind him when the stars began to fade and the first crack of light showed on the horizon. He made straight for it. The stony ground turned to sand under his feet as the sun cleared the shimmering horizon, but Nathan averted his eyes and continued to wander south. Soon he was warm, then hot, finally sweating. It meant nothing to him: just another discomfort, of which he'd had enough. At least this would be the last.

He came to cliffs of sandstone rising out of the desert, and at last looked back. And saw nothing but sand or perhaps, in the far faint distance, a dark wrinkle where blinding blue met dazzling yellow on the shimmering rim of the world. The barrier range? Possibly. But now Nathan had his own barrier to cross. And after that the greatest barrier of all . . .

The sandstone cliffs were high and sheer. Nathan could not climb them so must skirt around, and so proceed towards the sun and his inevitable end. He turned east, walked a mile in the cool shade of the escarpment, and came to a great gash where the cliffs were split open into a gorge. Perhaps at the back he would find a way to climb the cliffs. He entered the gully and followed its wall half a mile to the rear, then in a semicircle, and finally back to the entrance but on the opposite side. He had discovered no way to climb the cliffs, but what did it matter? This would make as good a place as any to die.

He was hungry now and thirsty, more so than he had ever been in his entire life. If there had been food he would eat it, and if there was water he would drink it, naturally. But there wasn't. And no way back to Sunside's forests now; for the sun would sear him in an hour, crush him to the earth in two, and shrivel him to a stick by midday. Which was all according to plan.

Nathan stood in the shade at the foot of the cliffs in the eastern lee of the gorge and looked around. In the otherwise sheer face of the cliff, a narrow ledge or fault climbed diagonally a third of the way to the top. Shading his eyes, he saw the mouths of many caves cut into the cliff where the split in the sandstone petered out. Perhaps this was a natural feature carved by water two or three or ten thousand years ago, in an age when the gulley was a watercourse; or perhaps the caves had been cut by men when the desert was more hospitable. As for now, they could only be homes for lizards and scorpions.

While Nathan thought these things, still they were neither curious nor even conscious thoughts; they were simply the activity of his human brain, which for all his traumas functioned as before. For in fact, even as he considered the origin of the precipitous caves and 'wondered' at their meaning, he couldn't really give a damn. After all, they made no slightest difference to his plan one way or the other.

For his plan was simply to die.

But Nathan had grown cold in the shade and desired to die warm. Stumbling now, he came out from the shadow of the cliffs into the blazing heat of the sun, and stood shivering until it burned through to his bones. Finally he returned to the shade, wrapped himself in his blanket shroud and lay down. And with a stone for a pillow he went to sleep.

With any luck he would not wake up but if he did . . . hopefully it would be to a painless and terminal delirium.

*

Nathan dreamed of the numbers vortex. He floated in black and empty space and the vortex rushed upon him out of the void to sweep him away to other places. But he was determined to stay here and die. He heard the voices of his wolves calling to him out of the spinning core of the maelstrom of numbers, but they were too far away and the din of clashing equations and mutating formulae was too loud; he couldn't make out what they were saying. Something about Misha? About his mother? About death?

Nathan supposed they were commiserating with him, but he didn't need that. 'I know,' he called out into the vortex, and hoped they would hear him and leave him alone to die. 'I know they're dead. It's all right. I . . . I'm going there too.'

The wolf voices became impatient, frantic, angry; finally they snapped at him. But why? Did they consider him a deserter? Or were they angry because he refused to understand? Whichever, the numbers vortex had given up trying to snatch Nathan and was shaking itself to pieces, disintegrating into fractions which it sucked into its own core. It snapped out of existence and left him alone, suspended in his dream.

Or perhaps not quite alone.

Did I hear you talking to . . . to wolves just then? The question startled Nathan. So much so that he shot upright in his blanket, awake!

'What?' He looked all around in the shade of the cliffs, whose shortening shadows told him that he had been asleep for only an hour or so. The voice had been so real, so close, that he felt certain someone must be hiding behind a boulder close by. Or maybe this was that terminal delirium he had hoped for. And less energetically, forcing the word up from a throat dry as the desert itself: 'What?' he croaked again. But of course he was talking to himself, for there was no one there.

Oh, but there is someone here! The 'voice' spoke again in Nathan's mind, from as close a source as before. *Indeed, there are many someones here.*

Many someones ...? The short blond hairs at the back of Nathan's neck stood on end and his skin pricked up in gooseflesh. For now he 'knew' what this was, and where he must be. And of course there would be a great 'many someones' in that beyond world called death: more than all the living in all of Sunside. Indeed, a Great Majority!

Are you dead then? the voice inquired, puzzled. *If so, it's a strange thing. You don't feel dead. But on the other hand, I can't see how you can be alive. I never before spoke with a living creature. Well, not since my own time among the living.*

Nathan had meanwhile stood up: slowly, achingly, as if all the oils of his body were already dried out. But he felt the pain of it, the emptiness of true hunger and the desiccation of thirst. That was what would kill him: his thirst. But he wasn't dead yet, just delirious. He must be, surely. For he knew that the dead shunned him. And yet here was one who spoke to him with no slightest hint of fear or shyness. It was wish fulfilment, nothing more.

For both of us, perhaps, the voice agreed.

Nathan's throat felt raw as freshly slaughtered meat. His lips were cracked, beginning to puff up. He tried to speak, to say: 'What, and did you also desire to speak to the dead?' But only the first three words came out. It made no great difference; the thought was sufficient in itself.

Did I wish to speak to the dead? No, for I can do that already. Being one of them, of course I speak to them. But to be able to speak to one of the living ... ah, that would be a precious gift indeed!

Nathan sat down on a boulder and thought: *I'm delirious!*

But I am not, said the voice. *And I don't think you are, either. And you're certainly not dead. So who are you?*

Nathan looked down at himself, visible, solid, unwavering. He was real. The voice in his head was the unreal thing. Surely it should be answering the question who are you?

First and foremost, I am Thyre, said the voice at once. *But I see that you doubt my presence. You believe me to be a figment of your own imagination.*

Nathan forced spittle down into his throat for lubrication. 'Your name is Thyre?'

My name is a secret, to any creature who is not Thyre. My race is Thyre. I am – or was – of the desert folk. But you are not. I perceive now that you are Szgany, of the forest and hill folk. You can only be, for if you were Wamphyri, then by now the sun must have melted you away. And the trogs likewise prefer their darkness. So, what is your *name?*

Again Nathan looked all around, satisfying himself that no one was playing some grotesque, macabre trick on him. 'I'm called Nathan,' he finally answered, speaking more to himself than the unbodied presence, and thinking: *how strange, to be a presence without a body!* While out loud: 'Nathan Kiklu, of the Szgany Lidesci.'

And you came here to die? Ah, yes, I know! For I've been listening to your thoughts for some little time. But when you talked to wolves, and them so far away ... then I knew I must speak to you. For even though you are Szgany, still you have the secret talent of the Thyre!

A talent? Nathan wondered.

To speak mind to mind with other creatures – telepathy!

'Or to mumble and mutter to myself,' Nathan said out loud, nodding wryly. 'Delirium – or madness!' But at the same time he knew that it was partly true. How often had he listened to the whispers of dead people in his dreams, and sometimes when he was wide awake? And what of the thing he used to have with Nestor? Or had all of that, too, been madness?

To which the voice answered: *And am I also mad?*

'Not mad,' Nathan shook his head, 'but probably not real, either. You're a mirage, heat haze over a tar pit, an hallucination. When I was a child and ate toadstools, I saw things which weren't there. Now, because I'm hungry, hot and thirsty, I've started to hear things which aren't there.'

Wrong, said the other. *For I can prove that I am. Or if not that, I can at least prove that I was.*

'You don't have to prove anything,' Nathan shook his head. 'I only want you to go away. I have to sleep and not wake up.'

Oh, you'll do that soon enough, if you don't let me help you!

Nathan was curious despite himself. 'Why should you want to help me? What am I to you?'

A boon! said the other at once. *A miracle! A light in the darkness of death! The chance to exchange thoughts, knowledge, legends, with living Thyre! That is what you are to me! There were others before you who spoke to dead men; they dwelled in Starside and talked to the spirits of Szgany and trogs. They didn't come here and in the end never could, because by then they were Wamphyri!*

Nathan nodded. 'I've heard that: that sometimes among the Wamphyri there would be a necromancer.'

What? The other was aghast. *No, no – not that! The ones of which I speak merely talked to the dead; they were beloved of the dead; they didn't torture them!*

Beloved of the dead? But hadn't Nathan heard that expression before, as used by Lardis Lidesci in respect of certain hell-landers he'd known? The old Lidesci had never been too explicit with regard to The Dweller and his father, however, and had always spoken of them in hushed tones. It was a subject Nathan might like to pursue, but suddenly . . .

. . . His senses were spinning! He swayed dizzily, staggered, and sat down with a bump. He pictured himself standing under a waterfall, letting the water flow over him. It was an entirely involuntary thing: an instinctive longing for old, irretrievable pleasures. But it was easy to see how, under extremes of deprivation, a man's mind might turn to the conjuring of false comforts in his final hours. Except in Nathan's case, his mind seemed to have called up a personal devil to torment him!

So that in answer to what this – this what? mental mirage? – had just said to him, he croakingly replied: 'Why does the idea of the living torturing the dead shock you so? Can't you see how you've reversed the process, so that now the dead torture the living? But for you I would be sleeping my last sleep, dying. And you are keeping me from it, prolonging it, making it worse.'

The other was horrified at Nathan's determination. *What has brought you to this? The most precious thing any creature can have is life. And you, so young, reject it? The abnegation of all earthly responsibility? Best be warned, Nathan: give up your place among the living – go willingly to an unnecessary death – and you'll find no solace among the Great Majority. What extreme is this you've been driven to, and why?*

Nathan took his head in his hands and stared at the sand between his feet, and despite himself the events of the recent past were mirrored in the eye of his mind, where his inquisitor saw them. So that in a little while:

In the Thyre there is no urge for vengeance. The 'voice' was quieter now. *When we are hurt we move away from it, and never go back there.*

'So would I,' Nathan told him. 'If you would let me.'

But in the Szgany (the other ignored him), *there is this deep-seated need for revenge upon an enemy. Just as there was in you. So what happened to it?*

'My vow against the Wamphyri? Perhaps I saw its futility: they are indestructible. But I am Szgany, and if I've allowed my vow to die within me, then I might as well follow it into oblivion. No great loss, for what use is a man who can't even honour his own vow?'

Self-pity? (The shake of an incorporeal head.) *And in any case, you are mistaken. What, you? No great loss, did you say? But you must believe me when I tell you that you would be the greatest loss of all! As for the Wamphyri: they are not indestructible. They were destroyed, upon a time, some of them. And by others like yourself. And . . . I perceive . . . that what was in those others is also in you! You thought I spoke of necromancy, but you were wrong. There have been – will always be – necromancers among the Wamphyri, that is true. But these were men who talked to the dead before you, Nathan! By no means ordinary men, no, but certainly not necromancers! Neither are you a necromancer. But you are . . . a Necroscope!*

Nathan had given up answering with his voice. He didn't need to, anyway. *Necroscope? I don't know the word.*

Neither did I! It is one of their words. As I am Thyre and you are Szgany, and the great vampire Lords are Wamphyri, so they were Necroscopes. And so are you. Its meaning is simple: you talk to the dead. And I am the dead proof of it.

Then why don't they talk to me in return? Nathan's

question seemed perfectly logical. *I mean the Szgany, of course. Why don't the dead of my own kind talk to me?*

Perhaps later there will be time to ask them, the other told him. *Some of them, your people, have spoken to me from time to time; those of them who have graves at least. But you Szgany have strange ways: you've burned so many of your dead, and when they are burned it is that much harder. Harder still if their ashes are scattered. Perhaps that is why your people scatter the ashes of vampires: to deny them even the slightest chance of some monstrous nether-existence.*

'I suppose it is,' Nathan answered thoughtfully, reverting to the use of his physical voice again, which after all came more naturally to him. 'But what of the Thyre when they die? What is their lot?'

We are not put down into the darkness of the earth but elevated, the other told him. *Neither are we scattered but gathered together. Eventually we are dust, but not for long and long . . .* He paused, and in the next moment suddenly gasped: *Ah, you see! Proof that you are a Necroscope! You asked me a question whose answer is a great secret, and yet I made no complaint but merely answered you. For I know that you are good and would never torment me, or use the knowledge to any evil advantage.*

'What knowledge?'

Of the last resting places of the Thyre.

'But you've said nothing, only that they are brought up instead of being put down. I didn't even understand you.'

You would understand if you tried to, the other insisted. *You Travellers live on the surface, in the woods and hills of Sunside, and when you die you are put down into the earth. Or you were upon a time, until recently. And you would be again, if the Wamphyri should be driven out or destroyed. You spend your lives in the air and the light, and your deaths in the earth and the dark. But among the Thyre the opposite is the case. Our lives —*

'— Are spent in the earth?' Nathan finished it for him. 'And your deaths . . . where?'

You have seen the place, the other answered, reverently. *One of the places, at least. One of many such places.*

A picture formed in Nathan's mind, which he recognized at once. He looked up, at the stairway cut into the precipitous sandstone cliffs, and the gloomy mouths of caves leading off from it into unknown darkness. 'The tombs of the Thyre?'

Indeed, and much more than that. For this is one of the places where our world enters yours.

Which was something else Nathan didn't understand. He thought back on what he knew of the desert folk: very little, actually. Only that they were thought of as primitive nomads who wandered at the edge of the furnace desert and occasionally crossed the grasslands to trade with the Szgany. It had always been assumed that they lived above ground, perhaps in caves or tents, but apparently . . . and there he got a grip of himself. For without even realizing it, suddenly he had begun to believe.

That I am real, an incorporeal mind? That I was real, upon a time? But didn't I say that I could prove it? Well, and the proof lies up there.

Nathan was tempted, but he was also sceptical. Was this really the mind of some dead creature, or was it his own mind trying to provoke him into a futile attempt at saving his life? 'Are you telling me that your bones — your remains — are up there?'

Yes.

Though it was something of an effort, and probably wasted at that, Nathan stood up again. And knowing that it would take a far greater effort to climb the sandstone stairs, nevertheless he made his way to the foot of the cliffs and looked up at the mouths of the caves.

The place is sacred, the Thyre voice sighed in his mind. *Only go there and my people will know, and eventually come to see what you are about. In this way you can save yourself.*

'But if it's a sacred place,' Nathan answered, starting up the steep climb, 'surely they'll kill me?'

The Thyre don't kill.

'Then they'll chase me away, or carry me into the desert to die.' Suddenly giddy, he closed his eyes for a moment and clutched at the sheer face.

In which case you have nothing to lose, said the other, grimly, *since that is why you came here.* But then, knowing his answer had been cruel: *No, they won't harm you in any way. Not if you tell them you were speaking to me. Not if you speak my secret name!*

Already a third of the way to the top, Nathan dragged one leaden foot after the next up the ancient stairway. The ledge was narrow and the sandstone badly weathered. One slip ... and none of this would matter anyway. 'But I don't know your secret name,' he said.

It is Rogei. Ro-gay. Now you know it.

'You have a good deal of faith in me, I can tell,' Nathan told him. 'Perhaps more than I have in myself. And I thank you, Rogei, for telling me your secret name. But can you also tell me why it was secret?'

It is our way. The other offered an unbodied shrug, which Nathan sensed. *In life all of the Thyre are telepathic, among themselves and sometimes with the creatures of the desert, too. Yes, and very rarely we may* even 'hear' one of you Szgany whose mind is similarly gifted – like you, Nathan. And very often we hear the great shouted thoughts of the Wamphyri! But unlike the Szgany we don't fear them, for they would never come into these lands which are closest to the sun. Being telepathic our minds are open, yet we would remain private unto ourselves. Wherefore our secret names are known only to those who are closest to us. This way, if a person does not know your name he won't pry. And thus we remain individuals. It is our way, and that is my best explanation.

'I think I understand,' Nathan said. 'Your secret names protect your privacy.'

That is correct. But . . . be careful!!!

Almost at the top of his climb, Nathan's foot had slipped and he had very nearly fallen. He clutched at a knob of projecting sandstone, regained his balance and clasped himself to the sheer face. And even without lungs, still Rogei gave a sigh of relief:

What, and are you trying to frighten a dead creature out of his wits?

Nathan shook his head, stilled his trembling, and gradually straightened up. 'No need to be . . . to be frightened on my behalf, Rogei,' he gasped, his words a tortured rasp. 'Do you see what has happened? I stopped myself from falling. Just an hour ago I thought I wanted to die and might even have been glad to fall; but having spoken to you – perhaps there's some purpose to my life after all. Anyway, I no longer wish to die. I only hope my living will prove to be worth it.'

For my purposes it will be, certainly! (The other was eager.) For through you – only through you, Nathan – I can talk to my children, to their children, and theirs, and know what is become of them in the land of the living. I will talk to all the Elders of the people, and *explain to them the truth of our world beyond life; they always suspected it but had no proof. Now they shall have proof! And I can tell them the secrets of this place, so that when their time is come they won't fear it. All through you, Nathan, only through you.*

Nathan had reached the place where the ledge became horizontal and stood in the entrance to the first cave. 'Secrets? In death? But ... what can there be to know? Immobile, incorporeal, doomed to everlasting darkness, what do the dead *do* in their afterlife?'

But that is one of the secrets! His dead friend answered at once. *However, since you are the Necroscope, I can tell you. I must, for who else can I tell? Ah, and these are things which I have longed to say! Now listen:*

Whatever a man was, thought, and did in life, so he continues to be, think, and do in death. The storytellers make up new stories, which they can only ever tell to the dead. And I have heard some wonderful stories, Nathan! Great thinkers and philosophers — of which, in all modesty, I was one — pursue their thoughts and beliefs to logical conclusions, then exchange their ideas with others of similar leanings. The mystics among us think the deepest, subtlest thoughts of all, and may not be disturbed where their minds fly out beyond the world's rim; by which I mean they are lost in their own conjecturings. In life, I had a friend who fashioned leather buckets for the wells; now he designs the most wonderful machines, driven by the rivers of the underworld itself, to carry precious water into all the caverns under the desert!

'You have purpose, then,' Nathan nodded. 'Yes, and you achieve.'

But of what use achievements which bring no benefits? The other drove home his point. *Don't you see?*

Through you we can pass on this secret knowledge — which is only secret because we have no way to tell it — to all of those we left behind! And so you, too, may achieve and have a purpose.

Nathan had gone a little way into the first cave. It was more a tunnel, narrow and low-ceilinged, so that he must bend his back. In there, it had quickly grown dark and cold. Uncertain, he paused and felt Rogei looking through his eyes, even as his brother Nestor had once been able to look through them. And: *Stop!* the other cautioned. *This is not the Cavern of the Ancients. The entrance is the next cave but one. You will know it from its ornamentation.*

Retracing his steps, Nathan groped his way backwards out of the cave into sunlight. Almost spent, his thirst was a constant agony; each rasping breath he took sucked more moisture out of his throat, his entire body. Turning, he looked out and down at the gully's rocky floor ... an error; the world seemed to rotate and his head swam dangerously! He went to all fours, waited until he'd regained his balance, then crawled the rest of the way along the ledge to the entrance of the unman fane.

Unman? Rogei queried. Yes, there have been times when we were called that by the Szgany. For they consider that of all thinking creatures, they alone are the true men. Nathan sensed a shrug. *But then, so do the trogs! Aye, and so do the Thyre, I suppose. We all have our pride; but pride is only one thing, and we are alike in more ways than one. The main difference is this: that in our becoming, we followed different paths.*

Nathan could no longer speak; his thoughts had to speak for themselves. *I mean no insult,* he said, *but there's no help for it. Each and every thought I think, you hear it — everything! There's nothing I can hide from you.*

He sensed the other's nod of understanding. *It seems unfair, I know. But I was born with my telepathy and practised it all my days, while in you it is a fledgeling thing. And as a Necroscope you are likewise a novice. But these are skills which may well grow in you with time.*

Nathan snorted, perhaps bitterly. *Granted, that is, that time is on my side!*

Rogei continued to sense his needs. *Of food there is none. But water ... there may be a little. Except you must get to it.*

In here? Nathan looked at the cave's entrance, much larger than the others.

Perhaps, but deep inside, a long way. And that delirium you so desired is much closer now. Rogei's mental voice despaired. *I can feel the flickering of your flame.*

It would be a shame, Nathan thought wanderingly, *to die now when I no longer want to!* He stood up, leaned against the arched entrance to the cave, peered with swimming eyes at its weathered carvings. The bas-reliefs were almost as old as the desert and sand-blasted to obscurity, but his trembling fingers could follow their still flowing contours in the stone.

And for the first time he knew something of awe to match the sensation he had known when he stood on the crater rim of the Starside Gate. From out of the cave, an aura of antiquity flowed over him; from unsuspected deeps a cool breath of air carried a not unpleasant musk and a hint, the merest suggestion ... of moisture?

Water, yes, but deep down below, Rogei said again. *Beyond the Cavern of the Ancients. Come in, Nathan Kiklu, Necroscope. We welcome you.*

From some secret inner well, Nathan forced the last drop of spit down his throat, and with it croaked: 'We?

How many of you? And why are you the only one who has spoken to me?' Staggering out of the glaring sunlight into the cool shade, for a moment he was blind, but in the next he saw the walls of the tunnel extending before him into deepening gloom.

When we sensed your presence and heard your thoughts and dreams (Rogei answered, from very much closer now), *and when we heard how you spoke to wolves so far away – which was not a dream – then we decided upon a spokesman. Since it seemed you were Szgany, and since in my life I occasionally had dealings with the so-called Travellers, I, Rogei, was honoured.*

Nathan leaned forward until he felt he was falling. Then, mustering his feet into reluctant life, he went weaving, stumbling down the high, wide tunnel. Weightless, it seemed as if he floated from wall to wall. But for all that his body was suddenly light, he knew that in fact he was sinking, and each step threatened to be his last. *I feel . . . that I should rest now,* he thought. *I feel I should rest for a very long time. Except now that it's time, I'm afraid to do it.*

Then don't! Rogei's mental voice was vibrant with alarm. *Take it from us, Nathan: while death is not the desert which living men believe it to be, life by comparison is an oasis!*

Nathan nodded deliriously. *But this oasis is drying up.*

The passage widened out, became a cave, a cavern. Nathan entered from gloom into light and fell to his knees in drifted dust. Lolling there, knuckles on the floor, shoulders slumped and head swaying, he knew that this could only be the Cavern of the Ancients, a Thyre mausoleum. And from the look of it, it was probably the greatest of them all.

He craned his neck to look up.

Across the centre of the sandstone ceiling wall to wall, set into the yellow rock like the slit pupil of a cat's eye, a gash of white quartz seemed carved from light. The cavern was riven right across its width, which was huge, but the seepage of centuries had filled the gap with crystals which had hardened to stone. Crystal stalactites hung from the ceiling, and glowing humps of it like shining candles reached up from the floor. And all around its perimeter – in alcoves and niches, on shelves and ledges carved from the stone itself – lay the mummied ancients of the Thyre, whose socket eyes gazed back at Nathan where he observed them.

And: 'Here I am,' he croaked, rolling over onto his back, surrendering to the weirdness of it all without further question.

Again Rogei was anxious for him, telling him: *Nathan, you may sleep, but you may not die!*

Oh? he thought back. *And will you stop me again? It might not be so easy a second time.*

Brothers! Rogei cried out, this time speaking to his dead companions and not to Nathan. *And were we not right? Only feel the warmth of his thoughts? Is he not a light in the darkness? We dare not let him die!* And they knew that he was right.

The massed voices of more than a hundred dead Thyre rose up in a tumult at first, and sighed like a wind in his strange mind: *Nathaaan!* But they soon saw the error of that and began to speak as individuals, so that shortly he could distinguish them one from another:

You must not die, Nathaaan . . .

Rogei is riiight . . .

Szgany youth, you are the light. Continue to shine for us, Nathaaan . . .

You are like a bridge between worlds, Necroscope: should you fall, one world is cut off foreeever!

On and on, so many of them . . .

Much like Nathan's own thoughts, those of the dead Thyre were warm as blankets; they wrapped him where he lay. And with their warmth surrounding him, comforting him, he began to drift into sleep. But Rogei was concerned that Nathan might possibly drift *beyond* sleep, and even in death the anxiety of the Thyre spokesman was such that it gnawed at him. He must be sure, and take whatever measures must be taken.

Nathan thought he heard a groaning of antique leather and a clatter as of dry sticks rattling together. It was a curious sound, but not enough to lure him back from what might well be his last sleep. Neither was the hand which at the last clasped his hand. They were small and shrivelled, those fingers, cool and dry . . . and dead. But the thoughts which accompanied them were warm, so that Nathan was not afraid, as other men would, assuredly, have been.

The final proof, Nathan Kiklu, Rogei whispered, his awed voice trembling with the wonder of it. *A secret which not even I knew! And now rest, Nathan, rest.*

Aye, rest, Nathaaan, the others sighed in unison from their many niches and benches in the walls. *Your flame is strong and will not die. But should the spark burn low, we will be here to blow on the embers. And so you may sleep, Necroscope, sleep . . .*

III

The Thyre were not people to desert their dead and leave them unguarded against scavengers; a fox or mangy dog might wander here from the grasslands, or a vulture discover the way in. But as Rogei had been well aware from the start, the Cavern of the Ancients was a natural sounding-chamber. Only let a footfall sound within – the snuffle of a beast's snout, the tearing of old leather or breaking of centuried bones – and its echoes would find their way below.

Down there, beyond a labyrinth of natural and carved passageways, caves and grottoes, the guardian of the place already knew there was an intruder. Nathan's rasping words, 'Here I am,' had thundered down to him like the shout of a giant; the *slap, slap, slap* of his sandalled feet had reverberated, and . . . there had been other sounds, more dreadful sounds. Plainly the ancients were discovered and molested.

Throughout his long watch the guardian, out of respect for his ancestors, had sat in an antechamber within sight of the sacred cavern. He had not entered it, for even the dust was fashioned of men and thus holy. Towards the end of his watch, hearing the signal trill of a whistle blown far, far below, he had set out to meet his relief half-way. But now, before they could even come together, exchange a few words of greeting and pass each other by, there was this: an intruder had entered the Cavern of the Ancients. Worse, a human intruder, but not of the Thyre breed of humanity.

Whistling an alarm, a shrill warning which he knew

would be taken up by his relief and passed back into the more populated underworld, and sending a thought – *Someone has entered the Cavern of the Ancients!* – the guardian turned on his heel and sped back silently the way he had come, along a well-worn path climbing through bedrock, limestone, finally into the upper sandstone. And approaching the sacred cavern, he fitted a long arrow to his bow.

All was silent now; the intruder was still; perhaps he had heard the guardian coming and was lying in ambush! The guardian went cautiously, allowed time for the huge green pupils of his eyes to shrink commensurate to the light in the quartz chamber, and finally entered. He stood stock still, bowstring drawn and arrow pointing ahead, and saw . . .

. . . A man – the intruder, Szgany! – collapsed there on the floor, but not alone. For with him lay a harmless old mummied thing, a clutter of rags and old bones. It was one of the ancients. Desecration!

The guardian crept closer and aimed his arrow directly at the young man's heart. He did not know him, but he knew that he should die – for what he had done to the old one, whose smallest bones lay scattered in a thin trail across the dusty floor. The Thyre do not kill men, but this one *should* die! Except . . . what *had* been done here?

The two were together, sprawled, feet pointing away from each other, right hands touching, indeed clasped. One of them was very dead and had been for, oh, a long time, and the other one was not quite dead. But the Thyre guardian was a skilful tracker who hunted in the desert and often at night, and the tracks in the Cavern of the Ancients were plain for any man to see. The dust lay thick and mainly undisturbed, and the guardian could not be mistaken.

And putting up his bow he backed off, walking slowly and in his own tracks, and returned to the ante-chamber to wait for his relief and others of the Thyre, by now alerted. And on his way out, he could not take his eyes off the tracks in the dust of the chamber: one set of footprints coming from the passage to the outside world and leading to where the Szgany youth had fallen to the floor, and the other . . . was scarcely a trail at all. Just a few scuff marks in the dust, where something light and thin had dragged itself towards the fallen youth, shedding its bones as it went . . .

Time to wake up!

Nathan heard the 'voice', so much like spoken words that he couldn't differentiate, and felt a gentle hand on his shoulder, shaking him awake. For a moment he thought it must be his mother, come to get him out of his bed; it had the same kind of warmth. But then, all of the voices which had tried to speak to him recently had been like that. He remembered them very dimly, as if he had dreamed them: their careful probing and question-ing. Only that, with nothing of any detail, except that they had all been warm.

But as he stirred and mumblingly protested his awak-ening, and the void of his mind began to come alive with true memories, Nathan knew that this couldn't be Nana Kiklu's voice for she was dead. At which, acti-vated by the sad thought, the cool hand at once trans-ferred from his shoulder to his brow, where it smoothed away the furrows with gentle strokings.

'And now you hear me,' the voice said – actually *said* it – a throaty rasp which nevertheless conveyed both a nod and a smile. A female voice. That of a Thyre female! And all of Nathan's memories came flooding back at once.

Even as he gasped, lifted his head and opened his eyes, so the hand moved to cover them. And: 'Don't start so!' the husky voice chided. 'There's nothing harmful here. But . . . it will be strange,' she warned.

Nathan tried not to swallow and was reluctant to test his voice; but he must, for his question was instinctive. 'Where am I?' Then: relief as the words came out without pain! His throat was moist, flexible, responsive. Which prompted a second question: 'How long was I asleep?'

'Sleep?' she said, slowly removing her hand, knowing now that *he* knew she was not one of his own. 'Is that what it was? More like death's doorway, Nathan – and you upon the threshold! But now you are in the Place-Under-the-Yellow-Cliffs.'

He looked at her . . . and looked away, beyond her. In a way the experience was shocking, in that he had never before seen a living female of the Thyre and had not known what to expect, but in another it was less strange than when he was with his wolves. At least his nurse was – what, human? Well, not animal, anyway. Never a wild creature. Nathan checked himself: that was a line of thought he'd do well to avoid. What had Rogei told him: that even trogs consider themselves true men? This Thyre female *was* human, of a sort. It was just that she wasn't Szgany. Another line of thought best avoided.

And so he looked at the Thyre female again; also at the – room? – in which he now found himself. And she was right: his surroundings *were* strange! He must give his mind time to absorb them, and slowly.

Seated on a stool beside his bed, the . . . *girl* was alert and her demeanour erect, graceful, somehow regal. Nathan saw that standing she would be quite tall. Her youth shone out of her eyes: young eyes are self-apparent in all creatures; they shine and have a brilliant clarity. She was also brown as the kernel of a freshly cracked nut but not at all wrinkled, and like all of the Thyre she was slender to the point of emaciation. The highly sensitive pupils of her large eyes were lemon green against a background of olive irises, and were shaded by the horny ridges of her eyebrows.

She wore a red skirt and sandals, nothing else. Her small breasts were loose, pear-shaped, slightly pendulous; not at all 'deflated paps', which was how Nathan had heard Lardis Lidesci describe the breasts of trogs. Her ears were large, her mouth and chin small, her nose wide and flattened, with dark flaring nostrils. The odour of her body was a light musk, but she also carried a pleasing scent of lemons.

'Is there something?' she said, tilting her head a little. And Nathan was surprised to recognize the source of the sweet lemon smell: it was her breath. Somehow, he had not expected it to be so clean and refreshing. But ... if she was reading his thoughts that, too, was one which she might easily find offensive.

He sighed and shook his head. 'Nothing I think comes out the way it was intended,' he said. 'Each time I give my brain free rein it issues insults which then require apologies. I'm sorry.'

'But your thoughts are your own,' she told him, seemingly taken aback. 'I would not enter unless it was necessary. That is an unspoken rule. You, too, have the talent. And would you come into my mind uninvited?'

'Rogei said much the same thing,' Nathan answered, 'that I was gifted. He said it might grow in me. But right now your mind is a blank to me. When I was young I would sometimes read my brother's mind, and ... I have a knack with certain wolves of the wild. But I am not a telepath.' He shook his head.

'You will be,' she said. And then, obviously curious:

'But this ... Rogei? Who is he? And for that matter, how do you know that the Thyre are telepathic? That is one secret which we have kept well. Or so we thought.'

Nathan was cautious. It might – just might – have been delirium, all of it. But if so his feverish mind had forecast all of this with remarkable accuracy. And so it seemed he must accept what had taken place as fact: he had indeed talked to a dead creature (no, a dead 'man'), and so discovered the things he knew about the Thyre. He was ... a Necroscope? That being the case, it seemed Rogei had supplied him with a real reason for living; the Thyre Ancient had not only saved his life but had given it meaning – but had also made it meaning*less*, if he couldn't pass the knowledge on.

'Rogei is the one who told me about your telepathy,' he finally answered, aware that she was listening intently and sitting up that much straighter. 'He demonstrated it to me. Except his talent is different now. As Rogei has suffered ... a change, so has his telepathy, which in turn allows me the use of my talent. For where the Thyre mind-talk with the living, I ...'

'Yes?'

'... What is your name?' He stalled.

'That is a secret!'

'Of course it is,' Nathan sighed, shrugged. 'And so are the things which you have asked me. But you've been my nurse and I thought that made us friends.'

She understood his comment: faith and trust is a two-way system or it doesn't work. 'My name is Atwei – At-we-ay. Now then, who is Rogei?'

Nathan took a deep breath. 'Rogei's body lies in the Cavern of the Ancients, Atwei,' he said. 'He was Thyre. Now he *is* an Ancient! And I ... am a Necroscope and talk to dead people. My talent lets me talk to the dead of the Thyre.'

If Atwei was surprised it scarcely showed. Nodding, she answered quietly: 'There are desert folk who practise such an art. They are a far-away tribe, not Thyre, and do other things which are unseemly. Once, when they would spread into the lands of the Thyre, they made war with us; their warriors invaded our colonies under the earth. The Thyre trapped them there, opened floodgates and drowned them all. Since when they have sent no more armies against us and we no longer kill men, for the mind-cries of the dying are awful! Instead, they are satisfied with their lands beyond the Great Red Waste and the Last Mountains. They are called necromancers, after that art which they use to torture the dead for their secrets.'

'Rogei the Ancient called me a Necroscope,' Nathan told her. 'He knew the word from the dead of the Szgany, with whom he had spoken mind to mind as you speak to the living. Upon a time, not long ago, the Szgany had known just such men as I am. They were not necromancers and neither am I. I've tortured no one, Atwei, neither the living nor the dead. But if you're not convinced, only look inside my head. It is that I *hear* the dead whispering in their graves, and on occasion they hear me. Rogei was one of them who heard and talked to me. He saw that I had problems and guided me to the Cavern of the Ancients.'

She nodded. 'So, you are not deranged. The Thyre elders have read certain of these things in your mind. They could not be sure but thought you might be mad. If what you say is true, plainly you are sane and have a weird, unique talent. And who am I to decide if it is for good or for evil?'

Nathan frowned. 'It seems I remember something of that: voices which questioned me while I slept. About the Cavern of the Ancients and what happened there.

Also about my past. But ... did I invite them into my mind? I don't think so. Which is strange, for as I recall you mentioned an unspoken rule. Also, you awakened me with a mind-call! Do you make and break these rules of yours so easily then, Atwei?'

She drew back from him. 'But several strange things had happened, and there were matters which the elders required to understand. At first it seemed you might not live. Before you could die, it was *necessary* that they look into your mind. As for myself: how could I determine your progress, without that I first inquire within?'

He nodded but this time made no apology. 'And did they get what they wanted, the elders?'

'Not everything. Your mind is closed to the past, locking out all of the pain which lurks there. There is a great deal of pain in you.'

'I no longer feel it.'

'Because it *is* locked out – or in! This is not a physical thing, Nathan.'

He changed the subject. 'What will become of me?'

'That is for the elders.'

'Then you should call them, or take me to them.'

'I have called them and they will come, soon. Before then you should eat. Will you eat with me?' She seemed eager now to make up for any possible misunderstandings. And after all, she had told him her name.

'Here?'

'Oh, yes. For it will be a while before you can get up. A long day has passed, and a night. Up above, the sun is freshly risen. And all while you have lain here.'

An entire cycle! Nathan thought, easing his bones a little and stretching in his bed. But he wasn't surprised: it felt at least that and more. And Atwei was right: he was hungry. 'I'll gladly eat with you,' he told her.

'Food has been prepared,' Atwei nodded, stood up, backed away and out through an archway. 'I shall return.' Left alone, he studied his surroundings.

The place where Nathan lay was a cave. Despite its rudimentary furniture, whitewashed walls, and crude mosaic floor of white and green flagstones, which gave it something of a room's appearance and made it habitable, it was still a cave. Central in the high ceiling, an irregular shaft three feet in diameter and possibly artificial ascended out of sight. But in an apparently subterranean room without windows, the most surprising features were the light and the warmth.

Down through the shaft in the ceiling streamed a beam of light, catching drifting dust motes in its ray in exactly the same way as sunlight coming into a barn through a gapped roof. Not solid sunlight, no, but light diffused and scattered, so that it emerged into the room almost as a haze. And falling onto a table near the foot of Nathan's crude wooden bed, the beam or shaft of soft yellow light struck against polished mirrors of gold to further permeate the room.

While Rogei had caused Nathan to believe that the Thyre colonies went deep indeed, as yet he had no idea how far he'd actually been carried underground. With sunlight like this to warm and light the place, however, he was sure it couldn't be far. Perhaps there were passageways leading from the Cavern of the Ancients to caves in the foot of the cliffs. In that case the shaft of light was nothing more than sunlight penetrating through some ancient chimney, and the warmth was residual of the desert.

Wrong! said a voice in his head, one which he recognized at once as Rogei's. *The Place-Under-the-Yellow-Cliffs is very deep, Nathan. But the temperature in the Thyre colonies is a constant. It is a natural thing and a*

504

great many of the caves under the desert are like this. Why would we dwell in the cold places, or for that matter the hot ones, when so many temperate labyrinth systems exist for our habitation?

Used to this thing now, Nathan sat up in his bed. He saw that under his quilt of furs he was naked. His clothes, washed and mended, lay folded on a shelf at one side of the room. Now, with some effort — leaving his bed and dressing himself on the one hand, and on the other concentrating upon Rogei — he said: 'Well, it appears you were right. I was rescued from the Cavern of the Ancients and brought here. And now the elders are coming to question me.'

Like me, Rogei answered, they've waited patiently for you to wake up. But you must be careful how you answer their questions. They demand respect, elders, and until you prove otherwise they will doubtless accuse you of desecration. Merely to enter a forbidden place is bad enough; and as for the rest of it ... Nathan sensed the other's shrug.

'The rest of what?' He was mystified. 'You welcomed me in and I entered; I could go no further and collapsed; I spoke to the old ones dead in their niches and upon their shelves. Then, at the end, I dreamed you came to me and comforted me.'

And touched you? Took your hand in mine?

'Yes.'

No dream that, Nathan.

'I don't understand.'

Probably as well, for the time being. Anyway, all is back to rights now.

Nathan frowned but didn't press him; there were too many other things he wanted to know. For example: 'If this place is so deep underground, where does the light come from?'

From the surface.

'The shaft falls straight? Like a well? In that case the sun would have to stand directly overhead, which it never does.'

I doubt that the shaft falls straight, Rogei answered. No, for the cracks of the earth are like a maze. But some of these mazy cracks have mirrors at every junction!

'Mirrors?'

Where the bedrock breaks through the desert sand, Rogei patiently explained, there, in certain protected places, the Thyre tend and polish their mirrors. The sunlight falls upon them and is deflected into the earth's potholes and passageways. Passed from mirror to mirror, it descends into the dark places under the desert. Thus the Thyre bring a little light into their colonies.

Nathan nodded. 'Else you'd all be blind down here.'

No, for our eyes are like trog or Wamphyri eyes ... or perhaps not like the latter's, for the night is their element. But given even a little light, the Thyre see well enough. It is just that the light is a special comfort. Down there in the hollow earth, it is treasured.

Nathan would ask next about the Thyre talent for tongues. Apart from some small initial hesitation, Atwei's conversation had been in perfectly good Szgany. He knew of course that the Thyre traded with Travellers from time to time, but would find it astonishing if they shared the same native tongue.

Seeing the question coming, however, and perhaps far too many more of them, Rogei cried: *Wait! Enough of these questions for now, Nathan. There are more important matters. First we must talk about the Thyre elders ...*

But before he could continue, Atwei returned with a yoke round her slender neck from which depended a pair of thin silver trays laden with small wooden bowls of various edibles. And looking at the bowls as she transferred them from the trays to the table, Nathan found his mouth watering. For the first time in a very long time he knew which matters were most important to him. Most *immediately* important, anyway.

Seated on tiny stools on opposite sides of the table and between the mirrors, Nathan and Atwei ate. There in the shaft of diffused sunlight, she looked more golden than brown, and he noticed how her pupils shrank to match the light's greater intensity.

The foodstuffs were fascinating, even exotic. Nathan had never imagined that these 'primitive' desert folk enjoyed such variety. Insisting that the food was for him, Atwei took only a little; she was simply keeping him company while he ate. And at that Nathan felt privileged. He rightly supposed himself to be the first of the Szgany to ever learn of such things. Certainly he was the first to ever taste them.

There were walnuts marinaded in vegetable oils, yellow bladder-roots with a bittersweet taste which stung the mouth as the vegetable was crushed, fried slivers of meat in aromatic sauces, several varieties of mushroom, and small, eyeless fishes baked whole. Various fruits followed: tangy cactus apples, figs and round ripe lemons, a bunch of small grey grapes. Everything was delicious, but Nathan had found a sort of small sausage especially succulent and asked Atwei what it was made of. That was a mistake.

'Grubs of the earth,' she answered.

And after a pause: 'Worms?' He cocked his head a little, inquiringly.

'Of a sort. We breed them . . .'

The meal was at an end.

They cleaned their hands in tiny fingerbowls, following which Atwei closed her eyes, placed the fingertips of her left hand upon her brow, and sat still for a moment. Then she smiled and asked: 'Did you enjoy?'

'Greatly. I thank you.'

Again she smiled. 'And I have thanked Him,' she said.

'Him?'

'Whoever listens.'

'Do you believe there is some One?'

'Don't you?'

'Many of our beliefs died in the day of the white sun,' he quoted Szgany 'history', of which there was little enough. 'Men had writing, numbers, science, and some believed in a god. Very little of science survived, and almost nothing of religion. In the close vicinity of the Wamphyri, it's hard for men to have faith in a merciful god! Now when the Szgany pray or give thanks, they offer them to their stars, which are remote even beyond the influence of the vampires.'

Then if I were you, Rogei said in his mind, *I would seek out my guardian star right now! Nathan, I have kept apart out of common decency; the Thyre require privacy for eating; Atwei has honoured you greatly. But finally the time has come when we must talk about the elders!*

'Very well,' he answered.

'Your pardon?' Atwei lifted an eyebrow.

'I was talking to Rogei,' he told her.

Her eyebrows went up higher yet, worriedly. 'You should not have got up and dressed yourself. I told you that you must wait, until you had your strength back. You were delirious for a long time and . . . you could be again!'

Nathan sighed and shook his head. 'I'm a little weak,' he said, 'that's all.' But then he had an idea. 'Atwei, listen to me: could you be delirious, too?'

'I? Now? Of course not!'

'Good! Now tell me if I'm correct: while I am limited in my ability to read minds, you are not. Right?'

'If a mind is telepathic, I can read it,' she said, frowning. 'Also, I can partially block another mind trying to read mine. These things come with practice. As yet, your talent is undeveloped. But your mind has the capacity.'

'I was wondering,' he said, 'if you could talk to Rogei through me? If you were to enter my mind right now, would you be able to overhear our conversation?'

'Eavesdrop on an Ancient?' She sat up straighter, looked more worried yet. 'Even an elder would think twice!'

'You believe me, then?'

'We are friends,' Atwei hesitated a little, 'you said it yourself. It takes two to build a friendship. If one lies it may be broken and have no value. This is proven; not only among the Thyre but also the Szgany, I think? And so I must believe you – at least until you are a proven liar.'

Rogei sighed in Nathan's mind. *Very well, try your experiment. Get it over with. Actually, it has merit. It will save a lot of time if it works.*

'There,' Nathan spoke to Atwei. 'He has nothing against it. And you needn't fear him for after all he's Thyre, one of your own. Also, Rogei's a dead creature and harmless.'

A dead 'man', Nathan, Rogei reminded. *And not all dead things are harmless, believe me! Well, will she or won't she?*

'Will you or won't you?' Nathan repeated him.

'If you wish it,' she said. She came round the table and he made to stand up. 'No, remain seated, and . . . *talk* to this Rogei.' She placed a small, trembling hand on his brow.

Atwei, I am Rogei the Ancient, once Rogei the elder. His mental voice was suddenly stern.

She snatched back her hand and placed it on her breast. Nathan got to his feet. 'You heard him?'

Her mouth had fallen slightly open. She closed it, shook her head and said, 'No . . . but I felt something. A presence!'

An echo, said Rogei. *Atwei sensed the merest trace, the smallest ghost of me, amplified by your mind. It doesn't work, and I didn't think it would. You are the Necroscope, Nathan. Such talents are not commonplace.*

Soft, padding footsteps sounded from outside the room. Atwei backed shakily away, turned and went to meet the elders. Rogei read Nathan's concern and said, *Well, too late for that now. We must deal with it as it comes. More ways than one to strip a cactus.*

The elders entered.

There were five of them, not all 'old' by any means and certainly not decrepit. Nathan calculated their ages on what he knew of the elderly among his own people. The youngest of the five was possibly forty-five, while the oldest would be well into his seventies. *Revise your estimates upwards by at least fifteen years,* Rogei told him. *The Thyre are long-lived. Since each colony has only five elders, a man cannot even aspire to become one until he is at least sixty.*

Nathan looked openly, respectfully, at each of the elders in turn. The youngest of them was spindly and quite bald, but as yet largely unwrinkled. His eyes were somewhat smaller than those of his companions; their pupils were grey, dartingly alert and (Nathan felt sure) more than a little suspicious. Three of the remaining four were quite simply Thyre; dressed in knee-length, pleated, belted yellow skirts, apart from the difference in their ages there was nothing to distinguish one from the next. The final member of the group was the one anomaly: bearing a torque of gold around his neck, he was heavily wrinkled, bent, and wore flowing white hair to his shoulders. His eyes were huge, moist, and uniformly yellow as the gold of his torque. He was at a glance the Elder of elders.

They peered at Nathan obliquely, blinkingly as they gathered to the table and their eyes adjusted to the extra light. Each carried a small stool, which they placed in a semicircle to enclose him. Then, straightening, they stood facing him.

Atwei, standing behind them, said, 'Nathan, please sit.' And as he sat down, so did they. And without pause the interview and question session got underway.

'We shall dispense with formalities,' said the youngest of the five in a high-pitched, superior tone. 'You are after all Szgany and cannot know the ways of the Thyre.'

Excellent! said Rogei. *This spokesman thinks he knows it all, a common failing among the young. So you must prove him wrong. Bow your head twice to him, then three times — but more slowly — to the Elder.*

Nathan did as Rogei instructed and the Thyre, including Atwei, sat up straighter. Then the five turned their heads to look at her, until she huskily protested, 'No, I have not instructed him!' In this way, and without saying a word, Nathan had their attention. But more than that, he had apparently earned himself the enmity of their spokesman.

'So,' said that one, frowning, 'your telepathy is not as embryonic as we thought, for patently you stole this greeting from my mind. What is more, I failed to detect the theft! Yet in your fever these unseemly skills of yours were not obvious, which tends to show a naturally deceptive turn of mind.'

Rogei was quick off the mark. *Point out how a man, even an elder, who jumps to conclusions to prove an elusive point may well deceive himself!*

Nathan did so, and added: 'One who investigates the mind of another while he is feverish risks discovering phantoms.'

At which point the Elder himself took over. In a voice which creaked like the branch of an old tree in the wind, he asked: 'And how many of these phantoms are there in your mind, Nathan of the Szgany?'

A great many, Rogei whispered in his inner ear, speaking now as Nathan himself. *Some of them are the ghosts of my past, which are mine alone to reveal or hold at bay as I see fit. But there are also the voices of an hundred Ancients of the Thyre, who would gladly speak through me to prove my innocence − if the Elder of elders so desires.*

Nathan repeated it.

'That is a blasphemy!' the spokesman made to stand up, but the Elder took his arm and held him down. The spokesman glanced at the venerable one and frowned, saying, 'But plainly he is a necromancer! He entered the Cavern of the Ancients in order to molest and torture our dead for their secrets!'

'If so,' the Elder nodded, patiently, 'the more we let him speak the more his words will condemn him. So far he is correct in one respect at least: namely that some are too quick to jump to conclusions! Let him say on.' And again he turned his great soft eyes on Nathan.

Tell them your story in brief, said Rogei, *while I spy on them through your eyes.*

Nathan complied. 'The Wamphyri have returned to Starside where they inhabit the last aerie. They raided Settlement, my home in the west of Sunside. During the raid, my mother and ... and a Szgany girl were stolen

512

and my brother went missing. Searching for him, I followed his trail east where I met a band of Travellers and determined to join them. But first I had to try one last time to find my brother. Finally, learning that he was dead, I tracked my Traveller friends to their camp at the edge of the grasslands and discovered that they were –' He paused and shook his head. '– They were no more. The Wamphyri ...' He hung his head for a moment to drive out the memories of these very real phantoms, then looked up.

'I had nothing left in the world, and no longer wished to live. But remembering how I sometimes overhear the dead whispering in their graves – a strange gift, I know, and one which I had kept hidden – I thought that I might join them in death. Perhaps then I would be able to talk to my mother again, to my brother, my girl. Wandering beneath the stars, I crossed the grasslands into the desert, where sunup found me at the foot of sandstone cliffs. There I decided to die.

'But as I lay down to sleep I heard the voice of a man, an Ancient of the Thyre, who called himself Rogei. He told me certain things, led me to the Cavern of the Ancients. By then I was weak and fell unconscious. I woke up and was here. And now I'm accused of desecration and blasphemy.'

The elder spokesman was angry again. 'Despite that Rogei is a revered name among the Thyre, it is not uncommon. There is more than one Rogei in the Cavern of the Elders, as this Szgany necromancer guessed there would be. He must have learned the name from our traders, and remembered it to put to evil use.'

'How so?' The Elder looked at him. 'Who among the Thyre would reveal his secret name to a Szgany youth met briefly at the trading? For what good purpose? No, I think not.' He shook his head. 'Also, if it were so, does it mean you have changed your accusation? If so, then what is this man's crime? Is he a vile necromancer or merely a clever liar?'

The other pursed his lips. 'I say we should speak in our own tongue,' he said sharply. 'He listens; he is intelligent; he is a talented deceiver!'

'I say again: you deceive yourself,' Rogei prompted Nathan into speech. 'I can prove what I've said.'

'Then do so,' the spokesman snapped, 'and so condemn yourself!'

I do believe I know this one, Rogei spoke to Nathan. *Yes, and also the Elder. Even under the trappings of his great age, still I know him. But the Spokesman: he has the looks and mannerisms of my own son. Why, it could be that he is my grandson! It would explain his vehemence, which is rare among the Thyre. Don't you see? He believes you interfered with the remains of his grandfather!*

'But I didn't!' Nathan burst out – and the Thyre elders drew back a little on their stools, staring at him curiously.

No, but I did touch you! No dream, Nathan. You are the Necroscope which I named you, beloved of the dead. In the Cavern of the Ancients, when I thought you were about to die, I was – moved – to come to you! And rising up, I was beside you, to comfort you in your fever!

'You ... came to me?' Nathan wasn't able to hold back from blurting it out loud. 'But you're a dead man!'

'Hah! He speaks nonsense!' The spokesman sneered, and went on to add some choice invectives in the Thyre tongue. But the Elder had read something in Nathan's strange eyes, causing him to caution his chief accuser:

'No, make yourself understood to him also. For if we desire to bring charges, he must have the benefit of the doubt.'

Rogei came to Nathan's rescue, telling him what to say and how he must say it. And looking at the Thyre spokesman he repeated Rogei word for word, faithfully, only leaving out his acid sarcasm. 'Ah, but your grandfather recognizes you at last, Pe-tey-is!' he said, gazing directly into the spokesman's eyes and nodding slowly. 'Petais, son of Ekhou and grandson of Rogei the Ancient, born in that same hour that your grandfather took to his sickbed. But before he died he saw you in your mother's arms and was proud of you, just as he is proud now to see that you're an elder! Rogei knows you not only from your premature loss of hair, familiar features and bearing in general – which is to say, moulded in an almost *exact* likeness of your father, his son – but also from your abrupt mannerisms and the heat of your argument. As Ekhou was ever the fiery one, so are you!'

Petais's mouth had fallen open. He couldn't speak and so gurgled a little, his eyes bulging. Under Rogei's expert guidance, Nathan gave him no time to recover but carried on. 'Now tell your grandsire, do you accept that these are his words? I hope so, for if not we must summon Ekhou your father and Amlya your mother, who will know me better. I know that they are not dead, for if they were I would have spoken to them in the Cavern of the Ancients!'

Petais shook his head wildly, stood up, sat down again. He was still lost for words. But the Elder of elders was not. 'Who is it speaks, you or Rogei?'

'A little of both,' Nathan answered. 'I repeat his words, faithfully if I can.'

The Elder nodded, reached out a trembling hand to touch Nathan's arm. 'I perceive that it is true,' he said, his eyes rapt on him and unblinking. 'Plainly a great wonder has come among us!'

Petais groaned and said, 'Still we must be sure!'

'I *am* sure,' the Elder answered him. 'You do not remember, Petais – of course not, for you were a child newborn – but I too was there when your mother took you before the dying Rogei, and indeed he was proud of you. I know, for I was Rogei's nephew, the son of his brother!'

Nodding, Petais seemed to sag a little. 'What must be must be. But it had to be decided, one way or the other.'

I was right, Nathan, Rogei sighed. *The Elder is my nephew, Oltae!*

Even as he spoke his ethereal words, the one he had named turned from Petais to Nathan. 'I know you will understand that Petais is correct,' the Elder said. 'We had to be sure. Even now, we *must* be sure.'

'Test me however you will, Oltae,' Nathan told him.

The Elder gasped, gave a small start, and his hand tightened on Nathan's arm. 'That is my name, aye,' he nodded. 'And I know you did not steal it from *my* mind, for I have built a wall there which is impenetrable! Wherefore, one final test, and I shall be satisfied.'

Rogei prompted Nathan to say: 'Now I speak as Rogei. Let me guess this test, nephew. Has it to do with your examination for a place among The Five? You were a young man then, as Petais is now, but I remember your examination well for I was your examiner! I had many questions for you, but your answer to one of them won exceptional marks! Do you remember it, Oltae?'

'I do indeed,' the Elder whispered.

'And I asked,' Rogei spoke through Nathan, ' "When will we know if The One Who Listens exists?" And you answered –'

'– My answer was this,' Oltae the Elder cut him short. ' "We shall know that He exists when finally He speaks, which will not be until we are better capable of knowing and understanding Him." ' And as he gazed deep into

Nathan's eyes, for a moment Oltae thought he saw an image of Rogei looking back at him, smiling. But as the Necroscope blinked, it was gone.

The Elder sighed, nodded in his fashion, and creaked to his feet; likewise his four colleagues. But before they left, Oltae said to Nathan (also to Rogei): 'It is my thought that today, perhaps we *are* one step closer to understanding Him!'

And then to Nathan alone: 'Rest, get back your strength. We shall talk again . . .'

In the long days which followed – days which would each have been as long as a 'week' in the time-scale of Nathan's unknown hell-lander father – he learned a great many things and did a great deal of 'teaching'. The Thyre called it teaching, anyway, though to Nathan it seemed he merely passed on the messages of the Ancients. But certainly the previously irretrievable knowledge of the dead was of enormous advantage to the living.

Long sessions were spent with The Five in the Cavern of the Ancients, where Nathan's talent as a Necroscope was proved beyond any further doubt; and as the living of the Thyre warmed to him, so did the Ancients themselves. And just as Harry Keogh had been a lone, bravely flickering candle to the dead of a far distant world, so now his son became a light in the darkness of the Thyre beyond.

Much like the Szgany, the Thyre had very little of true writing; rather than words, they used a system of complicated glyphs to illustrate whole ideas, so that a lot of the detail was inevitably lost. Most of their 'history' had come down to them in this way, and in the form of myths and legends passed mouth to mouth (or mind to mind), from generation to generation; out of which had sprung their art-form of storytelling. Foremost amongst makers of Thyre romance had been one Jhakae, dead for more than two hundred and eighty years. Now, through Nathan, Jhakae could relate all of his best stories, created for a limited audience of dead Ancients, and know that they would be passed down to thousands of the living.

Nathan relayed tale after tale, each of them furiously scribbled down and recorded as best as possible in the Thyre glyphs: the *Story of the Fox and the Kite*, the *Fable of the Gourd and the Granule*, the *Tale of Tiphue and the Dust-Devil*. Twenty of them, then thirty, finally forty, and all jewels of Thyre fantasy. But Jhakae's latest and greatest tale, as yet unfinished, would be that of the *Szgany Youth in the Cavern of the Ancients: a Parable*. And so Nathan was honoured.

In everything Nathan transcribed from death into life, and vice versa, he had the invaluable advice and assistance of Rogei. But such was the body of information to be passed on, the enormous bulk of questions from both sides, that priorities must be decided, time apportioned, and the practical take precedence over theoretical, philosophical, and theological subjects. Within the comparatively narrow confines of Thyre existence, all such subjects were limited forms anyway; far more important and immediately applicable were ideas and devices such as Shaeken's 'Water Ram', his 'Hydraulic Hoist' and 'Wheel of Irrigation'.

Shaeken was that Ancient whose name Rogei had mentioned at their first meeting, who once designed leather buckets for the drawing of water from the wells. Pursuing his obsession in death as in life, Shaeken had proceeded to far greater things; but even without the benefit of his genius, Nathan might have brought the principle of the water wheel to the Thyre. Desert folk, they had never journeyed beyond the grasslands to such townships as Twin Fords, and had not seen how the Szgany used the raw energies of the river to assist them in their work.

But they were the Thyre; the better Nathan knew them the more he understood their pride; making nothing of his own (in any case limited) knowledge, he spent long hours with a graphite stylus and the skins of lizards stretched on frames, creating meticulous sketches of machines direct from Shaeken's mind. And joiners of wood and other artisans pored breathlessly over each drawing as it was completed, so that as his work progressed the principles were grasped and the first models began to be carved.

There were times when Nathan grew tired but he made no complaint. His life had purpose; his mind was so occupied as to hold at bay all the mourning and miseries of his past; he had a deal more of respect from his new friends than his own had ever shown him. He was satisfied, or *believed* he was satisfied, for a while at least ...

He was pleased to perform personal favours. Rogei felt compelled to discover the fortunes of various kith and kin; Nathan stood in his debt and so made inquiries on his behalf; Rogei was enabled to 'speak' with those who were here, still alive. Others however had moved away, to far colonies beyond the range of Thyre deadspeak. For just like the telepathy of the living, that of the dead had its limitations, too. Many of the ones Rogei sought were dead in distant places, beyond his reach.

Meanwhile Nathan's fame had spread abroad; Thyre from other colonies began to arrive at the Place-Under-the-Yellow-Cliffs, all bearing invitations from their elders. Invariably they would seek audience with

Nathan and let it be known that he would always find a welcome should he ever decide to visit. He promised Rogei that if ever he accepted such an invitation, he'd be sure to seek out his old friend's relatives en route, wherever his travels took him.

But in the interim he worked . . .

With the exception of trivial items vetted out by Rogei, first Nathan satisfied all the personal queries of the dead in the Cavern of the Ancients, and of the colony's living alike, before setting to with a will. Then:

He made known all of the gourmet Arxei's myriad secret recipes, which that one had never revealed in life; he delivered a formula of preservation from the mirror-polisher Annais, a vegetable varnish to protect the Thyre mirrors and keep them from tarnishing; he gave voice to the gardener Tharkel's conclusions on bees, pollination, and the keeping of hives. In life Tharkel had made an oasis with his own hands, which had failed only through the lack of an adequate water supply; since when he'd planned bigger and better ones. Now, with the advent of Shaeken's Hydraulic Hoist, they could be real!

Nathan did all of these things, and as the work gradually slackened off even found time for a little local travelling and studying among the Thyre. And since the elders did not consider it fitting that a person of Nathan's importance should concern himself with the basic requirements of life, Atwei became his aide among the living just as Rogei was his spokesman among the dead. Dealing with all mundane matters, she left Nathan free to explore the possibilities of his unique talent.

In fact he was given too much freedom and failed to use it to his best advantage. For as the furious pace of his life slackened, so he allowed a host of dreams and memories of past, unbearable things to creep back in to plague him. He dreamed of Canker Canison's barking laugh as the loping dog-thing carried Misha away to the horror of some unthinkable future; and of his mother, a flame-eyed thrall in the service of a hideous vampire Lord; and of Nestor rotting in the river, a thing of weeds and sloughing grey flesh, dissolving into the mud. Nightmares such as these invariably brought Nathan gibbering awake, and Atwei would come running to comfort him . . .

In black bowels of earth beneath the colony, where even the fishermen of the Thyre must cast their nets by flaring torchlight, Atwei showed Nathan a section of the Great Dark River and explained as best she could its source and destination.

'As Sunside's rains roll down off the barrier mountains,' she said, her husky whisper echoing into the darkness and back from unknown places, 'and as storm-clouds burst less frequently over the furnace desert itself, so great bodies of water find their way underground. Many major tributaries may be found in the west, and others to the east, between the desert and the mountains. And so the Great Dark River under the earth is the sump of the world!

'The hard bedrock of the underworld is tilted eastwards; likewise, naturally, the course of the river. Where the rocks are softest, the rain of centuries has formed many cavern systems. Of these, the safest and most suitable have become Thyre colonies. The underworld is as important to the Thyre as your forests are to you Szgany. Temperate, it provides shade from the sun in the heat of the long day, and is a refuge from the bitter chill of desert nights. We could not live without it, or without the river which is its dark lifeblood.

'During its life the river has carved wide ledges in the rock. Of these, the driest and safest are used as paths along which we may follow the water's course where it rushes through dark gullies. In parts the river is navigable over long miles, forming vast sunless lakes where the blind fishes swim; but in other places the way is tighter and the water roars furiously!

'As for its length: the river parallels the barrier mountains; it passes under the Great Red Waste, and meanders past a range of lesser mountains where dwell people much like yourself . . . or perhaps unlike yourself, for they give of their young to the Wamphyri. And so the river flows into the unknown. Some say it journeys to a sea far in the east, beyond the caverns of the necromancers; but this is rumour, because no one of the Thyre has ever been there.'

Nathan listened attentively to Atwei; he looked at the ledges carved by the river in the canyon walls of the channel through ages immemorial, at the blackly gurgling water flowing swiftly by, and the catches of the fishermen wriggling in their nets. And at one and the same time the river both repulsed and fascinated him. Merely to think of its sheer *length* was an awe-inspiring exercise in itself: more than three thousand miles of subterranean waterways, if Atwei was right, and Nathan was sure that she was. Why, Sunside's rivers were streams by comparison; the Great Dark River covered more miles than Nathan had seen in his entire life!

And yet it wasn't so much the river's size as its course which most affected Nathan's imagination: a course that followed the mountains east into that region beyond the Great Red Waste where the Wamphyri held sway, out of which they had returned into Starside. And as the river was a road to the Thyre, which they might follow on foot and by boat, colony to colony for all its many leagues, so might Nathan follow it . . .

*

Sunups came and went; Nathan's work in the Cavern of the Ancients neared completion; he told The Five that he planned to move on, and they swore him to secrecy. He promised that whatever the future held, he would never tell his brothers in the outside world what he had learned of the Thyre and their ways.

In the meantime his nightmares had got no better; if anything they were worse. Over and over Nathan lived through the hell of that night and morning in Settlement, the time of the Wamphyri raid. Also, he was aware of time fleeting by, and wondered how Lardis and the Szgany Lidesci fared now. Often in the Cavern of the Ancients he would sense his wolves trying to contact him. But they were distant and he was shielded by massive walls of rock; and anyway, what would they have to say except – it seemed likely – things he did not wish to hear? For by now, surely the Wamphyri were mighty again, a plague throughout all of Sunside.

Once (for once on his own), he fell asleep in the Cavern of the Ancients and dreamed that the numbers vortex waited for him. That mighty, bottomless whirl-pool of figures tugged at him insistently; he felt that if only he knew the meaning of all of these rapidly mutating symbols . . . they could open up whole new worlds to him. Any world would be better than the one he'd left behind, providing that it let him live among his own kind. And again he felt like a traitor who had turned tail and fled from his enemies, his friends, even from himself.

And now he must flee again, put greater distance between himself and the past, go searching for some shadowy fulfilment just around the corner of to-morrow . . .

In the Cavern of the Ancients he said his farewells. The dead were silent for a while. They would miss him.

But ... he might return, one day? He couldn't say for definite, but possibly. Well, they had had their fair share of him, and the dead of other places were eager to meet him.

Nathan spoke to Shaeken. Working so much together, they had developed firm bonds, a warm friendship and understanding. And: 'In time, your works will be a blessing to the Thyre,' he told the great engineer.

They were nothing without you, Nathan, the other was flattered. But in a moment, and much more seriously: *Nathan, these numbers which plague your dreams ...*

'Oh? You've been spying on me?' Nathan knew it wasn't so.

Hardly that! We can't help it. After all, you are the Necroscope. But the numbers: I've seen them, it's true. And as you know I have a small understanding of numbers.

'You understood the vortex?'

He sensed the shake of a head. *Did I understand it? No. Was I afraid of it? Yes: even as a child fears the lightning! By comparison, my own calculations are ant tracks in the sand – quickly blown away – while yours are alive and work towards an end. And just as your deadspeak is unique among the living, so is the vortex yours alone. It is a part of you, Nathan! I'm no philosopher; my thoughts are shallow, mechanical things; but I sense that if one day you should fathom it, then you will be that much closer to your destiny. In Open-to-the-Sky there was upon a time an elder who was a mathematician. He is dead now, but what is that for a barrier? Perhaps you should seek him out.*

'Maybe I will.' Nathan was grateful.

Finally he spoke to the one who would miss him the most, Rogei, and discovered himself incapable of even a small white deception. 'This will be my last visit to the Cavern before I leave,' he told him. 'And I don't think I'll be back.'

I know it, the other answered, trying to make light of it. *Only think of me now and then; reach out with your mind and . . . who knows? I might be there. But if you can't speak to me, try speaking to Him Who Listens, for I feel sure He would listen to you. As for what Shaeken told you: will you seek out this mathematician? I think you must, for I am a philosopher and believe a man should follow his destiny.*

'I'll probably seek him out,' Nathan nodded.

Also, Rogei said, *there is that which you should know. In your time here you've proved yourself a friend, to both living and dead alike, and I have tried to be the same to you. I have spoken to the dead of the Szgany on your behalf, to tell them what an opportunity they have missed. Alas, only mention your powers, they withdraw. For whatever reasons, they are afraid of you.*

'I knew that,' said Nathan.

The reason is simple: the dead have always feared necromancy, and now that the Wamphyri are back in the land they fear it more than ever. Somehow, they associate you with necromancy. Now . . . they will no longer speak to me! But you Szgany have a saying: 'like father, like son'? Well, I kept reading that thought in their minds before they closed me out. And so I am given to wonder – I hesitate to ask – but could it be, perhaps, that your father did something to alienate the Szgany dead, which now causes them to shun you?

'My father, Hzak Kiklu?' Nathan frowned. 'But he was just a man, murdered by the Wamphyri like so many before and since. Why, I never even knew him . . . I wasn't born . . . what could he have done?'

Rogei's baffled shrug. *I could only try; I failed; I*

know no more. However, there is one other matter on which I would advise you.

'I will always value your advice.'

Nathan, I know you have put this thing from your mind. The elders have not mentioned it; the subject has never come up; men are wise to leave well enough alone. But the fact is that when you needed someone I came to you. Your power goes beyond simply speaking to the dead. Do you understand me?

'I think so, yes. What is your advice?'

Simply this: beware what you call up to a semblance of life, Nathan, for some things may be harder to put down . . .

Nathan wasn't sure he did understand, not fully, but he thanked Rogei anyway. And then he said good-bye . . .

I

Equipped with new clothes, a good leather belt and a polished ironwood knife with a bone handle, Nathan was ready. He would journey east downriver, for west would take him too close to home, or to what had once been his home. Only go that way ... it would be very hard to resist returning to Settlement, and he dreaded the thought of what he might find there now.

Atwei accompanied him upon the first leg of his journey; she took the lead, striding out along the stone-carved 'banks' of the Great Dark River.

Ostensibly he went to visit other Thyre colonies, to talk to their elders and their dead; but there was a lot more to it than that. Now that he was possessed of talents (his deadspeak, full-fledged among the Thyre, and his telepathy, as yet inchoate but promising, at least according to Atwei and others of her people), his confidence was that much greater. Where the past must remain a wasteland, anathema, it seemed the future might hold something of fulfilment at least. He had things to learn and people to talk to; whether they were living or dead ... that no longer made any difference.

Nathan's new clothes were quite remarkable. Fashioned in the Szgany style generally but of soft, sand-coloured lizard-skin, the cut was all Thyre, the work of a very high standard, and the fitting exact. In short, the Thyre of Place-Under-the-Yellow-Cliffs had dressed Nathan tip to toe much as they saw him: as a person of very special qualities. His fringed jacket had a high collar and wide lapels; his trousers were flared to fit snug over soft leather boots; his silver belt-buckle was scrolled to match the ornamentation on the sheath housing his knife.

All in all, with his startling blue eyes, and his yellow hair grown shoulder-length (outrageous colours in a man of the Szgany, and impossible among the Thyre), the ensemble gave him a mystical, even alien look in keeping with his standing. The only irony was that having done so much for the Thyre, gained so much in the way of respect, he should remain impotent to do anything for his own people. But they were not forgotten, and perhaps there was time yet.

For the first time in his life, Nathan was a person of substance, albeit in a world remote from his largely insubstantial previous existence. And he could not help but wonder: while his stature was vast among the Thyre, what would it be outside their limited sphere? What would he be now among his own kind, the Szgany Lidesci? Would he still be a freak, a mumbling fool, or were those days gone forever? And what of Sunside's Travellers themselves: all of them, the Szgany as a race? What were they now to the Wamphyri?

Cut off from them in self-imposed exile, he could not know. But two thousand miles away down the Great Dark River, where others of his kind cowered under the tyranny of grotesque Wamphyri masters, he might yet find an answer. For as they were now — stumbling serfs, cattle, scarlet sustenance for hideous vampire Lords — so must his own people inevitably become! Horrific as the thought was, it was also fascinating. And the more Nathan dwelled upon it the more he saw his obligation unwinding before him, much like the black canyon walls of the serpentine river . . .

Every half-mile or so along the way, Atwei would pause to point out caches of tarry torches wrapped in oiled skins in niches in the damp walls. The torches were long-lasting; she would let two or three of these replenishment points go by before renewing her own and Nathan's brands. Torches came and went like fireflies through the utter dark on both sides of the black river, as other Thyre passed them along the way. Nathan strained to hear the thoughts of these torchbearers in this blackest of black nights but heard nothing, only the far faint whispers of the dead . . .

Only fifteen miles to the east along a course that wound a little deeper into the desert, Open-to-the-Sky was the next colony. Nathan and Atwei were there in less than five hours. As to the colony's name: the reason for that was immediately apparent. The place was, quite literally, open to the sky.

The first indication that they approached their destination came in a stirring and freshening of the air; the light improved and the sputtering flames of their torches were buffeted; ahead of them, the way seemed shrouded in a misty haze. Soon they were able to extinguish their brands and proceed in the gathering light. As the far bank receded, so the pace of the river slowed to a crawl. Then the swirling waters widened into the neck of a lake, and the scene which gradually opened to Nathan's eyes was such as he could never have anticipated.

For suddenly . . . it was as if an oasis flourished underground! At first there were only ferns and mosses growing out of cracks in the walls, then small bushes overhanging the high ledges, eventually trees, vines and creepers, all straining for the indirect but beckoning sunlight. And where the river's roof opened at last into a real canyon and the light of day streamed down from overhead, finally there was lush foliage springing up on every hand.

Here the river had shingle beaches and timbered jetties; true banks of red silt rose up to level ground on both sides of the water, where rudimentary stone wharves had been built to defend against flooding. All of which lay in the forefront of patchwork fields and allotments; while at the rear, houses on stilts rose in terraces where the higher ground backed up to the cliffs. Between and beyond the houses, dizzy pathways climbed vine-shrouded scree slopes, faults in the canyon wall, and cliff-hugging ledges, zig-zagging up and across the rising rock from cavern to cavern and ledge to ledge. And the Thyre came and went along these paths and causeways like ants about their daily business. While high overhead —

— A marvellous sight! The canyon walls reared up two hundred feet and more; the light where it came slanting in from the south to burst against the opposite wall was blinding after the Stygian dark of the river; despite that Nathan knew the surface must be mainly desert, still he saw the silhouettes of palms crowding the canyon's rim. And so Open-to-the-Sky was an astonishing place.

Thyre elders met them where the worn-smooth granite of the river path met the rudimentary paving of the access road into the community. Nathan would have preferred to speak for himself from the onset, but by now well-versed in their code of conduct, he let Atwei act on his behalf; it was Thyre custom to open proceedings through an intermediary. His own name had been known in advance but theirs, of course, were secret. No introductions of that sort were necessary.

Nathan found himself greeted by a good deal of gravity, tempered with (he suspected), a small measure of scepticism; while Atwei, acting as his aide and spokeswoman — his dupe? perhaps his colleague in deception and blasphemy? – suffered an initially cool reception indeed.

As they passed through the lower levels of the colony and climbed a walled pathway to the Cavern of Long Dreams, a Thyre mausoleum one quarter of the way up the cliff, something of the stiffness and formality went out of The Five and they conversed with Nathan in cordial if restrained monotones. He continued to sense their hesitancy, however, and suspected there were those among them who thought he had somehow made fools of their colleagues in Place-Under-the-Yellow-Cliffs. Once inside the tomb he felt more at ease, and commenced to verify his credentials in very short order.

The Five had worked out a series of questions for Nathan to ask their dead ancestors, whose answers would permit of no deception or obfuscation. The dead, for their part, had heard faint rumours of the Necroscope's coming from the Ancients of Place-Under-the-Yellow-Cliffs, and immediately recognized the purpose of these opening questions: that they were designed to detect any charlatanry in Nathan. For which reason, once rapport was established and they felt the Necroscope's warmth, the response of the dead was accurate and not without a measure of Thyre sarcasm directed at the elders themselves.

The most 'junior' of The Five, perhaps irritated by Nathan's dry and very un-mystical delivery of answers allegedly from beyond the grave, brought about an early interruption by asking: 'Perhaps you could tell us why our ancestors converse so readily with you but not with their own kind?'

At which Nathan lost patience. This one reminded him of Petais, and he wasn't about to go through all of that again! He might have answered in his own way, without prompting, but a voice in his head cautioned him against it and in a moment supplied the perfect answer:

'Quatias, your father Tolmia begs you to remember a time in your childhood – you were five? – when you lost your way in the desert just a mile from Open-to-the-Sky. All you had to do was climb a dune and you would have seen the oasis clearly, you were that close. But no, you were only a child and afraid; you sat down and cried. Be sure not to lose your way again, in the maze of your own doubts, now that you are even closer to a great truth.'

Quatias opened his mouth, closed it and made a strangled sound in the back of his throat. Finally, in a broken voice, he said: 'Only my father Tolmia could have known ... thought ... said ... that which you just said. Wherefore I no longer doubt. Nathan, please tell him that I love him very much!'

'He knows,' Nathan answered, all anger fled in a moment. 'And he loves you in return, even as he did in life.'

Shortly after that the initial session broke up. Shaken, The Five must now reconsider things, think how best to employ Nathan – *if* they still had his good will. So they made to go off to their council chambers and discuss his awesome talent. But before he let them go:

'I want you to know,' he told them, 'that the girl Atwei is my dear friend. She was my nurse and brought me to health when I was sick. Now, I understand why you had doubts, about both of us. Of course you did and I don't hold it against you. But that is over now, and you should know: he who dishonours Atwei dishonours me.'

He couldn't know it, but from that time forward she would be part of his expanding legend. Atwei of the Thyre, friend of Nathan ...

*

And so, as in Place-Under-the-Yellow-Cliffs, once again Nathan became a bridge between two worlds: that of the living, and the darkness of those who had continued beyond it. But before that there were certain priorities: for instance, Shaeken's inventions.

In accordance with the Ancient's wishes, he passed on to the artisans of Open-to-the-Sky detailed drawings of his water wheel, ram, and hoist, all of which were of especial relevance here. Once constructed, Shaeken's Hydraulic Hoist should provide effortless irrigation for the oasis high overhead; and so the Thyre would prosper.

Then, as soon as these technical details had been passed on and understood, for five more sunups Nathan channelled all of his energies to the task of communication between the living and the dead. And as in Place-Under-the-Yellow-Cliffs, so now the results of his work were uniformly beneficial; exactly as before, word of the Necroscope spread abroad and emissaries from Thyre colonies further down the river came to see him.

But now that the work was no longer new to him it became ... simply work. Despite that it was satisfying in its way and the number of his friends among the dead grew apace, Nathan no longer took pleasure in it. Also, time seemed to pass by ever more swiftly, and he felt he should be elsewhere, doing other things.

It was time to move on.

Atwei sensed it in him. She may even have read it in his supposedly 'inviolate' mind. But seeing how she was saddened, Nathan made no complaint ...

One day they went up to the oasis, and there in the living sunlight Nathan saw how pale he had grown. He was pensive and gave voice to an idle thought. 'Why are you so brown,' he asked her, 'when you spend so much time in the deeps and the dark?'

'But before you,' Atwei answered, simply, 'I spent a good deal of my time in the light. The Thyre are desert folk, after all, and most of our work is done on the surface. Also, I was born brown. But why are you so pale, when you were born in the woods and the sunlight?'

He shrugged. 'So, we're different.'

'Are we so different, Nathan?'

He looked at her and wondered, *Are we?* And almost before he realized it, he knew – he heard – what she was thinking:

If I were Szgany, or he were Thyre, we would be lovers. He would lie in my arms and I would feel him pulsing within me. And I would stroke his back, while my thighs squeezed him for his juice.

Telepathy, or . . . did she do it deliberately? No, never the last, for she was Thyre and it would be unseemly. And now, as Atwei's thoughts continued, she too was pensive. *But Nathan is right: we are different. And I must love him as if he were my brother.*

Then . . . his look must be curious, wondering; she noticed it and quickly looked away. In order to save her embarrassment, he immediately acted as if nothing had happened, as if he knew nothing. In any case her mind was covered now; she had drawn a blanket over it, and he must assume that she suspected. But at the same time, suddenly, there came a second flash of inspired understanding as a riddle was solved. From the beginning he'd wondered how the Thyre, the living Thyre, knew and understood his tongue so well. And now he knew the answer:

When Nathan talked to the Thyre dead it was in deadspeak, but behind their mental voices and pictures he'd always sensed echoes of their spoken tongue, too. And now he saw how easy it was for a telepath to be a linguist. When thoughts are backed up by the echoes of words, a language is quickly learned. That was how it worked for the living Thyre: they had not stolen the Traveller language from his mind, not directly (they had always traded with the Szgany and so knew something of his tongue from the first). No, they'd not stolen it but read it in his expressions, seen it in his eyes, and — despite certain taboos and 'unspoken rules' — heard it in the echoes of his thoughts!

And he knew, too, why suddenly he understood large parts of the Thyre tongue when he heard it spoken all around him — because he had learned it the same way! And Atwei was right: he *would* be a telepath, in time.

But all of this coming at once ... it was a shock, a revelation to Nathan! Especially Atwei's feelings for him. And it was that more than anything else — the way she felt about him — which served to convince him that indeed the time had come to move on, while yet she thought of him as a brother ...

In the Cavern of Long Dreams, alone with the mummied dead and sharing their thoughts, Nathan spoke to Ethloi the Elder, who knew numbers. They were firm friends from the moment he mentioned Shaeken's name, for in life Ethloi and Shaeken had been colleagues.

How may I help you? Ethloi was eager to assist in any way he could.

'I have dreams,' Nathan told him. 'I dream of numbers. I have always thought they had meaning, and so did Shaeken. You are the expert, or so I'm told. Perhaps you can fathom them.'

An expert in maths? Is there such a thing? Ethloi seemed vague on the subject. *Shaeken required maths to calculate the numbers of cogs in his wheels, it's true, but his was a practical application. I was able, through* trial and error, to help him somewhat. Not a lot. As for me: I only know that like yourself, I too have dreamed of numbers, in death as in life. They are some of the several things I continue to explore, but not in depth. For since all such knowledge is useless (no one may confirm or deny my findings, because no one understands them), how may I determine if the things I know have value? There is no source of reference. And as for helping you ... we do not even know that Szgany and Thyre numbers are the same. Explain to me your system.

'The Szgany system?'

Yes.

'Do you mean, how do we count? But surely all creatures count the same?'

Not so. A bird has only two numbers: the number One and a number larger than One. If it has an egg in its nest it has an egg. If it has two eggs, three, or four, it has more than one. So how do the Szgany count?

'We count in fives, the number of fingers on a hand,' Nathan told him. 'We make gates,' (he showed the other a picture), 'like so:'

$$\text{I, II, III, IIII, } \text{IIII}$$

The Thyre have the same system, Ethloi replied, but as for me, I count in Tens! The picture he displayed to Nathan's mind was of two gates struck through.

Nathan frowned. 'But that is simply a count of the fingers on two hands. Is there a difference?'

Oh, yes, the other answered. The difference is simplicity! Now look:

1, 2, 3, 4, 5, 6, 7, 8, 9, 10,
11, 12, 13, 14, 15, 16, 17, 18, 19, 20.

The numbers he showed to Nathan were not these but symbols of his own, which had these values. Nathan studied them a while — sufficient that he understood that the last of these numbers was the equivalent of four gates — and shook his head. 'A different shape for every number? Simplicity? But this seems to me a complicated thing.'

Ethloi was frustrated (a great many mathematicians are), and sighed. But in a moment: *Now tell me,* he said, *how do you divide?*

'Divide?'

How many of these: | |, *are there in this:* ⊥⊦⊤ + |?

'| | |,' Nathan answered at once.

And how many of these: ⊥⊦⊤, *in this:* | | |?

Again Nathan frowned. 'There are only parts,' he shrugged.

And again Ethloi sighed. *As I supposed: you cannot divide.*

It was Nathan's turn to be frustrated, and: 'I know enough to divide a large orange between friends,' he blurted. 'Because it has segments!'

Yes (the nod of a wise although incorporeal head), *and so does my system. Infinitesimally small segments, and infinitely large numbers. Just as I count upwards in tens, so I may count down into the single unit. Into tenths, and tenths of tenths! But listen, about your orange: what if it has eight segments and there are only six friends?*

'Then two of them are lucky!' Nathan's thoughts were sour now, because it was beyond him. Already he was tired of this.

Ethloi felt it in him and shook his head. *Numbers are not easy, Nathan. Oh, I could show you a great many — and a great many tricks to play with them, too — but without an explanation they are only symbols. Such knowledge won't come instantly but must be learned. And somehow I don't think you will make a good pupil.*

'Show me some more numbers anyway,' Nathan begged him. 'So that I may at least consider them.'

Ethloi did as Nathan requested and sent his calculations rolling across the screen of the youth's mind. Decimals, fractions; a little basic algebra and trigonometry; calculations to determine the size of the world, the distance to the moon, the sun, and the stars. It was impressive, but it wasn't shocking. Nathan might not understand it, but he knew it for pretty rudimentary stuff compared with some of the things he had seen.

It did have something of an effect upon him, however; for as if conjured by this lesser display, now he felt the numbers vortex churning within his mind like some incredible mathematical dust-devil, just waiting to blast these intruding calculi to infinity. Ethloi detected nothing of the latter through his effort of mental projection, but he did note the Necroscope's unguarded thoughts: his apparent lack of regard for the display. And the images he transmitted to the screen of Nathan's mind were shut off at once.

Very well, Ethloi growled then, *now let's see what numbers you have dreamed.*

'Usually they come to me when I'm asleep,' Nathan told him. 'But my time here grows short. And when you produced your numbers for me, I ... I felt my own inside of me, almost as if they waited to be summoned.' He closed his eyes. 'Perhaps I can call them up.'

What happened then was ... swift as thought! The numbers vortex seethed with power; it sucked mutating calculations into its core as quickly as they formed on the rim; incredible metaphysical equations were fired in bursts from its rotating wall, like shooting stars in a meteorite shower! Until:

Shut it off! Ethloi groaned.

Nathan did so, opened his eyes, said: 'That is what I

have dreamed.' He took no pride in it; he only wanted to understand it, desperately. And Ethloi read that in his mind, too.

But how can you have such a thing, without understanding it? His question was in the form of an awed whisper.

'Just as I have feelings,' Nathan answered, 'in my heart and in my head, without understanding them.'

Ethloi nodded slowly, and said, *Aye, and perhaps you have answered your own question. For as telepathy is in the Thyre — come down through the blood of Gutawei the Seer, the First Remembered, and spread by his children, and theirs, throughout all the Thyre — so the numbers vortex is in you. It seems as much a part of you as your blue eyes and yellow hair. And spawned in some awesome ancestor, it came down to you the same way as they did!*

'I inherited it?' This was much the same as Rogei had told him. 'But from whom? Not my father for he was an ordinary man.'

Then from that same ancestor who gave you your deadspeak, Ethloi answered.

'But my deadspeak is a talent while this ... is a curse!' Nathan shook his head. 'It plagues me! I can't fathom it!'

Ethloi was obliged to agree. *Not all inherited things are for the good, it's true. In me it was my father's poor hearing, which turned me deaf in the end, much as he was deaf before me. A small trouble: I had my telepathy.*

'The numbers vortex baffles you then?' Nathan was disappointed. 'You don't know what it does?'

What it does? Numbers are, Nathan. They don't necessarily do things. And yet ... I sensed something behind it, yes. What it was, I can't say. Perhaps the vortex is a key.

'A key? To what?'

To a door, or to many doors. I sensed them there, in your mind. Doors to far, far places – even to far times! – all of which lie in the swirl of the vortex.

'But first I must understand the numbers?'

And control them! Ethloi nodded. *When you can bring them to heel, like a hunting dog – show them ordered on the screen of your mind, as I showed you my puny figures – then the key will be yours.*

Nathan was silent for long moments. Everything Ethloi had said was much as he'd long suspected. The numbers vortex hid a key which he must find. And then he must find the door in which to turn it. But as yet he was like a babe in arms who wanted to run before he could walk.

Ethloi remained silent, waiting.

And finally Nathan sighed and said, 'Perhaps you should show me some more numbers, and explain to me your system. I'll probably make a poor pupil, as you rightly said, but who knows? Something might sink in. Anyway, I have to start somewhere.'

He stayed for an hour until, head reeling, he could take no more . . .

Nathan slept one more time, ate a strangely tasteless, silent meal with Atwei, then told the elders he was leaving. They came down to the river route to see him off. Quatias, who was still spry, volunteered to go with him to the next colony just eight miles away. But in a garden of yellow flowers, where hazy sunlight fell dappled through leaf and vine, he begged a moment's privacy with Atwei.

She gave him a slender silver chain and a locket, which he opened. Inside, a tight coil of jet black hair. 'It is a custom of the Thyre,' she told him. 'A secret thing which siblings do when they are parted.'

He drew her to him and kissed her forehead. 'And this is how a Szgany brother parts from his sister.' Then he hung the locket round his neck and said, 'I'll never forget you, and I thank you for this lock of hair from your head.'

'My head?' she said, lifting a coarse eyebrow. 'Ah, no, for that would be unseemly!'

He raised his own eyebrows in a frown, looked at Atwei again, then at the locket, finally shook his head and smiled. The Thyre and their strange and 'secret' ways, their 'secret' things! Then, while she remained standing there, he went and said his farewells to the elders ...

'You waste your time with that one,' Brad Berea spoke gruffly to his daughter, Glina. 'He can fish, fetch and carry, hit a bird in flight, and eat – oh, he can eat! – but make sense? You ask too much of him. He spoke to me only once, to tell me he was the Lord Nestor: but what sort of a "Lord", I ask you? Since when, nothing.'

To be kind to her, Glina was only very homely. And Nestor, man or Lord or whatever, was a handsome specimen. He was a natural hunter, too, and upon a time had doubtless been a valuable member of a Traveller band, or citizen of some Szgany township. But now: Brad had seen more activity, more urgency, understanding, intelligence, in the geckoes which inhabited the rafters and chased flies when the sun fell hot on the roof. They, too, were hunters, but they didn't need to be told how to do it! It was instinct in them. But this one – *hah!* – it surprised Brad he knew enough to wake up after sleeping! Beggars can't be choosers, however, and Glina would lure him to her bed if she could. And what then, Brad wondered? Idiots in the camp? Better perhaps if he'd left Nestor in the river to drown.

'What happened to him, do you think?' Glina glanced at her father across the smoky room, where he took a taper from the fire to light the wick of the first lamp of evening. The fire would be allowed to die down now, as night came on. For if not its smoke, going up through the quiet forest into the air, would be like a beacon to ... well, to anything which might pass this way, over-head. But the cabin in the trees was warm and a lamp was enough. With blankets at the open windows, to keep the light in and the night air out, the Bereas were safe and snug.

'Happened to him?' Brad grunted. 'If you'll just feel the back of his head, above his right ear, you'll know well enough what happened to him. He received one hell of a clout from something or other, a blow that very nearly caved in his skull! The bone has knitted now but it's left a fat, hard knob just under the skin, and prob-ably on the inside, too. Also, he was shot and lost a deal of blood. The scars are clear enough in his side. Finally, he fell or was tossed into the river, and very nearly drowned. And all of this occurring about the time of the first vampire attacks on Settlement and Twin Fords. I didn't know about those when I dragged him out of the water, else I mightn't have been in such a hurry. What? Why, for all I knew he could have been a victim of the Wamphyri! But if so, well, it would have showed before now. So that's what happened to him. All in all, he's a simpleton with a damaged brain, and only his natural instincts seem in order – some of them, anyway. But even *they* might be a bit askew, else he'd know for sure you were after his parts!'

'Brad Berea?' His wife's voice came from the curtained platform which was their bed under the rafters. 'Come to bed and leave the young ones be.' After a hard day she'd retired early; but she would be up early, too, in the first hours of true night. It was as well to be awake in those most dangerous of hours, when the sun was down and the stars bright over the barrier range, and the vampires thirsty after their long sleep.

'Huh!' Brad grunted, and thought: *Aye, go and do your duty, Brad my son.*

But in fact Irma was a good woman and had stood by him uncomplainingly for twenty years and more, living a solitary existence out here in the forest. Brad had been a loner when she ran away from her Szgany band to be with him, and he was a loner still. A trip into Twin Fords every so often: it was the only pleasure Irma ever had out of life; that and Brad's love, and the knowledge that he would look after herself and their daughter all his days. In days like these, it was more than enough. As for Twin Fords: nothing there now but ruins, empty streets, and doors slamming in the wind like shouts of denial. And so no reason to visit.

'And you two?' The bearded Brad looked at Glina and Nestor sitting by the open door. 'Will you sit up again all night, girl? To be with that one? A pointless exercise! For I wonder: does he sit and think? Or does he just sit?' He took off his jacket and went to the foot of the ladder-like stairs climbing to his bed.

Glina looked at Nestor, whose eyes followed Brad where he began to climb. There wasn't much in those eyes, but they did have soul. Brad was hard-voiced, but he was soft-hearted, too, and Glina believed Nestor knew it. 'I'll sit and talk to him a while,' she said. 'I think he knows what I'm saying, but it doesn't mean much to him, that's all. Maybe we'll walk down to the river under the stars. Nestor likes that.'

Brad thought: *Oh, and what else does he like?* 'What, the strong, silent type, is he?' He called down, grinning despite himself. He went through the curtains to take off his clothes, and hung them on pegs in the rafters. Shortly he was in bed.

Down below, Glina listened a while to the creaking of her father settling himself, the low, murmuring voice of her mother cautioning him to: 'Shhh! Be quiet ... the young 'uns ... here, let me.' And then the rhythmic sounds of their sex. Little privacy in a timbered cabin.

Then Nestor's arm went around her waist, and his hand up under her blouse, to squeeze her large breasts. It was an automatic response to being left alone with her; something which he had learned to expect, to enjoy; something which Glina had taught him. 'Yes, yes,' she breathed in his ear, stroking him through his trousers with her fingertips. 'But not here.' And he followed her out of the open door and into the night.

The night wasn't yet cold; they walked slowly at first in bright starlight, then more hurriedly, finally breathing heavily, almost panting along a well-worn path to the river. And on the sand and shingle bank they threw off their clothes and fell on top of them, and she guided him jerking into her flesh. She knew how it would be but surrendered to it, as she had since the first time. But since Glina had been the one to lead him on right from the start, she could hardly complain. And he *was* a man, and filling her he filled the loneliness, too.

The first time ...

That had been when he was back on his feet again, five or maybe six sunups after her father had rescued him from the river. Until then Glina had washed and tended his wounds, fed him, cared for Nestor generally. And she'd rocked him in her arms when, in a fever, he'd called out strange names, shouted his passion at unknown persons and wept bitterly over obscure grievances and disappointments. Despite what Brad Berea said about him now, then there had been fire in Nestor.

But as the fever went out of him so the silence entered, and for a while his eyes had been empty.

In a little while he'd been strong and made no complaint about work. He hunted with a crossbow, fished, used an axe and carried wood and water well enough. Twice a week, when he went to bathe in the river, Glina spied on him. He was big and stirred her inside.

Once, three years ago when she was sixteen, the Bereas had gone into Twin Fords. Brad required new tools; her mother wanted a new dress, pots, pans; Glina just wanted to see and be seen. Then some boy might make inquiries, and find his way to the cabin to see her. Forlorn hope, for even then she had known she was homely: her brown, lustreless hair, nose just a little too sharp, heavy buttocks. She'd been to Twin Fords as a child, often, and had seen the many pretty girls there.

That time when she was sixteen, some young couple had got married. There'd been a party, music, laughter, and in the evening there would be drinking and dancing. An old friend of her father's had said they could stay the night. Well, Brad Berea knew how to drink and dance, and he had seen how Irma needed it. It seemed only fair.

But while Brad and Irma whirled to the wild music, Glina was simply . . . whirled away! A Gypsy lad shared his wine with her, and walked her behind a tree where the branches came down low. Now, she couldn't even remember how he'd looked. But then he had been the handsomest boy in town, and unlike Nestor he'd known exactly what to do. His mouth had sucked the breath from her lungs, and lifting her skirts he'd slipped into her slick as an eel. Afterwards . . . he was gone as quick as he came. No one had known but Glina – oh, and the boy, of course – but she'd dreamed of him almost every night since, right up until Nestor came. And then she'd dreamed of Nestor.

One day when her father was off hunting, and her mother washed clothes and stored vegetables, Glina had finished her tasks about the cabin and gone down to the river where Nestor was fishing. She deliberately wore a short dress and a blouse buttoned to the waist. And as soon as she was out of sight of the cabin, she'd quickly unbuttoned the top of her blouse to show the inner curve of her soft breasts.

Sitting down beside Nestor, she'd made a great play of lifting her dress so that her thighs would show, and talking to him she'd held his face towards her and leaned forward, tempting his eyes to her cleavage. And he *had* looked at her. There had been something in his eyes at least, even if she couldn't say what. But despite that while she talked to him she leaned her hand on his thigh and squeezed it, always when she stopped speaking and relaxed, his attention would return to the river and his line.

Committed, finally Glina had stripped naked, waded into the water, and bathed there right in front of him. He wasn't likely to tell anyone, after all. No longer able to fish, Nestor had watched her; and as she came out of the river gleaming wet, breasts lolling, at last he had stood up. Then ... she'd definitely seen something in his eyes, and a little more than something in his hand.

Hurrying him out of his clothes, she had kissed him all over that body she'd so cared for, and guided his hand to her aching flesh while she sucked on his rod. And Nestor: he might be damaged in his mind, but his body was whole; it wasn't long before the fire in his loins sparked faint, fleeting, disjointed memories in his head. And then ...

... It had been as it was now, as it had been ever since.

In the sun-dappled shade of a willow, driving into

her as if to split her, Nestor's face had been a mask of – what? – hatred? Oh, he had wanted her body, desperately desired to pour all of his angers, his frustrations into her, and so empty himself of them for a little while at least. But it wasn't love or even lust that he felt. No, for if anything Nestor took revenge against something which even he had forgotten, something which he had never understood in the first place.

His hands had crushed her breasts, which were scarcely hurt but yielded to the pain, the pleasure, and his mouth had crushed her mouth. And Nestor had moaned as he came again and again into her, and she felt the burn of his hot spray deep in her core. He had moaned a name – Minha? Minya? – Misha! And it was like a curse coughed from his damp slack mouth as his right hand left her breasts to tighten on Glina's throat.

But Glina was no weak little thing to be throttled. Now as then, she took his hair, yanked back his head, grasped him with her sex and sucked the last drop of loathing out of him; until he fell exhausted on his side, and rolled over on to his back. And then she hugged him, and sobbed while she worked his shrivelling flesh in her hand. She sobbed for herself, because she wasn't this Misha who had hurt him so much – whom he must have loved – and for Nestor himself, *because* he had been hurt so much . . .

And so Glina loved him, and was in turn 'loved'.

Later she used him, sat on him where her hands had brought him back to life. But because his eyes were dull again and his body's responses simply that, responses, she took cold pleasure in it . . .

On their way back to the cabin, suddenly Nestor paused and his face turned up to the sky. He sniffed – an animal sound – and his dark eyes flashed starshine. A moment later and Glina felt, sensed, heard it too. And gasped!

The moon was floating low over the distant barrier range. But there was more than moon and stars in the sky. Small dark shadows flitted high overhead; they blotted out the starlight and passed on. Then larger, more sinister manta shapes came gliding behind, while bringing up the rear –

– Something pulsed and throbbed, faint at first but growing louder.

'Down!' Glina whispered, dragging Nestor to his knees in a clump of night damp bushes. And a pair of Wamphyri warriors went spurting and pulsing overhead, their chitin armour tinged blue in the glitter of the stars.

A breeze had come up; it formed the blue-grey exhaust gases of the warriors into a veil across the sky; it fell on the forest in an acrid stench of something dead and crawling with maggots. Glina held her breath, but Nestor breathed deep. And suddenly ... he was alert! Brushing her hand away, he stood up, came slowly erect as the shapes of nightmare passed from view. He saw the sentient, liquid eyes of the warriors swivelling and scanning in their underbellies, and never knew how lucky he was that they didn't scan him. The hunting party sped off into the deepening night, heading north and slightly west.

And: 'Wamphyri!' Glina breathed, when they had gone.

Wamphyri! The word burned like cold fire.

Nestor looked at her. He was pale; there was recognition, a question in his eyes. His mouth twitched a little, and spoke at last. 'Wamphyri?'

'*Shhh!*' she cautioned, despite that they had gone.

Seconds passed and he spoke again, urgently. 'Wamphyri?'

Brad Berea came rushing along the path from the cabin. He was buttoning his jacket, his breath forming plumes in the suddenly cold air. 'Nestor ... and Glina!' He brushed Nestor aside, fell on his daughter and hugged her. 'We heard them – their warriors – and I knew you were out here. But we're well hidden away in the trees and they passed us by, again ...'

Nestor took his arm, and Brad looked at him in surprise. 'Eh?' he said. 'What's this? Life in the dummy? Has it scared some wits into him, then?'

'Again?' said Nestor. 'They've passed us by, again?'

'A yellow mocklark!' Brad grunted. 'He repeats my words like a bird, without understanding a one of them!'

'Wamphyri!' Nestor suddenly shouted, and grabbed Brad by the throat. But Brad was strong, and now that the danger was past he was also angry. He tripped Nestor and knocked him flying into the bushes.

'Father!' Glina cried. 'He was only frightened!' But she wondered ... Nestor's eyes had been so strange watching those monsters fly overhead ... she had sensed his fascination.

Nestor stood up and she took his arm. 'Aye, look after him,' her father grunted, turning back toward the cabin. 'For if he goes for me again you'll be tending his cracked skull a second time!'

As he faded into the darkness, Nestor whispered: 'Again? Have they passed ... before?'

'When you were sick,' she told him. 'It was like tonight, just an hour or so after the sun was down. They had been doing some early hunting. We saw them heading home again, toward the Northstar, which shines on Starside's last aerie.'

'The Northstar!' he said, turning his head unerringly in that direction, and gazing at the evilly glittering star, frozen like a chunk of ice over the barrier range. 'Heading home. The Wamphyri . . .'

'Come on,' she said, almost dragging him along the path. 'Let's get in.'

But not far from the cabin she pushed him against a tree and felt to see if there was life in him yet. There was still time, barely. Sometimes, even though she'd had him more than once, he would be ready; but not tonight. And as she took his hand again and led him back to the cabin, still his eyes were fixed on the low silhouette of the mountains, and the star of ill-omen which lit them. And in Nestor's mind, all unheard:

Home – the Northstar – the last aerie – the Wamphyri! Compared to which, the lure of Glina's body was nothing . . .

He left the cabin silently, in the long night. And when Glina woke up to answer a call of nature she saw his bed, empty.

Such a howling then! It woke up the two in the loft. Her father came down and told her: 'What, gone? But he'll probably be back . . . if not, good riddance! Only one master here, Glina, and I don't much care for a dog that bites his master's hand.'

Then, seeing that Nestor had taken a crossbow and knife, he cursed him long and loud. But what the hell: it wasn't his good crossbow. And certainly the idiot would need *some* protection, out there on his own in the night.

In a while Brad went back to bed, and even through Glina's sobbing he slept like a baby . . .

Lured irresistibly by the Northstar, Nestor travelled through the night-dark woods. Where streams were shallow he waded them, and where gullies looked dangerous he skirted around. But always his point of reference was the ice-chip star glittering cold on the barrier mountains. Beyond those mountains lay Starside, the last aerie, home of the Wamphyri. And now that he had seen *them* again, soaring dark against the night, at last everything had seemed to come together.

Nestor knew he'd been there before; he couldn't remember the circumstances, but he *had* been there. Perhaps Starside was his source, his origin. Certainly it was his destiny. Maybe he was an outcast, a changeling freak banished from his own kind to make his way as best he might in the world. Well, and now he was on his way back again.

As for Sunside:

He had enemies here; he must be careful along the way; men had pursued him, hurt him, would kill him if they could! He had scars to prove it. And he remembered ... things. All of his time with the Bereas, he had remembered them but could not, dared not, speak of them. Once, without thinking, he had told Brad Berea, 'I am the Lord Nestor.' But after that he'd said no more. For like his many unfocused thoughts and memories, his tongue was a traitor; it would betray him; there had been enough of betrayals already.

Once, he had a friend, a so-called 'brother', a child who played with him when he himself was a child. But he had been a traitor whose cheating thoughts were hidden behind a screen of numbers, which he'd used like a plague to torment Nestor, even in his dreams. Now: that one was his greatest enemy!

Once, Nestor had loved a girl, who did not love him back. She, too, was treacherous. But like it or not she *would* 'love' him one day. And she would die loving him. It was his vow.

Once, he had had a flyer. He remembered its fate: boiling away into rottenness in the hills. He also remembered taking a bolt in his side; and the river whose cold caresses had nearly drowned him; and Glina, whose warm caresses had given him his manhood. If she had known who and what he was ... perhaps she would not have been so eager. Not even the homely Glina.

I am the Lord Nestor, of the Wamphyri!

But a Lord in exile, stripped of his powers, who was now returning home ...

He trekked through all the hours of night, effortlessly. Given purpose, he was tireless. But there would be time enough for sleep in the daylight, before moving on again towards his Starside destination. And always the Northstar tugging at him, and the miles flying under his feet.

He let instinct guide him. Only set his sights on that bright blue ice-shard in the sky, and let his body take over ... the *idea* itself would do the rest. The hours sped by to match the miles; eventually his footsteps faltered; his body was not as tireless as he'd thought.

He drank from a stream, washed the grit of the forest from his eyes, sat down with his back to a tree. Almost without knowing it he slept, and woke up shivering, lost, wondering where he was. But the Northstar was there, and the *idea* lived again. As he got his limbs in motion, so his hot blood pounded and soon he was warm.

He came upon an encampment of Szgany. There were guards out, with at least one wolf. No doubt alerted by their watchdog, the men heard him, called out a password; Nestor made no answer but hurried on. They released their animal, which came bounding in his tracks and found him at once. He turned snarling, aimed his bolt right down its throat. But ... the wolf wagged its tail, came sniffing, jumped up to lick his face! Dimly then, Nestor remembered how he and ... he and ... one other (someone close? But he had no one who was close!) had had a way with canines. As a child, wild dogs had come out of the woods to play with him; domesticated wolves, 'guard dogs' like this one, had permitted the very roughest of games without turning on him; wild wolves in the hills had moved cautiously, but without animosity, out of his path.

He'd never made anything of it. Nor did he now. Indeed, he saw the wolf's friendliness as a stupid mistake. He wasn't Szgany. He was the Lord Nestor! But he was one and they were many, and they would be smarter than their tame wolf.

He moved on . . .

In the night he wasted a deal of time: sleeping, trekking around obstacles, getting mired in this or that bog. But seen through breaks in the trees, black against the dark-blue sky and ice-blue stars, the mountains drew ever closer. Likewise the dawn.

Where the forest thinned out and grew into foothills he rested a while, gazed out over Sunside and saw the first pale blush of light on the horizon. Hours yet to the true dawn, and more to go to sunup, but this was the start of it. Nestor had no fear of the sun: it was part of his freakishness, that the sun had no power over him. His flyer had not been so fortunate. That . . . puzzled him, but it was so.

He seemed to remember a pass through the mountains. But where would that lie? To the east or to the west? He thought east. But as he made to follow an old and half-familiar trail through the foothills –

– A sound, even movement up ahead! Grey shadows in the pre-dawn dusk, which was as yet much closer to night than day. Nestor loped silently through a ground mist swirling round his ankles like a disturbed shroud. On his right hand, the forest, and on his left the foothills rising towards the barrier range. But up there where the way was steep: something huge, grey and weird, projecting over the rim of a bluff, nodding and swaying against the dark-blue sky. It scanned the night with dull, disinterested eyes in a diamond-shaped head at the end of a long, tapering neck. An unmistakable design: a flyer! Ideally situated for launching, it waited there. Which could mean only one thing: that somewhere down here its vampire master, a Lord or lieutenant of the Wamphyri, was even now abroad in the night!

Night for the moment, aye, but dawn was fast approaching. Whoever was the beast's keeper, he'd have to be back soon. If he was not already here . . .

Desiring to see without being seen, to know without being known, Nestor went more quietly yet. He moved like a cat along the trail, and keeping to the darkest shadows passed under the flyer in its launch site. But in a while, higher up the slope and vague in the deceptive light, he saw a second creature. So, two of the flying beasts, and apparently no one in attendance. It could only be a small hunting party.

Though it seemed unlikely that such dull, stupid creatures would be used as observers, still Nestor took no chances but kept himself hidden anyway. A further fifty paces, and . . . what was that down there, where an outcrop of boulders tumbled to meet the trees? A fire?

It *was* a fire, flickering red and yellow in the lee of boulders; smoke rising in a grey spiral, carrying a whiff of roasting – what, rabbit? – to Nestor's nostrils and making his mouth water. And . . . was that a figure hunkered down, as if turning a spit? Some Szgany loner, fixing himself an early breakfast? It was surely so; for the Wamphyri weren't keen on roasted meat. And they weren't much for rabbits, either! But didn't this idiot know there were vampires about, two of them at least; or three, if Nestor included himself?

He glanced back over his shoulder. The pre-dawn mist was rising, obscuring the trail. No sign of the creatures perched on the hillside now; they were there, of course, but had disappeared utterly in mist and gloom. This fool at his fire was surely unaware of them. But the Wamphyri must return soon. And Nestor had no doubt but that they would be aware of him!

The man had food; Nestor was hungry; he could warn him, share his breakfast. And no treachery to the Wamphyri, his own kind, in this. He was an outcast after all. And his appearance would fool this loner even as it had fooled Brad Berea. But in any case, best to take precautions.

Nestor's crossbow was ready, loaded. Taking care to avoid loose pebbles which might be dislodged, he climbed down boulder to boulder; while below him the fool at the fire coughed where he turned his spit, grunting and grumbling to himself as if he were the only man in the world! Nestor got close, very close, until suddenly the hunched figure fell silent and sniffed the air, looked up and began to turn his head.

The man would be armed; Nestor didn't want another bolt in him; he ducked down behind rocks, waited, gradually nerved himself to look out, even to cry out, and so warn the other of his presence. The mist was thickening, and it had a slimy feel to it. Nestor felt his flesh creeping as he looked out between a 'V' in the rocks.

The loner was still there, crouched down. But –

– He was no longer alone!

Emerging from a dark copse to one side, and flowing like some swift and deadly shadow over the mist-wreathed ground, a second figure approached him. But there could be no mistaking this one – or his intentions. He was Wamphyri, and his mind was full of murder! Even in silhouette and little more than a dark blot, still his face was freakish; a jutting bulge of a head with a stunted, vibrating tentacle extended towards his victim.

Nestor scarcely required it, but as if to finally prove this creature's nature it glanced at him – the merest glance – where it sped silent as smoke to its target. Its eyes were red as coals, burning in the hideously misshapen, quivering mask of its face!

Unable to contain himself – jerking with an involuntary, spastic movement – Nestor stood up, and a pebble was squeezed out from beneath his sandal! The man at the fire heard it clattering in the rocks; he swivelled on his heel, came to his feet in one smoothly flowing movement. But in so doing he turned his back on the thing bearing down upon him!

Without conscious thought – all instinct – Nestor cried out a warning, aimed his crossbow, discharged the weapon at the vampire. It seemed he knew, again by instinct, where his loyalties lay. He reacted as a Traveller, Szgany, and not the changeling that he thought he was. Or perhaps it wasn't as complex as that. Maybe it was simply that when the tentacle-faced monster had looked at him with its scarlet eyes, Nestor had *known* that he was next!

Almost within striking distance of his intended victim, the vampire Lord was hit in the neck, sent staggering. And as Nestor lost his footing and came sliding over the dome of the last great boulder to crash down on his back, so the would-be 'victim' snatched up a brand and turned towards his attacker. Nestor lay there on his back, winded, gaping at the two. For now in the full firelight he could clearly see his mistake: that *both* of these creatures were Wamphyri!

II

The Wamphyri Lords Wran (the Rage) Killglance and Vasagi the Suck glared at each other red-eyed across Nestor where he lay on his back, winded. They ignored him; they would not let him distract them from their quarrel, their duel, their mutual hatred. Now that he had shot his bolt he was nothing to them anyway. But from Nestor's point of view, *they* were awesome, huge – and hugely malevolent.

'Treacherous bastard!' Wran snarled at Vasagi, waving his sputtering brand in the other's hideous face and kicking Nestor out of the way. 'So, you thought to come upon me under cover of this fool's blundering approach, eh? What, and did you think it likely I'd mistake his clatter for your own oily slither?' (In point of fact he had done just that.)

Vasagi's wet, glistening siphon was like the piston shaft of some alien penis; it made an almost sexual, sucking sound as it slid in and out of its sheath in the tip of his defensively mobile trunk or tentacle. He tugged at Nestor's bolt, which had penetrated the base of his thick, corded neck above his left shoulder and emerged at the back, having missed the spinal column by a hair's-breadth. He made no answer that Nestor could hear, but Wran the Rage heard it well enough:

Killglance, you spotted dog! Only good fortune and this Szgany scum together saved you from my single, clean, killing thrust. So now you face my gauntlet – before I ram my probe deep in your spine, to drain your cringing leech!

He was more voluble than was his wont; it was bluff and Wran knew it; Vasagi dared not let him see the true colour of his secret thoughts. His wound was not serious: an inconvenience, at worst. But even a bee sting can swing the balance of a fight, and the youth's bolt was more than a bee sting. Wran knew that the Suck was off balance, so why prolong it?

Holding the blazing firebrand awkwardly in his left hand, he flicked back his cloak from his right side and so displayed his gauntlet. It glittered red and yellow in the firelight as he flexed his hand within its metal sheath. Vasagi feinted to the left, the right; his movements were quicksilver; even with the ironwood bolt skewering his neck at an angle from side to back, still he was no mean opponent.

Still sprawling on his back but no longer winded, Nestor attempted to scramble away from the two. But the Suck was moving in the same direction. As Vasagi made a lunge at Wran, his feet got tangled in Nestor's threshing legs. That was the opening Wran needed. While Vasagi stumbled he moved in, hurled his torch into the Suck's writhing face and shrinking eyes, grasping his facial anomaly behind the wad of muscle which propelled its siphon. And with Vasagi's gauntlet tearing his back open to the ribs, Wran aimed a blow at his enemy's proboscis.

Wran's mind telegraphed his grisly intention; Vasagi saw it coming; he had no answer except to scream a desperate mental denial: *Nooooo!*

Such was the force of the Suck's telepathic terror that even Nestor heard it. With Harry Keogh's blood running in his veins, and with his own share of his brother's as yet undeveloped mentalist talent, Vasagi's mind-shriek got through to him and froze him to the marrow. Somehow he lurched upright, but incapable of flight he simply fell back against the outcrop.

While Vasagi had somehow avoided his enemy's first blow, still Wran had not relinquished his hold on the Suck's proboscis. Now the Rage flexed his metal-clad hand in a certain way, and in the moment before he struck a razor spine like the curved frill on a lizard's back sprang erect from his gauntlet's knuckles to Wran's wrist. And Nestor saw the rest of it as a blur of bloody motion.

Wran's gauntlet sliced into the Suck's shuddering snout and cut it half-way through, and with a tearing, sawing, snatching action, Wran quickly completed the job. Then he stepped back a pace to toss the severed trunk and its siphon tip hissing into the fire, and laughed at Vasagi where he staggered to and fro, clawing at his crimson face.

Despite Wran's own agony – the fact that the back of his cloak had been torn open, and bloody tatters of meat hung from his gouged ribs – he laughed! 'Ah, and what shall they call you now?' he crowed. 'Vasagi the Slobber?'

Vasagi's face spurted blood from the sleeve of raw flesh which had housed his probe. His pain was greater than Wran's, so much so that tears of agony started out of eyes half-blind from the other's torch-thrust. He held out his gauntlet before him, waving it to and fro like a blind man's stick. But there was no mercy in Wran the Rage. Still baying with laughter, he moved in and snatched up the blazing brand again. Vasagi turned to flee, stumbled blindly over sharp, jutting rocks, and went down.

Wran was on him in a flash; he leaped . . . came down massively with both booted feet on Vasagi's outstretched gauntlet forearm. Bones snapped sickeningly, and even Vasagi managed a gurgling shriek – an actual sound – through the scarlet orifice which was his ruined face.

Nestor's mouth was dry as kindling. He glanced here and there in the oh-so-gradually brightening air, looked for his crossbow. It had tumbled with him from on high, gone clattering into the scree. He saw a dull gleam among the rocks and edged towards it, but yet continued to watch the now totally unequal fight.

Wran kicked at Vasagi's gauntlet hand until the weapon came loose, then booted it out of reach. Half-blind, siphon-severed, ungauntleted, and his arm flopping loosely, still the Suck tried to stumble to his feet. Every time he almost got up, Wran kicked his feet from under him again. Finally, close to exhaustion, Vasagi flopped and jerked on the ground. Then Wran went to one knee beside him, grasped the ironwood bolt in his neck, and twisted it until the other's writhing was almost a vibration of sheerest agony.

Nestor's trembling hand dragged his crossbow out from a crack in the rocks. He primed it two-handed, unclipped the spare bolt from its housing under the tiller. And –

'Aye, load your weapon,' Wran's deep bass voice growled from only four or five swift paces away. 'Load it, and bring it here.' Nestor obeyed the first instruction, but as for the second: he aimed the crossbow at Wran. The other straightened up but kept a booted foot on the writhing Vasagi's neck. 'Well then,' he said, his scarlet gaze rapt on Nestor, 'and what are you waiting for? Shoot me, if you're sure you can hit my heart. But if you're not, best do as I say.'

Nestor found his voice. 'You . . . are Wamphyri!'

Wran nodded. 'And you're a fool! But a fool who probably saved my life. Who saved me a deal of trouble, anyway. I owe you for that. But only fire that bolt into me, I'll owe you a great deal more. And I'll pay you back bit by bit, until your screams ring out so loud as to bring down the avalanches! Now then, boy. Don't make me wait but put your bolt in this loathsome thing's heart.' He took his foot off the other's neck and Vasagi sat up.

Nestor looked at him, and was more frightened of him now than he'd been before ... such a hideous, pitiful sight ... it would be a mercy to kill him. He had only one bolt. He looked at the ugly, broken, bleeding Vasagi, and at Wran. The latter was more the man; he was – what, handsome? Handsomely dressed, anyway. He looked every bit the vampire Lord that Nestor had always pretended, imagined, and now believed himself to be.

'*Hah!*' Wran snorted. 'No guts for it, eh? But when I give orders, I expect my thralls to jump!'

'Thrall?' Nestor growled back. 'I ... am the Lord Nestor!'

'Eh?' Wran frowned, stepped away from Vasagi, took a pace towards Nestor. 'You're what? A Lord, did you say?' Behind him, Vasagi took up a jagged rock in his left hand, came flowing to his feet.

Nestor yelled, 'Look out!' And Wran hunched his shoulders, ducked down, stepped aside. An instant later, Nestor's bolt was sent thrumming through the air to bury itself to the flight in Vasagi's already scarlet tunic. Except this time when the Suck was knocked down, he stayed down ...

The bolt had struck close enough to Vasagi's heart to paralyse him. With Nestor's aid, Wran dragged him by the legs, flopping, away from the rocks and up the slope to a place where the hard earth faced squarely south. There he pegged him out face-down, to await the rising sun.

'Of course, we shall be long gone from here by then,'

Wran said. 'A pity, for I fancy I'd relish the Suck's screams as the sun reduces him to so much smoulder!'

'His screams?' Nestor looked in horror at the pegged-out thing. 'But how can he scream?'

'With his mind,' Wran explained. And Nestor remembered how he had 'heard' Vasagi's shriek of denial as Wran went to sever his proboscis.

'Ah!' he said.

Wran turned his scarlet gaze upon him and snorted. '*Huh!* You don't know too much for a "Lord", do you?' He grinned, in his way. 'And just what sort of a "Lord" are you, anyway?'

'An outcast,' Nestor lifted his chin. 'Cast out of Starside. And now I'm on my way back.'

'Really!' the other nodded, fingered his wen soberly. The lad amused him. 'Cast out, you say? For some heinous crime or other, perhaps? Against the Wamphyri?'

'I don't know,' Nestor shook his head, ran a hand through his hair, felt the plate of new bone where his scalp was thick and rough at the back. 'I don't ... remember.' Wran looked deep into his dark eyes; they seemed dazed, and the mind behind them not entirely there. Obviously this one had survived some raid or other – barely! But he was well enough now, physically at least.

'So, you'd be a Lord of the Wamphyri, eh?' Wran nodded again. An amusing scheme was taking shape in his mind. How it would work out he didn't know, must wait and see. But as far as Vasagi the Suck was concerned, certainly it would give Wran the last and loudest laugh. 'Well, it's not everyone who gets to be a Lord,' he said. 'But in your case – maybe I can arrange it.' Then he glanced south and saw the pale stain blossoming on the horizon, and his red eyes narrowed at once. 'Except we must do it quickly.'

'Do what?' Nestor was innocent as a child. He started as Vasagi made a slobbering sound and blew red bubbles, and began to come awake.

Wran made no answer but his eyes were totally evil, menacing – inviting? – when he asked: 'Are you ... hungry?' He glanced at Vasagi. 'Me, I'm hungry, and this one has a leech in him. If our roles were reversed, he'd do the same to me.'

Again Nestor felt prompted to ask, *Do what?* But he kept the question to himself and backed away. For Wran had gone to his knees, and his metamorphic face was less manlike now. His mouth was a gash that opened like a trapdoor, impossibly wide. Teeth grew visibly in that crimson hole, elongating, curving like white daggers from the ruptured ridges of his jaws. They were fangs, with eye teeth like knives; their 'blades' were long as Nestor's own knife, and overlapped Wran's trembling lower lip! His nose – dark and squat before, with large black nostrils – grew yet more convoluted, quivering, sensitive as a bat's. And his eyes seemed almost to drip blood.

'Aye, leave me now,' he coughed the words out, shooting Nestor a look that brooked no argument. 'But not too far. And when I call out for you, come at once.' His blunt fingers tore Vasagi's tunic open, and commenced to knead the ridge of his exposed spine.

Nestor left him, went stumbling back down to the trail, and along it to the dying embers of Wran's fire. The roasted meat smell was heavy in the air now. Some wild creature moved there, a fox or feral dog, scurrying at Nestor's approach. It grabbed up the spit and meat entire from where it lay toppled to one side, dropped the hot food and slunk into the shadows, returned in a moment to snatch up the meat again.

Nestor had not looked at Wran's roast before; but

now, as it lay there smoking, and as the fox – it was a fox, yes – snapped it up a second time, he saw what it was. At least, he *believed* he saw what it was. And then he no longer *wished* to know what it was, except its shape was something his mind couldn't erase: the blackened form of a tiny Szgany infant! The 'bait' which Wran had used to alert Vasagi to his presence here and lure him to his doom.

'Nestor, attend me now!' Wran's shout drifted down to him through the thinning mist. Nestor looked up, saw how the dawn was advancing. Above the barrier range, the Northstar's glitter was much reduced. Ah, but as he saw that star of ill-omen the *idea* returned to burn as brightly as ever, and his horror shrank down. What, fear? Trembling? Trepidation? No, for this was his legacy. He was the Lord Nestor, and he was going home.

He returned to Wran and saw what he had done, what he was even now about: a nightmarish act or acts! But Nestor's sensitivities were severely blunted, reduced, even reversed. What would so recently have horrified him merely fascinated him now. These were things which he had somehow forgotten or been caused to forget, which he must now remember, re-learn, if he was to be successful in Starside. Perhaps his failure to appreciate such things *in the first place* was responsible for his current privations!

Wran saw his morbid fascination and nodded. 'Well, you're a rare one, I'll grant you that. I gave you the opportunity to run for it – it's almost dawn; I have to go; I would not have pursued you – but you're still here. You really *do* want to be Wamphyri.'

Nestor only half heard him, glanced at him, saw that his face and mouth were more nearly 'human' again, however bloody. But mainly he gazed at Vasagi: his back laid open to the naked bone, and something black – his leech? – writhing there, but feebly, like a dying snake of black muscle, half welded to his spine within his body. The black thing had been punctured and leaked crimson, the richest colour Nestor could imagine, whose shade matched precisely the blood on Wran's face and lips.

In a voice filled with wonder but little or no fear, finally Nestor asked: 'What caused you to fight? For plainly you are both Wamphyri.'

Wran laughed. 'Isn't that enough reason?' And then, more soberly: 'He insulted me.' (He shrugged.) 'Well, we insulted each other. Our rivalries were various and couldn't continue. We dwelled too close together and crossed each other's paths too often. When it came, the challenge was mutual and could only be resolved like this: one of us must die. But even so, we had no desire to entertain our "brothers" and our "sister" in Starside's last aerie. And so our duel would be a private thing and take place here, on Sunside. No rules except that we come on our own, with all the length and breadth of Sunside for a battleground, and the long night from sundown to sunup for duration.'

'What if he had not come to you?' Nestor's eyes stayed rapt upon the black thing's spastic movements where it gradually detached itself from Vasagi's spine.

'Then there was always tomorrow night,' the other answered. 'But that was unlikely. For to live another night here meant living another day here. Which was the other proviso: that once we set out from Starside, we could not return until it was finished. Aye, and only one of us could go back. Anything else would be seen as – what? – half-hearted at best, cowardice at worst. But we were not cowards, the Suck and I, nor were we half-hearted.'

'That . . . *thing*,' Nestor nodded towards the maimed, tortured, outstretched form of Vasagi, 'is coming out of him.'

'His leech?' Wran answered. 'Indeed it is! For it knows he is a loser. Perhaps it will have a better chance . . . elsewhere?' Grinning hideously, he cocked his head on one side.

'Elsewhere?' Nestor watched the thing's struggles as it emerged like a long, corrugated slug from Vasagi on-to the hard earth. Blind, indeed eyeless, still its 'head' turned in Wran's direction as it sensed him there. And it lingered like that a moment, swaying this way and that as if it were exhausted and about to collapse. The thing was all of eighteen inches long, ridgy, shiny black and mottled green, and red from the Suck's spilled blood.

'A strong new host,' Wran's chuckle was a clotted gurgle, 'whose precious blood would save its life. Except I can't allow that, for there's far too much of Vasagi in it. So . . . give me your knife.'

Nestor handed over the knife, and as he moved so Vasagi's leech turned towards him. Wran had been appraised; he already had a leech; he'd been rejected as a possible host. But Nestor . . . had not. And with slow, painful contractions of its underbelly, it commenced to glide towards him.

But: 'Ah, no, my friend!' Wran cried. He fell on it, grasped its body with an iron hand, quick as a flash detached its six-inch 'head' and hurled it away, out over the misted trail. There was very little blood left in it to bleed, and very little strength. At first it flexed and whipped like a fish fresh from the river, but then in a moment lay still. Wran stood up from it and grunted: 'Now . . . watch!'

Nestor scarcely needed telling; he couldn't take his

eyes off the thing, which had turned a sick, glistening grey. It lay on its back now, more slug-like than ever, its belly silvery in the rapidly improving light. Something like a blister formed in the slit which might be a reproductive organ, and Wran pointed, saying: 'Ah, the very thing! Newborn, it knows nothing. In its way, why, it's much like yourself, Nestor! Aye, Vasagi's egg is all instinct. See!'

The blister was now a small grey sphere no larger than a man's thumbnail, which detached itself from the parent body and slid down the thing's belly to the earth. Nestor saw that there was something mobile within it. He had watched tadpoles emerging from frogspawn when he was a child; it was like that, but the casing of the egg was more like a film than a jelly. Suddenly it popped like a bubble, releasing its contents. The small, silvery sphere which emerged was frantic; covered with hundreds of flickering hairs, it skittered to and fro among the pebbles.

Wran said: 'Can you believe it? Can you understand, Nestor? For this tiny, harmless thing ... *is* what you would be! It *is* Wamphyri!' He went to one knee again, reached out his hand to touch it – and the sphere ran along his finger on to his palm and spun there like a top. He held it out so that Nestor could see it more clearly: this whirling thing in his palm – which suddenly grew motionless! And:

'Ah!' Wran said. 'It would test me. Watch closely.'

Nestor moved closer, gaped; his eyes were wide and his jaw hung open. The egg put out a single red thorn which sank effortlessly into the horny flesh of Wran's hand. And it tested – it *tasted* – him! Then ... the stinger was withdrawn in a moment, and the egg commenced spinning again.

'Ah, shame!' Wran cried. 'It rejects me! Only enter my

body . . . it would be devoured in a moment, and knows it. But *your* body is an entirely different thing!' Wran stopped smiling; his eyes were suddenly huge, blazing with hell's fires; he blew the vampire egg off the palm of his hand like blowing a kiss – directly into Nestor's face!

Nestor closed his mouth, turned his face aside as the stench of Wran's breath hit him. But the egg hit him at one and the same time, and clung like spittle to his cheek – for a single moment. Then he felt it mobile on his flesh, inside his shirt, moving to the back of his neck. And Wran was right: from then on it was all instinct. Instinct told him to crush this thing, remove it, kill it, before he in turn was tested, tasted. Too late, for in his case that wasn't necessary. The egg had instincts, too, and knew that Nestor was innocent.

In position, the shimmering pearly sphere turned scarlet. Requiring no ovipositor, it soaked into him, was absorbed into Nestor's flesh like water into sand. Settling to his spine, it made contact and fused with his shrinking nerve cells. Until which time, Nestor had never really known what pain was. But now he knew.

He started, cried out, leaped, gave a reflex bound into the air with his limbs flying in all directions. He came down on his back among sharp stones and didn't even feel them, but he felt the thing exploring his spine. He jumped up, bounded again, as if to shake it loose. And the pain, which was now spreading through every part of his body – back, skull, all of his limbs – increased. There was a fire in his veins, which burned worse than vinegar in an open wound.

He tripped, fell, rolled among rocks which cut him, and felt nothing of it. For his cuts were like scratches compared to a lashing whip, except there were a hundred whips and they were all lashing inside him.

Through all of this Wran the Rage laughed like a madman – a mad thing – laughed, danced and held his sides, and finally sat down, rocking this way and that in hellish glee. He laughed until tears streamed from his red eyes, ran down his grey cheeks to drip from the wen on his chin; laughed till he leaned back against a rock and the raw flesh of his back was rubbed. And at that ... perhaps at last he appreciated something of Nestor's pain, too.

Nestor had passed through panic and desperation and was well on his way into hell. He thought he was dying, that his agonies must soon kill him, but not soon enough, and knew he would welcome Death as a friend, a merciful release. His skull was bursting; his spine was on fire; acid coursed in his veins where he rolled and writhed upon the ground. But as Wran approached him, he summoned strength from somewhere and jerked to his knees, and begged him, 'P-p-please!'

'Aye, enough,' Wran nodded, and hit him just once ...

'Wake up!' A hand hard as old leather slapped Nestor's face, rocking his head to and fro. He sat propped against a boulder, exhausted, with the agony of his internal conflict gone now but all of his new cuts and bruises burning and throbbing. Opening his eyes, he saw Wran of the Wamphyri standing huge against the dawn. Dawn, yes, for the vampire Lord was a silhouette with Sunside for a backdrop; while beyond him on the rim of the world, a fan of golden spokes was already probing the sky.

'I go now,' Wran grunted. 'Up there on the bluff,' he jerked his head, 'two flyers are waiting. One of them was Vasagi's. As you're aware, he no longer has need of it. You have his egg, so why not his flyer too, eh?

Earlier, as you approached me in the night, my ears followed you along every inch of your route. Unless you were blind you saw the beasts. Am I right?'

Nestor nodded, which was as much as he could do.

'Well then, my Lord Nestor, the rest is up to you,' Wran told him. 'If you would come to Starside, the way stands open. Command Vasagi's beast and fly it home. Or if you're too weak, then it's best you stay here. Except I would warn you, the egg is sensitive: when it feels the sun upon your flesh its frenzy may well kill you. So fly or die, it's simple as that.'

Again Nestor nodded. But his eyes were less vacant now; indeed they were unwavering, hard, fixed upon Wran's face as if to remember every last line and pore of it. 'The night is flown,' Wran said. 'An hour at most before a golden blister bursts on the world's rim, and splashes these barrier mountains with yellow pus. But in Starside, all is safe and dark.'

He turned and strode away, and could feel Nestor's eyes burning on his back as he climbed the rugged slope towards his flyer . . .

Nestor couldn't walk, so he crawled on hands and knees. But as he passed the pegged-out form of Vasagi, something spoke in his head: *Boy, loosen these pegs.*

It was a whisper, faint, tortured, pitiful. As yet, Nestor could still pity. He looked at Vasagi where he lay: his bloody, mutilated face blowing scarlet froth into the dust; his broken arm and ravaged spine; a bolt projecting from his back, and his neck a gaping mess where the first bolt had been wrenched free and tossed aside. Yet still alive!

Aye, but dying, the voice came again. *Wran hurt me sorely, but it was you who brought me down. So perhaps you're worthy to be Wamphyri at that. But you* have my egg, my flyer ... must you take my life, too? It is finished anyway — but not like this, I beg you. Pull out the pegs, and let me crawl away into some cave to die. But not in the sunlight, for you can't know what it is ... for one like me ... to die in sunlight ...

Nestor knew well enough. Hadn't his flyer gone the same way, melting into stench and evaporation? But to pull out the pegs ... what if this creature were still dangerous?

The laughter which swelled in his mind then was bitter, and filled with a painful irony. *Dangerous? Oh, I was, it's true! But now? I have no leech; I am broken, gutted, an empty shell. But you ... you are, or you were, Szgany. And you have things in you other than the morbid emotions of the Wamphyri. For a little while longer, at least. Which is why I beg you one last time: pull out the pegs.*

Nestor did it, and crawled on. In a little while he could get to his feet. He looked back, and Vasagi was still stretched there; he hadn't moved; perhaps he couldn't. Nestor put him out of his mind and went to his flyer.

The beast saw him coming and looked at him through stupid, lustreless eyes. He approached it carefully, for he saw how it could roll or flop on him and crush his life out. But it was of vampire stuff and sensed the vampire in Nestor; it blinked its great eyes nervously as he took hold of its trappings, no more than that. Then, as he dragged himself up into the saddle, he saw Vasagi's bloody gauntlet hanging from a strap, where Wran had left it for him. Of course, for what's a Lord of the Wamphyri without his gauntlet?

Sunside was all hazy grey and green now, with mists rising out of the dark forests and blue smoke from distant campsites and townships, and all the birds waking up, commencing their dawn chorus. Central on the southern horizon, a yellow glow threatened at any moment to become a golden furnace.

Nestor dug his heels into his mount's sides at the base of its swaying neck, and gave a tentative jerk on the reins. 'Up,' he grunted. 'Let's be away.'

The creature craned its neck, looked at him curiously, stretched its manta wings – and did nothing. Nestor slapped its neck and the grey flesh twitched a little – that was all. 'Up!' he shouted, digging harder with his heels where rasps on Vasagi's boots had furrowed the beast's flanks. It grunted and quivered, but sat still. The answer was in Nestor's head, and finally he found it there.

I want you to fly! he told the creature. *Up, now, into the sky, and home to Starside. Or would you rather melt when the sun comes up?* Metamorphic muscles bunched then, and the flyer's thrusters coiled themselves as tight as springs. But still the beast would not, could not obey him. Till suddenly Vasagi's almost exhausted 'voice' joined Nestor's:

Aye, you were ever a faithful beast. When I told you to stay, you stayed. But now you are his. It pleases me to give you to him . . . for a while, at least. So fly – fly!

The beast's wings extended from its sides as alveolate bones, membrane and muscle stretched and flowed in metamorphic flux. A moment more and it tilted forward on the rim of the bluff. Nestor clung with his knees, gripped hard on the reins. The flyer's thrusters uncoiled to hurl it aloft and forward . . . it flew!

Wind whipped in Nestor's face as his weird mount glided out over Sunside, gaining height. But Sunside wasn't the way to go. And: 'Starside!' he shouted, with mind and mouth both. 'Starside!' Until the flyer arched its manta wings into vast scoops or air-traps, turned in a rising thermal, and climbed for the peaks.

And down in the misted valleys and forests, everything Nestor had been and done — everything which he'd known and had now forgotten, forsaken — was left far, far behind . . .

Nathan followed the course of the Great Dark River, visiting Crack-in-the-Rocks, Many-Caverns, the twin colonies Lake-of-Light and Lake-of-Stars, and Place-of-the-Beast-Bones. Mostly he travelled the river route, deep under the desert; on occasion, where the river became a borehole with no path as such, he must be ferried through black bowels of earth; sometimes he went on the surface, from oasis to oasis, where wells or potholes connected the drifted sands to the subterranean silt of the river.

There were many Thyre colonies, though few of them accommodated more than a hundred or so individuals. Even Open-to-the-Sky, which was the largest so far visited, had only supported some two hundred and sixty inhabitants. According to Atwei, the total count of Thyre did not exceed five thousand. To expand in excess of that number would be to reduce their living standards in the limited space available.

Nathan passed on lore and learning wherever he went, firmly establishing himself as a friend of the Thyre, never once forgetting the humility which the desert folk — and their dead — so admired in him. And in the process of teaching, Nathan learned.

He came across others who said they 'knew' numbers, but no one whose understanding surpassed Ethloi the Elder's rudimentary grasp. He studied what Ethloi had shown him, worked with his 'Tens System' and explored division, multiplication, even decimals; all without knowing his purpose or even if he had one beyond that he had been told it was important to him. And sometimes he conjured the numbers vortex, trapping whole sections of its fluxing configurations and bringing them to immobility on the screen of his mind, so that he might examine them. They revealed nothing but remained as alien as the farthest stars. Only relax his concentration for a moment ... they would flow, mutate, rejoin the vortex and be sucked back into an infinity of fathomless formulae ...

The Thyre gave him news of the Wamphyri. Here, far to the east of the great pass into Starside, their works were less in evidence. What Nathan was able to learn fitted well with what he already knew: that only a handful had crossed the Great Red Waste into Starside, and that they had settled in Karenstack, the last aerie. There they consolidated their position, built their army, created vampires. Since all of the 'makings' could be found just across the mountains, an hour's flight away, as yet they'd felt no need to strike east; for the moment it satisfied them merely to scout on the eastern territories; coming in the dead of night, they'd been seen as shadows against the moon and stars, mapping out the land from on high, and gazing down rapaciously on the human wealth of tomorrow's conquests.

West of the pass, however – among the displaced and dispossessed, ensieged and embattled people of Settlement, Tireni Scarp, Mirlu Township, a half-dozen more towns and encampments, and all of the Szgany tribes which now wandered there – things were different. For there could be found the first real victims of the scarlet plague, but *only* the first. For just as soon as the Wamphyri had recruited sufficient thralls and lieutenants, made enough of flyers and warriors, and established themselves as an utterly incontestable conquering force, then it would be time to advance their borders east. The rape of Sunside would continue, expand, and finally engulf all. The old order would fall, and the Szgany . . . would be as cattle . . .

En route east, Nathan spent less time in each new Thyre colony; he felt himself *drawn* east, to the very roots of the cancer which was even now spreading through Sunside. Perhaps that was the main attraction: no longer satisfied to run from the plague, he had determined to meet it head on. For unless he was prepared to spend the rest of his life with the Thyre, eventually it must overtake him anyway. Why, given time, it might even overrun the Thyre themselves!

Thyre place-names became a blur in his mind as weeks grew into months underground or in the seemingly trackless sands of the surface: Eight-Trees-Leaning, Glowworm Lake, Garden-Gorge-Over and Garden-Gorge-Under, Seven Wells South, Place-of-the-Hot-Springs, Big Swirly Hole and Crumble Cavern. Until, from the dead of Saltstone Sump, he learned the name of an Ancient in River's Rush beyond the Great Red Waste: Thikkoul, who had read men's futures in the stars. Alas, Thikkoul had gone blind before he died, and the stars had become invisible to him. But now, through Nathan . . . perhaps it was possible he could read them again? Perhaps he might even read Nathan's future in the stars.

Nathan determined to speak with Thikkoul, but many miles yet to River's Rush, and a great many colonies in between . . .

On the fertile rim of Crater Lake, rising like a false plateau from the surface of the furnace desert, Nathan spoke to his guide Septais, a young Thyre male only five or six years his senior. Septais had been with him now for a three-month; they were firm friends and felt little or nothing of strangeness or alienage in each other's company. Nathan's voice was hushed, even awed, as he asked: 'How can it be that Szgany and Thyre don't know each other? We've dwelled so close, so long, and yet apart from the occasional trading contact, we're strangers!'

'But ... we do know you,' Septais answered, blinking.

'Yes,' Nathan nodded, 'you know us – you know something of us, anyway – but the Szgany have never really known you. And they certainly haven't known this!' He held out his hands as if to encompass all of Crater Lake.

The place was simply that: a giant crater a mile across, with a raised inner caldera. The river entered through caverns in the base of the west wall; it formed a great blue lake which emptied through a gap in the reef-like central node of jutting rocks, and from there down into the sump of a whirlpool. After that, deep in the earth again, the Great Dark River ran east as before. And so the colony was an oasis, but vast and very beautiful.

'You mean our oases, our secret places? But if you knew of them they would not be secret. And if you knew of them ... how long before the Wamphyri learned of them, too?' Septais gave a shrug. 'You Szgany have your places, the forests and the hills, and we desert folk have ours.'

'I don't blame you for not wanting to share this,' Nathan told him.

'Perhaps different men should live together,' Septais answered. 'But our experience is that they can't. Upon a time, the Eastern Necromancers invaded. In aspect, they seemed much like the Thyre – far more like us than you Szgany – but they were not. For one thing, they did not have our telepathy. But they did have ... *other* arts.'

'I've been told about them,' Nathan nodded.

Again Septais's shrug. 'We trade a little with the Szgany, so that they may know us for a peaceful people. It is enough.'

'I understand,' Nathan said. 'But I still can't understand why *we* don't know about you. So close, and yet so ignorant. And your telepathy: I know that certain men of the Szgany have had such talents before me. Did they never hear your minds conversing? Did they never wonder?'

'Our thoughts are guarded,' Septais said. 'From birth to death, we are careful how we use this skill. Among the Szgany, telepathy is rare. But among the Wamphyri – it is not!'

Nathan nodded. 'That makes sense, for I couldn't bear the thought of *them* here!' Giving an involuntary shudder, he fell silent for a moment. But he was still curious, puzzled. 'That aside,' he said in a while, 'we *are* very close – I mean physically, geographically – with nothing so vast as the barrier range to separate us. It surprises me that men, Szgany loners, haven't stumbled upon your oases.'

'Really?' said Septais. 'You are surprised? Well, your geography may be sound in Sunside, Nathan, but it lacks something here in the furnace deserts. You ask, why have men not stumbled upon us?' He pointed north and slightly west. 'Over there, some sixty miles, lies the eastern extent of the barrier range, where the mountains crumble to the Great Red Waste.' Keeping his spindly arm raised, he turned slowly east through ninety degrees. 'And all of that, for a thousand miles, *is* the Great Red Waste. Beyond it lies a continuation of Sunside, the mountains, the Szgany and the Wamphyri: an unknown or legendary land, to you. Men, Szgany, have not crossed the Great Red Waste. How could they, when even the Thyre have not crossed it on the surface? You shall be the first of the Szgany, but you shall pass around and beneath it!'

Nathan looked where Septais had first pointed. 'Sunside, only sixty miles away,' he mused. 'And not even a crag showing on the flat horizon, because the mountains lie beyond the curve of the world. And of course you are right, Septais: why should any sane man of the Szgany ever venture out here? The forests blend into grasslands, which turn into scrub and sand, and the deserts sprawl sunwards forever. Only the strange, thin, dark-skinned nomads may dwell in the desert, and theirs is a fragile existence among the sun-bleached dunes, the rocky canyons and barren mesas. So we have always supposed; little we knew.' He pulled a wry face. 'But I wonder: if my people are to die out, killed off or ... *changed*, by the Wamphyri, mightn't a few be saved, out here in the desert?'

'That is for the elders,' the other sighed. 'If I were one of them ... you know I could never deny you but would try to arrange it. For I have felt your sadness: how it washes out from you in great waves. A great deal of sadness, but hatred, too – for the Wamphyri!'

'You "feel" it?' Again Nathan's wry smile. 'Do you spy on me, then?'

'No need for that!' said Septais. 'But I think: perhaps you should learn how to guard your thoughts, Nathan, like the Thyre. Why, sometimes they are so strong I must steel myself against them, unless they repel me!'

That strong? He looked at Septais and nodded, but grimly now. *Aye, maybe, but I wish they were stronger: so strong that I could think all of the Wamphyri into extinction! Especially the one called Canker Canison.*

The other shook his head, took Nathan's arm. 'The will is not enough,' he said. 'No man can *think* something into existence, Nathan, or out of it. Nor would we like it if we could. For as well as good, there is evil in all men. Who knows what a man might think, in some sad, frustrated moment?'

'Evil in all men,' Nathan answered. 'Yes, you're right – but more of it in the Wamphyri! I know, for I've seen it first hand. And you may believe me, I *would* drown them in my numbers vortex, or think them to death, if I could!'

'Well then,' said Septais, 'in that case you have a great deal of studying to do, for as yet your numbers are weightless and could not drown a fly. Likewise a great deal of thinking; for while your thoughts are passionate, they are also ungovernable, and you are the only one who is likely to die of them!'

And in this Septais showed wisdom far beyond the range of his two-score years . . .

Nathan had been with the Thyre for a year and five months – some seventy-three 'days' – when he surfaced through Red Well Sump on the edge of the Great Red Waste. He had parted company with Septais eleven sunup cycles earlier, since when he'd had various Thyre guides along the course of the Great Dark River. But from here on in the name of that subterranean torrent would be different: it was now the Great Red River, after all of the mineral wastes washed into it from the rusty, ruined earth.

Nathan's new guide was a spry Thyre elder called Ehtio, whose knowledge of this entirely uninhabitable region was as good as anyone's: at best rudimentary. In the ghastly glow of a crimson twilight, Ehtio showed Nathan a map drawn on lizard skin, which detailed the course of the river from their last stop, Ten-Springs-Spurting, to their current location.

'The river has swung north,' he husked, 'taking us under the Great Red Waste. And this —' he gazed all about, his soft Thyre eyes blinking, '— is the Great Red Waste, its southern fringe, anyway. Aptly named, as you see.'

They had come up steps cut in the wall of a vast well. A hundred and fifty feet below them, their boat was moored where Thyre oarsmen waited. There was no colony here; their stop was to be of the shortest duration, just long enough for Nathan to see and loathe the place. And from his first glance, he did loathe it.

Standing on the pitted wall of the well, behind its parapet, he turned in a slow circle and gazed out across the Great Red Waste. And in every direction he saw the same thing: wave upon wave of red and black dunes, with areas between like massive blisters which had burst and turned brittle, and crumbled back into themselves, and others which were lakes of seething, bubbling, smoking chemicals. Nathan smelled tar, sulphur, the overpowering reek of rotten eggs, the stench of mordant acids. The contours of the dunes were like wrinkles in diseased skin, as if this entire landscape were the body of some cosmic corpse dead of its lesions and infections, its flesh torn and rotting, and Nathan and Ehtio standing in its navel.

It was the twilight of evening. South, the horizon was a sick, shimmering, smoky ochre: the sunset seen through a smog of rising vapours. North, the horizon was black, humped, alien. Overhead, the stars wavered; they blinked on and off like sick fireflies, dying in the rising reek.

'The air is bad,' said Ehtio. 'We can't stay.'

'A thousand miles of this?' Nathan shook his head, turned towards the stairwell. 'I don't want to stay ...'

The damp, musty air rising from the well seemed

sweet by comparison. Descending in flickering torch-light, Nathan asked: 'What happened, up there? Does anyone know?'

'Not for sure,' Ehtio shook his head. 'Too old to be part of history, it is myth, lore, legend. I cannot guarantee it.'

'Tell me anyway.'

'One day in the long ago, a white sun fell from the sky. It skipped over the world like a flat stone bouncing on water. This was one of the places where it bounced; such was the impact, its iron shell was broken and fell on the land in so many pieces they could not be counted. The land became hot; chemicals in the soil gathered into pools; acids ate the white sun's metal skin into rust. It is a process which continues to this day. But the core of the white sun made one final leap. Shrinking, it sped west and slightly north; such was its fascination, it drew up the mountains to form the barrier range, and was in turn drawn to earth.'

Nathan nodded. 'We have much the same legend. The white sun fell on Starside and fashioned the boulder plains. It sits there even now – I've seen it – like a cold blind eye, glaring on Starside. But that's not all, for Szgany legend has it that this sphere of cold white light is a kind of doorway, to hellish lands beyond.'

'Beyond what?' Ehtio looked at him.

'Beyond itself, beyond this world.' Nathan shook his head. 'Beyond my powers to describe. But ... it's not just a legend, for men have come through that Gate from the world beyond. And creatures from Starside have likewise crossed to their side.'

'Creatures?'

'Wamphyri! I've heard it said that sometimes they would cast one of their own out – cast him *into* the Gate.'

'Indeed,' said Ehtio, offering a sad, slow, very thoughtful nod. 'And so vampires have passed through this "Gate", eh?' He nodded again. 'Well then, it strikes me that if these lands "beyond" were not hellish before, they are now.' Which reminded Nathan that Lardis Lidesci had once said much the same thing . . .

From Red Well Sump the river swung south again and back under a comparatively healthy desert. Such was its load of rust, its waters would run red for a further hundred miles.

Forty miles east of Red Well Sump and eighteen south of the Great Red Waste, the next Thyre colony was called Place-Under-the-Orange-Crags. It reminded Nathan of Place-Under-the-Yellow-Cliffs; also of Atwei, his Thyre sister. The Cavern of the Ancients was similar, too, except there was no Rogei and no crystal ceiling.

Place-Under-the-Orange-Crags fronted a sprawling plateau lying roughly east to west. Looking north from its summit towards the Great Red Waste, Nathan saw that the entire northern horizon was a dirty red smudge. The barrier range lay far to the west; likewise Sunside and Settlement, which through all of his formative years he'd called home. He was homesick; no, he was sick for *anything* Szgany. Once, he'd been a loner even among the Sunsiders; he'd wanted nothing so much as to escape to an alien world, while in this one Misha had been his only anchor. Now Misha was gone and he actually lived in an alien world, which palled on him more every day.

'Men are contrary,' Ehtio husked from beside him. 'Aye, Szgany and Thyre alike.' His voice drew Nathan back to earth.

'Oh? Was I thinking out loud again?'

'Often,' said the other. 'Do you no longer practise your mind-guard?'

Nathan thought of Misha's face — he couldn't help it; it flashed into his mind — but just as he had been taught by Septais during many an hour of trial-and-error instruction, so now he 'cloaked' both the thought and the picture. And: 'There,' he said. 'How's that?' He felt Ehtio's probe: a tingle on the periphery of his awareness, which he held at bay.

'Quite excellent,' said the elder after a moment. 'But now that your thoughts are in order and guarded, you must concentrate more on your emotions. The two are closely linked.'

Nathan nodded. 'I've heard much the same before.'

'Nathan,' said Ehtio, 'I have been asked to tell you that should you desire it, there will always be a place for you with the Thyre.'

It was a great honour and Nathan acknowledged it. Except: 'First there are things I must do,' he said. 'And even then ... afterwards ... I don't know.'

'Things you must do? Put your life at risk, do you mean? Go among the eastern Szgany, who give themselves — and their children — to the Wamphyri without protest? Oh? And how then shall they deal with you?'

'It's hard to believe they do that to their own,' Nathan shook his head. 'Not without protest. As for me ... I have to know how it is for them there, and how it's yet to be in Sunside.'

Ehtio made a hopeless gesture. 'But what good will it do? What can you change? You have nothing to gain, everything to lose. Yes, and we too, the Thyre, have everything to lose.'

'In me?'

'Of course.'

'You value me too highly.'

'How so? You are invaluable!'

'I have to go,' Nathan was determined. 'But I'm grateful to the Thyre for all I've learned from them. And I *will* work on my telepathy – yes, my emotions too – and on the numbers shown to me by Ethloi. It strikes me there has to be a reason, a purpose, in all of these things. But I *must* go east, if only to speak to Thikkoul in River's Rush and discover my future in the stars.'

'The first two are things you can do without risking yourself,' Ehtio answered. 'And the last is an excuse, or at best a forlorn hope. It seems to me you go to sacrifice yourself.'

'No,' Nathan denied it. 'I go to improve myself. Some time ago – it seems a long time now – I made my Szgany vow. It may be I made it in anger and horror, but it was still my vow. If I forsake it now, that would be ... unseemly. Perhaps these gifts of mine are tools, which I must learn to use in order to fulfil my obligations. In which case it will be a useful thing to know my future.'

'You are stubborn,' Ehtio told him, but without rancour.

'I'm Szgany,' Nathan answered, simply ...

A further twelve sunups and Nathan reached River's Rush. Here the Great Red River's course became a borehole, and the river itself a solid chute of water hurtling through eleven miles of narrow, subterranean sumps before widening out and being reasonable, placid again. Below ground those miles were unnavigable; it made little or no difference to Nathan, whose route now lay to the north, across the surface.

As for the Thyre: there were only two more colonies to the east, beyond which the river flowed on into myth and mystery. But the two must remain unvisited; River's

Rush was Nathan's last stop at the end of a journey which had carried him more than two thousand miles from his birthplace.

On the surface, the place was a small oasis twenty miles south of 'Sunside' (the Sunside of these unknown eastern regions, at least). Beyond Sunside were mountains, and across the mountains 'Starside'. There the Wamphyri dwelled in a mighty gorge, whose name Nathan had learned from the Thyre: Turgosheim. But even though the vampires were the undisputed masters here, still the restrictions upon them were the same: the night was their element, but the sun was their mortal enemy.

Upon a time the Thyre had traded with the Szgany in the grassland fringe between desert and forest, much as they did in the west; all that had come to an abrupt, bloody end some three years ago. For the Szgany of this region had become a gaunt, greedy people. Worn down by the Wamphyri, their sensitivities had been eroded away until they were little more than feral creatures, no longer trustworthy.

When the members of a Thyre trading party had seen how they were being cheated, even threatened by the Szgany, they had tried to withdraw back into the desert. The Szgany fell on them and murdered them; their few goods were stolen; they paid with their lives for a handful of medicinal salts and a few polished lizard skins. Only one man, wounded in his side, had returned to River's Rush to tell the tale.

The story made Nathan afraid, and not a little ashamed. For these were Szgany, his people. Also, he had intended to visit among them. Maybe now he would change his plans . . .

In any event, his work came first, and for the duration of a single sunup he proved his credentials in the mausoleum called the Hall of Endless Hours. There, when at last his time was his own, he spoke to Thikkoul: a bundle of venerable rags in a niche lit by a constantly flickering candle.

And so you've come, that one's deadspeak came as a whisper in the Necroscope's mind. *Well, it should not surprise me, for I remember how, before I went blind, I saw it in the stars: a visit from one who would make me see again, however briefly. Then I died and still you had not come. And I thought: so much for my astrology! And all my life's work was in doubt. Ah, how could I know that even in death there may be light!*

'Did you really read men's futures in the stars?' Nathan was fascinated.

Do you doubt me?

'It seems a strange talent, this astrology.'

Oh, and is it stranger than telepathy? Stranger than this deadspeak which allows me to communicate with my myriad colleagues among the Great Majority? Stranger than your own unique talent?

'It's not that I'm without faith,' Nathan answered. 'But even the Thyre bolster their faith with fact. Show it to me.'

The other chuckled. *Gladly! Only show me the stars, and I will show you the future.*

Nathan nodded. 'But there are no stars in the Hall of Endless Hours, Thikkoul. I'll have to go up into the desert. Stay with me . . .'

Above, it was night. The stars were diamonds, but they shone softer here than over Starside and the barrier range. Nathan walked out over sands which were cool now, away from the oasis. And in the silence and aching loneliness of the desert, Thikkoul's thoughts came more clearly into his inner mind. *Lie down, look up, gaze upon the heavens. Let me look out through your eyes* upon all the times which were, are, and will be. For just as the light from the stars is our past, so is it our future. Except . . .

'Yes?' Nathan put down a blanket, lay upon it, and looked up at the stars. Likewise Thikkoul.

Except . . . first I should warn you: things are rarely as I see them.

'You make errors?'

Oh, I see what I see! Thikkoul answered at once. But how the things which I see shall come to pass, that is not always clear. The future is devious, Nathan. It takes a brave man to read it, and only a fool would guarantee its meaning.

'I don't understand,' Nathan frowned, shook his head.

Thikkoul looked out through Nathan's eyes at the stars – looked at them for the first time in a hundred years – and sighed. Ahh! he said. Boy and man, they fascinated me, and continue to fascinate me. I am in your debt, Nathan Kiklu of the Szgany. But repayment may be hard, for both of us.

'No, it will be easy. Read my future, that's enough.'

But that was my meaning. What if I read hard things for you? Must I tell you your fate as well as your fortune?

'Whatever you see, that will suffice.'

I shall do as best I can, the other told him, and for a while was silent. Then . . . it came in a flood, in a flash, a river bursting its banks. So fast that Nathan could scarcely cling to the words and images as Thikkoul threw them into his mind:

I see . . . doors! Like the doors on a hundred Szgany caravans but liquid, drawn on water, formed of ripples. And behind each one of them, a piece of your future. A door opens. I see a man, Szgany, a so-called 'mystic'.

589

His name is – Io ... Io ... Iozel! And his game – is treachery! Now I see Turgosheim; the manse of a great wizard; you and he together. He would use you, learn from you, instruct and corrupt you! The door closes, but another opens ...

The sun rises and sets, and sunups come and go in a blur where you wander in a great dark castle of many caves. I see your face: your hollow eyes and greying hair? Now I see ... a flight to freedom, yes! But ... upon a dragon? One door closes, and another opens. I see ... a maiden; the two of you – three of you? – together. You seem happy; doors continue to open and close; and now you seem sad ...

Some hours are long as days; others fly like seconds; long and short alike, they draw you into the future. And always the doors of your mind, opening and closing. I see ... a battle – war! – Szgany and Wamphyri! You win, and you lose. Now I see an eye, white and blind and glaring, much like my own before I died, but vast as a cavern! You stand before it and the eye ... is another door! It blinks! And in the blink of a great blind eye, you ... are ...

Thikkoul paused, like a man breathless.

'Yes?' Nathan's real voice was hoarse with excitement ... but Thikkoul's deadspeak was hoarse with horror as finally he continued:

You are – gone!

III

In the chill, cheerless hours before dawn, made all the more cold and lonely because he was on his own now, Nathan walked away from the oasis over the blown sands which kept the subterranean caverns of the Thyre secret. He had been told that the going was firm between here and Sunside; but in any case, he'd grown used to walking in the desert and found it no great discomfort. The night was bright and the stars clear; Nathan's shadow walked behind him, cast by the moon as it hurtled over the mountains of the barrier range, whose serrated ridge made a scalloped horizon in the far dark distance. Frequent meteorite showers left brilliant, ephemeral tracks across the sky.

After so much time spent underground, Nathan's night vision was much improved; he could see almost as well as in full daylight. As for direction: no chance that he could lose his way. No one among the Szgany knew the stars as well as he did; not even among the Thyre, that he knew of ... except Thikkoul. And as he went at a brisk, long-striding pace across the featureless desert, Nathan thought back on what Thikkoul had told him, the conversation which had followed fast upon the dead astrologer's reading:

'What does it mean?' He had wanted to know.

Everything. And nothing, Thikkoul had answered, a little sorrowfully now.

'I can ignore it?'

Of course. But alas, it won't ignore you.

'Can't you make yourself plainer?'

Thikkoul had sighed. *Didn't I warn you? The future is a devious thing, Nathan. This is the problem: will what I have read in the stars come to pass because, believing it, we make it come to pass? Or will it happen whether or no? And what if we should try to avoid it, how then? Could it be that our actions will cause the very event we seek to avoid? But in fact* (Nathan had sensed the other's incorporeal shrug), *there's no riddle – nothing contrary – in any of this. The answer is simplicity itself: what will be will be! And that is all.* 'I can set about making it happen,' Nathan had scratched his chin, repeating what the other had said but in his own way, 'or take steps to avoid it, or simply let it be. But whichever I choose, it will make no difference?'

Exactly. But there is one other complication. My readings are often symbolic. I don't understand the doors I saw in your future: they seemed to be part of you. Nor do I understand the dragon-flight, or the vast eye which swallowed you in a blink. For these are things of your future, which are perhaps linked to your past. And so it's for you to know and understand them. If not now, most certainly later . . .

Nathan had frowned as he held to one of the things Thikkoul had told him. 'How may a thing come to pass *because* I try to avoid it? What if I know of this blind white eye which you mentioned – for indeed I believe I do – and make sure I go nowhere near it? How then can I be swallowed by it?'

There was a man, the other had answered. *He feared water and had bad dreams, premonitions, about his death. He came to me that I would read his stars. I told him the dangers but he insisted. The forecast was this: that in the course of a single sunup he would drown in the borehole of River's Rush, and his body never be found!*

I did not want to tell him but he insisted. Then, when he knew the truth he left River's Rush and climbed to the surface, and travelled west, alone, into the desert. He would escape his fate, do you see? Well, he found himself a little shade and sat out in the desert for all of that sunup, until the evening was nigh. Then, making to return, he stumbled and took a fall which broke his skin of water. Close by was a well; he went to it and lowered the bucket. But then, when he hauled up the water, the wall crumbled and he fell in.

The well was fed by the Great Red River; the river swept him away; he was seen, alive, lifting his hand up from the torrent, before being swirled into the borehole, lost forever . . .

At the end of his story Thikkoul had sighed again before lapsing silent, waiting for Nathan's response.

'But if he went into the desert alone,' Nathan had queried eventually, 'how can you know the sequence of events?' At which, once again he had sensed the other's simplistic shrug, enabling him to guess the answer even before he heard it. It was deadspeak, of course: the ability of the Great Majority, and of Nathan, to converse among themselves in their graves.

Because he told me all on the day I died! Thikkoul confirmed it. *And his is a singularly awful 'resting place', Nathan, where in fact he knows no rest at all! For he was trapped in a swirling sump, where to this day his body remains, rotated and whirled in the frothing tumult. And all of his flesh long sloughed away; his bones all broken and reduced to rounded marbles, from the action of the waters. But at least he no longer fears the water, which has done its worst . . .*

Later, Nathan had asked The Five of River's Rush if they knew of a man – Szgany, a 'mystic', perhaps – who dwelled in Sunside. Indeed they did: his name was Iozel

Kotys, who upon a time had had dealings with the Thyre. He had traded with them: low-grade iron knives for their good skins and medicines. But a mystic? That was a device which Iozel had used all his days to avoid being taken in the tithe, until now he was well past his prime and had no need of it. But he was still the cunning one, Iozel Kotys! Why, it was rumoured among the Szgany that he had even been to Turgosheim in Starside! If so, then Iozel was the only man who ever returned unchanged from that dreadful place.

After that, there had seemed nothing for it but that Nathan must go into Sunside. For quite apart from Thikkoul's predictions – even despite them, anticipating or pre-empting them – he had after all travelled the length of the known world in order to do just that. His original intention had been to see how the Szgany of these parts lived, and so discover how his own people must live one day, in the shadow of the Wamphyri. But beyond that, his reasons were now several.

The things which Thikkoul had told him had come thick and fast, but among the purely verbal had been blurred, indistinct scenes, even as the astrologer had seen them for himself. The impression of insubstantial doors opening and closing; dim figures (chiefly Nathan's) weaving in and out of a succession of situations and locations; strange faces ogling and peering. Except ... two of the latter had not been strange at all but loving, and beloved.

Nathan remembered Thikkoul's words, and the fleeting scene which had accompanied them. *I see a maiden; the two of you – three of you? – together. You seem happy* ...

Of course he would seem happy, if such were true. But how could it be? For those dim, wavering female forms had worn the glad shining faces of his mother, and of Misha Zanesti! Which was why, at the end of Thikkoul's reading, Nathan's voice had been hoarse with excitement. Ah, but now, thinking back on the rest of the astrologer's words, his excitement was replaced by doubts and uncertainties.

Nathan had always assumed that his mother and Misha were dead, or worse than dead, even though he had never seen their bodies or known for sure their whereabouts. And how should he think of them now? Thikkoul had told him: *These are things of your future, which are perhaps linked to your past. And so it is for you to know and understand them.*

But *how* was he to understand them? Had the faces of those loved ones out of past times been simply that: scenes from the past, which yet influenced his future? Of course they had influence over him; they always would have. Or ... was there more to it than that? What if they were alive even now: not as monstrous Wamphyri changelings but as simple slaves, thrall servants in some Starside aerie or craggy mansion? And if so, how to find them?

Which was why he walked to Sunside in the brightening air, with the stars gradually fading overhead, and the barrier range growing up before him like a mirage out of the desert. For his future was right here; time bore him forward into it with every passing second; and since he couldn't avoid it, he might just as well meet it head on. And somewhere along the way, all unsuspecting, Iozel Kotys was waiting for him. Which seemed as good a place as any to start ...

In the Sunside of Nathan's infancy the Szgany had preferred to stay close to their mountains. Most of the Traveller trails had been in the foothills, rarely in the forests. The reasons were several: clouds breaking on the peaks provided good water; wild life was plentiful on the slopes and the hunting was excellent; the roots of the mountains were riddled with hiding places in the rocks, where cavern systems abounded.

Here things were different. While these eastern people were Szgany, or of the same basic stock, they were not Travellers. Perhaps – almost certainly – they had been in the long ago, but no longer. Now, under total Wamphyri domination, they lived in sorry townships (corrals or pens, in effect) and wandered no more. In the Sunside Nathan knew, in the old times, his people had become Travellers in order to avoid and defy the vampires, and had only settled after their supposed 'destruction'. But here the people had settled because the Wamphyri ordered it, which had marked the beginning of the infamous, immemorial tithe system. And so their towns were spread out evenly and in the open, like market places, where the Starside Lords and Ladies sent their lieutenants on regular, long-established errands to replenish their spires and manses. Except that unlike a market, the Wamphyri 'purchased' nothing, but took what was deemed to be theirs by right of conquest. Which amounted to a percentage of everything, from grain and oils to beasts and blood – but mainly blood, and human.

North of the grasslands at the edge of the forest, some twelve townships out of a total of around fifty stood roughly equidistant: four in the west, and eight towards the sprawling morass which lay beyond the habitable region to the east. The Thyre estimated that the distance between the Great Red Waste on the one hand and the swamp on the other was more than six hundred miles; and so Nathan considered himself fortunate that the first of the four towns to the west, a place called Vladistown after its founder, was the origin and last known home of Iozel Kotys.

Dressed in his good rich clothes, and with the first rays of the sun warm on his back, Nathan came out of the desert and crossed the savannah, and saw the smoke of morning fires going up in lazy blue-grey spirals along the forest's rim. Angling a little to the left, he headed for the closest huddle of houses where the woods had been cut back into a clearing.

The first man he met was in the grasslands at the very edge of the forest: a hunter, he was shooting rabbits with a crossbow. Nathan heard the deceptively soft *whirrr* of a bolt and ducked, saw a rabbit bound spastically and fall back dead in the grass. Then ... he saw the man with the crossbow, where he rose from his knees in a patch of gorse; and a moment later the hunter saw him. At first, facing each other across a distance of no more than a dozen paces, they froze; then the hunter's jaw dropped, and his face turned pale.

Nathan approached him fearlessly. The man was Szgany after all, and the Thyre had told him that although these people were not trustworthy, they could at least be trusted *not* to take his life. No, he was far too valuable for that. They might *give* his life away — give it to the Wamphyri, in return for their dubious favours — but they would never dare to take it for themselves. Also, apart from the ironwood knife he carried, Nathan was unarmed; he posed no obvious threat. But from the reaction of the other, one might very easily suppose that he did, and an extreme threat at that!

The man dropped his weapon, fell to his knees again, and shivered like a naked child in morning sunlight which was warm and bright. He choked out some inarticulate greeting, an apology, and a question all in one. His speech was Szgany but the accent was difficult. Nathan frowned, looked into his eyes ... and suddenly the man's words and their meaning gained resolution.

But even assisted by his as yet immature telepathy, still Nathan found the other's thoughts a kaleidoscopic jumble, and his speech even more so:

'Morning!' the other gasped. 'You are early ... the tithe is not until sundown! I mean ... why are you here? No, no,' (he fluttered his hands), 'for that's no business of mine! Forgive me, Lord, I beg you! I'm a fool taken by surprise, whose words fall all wrong. But ... the sun! Come, take cover in the woods! Hide yourself in the shade!'

Now all was apparent. The man thought Nathan was Wamphyri, a lieutenant at least! Comparing himself with the other, he could see how easily the mistake had been made: his clothes of fine leather, yellow hair and strange eyes; but most of all his pale, unblemished flesh, which, seen in silhouette against the sun, might even appear grey. As for the hunter:

The man was Szgany, certainly, but not like any other Nathan had ever seen. Where was his personal pride? Where was any sign of pride at all? Maybe twenty-seven or -eight years old, he was dirty, ragged, grovelling; his hair was matted and full of lice, and there were open sores on his face and hands. Why, even the wildest old loner of olden Sunside had cared for himself better than this one! Perhaps he was an idiot; but if so, why did they trust him with a crossbow? Certainly he knew how to handle the thing.

'Get up,' Nathan told him, shaking his head. 'I'm not Wamphyri.'

'You're not ...?' A puzzled frown crossed the other's face; only to be replaced in a moment by narrowed eyes which glittered their suspicion. 'But you are one of theirs.'

'I'm nobody's,' Nathan said, stepping closer. 'I'm my own man, free, and you have nothing to fear from me.'

He went to take hold of his shoulder, draw the man to his feet. But the other fell backwards away from him, terrified in a moment.

'Your own man,' he babbled. 'Yes, yes, of course you are! And I'm a fool who says and questions too much, when in fact *you* are the one who should question, and I should supply the answers!'

Nathan felt sick with disgust. Perhaps this creature was the village idiot after all; but at least his words had given him an idea. 'You're right,' he said, nodding. 'That's what I need: a little shade and a few answers.'

'Then ask away!' the other cried, coming to a crouch and backing away towards the forest, and leaving his crossbow where it had fallen. 'Whatever questions you like, Lord. And if I can answer them I will, be sure!'

Nathan took up the weapon, loaded it with the spare bolt from under the tiller and applied the safety; and the other at once groaned and put up his trembling hands, as if to ward off a shot. Nathan looked at him, then at the crossbow in his hands and frowned again. 'What?' he said. 'Man, I won't *shoot* you! Do you always greet strangers this way?'

'Strangers!' the other was almost hysterical. 'Do I greet strangers this way ... always? But there are no strangers! Who would come? Who *can* come ... except such as you? As yet you are unchanged ... but soon, ah, soon! You're one of theirs, I know it, come to practise your deceptions among your slaves!'

'Deceptions?'

'Ah! *No!* I did not mean it!' The other threw his arms wide and fell to his knees for a third time in the dappled shade of the trees. 'Forgive me! I am confused!'

'You're ... a *fool!*' Nathan couldn't contain himself. The hunter burst out sobbing at once, crying:

'No, no! I was not taken in the tithe! Please don't take

me now! Whatever you want, only ask it of me, but let me be a man all my days and not . . . *not* a monster!'

'Now listen to me,' Nathan hardened his voice. 'You are wasting my time. There's something I want to know. And that's all I want with you.' He tossed the crossbow aside.

'Ask away! Ask away!'

'Iozel Kotys — where can I find him?'

'Eh? Iozel the mystic? Iozel the hermit?'

'If that's what you call him,' Nathan nodded.

'Iozel, aye!' the other's eyes started, as if he made some connection. 'For he has been there, of course!'

'Do — you — *know* him!?' Nathan's patience was exhausted; he spoke through clenched teeth.

'Yes! Yes, of course!' The hunter turned, pointed north across the forest to where a steep, thinly clad knoll or outcrop reared above the trees. 'There . . . a mile . . . the knoll. And at its foot, a cave. Iozel lives there, alone. Only head for the knoll, through the woods, you'll cross a path, well-worn, which runs between the town and his cave.'

'Show me,' said Nathan.

'Indeed, yes, of course!' The hunter made to set off at once, but Nathan stopped him.

'Pick up your crossbow.'

'My weapon, aye!' the other licked his lips, trembling as he did as he was told . . .

Along the way were other hunters; glimpsed dimly between the misty trees, they were like wraiths drawn out of the earth by the warmth of the new day. No one approached, and in a few minutes Nathan's guide found the path: a narrow way cut through the woods. By then it was almost full daylight, and Nathan had had more than enough of the cowed hunter's company. 'You say this path will lead me direct to Iozel's cave?'

'Indeed, Lord. Indeed it will.'

'I thank you,' said Nathan. 'From here on I go alone.'

'I . . . can go?'

'Of course.' Nathan turned his back on him and followed the path. But he was aware that behind him the hunter backed off — slowly at first, breathlessly — then turned and tiptoed away, and finally ran for Vladistown. Shaking his head, Nathan went on.

Iozel Kotys was up and about. In the mouth of his cave, the hermit braised slivers of skewered pork on hot stones at the rim of his fire. Becoming aware of Nathan's approach about the same time as Nathan smelled his cooking, Iozel looked down from the elevated shelf in front of his cave and saw a vague, grey figure where his feet stirred the lapping mist.

'Now hold!' the hermit's voice rang out, wavering and a little infirm. 'Who comes and why? I receive no casual visitors here . . .'

'But you'll receive me,' Nathan called back, coming on without pause. And if Iozel wouldn't receive him . . . so much for Thikkoul's stargazing!

There was a ladder at the foot of the rocks. As Nathan strode closer Iozel went to draw it up. Nathan caught at the lower rungs and held on, and gazed up at the other's furious face scowling down on him. Against the strength of Nathan's arms and the weight of the ladder both, the hermit could do nothing. Anyway, he'd noted his visitor's dress and curious colouring, and as the anger drained out of him something of anxiety, fear took its place.

'Who are you?' he gasped, releasing the ladder and backing off a pace, until only his grey-bearded face was visible. Nathan fixed him with his eyes, and climbed.

'I'm a Traveller,' he said. 'And I've travelled a long way to see you, Iozel Kotys.'

Iozel was small, wrinkled, middling clean and reasonably clothed in well-worn leathers. While he wasn't extremely old, he did suffer from some infirmity which caused his limbs and voice to tremble. And his dark eyes ran a little with rheumy fluids. 'Eh? A Traveller?' he said, his eyes darting, taking in all they could of Nathan where he stepped off the ladder on to the shelf. 'And you've come a long way, you say? How is it possible? Unless — from Turgosheim?' And now his voice, fallen to a whisper, was hoarse.

Nathan had learned something of the ways of these people, and something of their fears. 'Iozel,' he said, 'I'm not here to harm you. I'm simply . . . here!' It was difficult to find a reason for being here. He didn't have one, except that Thikkoul had foreseen it, and beyond it to a possible reunion with loved ones whom Nathan had long thought dead and passed from him forever. That alone would be reason enough, but how to explain all that to Iozel?

'Simply here?' the hermit repeated him, shaking his head. 'No, if there's one thing I've learned in life it's this: that nothing is "simply" anything, and no one is "simply" anywhere. You were sent — by him!'

'Him?'

'Maglore! You are my . . . replacement!'

Nathan sighed. Nothing these people said made any sense. 'I don't know this Maglore,' he said.

'Maglore of Runemanse — in Turgosheim!' the other told him.

Things began to connect. Nathan said: 'That makes twice today I've been mistaken for Wamphyri, or one of their changeling lieutenants. But I'm not. I'm Szgany.' He decided to tell it all. 'I'm from the west, beyond the Great Red Waste. Upon a time the Wamphyri were there, but they were driven out, beaten in a great battle.

602

Now they've come back — from here. Or rather, from Turgosheim. I came to see how you people lived here in this land of vampires, so that I would know how best to advise my own people in the west.' He shrugged. 'Well, and it seems I must tell them to fight on — even to the last drop of blood! For obviously you don't "live" at all but merely exist, like goats fattened for the slaughter.'

While Nathan talked he scratched vigorously at his left wrist. A grain or two of sand must have got under his strap to irritate him, and he still felt lousy from having walked too close to his hunter guide. But as he paused from speaking, finally the itch became too great. In order to scratch more freely, he rolled the leather strap from his wrist and slipped it free of his fingers. Circling his wrist, a band of white skin showed glassy grains embedded and inflamed. Nathan got them out with his fingernail, rubbed spittle into the red patch, and went to pick up his strap.

Iozel had been watching closely, however, and beat him to it. Frowning, he took up Nathan's wristlet strap and looked at it — curiously at first, then with studied intensity. Finally his eyes narrowed in what seemed to be recognition, and nodding knowingly, he gave the strap back.

Nathan said: 'Is there something . . .?'

The other shrugged. 'A strange thing to wear as orna-ment, that's all. Some weakness in your wrist, that you need to keep it strapped up, "man of the west"? Or is the twisted loop some sort of sigil? Your brand, per-haps?' There was that in Iozel's quavering voice which Nathan didn't like, which more than suggested that the hermit considered his visitor a liar.

'You people are suspicious, full of fear,' he said. 'You meet strangers like dogs: yapping and snarling. It was a mistake to come here. Even if I could help you, I can't see that it would be worth it.'

Iozel looked beyond him, down at the trail where sunlight came filtering. But more than sunlight had come. And: 'Oh yes, you made a mistake coming here, all right!' the hermit said.

Nathan looked, felt his first pang of apprehension as he saw a handful of men approaching. They were led by the ragged hunter. 'There! That's him!' the hunter pointed. As the party arrived at the foot of the ladder, Nathan climbed down; Iozel stayed where he was, up on the rim of the ledge. Nathan faced the newcomers, and saw that they were much of a likeness; inbred, ugly, rough and ragged. The hunter was no village idiot: they were all cut of much the same cloth. And all of them were armed.

'My name's Nathan,' he said, perhaps lamely. 'I've come from the west, beyond the Great Red Waste, as a friend.'

'He has come from the north,' Iozel called down. 'Rather, he is *fled* here from the north — from Turgosheim — and comes as an enemy, albeit unwitting . . . maybe! They'll be after him in a trice, and if they find him here . . .'

The men ringed Nathan about, looked at him, fingered his clothes. One of them took his knife. Nathan stood tall, tried not to appear afraid. He turned to their obvious leader, a man who was burly and big-bellied; the only one who looked as if he ate well. His eyes were piggish in a red, puffy face. Nathan spoke to him. 'Iozel is wrong. I'm from the west.'

'Aye,' Iozel called down again, his voice heavy with sarcasm. 'And he's come across the Great Red Waste. Why, certainly he has! Only see how desiccated he is, all poisoned from the wasteland's gases. And his clothes all in tatters.' His voice hardened. 'He's fled out of Turgosheim, believe it. Some Lord's unwilling pet, and I think I know which one. Why, he even wears Maglore's sigil upon his wrist!'

The burly one nodded, scratched his chin, looked Nathan in the eye and gave a musing grunt. 'Iozel's right,' he said. 'No one has ever come out of the west. In any case, the lands beyond the Great Red Waste are legendary: we're not even sure that they exist.' He frowned. 'But I'll grant you one thing: you don't look Szgany.'

'One of Maglore's experiments,' Iozel interrupted again from the safety of his ledge. 'This one's a changeling!'

'Eh?' The leader of the bunch at once drew back from Nathan, likewise his companions. 'A vampire thing?'

'Not him,' Iozel shook his head. 'And that's puzzling, I admit. But I was cooking and my hands are smeared with oil of kneblasch, which I rubbed into the leather of his strap. If he were Wamphyri we'd know it: he'd be in pain from that strange strap of his. Also, he carries silver on his person. Last but not least, sunlight falls on him and he suffers no ill.'

'It's true!' the scabby hunter put in. 'He came from the grasslands, with the sun full on him!'

'So,' said their leader, eyeing Nathan up and down. 'And what's to be done with you?'

Nathan glanced at him in disgust, then looked up at Iozel until their eyes met and locked. And: *What are you thinking, you scruffy, treacherous old dog?* Nathan wondered. Treachery, yes – just as Thikkoul had warned.

Iozel's thoughts were easy to read; his mind had been opened before, often, so that he couldn't close it. Even Nathan's small talent found no difficulty in breaching his mental defences. Or perhaps it was simply that Nathan was desperate to read the other's thoughts.

He is or was Maglore's, I'm sure of it, Iozel was thinking. *But is he a runaway, or was he sent? Is he here to replace me, or did he hope to enlist my aid in hiding himself away?*

'So,' Nathan said, 'what I've heard about Iozel Kotys is true.' (Two could make accusations.)

'What's that?' the burly one was interested.

Nathan glanced at him again, contemptuously. 'Why, that the Wamphyri use him as a spy against the Szgany. Against you! Except he blinds you with the lies of a so-called "mystic", so that you don't see him for what he really is. Now tell me, who else have you ever met who returned out of Turgosheim?'

'Don't listen to him, Dobruj!' Iozel screeched. 'What, me, a spy? I spy on no one. To what end? Why, all I ever ask is to be left alone. But this one: just *look* at him! His clothes, his alien colours, his story! *Hah!* From beyond the Great Red Waste, indeed! His lies are obvious.'

Dobruj was the burly one, the chief. Craning his neck, he scowled up at Iozel. 'Aye, and this isn't the first time you've been suspicioned, old hermit! If I had the proof of it, one way or the other ... *huh!*' He fingered his chin again, and looked at Nathan. 'But meanwhile, what's to be done with you?'

'Only listen to me,' Iozel had managed to compose himself, 'and you'll know what to do with him. Put him in the tithe and so save one of your own! Vormulac's tithesmen come tonight, and already your tally is short, because of deserters. So why not let this one make up the numbers, eh? If he, too, is a runaway – from Turgosheim – they'll surely take him back again. Which will stand you and Vladistown in good stead, Dobruj. Ah, but if he's a spy, they'll find reasons *not* to take him! And then . . . there will be time later, to deal with him. Either way, you've nothing to lose.'

Dobruj thought about it, cocked his head on one side and glanced yet again at Nathan before making up his mind. Finally he nodded and said: 'It makes sense.' At which, two of his men grabbed Nathan by the arms. He tried to fight them off until a third held the point of his own knife to his ribs. But:

'None of that!' Dobruj commanded. 'If he's going in the tithe we don't want him damaged. Right, enough of this. Back to town . . .'

As they bundled Nathan along the path, Dobruj called up to the hermit: 'You, Iozel – be sure you're close to hand in town when the tithesmen come. For should these accusations of yours make a fool of me, I'll be wanting words with you . . .'

'Hah!' the hermit called out, shaking his fists from on high. 'You'll see! You'll see!'

Dobruj paused a moment and narrowed his piggish eyes at him. 'Aye, we'll see what we'll see,' he said. 'But make sure you're there anyway.' It was a command, not to be denied. And it was a sure threat.

Iozel watched them out of sight, then went to a ledge in the cave and took up a sigil shaped in gold. It had been given to him by the Seer Lord Maglore of Runemanse. Maglore's sigil: whose shape was the very image of the strap on Nathan's wrist, but moulded in heavy metal. Muttering curses, Iozel carried it to a dark corner, sat down on the edge of a stool, and closed his eyes. And just as Maglore had instructed him, so the hermit held the golden shape warm in his hand and felt its weird contours, and sent his thoughts winging, winging, winging –

– All across the mountains to Turgosheim . . .

*

In Vladistown – a huddle of maybe one hundred and twenty drab dwellings of timber, sod, withes and skins; nothing so sophisticated or large as Mirlu Township, Tireni Scarp or Settlement – Nathan was detained with six other young men in a timbered pen which was largely open to the sky. On the inside, a few narrow awnings kept the sun off the prisoners. These were not criminals but tithelings: the 'legitimate get' of vampire tithesmen, who would arrive out of Turgosheim after sundown to collect their miserable flesh-and-blood levy. Since male and female tithelings were kept apart, there were two such stockades.

Nathan's belt had been taken from him and replaced with a length of twine. To offer him up to a lieutenant of the Wamphyri bearing silver upon his person ... the consequences would be unthinkable! He would never see that belt, buckle or sheath again. As for the silver locket and chain given him by Atwei at their parting: they went unnoticed under his flowing hair and soft leather shirt. After dark and before the tithesmen came, he would secrete them in an inside pocket.

Nathan was mortally afraid but tried not to show it. The others penned with him were less reticent. Listening to their whispers, it was plain they'd given up all hope. They saw themselves as fodder for the Wamphyri; even when loved ones came to speak to them through the perimeter fence, they could scarcely be bothered. The place was heavy with depression, rank with the acrid stench of fear. A tented privy in one corner did nothing to improve the atmosphere. Nathan would like to shut the hushed conversations out and think his own thoughts, but could not. In the end he listened however listlessly, gleaning what scraps of information he could.

The tithesmen would come an hour or so after sundown, when the last soft flush lay low on the southern horizon. Should all go well they would take Dobruj's tribute of flesh and be out of here in less than one hour; but if anything was amiss ... someone must be made to pay for it. Dobruj was the town's headman, whose back bore the scars of past failures, when the tally had been short now and then. He wasn't likely to make that mistake again. Yet even now a pair of defectors had brought the count down: the tally was two men short — or one man, now that this flashy stranger had been taken — so that Dobruj must find one more, when the tithesmen came.

The day was no shorter than any Sunside day, yet somehow time flew. Nathan likewise thought of flight, but outside the stockade the guards were cautious for their lives; only let a titheling escape ... who would take his place? When water was brought Nathan drank it, but he refused the tasteless food. It was snapped up by the others as if they hadn't eaten in a week. Well, things were not that bad, but neither were they good. He continued to listen to their stories ...

For a year and nine months now Wamphyri demands had been on the increase, tithe collections more frequent, the sack of Sunside's resources more utter. The Lords of Turgosheim were draining the townships as never before; they seemed unable to get enough of anything; there was such a thirst, a hunger and fire in them as to outdo all previous greed. As for its cause or source: who could say? What man would ever dare to ask? But one thing for sure: their monstrous works across the barrier mountains were grown more monstrous yet!

Things had crashed in the foothills — gigantic, hideous Wamphyri constructs; mad, mewling, ravaging carnivores — word of which had found its way through the forests to the towns on the rim. The Wamphyri made aerial monsters in Turgosheim, from innocent flesh and blood! But these were creatures far removed from their doleful, nodding manta flyers. As to their purpose: again, who would dare ask?

Nathan didn't need to ask; for remembering only too well that night almost a hundred sundowns ago, when a . . . a *creature* called Vratza Wransthrall had died on a cross in Settlement — and the things that creature had told to Lardis Lidesci — Nathan knew! Wratha's raiders had been first to fly the coop, yes, but others would soon follow her. And they were preparing even now, in Turgosheim. If the quality of their warriors was such that they were still crashing in the hills, however . . . well, obviously Wratha had a head start. And how dearly Nathan would love to get *that* information back to Lardis Lidesci, if Lardis was still alive. Somehow, Nathan fancied that he was . . .

In the heat of the day Nathan drowsed, and when the flies would let him he slept; it seemed as well to conserve his energies for whatever was to come. Sleeping, he dreamed of several things, most of which were forgotten whenever he started awake. Dimly, he remembered the mournful howling of his wolves in the faraway. And certain of the Thyre dead, whose sad thoughts had reached him even here.

Midday came and went; more water and a crust of bread; the stockade guards changed and changed again. Nathan slept, jerked shivering awake in the shade of his awning, put out an arm into the waning sunlight to absorb a little warmth. Waning, yes — already. For all that Sunside's day was like half a week in the world of his unknown father, still time's inexorable creep was the same in both worlds.

Later . . . Nathan was hungry. This time when food came he ate it, and appreciated it. Already his perspective was changing. Once, he read the mind behind a child's sad eyes peering in at him through the stockade fence: *When will it be my turn? Not for a long time, for I'm only six.* Aye, but soon enough, soon enough.

Another 'visitor' as evening drew in was Iozel Kotys. His mind was loose as ever; it overflowed with venom, but also with wonder and not a little fear. *Who are you, and where from? Out of the west? Is it possible? Not Maglore's man, as I've discovered, though he wants you badly enough now. But who? How? Why?*

Nathan looked up at the glaring eyes in the bearded face, which glowered at him through the gapped fence. 'Oh?' he said, in a low voice. 'And have you spoken with your master, then? Are you his thrall, in mind if not in body?'

And Iozel gasped and went away . . .

Nathan slept again, long and deep, and woke up cold and cowed. The first stars were out, and beyond the stockade's wall a fire blazed up. Tables had been set, where barrels of wine stood in a row. A low platform had been erected, with a number of great wooden chairs at its centre. Dobruj was there, striding nervously this way and that, waiting.

Then: it happened all at once.

The stars were blotted out; they blinked off and on again as something black, several things, passed between. There came the throb of powerful wings to fan the fire, as shapes of midnight flowed overhead, settling to a rise in the near-distant grassland border. And finally the tithesmen, Wamphyri lieutenants, were here.

They came striding, four of them – tall, powerful, cruel, arrogant; certain of themselves, showing nothing of fear, only scorn – with lesser vampire thralls bringing up the rear. Nathan saw them through the stockade fence, and knew where he had seen such before. They were much of a kind with Vratza Wransthrall.

No time was wasted: Dobruj met them grovellingly, and was pushed aside. He followed them to the platform where they took seats. And: 'Bring them on,' one of them, the chief among them, commanded. His scarlet eyes glanced towards the stockades. 'But quality this time, if you please, Dobruj. For I was here a year ago, remember? You won't be foisting any more scum on me this time!'

The tithelings were paraded, females first. One at a time, eight girls were taken up on to the platform, where the lieutenant ripped their blouses to the waist, exposing their breasts, and lifted their skirts to admire their thighs. And while they stumbled there in tears, trying to cover themselves, he licked his lips and sniffed at them lewdly, like a dog, but without seeming much impressed. In any case: 'They'll do,' he grunted shortly, grudgingly. 'And the men?'

As the girls were led away, Nathan was brought out along with the six other young men. He was the fourth put up on to the platform. 'Oh?' said the lieutenant. 'And what have we here?'

Dobruj answered breathlessly: 'A stray – we don't know from where. I thought maybe he'd come ... out of Turgosheim?'

The lieutenant was all of six inches taller than Nathan; pinching his face in a massive hand, he squeezed until Nathan opened his mouth and displayed his teeth, much like a shad examined by a man. 'What?' The lieutenant released Nathan, sent him staggering, and turned to Dobruj. 'Eh? Out of Turgosheim, did you say? How so?'

Dobruj flapped his pudgy hands. 'His clothes, Lord, and his colouring. He's not a man of these parts. We thought perhaps ...'

'Be quiet!' the other told him. 'You're not supposed to

think. We don't need you to think. But this one was never in Turgosheim, believe me! However, he is the best of what we've seen, so I'm not displeased. Now, let's see the rest.'

The other three were brought up together; the lieutenant merely glanced at them, then at Dobruj. 'One short,' he growled, warningly, his eyes reduced to crimson slits.

'The eighth comes now,' Dobruj answered, as a scuffling sounded from the edge of the firelight. His men dragged Iozel Kotys into view, kicking and screaming. But as soon as he saw the vampires he fell silent, gasping.

The chief lieutenant looked at him for several long seconds, then at Dobruj. Until from deep in his throat, soft and dangerously low, 'Some little joke, perhaps, Dobruj?' He took hold of the headman in the armpit, squeezing him hard there as he drew him close. 'I certainly hope not.'

Dobruj gulped, gasped his pain and fluttered his free arm. 'Lord,' he cried out for his life. 'Please listen! All of your provisions have been put aside on travois, exactly as required. Fruits, nuts, honey in jars, grains, beast-fodder by the bale, and wines. As for the barrels you see on the table there: they are *extra* to the tithe – for you! Take a sip, a taste, I implore you!' One of his men ran forward with a jug. The lieutenant grabbed it up, drank until it swilled his face, and spilled the rest over Dobruj's head.

'Aye, it's good!' he said, tossing Dobruj aside. 'But what shall I do with this?' He pointed at Iozel, grovelling in front of the platform.

Iozel looked up. 'Take me to Maglore!' he cried. 'He will have me. I was his upon a time, until he returned me here . . .'

'Ah!' the lieutenant's eyes opened wide. 'So you are that one! The Seer Mage mentioned you, of course – his spy!'

'There! There!' Iozel grinned, however lopsidedly, aware of Dobruj's eyes – and the eyes of many another – burning on him. 'I knew it would be so.'

'Indeed,' said the lieutenant. 'And Maglore told me: "If Iozel is offered in the tithe, by all means bring him in, but *don't* bring him to me. For if he is a traitor to his own, how then will he serve me? Ah, but the manses will always require provisioning, and even offensive meat is still meat!" So spake Maglore!'

'No – *no!*' Iozel jumped up, turned to run.

'Still him!' Dobruj ordered it, grimly and with some satisfaction. And one of his men cudgelled the hermit behind the ear, so that he fell asprawl. With which it was over.

The chief lieutenant came down off the platform and went among the tithelings. He singled out the two comeliest girls, plus Nathan and one other youth, then spoke to the lesser vampire thralls who accompanied him. 'These four go with us. The rest are for the march through the pass. Be sure not to lose any on the way.'

He saw them off with their laden travois along a forest track, and without another word headed out of town across the plain to where the silhouettes of flyers nodded grotesquely at the crest of a rise. Nathan and the other youth were each given a small barrel to carry; they and the girls were shepherded ahead; the lieutenants brought up the rear, carrying barrels as if they were weightless. And the rest was dreamlike:

The great grey beasts nodding in the night; the barrels loaded into their fetid pouches; the tithelings made fast at the rear of long saddles, where they were warned: 'One false move and we'll ditch you into space, and see if you can fly like the Wamphyri!'

Then the launching and dizzy climb as hugely arched wings trapped wafts from below; the sick, soaring flight over twelve or thirteen miles of forest, foothills, ragged peaks; finally the sighing, slanting descent between crags, spires, flaring orange and yellow gas jets and reeking chimneys. Down, down into a vampire realm, past grim battlements, ruddily glaring windows and balconies, towards communal landing- and launching-bays in the great dark gorge which was Turgosheim . . .

In normal circumstances, Maglore would rarely if ever lower himself to attend a draw and allocation of common tithelings; he would send a thrall, to collect his get on his behalf. But these were scarcely normal times, and if Iozel Kotys could be believed this 'Nathan' was no common or ordinary Sunsider.

Three 'lots' of tithelings had been brought in: four from Vladistown, five from Gengisheim, six out of Kehrls-crag. These were the so-called 'cream', flown in for special treatment; the commoner stuff would follow on foot. But the draw was the same for all: bone sigils in a bag, and luck the only arbiter.

The draw for the best of the batch was worked on a strict roster. Maglore must consider himself fortunate that it was his turn in the round, else he must do some serious bargaining and even then be lucky to obtain this oddity, this Nathan, before it could be . . . damaged. But his luck was out (his sigils had already been drawn; he'd got two middling girls and a loutish youth), and so was obliged to wait and do a little bargaining after all. Which was his reason for lingering until Nathan had been 'won' by Zindevar Cronesap.

Zindevar wasn't at the fatesaying in person; neither were the Lords Eran Painscar, Grigor Hakson, and Lom Halfstruck of Trollmanse. All were busy elsewhere —

occupied or preoccupied with their various creative endeavours, most likely – but lieutenants were there in their stead. Eventually Zindevar's man had his three – two more males, to go with that 'item' which Maglore found most interesting – and headed for the launching bays. Maglore left one third of his get (the surly youth) in the care of one of his two thralls, and with the half-naked, whimpering girls in tow caught up with Zindevar's unhappy-seeming lieutenant in an antechamber.

'No luck, then?' he said, coming up behind him.

'Eh?' Taken by surprise, the man turned, saw Maglore and said, 'Oh!' He bowed clumsily. 'My Lord Maglore!' His confusion was understandable; it wasn't usual for Wamphyri Lords to pass the time of night with the lieutenants of other Lords or Ladies; even one's own lieutenants could scarcely be considered worthy persons. Then Maglore's query struck home.

'Luck?' the man's face turned sour as he eyed Maglore's girls. 'It appears that you at least have more than enough! As for Zindevar . . .' He shrugged sorrily.

Maglore nodded. 'She won't be happy with just three lads, be sure.'

'Huh!' the other scowled, then rounded on his charges and glared at them for being male.

Nathan, no less uncertain and afraid than his fellow prisoners, was nevertheless fascinated to recognize Maglore from two separate sources: one was his name (Iozel Kotys had mentioned him as a former master); the other was his awesome and awe-inspiring aspect. He was without question that same 'mage' glimpsed however mistily in the eye of Thikkoul's mind as he gazed on Nathan's stars to read his future: the one of whom he'd warned, *He would use you, learn from you, instruct and corrupt you!*

So that where the other captives cringed back, averting their eyes from Zindevar's lieutenant as he rounded on them, Nathan continued to stand tall and gaze upon Maglore. It was merely his way – the Szgany way, innocent and even naïve – and never intended as a slight or an insult, neither to Maglore nor even to the bullying lieutenant. But that one's eyes blazed up like fires as he mistook Nathan's natural curiosity for dumb insolence.

'What?' he roared, catching Nathan up by the front of his jacket and shirt. 'Why, you – !' He held him like that a moment, then hissed and thrust him violently away, and snatched back his hand as if he'd been stung. Nathan's jacket was torn open; a button popped at the neck of his shirt; Atwei's silver locket, which he had replaced around his neck, dangled into view. And the lieutenant still astonished, gazing at his huge, iron-hard hand. Then:

'*What?*' he said again, a whisper this time, as finally he noticed the locket at Nathan's neck. 'Silver? Can I believe it? Would you poison me, then? You ... prissy ... little ... !'

Pointing a shaking hand at the locket, he grated: 'Take it off! Throw it down!'

Nathan did so, and stood with his back to the hewn stone wall. The lieutenant stepped forward snarling, stamped on the locket with a booted foot. It flew into several pieces, and a tight curl of hair sprang free. '*Hah!*' The man pounced, snatched up the black wisp and showed it to Nathan. 'And this?'

'A ... a keepsake,' Nathan gasped. 'The pubic hair of ... of a maiden.'

'Indeed!' The man grinned, kicked bits of locket in all directions, held out his free hand palm up for Nathan to see. The flesh of his palm was grey, calloused, horny. Even as Nathan watched, it formed sharp scales or rasps like some hideous flensing weapon. Then the lieutenant clasped his hands together, crushing the lock between them. And with a grinding motion he reduced the tight coil to so much black snuff, inhaling it with gusto, in pinches, into eager, quivering nostrils.

'Hah! Delightful!' he crowed then, smacking his lips. 'And was she beautiful?'

'She was Thyre,' Nathan at once answered him, with a great deal of bravery and more than a little satisfaction. If he was going to die it might as well be now. 'She was a desert trog!'

For a moment there was a silence broken only by the whimpering of Nathan's fellow tithelings. Then ... the lieutenant's grey-mottled face turned greyer still as he swelled up huge as if to burst. He grabbed Nathan by the throat with one hand, and drew back the other to slap him. Just one such slap would ruin Nathan's face forever. Except –

'Now, hold,' said Maglore, quietly, yet in a voice which brooked no argument. 'Only damage him and it's no deal. And I shall tell Zindevar you lost her a pair of lovely little playmates for her bed.'

The lieutenant's hand froze in mid-air; his head swivelled on his bull neck and he glared at Maglore, then frowned and said: 'What deal?' Finally he remembered his manners, blinked and relaxed a little. And: 'Lord Maglore,' he said, 'I mean no disrespect, but it is the Lady Zindevar commands me, not you.'

'Aye, and she'll command that you are disembowelled!' Maglore chuckled, however humourlessly, '– If you don't take these girls into Cronespire in exchange for that one foppish youth. Make up your mind, quick!'

Now the other was suspicious. He glanced at Nathan again. 'Oh? And what is it with him? Why would you want this one, who is either an idiot, or just plain insolent, or both? Bringing silver into Turgosheim, indeed! What madness! Don't the Szgany teach their Sunside brats anything these days?'

Maglore shrugged, and answered mysteriously, 'There is Sunside and there is Sunside, and Szgany and Szgany, and what is taught in one place may not be deemed necessary in another . . . not yet. But this one —' he shrugged again, '— I like his colours, which are weird. Also, he seems stupidly docile, dumb, even innocent; he shall follow me around Runemanse like a pet. As for Zindevar: she shall have these girls to tweak, which is bound to stand you firmly in her favour.'

A moment's pause for thought, and: 'Done!' Zindevar's lieutenant released Nathan, sent him flying along the wall and out of his sight behind Maglore. And the Mage of Runemanse told his girls:

'Go with this gentleman and he will take you to your new mistress, a very lovely Lady who will show you many *wonderful* things!' Hearing which, even Zindevar's 'gentleman' burst into baying laughter, as Maglore took Nathan's shoulder and quickly walked away with him . . .

Along the way to Runemanse — a route covering almost two and a half miles of caves, crags, causeways; often climbing internally through communal cavern systems, or externally over vertiginous chasms and up dizzily spiralling walkways of bone and cartilage — Maglore kept up an onslaught of seemingly innocuous questions. But Nathan knew for a fact that his interest was any-thing but innocent, which was made obvious by the veritable barrage of mental probes which Maglore used in a prolonged simultaneous attempt to penetrate the shield around Nathan's secret mind. Given the chance (if Nathan were to relax his guard for a single moment), he knew that these probes would at once enter and explore the innermost caverns of his brain.

Even before meeting Maglore, Nathan had known that the Wamphyri Lord was a telepath; however stupidly – unwittingly, whatever – Maglore's spy Iozel Kotys, the so-called 'mystic', had given him away. But Nathan could never have anticipated the full range of the Seer Lord's mind, whose insidious energies seethed in his vampire skull like the smoke of balefires, sending out curling black tendrils of thought in all directions.

In order to maintain and reinforce the telepathic wall with which Nathan had surrounded himself, he used the subterfuge of asking questions of his own: he knew how difficult it would be for Maglore to scry upon his mind and construct meaningful answers to his questions at one and the same time. And why shouldn't he question? Nathan knew that Maglore would not harm him, not yet at least and perhaps not ever. No, for Thikkoul had foreseen a long stay for him in Runemanse, but nothing specifically harmful that Nathan could remember.

The sun rises and sets, Thikkoul had read in his stars, *and sunups come and go in a blur where you wander in a great dark castle of many caves. I see your face: your hollow eyes and – greying hair?*

Well, that last was ominous, admittedly. But now that Nathan was here, what had he to lose? Very little of his own, for in Turgosheim his life *was* nothing; but still there were certain interests he must protect. His knowledge of the Thyre, for instance: their secret places over and under the desert; also his familiarity with old Sunside, where Wratha and her renegades (and in a little while the vampires of Turgosheim) would do to his people what had been done here. He must give nothing of such knowledge away to benefit the Wamphyri, not if there was a way to avoid it.

'Why didn't we fly to Runemanse?' he asked Maglore

where they crossed a swaying bridge of sinew and arching, alveolate cartilage. 'Do you have no flyers?'

'I have one, aye,' Maglore answered, offering him a curious, perhaps indulgent glance. 'It is in use now, where a man of mine flies back a surly Kehrlscrag youth to Runemanse. But flyers are for the younger Lords, my son, and for the generals to ride out and command their armies. Oh, I have made a flyer or two in my time, but mainly I prefer to walk. When I can go on foot I do so, but where the way is too sheer or distant I fly. Personally, I dislike great heights; for gravity is a curious force and insistent. I have never flown in my own right, as certain Lords are wont to do, for that requires an awesome strength, and alas my body is feeble – by comparison.' But he did not say with what.

They were in the middle of the span. In the dark, distant sprawl of the gorge, the lights and flaring exhausts of some of the spires came up level with their eyes. More than a thousand feet below, Turgosheim's depths were lost in dark velvet shadows. Maglore paused and drew his charge to him, and with an arm around his shoulder leaned out over the fretted cartilage wall to look down. Behind Nathan and Maglore, one of the mage's vampire thralls waited silent but alert.

And: 'About flying,' said Maglore quietly, huskily, with a scarlet, sideways glance at Nathan. 'Can you imagine flying from here? To leap out upon the air, and form your flesh into stretchy scoops like the wings of a bat? To trap the currents rising out of Turgosheim, and so glide from peak to peak? Ah, but what an art that would be! Even though I've never used it, I have it, for I am Wamphyri. I probably could do it even now, despite the lack of that special strength which could only be mine by virtue of ... a certain lifestyle. But you: you would fall like a stone, and splash like an egg ...'

Maglore drew Nathan closer in an arm which contracted like a vice, crushing his shoulders. Nathan felt
the other's awesome strength, and for a moment thought
it was his intention to lift him up and throw him down.
For all his protestations about his 'feeble body', the
vampire Lord could do it ... just so easily. Nathan
looked at his hideous face, so close – that long-lived,
evil face, grooved as old leather; its white eyebrows
tapering into veined temples under a lichen-furred dome
of a skull; the crimson lamps of Maglore's eyes, set deep
in purple sockets – and tried not to be afraid. Perhaps
Maglore sensed it: the bolstering of Nathan's resolve,
his determination, and perhaps he admired it. At any
rate he released him, and said:

'Go on, cross the bridge and I shall follow on.' And
as Nathan set out: 'Aye, there's a great art to flying,'
Maglore repeated himself from close behind, but in a
lighter tone now. 'One of the more physical arts of the
Wamphyri, called metamorphism. But there are arts and
there are arts. Arts of the body, of the will, and of the
mind. Indeed, for will and mind are not the same. I have
known splendid minds with little or no will at all, and
creatures with a rare and wilful tenacity but hardly
anything of mind!'

Nathan walked on, across the bridge of bones, the
fossilized cartilage of mutated men, and spied ahead at
the end of the span a walled staircase carved from the
face of the gorge itself. It went up a hundred, two
hundred feet, to where Turgosheim's rim had been
notched and weathered into wind-, rain- and time-
sculpted battlements. But there were landings, too, with
dark-arched passageways leading off to rooms and regions within that vastly hollowed jut of rock, that massive promontory turret, Maglore's manse over an abyss
of air and darkness. And there were also gaunt win-

dows – some of them aglow with fitfully flickering lights, and others dark as the orbits of a skull – which gloomed out from it.

'Runemanse!' Maglore whispered in Nathan's ear, when his charge came to a stumbling halt. 'In which I practise my arts. And where you will practise ... yours?'

At the end of the bridge, as he stepped up into a walled landing or embrasure, Nathan turned to Maglore. 'My arts?'

Peering at him through red-glowing, slitted eyes, Maglore grasped his shoulder in a hand like iron. 'I have sensed arts in you, yes,' he said. 'Undeveloped as yet ... perhaps. Do you understand mentalism?'

Nathan was almost caught off guard. 'Mentalism?'

'Call me master,' Maglore growled. 'When you answer me, you must call me master. Here in Runemanse I have creatures, thralls, beings which are mine. I shall require of you what I require of them: obedience. If your ways are seen to be slack, so might theirs grow slack. Wherefore you will call me master. Do you understand?'

'Yes, master.'

'Good.' And returning to his previous subject: 'Mentalism, aye. Telepathy. To read the secret minds – the thoughts – of others, and so discover their wily plots and devious devices.'

'I know nothing of it,' Nathan shook his head. His guard was solid now, or as near solid as he could make it. But Maglore's eyes grew huge in a moment as for one last time he tried to enter his charge's mind. Nathan could almost feel his disappointment as he failed and withdrew.

Then Maglore nodded, and: 'Perhaps you don't at that,' he said. 'But you do have a capacity for strange arts, believe me. Yes, for I sense them in you. Perhaps we can develop them. One such is the opposite of mentalism: it is to create a wall which shields the user's mind from outside interference. In some rare men it is a natural thing. One *cannot* read their minds, however crafty one's skill.'

Nathan shrugged and tried to look bewildered. 'I am trying to understand, master.'

Maglore relaxed, sighed, and said, 'Let it be.' He indicated an arched entrance across the landing. 'This is to be your home. Enter now and be with Runemanse as you have been with me: unafraid. For to walk with fear is to fail, especially here.'

Nathan held back a little, pausing there on the external landing. But in fact it wasn't fear this time, more the oppressiveness of the place, like the pause before lowering oneself into some deep and lightless hole. Or perhaps it was the sigil carved in the virgin rock of the arch which held him back: the twisted loop which Nathan had known all his days, which indeed was part of him and was now to be even more a part of his life. And so he stood there, looking up at it; until, but impatiently now: 'Enter!' Maglore commanded again. 'Enter now, of your own free will, into Runemanse.'

Nathan could only obey, while in his secret mind he wondered: *But at the end of the day, will it be so easy to leave, 'of my own free will'?* And as Maglore's hand closed like a claw on his shoulder, guiding him forward into the perpetual gloom of Runemanse, he supposed that it would not . . .

PART EIGHT:

Runemanse − Flight − In the Blink of an Eye

———————

I

Within, there was no lack of activity. Huge sighings (animal or mechanical, Nathan had no way of knowing) issued up from the bowels of the place; draughts of air, some warm and others bitterly cold, blew busily here and there as if out and about upon missions of their own; there were sounds of vast, animal exhalations, gasps and grunts, and other echoes which seemed of entirely human origin: voices and/or sounds of thrall work in progress. In the weird acoustics of the place it was difficult to locate any specific source; the sounds penetrated from above, below, around. Eerie snatches of conversation, the slap of sandalled feet on hollowed flags, the *chink, chink* chipping of cold stone, or the reverberating, nerve-shattering clanging of a door slammed shut. Occasionally, shadows would flit apace in parallel corridors, and Nathan would glimpse feral eyes turned in his direction. Once, a hulking lieutenant loomed large, only to shrink back as Maglore's presence dwarfed him.

Extensive, Runemanse filled the honeycombed rock like a warren in a bank of earth. Innermost was a huge hall illumined by flaring gas jets, leading off from which were the rooms of Maglore's various aides: his two lieutenants, his thralls and women. The vampire Lord's own apartments were reached up steps which spiralled around a central core, and had balconies overlooking the hall as if it were an amphitheatre. At the foot of the steps a ... Thing was chained, manacled to the natural pillar. Unseemly by any standards, it had its own place behind a curtain of ropes, out of sight in a small cave in the central stem. But as Nathan, a stranger, approached the foot of the stairs . . .

. . . It burst out, mewling, towering eight feet tall and shaped – very much like a man! Yet paradoxically and appallingly, not like a man at all. Not any longer. Nathan felt himself shrinking back, unable to proceed, and felt Maglore propelling him irresistibly forward. And as they went the Wamphyri Lord told his guardian creature: 'This man is mine. Who harms him harms me, and will answer for it. Now begone, for you are ugly.' At which the awful thing fell to all fours and scurried backwards, grovellingly, through the curtain of ropes. Nathan could hear it panting and rumbling in there as they passed by and climbed the spiral staircase.

In Maglore's rooms, food had been prepared. Nathan could scarcely contain his suspicion of the contents of the various platters. They looked innocent enough – steaming portions of rabbit and partridge, roasted vegetables, and bowls of fresh fruit – but on the other hand . . .

'What?' said Maglore, noting Nathan's expression across the table, and chuckling darkly to himself as he dined delicately on thigh of rabbit and red wine. 'And did you expect raw flesh, possibly Szgany, and perhaps still alive? Well, I have to admit that in certain spires and manses you would not be disappointed – but this is Runemanse. Certain of my thralls and creatures have their "requirements", but in the main I've learned to curb my own appetites. You need not concern yourself, Nathan: your food will not disgust or harm you, nor will I give you cause to throw it up; not here at least. For when I have need of . . . coarser sustenance, I take it in private. And even then I'm no great glutton. So have no fear; for unlike the raw red *regimen* of some of Turgosheim's Lords, you'll not hear *my* food screaming!'

Despite the terrible pictures Maglore's words conjured, Nathan tried the food and found it very good. And as his hunger took hold, so a little of his natural caution deserted him. 'Aye,' Maglore nodded approvingly. 'Eat, and when you've eaten explore the manse. Step boldly and no harm shall befall you. But before then and while you're about your meal, we have a chance to talk.' He put aside his own plate. 'On our way to Runemanse I asked you many things: your age, full name, birthplace; I inquired especially about the colours of your eyes, hair, skin, which seem scarcely Szgany colours at all, and yet are not so weak or freakish as the pallid pastels of an albino. Patently they are not the result of disease, deformity or experimentation, and so must be inherited. But from whom, mother or father? Your previous answers were vague at best.'

Nathan swallowed scooped-out oyster of partridge from his index finger, and washed it down with a sip of wine. 'My mother was Nana, a Szgany woman of course, and my father was Hzak Kiklu, a common Traveller.' He shook his head. 'I didn't get my colours from them.'

Just looking at him, Maglore could see that he told the truth. He frowned and said, 'Let it pass, for now.' But Nathan's answer had prompted another question. 'Your father was a . . . a "Traveller", did you say?'

'I came out of the west,' Nathan answered, 'which I also told you.' (No harm in it, since Iozel had probably told him the same thing in advance.) But remembering himself in time, Nathan quickly added, 'Master.' And continued: 'There in the west, the Szgany of Sunside don't live in towns but travel by day and hide by night. The word "Szgany" means, among other things, "Traveller". Which is what my people are. Perhaps your own Szgany were Travellers, upon a time?'

'Oh, they were!' Maglore answered, 'in those early

days after Turgo Zolte brought his people here out of the west. Aye, they travelled, before the Wamphyri brought them to heel, as it were. *Hmmm!*' He stroked his chin. 'How is it, then, that while *your* Szgany do not live in "towns", still you know the word?'

Nathan shrugged, and thought quickly. 'But I know it as in "Vladistown", master,' he said. 'Also as an old word of my own people. Though I was only a child of four or five years on the night of the burning clouds and the thunder over the barrier range – when the last of the Wamphyri were destroyed, or so it was supposed – I remember that some of our leaders said we should build "towns" again. Others, however, were against it. No, they said, for the vampires would return one day, out of the swamps or from other places.' His answer was deliberately confused and confusing, to throw Maglore off the track. And to distract him even further, he scratched for a moment at the leather strap on his wrist, then took it off and placed it on the table where Maglore could not help but see it. And continuing to scratch at his imaginary itch, he watched the Seer Lord's scarlet eyes grow large as he pounced.

'A-ha!' Maglore cried, snatching up the strap. And just for once his telepathic mind was so open that Nathan clearly 'heard' the thought: *Just as that old Sunside fraud informed me! Why, I had almost forgotten – till now!* Then, a moment later, his thoughts were guarded again. But not nearly as close as Nathan's. And: 'What are we to make of this?' Maglore said. 'Where did you get it? And do you recognize it?'

'It is my wrist strap,' Nathan shrugged, '– master.'

'Of course it is!' Maglore shook his head – then glanced at Nathan sharply, suspiciously. 'Do you play word games with me? If so you should know: I'm good at them.'

Nathan looked blank, and again Maglore grunted, 'Hmmm!'

And: 'Ah!' Nathan said after a moment. 'The sign over your doors! I recognize it now: your sigil! And mine, it would seem. Except ... it's nothing but a strange coincidence, master.'

'Perhaps it is,' Maglore nodded. 'And strange indeed – or would be, if I believed in coincidences. But on the other hand, I am *fascinated* by mysteries! So tell me now, how did you come by this thing?'

'But I've always had it,' Nathan answered truthfully. 'I think I first remember it ... on the night of the thunder over Starside, and the fire in the clouds.'

'How long ago?' Maglore hunched forward in his chair.

'Nearly sixteen years,' said Nathan.

'*Ahhh!*' Maglore sighed. And again his mind was open. *The night of the Light-in-the-West, the tremors in the earth, when I dreamed of the sigil and found it potent, and took it for my own! This is a mystery; there is an affinity, between this man and myself!*

Then ... perhaps he knew he was read. At any rate he sat up straighter and glared at Nathan. 'There *are* talents in you, hidden, I sense them,' he insisted for the third time. 'When I have an hour or two to spare, we must dig them out. Perhaps we might even make a start now.'

Footsteps sounded at the top of the spiral staircase, and a hulking lieutenant appeared on the landing. He paused uncertainly. Maglore scowled at him. 'Well? Is it urgent?'

'Your creature waxes in its vat, Lord,' the lieutenant reported. 'Alas, it has wrenched loose the breathing tubes and so may drown in its fluids.'

'What!' Maglore sprang up. 'Why did you not re-connect the tubes?'

'Go *into* the vat?' The lieutenant fell back. 'But the creature is voracious, and ill-humoured!'

'Take me there, now!' Maglore shouted. 'If aught befalls that construct of mine ... by Turgosheim, you'll know the meaning of ill-humour!'

Half-way across the floor he paused and looked back. 'You, Nathan. Explore the manse. If you are weary, ask any thrall to show you your room. Nowhere is forbidden to you, but avoid the women ... at least until I have spoken to them. Now I must go, but one last thing: I shall keep you as a friend, for I value you for yourself and not as a cringing vampire thrall. But let me make myself plain: I will take it *very* hard if you should try to run away. And always remember, a man without legs cannot run very far at all ...'

He *had* made himself plain. In any case, Nathan couldn't see where he might run. What, into Turgosheim? Or up on to the roof of the manse and the rim of the gorge, and so across the mountains to Sunside? To be picked up and brought back again? No, for his stay here was to be a long one. According to Thikkoul, anyway.

Nathan remembered Maglore's words (it seemed as well to remember *everything* the Seer Lord said): 'Nowhere is forbidden to you.' But did that include Maglore's chambers? Whether or no, he explored his master's rooms first. At least he felt comparatively safe here, which was probably more than could be said for the rest of the place.

As a powerful Lord of the Wamphyri, Maglore didn't stint himself: his apartments were huge. While some of the rooms were natural caves, massive cysts in the volcanic wall of the gorge, others had been carved from the virgin rock. And above every doorway Maglore's familiar sigil was plainly visible: the loop with a half-twist, chiselled in bas-relief into arch or lintel.

Maglore's bedroom faced north, away from the sun. There Nathan looked out through narrow windows on the blue-glittering rim of the world, where strange auroras wove over a coldly distant horizon. But while the windows were wide enough to take a man, he made no attempt to step up and pass through the thick exterior wall; it was enough to simply put his head out. For out there where a precarious ledge or balcony clung to the face of the turret, and a low wall of grafted cartilage was the only protection against a fall of what must be at least twelve hundred feet . . . the whole affair seemed very unsafe! In any case, the view was mainly away from Turgosheim and so uninteresting. That was Nathan's excuse, anyway . . .

As he explored Maglore's kitchen, a vampire thrall came ghosting, making the place clean. Once-Szgany and male, he was small, thin, ghastly pale; only his eyes contained a spark, and they were yellow, feral, dangerous. When he saw Nathan he gave a start, and then was curious. 'You'll be the new one,' he nodded. 'Well, and you've a lot to learn. For one thing, you're in the wrong place. A room has been set aside for you. If Maglore were to find you here . . .'

'He left me here,' Nathan answered. 'There are no restrictions upon me.'

'Oh?' The other raised an eyebrow, offered a half-sneer. 'Then you must consider yourself fortunate – for now!' He busied himself about the room. 'At any rate, you've been warned.'

Watching him at work (he worked hard, making the kitchen scrupulously clean), Nathan thought: *This man was Szgany, like me. Now he's a thrall, a vampire, the next step between Szgany and lieutenant. Except he's reached his limit because he isn't . . . the right stuff? In Settlement, Lardis Lidesci burned such as him, before*

they could head for Starside. Should I pity him, or
should I be afraid of him?

'Why do you watch me?' Nostrils gaping, eyes glaring,
the other rounded on him; and Nathan saw that he
really should not pity him. It was much too late for
that.

'You must know this place well,' he said, mainly for
something to say.

'Runemanse? Turgosheim? I know them well enough,'
the vampire answered. 'I know what I may do and what
is forbidden, the places where I may pass safely and
those where I must never go. For unlike you I am not
"privileged" in that respect.'

Nathan climbed wooden stairs to peer out through a
high, round window. Looking west and a little south, it
gave him a good view of all Turgosheim. 'Maglore says
he will not change me,' he said, half to himself. 'He
wants me for a friend. It seems he desires that I should
retain my Szgany initiative.'

Sniggering, the other followed him up the stairs.
'What?' he said. 'You're to be his friend, you say? Well,
and he's had "friends" before, has Maglore. I'm not so
sure I envy you your clean blood after all. Here in
Runemanse . . . some things are easier for a vampire.'

Nathan read his mind, however loosely. There was a
great red hunger in him, and also a great fear, of Maglore. But there was pain, too, and curiosity, and a longing like the ache for a loved one who is far away,
or lost forever. Which Nathan understood only too well.
'Have you been here long?' he said.

'Who counts the time?' the other shrugged, and
looked at Nathan through seething eyes. 'We seem of
an age, or I might be a year or two older. But I came
here when I was sixteen, out of Sunside. Perhaps I
might live so long again. And how's *that* for a night-

marish thought? Why, if I were not a vampire, I would throw myself down from this window for the guardian warriors to find broken in Turgosheim's bottoms when the sun lights on the barrier mountains! Ah, but I *am* a vampire, and tenacious! *I* might do it, but my weird blood won't let me.'

'Do you drink the blood of innocent men?' Nathan supposed he was taking a chance with a question like that, but asked it anyway.

'Rather the blood of girls and women!' the other answered gurglingly, out of a phlegmy throat. 'Sometimes, when the tithelings come, we are given our share. Maglore tries to keep his creatures happy, at least. The females will pass from hand to hand; we share their blood and bodies, until their lust is as great as our own. And the males are shared by Maglore's women. Those who are to be kept are then given employment under the supervision of Maglore's lieutenants or senior thralls, while any who are deemed unworthy ... are drained, and their bodies go to fuel the manse.'

'Fuel?'

'The provisioning,' the other nodded, flame-eyed and grinning, however grimly. 'A manse can't run on air and water alone, you know. But why waste time with questions? If as you say your movements are to be unrestricted, and you'll have access to all of Runemanse's chambers, workshops, and storerooms, why, you'll soon enough see for yourself!' His answer seemed like a threat in its own right, so that Nathan didn't ask him to elaborate but looked out through the great round window.

And after a moment: 'Do you have a name?' he inquired.

'Nicolae,' said the other. 'Nicolae Seersthrall ... now. And you?'

'Nathan. Nathan Kiklu.'

'Ah, no!' the other grinned again. 'You are Nathan Seersthrall. For here in Runemanse, we are all brothers and sisters. To keep your second name would mean you were a free man, which you are not. No one in Turgosheim is free.'

'Turgosheim,' said Nathan musingly, continuing to scan the gorge through the empty window. 'All of its spires and manses. Can you name them?'

'Why should I?'

'Because I would consider it a favour,' Nathan answered. 'Which one day I might return.'

Nicolae Seersthrall shrugged. 'I doubt that you'll be in any position. Also, it's a waste of my time. But on the other hand — and as I believe I said before — who counts the time in Runemanse?'

He settled down on the great stone windowsill, where his arm touched Nathan's — the merest touch. But: '*Ahhh!*' he said, half-sigh, half-gasp, and Nathan knew why. For where Nathan's flesh was warm, vibrantly alive, Nicolae's was cold as clay.

'And yet you are not undead,' Nathan said, drawing a little apart.

'No,' the other shook his head. 'I have never been "dead". I am merely changed, the lowest of the low. Vampire blood has contaminated my blood, that is all. But to touch one such as you, whose blood is clean ... is *thrilling* nevertheless! And it will be even more so for Maglore's women! That's something for you to avoid, if you can, Nathan Seersthrall.'

'I know nothing of women,' Nathan shook his head. 'Or ... very little.' Half apologetically, he shrugged.

'What?' Nicolae laughed. 'You are a virgin?' But his face went deadly serious in a moment. '*Never* tell them that, do you hear me? For if you do, they'll not let you alone for a minute but seek to suck you dry of more than just your blood! And despite all of Maglore's commands, they'll get you in the end!'

Nathan said nothing but simply nodded, and after a while Nicolae looked out over Turgosheim. 'Very well,' he said. 'And so you would know about this place . . .'

He pointed to the east, right across the three-mile mouth of the gorge to where the mountains fell down to the Starside plains. 'As you see, the barrier range was like a long, edible root, out of which some giant took a great bite – or a bight? But several of his teeth were stumps and others were missing entirely, and so a number of stacks and spires were left standing in the "bight" of the gorge, like pulp in the "bite" of an apple.' He let his arm swing to the right, south-east through an arc of thirty degrees. 'There against the far wall of the ravine, the scrapings which those great teeth missed:

'In fact they are stacks weathered from the old face of the gorge. Stacks, spires, and sometimes chimneys, where the fault has not quite managed to break away from the bulk of the cliff. Tonight, despite that the vats of the Wamphyri are bubbling with a vengeance, the light is good; smoke and steam have not obscured the view; a wind over Starside's plains is drawing the vapours away. But in any case it would make no difference; I would know the various spires and manses from their shapes alone, or from their fires, whose colours are distinct.

'To the left of the group, that one with the flaring yellow gas jet is Cronespire, the lair of the Lady Zindevar. Aye, and from the brightness of the flare you can see how hard she works tonight . . .'

Nathan looked at him. 'At what does this Lady . . . work?' He had guessed it but desired corroboration.

'At her vats, of course,' Nicolae's glance was scornful. 'At the shaping of human flesh into other than human flesh. At the making of monsters – out of men!'

'Warriors?'

'Warriors, flyers, creatures,' said the other. 'The Wamphyri are building an army! But . . . do you want to know about Turgosheim, or don't you?'

Nathan nodded, and Nicolae continued. 'Next in line after Cronespire, a hand's span south, or so it appears from here – that great stack of stone standing all askew in a lesser bight of its own, haphazardly piled as by an infant balancing shards of slate – is melancholy Vormspire. Note the paleness of its lights, like glow-worms, or the foxfire on a corpse left unburied. Vormspire is the aerie of Lord Vormulac Unsleep, perhaps the mightiest of all the Wamphyri. But the stack's illuminations are ever dim, its aspect shrouded, and its vampire master morose. Vormulac and Maglore are "friends", or as friendly as the Wamphyri ever get to be.'

Nicolae's arm traversed south. 'There, where the bight curves west along the rear wall – that series of caverns like sockets in some weathered, freakish skull carved from the face of the hollow cliff itself – is Gauntmanse. Its lights, fires and smoke have a uniformly purple tinge, which among the Wamphyri is the colour of sexual prowess. Lord Grigor is the master there, or "Grigor the Lech", as he's better known. One of the "younger" Lords, Grigor's cognomen says it all: for as fast as the Lech acquires female tithelings, so he wears them out! In Gauntmanse, young girls have withered to hags in the space of one long night . . .'

So it went: Nicolae pointed out the more prominent spires and manses, naming them all and detailing many of the characteristics of their masters and mistresses. His discourse covered Zunspire, Masquemanse, Tormanse, and many others along the rear wall, until the angle of observation became too acute. Then he looked into the gorge itself, where numerous lesser stacks and knolls made gargoyle humps among the shadows of Turgosheim's lower reaches. 'Down there dwell the lowly Lords and certain newcomers, and others who merely aspire. Yet even in the depths some Lords are well-established and powerful among the Wamphyri, who have chosen to live there for reasons of their own. One such is Lom Halfstruck, master of Trollmanse. His place is that square, squat knoll there, with turrets in its corners and red lanterns in their windows. Lom is a dwarf among the Wamphyri, whose legs are stunted. He says that since he was born close to the earth, it suits him to stay there, and he scorns the soaring aeries of the others . . .

'. . . But there,' Nicolae Seersthrall blinked twice, and turned his feral gaze from the gloomy gorge of Turgosheim inwards upon Nathan. 'There's a lot more, but that's enough for now.'

Nathan nodded and said, 'Despite that you're no more than a prisoner here, you seem to have acquired a great deal of useful knowledge.'

Nicolae's turn to nod and sigh. 'I've spent many a long hour at windows such as this one, overlooking Turgosheim,' he said. 'But in Runemanse there are things to look *into* as well as out of. I tidy Maglore's rooms, all of them. In one of this workshops he keeps an amazing model of the gorge, where all of its spires and manses are represented. For the Lord Maglore is a mage and seer, and believes in the magical, mystical things. If another Lord is spiteful towards him, Maglore utters curses against the likeness of his manse, to bring down a doom upon it! Also, being a mentalist, the model helps concentrate his mind when he sends out his thoughts to spy upon his contemporaries. It provides the targets for his mind-darts.'

'You should be careful,' said Nathan, 'that he does not look in your mind!'

'Why would he?' said the other, with a small start. 'For what am I, after all? I am nothing!' But still he drew back a little, in sudden alarm. Then: it was as if a wind had blown in through the window; the pair felt an inner chill; and in a moment Nicolae's alarm was very real. '*Maglore!*' he snatched a breath.

There was a shadow in the room, at the foot of the stairs, one of many cast by the flaring of the kitchen's gas jets. This one had been there for some little time, though neither Nicolae nor Nathan had noticed it until now. But it wasn't just a shadow, for as finally their eyes focused upon it, they saw that its own were scarlet. And: 'Maglore, indeed!' it said.

Nicolae was on his feet in a moment and flying, gibbering down the wooden stairs so quickly as to shake them. But Maglore trapped him at the bottom, gripped his shoulder in one clawlike hand and drew him yelping to a halt. 'Not so fast,' he murmured in a doomful voice. 'For one who talks so readily to strangers, Nicolae, you don't do nearly enough talking to your master.'

'My tongue ran away with me!' The other was in a state.

'Oh?' Maglore answered. 'Well, and now it may run away *from* you entirely. Indeed, I might bite it right out of your face!'

Nathan had stood up. Looking down on Nicolae and Maglore, he could read the Seer Lord's passion. Despite Maglore's quiet tones, his anger was enormous. Starting down the stairs, Nathan said: 'Master, it was I who asked the questions. If I had not, Nicolae could not have answered them. I asked only about Turgosheim and meant no harm. And his answers seemed likewise innocent.'

Maglore glanced at Nathan as he reached the bottom step, then glared at Nicolae again. 'If he speaks so readily to you, perhaps he would speak with others — but of what? The room of the miniature, perhaps, where by use of small spells and conjurations I try to put right what wrongs are worked against me? Ah, but there are those among the Lords and Ladies of Turgosheim who would seize most swiftly upon that, whose belief in the magical, mystical things is no less than mine!'

'I would never work against you, master!' Nicolae denied it, wriggling like a worm in Maglore's grasp. 'But to talk to this Nathan ... why, he is yours! In Runemanse, we are all — each and every one of us — yours!'

'But we are not *all* so nosy,' Maglore answered.

Nathan took a chance and said, 'If Nicolae is in any way guilty, then so am I. But I say again, we are innocent, master.'

Maglore released Nicolae and thrust him stumbling away, but fixed him with his eyes and held him incapable of flight where he came to a trembling halt against the wall. And growling, the Seer Lord answered Nathan, 'You may be innocent — possibly. But this one ...?' He continued to glare at Nicolae. Moreover, his upper lip had wrinkled back from his eye teeth like the muzzle of a dog, and his fangs showed metamorphic growth where blood crept on ivory down from the ruptured gums.

'But since nothing is forbidden to me in all Runemanse,' Nathan spoke hurriedly, gasping the words out, 'what could he tell me which I cannot discover for myself?'

Slowly, very slowly, a little of the fire went out of Maglore's eyes. He had seemed huge, awesomely powerful, but now in a moment shrank down into himself and was merely ... old. Then, to his errant thrall, he said: 'Ah! Now see how he pleads for you, Nicolae. Yet if the boot were on the other foot, and if I were to give you leave, you would have his blood in a moment! What it is to have compassion, eh? Why, if I don't take care, I can see this Nathan beguiling all of Runemanse with his winning ways!'

Nicolae, cowering to the wall, nodded his eager agreement. 'Oh, he's a one to watch, master, be sure!'

Maglore gave a phlegmy chuckle, then stood up straighter. 'Oh, I *am* sure – but you're the one I'll be watching, my lad! Now begone, you scummy, treacherous thing!'

Nicolae licked his lips, slid along the wall, fled wailing past Maglore and out of the kitchen. His footsteps receded into distance, pattering through his master's rooms . . .

Nathan took the opportunity to repeat, 'I meant no harm. Nor do I think that Nicolae meant any harm.'

Maglore nodded. 'I'm satisfied that you didn't. But *that* one – is a beggar! This time I have let you intervene on his behalf. But let's have it understood: I don't welcome such interference. And I would advise you, Nathan: even one who is to be my . . . friend, should know when to step carefully.'

Nathan said nothing, and in a little while Maglore asked him, 'Have you begun your exploration of Runemanse?'

'Your rooms, yes.'

'My rooms?' Maglore arched an eyebrow. 'Do you always take people at their word?'

Nathan shrugged – he hoped not negligently – and said, 'Only liars may not be taken at their word, master.'

Maglore blinked and slowly nodded, then laughed and slapped his thigh. 'Aye! It must be true! Well, well

– and so you *are* good at word games! And we shall get along famously. I look forward to many long conversations with you, Nathan. Except now I have things to do. A creature of mine lies damaged in its vat and I have repairs to make, lest a deal of hard work is wasted. And so I say again: go and explore the manse, or seek out your room and rest, and when I call for you come to me. Ah, but *when* I call, then make haste! Never keep me waiting, Nathan. Now, do you understand all?'

'Yes, master.'

Maglore turned away, and at once turned back. 'Perhaps I have already warned you, but if not I do so now: avoid my lieutenants if you can, for they are impatient men and unkind. Aye, and you must also avoid my women, who are patient beyond words and only *too* kind! And if you follow my meaning and my advice, all will be well . . .'

Runemanse was a queer mixture of rocks, mainly volcanic, whose outer sheath was of quartz and feldspar fused to granite. Many of its caverns were natural, formed from cysts of expanding gas trapped in the ancient magma as lava cooled to rock. But where softer pumice had formed in the primal flux, there the Seer Lord's thralls were at work even now, tunnelling in the body of the place like maggots in an apple.

Nathan found his 'room' (a small cyst or cavelet, in fact, situated directly below Maglore's own expansive apartments but unconnected except through the central stairwell with its hideous guardian), set back from the perimeter of the great hall at the furthest reach of a corridor hewn through the fibrous pumice of an old lava run. There were several other rooms off that corridor; their low, arched entries lacked doors but were equipped on the inside with screens of animal skin stretched over cartilage frames, which kept their interiors private from the view of casual passers-by. Nathan's room, however, had a wooden door with a peephole and a latch . . . but no key. Still, it was privacy of a sort.

Directed there by a slender young female thrall – a waif-like creature no less than Nicolae, but a vampire for all that, whose eyes were luminous in the darker places and cunning when Nathan found them observing him – he quickly examined his accommodation, or more literally his prison: a room four paces by five, paved with featureless, irregular slabs, with a bed under the high window and a small curtained area containing a crude commode and chamber pot. Low-burning gas jets in the walls gave flickering light but very little of warmth.

From the bed he stepped up into the deep, curtained window embrasure, opened the drapes and found the gap barred. Just as well; beyond the bars the drop was vertical and terrific! Looking out, the view was almost exactly the same as from Maglore's kitchen window overhead, which solved the problem of orientation. Then, climbing down again, Nathan found his vampire guide sitting on the rough blankets of his bed. He had left her outside the open door, without indicating that he desired company. But these creatures had minds of their own, and came and went like smoke.

'Thank you for bringing me here,' he told her. 'But now I intend to sleep.'

'Well,' she indicated his bed with a languid hand, 'you have a bed. It's good for sleeping, among other things.' Her smile was enticing as she slowly unfastened her blouse, showing Nathan the inner curves of her breasts. But her flesh was sallow, and her eye-teeth long, white and sharp. Fascinated, he stared at her where she stretched like a kitten, and saw the stains of her aureoles under thin material forced up into sharp, twin peaks by the stiffening of her nipples.

He got down from the bed, looked towards the door. 'You had better go.' His voice was shaky.

'Or what?' Hers was sultry, hot, teasing. 'How will you punish me, if I don't?' She lay back, lifted her dress, showed Nathan how she was naked underneath, and everything displayed. Then, spreading her legs wantonly, she ran her fingers through her bush. Her dark flesh quaked and opened like a small mouth, moist and pouting, so that from where Nathan stood two paces away, still he could feel its sweet suction — and its venom.

'Go now,' he said, hardening his voice, 'at once, or risk Maglore's wrath!'

'Hah!' she was up on her feet in a moment. 'But we thought you were fresh from Sunside, a young lad bursting with seed. We did not know that Maglore had bought you from Zindevar, who has doubtless kept you as a gelding in Cronespire, where your sole duty has been to oil the creaking leather of her flaccid teats! And did she steal your dark Gypsy colours, too, as well as your manhood, you pale trembling whelp?'

'Out!' Nathan went to the door, held it open.

'What?' She was furious now: her nostrils flaring, eyes blazing crimson, mouth a writhing, hissing, cursing gash. 'Do you really spurn me? Do you dare? I see that you do! Fuck you then, you pallid, sapless freak!' She swept by him and out of the room.

It had been the first of Nathan's several encounters with Maglore's women; in respect of which, it seemed that both Nicolae and the Seer Lord were perfectly correct . . .

Nathan was mentally and physically exhausted. Fully

clothed, with all three of his blankets covering him, he did eventually sleep but it was a long time coming. In the end he only succeeded after reminding himself that awake or asleep Runemanse was a place fraught with terrors, and that like it or not and for as long as he stayed here he must sleep and replenish himself at frequent intervals. Then, as he felt himself slipping from eerie awareness into the darkness of equally weird dreams, he remembered to cloak his telepathic mind with the vast and incomprehensible swirl of the numbers vortex, hopefully to protect it from the incursions of other minds with similar abilities.

In this way he shrouded his secret mind at least, which in any case would be cluttered with the debris of his waking hours and hard to decipher. But where telepathy is communication between living, physical minds, deadspeak is something else entirely. Only the minds of the dead were tuned to it, and Nathan's mind, of course . . .

Nathaaan! The dead voice was only a whisper at first, a sigh in the dark, uneasy drift of subconscious wandering. But as Nathan heard it, focused upon it, and drew closer to its source, so all other memories, pseudo-memories and dream-clutter were brushed aside; and the voice grew stronger. *Nathaaan?* It was a clotted gurgle, a dead and rotten thing, and despite its incorporeality, it was still the very 'embodiment' of evil. So that Nathan was instinctively aware that this was a voice from the pit.

'Who are you?' he asked it breathlessly, as his sleeping body grew cold and the short hairs stood erect on the back of his neck. 'What . . . are you?'

Ask what I was, the thing answered, its voice mournful now and racked with a sob. *For that is something I can tell you, aye, and perhaps even show you. But as for what I am ... why, I am no longer anything! Or if anything at all, an old dead thing in his lightless grave, blind and shrivelled and leathery as the mummified Thyre in their cavern mausoleums. That is what I am.*

'The Thyre? What do you know of them?' Nathan remembered his vow: he would never reveal his knowledge of the desert folk to the outside world. But it seemed that this one already knew of them. Something of them, at least.

Do I know of them? Ah, better than you think! Why, for fifty long years I have lain here in my solitude and listened to them through the long blind night: the echoes of their dead thoughts, drifting in from their dusty tombs, over Sunside and the barrier mountains, and down into Turgosheim. They are dead things no less than I myself, and so in my solitude I am privy to their thoughts. Except they are unkind and will not speak to me, and I no longer try to speak to them. But you ... are different. You are alive, Nathan! Your works have definition in the land of the living. You can make change, can bring things into being! Whereas I myself and all the dreaming Thyre, because we are only dead things, can change nothing.

Nathan was wary of the thing, whose evil was a miasma in his mind. 'You know my name, knew that I was here. How could you know these things, without that we've met before?'

How could I know? But I feel your trembling footsteps in the rock, which reverberate down to me like thunder! By comparison, Maglore's comings and goings are a patter of raindrops, and his thralls' a slither of leaves. Also, I hear your dreaming thoughts, called deadspeak, which are solid as spoken words to me, while the living hear nothing at all. Ah, you can build your barrier of numbers against the living, Nathan, but you may not

657

shield your mind from the dead! We know you, Necro-scope!

The thing seemed to know altogether too much. 'We?' Nathan answered. 'But the Thyre shun you, you've admitted as much. And you talk about your "solitude", which would seem to imply that all of the dead shun you. You can only be Wamphyri!'

Wamphyri, of course! said the other. It's no big secret. I am what I am. But I'm also dead, and you are the Necroscope. Or does your pity exclude such as me, as I have been excluded from light and life and existence itself, except as an old and crumbling thing in the rock?

Despite his instinctive caution, still Nathan was curious. 'Where are you — exactly?'

Where I dwelled for an hundred years; where I was blinded by treacherous sons and buried; where even now I stiffen to a stone, to become one with all the stones of Turgosheim. Upon a time my home was Madmanse. Now it is only my tomb . . .

Madmanse? Nathan didn't know about Madmanse.

Ah, no! The thing at once explained. Despite that Maglore and I were neighbours, you won't see Madmanse from his windows. For he was above and I was below.

'In Turgosheim's lower reaches?'

Look you, said the other. You know that Runemanse is like a turret, a hollow promontory of rock jutting from the rim of the gorge? Well, its column goes down into the roots of Turgosheim itself. The upper levels are Maglore's, but down below . . . is Madmanse! You must visit me one day. Maglore knows the way: an old stair-well, winding down, down. We shared the same wells, upon a time . . . The other's voice had sunk to a ghastly gurgle, suggestive, insinuating, inveigling. It was over-powering, very nearly hypnotic . . .

But even dreaming, still Nathan sensed his danger. 'Very well,' he said, pushing back the reek of mental contagion. 'So now I know where you are. But I still don't know *who* you were. Did you have a name?'

A name? Oh, indeed! The other's oozing, poisonous voice was more ghastly yet, like an evocation of immemorial horror, shuddering into life from beyond the grave. *My name was much feared in its time, even among the Wamphyri. I was Eygor Killglance, whose very eyes were instruments of death — which was the reason my twin bastard bloodsons blinded and destroyed me! Also why they fled in the end; for they knew that I was still here, and they feared the dreams I sent them, to plague them all their days. Well, now the dogs are gone, even beyond the reach of my dreams. But they'll be back one day, and I shall still be here, waiting . . .*

A little of Eygor's loneliness, his helplessness — but a great deal more of his bitterness, hatred, and frustration — touched Nathan's metaphysical mind, clinging there and burning like hot tears, or perhaps like acid. In the moment of its passion, the old thing in its long-forgotten vault had become more than just a disembodied mind; now it was more truly a Being in its own right, and Nathan took the opportunity to look deeper at what the once-master of Madmanse had been like towards the end of his time.

The other sensed the extension of Nathan's mind and knew that he had drawn closer. *Aye, seek me out,* he said. *First in dreams and then in life. Here I am, here — in the dark and the dank and the drear of my prison, where I died in the mire of Madmanse . . .*

Nathan could see, but dimly. He stood in a gloomy cathedral of a cave, vast and high-ceilinged, whose walls dripped slime and nitre. The floor was a clutter of anomalous debris, humped, fibrous, boggy. Spongy bones and white-shining cartilage gleamed everywhere, like a boneyard of monsters. The place was a vampire refuse pit, diseased, disused, and sealed up forever. But not everything here was refuse. Or perhaps it was – now.

Something leaned or slumped against the wall. At first Nathan took it for some strange stalagmite formation: a fantastic dripstone creation of nature. But he saw that its shape was much too irregular, and its texture darker than the salty, nitre-streaked stone. Lured by a morbid fascination, he willed his dream-self into motion and approached until the thing towered over him, clinging to the curve of the cavern's wall. And as Nathan's perspective changed so details stood out clearer, and the true nature of the thing was known.

It was ... a monstrous *amalgam*, a welding together of everything unwholesome! Like Maglore's guardian creature in its curtained niche under the central staircase in Runemanse's great hall, this thing's general outline was manlike. But the Seer Lord's creature was not eighteen feet tall and composed of fused bone, black mummied flesh, knobs of gristly cartilage, and plates of gleaming-blue chitin. Nor did Maglore's guardian have additional mouths in its bloated body and rubbery limbs, as well as the one in its face!

Nathan's dream-self drew back a pace. His fevered eyes scanned the *size*, the *shape* and diseased *design* of this thing slumped in a kneeling position against the wall. Its horny fossil feet and shrivelled, leathery thighs; its arched back and shoulders, and misshapen, screaming skull. Fused to the wall by nitre, the great head was thrown back, jaws frozen in some everlasting rictus. A withered arm lay along a ledge of rock, terminating in a talon that drooped from a wrist almost as thick as Nathan's thigh, where blackened bones protruded from dusty, fretted, crumbling flesh. Or at least, from the desiccated stuff which once had been flesh.

And: *Welcome to Madmanse*, the awful voice said, and Nathan knew that it was this gargoyle who spoke to him. *You entered of your own free will, and I shall make you heir to all of my mysteries – if you so desire. For I had powers in my time, Necroscope, just as you have powers now. And who knows but that one day we might trade something for something, and so benefit mutually from our . . . transaction?*

Nathan knew he should leave, and now. But this was a new experience. This dead creature – this otherwise extinct mind – was no innocent Thyre ancient dreaming incorporeal dreams of the past, but a Lord of the Wamphyri still hoping against hope and scheming for some highly improbable future! Indeed an entirely impossible future, without Nathan. Eygor's tenacity was that of the vampire, and Nathan was his one thread of contact, his one chance of continuity.

'There's nothing I want from you,' he said, backing off farther yet. 'All you knew in life was horror, of which I've had more than enough, and probably a great deal more to come. All thanks to the Wamphyri.'

But can't you see the irony in it? The other was insistent. *That I could be the instrument to right all of the wrongs you've suffered?*

Was it possible, Nathan wondered? To fight the Wamphyri with their own evil? Was that the way to go? But what power did this creature have? And how, now that Eygor was dead, might Nathan become 'heir to all of (his) mysteries'?

Ah, there! The other sighed in Nathan's mind. *Now see how I have sparked your interest, Necroscope. Aye, and I fancy we shall speak again, and soon. But for now – 'ware! For I know the patter of Maglore's sly, slippered feet. And the Mage of Runemanse approaches even now. Until the next time, then . . .*

Abruptly, the cavern and its occupant disappeared; the numbers vortex sprang up in its place; Nathan felt the familiar, furious tugging of alien formulae, and also Maglore's mind-probes recoiling from the whorl and suck of his mental barrier.

'*Nathaaan!* Nathan!' The transition from one evil voice in his metaphysical mind to another in his entirely physical ears was confusing . . . until a claw-like hand grasped his shoulder and shook him, rocking him in his bed.

'Who? What . . .?' He came gasping awake.

'Who indeed?' Maglore's face was hideous — and accusing? — in the yellow-flaring light of the gas jets, where he leaned over him. 'Who is it comes to visit you in your sleep, Nathan? Who do you talk to, secretly, in your dreams?'

'My dreams?' Nathan's guard was firmly in place. Quickly awake, he tried to sit up and Maglore withdrew a little to let him. 'Was I dreaming?' His brow was feverish and he was trembling. 'Yes, yes I was! But not a dream, a nightmare, which now has gone.'

'Ah, a nightmare!' Maglore nodded curtly, his red eyes swivelling this way and that, as if seeking out some vestige of the unknown visitant. 'That which comes in the darkness to terrify the sleeping mind. The memory of some fearful event out of the past, perhaps, or the prescience of that which is yet to befall.' He cocked his head in a listening attitude, sniffing at the air like a hound before seating himself on the edge of Nathan's bed. 'The result of gluttonous overeating, or merely a case of conscience. But . . . guilty conscience, perhaps?'

Nathan kept his mind shielded and played the innocent. It wasn't difficult, for after all he was innocent. 'Did I eat too much, Master?' He ignored the implied accusation.

Maglore narrowed his eyes, but still Nathan saw right into them. The master of Runemanse was thinking, *Does he continue to play word games with me? One thing for sure: he's no fool, this Nathan.*

But as Maglore stood up, so he made inquiry: 'And are you hungry?'

Nathan threw back his blankets, thrust his feet over the edge of the bed and joined the Seer Lord on his feet. 'I think I am,' he said. He glanced out of the high window and noted the orientation of the stars. And so he should be hungry, for he'd slept half-way through sundown!

'Then you did not eat too much,' Maglore told him. 'And so we're left with a case of conscience; or perhaps some real however intangible thing, which came to you in your sleep. Do you believe in ghosts?'

'Yes,' said Nathan at once, relieved that he could speak the truth. Of course he believed in ghosts, for he of all men knew that they were real, even though they were not always the dark phantoms of myth which men supposed. But Maglore, for all that he was a mage, didn't know that.

The Seer Lord nodded. 'And so you should believe in them, and especially here. Let me advise you, Nathan, that Turgosheim has known a variety of terrible men and creatures. Though they themselves are gone, their auras dwell here still. And in Runemanse, you are not the only one who dreams dark dreams.'

He looked Nathan up and down. 'But tell me, why are you dressed? You did not simply fall asleep on top of the bed, for I saw you under the covers. Is there something here which you fear? Has someone ... bothered you?' His frown brought his eyebrows crushing inwards under a warp of wrinkled forehead. And once again he glanced this way and that, and sniffed the air. Until, in a moment: 'A woman!' he said.

'She did me no harm,' Nathan shook his head. 'She showed me the way here, that's all.'

Maglore glared at him furiously. 'What? She showed you the way? Oh, she would do that, all right! Any one of them would do that!' He grasped Nathan's arm. 'Who was she? Did she touch you, kiss you, offer you her body? Speak, fool! Did you take her?' But even as Nathan began to shake his head: 'What? Do you lie to me? Why, there's not a horny red-blooded man born of woman who could deny those whores of mine, except maybe a whelp who doesn't know what a woman is!'

Nathan felt his ears burning red . . .

Astonished, the Seer Lord gazed deep into his eyes, and saw the truth written there. 'What?' he said. 'A strapping man, Szgany, almost twenty years old and never bedded a woman? *Hah!*' He slapped his thigh. 'Little wonder they're prettied up and on the prowl! I've never seen them so agitated! But . . . can it be true? You're a virgin?'

'I . . . I had a . . . g-g-girl, Szgany,' Nathan answered. It was the first time he'd stumbled and stuttered in a long time. And now he resolved never to do it again. 'She was stolen away by Canker Canison, into Starside,' his voice hardened. 'Perhaps she would have been mine, if things had been different. Anyway, we kept apart from taking lovers, and waited for each other.'

'Ah, true love!' Maglore fluttered long, almost furry eyelashes and sighed sarcastically. 'The dog Canker got her, yes?' He shook his head, made sympathetic clucking noises. 'I trust you have forgotten her? If not, you may safely do so.'

Nathan was not required to reply.

'Now, try to understand my concern, my anger,' Maglore's tone was conciliatory. 'If you are seduced by some creature of mine, you will no longer be your own creature, and therefore of no earthly use to me. It is my desire to keep your blood, body, and very mind clean and free of other influences — except my own. For I have enough of vampires, and at times the fawning of thralls becomes an annoyance. This is no unique situation, however; you will not be the first entirely human being who ever stayed in Runemanse ...' He paused, and in a little while continued:

'Well, and no doubt you are wondering why I'm here. Since I was passing this way I thought to look in on you, and if you were awake bring you to table. You shall take all of your meals with me, for sometimes I crave the company of common men. Also, it seems I must keep you safe — for the time being, anyway — until I can make other arrangements.' He spoke musingly, almost to himself. But then:

'Come,' he made for the door. 'You can wash in my apartments, and while we eat we shall continue our conversation. I desire to know you better, my son. For after all, your welfare is in my hands ...' Maglore glanced at Nathan sideways where he hurried to keep up, but the Seer Lord's thoughts were now as inscrutable as his expression ...

Entering the great hall from the corridor, Nathan came face to face with the vampire girl who had attempted his seduction. She turned her face away immediately but Maglore had seen. He paused in his striding, nodded grimly, and called her back. She came smiling, eager, but ghosting in the awful flowing fashion of a vampire.

'So,' said Maglore. 'It is Magda. You were the one.'

She glared at Nathan and faced up to Maglore, determined to brazen it out. 'But he's one of yours, master, which you have brought into Runemanse. I thought to have him before the others, that's all, and he gave me the opportunity by asking me the way to his room. But as it happens, he's one of three things: a eunuch, or queer, or a child who still thinks it's for pissing! Me: I like a man with backbone. And so no harm done. Besides which, I had no instructions to the contrary.'

'Perhaps not, at the time,' said Maglore nodding, chucking her under the chin almost affectionately.

She rubbed against him and brushed his shoulder with her cheek. 'Then I have not offended?'

Maglore had been half-smiling. Now the mask slipped from his face and he called for one of his men. At the sound of his voice, a silence fell on the great hall. Then a lieutenant came striding, and Magda tried to back away. But Maglore held her.

Nathan glanced around the great hall. Nearby, a squad of pallid thralls gouged with heavy flint chisels at a wall of pumice; but work stopped as gaunt, hollow faces turned inwards on the drama. Feral eyes lit with morbid fascination, and perhaps with something of grim anticipation, too. A small group of women, pounding washing at a trickling water sluice, looked up and nudged each other, and grinned. They were drudges, most of them, older than Magda and perhaps jealous of her.

Maglore saw that, too. 'Did you wager for him?' he asked her as his lieutenant approached.

'We drew straws,' she snarled, still struggling. 'And I won.'

'Fool!' Maglore told her. 'You lost! Where orders exist you obey them, and where there are none you do nothing. That is the rule, in Runemanse. The others know that, and so they let you win. They were baiting you, trying Nathan, and testing ... *me!*'

He tossed her into his man's arms, grew taller and glowered all about the cavern. 'Testing me?' he shouted, his face livid with a fire which seemed to burn through the very bone. 'Well, and let this be a lesson to all of you. I need not say more than this ...' He glanced at his lieutenant, and twitched his head in a negligent gesture: '... Magda is for the provisioning!'

The girl screamed once and clawed for the lieutenant's eyes; he jerked back his head, struck her with a massive fist that broke her jaw and knocked her senseless. And the last Nathan saw of her, she was being carried away.

For a moment the silence seemed to ring ... then Maglore headed for the spiral staircase with Nathan following on. But this time he knew better than to plead for the girl, for the Seer Lord's mind was seething like a cauldron full of poison. And as they climbed the central stairs, slowly the great hall came back to life behind them ...

At Maglore's table, Nathan had no appetite. He picked at his food when the Wamphyri Lord insisted, but his spirit felt so weighted, depressed, that the morsels would not go down. And he wondered about Magda. Perhaps he'd left his mind unguarded; in any case he was jolted and learned a lesson from it, when Maglore said:

'Forget about her. You won't see her again. And anyway, why concern yourself about someone who would have drained you in a trice?'

'Because I feel it was my fault, master.'

'It was no one's fault. It was Nature's fault: the nature of the vampire. But I am glad you refused her. So should you be glad, for your continued existence.'

'Everything in Runemanse appears a threat,' Nathan answered before he could control his thoughts or words. 'There's no innocence here.'

'Well, there is now,' Maglore contradicted him. 'Aye, and there was before. Perhaps not *entirely* innocent, but certainly human. Didn't I tell you that you weren't the first human being to stay in Runemanse? If I let my . . . *ladies* see you and she together, then perhaps they'll leave you alone. I have sent for her and she will join us in a little while.'

'She, master?'

Maglore waved a dismissive hand. 'Ask no more. Now I have questions for you. For instance: you say you don't know women, yet wore a locket with a curl of pubic hair. And Thyre hair at that! Explain it, if you will.'

Nathan shrugged. 'It's a custom of the Thyre when brother and sister part. Atwei was like a sister to me.'

'And how did you know her so well?'

'I got to know her, in my long wanderings in the desert.'

'Ah, yes, I remember,' Maglore nodded. 'You told me about that on our way here. After Wratha and her renegades fell upon your tribe and destroyed it, you walked out into the desert to die. But the Thyre found you and you joined them, and wandered east with them from oasis to oasis. You skirted the Great Red Waste and lived like the desert trogs themselves, on the flesh of lizards and the juice of cactus plants.' Maglore blinked and shook his head. 'So much sunlight and so little colour. Why did you not burn?'

'I wore a cowled Thyre robe,' Nathan lied, 'and kept to the shade wherever possible. Then, when I came to Turgosheim's Sunside, I lived on the fringe of the forest a while before I heard of Iozel and sought him out. In the forest's shade, my skin grew pale ... which in any case had never been dark.'

'Why did you seek Iozel out?' Maglore's questions were coming closer to the mark. Nathan must think fast, and guard his thoughts at the same time.

'I heard he was a mystic who understood strange things. Perhaps he could explain the numbers which plague my dreams, and the reason I feel like a stranger in the presence of my own kind.' He tugged at the twisted strap on his wrist. 'He might also know why I wear this, which has become a part of me.'

'Ah!' Maglore was distracted, fascinated at once, just as Nathan had hoped he would be. 'Take it off. Let me see it again.' Nathan did so, and Maglore picked it up and said: 'So, the sigil puzzles you even as it puzzles me. Why did you not say so?'

'I have lived with it,' Nathan answered. 'I wear it like my hair. Yet while it seems nothing special, I know that it *is* special, for it is also your sigil. It seemed presumptuous of me to claim it for my own.'

And at last Maglore chuckled. 'Not to say dangerous, eh?'

'That, too,' Nathan answered.

'Well, and we learn more about you all the time,' the Seer Lord nodded, tossing the strap onto the table. 'You're not so naïve after all. And did Iozel know the sigil? Could he tell you anything about it?'

'Oh, he knew it, master,' said Nathan. 'But did he know *about* it? – no, nothing. He was a fraud! I myself know more.'

'You do? Explain.'

Nathan took up the strap. 'I have ... noticed things. In quieter moments, I have studied this device.'

'A device?' said Maglore, raising a feathery eyebrow. 'Oh, really? Do you think so? Ahhh!'

'How many sides has it?'

'Eh? A question?' Maglore leaned over the table and tested the leather between thumb and forefinger. 'Sides? Why, two, of course.'

'One,' Nathan shook his head. 'For it defies the eye, do you see?' He brought a sliver of charcoal from the fireplace and drew a line on the brown leather, down the centre of its width. As the line lengthened he turned the strap on the table, until the head of the line met up with its tail.

'*Ahhh!*' Maglore's great jaw fell open.

And Nathan asked him: 'How many edges has it?'

'Eh? Edges?' Maglore's eyes darted from the strap to Nathan's face and back again. 'Why, two, plainly. What is it but a strip of leather, after all? There *must* be two edges, if only to separate the space between them!'

'One,' Nathan said again.

'No!' said Maglore, astonished. 'Let me try it!' He blackened the strap's rim with charcoal, until 'each' edge (in fact there was only one, as Nathan had pointed out) was smudged with soot. Then . . . the Seer Mage's eyes were very wide as he carefully put the strap down. And:

'For all of sixteen years I have known this thing,' he said, 'even taking it for my sigil. Yet I have never "known" it! But now, through you . . .' He gazed at Nathan in something approaching wonder. 'Well, in alerting me to your presence, Iozel Kotys has paid his dues at last. For indeed there is this bond between us.'

He might have gone on to say more, except that was when 'she' arrived . . .

II

She was beautiful in a wan, subdued sort of way, but it was obvious that she was not a vampire. Her eyes were as black as any Szgany eyes Nathan had ever seen, and despite the lack of sunlight — or perhaps because of it — her flesh had taken on a unique creamy texture. No longer the tanned, natural, light golden brown of a Gypsy, still her colour appeared healthier than Nathan's, and it could never be mistaken for the pallor of a thrall or the sickly grey of an undead vampire thing.

Long-legged and dressed in a black sheath split up the sides to mid-thigh, and in a gauzy blouse which scarcely concealed the elastic globes of her breasts, she approached the table and bowed from the waist. Her hair, straight, black as jet, and cut in a fringe over her eyes, was long at the sides and fell forward to frame her oval face. But as she straightened her back and stood tall, waiting for her master's command, her eyes were only for Maglore. So that Nathan supposed she dared not look at him, not in the presence of her Wamphyri Lord.

'Orlea,' Maglore acknowledged her presence with a smile, indicating that she should take a seat at the table. 'Eat with us.' And, as she sat down: 'This is Nathan, and you shall know him well. He is new here and Runemanse is very strange to him. I shall require you to show him all of its levels, rooms, and functions. Nowhere shall be forbidden. He shall be as you are, a free person — within those limits which I impose.'

While Maglore placed some choice tidbits on a plate

and passed it to her, Orlea glanced at Nathan, perhaps curiously. Then, lowering her eyes, she picked at her food.

Nathan thought it might be as well to make conversation. 'Despite my colouring,' he spoke to Orlea, 'I am Szgany. But I came here out of the west, from beyond the Great Red Waste.' Perhaps she, and Maglore too, would take it that there were other anomalies of pigmentation in those distant regions. In any case, it was an opening.

She looked at Maglore for his approval, and he nodded. And turning a little more towards Nathan, she asked: 'How is it now, on Sunside?' Her voice was soft, pleasant, but completely lacking in animation; and never a smile to betray her emotions. In fact she seemed drained of all emotion. Nathan could well understand that.

'My Sunside, in the west, or yours?'

'My own,' she answered.

'Do you miss it?' Maybe he was taking a chance. Perhaps she would also take a chance, and answer him truthfully. But she didn't, or so he believed at that time.

'No,' she said. 'My life was hard there.'

'Then why do you ask after it?'

Maglore interrupted. 'Good! And so you'll converse and find things in common. But I suspect my presence inhibits you, and anyway I have things to do. Orlea, first I would speak to you . . .' He stood up and moved apart; she went to him and they talked a while in lowered tones; finally Maglore left the two on their own and went about his business.

As they made an end of their meal, Nathan looked at the spread table. 'What about these things?'

'Just as you and I have our duties here, so others have theirs,' Orlea answered him. She indicated the table. 'All of this will be attended to; but for now Maglore has tasked me to show you Runemanse, and tasked you to observe closely and remember the things you see. No great difficulty in that; I *know* you will remember, just as I remembered in my time. Indeed, I cannot forget.'

He followed her to a room with a staircase, which they climbed to Runemanse's highest level. 'The topmost fang of the aerie,' she told him without looking back. 'We'll start there, and work our way down.'

'Why *did* you ask after Sunside?' Nathan was curious.

'Because you were making conversation,' she answered. 'If I had not answered, Maglore would have made me. He admires that such as you and I are civil towards each other. It pleases him that within the limits he imposes we govern our own bodies and minds, and that we temper ourselves and are matched on an emotional level — unlike vampires, who are commanded by powerful, alien urges to argue and fight at every opportunity, often for the sake of it!'

'Is that the only reason?' They had arrived at the topmost landing.

'No, for it was also my thought to ask ... after the children.' She waited for him to step up beside her.

'The children?'

'My life on Sunside was hard,' she said, 'but I remember the little ones. They were sweet, pure, innocent.'

Nathan shrugged. 'All young things are.'

'Ah, no!' she answered with a small shudder. 'The young of the Wamphyri are not ...'

'And are there young ones here?'

'In Runemanse? No. Maglore cannot abide them. But when I asked him once for a child, he showed me the nurseries of the Wamphyri. The children of Sunside take milk from their mothers or wet-nurses, but in Turgosheim ... they take other than milk. If Maglore could be sure he would father other than a vampire, then he might give me my child, but until then he won't spoil me for the sake of "some usurper brat!"'

'You asked Maglore for a child?' Nathan couldn't believe it. 'Do you mean ... you wanted to bear *his* child?'

'Yes,' she answered, leading the way through a labyrinth of empty rooms to one with a window and, set back in an alcove, a curtained area. There, for the first time, she looked Nathan full in the face. But her chin was raised and her eyes defiant. 'You have not seen Maglore when he's young. You're not a woman. You do not know what it is to be with a vampire Lord. You have no understanding of the word "fulfilment".'

'No,' Nathan replied, drawing back from her. 'But I have seen what remains *after* women have been ... fulfilled! And if they're not dead, they're doomed!'

She nodded, looked away. 'Yes, you are right. But with me ... Maglore has been careful, and gentle. I am not changed. Or if I am, it is that I hated him and now love him. A woman can be in thrall to a man in more ways than one.'

'You actually love him?' It seemed impossible.

'I love *Maglore!*' she snapped. 'Not his works or the thing inside him, but *him!*'

It was beyond understanding. For a moment, lost for words, Nathan shook his head. Then he said: 'But surely, it's his vampire that makes him what he is?'

'And that is the paradox,' she answered, 'which tears me like rotten cloth. I *hate* that thing inside Maglore as much as I love its host! For where he is my master, it is *his* master! And I am jealous of it and hate it because it shares him with me. Also, it shares *me* with him! But when he is with me in the guise of a young man, then I cannot help but love him.'

Nathan had backed up to the curtained alcove; Orlea had followed and was standing close to him, with her hand on the curtain rope, when he said, 'I think . . . that I pity you!' He spoke before considering his words, perhaps without even meaning them; for he had no way of knowing what her life had been like before Rune-manse. It was simply an expression of his horror. But whatever else she'd lost, Orlea still had her pride. Her dark eyes blazed as she told him:

'Save your pity for yourself, Nathan, for you've not yet seen Runemanse.' With which she pulled the rope. The curtains swished open, and Nathan saw . . . Mag-lore's siphoneer. At first he did not recognize what he was looking at, but then he did, and staggered away grimacing and gasping.

'So you see,' she let the curtains fall and followed him, taking his arm to steady him, 'there are times when it's useful to have someone to love and cling to in a place like this. Aye, even a thing like Maglore.' Looking into her eyes, Nathan saw nothing of the feral yellow of a thrall's evil intelligence, or the scarlet of tumultuous Wamphyri passions. But perhaps he did see something of the vacancy of madness . . .

Next on her list, Orlea showed Nathan Maglore's study or 'room of meditation', to which only a few trusted thralls had access. His eyes were drawn at once to a heavy golden model of the Seer Lord's sigil upon a slender onyx base, and he wondered at its use; or perhaps it was merely ornamental. And seated for long hours before a marvellous model of Turgosheim, he absorbed what Orlea told him of the vampire gorge. This was a great deal more than he'd learned from Nicolae

Seersthrall, and went a long way towards completing his knowledge of the geography of the place and the history of its inhabitants. More than two-thirds of Sundown had passed by the time they were finished there.

'Are you tired?' she asked him. 'Or do you wish to continue?'

'I don't know if I am tired,' Nathan answered truthfully. 'There's so much to see, learn. And what I've seen already will keep me awake, I'm sure. Anyway, I need to be fatigued in body as well as mind, to sleep soundly.' But inside he knew that he really should sleep, and do as much of it as possible, at every opportunity. For if he should allow himself to become overtired, sooner or later he would let his guard down. His secret talents must remain secret; his knowledge of the Thyre and their desert places was a trust he could never break; he must see about the fabrication of a false geography and lifestyle for that olden Sunside in the west, which he'd left so far behind. For eventually Maglore would want to know about it, he was sure.

'Now would be a good time for sleeping,' Orlea told him as if reading his thoughts, though in fact she had not, for he kept them guarded and could sense nothing of telepathy in her. 'For the deep sleep which you require, if you'd stay strong in Runemanse. Fear saps your strength here – everyone's strength, except Maglore's. One's nerves are stretched to breaking point; breathing and heartbeat fluctuate; will withers to a husk, even as Maglore's grows stronger. For it's not only blood that vampires suck, Nathan. They suck everything.'

He followed her back down to the great hall, where there was little of activity now. Several female thralls were still out and about, however, and a group of them stood in secretive conversation. Seeing Nathan and

Orlea together they fell silent, frowning, and apparently frustrated. Then, when he would have made for his room, Orlea took his elbow and guided him in a different direction, down a passageway carved in pumice.

'Where are we going?' Nathan inquired.

'To a place where those women won't bother you,' she told him. 'For they fear me almost as much as they fear Maglore.'

'And where is the Seer Lord now?' He felt uneasy, but was not quite sure why he wanted to know.

'Asleep,' she answered. 'He has his routines. This is one of the times when he sleeps. Sunup will rouse him from his bed, when he'll retreat to his workshops in the lower levels. Unlike the other Lords, most of which work only at night and cower in the dark when the sun stands on high over Sunside, Maglore has regulated his sleeping evenly between day and night.'

They reached the outer wall where a narrow window looked towards the north-east, and stone steps spiralled down around a mortared stone core. At the bottom was a lesser hall like a warren, with passages leading off. She led the way down one of these to a room with a door like Nathan's. It was Orlea's room, but inside . . . the door was fitted with a bolt. This wasn't the only difference, for her apartment was very well appointed. She had a bath, furniture, furs on the floor, and tasselled drapes at a tiny window punched through the massive wall; and her bed was curtained with gauzy drapes, which hung to the floor from rails between the posters.

There were several gas jets with low yellow flames. She went about the room plugging them with bone dowels, until the light was reduced to a smoky dusk. And as Nathan's imagination began to run rampant, she said: 'No one will bother you here. Here you may sleep safely.'

'Orlea,' he headed for the door, 'I appreciate your concern for me, but I fear that if Maglore knew I was here ...'

'He does,' she cut him short, stopped him in his tracks. 'Do you think I would dare if he did not? He ordered it.'

Mind whirling and senses numb, Nathan faced the door, his hand reaching for the bolt. But hearing the rustle of curtains, he turned and looked back. Her clothes lay where she'd tossed them on a stool beside the bed, and the drapes were still mobile, shivering into stillness.

Tingling with an electric awareness, scarcely daring to breathe, Nathan asked, 'What ... did he order?'

'Everything,' her voice came back to him, very small and somehow sad. 'I'm to take your innocence, until there's nothing left for them.'

'His vampire women?'

'Yes.'

He went back to the bed. 'Orlea, I know better now. I know that I'm to avoid them, which in turn makes this unnecessary.'

'Do you spurn me and defy Maglore?'

'No, I don't spurn you,' he said, trying hard to make her understand, without belittling himself. But in the end he knew there was only one way, which was to tell the truth. 'It's just that I have no experience of women,' he finally blurted it out. 'I don't know ... anything!'

'Well,' she answered, 'and weren't we all innocent, upon a time?'

Even as she spoke, Nathan's fingers were trembling as if they were some other's where they removed his clothes. 'I mean it,' he said. 'I really don't know anything at all.' Even now it wasn't the whole truth, but close enough.

'But you will,' she whispered, 'you will. Even as I know, so shall you.'

He was naked. 'Orlea, I . . .'

'Come to bed and warm me,' she told him. 'At least I'll know that there's only one of you, that your actions are your own and not directed by some other. At least it will be you, and not some slimy-black thing inside that drives you on.'

He passed through the curtains to where her slender hand greeted him. She turned back the covers and he slid in beside her. She covered him with the blankets, then with her strange cold love . . .

Later, in the dusk of the curtained bed and the musk of their bodies, Nathan asked: 'How did you come here?'

'I was a child on Sunside,' Orlea told him, 'just fourteen years old, when the headman of my village, Gobor Tulcini, noticed me. He was a brutal man, Gobor, with a frail and much abused wife. But then, he abused everything: his position, his people – *phah!* – the very air he breathed. Why, wild dogs are better behaved! One tithe time, he engineered a deficiency, and at the last moment chose my father to make up the number. After my father was taken, my poor mother died of grief. Then Gobor took me into his house, so that he might "bring me up as his own". So he said . . .

'My duties were to look after the village children, which I loved. For after all, I was only a child myself. But while I looked after them, Gobor . . . looked after me. His wife knew but feared him terribly, and so made no complaint. Twice in a year, by his order, she helped me lose the child he had made in me.

'I bided my time, until I could stand it no longer. Then, one night when the tithesmen came out of Turgosheim, I crept to the square and offered myself for the taking. Gobor would have snatched me back and beaten me, but a lieutenant, seeing that I was more comely than some of the girls on offer, questioned me. I told him my mother was dead and my father had been taken by the Wamphyri, and Gobor had kept me for himself, out of sight of the tithesmen. Well, the truth was that I was too young for the tithe, but most of what I said was true.

'Also, I said that I vastly preferred Turgosheim to the great brute Gobor, which *was* the whole truth. Even death was preferable, though that was not the entire reason. But being a child and still naïve – in my thinking, at least – I also thought I might find my father here. And despite that I was young, I was brought into Turgosheim.

'Luckily, a man of Maglore's drew me in the fatesaying, and so I came here. I had learned the ways of men from Gobor, and used a woman's wiles on Maglore. He was fascinated to know how I, a child, was such a woman. And when he knew ... then he arranged for men of his to be tithesmen for a spell, going into Sunside to collect the pitiful human tribute of the Szgany. And he instructed his men to choose a new leader for the people of my village, and to bring Gobor back with them. Thus the great brute met his end in the provisioning of the Lord Vormulac's melancholy Vormspire, which I believe was my father's fate before him . . .'

As she finished her story Nathan slipped out of bed and began to dress himself. She watched him through the curtains a while, then said, 'You don't have to go.'

'But I do have my own place here,' he told her, 'which I had better get used to.'

'As you wish. And there will be another time, when you will be more at ease. Then I'll show you the things you still don't know.'

'By Maglore's command?' Even as he said it, Nathan knew that it was churlish of him. Especially now that he knew what her life had been. But with the words already out, it was too late to make amends.

And after a moment she answered quietly, 'Maybe . . . and maybe not. We all must do as we're told, but the way in which we do it is our own concern . . .'

He left and made his way to his room. There were several vampire thralls in the great hall, a handful of women and one or two males. The latter glanced at Nathan, perhaps enviously, but he was pleased to note that the females ignored him. They had learned Maglore's lesson. And anyway, he was no longer an innocent. Oh, he was, in many ways, but not in that way. That part of him was gone forever.

In one way he felt more the man, but in another he felt dejected, made small. And he remembered what his mother Nana had used to tell him when he'd been hunting, that good meat is always the tastiest when you've caught it yourself . . .

From then on time passed quickly, and as Nathan got to know Runemanse, so its menace receded a little, but never entirely. And Orlea had been right: there were times when he would wake up in the night (even during the long days), with his nerves screaming and his heart pounding in his chest. It was simply the knowledge that terror and morbid works were all around, and that every other creature in Runemanse, and indeed Turgosheim, was a plague-bearing vampire. With the sole exception of Orlea herself.

And as for Orlea: she was as good as her word and showed Nathan those things he still didn't know. She took him to her room a second time, and on a third and final occasion he made his own way there by prior arrangement. And again he saw how she had been right, for he was more at ease and pleased to take the initiative. Being young and potent, he enjoyed her slender body and might easily have fallen in love with her, except she warned him against it.

'I *am* Maglore's,' she told him, when on that third occasion he proved hard to drive from her room. 'And I have done my duty by him and obeyed his orders.'

'Maybe,' he said, at her door. 'But you've loved me anyway, and you found it pleasant.'

'No,' she shook her head, 'but I made you think so.' And as his face fell: 'From now on you must never look at me with those eyes, Nathan, for if he sees it he'll punish both of us, which in my case would be unfair. You mean nothing to me, not as a lover. But as a friend . . .?'

'Shall we be friends, then?' She was closing the door on him, for good.

'Best if we are,' she answered. 'There are a hundred rooms and workshops in my master's house, and he wants you to see all of them. But if you would prefer the company of some other . . .?'

'No,' said Nathan, as the door closed in his face, and he heard the bolt slide home. 'No, but I'll always be grateful for your company, and for your friendship.'

'So be it,' she whispered from beyond the door . . .

After that she was cold and withdrawn as ever, and Nathan made no further advances towards her. But when it was Maglore's time for sleeping, and when Nathan would see Orlea on her way to her master's apartments . . . sometimes he felt embittered.

Maglore called for him often during that early period, and whatever Nathan was doing he must rush to the Seer Lord's side. Once, entering Maglore's apartments, he found a handsome, slim, broad-shouldered vampire Lord waiting there. But as this stranger spoke to him he started, and actually staggered from the shock. For the voice, if not the vibrant body it came out of, was unmistakable: it was Maglore's!

'How do I look?' Maglore inquired, when Nathan had recovered.

'Young!' He blurted out the first word that came to him. 'A man in his prime, forty or forty-five! You look . . . like a Lord!'

'Like a "real" Lord, do you mean?' Maglore chuckled. But his amusement was brief, and in a moment his brow clouded over. 'All my life I've denied the thing within,' he growled. 'Except when I may no longer — when I *cannot* deny it! Then, briefly I am as you see me now. For this is how I am "rewarded" for my co-operation. Which only goes to prove that however much I deny my creature, and myself, still the blood *is* the life. Now go, my son, and reflect on the wonder you have seen, and how it was achieved. And always remember, I *am* Wamphyri!' And to give his words more emphasis yet, he yawned his jaws to show Nathan the forked tongue that flickered in the red vault of his mouth.

But as Nathan headed for the spiral stairwell, so Maglore called after him: 'My son!' He looked back, and the young Seer Lord stood there smiling. 'Now tell me, do you understand the provisioning?'

Nathan shook his head. 'There's a great deal of Runemanse I've not yet visited.'

'Then do so, today, now.'

Nathan nodded. 'And shall Orlea take me there?'

'Ah, no — not this time. Take yourself there, or go with one of my men. But along the way, you may tell Orlea that I am waiting . . .'

Nathan did as he was told. The last had been a cruel

command and Maglore knew it, but not as cruel as ordering Nathan to visit the rooms and workshops of the provisioning.

He went there with Karpath, a thrall of Maglore's for three years, a lieutenant for eleven, and now the Seer Lord's right-hand man. Karpath was interested in Nathan, and as they descended through the many levels asked him: 'How do you find our master?'

Nathan looked at the other. Two inches taller than Nathan, Karpath was broad as a door, heavy-jawed, grey as slate and more than three hundred pounds of solid vampire flesh. His eyes held an inner fire which, however mutely, spoke volumes. No common thrall — nor even an ordinary lieutenant — it was obvious that Karpath had known the virulent bite of a true Wamphyri Lord, and often. Something of Maglore himself was in his blood.

'How do I find Maglore?' Nathan repeated him. But then, remembering the Seer Lord's emphasis, he replied: 'He *is* Wamphyri, and I'm not even a thrall. I find him awesome!'

'You would like to be like him, then?' Karpath kept his voice low, but it was full of some inner passion. Nathan read his mind, made open and receptive through previous invasions of Maglore's. He was thinking:

This one grows close to the Seer Lord. But is he a rival? I crave Maglore's egg and will have it, come what may! There may not be room for the two of us — this Nathan Paleblood and Karpath Seerson — in Rune-manse.

Nathan had to work hard to avoid recoiling from the several vicious, bloody, and terminal scenes which came seething out of Karpath's skull then, and knew he must take care how he answered. Not only had Karpath chosen his own name in advance of his anticipated succession to Maglore's seat, but that of his supposed rival too!

'Be like him? Like Maglore? Wamphyri?' Nathan's shudder was only half-feigned. 'I think I would prefer to die first!'

And you would, most assuredly! Karpath thought. *But ... perhaps I concern myself unnecessarily. This Nathan's blood is indeed pale, and weak as water.* Out loud, he said nothing.

They reached the lowest level of Runemanse. Below lay Madmanse, and Karpath showed Nathan the dank, disused steps: 'an old stairwell, winding down, down', just as Eygor Killglance had described it.

Nathan wanted to know: 'Can we go down there?'

Karpath looked at him. 'We can – but we won't. Now that Wran and Spiro are flown, it is an empty place. Only a ghost dwells there now.'

'A ghost?' Nathan played the innocent, but knew very well who Karpath meant.

'The ghost of Eygor Killglance,' the other confirmed it. 'The Seer Lord suspects that he was murdered but no one knows the truth of it, except perhaps his murderers. Eygor was very powerful and had the Evil Eye: he destroyed his enemies with a glance! His ghost is strong, too, and wafts like a giant shadow in Madmanse. When Wratha and her traitors fled from Turgosheim, their spires and manses were sacked and offered to others. Several tried to dwell in Madmanse, but all felt Eygor's presence there and could not stay. The place is hollow and echoing now. Maglore goes there from time to time, but alone.' Karpath gave a shrug. 'Perhaps he will extend his holdings downwards. I do not know ...'

Then Nathan was shown the provisioning:

The granary, where grain, fruits, wines and other produce out of Sunside were stored; the mill and mixing rooms where the raw materials of food were ground down and prepared in various ways, for many of Maglore's creatures had special requirements; the bakery and kitchens, and finally ... the slaughterhouse and storerooms. The first of these was not in use at the time. Nathan saw huge stained chopping blocks, saws, cleavers and other implements, buckets for blood and troughs for offal, that was all. But it was enough.

He had already visited the odious pens in a high, south-facing flank of Runemanse, from which at sunup goats and pigs were driven out on to a false plateau to enjoy a few brief hours of sunlit freedom in a small field of shallow earth, scrub, and coarse grasses behind a low stone wall. And there, where a handful of rabbits ran wild, such animals spent the last of their days. For these larger beasts were hard to breed; they sickened quickly in Turgosheim and could not be kept alive. That was no great problem; the provisioning was an ongoing process; Runemanse's turnover was swift.

Karpath took him into a cold-storage room with huge windows open to the north, where the draughts were freezing cold. In there, rows of heavily salted carcasses hung from hooks – but not all the cadavers were of animals. Suddenly and without warning, Nathan came upon two which were not ...

Then, as he choked and reeled dizzily from the room, he found himself caught up under the arm, and supported until his stomach had stopped churning. Finally Karpath released him and said, 'This is what Maglore wanted you to see. It is something of an incentive if men see what might befall them, should they fail in their duties.'

'In there,' Nathan choked the words out, 'I saw two men. One of them was a surly youth out of Kehrlscrag. He was taken in the tithe at the same time as I myself, so that we came to Runemanse together. And the other –'

'– Was Nicolae Seersthrall, aye,' Karpath grunted. 'The first was *too* surly, and the second – too talkative, I think? Had you stayed long enough, you might also have seen the girl Magda. But obviously you've no stomach for it.'

Fighting to control his gagging, Nathan said, 'I take the water which I use for drinking and bathing from the catchment sluices in Runemanse's outer walls. So does Orlea, Maglore's woman. It's rainwater, pure and simple. But I also know that the majority of Maglore's thralls and creatures drink water which has been passed through and purified by a . . . a *man*, or what's left of a man, a siphoneer. Then there's . . . my food?' He looked at the lieutenant pleadingly. 'Karpath, I've got to know. Have I eaten food which was prepared here? Just how are those human bodies used?'

The other grinned. 'Don't you trust Maglore, then?'

'Trust him?' Feeling desperately ill, Nathan leaned his upper body out of a window embrasure.

Karpath was right behind him, whispering, 'Can you trust any of us, in Runemanse?'

Nathan saw a picture in the other's mind: one of himself, tumbling, turning, rushing to earth! But it was whimsical and meant nothing. It was simply wishful thinking, accompanied by the thought: *No, for it would only jeopardize my future. This Nathan is weak, a freak, nothing. Maglore's egg would wither and die in him.* While out loud he continued:

'Your fears are empty, Nathan. Nothing of nasty vampire stuff will get into you via your food. Why should Maglore wish to poison you that way, when a simple bite would suffice? Aye, and there are other ways: a fond fatherly kiss or a little sodomy, or simply by giving

you to his women for a night . . . or to his men? No, only
the lowliest thralls – who lack the power of infection,
except by direct contact – prepare food for my master's
table. And as for Maglore: except when he requires
blood, he is satisfied to eat the meat of beasts and
birds. But then, so do we all in Runemanse . . . mainly.'

Nathan stood up straighter, glanced towards the cold
room, and said: 'How . . . was it for them?'

Karpath shrugged. 'The men, if you would call them
that – personally I prefer to call them boys – were given
to the women of Runemanse for their pleasure, to be
drained of their sex and their blood, and Magda was
given to the younger male thralls. Dead, all three would
soon become undead, which was not desirable. So while
they lay in their vampire sleep, they were butchered,
quartered, and their parts hung up for keeping. That is
how it was for them. As for how it's yet to be:

'Maglore may well require flesh for the fashioning.
Also, there's meal and bone to be ground down for the
manse's flyers, its gas-beasts and emergent warriors.
The flyers and gaslings consume grain, mainly, and a
little Sunside honey for energy, and blood or flesh naturally; for they are vampire creatures, as are all of Maglore's constructs. But warriors, especially young ones
fresh out of their vats, must have it red! As for Maglore's
lieutenants and thralls: well, it's good to have a roast
now and then. All of these uses are in order . . .'

'A . . . roast?' Feeling his blood draining again, Nathan
turned away. 'Cannibalism!'

Karpath grabbed his shoulder, spun him around,
snarled: 'No, vampirism! If ever you get to be one, *then*
maybe you'll understand.' *Except the knowledge will
come too late, for I shall not suffer a rival in Runemanse!*

Nathan shut out Karpath's murderous thoughts,

pulled himself together, stood up straighter and remembered what Maglore had told him: to walk boldly and without fear. Then, shrugging the grinning lieutenant's huge paw from his shoulder, he said: 'Are we finished here?'

Karpath sensed his resolve. The grin slid from his grey face as he growled, 'I've nothing else to show you.'

'Then I'll be on my way.'

'Where to?'

'Wherever I wish. For as you know well enough, Maglore has given me access to all of Runemanse, and I even eat with him. I shall go to him; perhaps he already misses me; he worries constantly, for my safety.' He said these things deliberately.

Karpath was suspicious at once. Waves of jealousy flooded out from him. 'What will you tell him?'

Nathan looked him straight in the eyes. 'Karpath, listen to me and listen carefully. Maglore prizes me for my colours, and for my "innocence". Well, I'm no longer entirely innocent, but he'll keep me free of vampire influences, if he can; you've said as much yourself. But on the other hand he prizes you for your strength and for your ... loyalty? And so we're not rivals, you and I. But think about this: if he is forced to make a life or death choice between us, which of us shall live?'

'What?' Karpath's brows gathered like thunderheads as he considered it.

Nathan shrugged. 'Maglore can always make himself a new lieutenant, but where would he find another familiar like me? Now, I say again: we are not rivals, but if you're determined to be my enemy –' he turned and walked away, '– so be it.'

And behind him, Karpath made no reply but let him go ...

*

Time passed. Nathan spent a great deal of it asleep, conserving both his physical and mental reserves. When he was awake, however, he scarcely went short of exercise: Runemanse was a far more vertical than horizontal place, and the stairwells seemed interminable.

Now that the provisioning was behind him, he felt fit to tackle anything; he didn't think Runemanse would contain anything worse than what he'd already seen or experienced. In a way he was right and it didn't, but in other ways . . .

He saw the Seer Lord's warriors 'waxing' in their hugely excavated vats. Apart from their armour plating, which reminded him a little of his deadspeak dream of Madmanse and Eygor Killglance's anomalous blue-gleaming *appendages*, the creatures in their loathsome entirety were like nothing else Nathan had ever seen before. But in any case, they were not things which a healthy mind would want to dwell upon, not if a man desired to sleep soundly. One thing he did notice: for warriors, they were a good deal smaller than those beasts of Wratha's which had ravaged in Settlement, and they weren't built for flying. However Maglore intended to use them, they wouldn't be taking part in any attack upon Wratha the Risen in olden Starside.

But the intentions of Turgosheim's other Lords were less ambiguous. From the window of his room, night after night, Nathan spied upon the training flights of monsters. Any excessive use of torches or brightening of the gas jet flares, or unaccustomed activity in this or that launching-bay along the wall of the gorge, would tell him where to look. And then he would hear again, even as he'd heard it in Settlement that time, the sputtering throb of propulsive vents as nightmare shapes went spurting through the rising vapours of Turgosheim.

Most of the Lords and Ladies tested their creatures

from time to time, but not all were successful. During a session in the twilight hours before sunup, Nathan watched one especially disastrous test-flight. Vast and lumbering, the creature flew out from Vormspire with the rumble of its propulsors echoing over Turgosheim, its armour glinting ruddily in the lights of the manses, and its exhaust vapours shaped by the winds into a fantastic, billowing slipstream. A monstrous and terrifying sight, it came throbbing across the gorge with a row of sentient saucer eyes flickering this way and that within the visor of its triple-horned, heavily plated prow. But it was perhaps too heavily plated, and its balance ill-aligned.

Tilting to avoid the jutting promontory of Devetaki's Masquemanse, suddenly its nose dipped and the tilt became too steep. It attempted to adjust its balance but overcompensated. There followed a lurching roll, then a shuddering, total capsize! Upside-down, the monster's starboard gas bladders were torn open on the jagged flank of Masquemanse; deflating in a moment, they fluttered like curtains in the wind as the damaged warrior was deflected out over the gorge.

Then ... the thing seemed to sense that it was finished. At the last an anguished howling was clearly audible. Mingling with the angry sputtering of propulsors, this formed a combination of alien, nerve-rending sounds which carried to Nathan as a groaning, echoing ululation: a death cry. And the doomed Thing spiralled down into deepening darkness, then plummeted, finally glanced from a corner turret of Trollmanse and slammed headlong into the rocky bottoms. Chunks of red, fleshy debris and shattered chitin armour flew everywhere, and the sounds of the crash echoed into silence ...

Failures of this sort were not infrequent at first, but as time passed and the Lords became more proficient in the making of aerial warriors, they were fewer. And always Nathan was aware that these living engines of destruction were destined for olden Starside, and that eventually they would rain terror on Sunside, too. *His* Sunside, from which he'd fled like a coward to die in the desert . . .

Nathan visited the gas-beast caverns located close to the refuse pits, and understood the *reason* for that proximity. But the gaslings themselves . . . were something else which he would try in vain to forget. The horror of the thing — of all Runemanse — lay not so much in the physical reality of the system, but in its morbid and pitiless efficiency; for all of Maglore's creatures had once been men and expendable. And whenever Nathan looked at them, always the *vestiges* of men remained . . .

Eventually, when he had lived in Runemanse through thirty-odd sunups, Nathan went to see Maglore's flyers penned in the yawn of the landing-bay. The reason he'd not done so before was that Maglore had warned him off it: the north-facing wall was notorious for treacherous updrafts and freakish, blustery winds; the polished rock of the launching ramps was slippery as ice; there were no protective walls to impede the flyers on take-off. The Seer Lord had lost a lieutenant there once, who stepped in the wrong place and shot himself screaming into eternity.

Two of Maglore's three flyers were recent constructs: he had fashioned them as an exercise preparatory to starting work on his warriors. Skittish (for they sensed that Nathan was no vampire), the pair rolled their eyes and reared their diamond-shaped heads as he passed carefully along a railed walkway in front of their pens. But Maglore's scent was on him, and they quickly settled down again.

The third creature was different, however. Housed to one side of the precipitous launching bay, beneath an overhang in the lee of the cavern, it was far less nervous. Something about the thing attracted Nathan's attention. He gazed at the flyer in its pen: huge, grey, mute and comparatively docile, its huge head nodding at the end of a swaying neck, with eyes large as fists, moist and gleaming black in a weirdly manlike face. Eyes which might well be . . .

. . . But here Nathan paused in his musing. What on earth had he been thinking about? Manlike? And eyes which might well be . . .? For of course there was no man*like* about it; those eyes were or had been human, Szgany! And again he reminded himself what he was looking at: a mutated, vampire thing – something that Maglore had changed – which, having undergone its metamorphosis, was human no more.

Leaning his elbows on the gated wall of the pen, he gazed into the great, sad, human eyes in the elongated, mutant head; gazed deep, and wondered: *Who were you?*

I was a youth upon a time, like you. The answer came back at once, shockingly, jerking Nathan rigidly upright against the wall! *Then I was a man, a titheling, and Maglore's thrall. But never a vampire thing . . . not until the end. Perhaps I offended him, though even now I don't know how. What does it matter? It is enough that what you see before you is all that remains of a man. Ah, but the Seer Lord of Runemanse was generous with my brain and made himself a crafty flyer this time – damn his black heart!*

Shaken to his roots, Nathan clung to the wall and whispered: 'He left you your brain, a man's brain . . . entire?'

Not entire, no. The flyer's thoughts were vaguer now.

But enough that I remember ... things. And among them my name. You asked me who I was. I was a thrall who knew writing and faithfully recorded the history of a race, according to the word of my master, Maglore. And my name was Karz Biteri ...

Later, Nathan would spend many a long hour with Karz, or what had been Karz, learning Turgosheim's history from its onset. But on that first occasion he had been far more interested to know how the – creature? – had read his mind and been able to answer him so lucidly.

That was the way of it with all flyers, he was told, for they were the aerial command-posts of the Wamphyri with immediate access to their minds, so that they might react instantly to any order. In the reshaping of Karz's mind, when Maglore had given it something of his own alien essence, telepathy had been the governing factor. Desiring something special, he'd let Karz retain much of his memory and all of his knowledge of old Turgosheim. Thus Karz Biteri, Maglore's flyer now, was also a reference library on all Turgosheim's morbid past.

You, too, are a powerful telepath, Karz had told him then, and so we may converse. But you must learn how to shield your thoughts, and you should always remember: a man is never alone in Runemanse. When you thought you were on your own down here, I read a good many things in your head which Maglore would not like. If I could read them, so could he.

'I have shielded them,' Nathan had answered, 'constantly, or so I thought. But you're right: I thought I was alone here. And when I saw you, and realized what you were ...'

You were shaken and forgot yourself, I know ... The

answer had been a sob, soliciting Nathan's pity; so that he'd said:

'You too should guard your thoughts, Karz, for I can feel your hatred for him. If Maglore should discover it . . .'

Ah, but he has, the other had cut him short. *He knows! Why do you think he won't ride out upon the air? Because he fears I would tilt him into space. And so he made these new creatures, but doesn't trust them either! For if I can have such feelings, perhaps they have them, too. Oh, he knows they do not, but will not trust them anyway. It seems I have given him a bad dream that won't go away, for which I'm glad!*

'Those are thoughts you really *should* watch,' Nathan had answered, 'and very carefully.'

He'd sensed a mental shrug as Karz answered, *Sometimes I do, and sometimes I don't care. What is my life, anyway? It were as well to launch myself at sunup, and cross the mountains into the sun!*

At which Nathan had remembered Thikkoul's reading of his future in the stars:

'Now I see . . . a flight to freedom, yes! But . . . upon a dragon?' And Nathan had wondered: a dragon, or something that looks like one? And the thought had entered his head: *why fly into the sun when there are other places to go and good works to accomplish along the way? Yes, and scores still unsettled?*

Perhaps Karz had 'heard' the thought, perhaps not. But his great head had stopped nodding for a moment, and his huge dark eyes had gleamed a shade brighter . . .

Maglore made more creatures and cocooned them away in forbidden vaults. The more he worked at the fashioning, the less time he had for Nathan. Apart from taking his meals with Maglore, Nathan rarely saw the Seer Lord, for which he was glad. But that was during his waking hours, while sometimes in his dreams –

– He often wondered about his dreams:

How he would start awake to discover his guard down and something other than his own thoughts oozing in his head, but something which always withdrew at once, leaving him his own man again. Maglore? But who else could it be? Not Eygor Killglance, for the old dead Thing in Madmanse made no bones about his presence but invariably introduced himself when he came in the night to wheedle and inveigle.

As for what Eygor wanted: some kind of bargain he wished to strike, some sort of promise to extract, and something evil to engineer from beyond the grave. So far Nathan had resisted him, but still he was curious and had long ago determined to go down into empty, echoing Madmanse one day . . .

Once, when the moon was full and floating outside his window, Nathan woke up and went to dash his face with water from a bowl beside his bed. But before he could lower his hands to the bowl, he saw the moon mirrored in the still water, and likewise his face. Then, as so often before, the stargazer Thikkoul's words had come back to him:

'I see your face, your hollow eyes and greying hair . . .' For indeed his eyes were sunken in dark orbits, and his yellow hair was flecked with grey . . .

Time passed ever more swiftly, and Maglore grew sparing in his use of thralls and recent arrivals out of Sunside. Now that he had enough warriors, it seemed he was conserving his energies and the raw materials of his metamorphic art in anticipation of some new endeavour.

One evening he called Nathan to him, asked for his wrist strap and snapped it into short sections. 'You with your fine clothes,' he said, 'wearing this scrap of leather like a brand! If you must be branded do it in style. Here . . .' And he gave him a sigil in solid gold, an inch long, whose design was the same familiar loop with a half-twist. Fashioned on Sunside, it was an earring, which Maglore told him to wear in his left ear.

By way of explaining his gift, the Seer Lord said, 'Since you're the very jewel of a lad yourself – and it being a well-known fact how much you Szgany like your jingly bits and pieces – I knew you would appreciate it.'

'I'll need my ear pierced,' Nathan said, without considering his words. Maglore feigned a coy look, then grinned and displayed eye-teeth as sharp as needles.

'If you were a lass, I might consider doing it myself!' he said. 'Why, I might do it anyway! Except I prize you for what you are, not for what I can make of you. You'd best have Orlea do it with a hot needle, and remain in your room until it's healed.'

Then, as Nathan was leaving, Maglore said: 'When Orlea's finished with her jabbing, send her to me. For while some jabs hurt, others are a pleasure. Oh, I follow Turgo Zolte's teachings, it's true, but even the strictest adherent has certain needs . . .'

Nathan chose his time carefully. And at the height of sunup when Maglore slept and the aerie was quiet, he made his way down into Madmanse.

I've been expecting you, Eygor's deadspeak voice came oozing in his mind, as he descended the cobwebbed stairwell to the uppermost, deserted levels of the stripped, haunted manse. *For plainly you're an inquiring youth who can't bear a mystery to go unfathomed.*

Even though a hazy light came in from the gorge, Nathan struck flints to a torch; the innermost rooms and passageways were dark, and the place had the feel of a tomb. *Ah, but it is a tomb!* Eygor told him. *That of a blind, blameless thing discarded like refuse into a pit, to die there and stiffen to a stone.*

'Blameless?'

I was Wamphyri! How can you blame a creature for acting out its nature? Is the wolf to be blamed for worrying rabbits? Or did you only come here to scold me for those deeds which I was obliged to perform, by reason of the monstrous leech which all my life controlled and corrupted me?

'All men have urges,' Nathan answered, descending another stairwell towards the source of Eygor's deadspeak, and checking that his footprints lay clear in the dust behind him. 'But we don't all give in to them.'

Which is of course the difference between us, the other came back at once. *For where mere men are not obliged to vent their passions, I was Wamphyri.*

'Tell me your story,' said Nathan. 'I've had some of it, from someone who knows all the history of Turgosheim, but not the end of it. That is the mystery. How did you die, Eygor?'

I died as I lived – as I was, yes, obliged to live – cruelly, even by Wamphyri standards. For I died at the hands of my own bloodsons. Would you hear of it?

'That's why I'm here,' Nathan told him.

Then I'll not keep you. It was like this:

I had the evil eye. Only show me a man, a target, Szgany, and I could crush him with a glance. Such was the energy of my Wamphyri mind, I could store it up and release it from my eyes like lightning – like a poisoned dart – to wrench my targets and stop their hearts! Do you believe me?

688

Nathan shrugged. 'Why should you lie – ?' he began.

Just so, Eygor cut him off.

'– You poor, "blameless" creature . . .'

The other's turn to shrug. *Well then, perhaps not entirely blameless. But . . . it was my leech! With a creature like that inside me, how might I deny myself? Why, even 'aesthetes' such as Maglore are still Wamphyri!*

And how well Nathan knew it! By now he had descended to the heart of Madmanse, where he paused in a hall with a walled well. But when he held his torch out over the low wall, he saw that the irregular throat of the pit was choked with boulders. The place could hardly be a real well, not this far from Turgosheim's lowest levels, but had more the look of a methane chamber or refuse pit. So why had it been sealed? Nathan's thoughts were deadspeak, of course, which Eygor heard and answered:

It was sealed to keep me down! The dead thing's nightmare voice was very close now, gurgling like a sucking swamp. *You've come as close as you can get to me, Nathan Seersthrall, except in your dreams. A stinking refuse pit, aye: the tomb of Eygor Killglance!*

Suddenly the darkness was alive with unseen presences. The smoke from Nathan's torch writhed into unearthly shapes as if he'd breathed through it, or as if some draught had come moaning into the room. Except his breathing was more or less controlled, and if there had been a draught, he hadn't felt it. A moment ago, he'd thought to feel the clinging touch of cobwebs where they hung in festoons from the low ceiling, but as the flame of his torch melted them away, they were replaced by the fingers of some invisible wraith which brushed him as gently and secretly as a lover. It was as if something tried to know him, to be sure of his presence, his identity.

Ah, yesss! Eygor's voice seethed in his mind. *And now you feel it, which all of the others felt before you. But you feel it more, for you are the Necroscope.*

'What ... was that?' Nathan had been holding his breath.

This place was mine, said the other. *The porous stone, the very air. I was part of it and it was part of me. My breath and my sweat seeped into it, so that even now it remembers me. What was it? Call it my spirit, if you will. It has no form and cannot hurt you. But it guards this place for me and no one else shall ever dwell here, until those sons of mine return.*

Nathan felt enclosed, strangled, dizzy. It was the smoke, the claustrophobia of the old, echoing place. He moved back a little from the choked pit. But at the same time, to keep the other engaged and know his mind: 'How did your bloodsons kill you?' he inquired. 'And why?'

Because they were cowards! And because ...

'Yes?'

Perhaps I was hard with them ... But it's a hard world (he was quick to defend unspoken brutalities) *in which I wanted my sons to be strong. And so they were strong in the end, but not as I intended. They were strong against me! I should have seen it coming: they were lieutenants and would be Lords, and their father was the one thing that stood in their way.*

Wran played the gentleman: he used his fine clothes as a shield against me, like the snobbery of a 'superior' whelp! As for Spiro: he dressed in rags, and made himself pitiful before me so that I would not strike him. Like a young male wolf, he wriggled on his back before the leader of the pack. But there was treachery in both of them. It was ... my evil eye. Above all else, they feared that. Having seen it used against common thralls, they believed that one day I might ...

'Use it against them?'

Eygor chuckled, as evil a 'sound' as Nathan ever heard. *One thing to kill a mere man with a glance,* he said, *but something else entirely to kill a true vampire that way. Occasionally I lashed out at them, I admit it, but against them my eye was like a whip on the shaggy backs of dogs: it made them yelp, no more than that. But they felt my power growing stronger day by day, and finally I stung them once too often.*

They gave me strong drink to deaden my senses, poisoned my food with silver, and while I lay in a coma . . . blinded me! Hot irons fried the surface of my eyes, until I leaped shrieking awake! And they taunted me as I followed after them in my agony, weeping acid tears and stumbling like a fool through the inky blind blackness of Madmanse.

Then . . . they were close and I sensed it. They stood right there before me, only a few paces away. I formed my hands into talons and rushed at them. And . . . they had brought me here, to a refuse pit! My legs struck the wall which you see before you; I fell! And while I lay at the bottom, broken in the mire, Wran and Spiro choked the pit with boulders.

For half a year I lived on muck and bones. And while my metamorphic flesh was still willing, I gathered to me the remnants of extinct creatures: the armour of warriors, and all of that which you saw in your dream. I made a giant of myself, my plan being to break out. But the pit was as deep as my 'food' was bad, so that my strength waned even as my size increased.

As for my eyes, I would repair them. But nothing I fashioned was nearly so good, and all of the evil had been burned right out of them. Finally I was starved. Too weak to struggle on, at last I slumped against the wall, where in the course of fifty years I commenced my stiffening. Thus Eygor Killglance became the mummy-thing which you saw in your dream . . .

Nathan, who was almost inured to horror now, nodded and said, 'Your just deserts.'

You think so? Ah, but you're a hard one! And what of my bastard bloodsons? Should they go unpunished?

'Punished? They should be destroyed utterly!' Nathan answered. 'Not for what they did to you but for what they've done – and what they're doing even now – to Olden Sunside in the west.'

Ahhh! said Eygor, and Nathan read approval in his sigh. *And so we are of a mind after all!*

Nathan's torch was wavering; he turned to go, to follow his own tracks back the way he'd come. *Wait!* Eygor begged him.

'For what?' Nathan kept going, putting distance between. 'We've nothing in common. There's no way you can help me. But I sense that you would help yourself, even now!'

Nathan, it can be yours . . .

With his foot on a bottom step, Nathan paused. 'What can be mine?'

The evil eye of Eygor Killglance. I've read your dreams, your wildest flights of fancy, and know that you'd make war on the Wamphyri. But only think . . . what a weapon it would make!

'To kill men with a glance? To be a monster as you were a monster?'

But you said it yourself: 'All men have urges, but some control them.' You, the Necroscope, would control this special urge. My power would be yours to use for good, not evil!

'I don't want it.' Nathan climbed away from the voice, through the hollow shell of Madmanse.

But now that you know it's there you will, eventually.

And now that you know where I am, you'll be able to find me always. I'll never be far away, Nathan, wherever you are.

'Suppose I did ... want it? What then? How would you give me your power? And what would you want in return?'

Oh, I would give it to you, never fear. And in return ... my freedom!

'Freedom? From what? You're a dead thing.' Away from the miasma of Eygor's mind, Nathan's dizziness quickly cleared. He went faster, and as he approached the outer wall and light came in from the gorge, so the other's deadspeak began to fade and break up. It wasn't so much that Eygor couldn't reach him, but that Nathan no longer desired to be reached. He felt that he'd escaped – but just in time – from something which would damn his soul forever.

My freedom from that, from death itself! Eygor was desperate now. *You can do it, Nathan. I heard it from the Thyre, carried on their dreaming deadspeak thoughts ... you, the Necroscope ... it for Rogei ... Cavern of the Ancients ... was a dead thing, too ... gave him life ... you willed it, you and Rogei together ... because you needed ... he was alive!*

Nathan had heard enough. 'Return you to life? Never!' His torch went out and he ran in near-darkness to the final stairwell. And the night-dark spirit of the place was right behind him, snapping at his heels.

Not now but ... some future time. If you should need me, I ... here. All I ask ... don't forget me ...

Panting, trembling, Nathan came up into Runemanse, which seemed a healthy place now – almost. But in his metaphysical mind, burning like ice: *Don't forget meeeeee!* It was Eygor's last word, for the moment at least.

Nathan fled to the great hall, slowed down a little and headed wearily for his room. But in the passageway he ran into Orlea, who caught his arm to steady him. She saw his condition but made no comment except to tell him, 'Maglore wants you . . .'

In his spacious apartments Maglore paced to and fro, not worriedly but perhaps contemplatively, as if he deliberated upon some course of action. Approaching him, Nathan wondered what was on his mind. He suspected that this would not be the best time to try reading it, which was confirmed almost at once.

'Mentalism,' Maglore said enigmatically, but as yet not threateningly. He came to a halt, crooked a finger, and beckoned Nathan closer. 'Telepathy. There was a time when I asked you if you knew the meaning of it, to which you answered no.'

Nathan's shields were up, his thoughts impregnable. 'I remember, master.'

'Ah!' Maglore sighed and shook his head sadly. 'You remember, do you? And so we are come to this. You my friend and companion, a liar who hides his every waking thought from me. And why? Because if I were to see inside your head, I would know the treachery you plan.'

Nathan shook his head. His mouth was dry as dust but he forced words out of it anyway. 'I have planned no treachery against you, master.' It was true, and because his words were simple they carried conviction. No treachery *against* Maglore, but merely an escape *from* him . . . Nathan clamped down on the thought at once. If Maglore were to suspect that he and Karz Biteri plotted flight . . . and again he screwed the lid down on the contents of his mind. The effort caused perspiration to break out on his forehead.

Maglore saw it and smiled. 'You are hot, my son.'

'I've hurried,' Nathan answered.

The other nodded, and thought: *Aye, and you're never lost for an answer, are you? No, for you are clever, and will serve my purpose ideally! You shall be my eyes and ears on the works of my enemies: those who exist now, across the world in Olden Starside, and those who are yet to be.*

Maglore's probes were groping at the slippery, rotating wall of the numbers vortex, trying to find purchase there and so form a link with Nathan's mind. But it was a one-way system: Nathan read Maglore, but the Seer Lord couldn't read him! His mentalism was *greater* than Maglore's; he read him effortlessly, without even trying to, and as yet without attempting to understand what he read. And with the knowledge of his mental superiority, something of Nathan's confidence returned.

'And so you've hurried here,' Maglore nodded. 'Indeed you have – but from where?'

Obviously he knew, and Nathan dared not lie about it. 'I went down into Madmanse, but there was something there. I felt it, a presence. I fled before it, and returned here.'

Clever. He will survive. Why, this one might even try to outwit Shaitan himself! Maglore withdrew his probes and turned abruptly away. And his voice was slightly sour as he said, 'In your dreams you are not so stubborn.'

'My dreams?' So it had been Maglore after all. Unable to spy upon Nathan's waking mind, he had attempted to invade his sleep. But how often, and how well had he succeeded? 'Have you looked upon my dreams? But what harm is there in dreaming? And is it treachery to dream of freedom? I have no control over my dreams, master.'

Maglore faced him. 'You have no sinister purpose, then?'

'None.' *Only a desperate desire to be out of here now; to convince Karz that we must flee; to get back to my own kind in Olden Sunside.* But his secret mind was shielded, of course.

'Then I've accused you falsely and you deserve an explanation,' Maglore nodded, however reluctantly; or was that, too, only part of the game which he played? 'Very well, I will tell you:

'The time rapidly approaches when I shall be master here. Not only in Runemanse, but the gorge entire, Turgosheim itself! You will have noticed how the Lords have perfected their flying warriors? I know you have. And for what? An attack upon Olden Starside and the renegade Wratha, who destroyed your tribe and in so doing sent you to me. Four months, sixteen sunups, until they set out. But Maglore stays here! I shall "keep" the gorge for Vormulac and be its caretaker, while the others go warring in the west. For I'm no warlord, do you see? And all the tribute of Olden Sunside shall be theirs, in that land you called home beyond the Great Red Waste.

'But here in Turgosheim: my responsibilities will be onerous, with much to watch over – all Starside and Sunside, too – and I'll harbour no dubious characters here in Runemanse to work against me while I perform my duties. Which is why I must be sure of my thralls, my lieutenants, my . . . friends? To that end I've visited you in your dreams, aye; for you're a strange one, Nathan, a most uncommon man. You say you have no knowledge of mentalism, and yet your thoughts are unreadable, as if kept behind closed doors. Perhaps it's a "natural" thing, inherited like your freakish colours. But it's hard to trust a man whose thoughts are like the breath of bats, invisible.

'What's more, your dreams are stranger still! Who is it you talk to in your sleep? I have watched you sleeping; I *know* that you converse – but with whom, with what? Or is it just a dream? I doubt it, for I've sensed the thoughts of others from *outside* striving to reach you here. Who are they? Why is it I can't read them? And often the thought occurs: was this Nathan *sent* here, to spy upon me, perhaps? Ah, but wouldn't *that* be a thing: the Great Watcher, himself watched!

'But enough; I doubted you; perhaps I still do and should study you more carefully, or draw you closer to me . . . in one way or another. I've neither bloodson nor egg-son, as you know. A man can't live forever; especially not a Zolteist. Who knows but that you could be my vehicle, my window on tomorrow? Would you make a fitting vessel, Nathan, to carry Maglore's egg into the future?'

He clutched Nathan suddenly, his eyes gazing scarlet into blue, his nostrils flaring under convoluted ridges. Nathan was rooted to the spot, frozen, near-hypnotized by Maglore's proximity. Behind his thin, cold, cruel mouth were jaws which could gape in a moment, a cloven tongue, and teeth – but *such* teeth – that could ruin a man's face, rend his throat or poison his blood forever . . .

. . . But Maglore released him, turned away again, and said, 'You see what a quandary I'm in? So much to do and so little time, before I'm left alone here of all the Lords. And in addition to caring for Turgosheim, my own works to consider. For instance: an unruly flyer to change, an errant creature whose loyalty is suspect. Perhaps I'll bring him to heel, or simply reduce him to fats and fluids and vampire stuff for the fashioning.'

Nathan was aghast. He could only mean Karz!

'Leave me now,' Maglore said. 'I shall continue to

trust you, for the moment at least. But for now I'm weary. We shall talk again. What will be will be.'

Nathan said nothing, made to creep away.

'But Nathan –' Maglore stopped him, as was his wont, '– I want you to think on this. I believe you would make a good son and a better Lord. You with your freakish colours and talents. It may not be your choice, but think on it anyway. Indeed, you must give it your most serious consideration . . .'

He need not concern himself: Nathan could think of little else. On legs heavy as lead he made for the central stairwell, and pale as death descended. But he did not see Maglore watching him, or the grin on that one's malevolent face as Nathan passed from view.

Aye, think on it, Maglore thought (but secretly now, for he was sure of one of Nathan's talents at least). *Think well on it, my son – on how you must flee from it – and so become my eyes on the great wide world beyond!*

III

Nathan waited out the long day and watched Maglore, but from a distance. The Seer Lord kept himself busy all day, and as night came down he retired. In this he was different from the other Lords; he took to his bed when he needed it, never on account of the sun alone.

But as soon as Maglore slept, then Nathan hurried to the launching bay ... and found Karz ready and waiting. *Say nothing, that great sad creature told him, for there's really no need. Maglore was here today and looked at me, and I read it in his eyes that my time was up. Since when I have waited for you. So let's be up and gone from here.*

The saddle was huge, heavy, and awkward. Karz assisted where he could: lowering his neck, offering advice in respect of belts and buckles. At any moment a vampire thrall or lieutenant – especially the surly Karpath, who had been hovering over Nathan like a hawk for weeks now – might appear out of one of the stairwells. But the worst fears of the pair were not realized; there was only the wind and the deepening twilight, and the morbid lights of Turgosheim spread below and beyond.

Nathan opened the gates and edged his mount out to the rim of the launching ramp, and shivered as he climbed up into the saddle. He had food, which he placed in a saddlebag to the right of the pommel. Karz felt him in position – and felt his fear, tangibly clammy – as he flopped forward on to the ramp.

Hold on, he warned, unnecessarily, and in the next

moment they were airborne. They soared out over the gulf, were buffeted into a steep climb on spiralling thermals, turned and passed high over the darkly jutting turret which was Runemanse. Nathan held his breath and looked down.

The wind was in his eyes, bringing tears; he could see nothing; the rearing west wall of the gorge was a blur. From somewhere in the east there sounded the dull rumble of propulsors: a training flight, it could only be. Then the gorge lay behind and the mountain range stretched ahead. 'Will we make it?'

I'm well fuelled, Karz answered, *well rested, and I have volition and motivation. I want to make it. In this I surely differ from any flyer who came this way before. We'll make it, yes.* Even as he fell silent a tail wind came up, driving them west with a vengeance. Nathan's eyes were clear now; he felt the exhilaration of his flight 'upon a dragon'; he breathed deeply, almost as if he had never really breathed before, of air which tasted clean and sweet.

And down below, behind, on the very plateau of Runemanse, Maglore and Karpath watched them go; and the Seer Lord said to his lieutenant:

'Two birds with one stone. I have rid myself of Karz, who in any case was problematic, and I've gained a window on a far new world. For Nathan *is* a telepath, and powerful. Awake he hid it for me, but asleep . . . oh, I found my way in, from time to time. Now, whenever his guard is down, I can be in again. Why, he wears my sigil in his ear, only six inches from the centre of his brain!' He glanced at Karpath. 'Do you understand?'

'No, Lord,' the other shrugged apologetically.

Disgusted, Maglore grunted, scowled and looked away. 'On the other hand, perhaps there'll be times when I'll miss him.' While to himself: *And I still don't*

*know who he talked to in his dreams, except that they
were not of this world . . .*

The night was long, but barely long enough. Only Karz's
will sustained him, while Nathan lolled in the saddle
like a zombie: awake one minute, drowsing the next,
then starting awake again. But as an amethyst dawn
crept in like some glowing tide along the rim of the
world, and secret watchers in the barrier mountains
yawned and relaxed after their long night's vigil,
making ready to go down into Sunside, so the great
grey shadow which was Karz went wafting overhead
on arched, aching manta wings, and dipped down towards the foothills over Settlement. He was seen, of
course; the blast of a shotgun sounded, not aimed at
Karz or Nathan for they were already gone into the
gloom; the echoes rolled down into Sunside, faintly but
loud enough, and the pair were guaranteed a welcome.

Nathan had not anticipated that there would be men
out and about in the pre-dawn heights. The sound of
the shotgun had come as a surprise. Several such
weapons existed, he knew, all in the hands of the
Szgany Lidesci. So then, the Lidescis had not succumbed to vampire domination. Good, and Nathan had
prayed it would be so; but the very fact of it made for a
change in those sketchy plans which he'd so hastily
prepared in Turgosheim.

'We've been seen,' he told Karz. 'I had hoped to go down
into Sunside on foot, in secret; show myself to the Szgany
in streaming sunlight; approach them as a man – *obviously* a man! Now . . . they will surely connect me with a
flyer seen settling towards the foothills. Namely, you.'

It's your problem, Nathan, the other answered, but
weakly. *I have played my part and for the moment can
do no more . . .*

They landed on a slope high in the foothills two miles west of Settlement, and while Karz munched on resin-laden pine branches, Nathan found flints and lit a fire under a hornet's nest in a patch of mountain gorse. Stung three times for his efforts, he didn't mind. He broke a small corner off the huge comb, chewed wax and honey alike for instant energy, then fed the rest to Karz.

That will get me where I'm going. The flyer was grateful.

'I've been giving it some thought,' Nathan told him, despondent for the other: that Karz, even a vampire changeling like him, should contemplate so hideous a suicide. For it seemed to Nathan that Karz's humanity was proven. 'Why don't you fly west, beyond the range of Wratha and her creatures in Karenstack? For you said it yourself: you're different from any flyer that ever was. You can find a Starside cave and make it your own, sleep out the days and forage for your food in the warm evenings or the long dawns before the sunrise.'

I'm a vampire thing and bulky, Karz answered simply. *Pine cones and honey are not enough.*

Down the slope someone stepped on a branch; there sounded a breathless, whispered query. Karz turned his huge soft eyes on Nathan and said, *Szgany, even as I was once Szgany but no longer. These are your people, and it's time I was on my way.*

Nathan slowly nodded. 'At least you are your own ... man.' Then he backed off, and Karz launched himself south for the sun and rose up into a bank of cloud heading in the same direction. For a moment he was a misty outline, then gone ... .

Nathan knew how it must be and wouldn't go rushing to his doom. But neither could he flee from it, for that would be to admit his guilt when in fact he was innocent. Waiting for them to come, he sat down on a flinty outcrop. But when he saw the first head bobbing in the gorse, and heard the climber's hoarse panting, he stood up to shout: 'You on the hillside, listen to me! I'm not Wamphyri! My name is Nathan Kiklu! I'm Nathan, of the Szgany Lidesci!'

'Oh, really?' a young voice, hoarse with fear and breathless from the efforts of its owner's climbing, came back. 'And you came here on a flyer out of Starside, right?'

Nathan was cold, tired; the wonder was that he was alive, that he hadn't died of exposure. Now that his feet were on the ground, all he wanted to do was rest. Wearily, he held out his arms and said, 'I have no weapons. Only look at me. Do I look like a Wamphyri Lord or lieutenant?'

Gorse bushes parted and an anxious face peered through; a youth shouldered his way into view; he looked carefully all around, then gave a piercing whistle. His crossbow was loaded, and now he aimed it at Nathan's heart. 'What do you look like to me?' he said, squinting down his sights. 'You look like a dead thing!'

In Nathan's entire body, there was no ounce of resistance left. But he tried one last time. 'I'm Nathan,' he said, 'Nathan Kiklu. I'm just a man.'

'You're a liar,' said the other. 'I saw you and the flyer together. Say goodbye to all this, Nathan Kiklu.'

'What?' A gruff voice sounded from behind him, and a wiry shoulder knocked him aside. 'Did you say Nathan Kiklu?' A face which Nathan knew stared into his across a distance of no more than nine or ten feet. Then, however slowly, recognition registered, and with his jaw hanging slack the other stepped forward. In his arms he cradled a weapon from another world: a shotgun, all gleaming for the care and attention he gave it. And finally: 'Why, I'll be . . . !'

Small, wiry, weathered, it was Kirk Lisescu . . .

In Old Starside's last aerie a young Lord came starting awake in a cold sweat. His dream had been very vivid, very weird, and very uneasy. For even the Wamphyri were men upon a time, whose dreams are like those of common men, with the power to transport them back to other times and places; so that the terrors they knew in their youth, before they were vampires, may rise up to trouble them again.

In this dream there had been no blood. Instead, the young Lord had battled through the ranks of a thousand dead men whose bloodless, crumbling bodies stood up again as quickly as he cut them down! But even though his every effort had seemed useless, still he'd fought through them to get to *That* which they protected, the *Thing* which they guarded, his Great Enemy from a youth which was now almost entirely forgotten.

And when finally he had stood upon a mound of crumbling, stinking human debris – *pieces* which yet clutched and clawed at him to pull him down – then the aerie of his alien foe had materialized: a rearing cone of whirling, mutating numbers! And within the rush and swirl of the cone, the infinitely sad face of a yellow-haired, blue-eyed giant; made sad, perhaps, by the sacrifice of his teeming dead army, but not by that alone. For strangely, inexplicably, he also felt for his vampire enemy.

Nestor had somehow known it, that his enemy cared for him. And that was when he'd been wrenched awake, as the sad sapphire eyes of the face in the numbers vortex had gazed right into his soul, or what was left of it . . .

Now, standing naked and trembling beside the thickly curtained windows with his hand on the rope,

Nestor's scarlet eyes stared almost vacantly west and a little south, as if his gaze might penetrate to the outside and over the boulder plains to the mountains, and across them into Sunside. The drapes were of black bat fur, thick and heavily weighted; not a chink of light passed through from the outside, and nothing of Nestor's gaze the other way. But he could imagine well enough. The peaks of the barrier range would be golden, and in a little while the sun would aim its beams this way, too, and shine on Wrathspire.

Wrathspire. That was what the Lady had finally named this place, these upper levels: Wrathspire, after herself and after the memory of another aerie which she'd fled from in the east. The Lady Wratha, aye: Nestor's Lady, now, for as long as that would last. Why, he might even love her, if he were capable of loving anyone. But all of that had gone out of him a long time ago; a dream which was wrenched from him, just as he had been wrenched from his dream. Except . . .

. . . Something of the dream remained, niggling there in the back of his wounded mind. The whirling wall of numbers, fading but – real? Absent for so long and only now – returned?

Returned . . .

The thought of that – of his Great Enemy, returned – made Nestor's vampire flesh tingle. And what of his stolen love? Was she out there even now, together with him? And were they lovers again, plotting against Nestor anew as once before they'd plotted in a time long forgotten?

'What's on your mind? Do you walk in your sleep?' Wratha's sleepy mumble reached him from their bed, or her bed, to which she invited him ever more frequently, until it was hard to remember when he'd last slept in his own. 'Have no fear but open the drapes if you want to look out, for I would know it if the sun were up. Oh, it is, and burning – but in Sunside! Not on Wrathspire, not yet. No, for I would feel it there, scorching the stone.'

He glanced at her sprawled unashamed, half-in, half-out of the sheets; then looked again, stared, and held his breath. One marble breast that lolled a little, tiptilted; a flat, dimpled belly; a pale, rounded hip; the curves of thigh, leg, ankle and delicate foot. And central, a tight black mass where her thigh joined her body, half-hidden by the sheet. He breathed again. She was a wanton, this Wratha, and beautiful.

'I don't need to look out,' Nestor told her, his voice already choked with lust, like his bruised manhood, reacting to the lure of her sex as if he'd never known her. 'For I know what's out there . . . and also what's in here.' The room was in total darkness; it made no difference, for they were Wamphyri. Wratha lifted her head and saw him as clear as daylight, his shaft rising and hardening as his red eyes fed upon her.

'Then come to bed and ride awhile,' she said. 'Or let me ride you, until you fire your juices into me. Or let my tongue tease the sweet nectar from you. Whichever way you will it, so long as we then may sleep. For though I'm weary, still I won't rest, not with you at the window like that.' And to herself:

You are young, strong, beautiful, and mine! And innocent? Oh, you were, you were! Not a virgin, not quite, but next best. Some dull Szgany cow had known you, without knowing how to handle you. Ah, but Wratha knew! A touch was all it took. Why, I remember how you almost came in my hand the first time I touched you, and how I brought you along like an infant learning to walk . . . since when you've learned to run! But to think of

*you running with someone else . . . I would kill her first,
or you, or both of you! Is that what disturbed you? Did
you dream of her again? Of Misha? Only let me come
upon a Misha – any Misha – among Sunside's sluts . . .
I'll throw her from the highest balcony!*

He went back to the bed and at once sank into her
flesh, which sucked at him as powerfully as the first
time. That was how it was with Wratha: always like
the first time. It was hot and it was cold and it was
pain and it was pleasure, and when he thought he had
nothing left there was always more. But it was not love,
and both he and Wratha knew it.

Before they slept he let his mind drift out, out across
the boulder plains to Sunside. But the searing sun was
higher now and he felt it on the mountains; it leeched
on his probe and weakened it, until he could feel its
heat even from here. If the numbers vortex was there, it
was shielded by an impenetrable veil of golden fire,
which would last even as long as the day. But when the
long day was done –

– There was always the night . . .

Two miles into the woods, in an area of freakish rock
formations, hot springs and volcanic blowholes, there
Lardis Lidesci and a team of tried and trusted men
worked hard and sweated in tropical heat and acrid
reek. Settlement lay to the north-east something less
than three miles away, and the honeycombed outcrop
of Sanctuary Rock stood half a mile closer, due north in
the foothills. But here where the sprawling forest
thinned out into an ugly scar or natural clearing, and
the earth was a treacherous, crumbling, steamy grey
crust streaked with ashes, sulphur and other mineral
deposits, Lardis and his team built warrior traps.

The morning was already a quarter spent when Kirk

Lisescu and three others, one of them a stranger, came out of the woods from the north. They hailed the old Lidesci where he supervised the lowering of the last framework of brittle poles into position over a lethal sulphur pit, to be covered with a camouflage of coarse nets and tufts of withered gorse dipped in sulphur to simulate life; the finished effect being to imitate firm ground. Tonight someone would stay out here, just one brave soul in all the empty miles around, to light small, discreet fires in the centre of this vast trap. The first would be lit an hour after sundown, the second when the first went out, and the last – if the others proved ineffective – midway through the night. From on high the place would have the appearance of a Szgany encampment, where some fool had forgotten to damp down the evening's fire. But as for any flyers or warriors who fell to earth here to investigate ... they'd very quickly discover that it wasn't earth!

Eventually Lardis was satisfied; he looked up, squinted his eyes and frowned inquisitively at Kirk and his party, then walked a well-marked path to the safe margin where they waited. And: 'Kirk,' he called out. 'But you should be at the Rock and resting by now! And a well-earned rest at that! So what brings you ...?' His query petered out, for in that moment Lardis had taken a closer look at the stranger.

'Someone I thought you'd like to see,' Kirk answered with a grin. 'For it's been ... what, almost a three-year?'

'Lardis,' Nathan smiled, however tiredly. They had slept on the way here, under the trees, but he was still bone-weary. His eyes were hollow and his flesh wan; there was grey in the corn of his hair, which was no longer cropped but fell behind his ears and over the back of his collar; he stood taller, and his voice was deeper. But still, of all the Szgany in all Sunside, there could be no mistaking this one. And yet ...

... For a moment Lardis stood stock still, blinking like a man struck between the eyes. For it seemed as if there were two men here, and that he should know both of them. Or was it simply that his mind made connections with times, places, and faces? No, for Nathan wasn't born then. What possible connection could there be between him and . . . Harry Hell-lander?

But in another moment the double picture swam into one as Lardis's eyes focused and finally goggled. And as his mental confusion receded, so his jaw fell open and his breath was expelled in a gasp of acceptance, recognition. 'Nathan Kiklu!' He choked on the words, staggered forward, grabbed Nathan and clasped him to his barrel chest.

'Careful, Lardis!' Kirk warned, only half-jokingly. 'It's Nathan, all right, but he came out of Starside – on the back of a Wamphyri flyer!'

'What?' The old Lidesci stepped back a pace, held Nathan at arm's length. 'You did *what*?'

'It's a long story,' Nathan nodded.

'Long and daft,' Kirk agreed. 'I know for I've heard it! But I believe it, because no one could lie like that! Why Nathan's been where Wratha and the others came from, and come out of it unscathed!'

'Unscathed?' Lardis had a grip on himself. Narrowing his eyes, he looked at Kirk more seriously, questioningly now.

'Oh, I've tested him,' the wiry hunter nodded his understanding. 'Silver, kneblasch, whatever. But the best test of all is sunlight, and here he stands soaking it up! He's pale as ever, is Nathan, but he's still one of us.'

Everything from three years ago came back to Lardis in a rush. 'Nathan! We sent a runner after you but he didn't find you. You don't know about your mother, and Misha, and –'

'— I know it all,' Nathan cut him short, laughing. But the laughter went out of him in a moment. 'And all that time wasted, when I could have been here with you ... with them.'

Unashamed tears filled Lardis's eyes and for a moment he couldn't speak. Then, gruffly, 'But now you're back, and you can make up for lost time. Man, you've been a trouble to me!'

'What?' It was Nathan's turn to frown. 'What makes you say that? How could I be a trouble when I've been away?'

'Aye, *and* left a broken heart behind you! I gave her a year, then suggested she should marry. Now hold on! — don't look at me like that! — for she, too, told me what to do with my suggestion! So she takes care of her father still, but only him now, for her brother Nicolae's been dead a year. Well, and he's one among many, but there are enough left to remember you and welcome you back. Your mother, too, brave women that Nana is. She never stopped hoping; she *knew* you would be back! Why, even now she's always talking about you ... and ...' He paused and fell silent, and something of the excitement went out of him.

Nathan understood and shook his head. 'I picked up Nestor's trail, but lost it in a river. I think he drowned.'

For a moment they were both silent, until Lardis said, 'Look, we're all finished here. We can talk on the way back to Sanctuary Rock. Then, this afternoon, I'll be busy again while you ... renew old acquaintances?' And the familiar grin was back on his face again.

The rest of Lardis's men had joined him; Nathan knew one or two of them; he clasped forearms with them Szgany style but was too choked up to speak. After that, until they were underway for Sanctuary Rock, it was all business again for Lardis.

'You men, get out into the woods and hunt,' he told them. 'Food for the people, and for the fire.'

'The fire?' Kirk Lisescu looked at him.

Lardis nodded. 'This place looks like a trap pretending to be an encampment. But if we leave some portions of meat to be thrown on the fires, then it will smell like an encampment! Should any Wamphyri or the like happen this way, they'll know there's food down here. And where there's food there's always . . . food. They won't look too close before coming in for the kill.'

As Lardis's men dispersed into the woods, he called after them, 'As soon as you're finished here, make for the Rock and get your heads down. We'll be at it again this afternoon.' He turned to one who stood apart. 'You, Janos Raccas: you volunteered to stay back and see to the lure. Well, I won't wish you luck, for I'm sure we'll be having a drink together tonight at Sanctuary Rock, or tomorrow morning at latest.' He clasped the other's forearm. And finally, to Nathan, Kirk, and his watchmen: 'Right then, let's be off. There's never enough sunlight, and it's too precious to waste just standing around in it . . .'

Nathan told his story, only holding back when it came to his mainly subterranean journey along the course of the Great Dark River. His debt to the Thyre was beyond value, and he wouldn't repay it in treachery. But in any case Lardis made no comment; obviously a man can travel a long way in three years; Nathan had simply skipped his uneventful trek across the desert.

Still, while Nathan talked, he did feel Lardis's eyes on him from time to time: frowning, wondering, speculating? But about what? He suspected that he would be able to read the older man's mind quite easily . . . but he wouldn't. He'd learned from the Thyre how it was as well to respect the private thoughts of others.

And indeed Lardis was thinking strange and speculative thoughts: about Nana, and a man called Harry Helllander out of another world, and about Nathan: about his origins. The son of Hzak Kiklu? Not this one. Lardis should have seen it before. But if not Hzak's son, whose? Harry's? Nathan had always been the strange one. But how strange? He had lived with vampires, and returned . . .

Then, feeling the lad's eyes upon *him* for a change, Lardis had snapped out of it. It was all speculation anyway, and only Nana would know the truth of it. Nana, aye. And now there were other things which Lardis remembered . . . but he must put them aside, for the moment at least.

Far more important was Nathan's warning of the bloodwar to come: the news that the Wamphyri of Turgosheim planned an invasion of Wratha and her colleagues in Starside, which they would launch just four months from now. In the aftermath of that war, no matter what the outcome, the shadow over Sunside must surely be that much darker, and the final dissolution of the Szgany as a free people so much more certain. For the vampires would be depleted, and could only replenish themselves in Sunside.

Then for a time Lardis was quiet, his thoughts shrouded, his mood gloomy where they strode out along a woodland trail. But in a while: 'Only if we're weak enough to let it happen,' he growled. 'In which case we would deserve it. But we're *not* weak, lad – far from it – and forewarned is forearmed. Now, let me tell you how it's been for us while you were away . . .

'The Wamphyri have raided Settlement eight times since then, but never so effectively as that first time and always to their cost. Does it surprise you that we're still around, still fighting back? It shouldn't.

Wratha and her bullies are a handful, it's true, but they're still *only* a handful. Me, I remember when I was your age, when the vampires were a plague! We fought back then, and we always will. And never forget, we have two great allies: the barrier range and the golden sun.

'Eight times they've been back, but a while now since the last time. That was when Misha lost her second brother, Nicolae. But as for the Wamphyri, they lost a great deal more. We have *weapons*, Nathan, and *intelligence*, and *humanity*! But all they have is their lust for blood and their mutual hatred. The first time they came — that night they took your brother, Nestor, and my own son, Jason — they were organized under Wratha; since when, they've become a rabble! They've split up and gone their own ways; they have no single leader as such but squabble with each other as in the old days, and with much the same result: vampire anarchy, disorder, fragmentation. Recently there have been rumours that they're working together again, some of them, but I doubt it.

'Do you remember Vratza Wransthrall, the night we burned him? I'm sure you do: how could you forget the things he said, when you thought that Canker Canison had taken Misha? Well, he as good as admitted that Wratha's plan was to build herself an army, with which to fight off the rest of them when they followed her out of Turgosheim. Or she might even use it to invade Turgosheim in her own right. Except it hasn't worked out that way.

'For now, as individual Lords — and "Lady", of course — they are lessened. Their raiding parties consist of a leader, two or three lieutenants, three flyers at most, and a warrior or two. They daren't keep more than a handful of lieutenants each for fear of treachery, of being usurped! Which has been to our advantage.

713

'I say again, they've raided Settlement just eight times since that first time, and each raid has cost them dearly! Do you remember the shotgun shells, the tubes of silver shot and black powder which provide the energy and killing substance of our guns? We exhausted them eighteen months ago, fighting off an attack. But then – a miracle! I sent a party of men across the mountains into The Dweller's garden, his armoury. The whole place has fallen into ruins; but in one of the little houses backed up to the wall of the saddle – in a cave at the back, snug and dry under dust and old leathers – they found a box of shells. A whole box! Perhaps it was handed out to someone at the time of the battle for the garden, someone who never got the chance to use it. But it was an important find for two good reasons.

'One: we had one hundred and sixty good shells for use as early warning devices – not to mention lethal weapons – against the Wamphyri and their lieutenants. Two: ever since I saw The Dweller's weapons in action, I knew that we must have them. Which is why I've kept old Dimi Petrescu hard at it all these years trying to duplicate that black powder. Now that we had these shells, I could give Dimi a little more of the original stuff to work with. Until finally he succeeded!

'. . . Or almost. Dimi's stuff isn't as good and it doesn't make effective cartridges, but it does make a bang! You remember the giant crossbows in Settlement? We still have them. But we also have rockets, and a lot of them! But dangerous? I've had a man blind himself, and another who blew an arm off. Ah, but on the other hand, when these things work properly, then they really *do* work! During one raid a year ago – Gorvi the Guile, it was, with a small handful of his lads and a warrior – *didn't* we make him pay? You can bet your life we did! Just you wait, Nathan, and you'll see! You'll see!

'And we've learned, lad, we've really learned. More than we ever knew before, and faster. Do you know what a flyer is? Certainly, for you flew one here out of Turgosheim. But do you know what a flyer *in a pit* is? No? Then I'll tell you: a flyer in a pit is a dead thing! Stick a flyer in a hole in the ground and it's useless; it can't launch itself, and has to be dragged free before it can get airborne again. So we dug pits in strategic positions in and around Settlement, with spikes in the bottom to impale their ugly bellies. That worked for a while, until the Wamphyri got the idea. Then they began crashing their beasts onto our houses, and launching them from the rubble. So we made dummy houses, fragile frameworks, with pits underneath! What's more, we left barrels of Petrescu's powder down there, all fused-up and ready to detonate! We've learned how to blast those wormy launching limbs right off them, melt 'em down hissing in their pits, and bury 'em for good when the stink has blown away!' Lardis smacked his lips, found relish in detailing the more gruesome aspects of his defensive systems.

'Their warriors are the worst, of course,' he eventually continued, 'but even they are not invulnerable. We used to run from them once, but not any more. If you can get an explosive device into a warrior's gasbag, that's half the battle. And if you can explode oil of kneblasch in there, that's even better! You see, warriors manufacture gas for lift, buoyancy, but when they're on the ground the gas soaks back into their systems and the bladders are retracted. So, if you doctor a warrior's bladders with kneblasch just as he's coming in to land – he's done for, poisoned! Oh, they thrash around a bit and they're noisy about it, but they quiet down after they've burned a while . . .' He gave a sharp, vicious nod.

'As for the Lords themselves, silver shot is the best

bet. If you could hit one in the eyes he'd be finished. We've taken out lieutenants that way, with our shotguns, no trouble at all. But a lieutenant isn't a Lord. They're just too damned clever, the Lords, and we haven't managed to stop a one of them as yet. It's their Wamphyri senses. With more than the five we've got, they can sense trouble coming. They send their troops in first to clear the way, and as often as not to die for them. But a Lord is different. He can breathe a mist and melt right into it ...' Lardis paused to get his breath, then said:

'Aye, and I've gone on a bit, haven't I? But I wanted you to understand. We haven't given in to them, and we're not about to.'

Finally the old Lidesci fell silent, which gave Nathan the opportunity to say: 'But you've done so well! It's all ... wonderful! And is it like this for all of the Szgany? Right across Sunside?'

Lardis glanced at him, shook his shaggy head and looked away. 'How can it be? Charity begins at home, son, and as far as I know it's only like this for the Szgany Lidesci. What do you expect? How far do you think we can stretch ourselves?'

'And the people of Twin Fords, Tireni Scarp, Mirlu Township and all the other towns and tribes?' Nathan's excitement was swiftly ebbing.

Lardis shrugged, but not callously. 'Should I give them gunpowder, so that they in turn may give it to the Wamphyri? How long before supplicant tribes started making it for them, eh? Or are you asking why I haven't gathered all of the tribes together? I'll tell you: because I've been through all of this before, Nathan, and small is safe. Now listen, Sanctuary Rock is only so big. Its caverns will take my people, but barely. And *only* my people know its secrets! Lad, why do you think I built

Settlement where it stands, or leans, now? Because it was close to Sanctuary Rock, that's why! I never did trust my luck all *that* much, and as it happens I was right not to. No, for I knew that if there was a way back, the Wamphyri would find it. You know how a lichen clings to a rock? Well, that's *nothing*, compared to the way they cling to their filthy, miserable existence!'

'And Travellers when they pass through?' Nathan's voice was much quieter. 'Do you still give them shelter?'

'If they come in daylight, and if I know them, aye. But in the evening, or the night ... you're making jokes, Nathan! Think, man! Things aren't like that any more. Would you harbour a leper in your camp? Of course not. Well, then, how much more virulent is a vampire?'

Nathan nodded. 'You're right, of course ...' And after a moment's silence: 'What about the other townships? How have they fared?'

'Badly!' Lardis answered at once. 'Karl Zestos leads the people of Twin Fords, what's left of them. They're Travellers now, a small band torn to pieces in the raids. Karl's no fool, though. He's learning, just like I had to learn when I was his age. They have caverns in the cliffs east of here; not as good as Sanctuary Rock and not so easily defended, but they're working on it.'

Nathan nodded. 'He asked me to join him that time when I passed through Twin Fords. I liked him well enough, but I was still looking for Nestor. What about Mirlu Township?'

'Swept away!' said Lardis. 'Scattered, gone! Four or five sunups after Settlement, then it was Mirlu Township's turn. We expected them to come back here, if only to punish us for what we did to Vratza. But they fell on Mirlu instead. The brothers Wran and Spiro. They must be madmen!' (And Nathan thought: *they are!*) 'Sent in a warrior to wreck the place, and waited outside for the people as they fled. Aye, and the bastards recruited a few that night! The survivors are Travellers now, like all the rest. Only me and mine, and the folk of Tireni Scarp, have managed to hang on to what was theirs. And then by the skin of our teeth.'

Through the trees Nathan could see the foothills and the dome of Sanctuary Rock. The morning was only a third done and he was almost home. Or if not home exactly, back among his own people at least. He felt his heart leap inside him. His mother was alive and well . . . and Misha! All weariness fled, he felt he must run the rest of the way; and Lardis sensed it in him.

'Can't let you go, lad,' he said. 'There'll be some who know you, but others who don't. And there's not much of trust in men these days. You go in there bragging how you flew home on a vampire thing . . .' He shook his head. 'Anyway, I'm just as eager as you, if only to see your mother's face.' He glanced at Nathan and grinned. 'Not to mention Misha's.'

Nathan grabbed his arm. 'Is she . . . is she . . .?'

'She's a beauty!' Lardis stopped him. 'Ask any one of the young, single men and they'll all tell you the same thing: that Misha Zanesti is beautiful.'

Nathan's face fell. 'The young men? But, does she . . . has she . . .?'

'Now hold!' said Lardis. 'What's all this? Are we back to stuttering again? And why ask me? I'm an old lad and past that sort of thing — well, almost. Anyway, another hour and you'll be able to ask the girl herself.'

An hour! It sounded like a lifetime.

But it wasn't . . .

On the final approach to Sanctuary Rock along dusty foothill trails, Lardis and the others stepped very carefully. 'Pits everywhere,' Lardis informed. 'Can you see them?'

'Now that you mention it, yes,' Nathan answered. 'A man would have to be a fool to fall into one.'

Lardis gave a grunt and shrugged. 'Well, people do forget from time to time, and then we have accidents. But flyers and the like aren't as bright as men —' (then, remembering Nathan's story about Karz Biteri) '— well, not usually. And anyway, at night they use their noses as much as their eyes.'

They climbed closer to the Rock, a gigantic outcrop jutting from the wooded hillside, bald and domed on top, but hollow as a rotten tooth in its base. 'And do you live here now?' Nathan had been inside the place as a child; it seemed a dire sort of existence, to actually live here.

'We *hide* here,' Lardis answered, 'but we still "live" in Settlement — because I won't let go! It's no great distance, and we always come back to the Rock at nights. But the Wamphyri? Territorial? *Hah!* They don't know the half of it!'

'But if you still live in town, why have we come up here?'

'Because right now this is where the work is. Enough for everyone. We're hollowing the place out, making it liveable, and charging the larger outer caves with Dimi's powder. Yet another way to kill a warrior: flatten the bastard under a hundred tons of rock!'

'Without flattening yourself?'

'We've tunnelled our way through to the back and far side. It's quite a maze in there. So that now the Rock's a sanctuary, a makeshift home, a lethal trap and an escape route all in one. The Wamphyri haven't discovered us yet and with luck they never will. If they do . . .' Again Lardis's fatalistic shrug, 'it will cost them as dearly as it costs us.'

In the main entrance a chain of people, men and women, passed heavy leather buckets laden with dirt and small rocks from the inside to the open, and there tipped them over the rim of a shallow bluff on to the scree slopes below. Sweating and grimy, the people looked much alike. Most of them merely glanced at Lardis and his party, nodded, and carried on working. But one of them dropped her bucket and the work came to a halt.

Then ... it was as if a whirlwind had struck! Nana rushed at Nathan so as to almost knock him down. He wrapped her in his arms, grabbed her up fiercely, kissed her dirty neck and hugged her like a lover. His *mother*! Alive and well! Finally they held each other at arm's length, and Nathan's eyes drank Nana in; he let her aura, her smell – no, her *scent* – wash over him, and thought, *She's so ... small!*

'You're so ... big!' she said. There were tears behind her eyes, but she wouldn't cry in front of people.

Lardis put an arm round each of them. And to Nana: 'Take him to your place in the Rock,' he said. 'Let the work go. No one here will grudge you that.' His voice was husky, too.

On their way inside, still holding each other, they found their way blocked as a huge, frowning figure stepped out of the line. It was Varna Zanesti, Misha's father. He clasped forearms with Nathan, nodded and said, 'Well, what a sight for sore eyes *you* are! And do I have a son at last, or what?' As ever, Varna was straight to the point.

At first Nathan didn't understand, so Varna prompted him, 'That conversation we had, in Settlement that morning?'

Then Nathan understood, sighed and said, 'I'm honoured.'

'Huh!' Varna grunted. 'Damn right you are! Very well then, I'll see to it – and at once!' Finally he grinned.

'Where is she?' Nathan asked.

'In the woods with the children, teaching, gathering nuts, fruits. Will midday suit you?'

'Eh?'

'To be wed, of course!'

Nathan looked at Nana, who nodded. And: 'Yes, whatever you say,' he answered Varna.

'Consider it done then,' said the other. 'Now be off, and enjoy what time you have left as a free man.'

Nana had a large cave close to the main entrance. There, where beams of sunlight shot in through holes in the perforated rock and dust motes drifted like specks of gold, she sat Nathan down on a blanket on a ledge carved in the wall. And while she saw to the needs of two old ladies in her care – in the course of preparing their food – she talked to him and questioned him over her shoulder. In a little while he stopped answering, and Nana saw that he'd stretched out and gone to sleep.

Then, as the old ones ate their food Nana sat beside him. She stroked the lines from his brow, cried all the tears she'd stored up for so long, and loved her son for all the lonesome times she'd missed loving him . . .

Nathan dreamed of Maglore, who in any case had never been far from his thoughts since his escape from Rune-manse; an image of the man, the vampire Lord, the monster, had seemed printed indelibly on his inner eye, but faintly, like an after-image.

Maglore in his aerie, in a darkened room, alone, with a smile on his ancient, evil face and his eyes half-closed, and spider hands with spindly fingers resting upon an image of his sigil, the hammered gold loop with a half-twist. Nathan dreamed of the Seer Lord, and knew that Maglore in turn dreamed of him, of Nathan!

He conjured the numbers vortex and washed Maglore away in its seething swirl – and saw the smile on his fading face turn to a scowl – before he drifted deeper into sleep . . .

He dreamed of his wolves. They had felt the swirl of the vortex and stirred in their mountain cave. He knew that their yellow eyes blinked in the gloom, and could feel their warmth and smell the musty heat of their curled bodies. But they were tired and he should let them sleep; it was sufficient that they acknowledged his return . . .

His freely drifting mind touched upon the deadspeak minds of Sunside's Great Majority: a living mind listening in on the dead. They knew him at once, but the message of their swiftly receding whispers was as vague and mysterious as ever:

'That one, Nathan!'

'But the Thyre speak for him; they say there's no harm in him, only good.'

'So was his father good, in his time. But in the end . . .?'

'We could tell him much.'

'We daren't!'

Among them was a voice which was very faint. 'I, Jasef Karis, could tell him most of all.'

'And be shunned among the dead forever?' The others were alarmed.

'You are cold and cruel,' the faint one replied.

'But not as cold and cruel as the Wamphyri necromancer who is his brother!'

'He is a vampire. They are not the same.'

'Can Nathan live forever, then? And what will he be when he dies? Ah, and will he stay dead?'

Finally, reluctantly: 'Perhaps you are right,' said Jasef Karis. With which their dead voices faded away entirely as the teeming dead fell silent in their graves and resting places . . .

At last it was Eygor Killglance's turn; the leathery amalgam which was Eygor, blind and dead in his pit in Madmanse. But Eygor didn't talk about Nathan, he talked to him. 'The killing eye, Nathan. It can be yours!' The clotted gurgle of his mind spanned all the miles between. 'Now look, and see what my sons did to me!'

Nathan stood at the feet of the Thing in the pit again, and stared up at its dead face, its closed eyes which even now, in his dream, creaked open! And a pair of blind white orbs huge as the eggs of swans, white as shining marble, wept acid tears on to a fretted, crumbling cheek!

'Only see how I cry,' said Eygor, 'because my eyes are blind and white. Ah, but upon a time the right one was filled with blood! See!' And at once, the right eye of the gargoyle dripped scarlet. 'While the left was full of pus!' And indeed the left one turned yellow, and swelled like a boil about to burst. And Nathan knew that if it did and the poison splashed him, then that he would be infected, heir to Egyor's eyes!

He came shouting awake . . . !

But the eyes were gone. The original great white blind glaring eyes (like the eye which Thikkoul had seen in Nathan's stars, perhaps?), the bloody eye and the yellow one, too: gone! Only his mother's eyes, Nana's, were there to greet him where he jerked violently upright. And gazing back worriedly into his, all they contained was love and concern.

For Nathan was more than ever like Harry Keogh before him, and she knew from his mumbling that he talked to . . . *people*, in his sleep; or at least listened to them talking to each other. But mainly she was concerned because of who these people were, and the fact that they were no more . . .

Aye, he was more than ever like his Necroscope father, which could be a blessing –

– Or a curse.

Nathan and Misha were married at 'noon', when the sun stood at its highest point far to the south and central over the distant desert. The ceremony was simple; Lardis presided; all of Sanctuary Rock's workforce was present, almost a hundred and forty of them. Times were hard but Lardis had done his best, providing bread and wine and a beast turning on a spit over a fire.

At the high point of the affair the old Lidesci gathered the couple and their parents to him – Misha in white, Nathan in his freshly cleaned Thyre clothing, which by Szgany standards was still exceptionally fine gear – and with Nana standing face to face with Misha, and Varna glowering at Nathan, then Lardis commenced to say the approved words:

'Varna Zanesti, what can you say of this girl, your daughter Misha?'

'That she's innocent, unknown by man or monster,' Varna growled. 'Also that she's obedient and good. Far *too* good for this one!'

Nathan was obliged to back off a step and lower his head. It was all part of the ritual.

'And Nana Kiklu,' Lardis turned to her. 'What have you to say to that?'

'No mere girl is good enough for a son of mine,' Nana answered, tilting her chin and sniffing at Misha. 'I can only hope that their children take more after him.' *But not too closely after their grandfather!*

Lardis turned to the couple. 'And do you love each other?' They answered yes. 'So you may, and from this time forward you have that right – to love with your hearts and your bodies – for you're now man and wife!'

They kissed; people applauded; everyone enjoyed a little food, and toasted the health of the couple in wine. There was music and the younger ones danced, those who had the strength for it. But at their first opportunity, Nathan and Misha slipped quietly away . . .

Their travois was waiting behind bushes under the south-west facing wall of the Rock. There Misha made Nathan look away – 'Three years is a long time, after all!' – while she changed into Traveller clothes and folded her dress into a pillowcase, and discreetly averted her eyes as he likewise changed. It was the Szgany way. Then, dragging the light-framed travois behind them, they went out into the forest. Heading south-east, they skirted the Rock along an old trail, but half-way towards Settlement turned off into virgin woods and found a place where the bracken stood tall.

In the heart of the bracken Nathan put up their shelter, a skin stretched over the bole of a fallen tree, made fast to projecting branches, while Misha cleared the ground and spread their blankets underneath. And with mixed feelings they stood looking at the finished job. Everything seemed to be melting into a blur now for Nathan. He still daren't believe that he had really escaped from Turgosheim; yet here he was, married to Misha, and their first bed ready for them. She didn't seem changed; it might be as if he'd never been away.

'Our home for half a day,' he finally said.

'And for part of a night,' she answered. 'For I won't go back till the stars are out at least. Tonight of all nights, I won't scurry and scuttle in fear of Them.'

Nathan looked ruefully at their rude shelter. 'Not much of a little house, is it?'

She smiled in a way he remembered and loved well enough – a smile she'd kept only for him, which was half-innocent, half-brazen – and answered: 'People have lived, and loved, in worse than this, Nathan. Anyway, you'll remember this "little house" for the rest of your days. I shall see to that.'

Following which . . .

. . . It was as it has always been and always will be between lovers. And for an hour, two, three, they excited, explored and exhausted each other. Misha was mainly innocent, for which they both were glad. And Nathan . . . if Misha suspected anything she said nothing. And anyway, he was careful not to 'know' too much. From now on they could learn together, or at least he must make her believe that it was so. It wasn't so much that he deceived her, rather that he would not disappoint her.

And he didn't, not in any measure . . .

In the time scale of the world of Nathan's father, the couple stayed in their love nest for an entire day, and one more to go before sundown. Like all young animals paired off, they loved and slept to excess; between times they replenished themselves on bread and cheese from a bundle in the travois.

Three years without each other; now each moment spent together filled the space of an hour apart, and the husks of empty years fell aside. They got to know each other all over again, but more surely now, more certainly: like a broken wall repaired and made stronger. And the extra wrinkle here or line there: all smoothed themselves out, or seemed to, until their faces were the same yet more than before. Nathan had used to think

Misha's shape was boyish; now it was all woman. She had likened his yellow hair to sunlight; now it was a misted morning, with some of the gold fading to grey.

Eventually they left their bower and walked to Settlement, which served to revive more old memories. A handful of people were working there; Nathan met some old friends, saw a few new faces. They wandered the forest ways they'd known as children, bathed in the same shingly pool at the river's bend, fell more deeply, truly in love than ever. Back in Settlement they ate a meal with friends, and Nathan stood for a while outside his old home under the stockade's west wall. Some repairs had been made but the place seemed like a shell now; at least there wasn't a flyer trap underneath it; maybe one day Nana would live here again. But *live* here, as she had used to in better times.

In the shade of the forest as they returned to the bower, suddenly Nathan shivered, paused, listened. There was only the cooing of pigeons. Misha looked at him curiously. 'What is it?'

Frowning, he touched the golden sigil in his ear. Then he shrugged and offered an awkward smile. 'Only the ghosts of memories.' *Or the feeling of someone listening, watching, waiting.* Instinctively he shielded his mind and conjured the vortex: two perfectly logical moves, of which only the first was a good one. For Nathan didn't know that where the vortex kept certain evils at bay, it lured one other more surely than crows are lured to a cornfield. And even if he did know it would make little difference, for that one was dead.

In any case, and long before they reached their love nest, the feeling had passed . . .

Evening fell on Sunside, and the first stars came out as the sky slowly darkened towards night. In their bower the lovers slept, touching all along their length, so close they might be one. In Settlement and other places the first fires were burning even now, lures for Starside's Lords. But the last vampire raid on Settlement had been a while ago; there was no reason why any monster should come hunting here now, and certainly not in this private place. In Nathan's metaphysical mind the numbers vortex whirled, and in its heart the mysteries of the universe were hidden behind countless mutating formulae; as were his secret thoughts. Thus the vortex was his protection —

— And his betrayal.

High in the mountains, in a saddle between peaks where the gold had faded to grey, a Lord and his lieutenant gazed down on Sunside, the first through scarlet eyes and the other with eyes which were feral. The latter was Zahar (once Zahar Sucksthrall, but no longer), and his master was the Lord Nestor of the Wamphyri, an awesome necromancer whose rapid rise to power had made him a living legend on all the levels of Starside's last aerie. Their flyers rested a little apart, nodding their great, slate-grey heads in that curiously vacant way of theirs.

Zahar knew why they had come here: it was a habit of Nestor's to rest here a while, this very spot, and gaze down on Sunside before a raid. Always here, over Settlement. But while he found a constant fascination with the place, he had never once raided in the town. In the past he'd always given the same reason: 'I think ... I *know* this place. But there's nothing here that I want, not any longer.'

Tonight was different. Wratha had suggested that she and Nestor might raid together, yet he had flown out early with just Zahar in attendance. Just the two of them, without even a warrior. And Nestor's gaze was very keen, even eager tonight as he looked down on the glow-worm flicker of the town's fires; and Zahar sensed within him an eagerness, a strange cold passion, and a purpose.

For a while the lieutenant fidgeted, then asked: 'Do we raid here tonight? Do we recruit? If so we should be careful, for these people have a reputation. Those fires could well be lures!'

Nestor merely glanced at him, but at least the question had drawn him back to earth. 'We hunt,' he answered.

'*Hah!*' Zahar snorted appreciatively. 'For women?'

'For a couple, male and female,' Nestor's voice was like a low wind out of the Icelands, cold and foreboding. 'A great enemy of mine who went away and is now returned. A treacherous Szgany dog and his bitch, who plotted against me. Even now they are hiding from me, in the woods where they always hid. But I shall find them now as I found them then.'

Zahar stared at him, feared him. Nestor had no background. There was nothing in his past to guide his future. Except this, perhaps, whatever it was. And he was pure as pure Wamphyri! All Nestor knew, he'd learned in Old Starside's last aerie. And despite that the ways of the aerie were hard, he'd learned fast. Add to this the fact that he was a necromancer ... the Lord Nestor's mind and his ways were unknowable.

Still, Zahar thought that he should make some answer. 'How will you find this enemy, Lord?'

Again Nestor's glance, and his grim smile. 'He sleeps and dreams,' he said. 'But I know his dreams, for they penetrate my own like darts.'

Zahar said nothing. He had been right: his master's mind was entirely unknowable.

'Now listen,' Nestor continued with more animation.

729

'In the twilight before the dawn I sensed his return, and dreamed that I went to fetch him into Starside to punish him. But my dream was ominous, and in the hour of my triumph I fell foul of some nameless fate. Tonight, leaving Wratha to sleep on, I rose early and came down to my apartments, from where I heard the Lord Canker Canison singing to the moon. Because they say he is touched with oneiromancy, I mentioned the dream to him. He howled like a wolf and told me that the future is inviolable; the only danger lies in trying to read or alter it; what will be will be. I agree with that last: what will be will be. Except . . .'

'Yes, Lord?'

'If aught befalls me, will my enemy go free? I can't bear the thought of that.' He shook his head. 'No, for if I'm destined for hell I want to know that my enemy got there before me, or follows close behind, at least! These are my instructions:

'He is mine and you shall take the girl. If all goes well we head direct for Starside. But if I should come to grief my order is this: drop the girl and take him! Do you understand?' His voice was suddenly sharp.

'Yes, Lord.'

'For I don't mind that she lives, only that he should not! And in no circumstance are they to be allowed to live together. Which is why you will take him and head for Starside. For I've heard of a certain legend, and I'm determined that he shall be the one to test it.'

He explained his meaning in more detail, then continued: 'Zahar, a dream is only a dream and I'm not afraid of it. Nor do I fear anything. But if aught *should* go astray, don't fail me. For I am the Lord Nestor and life and death are one to me, and even in the worst possible future, I *shall* be back!'

'I believe you, Lord,' said Zahar.

They went to their beasts and mounted up. And Nestor said, 'Now follow close behind, and I'll take you to them.'

Zahar kept his thoughts well guarded where he goaded his flyer into the air. But in the eastern foothills and along the peaks he'd seen banks of mist forming, and knew that the Wamphyri hunted there. While Nestor pursued dreams and ghosts out of his unknown past, they hunted for the good things of life: for the blood which *is* the life, for women and slaves, and for the sheer joy of it. *Huh!* Not much of joy in Nestor. But then, there'd not been a deal of it in Vasagi either! And this one had his egg.

Nestor 'heard' none of this; his damaged mind was full of other things and remembered only those which he wanted to remember. And as his flyer arched its wings and soughed down the wind towards the tree-line, he was maddened by the swirl of alien numbers rushing faster and faster in his brain. Now, at long last, he would track the maelstrom to its source and destroy it — destroy *him* — forever. As he should have destroyed him in the far, dim, all but forgotten past . . .

The mist on the mountains. Like Zahar, Nana Kiklu had seen it, too, and had gone straight to Lardis. Now they were out searching for the newlyweds, Nana in one direction and Lardis in the other. He was the one who found them, and with time to spare, or so he thought. But in fact he was just too late.

Arm in arm, they headed for the Rock along a foothill trail. Trudging and weary, they dragged their worldly goods behind them. Lardis saw them, sighed his relief and hurried forward . . . only to freeze as the night air throbbed and the starlight seemed to dim a little, and a shadow went wafting overhead! Lardis fell into a crouch, snapped his shotgun shut, and looked up. He saw them — flyers, a pair — banking against the hillside, and stooping towards the lovers like hawks! And now they too felt the throbbing of the air, looked up and saw the swooping flyers. Instinctively, Misha flew into Nathan's arms.

'This way!' Lardis bellowed. 'To me!' They saw him, ran towards him. The flyers veered a little and their belly pouches yawned open; their wings formed arches where they seemed almost to drift down upon the pair.

'Down!' Lardis yelled. 'Get down!'

The flyers were upon them, buffeting them apart; the one which pursued Nathan made to scoop him up; he stumbled and the flap of the thing's pouch sent him flying. It formed its wings into air-traps and hovered, following him where he tumbled down a scree slide.

Frantically, Lardis swung his weapon towards the other beast but daren't fire; Misha was in the way. The creature was almost upon her when suddenly ... she gave a scream and disappeared! She was the victim of one of Lardis's pits! But better that than the other. Far better! She might be injured, but she was safe for the moment. And the old Lidesci launched himself feet-first down the scree slide after Nathan.

Nathan was on his feet. He turned to look back up the slope — and the flyer was there, right behind him! He saw it, and saw that its rider was ...

... *Nestor!*

Nathan might not know the face — that twisted, snarling visage with its scarlet, glaring eyes — but he would recognize the mind anywhere, however warped and changed it had become. At close range there was no mistaking it; he *felt* its hatred, and knew that recognition was mutual. Nestor was a Power now, and Nathan's own telepathy that much more enhanced.

You! The word was a hiss, burning like acid as it flowed from Nestor's mind.

'Nestor!' Nathan gasped, as the flyer's head passed over him and its belly pouch yawned. He smelled its stench . . . and in the same moment heard Lardis's yell:

'Get down!' A split second later and the old Lidesci came skidding on his heels and his rump, collided with Nathan and sent him flying. The two of them rolled and tumbled; but relentless as a shadow and almost as close, the flyer followed after. They hit the bottom of the slope, and Lardis was first on his feet. Growling like a bear he turned his weapon on the flyer and discharged it pointblank into the creature's eyes – once, twice!

The thing screamed high and shrill, lashed its head left and right, and its wings pounded frantically, uselessly at the air. Then, as a wingtip struck the slope, the beast tilted to one side, which threatened to unseat its rider. Yelling like a madman, Lardis reloaded and aimed at the vampire Lord.

And even if Nathan would wish it otherwise, there was nothing he could do about the rest of it. Dazed and still trying to climb to his feet, he heard the twin shotgun blasts and *felt* Nestor's agony! And again he and Lardis were bowled over as the stricken flyer's thrusters uncoiled downwards and drove it out and away into the night, with Nestor lolling and jerking in the saddle.

By now Sunside lay under a blanket of mist, and because the main body of Wamphyri hunters were in the east, it could only be a natural mist rising from the woods and rivers of the region. Nestor's flyer dipped low and tore a soft hole in the stuff, which quickly filled in behind it.

Lardis was yelling, 'I *got* the bastard! I got him in the eyes, like I told you! If my aim had been better I could have taken his head off!'

The mist rolled up and covered them, and passed up the slope. And despite that Lardis had been talking about Nestor, there was only one thought in Nathan's mind now: 'Misha?'

'Come on,' Lardis growled. 'She fell into one of our own pits. And that other flyer may still be around, might even have landed!' Reloading his shotgun, he headed up the slippery scree slope. But even as they began climbing, so Zahar came gliding from above and fell on them. It was as swift as that: the mist opened and the flyer was there.

Lardis got off a shot before he was buffeted aside. He was on his feet again in a moment, aiming at a nodding, mist-wreathed head, squeezing the trigger. And the gun blew up in his hands! One of the old cartridges, a bad one, had finally let him down. Blown backwards and off his feet, he waited for the shock to pass, then struggled upright and looked for Nathan . . . and saw nothing but the mist. But in a little while he found the wind to climb the slope.

Misha was waiting at the top, shivering and dishevelled but otherwise unharmed. She took Lardis's hand and helped him up, then grabbed him and looked into his eyes. He could only lower his head and look away . . .

EPILOGUE

Unconscious from the flyer's gases, Nathan lolled in Zahar's arms where the vampire lieutenant carried him across the wormhole-riddled terrain surrounding the hell-lands Gate and tossed him down on top of its low crater wall. Beyond that wall, snug as an eye in its socket, the vastly glaring Gate shone with a cold white light, causing Zahar to lower his eyelids half-way shut and put up a hand against the dazzle.

He found a toe-hold and stepped up onto the wall, picked Nathan up and paced forward to the very 'skin' of the shining hemisphere of light. There he paused, looked at the man in his arms and shrugged. There seemed very little of a 'great enemy' in this one, and as any vampire would know, there were better uses for good Szgany flesh than this! On the other hand, his master's warning couldn't be ignored; Zahar dared not fail him who had sworn to return. For Nestor was a Lord and crafty necromancer, while Zahar was only a lieutenant.

Well, time now to get it over with. He cradled Nathan like a child in one arm, and slapped his face until his eyes flickered open. 'What?' Nathan groaned, rolling his head and seeing first Zahar's awful face, and then the blinding light spilling from the Gate! The hell-lands portal, which he knew at once, glaring like ... like 'a great blind eye'!

Zahar grinned at him and said: 'Courtesy of the Lord Nestor. Whoever you are, this world has seen the last of you. But I hope they make you welcome in hell!' And so saying he spilled Nathan out of his arms into the glare, which absorbed him in a moment, effortlessly and without a sound, like an eye blinking away the irritation of a dust mote . . .

Far to the east in a blocked pit in Madmanse, the gigantic monstrosity which was Eygor Killglance lay where he had died, slumped against a nitre-streaked wall, and groaned a vast and terrible deadspeak groan. *He* was dead, the physical Eygor, but his mind of course went on. Except there was no one now to know it, not with any certainty. For like the guttering of a distant candle in the ultimate darkness of death, Eygor had seen Nathan's light go out. Which could mean only one thing: that the Necroscope was no more.

In the higher levels of the promontory, called Runemanse, perhaps Maglore 'heard' something of Eygor's groaning; perhaps he 'felt' something of Nathan's passing. At any rate he rushed to his room of meditation and placed his trembling fingers on the sigil shaped in gold, and let his mind drift out from Turgosheim, then hurtle west at the unthinkable speed of thought, which is instantaneous. But the sigil was lifeless now, merely a strangely twisted mass of heavy metal, and Maglore's 'window on an unknown world' was closed. It was weird, because even though Nathan's aura was gone, the feeling persisted that he was not dead. What, then? Undead? Locked in that metamorphic sleep which precedes the vampire condition? Had he finally succumbed to the seduction of vampirism? Did Wratha or one of hers have him? And Maglore sighed. Better perhaps if he had made him his own after all . . .

In all the dreaming places of the Thyre, suddenly the darkness was that much deeper. For the ancients also knew of Nathan's passing from this world, but they knew a little more than the rest: that he was *not* dead. For if so he would be one with them, an honoured member of an élite, 'extinct' society, where his dead-speak voice would always be welcome. No, he was not dead but *removed* from them, taken away, transported to a place from which no one ever returned.

The teeming dead of Sunside knew it, too, and felt safer for it, however shamefully. But men reap what they sow, and in the child there is *always* that of the father. Perhaps Nathan had posed a threat, and perhaps not. Whatever, it made no difference now for he was gone. And of all of them who had passed into Sunside's air and earth, only Jasef Karis missed him and wished that he had spoken to him.

But not a one of them — not Eygor, Maglore, the Thyre, or all the dead of Sunside put together — could ever have dreamed that they would hear Nathan's dead-speak voice again, or see his candle burning in the darkness as before . . .

Nestor's awakening was slow and painful. His eyes were burning, his back had been very nearly broken, but his mind . . . was free of numbers! And with that, it all came back to him:

. . . His flyer, blinded, with its face half shot away and its tiny brain peppered with poisonous silver pellets. Nestor, too, reeling in the saddle with sightless eyes, his face a raw red mess and consciousness slipping as he fought to command his crippled beast up, away, back to Starside. He remembered a long low glide, and his inability to impress himself on the flyer's mind. The wonder was that the beast had stayed aloft so long.

. . . Then the crash; the whiplash as he was hurled from the flyer's back, his body somersaulting, smashing against the bole of a great tree, falling through branches

737

which snapped under his weight, down to the forest's floor. And the darkness.

Following which:

Ministering hands? Kindness? Ointments and bandages, to assist in the healing process which Nestor's leech had already commenced? Brief bouts of consciousness, in which he had known that people moved about him, caring for him, even feeding him a vile soup, which his body accepted readily enough despite that it was not his usual fare. It could only mean that he had made it back to Starside, where Wratha had found him crashed among the great hardy firs of the barrier range below the tree-line, and brought him into the last aerie.

But when he had tried to speak to her, it was not the Lady Wratha's voice which answered him. And because his eyes were so badly damaged and bandaged, he'd not seen the ones who covered his shivering body with blankets to keep him warm, and fed him, and pricked the silver shot out of his face, and generally succoured him through his fever.

Until now, finally, he heard their whispers, and felt once more the pain in his back, the agony of his ruined face. But he held still as they peeled away the bandages, and listened to their whispers tailing off as they sensed that he was awake. Then, despite the pain of tearing scabs, he gradually forced his eyes open and felt pus begin to ooze as something of sight returned. But –

– Was the room dark, or was it his eyes? It was both, he knew. He was healing, but not yet fully healed. For even a dark room would appear as daylight to one who was Wamphyri. But this room seemed full of a thick grey mist, and his eyes burned like fire when he blinked them to clear his vision. Except his vision would not clear. He was half-blind, and a long way yet to go before his vampire repaired him back to new.

He stirred, groaned, moved his limbs and tested his body. And like shadows the ones who had saved him backed off, melted away and out of this misty room of vague grey shapes and musty odours. Their movements seemed strange, stumbling, crippled as badly as Nestor himself and perhaps worse. For he was at least aware of his blood surging and knew that his limbs were his own again. He was weak but would be strong, and given time he would see as well as ever. But not yet for a while.

Now that Nestor was alone he put out a trembling hand to feel his bed, the wall, the edge of a table. All of wood, and warm. In no way the familiar cold grey stone of the last aerie. So what was this place? Where was he and what had awakened him? Deep down inside, some strange instinctive terror grinned and gurgled, and in the eye of memory showed him a picture out of the past:

Of a flyer, gouting smoke and steam and shrivelling as its hide split open; then spilling its loathsome fats as the sun ate into it like acid and reduced it to so much slop! The sun . . . ! Was that what had awakened him, fear of the sun? But why? Where *was* he . . . and what was the hour?

Someone entered the room and Nestor froze, then fought to control his fear as the grey shadow came closer and stood beside his bed. His fear? But of what? He was the Lord Nestor of the Wamphyri! 'What . . .?' he gurgled from scabby, tattered lips. 'Who . . .?'

'Ah!' The grey shape nodded. 'And so you'll recover and return to Starside. Good!'

But though the voice was warm and not unkind, still its tone was strange, bitter, and . . . satisfied? And what was that it had said? About a *return* to Starside? Suddenly, anger and frustration flooded Nestor. He struggled to a sitting position and focused his damaged eyes until the grey one's misty silhouette filled in a little and his features took on shape beneath the cowl of his robe. But they were still grey features, poorly defined and oddly ... incomplete? The wraithlike figure leaned a little on a crutch which fitted under his right shoulder, and his robe hung like a shroud from his insubstantial frame.

'It's so dark in here,' Nestor said stupidly, or perhaps hopefully.

The other shook his head. 'No, it's light enough. Or will be soon.'

Nestor's pain threatened to engulf him again. He was Wamphyri, but he was still learning their disciplines. As yet he couldn't suppress pain. He fought it back as best he was able, and asked: 'Who are you, and what is this place?'

'My name is Uruk Piatra, called Uruk Long-life,' the grey one answered with a shrug. 'But a misnomer, I fear. And as for this place ... it's a leper colony.'

For a single moment Nestor's brain froze: a leper colony! Leprosy, the great bane of vampires! – but in the next he was galvanized to activity. Then, swinging his legs out from under the blankets, he grabbed the dangling arms of the other's robe. But they were only empty sleeves and couldn't take his weight. They ripped at the shoulders and came away in Nestor's hands where he fell back again onto the bed. And he saw how Uruk's twig arms ended in swollen fungus nubs at the elbows!

After that: a rush of adrenalin – a madness of vampire-induced flight in which all of Nestor's previous agonies were forgotten – a blundering confusion of blind terror as he fled the colony out into the forest. And even then no respite, for in the south the light was improving moment by moment. Grey shapes stood gaunt as ghosts in the mist of Nestor's perception as he rushed this way and that under the trees, trying to avoid them. He crashed among a cage of squawking chickens and wrecked it, fell against a fence and tumbled over it, and felt no pain now but only fear as he careened deeper into the dawn woods in search of a place to hide.

A deep hole in which to find safety from the sun and wait out the long day. A sanctuary in which to rest and recuperate, sleep and dream ... and nightmare, certainly.

About what had been, and what was yet to be ...